Season of Hope

Season of Hope

Season of Hope
by Carol Cox

Sleigh Bells
by Judith McCoy Miller

Candy Cane Calaboose
by Janet Spaeth

For a Father's Love
by JoAnn A. Grote

HeavenSent
FROM
Crossings

Scripture taken from the HOLY BIBLE, NEW INTERNATIONAL VERSION®. NIV®.
Copyright © 1973, 1978, 1984 by International Bible Society. Used by permission
of Zondervan Publishing House. All rights reserved.

Season of Hope
Copyright © 2001 by Carol Cox

Sleigh Bells
Copyright © 2000 by Barbour Publishing, Inc.

Candy Cane Calaboose
Copyright © 2001 by Janet Spaeth

For a Father's Love
Copyright © 2002 by JoAnn A. Grote

This edition was especially created in 2003 for Crossings by arrangement with
Barbour Publishing, Inc.

Published by Crossings Book Club, 401 Franklin Avenue, Garden City, New York
11530.

ISBN: 0-7394-3738-0

Printed in the United States of America

Season of Hope

Season of Hope

by Carol Cox

Rejoicing in hope; patient in tribulation;
continuing instant in prayer.
ROMANS 12:12

*C*ome in, Rachel. Have a seat."

Rachel Canfield slid into the dark leather chair facing Ben Murphy's massive oak desk, her back straight, chin up, trying to exude an air of confidence she didn't feel. The bank manager's office was a familiar setting. Goodness knew, she'd been in there often enough with her father, but having to conduct business on her own gave the room an odd sense of unfamiliarity today.

"I want to tell you again how sorry I am about your father's accident."

Rachel nodded briefly, appreciating the sentiment, but not wanting to deal with the fresh wound of her loss right then. She cleared her throat, then hesitated, lacing her fingers into a white-knuckled knot. What was wrong with her? Ben Murphy had been her father's friend for all the time they'd lived in Arizona Territory. In her present hardship, she knew she could count on him to be an ally. She had absolutely no need to be nervous.

Ben leaned forward, giving her an encouraging smile. Rachel breathed a quick prayer for courage, squared her shoulders, and got right to the point. "The farm is doing well. *Very* well," she added for emphasis. "I fully expect to make a better profit than ever this year." Ben nodded, obviously pleased, and Rachel drew in a long, shaky breath. She had just given him the good news. Now for the hard part.

"Unfortunately, we've had a good many extra expenses, what with the doctor and the . . . the funeral and all." Rachel's voice shook, and she pressed her lips together for a moment, trying to regain her composure. "I'd like an extension on our loan payment—just for a few months," she added hastily as Ben's smile faded and his eyebrows drew together. "Just until we catch up a little bit." Her voice trailed off, and she sat speechless, hating the way her lower lip quivered, but powerless to stop it.

Ben looked at his hands, at his inkwell, at the Seth Thomas clock on the wall—anywhere but at Rachel.

What was going on? The Canfields had always paid their debts and always would. Ben knew that. Why did he suddenly look so unfriendly? Why did he refuse to look Rachel in the eye?

"I'm afraid I can't do that." His eyes focused on a Currier and Ives print across the room.

Rachel's breath came in short, jerky gasps. "But–but why?" she faltered. "You know you'll get the money."

Ben ran a finger back and forth inside his collar. "If it were up to me, Rachel, you'd get the extension. Your father was a man of honor, and you've always followed him that way. But the board of directors has already met to discuss your loan. They don't believe two young women can keep the place up by themselves, so if you and your sister have any problem making this year's payment—any at all—I'm supposed to hold you strictly to the terms of the agreement."

"I don't believe it!" Rachel slammed her palms down on the polished desk top, relishing the way the blow made her hands sting. The pain shocked her out of her confusion and helped her marshal her thoughts. "Do you mean to tell me that after all the years I've worked with my father, Doc Howell and Ed Silverton don't think I'm capable of making a go of the place now that he's gone?"

"It's—it's not Doc and Ed exactly," Ben mumbled.

"Then who?" Rachel demanded. "Who's left? Everyone around here knows I'm a hard worker and that I know what I'm doing. That makes me a good investment, Ben. Who would want to see me fail?"

Ben stared miserably at the rug as if fascinated by the floral pattern. "I don't know that Hiram *wants* to see you fail, exactly. . . ."

"Hiram? Hiram Bradshaw?" Rachel's voice rose to a screech. "What does he have to do with this?"

"He just invested in the bank, Rachel. He's on the board of directors now." Ben's gaze met hers at last. "In fact, he's the biggest investor in the bank, so he has the biggest say in what we do. And what he said about you was that I was to give you no leeway on this. None whatsoever."

"What about all the time you and Pa spent together?" Rachel hurled the question at him. "Didn't his friendship mean anything to you?"

Ben squirmed, looking more like an errant schoolboy caught in a misdeed than the manager of a financial institution. "I wish it were up to me," he said, shaking his head. "I really do."

Rachel rose from her chair and leaned as far over the desk as her five feet five inches would allow. "All right, Ben Murphy." She ground out the words. "We worked hard to build that farm up out of nothing but a hole in the forest—too hard to let it slip away to a scoundrel like Hiram Bradshaw. I don't know just how we'll manage it, but you can expect to have the full two hundred dollars right here on your desk December 15, and not a day later." She stood up and smoothed her skirt with trembling hands, preparing to make a sweeping exit. Ben's quiet voice stopped her.

"It's not two hundred, Rachel." At her sharp glance, he squirmed again. "Your father borrowed more money for mining equipment last spring. He signed a paper, promising to pay that in full, along with the loan amount. You'll need to come up with three hundred dollars."

Rachel's knees gave way, and she sagged back into the chair.

"Your father anticipated getting enough from this year's crop and his mine to pay it all off with no problem," Ben explained with a sympathetic look. "I know he never dreamed he'd leave you girls in the lurch like this."

Three hundred dollars! Rachel's mind whirled crazily, trying to calculate ways and means of coming up with that amount. Stiffly, she rose to her feet once more. "Then that's what you'll have," she said through taut lips. "I don't know how, but you'll get your money, Ben. Every penny of it."

Ignoring the pitying disbelief in the banker's eyes, Rachel pivoted and stalked out the door, her back ramrod straight and her head held high. No one, least of all Hiram Bradshaw, would take their land from them. And no one was going to see her look the least bit concerned about it! She climbed into the wagon seat and gathered the reins in one fluid motion.

Thumb Butte. Granite Mountain. Williams Peak. The familiar landmarks stood in the same places they had occupied for thousands of years. Rachel could gauge her location within a hundred yards just by a quick glance at her surroundings. Nothing had changed outwardly, yet everything was different, just because of Pa's passing.

Rachel viewed the passing landscape with shock-dimmed eyes, barely noticing the wagon turn when the road curved in the direction of Iron Springs and home.

How much longer would she and Violet be able to call it home? Her brave declaration to Ben Murphy had sounded fine inside the bank, but how on earth could she possibly come up with three hundred dollars in the space of three months?

"That prideful streak of yours is going to land you in trouble some day, Rachel." She could hear Pa's voice as clearly as if he'd been riding in the wagon seat next to her. How she wished she could turn and see him sitting there! She needed his calm guidance now, more than ever.

Rachel groaned aloud, and the wheel horse flicked one ear back, checking out the unexpected sound. With their lives suddenly turned upside down, raising two hundred dollars would have been challenge enough, but *three* hundred? "It's impossible," she informed the horses. "Utterly impossible."

With God all things are possible. Rachel gasped and spun about on the wagon seat, her heart pounding wildly. No one but she and the plodding horses were in sight. " 'With God all things are possible,' " she whispered, the verse from the Gospels sounding clear and fresh. "All things. Not everything but getting enough money to keep Hiram Bradshaw's greedy fingers off our land. *All* things." A way existed, and God would provide it. All she had to do was find out what that way might be.

The vague outline of a plan had begun to form in her mind by the time she turned off the road and into the farmyard. Wanting to share the idea with her sister before she lost her train of thought, she pulled the horses to a stop in front of the house and hurriedly dismounted from the wagon. "Violet!" she called. There was no answer. "Violet?" she tried again, louder this time.

A quick glance from the front door showed no sign of her sister. Rachel stood on the porch, hands on her hips, and tapped her foot impatiently. Wasn't that always the way? Here she had a perfectly wonderful notion just waiting to be shared, and Violet was nowhere to be found.

Rachel took a deep breath, ready to call out again, when a wail burst forth from the barn. "Violet!" she shrieked and raced across the hard-packed dirt, skirts held high, visions of mayhem flashing through her mind.

"Where are you?" she hollered when she arrived, panting, at the wide-open double door.

The dreadful yowling erupted again, just overhead. Rachel's head snapped back to scan the hayloft. What could her sister be doing up there? And what was happening to her to cause her to produce that inhuman sound? Rachel mounted the ladder leading to the loft. "I'm coming, Violet," she called breathlessly. "Just hang on."

"Thank goodness you're here." Violet's legs swung precariously near Rachel's nose to dangle over the edge of the loft. Bits of hay adorned her glossy dark hair and her skirt was rumpled, but otherwise she seemed in good condition—and remarkably unruffled for someone making such an unearthly noise.

Rachel stared openmouthed at her younger sister. "What on earth is going on?" she demanded, panic making her voice harsh. "You sounded like you were being murdered."

Violet blinked in surprise at her sister's accusing tone, then grinned. "Not me," she said, laughter gurgling in her throat. "Come on up." She scooted to one side and helped Rachel scramble from the top of the ladder to the loft.

Rachel wrinkled her nose at the hay dust she stirred up. She slapped at her skirt and sneezed violently when a cloud of the fine dust assailed her nostrils. "All right. What—*choo!*—is making that horrible noise?" Violet pointed to one corner. "I don't see any–any–ah–

9

ahh—" The discordant wail sounded again, cutting her off in mid sneeze.

"It's Molly," Violet explained, indicating the gray tabby cat that crouched against the wall, swiping her paw at a large orange-and-white tom. "Well, not Molly exactly," she said, watching the male visitor tilt his head back for another round of impassioned caterwauling.

"It's that tomcat of Jeb McCurdy's again!" Rachel fumed. "And after I've told him a dozen times to keep the mangy thing at home." Snatching the amorous cat by the scruff of the neck, she carried him down the ladder, ignoring his loud objections. "Where's that old sewing basket?" she asked Violet, who had followed her down, carrying Molly in one arm.

Violet reached behind a pile of grain sacks and pulled out the covered basket, which Rachel snatched gladly, depositing the lovesick tom inside and fastening the lid securely before he had a chance to escape. "There," she announced triumphantly. "That ought to hold him until I get him to McCurdy's place." She stalked off to the wagon, where the horses still stood in their harness.

Preparing to swing the basket onto the seat, Rachel paused to shade her eyes and peered at a distant figure coming toward them on the road. "Talk about timing!" she crowed. "There's Jeb McCurdy in his buggy now." With a grim smile, she grabbed the basket and strode off to intercept their neighbor.

Shielding her eyes with one hand, she waved her other arm in a wide arc. McCurdy slowed his horse to a walk, staring curiously. "Need some help, Miss Rachel?" he asked congenially, shooting a stream of tobacco juice neatly to one side of the buggy.

"What I need, Mr. McCurdy, is for you to keep your wayward animal at home."

"My what?" McCurdy rubbed his grizzled chin with a work-worn hand, a puzzled frown creasing his forehead.

"This wanton feline of yours." Rachel raised the basket and shook it menacingly in the surprised farmer's face, bringing indignant yowls of protest from the prisoner within. "I have asked you repeatedly to keep him from wandering onto our property, but he was back again today, tormenting our poor Molly."

The owner of the treacherous tom cast a bewildered look at Violet, who stood nearby holding Molly, then back at the avenging fury before him. "But I thought your sister's name was—" A second glance at the cat nestling comfortably in Violet's arms brought illumination to his weather-beaten face, and a muffled chuckle escaped his lips. "Molly— she'd be your cat, would she?"

"Of course she is," Rachel snapped. Her feelings raw after learning of the possible loss of the farm, she found a certain satisfaction in venting her pent-up anger. "The poor thing was cowering in a corner, trying to fend him off. Who knows what might have happened if we hadn't intervened?"

"Who knows, indeed?" McCurdy mumbled, rubbing a hand across his mouth.

Rachel pressed on, heedless of the interruption. "I want your word—your solemn word, Mr. McCurdy—that you will keep that beast on your own property from now on. We have enough to do to keep the place running without having to deal with the attention of unwanted intruders." She folded her arms and fixed McCurdy with a severe look, daring him to argue.

The faintest curve tilted one corner of McCurdy's mouth. "Has it occurred to you, Miss Rachel, that his attentions might not be totally unwanted? By Molly, that is," he hastened to add.

Rachel's fist tightened on the basket handle, fighting the urge to fling it, cat and all, straight at her neighbor and knock that infuriating smirk right off his face. "Mr. McCurdy," she said in icy tones, "I assure you that none of us, Molly included, have the slightest desire to entertain that creature. Please take your appalling animal and keep him at home. Or at least away from here!"

McCurdy caught the basket Rachel thrust at him and fumbled with the lid. "Oh, no," she told him, replacing the latch firmly. "Keep him in there until you get him home. You can return the basket later."

Nodding agreement, McCurdy snapped the reins and started his horse down the road. A rasping laugh floated back over his shaking shoulders to where Rachel stood glaring after him.

Hot tears stung her eyes, and she balled her hands into fists. How dare that old reprobate make fun of a serious situation! No wonder his cat behaved the way he did, she told herself; he was a reflection of his owner. Sniffling, she whirled purposefully toward the house and walked headlong into a tree that hadn't been there earlier.

2

*O*w!" Blinded by tears of pain, Rachel doubled over, with both hands clamped to her nose. Voices, one Violet's, one she had never heard before, floated above her.

"Rachel, are you all right? What happened?"

"I'm not sure." This from the strange voice, a mellow baritone. "She just ran smack into me." Strong hands took hold of Rachel's shoulders with a firm yet gentle grasp. "Are you hurt? Let's see."

Rachel raised her head slowly, still pressing her throbbing nose, to see two blurry figures before her. Blinking rapidly to clear her vision, she focused on the tall, sandy-haired man standing next to Violet. "Who are you?" she asked, her voice muffled by her hands. She threw a look at her sister, silently demanding an explanation.

Violet gave a nervous laugh. "We have company," she said helpfully. "You didn't hear us talking, because you were, ah, busy with Mr. McCurdy."

Jeb McCurdy! Rachel felt her cheeks flame, remembering the dressing-down she had given the grizzled miner. She must have sounded like a fishwife! What must this man, whoever he was, think of her? She turned back to him, pulling her hands from her face, and heard Violet gasp. Looking down, Rachel saw the bright red blood staining her fingers and a blotch of the same color on the front of the stranger's white shirt.

Mortified, she clapped her hands to her cheeks, regretting the action the instant she felt the sticky warmth from her fingers. She squeezed her eyes shut, wishing with all her might the man would be gone when she opened them again. Instead, he still stood before her, holding out a snowy handkerchief. Rachel took it without a word and held it to her nose, gratified that the bleeding seemed to have slowed.

"I'm Rachel Canfield," she said through the folds of fabric. "I take it you've already met my sister, Violet."

"Daniel Moore," replied the stranger. He held out his right hand, then appeared to reconsider and tucked it into his pocket. His gaze swept over Rachel from head to toe, and she felt as though she'd been appraised by his deep green eyes and found wanting. "I apologize for coming up on you like that. I thought you had finished your conversation, and I was coming to introduce myself. I didn't realize you were . . . preoccupied."

Rachel flinched at the reminder of her outburst. "I'm the one who should apologize, running into you like that. Look what I've done to your shirt! And your handkerchief," she added lamely, staring at the crimson-spotted square of fabric in her hand.

"Mr. Moore was a friend of Pa's," Violet said happily.

Then why haven't I seen him before? The day's upheaval made Rachel leery of putting her confidence in a total stranger.

"I thought maybe we could ask him to supper," Violet went on. Rachel opened her mouth to refuse but stopped when she saw the pleading look on her sister's face. What could it hurt? She didn't trust Daniel Moore—she didn't trust much of anyone at the moment—but she did owe him something after ruining his shirt. Besides, she could tell that entertaining a friend of their father's meant a lot to Violet.

"Will you join us, Mr. Moore?" she asked, attempting a gracious smile, but the taut feeling of dried blood on her cheeks reminded her of how she must look, and the smile faded. When he hesitated, she hastened to add, "If we get your shirt in some cold water right away, we might be able to get the blood stain out before it has time to set."

Daniel looked ruefully at his shirt front and gave Rachel a crooked smile. "I don't want to be a bother, but I did have something to discuss with you. That might be the best way to do it, if it's all right with you."

Daniel sat at the dining table, wearing one of Ike Canfield's shirts. His own sat soaking in a bowl of cold water Rachel had drawn. He wriggled his shoulders, trying to stretch the fabric a bit. Ike had been as tall as Daniel, but lean as a whipcord. Ike's arms had been shorter too, Daniel thought with amusement, looking down at his own tanned wrists extending well past the ends of the sleeves.

He scooted the chair sideways and stretched his long legs out before him, wondering how much longer Rachel would be. She had caught sight of her reflection in the front window when they entered the house, and Daniel had been hardpressed not to laugh out loud at her strangled cry of dismay. After putting his shirt in to soak and loaning him one of Ike's, she had immediately dashed off to repair the damage, Daniel supposed. Violet had gone out to feed the chickens right after that, leaving Daniel very much alone. He fidgeted again, wanting to get the upcoming interview over with.

Smoothing her light brown hair back from her face, Rachel walked into the kitchen, her expression contrite. She pulled out two loaves of bread and a sharp knife and began cutting the bread into even slices.

"Exactly how did you know my father?" The words tumbled out abruptly. "I mean, I never heard him speak of you. . . ." She pressed her lips together and eyed Daniel expectantly.

"My mining claim was next to his," he answered.

Rachel's hands froze in midslice. "Then you were there when the beam fell on him?" Her eyes widened, and the knife wavered in her hand.

Daniel shook his head miserably. "I was gone that day, that whole week, in fact. I had to go over to Camp Verde on business, and I didn't get back until it was all over. I didn't even make it to the funeral," he said in a dull voice. "If I'd been around, I might have heard the commotion and gotten to him in time."

And if you had, he told himself, *you might be sitting here now having supper with the whole family, instead of with two girls who have been left alone in the world.* It was possible, he reasoned. Old Ike had extended an invitation often enough. But for someone as skittish around women as Daniel, the mere mention of two unmarried daughters in the household had been enough to make him keep his distance.

He watched Rachel's mobile face as she digested the news that her father might not have died if only he, Daniel Webster Moore, had been close by. If he hadn't made the spontaneous trip to Camp Verde.

If he'd been around to hear and lend a helping hand, they might never have suffered this loss. And he would not now be in this unpleasant position.

This wouldn't be easy; he could see that already. Ike's description of his daughters had been remarkably accurate. "Violet's a frail little thing," he had told Daniel more than once. "Not sickly, mind you, just not sturdy like her sister. She takes after her mother, God rest her soul—dreamy and gentle, always concerned about the other person's feelings.

"Rachel, on the other hand," he would continue, "has an independent streak a mile wide. Nothing wrong with that in itself, but once she sets out to do something, that stubborn pride of hers won't let her change direction. And feisty? My land, that girl has a temper! Rachel isn't one you want to cross without a rock-solid reason."

Ike had been right on target. Daniel could see that, even after his brief acquaintance with the sisters, and it wouldn't make his self-appointed task one bit simpler. Violet would probably accept his offer as the sensible solution it was. It was Rachel who worried him.

Taking a deep breath, he decided to plunge right in. No use beating around the bush with this one. "You're going to need some help on this farm," he began. "You still have the corn and beans to get in and the late vegetables to harvest, not to mention needing to cut firewood and plow the fields before winter. Your father was a good man, one of the best. He helped me out more than once, and I'd like to do something to repay the favor." He glanced at Rachel, who eyed him narrowly.

"Just exactly what did you have in mind?" she asked in a tight voice.

"I can give you a hand with all of that. I'm a hard worker, and I'd like to do it in memory of your pa."

Rachel seemed to turn the proposition over in her mind while she melted lard in the skillet. To most, Daniel knew, it would seem a generous offer from a friend. But this stubborn, proud woman would likely be rankled if she felt beholden to a stranger.

The door swung open to admit Violet, cheeks tinged a rosy pink from the nip in the air, the hem of her apron gathered in her hands.

"Can you believe it? I found six more eggs when I fed the hens." She removed the eggs from her apron and set them gently on the counter, blithely unaware of the undercurrents in the room.

Rachel didn't answer her sister but swung around to face Daniel. "I appreciate your offer, Mr. Moore, but I believe God has already shown me a plan to keep things going here. We're going to be strapped for cash until our bank loan is paid off, so I couldn't pay you, and I certainly couldn't allow you to work for us for nothing. Thank you for your generosity, but the answer is no."

A knot formed in Daniel's stomach. It hadn't been easy for him to convince himself to approach Ike's daughters. Women, in Daniel's experience, were better left alone. But Ike had been a good neighbor—more than that, he had saved his bacon the time he'd run off those Yavapai Apaches that had Daniel pinned down. In Daniel's book, a debt like that couldn't go unpaid. He hadn't been there to help Ike, but he could step in now to do what he could for Ike's family. And Rachel seemed ready to throw his offer away without even discussing it.

In the six weeks since Ike's death, the girls had done a remarkable job of keeping the place going. The fields were well tended, and the livestock were in obviously good shape. It had probably been good for them to keep busy with a regular routine. But now they faced the prospect of bringing in the harvest, where they would make the bulk of their income. If that wasn't done right and on time, all the other hard work would have been for nothing.

Daniel noted the determined set of Rachel's chin, and the knot in his stomach tightened. Did she really believe she and her sister could do it on their own? He shook his head in reluctant admiration. Her father had her figured, all right—independence and stubborn pride enough for three people.

He nodded, outwardly accepting her decision. "It's your choice," he said. "Have it your way." Under his breath he added, "For now." He had a debt to pay, and a stubborn streak of his own.

Visibly relieved at his acquiescence, Rachel turned her attention to Violet. "Go ahead and add those eggs to the ones you brought in this morning and cook them up, will you?"

Violet rolled her eyes. "Eggs again?"

"We have to do something with them. Those hens are laying faster than we can use them up. Even with the ones you keep sneaking to Molly," Rachel added, clearly suppressing a chuckle when an embarrassed flush stained her sister's cheeks. "I hope you like eggs, Mr. Moore," she called over her shoulder, then frowned. "What's the matter?"

Daniel's mouth hung open in utter astonishment. "You're trying to get *rid* of your eggs?" he asked, stunned.

A crease appeared between Rachel's eyebrows. "It's not that we're ungrateful; we just have more than we can possibly use. What's wrong?"

Daniel shook his head in disbelief. "Just that most folks around here would give their eye teeth for an occasional egg, and here you are, throwing them away."

"Giving the extras to Molly isn't throwing them away," Violet retorted with a sniff.

"Wait a minute." Rachel stared at Daniel. "Do you mean you think we could sell some of these eggs?"

"Not some," Daniel corrected. "All. Why don't you take a basketful with you the next time you go into town and see what happens?"

"Maybe I will," Rachel said.

Rachel wrapped a length of binder twine around yet another armload of cornstalks and set the shock upright. She wiped the dampness from her brow with the back of her hand and shook her head. Even with the feel of autumn in the air, she was sweating. Harvesting the corn single-handedly made for slow going. Too slow. At this rate she wouldn't be done for weeks. And that would be much too late.

Her plan for saving the farm had seemed so simple. She and Violet would get the harvest in by themselves. Without hiring outside help, she reasoned, they'd save a lot, maybe enough to put a goodly bit toward the hundred-dollar difference in the loan amounts. They would do such a wonderful job that even the worst naysayers in town would have to admit being a woman wasn't the drawback some of them would like to believe.

Rachel knew what needed to be done and how to do it. After all, hadn't she worked with Pa on every job on the place? She still would be too if it hadn't been for the accident. If only that beam hadn't fallen just when Pa was underneath! But she was learning there was a vast difference between working alongside her father and being responsible for everything, the housework and fieldwork both.

She rolled her neck, trying to work out the kinks, and surveyed the waving corn about her. Nearly half of it had been put up. Over in the bean field, Violet moved methodically down a row, stripping the dried pods from the plants and placing them in the gunnysack she dragged along behind her. The vegetable patch, neat and weed free, was ready to yield the last crops of the season. Yes, she could be proud of all they had accomplished so far. But looking beyond that, she could also see what still needed to be done.

"I'm trying, Pa. Really, I am," she whispered, her voice catching in her throat. Tears pricked her eyes as the fresh pain of her loss tore at her once more, and she looked across the fields, aching to see her father's familiar figure striding along, a corn knife in his hand.

But Pa was gone, and no amount of longing would bring him back. An indescribable heaviness swept over her, and she felt far older than her twenty-one years. How could she possibly expect to make enough to keep her and Violet eating, much less earn enough extra to pay off the loan?

"What do I do, God?" The cry burst forth from her weary spirit. She no longer had her earthly father with her, but her heavenly Father was always near. "Even Pa had to hire workers at harvest time. And he had me to keep the house and cook for him and the crew. I've got no one except Violet . . . and You.

"If we hire men, we won't have enough money left to pay off the loan, and that miserable Hiram Bradshaw will waltz in and take the place. But if we don't get help, we'll never get it all done, and there won't be any money then, either.

"I thought I was hearing from You when I decided Violet and I would do this on our own . . . but it isn't working. We'll never get it done at this rate, and we're both so tired we're ready to drop in our tracks." She flung up her hands in despair. "All things are possible with You, but You've got to help me see the way clearly."

"If I have to eat another egg, I'll scream!" Violet's heartfelt protest rang across the kitchen.

"You'll eat them and like them, Violet Canfield. The less money we spend on food in town, the more we can set aside for the loan payment. Didn't you hear Mr. Moore the other night? Lots of people would appreciate those eggs. Be grateful."

"And I'm sick of hearing about the loan payment! That's all you seem to care about anymore." Violet's blue eyes were stormy.

"It's you I care about," Rachel retorted. "You and this farm. Pa worked hard to build it up for us, and I don't intend to lose it."

Violet crossed her arms mutinously. "At least while Pa was alive, we had decent food to eat."

Stung by the justice of Violet's remark, Rachel studied her sister's slight form with a critical eye. Violet had always been slender like their mother, but now her dress hung loosely on her slim frame—a frame that was far too thin, Rachel realized with a tinge of panic. Bread and eggs didn't make a hearty supper by any means, but they didn't have the energy to fix anything more ambitious after a day of working outdoors.

"Go on out and feed the chickens while I fix the eggs," she told Violet, trying to keep her voice level. "At least that way you won't have to watch them cooking."

Violet exited gratefully, looking contrite. Rachel cracked the eggs into a bowl, then squeezed her eyes shut and leaned her forehead against the cupboard door. "Lord, it's me again, and I need a word from You real soon. I've got to figure out a way to get the fieldwork done, and feed us decently, and tend the kitchen garden, and keep house, and . . ."

Overwhelmed, Rachel felt the hot sting of tears on her eyelids. She bit her lower lip and shook her head, angrily dashing the tears away with the back of her hand. She couldn't afford to break down now. Maybe when all of this was over. *If it's ever over,* she thought bleakly.

Immediately, she felt a sense of shame. Five years Violet's senior, she had been responsible for her younger sister ever since their mother's death back in Missouri. With Pa gone too, who could Violet depend on if she, Rachel, gave in to despair?

With a determined tilt of her chin, she squared her shoulders and proceeded to whip the eggs into a froth, then poured them into the waiting frying pan. "Lord, I'll just keep going one step at a time. But You're going to have to show me the way."

The shuffle of footsteps and the rattle of the door latch heralded Violet's return. Rachel gave her cheeks a quick swipe with the tail of her apron to make sure no traces of dampness remained. Hearing the door open, she cleared her throat and asked brightly, "How many more of those horrible eggs did you find this time?"

"Just two." Violet slipped them onto the counter and backed away quickly. Puzzled, Rachel turned to find her sister with the egg basket on her arm and a guilty look on her face.

"And what else do you have in that basket?" she demanded.

"Oh, Rachel, he looked so pitiful, I couldn't bear to leave him outside." Holding the basket protectively, Violet scooped up a small gray object and held it out for Rachel's inspection. The little squirrel in her hand took in its new surroundings with bright eyes. Even from across the kitchen, Rachel could see that one of its back legs bent at an unnatural angle.

Rachel moved the eggs off the stove and sighed in exasperation. The last thing she needed right now was another responsibility, no matter how minor.

The squirrel chittered nervously, and Violet cuddled it close, murmuring soothing words. Memories flashed through Rachel's mind— Violet bringing home baby birds fallen from their nest . . . tending a little cottontail with a broken leg . . . She shook her head with a wry grin. This nurturing instinct was an inherent part of Violet. Just as well try to change the weather. And if it helped her get her mind off their present difficulties, why fight it?

"Make him a bed in front of the fire while I dish up supper."

3

*V*iolet sat near the dancing flames, her fingers methodically splitting open the pods she had gathered earlier, her thumbs popping out the beans. With the squirrel curled on a bed of rags at her feet, she looked the picture of contentment.

Sitting opposite her, Rachel's hands worked just as efficiently, but inside her feelings churned. So much to do, and so little time! When Pa was alive, he and she had worked out an equitable system of sharing the responsibility for the farm. Now he was gone, and the burden was placed squarely on Rachel's shoulders. Gentle, fragile Violet couldn't be expected to carry out all Rachel's former duties. Just having her gather the bean pods had taxed her strength to the limit.

Eyeing her sister's delicate form, Rachel knew she had to do something to feed them better. But what? They couldn't spend time tending the stove when they had to be in the field harvesting. When they came in for the evening, they were far too tired to fix anything more substantial than bread and eggs. Eggs for breakfast, eggs for supper.

Rachel groaned. Violet was right—something had to change, but how? Even during the hardest parts of Rachel's life, she had never questioned God's loving care. Now, though, it was getting hard to see His hand in things.

Father, I don't mean to doubt You, but I do need an answer in a hurry. If we don't eat right, we won't be able to do all the other things we need to, so please help me figure that out right away.

One step at a time, remember? Rachel winced. She had never before addressed the Almighty so boldly, but these were desperate times. She hoped He wouldn't be offended.

Violet's voice broke into her thoughts. "Do you know where that

22

old dynamite box of Pa's is? It would make a good home for this little fellow, but I can't remember where I saw it last."

"I think it's up in the loft." Rachel tossed her last handful of beans in the bowl between them. "I'll go look for it while you finish up." She made her way to the loft over the bedrooms, frowning as she pushed her way between cast-off boxes and keepsakes. Pa hadn't been much better than Violet about putting things away neatly, and the resulting hodge-podge had gotten out of hand. It needed a good going-over, but she wasn't likely to have time for that for quite awhile.

Rachel tried to maneuver past an old packing crate, caught her foot on something, and fell sprawling to the floor. She swiveled her head to see what had tripped her and saw the corner of a trunk protruding into the walkway. Muttering, she got to her feet and braced herself to shove the offending trunk back where it belonged, then paused and looked at it appraisingly, scattered recollections from the past appearing before her eyes like images in a scrapbook. With a grin, Rachel flung open the lid and started piling the clothing inside onto a shelf.

"Good, you're finished," she told Violet as she backed into the room, dragging the heavy chest. She tossed a stack of papers on Violet's lap. "Take these and line the trunk while I go get some hay."

"Do what?" Violet's hand paused in the act of stroking the little squirrel on her lap, and she gazed at Rachel in astonishment.

"Make it several layers thick, and don't leave any spaces."

"Rachel, are you all right?"

"Just do it. I'll be right back." Ignoring Violet's look of concern, she hustled outside.

In the barn, she stuffed armloads of grass hay into a gunnysack and returned to the house, humming merrily. "Are you finished?"

Violet, on her knees beside the trunk, looked up warily. "Will that do?" she asked, smoothing a sheet of paper into place.

Rachel looked at it judiciously. "Put one more piece in the corner. We want it to be completely sealed." Violet obeyed, keeping a cautious eye on her sister. Rachel, still humming, rummaged through the linen cupboard and pulled out an old pillowcase with a jubilant cry.

"Good job!" she told Violet. "Now stuff that with hay," she ordered, flinging the case her way.

Rachel dropped to her knees and began packing hay into the trunk. Violet watched her nervously, then grabbed fistfuls of hay and rammed them into the pillowcase with trembling hands. "Are you sure you're all right?" she asked in a shaky voice.

Rachel didn't respond but danced across the floor to the kitchen, where she lifted the large stew pot from its hook and waltzed back to the trunk with it. Nestling the pot on the bottom layer of hay, she continued to pack hay around it.

"Rachel?" Violet said in a tiny voice.

"Oh, you're done." Rachel squeezed the pillow. "Yes, that feels fine. Now stitch it closed while I finish up here."

Violet reached for the mending basket and did as she was told.

Rachel continued stuffing hay around the pot, pressing it down firmly. Taking the pillow from a bewildered Violet, she placed it on top of the pot, then closed the lid with a flourish. "And there we have it!" she cried triumphantly. When Violet didn't reply, Rachel turned to see her sister watching her with worried eyes.

"You've been working awfully hard," Violet began, putting a comforting arm around Rachel's shoulders. "Why don't you climb into bed? I'll bring you a nice, hot cup of tea."

Rachel sputtered with laughter. "Violet, you ninny! Don't you remember the hay box we used back in Missouri?" Violet shook her head slowly. "Ma used it when she had a lot of canning to do. I'd completely forgotten about it until I tripped over this fool trunk.

"Look," she continued, dragging Violet over to the contraption and flipping the lid open. "Before we head out to the field in the morning, we'll heat some meat and vegetables on the stove. Then we'll pour it into the stew pot, cover it up, close the lid, and it will keep cooking all day while we're gone. We'll have stew tomorrow night, Violet. A real meal!"

"No more eggs?" Violet regarded the hay box thoughtfully, assessing its possibilities, then threw her arms around Rachel in an exultant hug. "Then hooray for the hay box!"

* * *

Rachel sat before the fire, her Bible open in her lap. Violet, reassured of Rachel's sanity, had gone off to bed. The squirrel, bedded down in the dynamite box with a splint on its injured leg, slept contentedly, and Rachel rejoiced in having some unaccustomed time to herself. She smoothed the pages with her hand, closing her eyes to reflect on the words from the Forty-sixth Psalm: "God is our refuge and strength, a very present help in trouble. Therefore will not we fear, though the earth be removed, and though the mountains be carried into the midst of the sea . . ."

Rachel smiled drowsily, her soul at peace for the first time in weeks. God was with her, and she would not fear. Not even if Thumb Butte and Granite Mountain parted from their moorings and sailed away. Not even if Hiram Bradshaw showed his ugly, threatening face on her property. God was her help.

A tentative knock at the door interrupted her reverie, and she sprang up, shaking her head to clear it. Late night visits only meant trouble. She approached the door cautiously, one hand at her throat, trying to recapture the serenity she had felt only a moment before. Opening the door a mere crack, she peered out into the darkness.

"I'm sorry to call so late." The voice belonged to Daniel Moore. "I saw the light and figured you were still up. May I speak with you for a moment?"

Rachel frowned, then backed away, allowing him to enter the room. She stood near the fireplace, not offering him a seat. Whatever he had to say, he could say it quickly and be on his way. If he tried to give her any trouble, Pa's Henry rifle hung over the mantel less than an arm's length away.

"I've been thinking," Daniel said, unaffected by her lack of hospitality. "I can understand your reluctance to accept free help. I guess I'd feel the same way in your place. How about if we work it another way?"

"What did you have in mind?" Rachel asked, eyeing him suspiciously.

Daniel licked his lips, choosing his words with care. What could it be about this woman that turned his usual assurance into self-doubt? And why did she want to be so all-fired difficult? He only wanted to help. "What if I work for you, just like I offered the other night, but you pay me for it?" He raised his hand when she opened her mouth to protest.

"What I'm thinking is that *after* the loan payment is made, you and I split any profit that's left. That way, you'd be assured of making the payment, and you'd know I was giving you my best so there'd be as much profit as possible for us to share." He pasted a confident grin on his face that didn't at all match the uncertainty he felt.

Rachel measured him with calm brown eyes that seemed to probe his innermost being, and Daniel's heart beat faster. Finally, she nodded.

"It's a deal," she said solemnly, extending her hand to seal the bargain. "After the loan is paid, we'll split what's left right down the middle."

Daniel started to object that he'd figured on giving her and Violet the bigger share but clamped his lips shut and took her hand. She had agreed to let him help; he wouldn't jeopardize that by quibbling over the split. Her grip was firm, but not at all masculine. As little as he trusted women, he felt that when this one gave her word, a person could take that to the bank.

"I'll see you in the morning," he told her and let himself out.

Rachel lay in her bed, looking up into the darkness. Had she done the right thing in striking a bargain with Daniel Moore? She truly believed God had shown her the way to save the farm by cutting out labor costs, but she now knew she and Violet could never do it alone.

Allowing Daniel to help should make it possible to save money like she'd planned, and paying him a percentage of what was left over would soothe her pride. There might not be much to divide between them, but that was a chance they would both take.

"You must have sent him, after all, Lord," she whispered into the night. "Thank You for giving me a second chance. And thank You for reminding me about the hay box. You really are leading me one step at a time . . . even if some of those steps cause me to fall flat on my face!" She chuckled and rolled onto her side, drifting off to sleep.

*　　*　　*

Rachel pulled the wagon to a stop behind Samson's General Store and smiled at Jake Samson when he came out the back door to help her unload. "Mornin', Rachel," he drawled, his genial face breaking into a mass of creases when he smiled. "What do you have today? I hope you brought more of those sweet carrots of yours."

"I have those, plus turnips, potatoes, and string beans." Rachel slid the sacks of vegetables down the wagon bed to Jake with a sense of satisfaction. Getting the harvest in on time might be a tricky proposition, but the vegetable business she and Pa had built up continued to flourish.

She pressed her lips together and took a deep breath. "I brought something else too," she said, trying to sound casual. "Would you be interested in some eggs?" She lifted the basket from its carefully padded resting place and held it out for Jake to see. The general store was her first stop today, and Jake had always been her favorite customer, but if he wasn't interested, she could always try the Prescott Mercantile and Grady's Market down the street.

Jake pursed his lips in a soundless whistle. "How'd you know folks have been clamoring for these?" He grinned and shook his head admiringly. "You're a shrewd one, all right, just like your pa. I'll pay you top dollar," he said, naming a price that took her breath away. "And I'll take every one you can bring, all right?"

Rachel finished her rounds in a happy daze. If the hens kept laying like they had been, she calculated the eggs alone would bring in enough to keep them going from day to day, leaving the vegetable money free to go into the loan fund. Raising three hundred dollars by the fifteenth of December still seemed an unattainable goal, but God had been faithful to meet their needs so far. Surely He would open other opportunities to keep the farm safe.

Elated by her newfound source of income, she treated herself to a small bag of lemon drops and had nearly reached the wagon when a rough hand grabbed her by the elbow. Whirling, Rachel found herself staring at a faded checkered shirt front. She tilted her head back and looked up into close-set blue eyes that regarded her coldly.

"Hiram Bradshaw, what on earth do you think you're doing? Let go of me this minute." She twisted her arm to escape his grasp, but he only tightened his grip.

"We need to talk," he told her and propelled her unceremoniously past the corner of the market and into an alleyway between two buildings.

More angry than frightened, Rachel spun around to face him. "Are you out of your mind?" she demanded, wrenching her arm free at last. She glared at him while massaging her elbow where his meaty fingers had dug in. "I have nothing to say to you. Nothing at all."

Hiram's beefy face turned a dull red. "You'll have plenty to say to me before I'm through with you," he rasped. He took a step toward Rachel, his massive bulk looming over her, filling the narrow confines of the alley. Rachel backed away, her nose wrinkling in distaste at the smell of stale liquor on his breath.

"I hear you're having problems coming up with the money you owe on your farm. Looks like your pa wasn't the slick operator everyone thought he was." Hiram's mouth twisted in a crooked grin. "It's a shame he left you girls in such a fix."

"You need to find a better informant. We're doing fine, just fine." Rachel glowered at him, daring him to disagree. Now that Daniel was helping them, they'd be able to make the payment with no problem. She edged away, intending to slip between Hiram and the board-and-batten wall, but he propped an arm against the building to block her escape. Rachel backed away, feeling the rough-cut wood behind her snag the fabric of her dress.

Hiram continued as though she hadn't spoken. "There's no way you and your sister will be able to come up with that kind of money." He leaned closer, his heavy breath stirring the loose wisps of hair at the sides of her face. "I'd like to help you out. I'll give you a thousand for the place, and you two can move to town. No more breaking your pretty little back doing all that heavy work. What do you say?"

"I say you're just one step above a common thief!" Rachel retorted, eyes flashing. "You know as well as I do our place is worth at least three times that."

"It's a thousand more than you'll get when the bank forecloses.

I'd hate to see you two sweet things out on the streets, penniless." He edged back, giving Rachel room to move again. "Think about it."

The cramped space barely gave her room to squeeze by him. She shrank back and slid past against the wall, preferring to risk a rip in her dress rather than any contact with Hiram. With his taunting voice echoing in her ears, she emerged from the alley and hurried to the wagon. "The nerve of that lout!" she fumed, heading the horses toward home.

Her earlier joy ebbed away, and an icy knot formed in her stomach. Was Hiram right? Could they really lose the farm? Despite his unappealing appearance and utter lack of manners, Hiram had a reputation as a canny businessman. If he honestly thought they wouldn't be able to raise the money in time . . .

"Nonsense! The man just wants to get his grubby hands on our land, and I won't let it happen." They had Daniel's help now, and they would be all right. The faint suspicions she first felt when he'd offered to work for them returned, gnawing at her, teasing her with questions. Why would he want to spend so much time helping them, especially when he had no guarantee of much, if any, income for all his efforts? Did he have some unspoken motive?

Rachel fretted over those questions all the way home and had worked herself into a foul mood by the time she reached the house. Molly met her on the porch, wrapping around her ankles with loud purrs. Rachel looked at the cat, looked again, and stomped inside.

"Violet!" she hollered, glad to be able to vent her pent-up frustration.

Violet appeared in her bedroom doorway, cuddling her furry patient. "Look how much he's improved. He'll be ready to be on his own again in a few—"

"What have you been giving Molly?"

Cut off in midsentence, Violet stared, her face a puzzled blank. "What do you mean?"

"Don't play the innocent. I can tell you've been slipping her extra food." Rachel swung the door open and pointed dramatically. "Look at her. She's positively fat!"

"But Rachel, I—"

"It better not be eggs again. We're going to need every last one of them to sell in town. I appreciate your tender heart, Violet, but you need to realize we're going to have to tighten up until this land payment is taken care of." She leaned forward, jabbing a finger in the air to emphasize each word. "We'll have everything we can do just to feed ourselves. We certainly can't waste food on the cat."

Instead of looking contrite, Violet took a combative stance and raised her chin. "I don't know what she's been eating, but it didn't come from me, not after the way you got after me last time. We've been clearing the cornfield; maybe she's catching extra mice." With that, she tucked the squirrel back into his box and stalked off toward the kitchen garden.

Rachel stared after her, unconvinced, although she knew Violet was not a devious person. She tilted her head and considered Molly, now washing herself with slow, deliberate strokes of her tongue. "Extra mice, is it? You must have found every mouse in this part of Yavapai County." Molly stopped her cleaning and regarded Rachel coolly, then walked away in the direction of the barn, tail held high.

"You too?" Rachel muttered. She leaned back against the doorjamb, then slid down until she was sitting with her arms wrapped around her knees. First her sister, then the cat. Was everyone going to turn away from her?

She stared at the solid outline of Granite Mountain and shook her head slowly. Honesty compelled her to admit that Violet had ample justification for leaving in a huff. Even though she had a soft spot for animals and spoiled them rotten, she had never lied to Rachel. There had been no earthly reason to upbraid her like that.

Rachel buried her head in her arms. This whole miserable situation had turned her into a cynical shrew, suspicious of everyone. Although, she reminded herself, some people positively invited suspicion. "Like Hiram," she grumbled. "I wouldn't trust him as far as I could throw him."

"Do you always sit around in doorways talking to yourself?"

Rachel sat up with a start, cracking the back of her head on the doorjamb. Daniel stood at the bottom of the porch steps, one corner of his mouth tugging upward. Rachel scrambled to her feet. Being on the porch while he stood on the ground gave her the advantage of height, and she scowled at him from her superior position.

"Do you always sneak up on people like that?" she countered waspishly. "Seems like every time you come around, I wind up banging into something." She touched the back of her head gingerly, wincing when her fingers made contact with the sore spot.

Daniel's half smile immediately disappeared. "Are you bleeding?" he asked with concern and mounted the porch steps. "Let me look."

"I can take care of myself just fine, thank you," Rachel snapped. "Now what was it you wanted, besides scaring me half to death?" She fixed him with a steely glare, and the hand he had raised toward her dropped back to his side.

"I just wanted to let you know I'm ready to take another wagon load of corn over to Fort Whipple," he said stiffly.

"Oh. That's fine. I'll see you when you get back." Rachel stepped off the porch and strode away briskly, silently raking herself over the coals. Daniel had come to help them of his own free will, for goodness' sake. How long could she expect him to stay if she jumped down his throat every time he turned around? Her steps faltered, and she realized she had no idea where she was headed.

To the garden? No, Violet had gone there to get away from her. The barn was out too—even the cat didn't want to be near her. Rachel sighed and turned toward the cornfield. Out there, at least, she could do something productive.

Daniel watched her walk away, easy grace in every stride. Why couldn't Ike have produced a quiet, easygoing daughter instead of this spitfire? On the other hand, a meek, docile woman wouldn't have the spirit needed to try to keep the place going. Rachel might be as prickly as the cactus that dotted the nearby hills, but he had to admit she wasn't afraid to get out and work hard. Most days she kept right up with him.

She didn't whine, either. He chuckled ruefully, remembering the way she'd lit into him, even though her head must have hurt like anything after that whack she gave it. He admired that kind of grit and determination, and she'd need every bit of it if she truly planned to make a go of this place.

He stared after Rachel's retreating figure, growing smaller in the distance. When he'd made the offer to help out, he wasn't sure whether she'd accept or throw him off the place. He was beginning to be glad she had taken him up on it. She might not be a delicate beauty like her sister, but she was one very intriguing woman, this Rachel Canfield.

*R*achel gave the clothes in the washtub a final stir, then straightened, pressing her fingers into the small of her back. She swiped at the dampness on her forehead with the back of her wrist and shook her head wearily. This time of year, a body expected crisp fall weather, not temperatures nearly as warm as summertime.

She rolled up her sleeves and set the washboard in place, preparing to give their clothes a good scrubbing. It galled her to lose the time she should be spending in the field to this chore, but it couldn't be helped. She ignored the laundry as long as she could, and the only relatively clean clothes she and Violet owned consisted of the ones they stood up in. Violet generously offered to do the wash, but they both knew she didn't have the stamina to carry out the strenuous chore. Rachel set her to mending instead.

No wonder Pa left the farm solely to Rachel. He knew that, try as she might, Violet would never have the staying power needed for the outdoor work. Even the heavier indoor chores sometimes taxed her delicate strength.

Over a year ago, Pa shared his misgivings with Rachel when she took him a cold drink in the field one midsummer morning. "I may have made a mistake bringing your sister out here," he'd said, rubbing his hand across his forehead the way he did when a decision faced him and he couldn't make up his mind. "The way things were back in Missouri, it seemed like the right thing to do."

He tilted his hat back and mopped his lined forehead, squinting at the cloudless summer sky. "Even with the war being over for more than a decade, folks still held so much hatred and bitterness in their hearts. Fellas would have come crowding around you girls one day, and I didn't like the looks of any I saw. Didn't know if I could trust a one of them. Out here," his gesture encompassed a region far broader than the farm they'd carved from the forest, "it didn't matter so much which side a man had fought on. Politics didn't amount to much. What counted was what he'd made of himself since then. I wanted you two to have a real choice when the time came. When the fever came and took your ma, I figured it was a good time to move on and make a new start."

Rachel nodded soberly, remembering the dark days of her mother's death. "You were right to do it, Pa." The words came out in a whisper. "Coming out here helped us all."

He flashed her a quick smile of gratitude before his face grew thoughtful again. "I'm not so sure about Violet. She's frail, like your mother. I should have seen that in her before we left home, I guess, but I thought she'd grow strong out here." He shook his head slowly. "When it comes time for her to think about a husband, we'll have to make sure she gets the right one. She's going to need a town man, Rachel. Violet isn't like you; she'll never make a farm wife." His eyes lit up again, and he looked at his older daughter with pride.

Rachel relived that moment, remembering how proud she'd been of his accolade. Looking around her now at the tub of clothes still awaiting her attention, the corn yet unharvested in the field, and the kitchen garden in need of weeding, her heart sank. What would he think now, to see the myriad chores still left undone? She closed her eyes, ready to admit defeat, then she raised her chin and squared her shoulders. Pa had believed in her. Somehow she'd find the strength to make a go of the place he'd worked so hard to build. She wouldn't let him down.

She reached for the washboard once more, then paused when she noticed the buggy out on the road. She puffed out an impatient sigh. With all the work ahead of her today, she just didn't have time for company. She watched the buggy, hoping it would pass by and continue on toward Jeb McCurdy's. Instead, it slowed and turned in to her place.

Rachel smoothed back the strands of hair that had fallen loose from her bun and pasted on a smile. Maybe she could get rid of whoever it was before they wasted too much of her time. With the sun in her eyes, she couldn't see more than just a silhouette stepping down and walking toward her. She shaded her eyes with her hand, and the smile froze on her face when she recognized Hiram Bradshaw.

"What are you doing out here?" she demanded, dropping all pretense at a cordial welcome.

Unabashed, Hiram strode toward her like he owned the place already, stopping only a foot away from where she stood. His bold gaze moved over her from head to toe and back again, and his knowing smirk made gooseflesh prickle all up and down Rachel's arms. If Daniel had been around, she would have hollered for him, pride or no pride, but he had left earlier to make another delivery to Fort Whipple.

With an uneasy glance toward the house, she considered her options. A cry of alarm would bring Violet outside in a hurry, but she couldn't bring herself to subject her gentle sister to Hiram's ugly leer. She would just have to brazen it out and get rid of the man as soon as she possibly could.

Hiram rocked back on his heels and regarded her thoughtfully. "You're looking right pretty today, Rachel. A trifle tired, maybe, but pretty, all the same."

Rachel stood her ground, determined not to give way before his insolent stare. She lifted her chin. "I asked you what you were doing here."

"Not very friendly today, are you?" Hiram's thin lips drew back in a grin. "I had some business out this way, so I decided to stop by and visit a bit." He studied the house and the outbuildings. "I'd forgotten just how nice a setup you have here. Old Ike knew how to do well for himself, and that's a fact."

"I don't have time for small talk," Rachel told him, trying to keep her voice steady. "I have chores to do, so if you'll excuse me . . ."

Hiram didn't take the hint. He stood squarely in front of the washtub, just where Rachel needed to be. She crossed her arms to give herself some measure of comfort. She could no more force herself to move that close to Hiram than she could pet a rattlesnake. Well, if he felt inclined to take up space there, she had a hundred other things to do. Without a word, she spun on her heel and set off in the direction of the barn with Hiram dogging her heels.

Rachel fumed and blinked back angry tears. He had no right to be there, none at all. If it hadn't been for his inflexible position on their loan, she and Violet wouldn't be working like slaves trying to bring the harvest in with only Daniel's help.

His presence only intensified the desperation that gnawed at her night and day. If she had the strength to throw the man off her property by brute force, she would. Failing that, she would just have to maintain her composure and wait until he tired of his game of cat and mouse and decided to leave.

Whatever she did, she mustn't show fear. That would only serve to fuel the flames of Hiram's bullying ways. A demeanor impervious to his provocative jibes was her only hope of protection.

In the barn, she forked hay to the milk cow, all the while keeping a wary eye on Hiram, who leaned against the center post, content to watch her work. Rachel couldn't help but compare his behavior with Daniel's. Daniel didn't try to stop her from working alongside him— *as if he could!* she told herself with a sniff—but he would never stand by and watch her labor alone.

A jumble of garden tools lay heaped in a corner near the wide door. Violet had neglected to return them to their proper places, she thought, pursing her lips in irritation. Not a surprising discovery, but definitely an annoyance. She bent to set the implements in some sort of order. Straightening up the hoes and shovels didn't rank very high on her growing list of things to do, but it did have the advantage of keeping her busy and able to ignore Hiram.

She picked up a three-pronged pitchfork. How did this one come to be in the pile with the tools from outside? It belonged up in the loft, ready to pitch hay down for the horses and cow. Rachel hefted it in one hand, hesitating at the thought of putting herself in a vulnerable position on the ladder or being cornered in the loft by Hiram.

Then she eyed the fork's sharp tines and grinned. She wouldn't be all that vulnerable. It would serve him right to be on the receiving end of the keen-edged points. She mounted the ladder rungs and climbed upward, almost hoping he'd try something.

Instead of pursuing her, Hiram began circling the interior of the barn, thumping the walls and trying to shake the uprights.

"Good and solid," he said with an approving smirk. "Nice to see it won't need much work."

Rachel clamped her lips together and resisted the impulse to fling the pitchfork straight at him. She could always say she'd dropped it. She clambered back down, picked up the egg basket, and strode out the door toward the chicken coop. Normally, Violet took charge of the chickens, but the chore gave Rachel the opportunity to keep occupied and keep moving . . . away from Hiram.

If only Daniel would come! He could set her free from her dilemma in short order. Her steps faltered when she realized the direction her thoughts had taken. When had she started looking to Daniel for protection? His only purpose in helping them was to repay the debt he felt he owed their father, nothing more. She couldn't get used to the idea of having him around for long. He'd be gone as soon as the harvest ended.

But the only reason she wanted him here today, her mind argued, was to get rid of Hiram. That didn't mean she wished to pursue a more personal relationship with him, just that it would be nice to have some masculine strength available when she needed it. The kind of protection she'd always taken for granted when Pa was around. She didn't need or want Daniel for anything more than that.

No point in dwelling on such thoughts in any case, she thought drearily. Daniel wouldn't be coming back any time soon.

"How's the harvest coming?"

Lost in her thoughts, Rachel started at the grating sound of Hiram's voice. "Fine," she snapped and resumed her brisk strides toward the chicken coop. "You can see for yourself." She nodded toward the cornfields off to her left where over half the crop had already been cut and delivered.

Much to her relief, Hiram stopped and stood gazing across the land. With a renewed sense of freedom, she hurried to the coop. She set the basket down and used an old can to scoop cracked corn into her gathered apron. The hens followed her to the end of the chicken yard, clucking in anticipation, then diving after the yellow morsels when she scattered them on the ground.

Rachel watched them bob their heads and peck at the kernels. "Eat hearty," she told them. "You need to get lots of food so you can lay lots of eggs. You're going to help me save the farm." She stood a moment, smiling at their awkward antics. How long had it been since she'd taken the time to do anything more than run from one chore to the next?

She shifted her gaze from the greedy birds to the hills around her. Their short-lived summer greenery had disappeared, to be replaced by the tawny tones of autumn. The fawn-colored grasses made a pleasing contrast with the muted green of the juniper trees. Rachel heaved a weary sigh. It seemed like ages since she'd had even a moment to appreciate the beauty of her surroundings, but she and Pa used to take time to enjoy the splendor of God's creation regularly.

She and Pa. The pain of his absence hit her afresh like the stab of a knife. They wouldn't share any more times of wonder together, at least not this side of heaven. She gave her apron a final shake and went back to collect her basket. She would collect the eggs while the hens were off the nest and occupied with their food. Surely seeing all that potential income and thinking of the promise of more to come would help boost her spirits.

It took a moment for her eyes to adjust to the dimness of the coop's interior. The comforting smells of earth and straw filled her nostrils, bringing a renewed sense of well-being. With her every waking moment spent trying to find ways to stretch their meager funds, she had almost forgotten how much she enjoyed working with the animals. Their easy contentment served as a lesson in taking life as it came and not fretting over what might lie ahead.

Once her eyes had adapted to the change in light, she scanned the nests and lifted the precious eggs into her basket one by one. Soft clucking sounds came from behind the corn bin, and she dropped to her knees to investigate. One of the hens huddled on a makeshift nest, watching Rachel with a baleful eye. Rachel clicked her tongue. Violet must have missed those eggs, and the biddy had decided to settle on the nest to hatch them.

Rachel reconsidered her initial indignation at the loss of income from those eggs. They had a steady supply now. It wouldn't hurt to have a new batch of hens coming up as replacement layers for the year ahead. She started to rise but stopped when she spotted an egg resting in a dark corner, then another. Finding every single egg could be something of a challenge, she admitted, reaching far beneath the roosts to extract the last one.

She wrinkled her nose at its dusty appearance. Evidently Violet had missed it too, and for quite some time by the looks of it. She set it gingerly atop the pile, planning to bury it before she took the rest of her booty into the house.

Grabbing the lid of the corn bin to help pull herself to her feet, she heard the door thump softly. "Thought I'd lost you." Hiram's voice came from directly behind her. She whirled, her heart pounding. How could she have forgotten his unwanted presence?

"Looks like you've been keeping right on top of things around here," he conceded. "Must be awful hard for a couple of women alone to deal with, though. You really need a man around here to keep the place going." He narrowed the gap between them to mere inches with one step.

Rachel felt her throat tighten. She tried to step back, but her shoulders collided with the wall. "It's time you left, Hiram," she said, trying not to let her alarm show in her voice.

"Remember the offer I made you the other day?" He leaned closer, as if she hadn't spoken. "I have another one." He lifted his hand and traced her jawline with a fleshy thumb.

Rachel shrank back against the rough boards, feeling the sharp splinters dig into her shoulder blades. With sickening clarity, she realized all too well the limitations of the coop's confined space.

Hiram's cold blue gaze bored into hers. He edged closer still. "You could keep the farm, Rachel . . . as my wife."

Her mouth fell open. "Your wi—" she began, but bile rose into her constricted throat, and she couldn't continue. Disgust and panic lent her strength, and she twisted sharply to one side. The move increased the distance between them but put Hiram between her and the door.

She tried to ignore the metallic taste in her mouth and ordered her heaving stomach to settle down. "Get out," she rasped, forcing each word through stiff lips. "This farm is not for sale . . . and neither am I." She took one step back, still clutching the egg basket.

5

*H*iram's hand flashed out and seized her arm in a pincer grip. Panic threatened to blind her. With a wild cry, she wrenched her arm free from Hiram's grasp, steadying the teetering basket. Her hand closed on the first egg she touched, and she hurled it at Hiram with all her strength.

The egg splattered across Hiram's face, and a putrid stench exploded through the coop. Rachel gagged and pulled the skirt of her apron over her nose and mouth. Through watering eyes, she could see Hiram bent double, raking at the slimy mess. Taking advantage of his distraction, she pushed past him and made her escape.

Away from the reek of the sulfurous fumes, she filled her lungs with sweet, clean air again and again. The door slammed open, and Hiram emerged, his face suffused with fury.

"You!" he snarled and started toward her.

"Not another step," she ordered. Of its own accord, her hand held up another egg, poised for throwing. She almost laughed out loud when Hiram froze in his tracks. "I told you you weren't welcome here. Maybe now you'll believe me. Now get!" She took several steps backward, then wheeled around and hurried toward the house, straining her ears to pick up any sound of pursuit.

"I'm going to enjoy seeing you hauled out of here kicking and screaming," he bellowed. "I'll be standing right here when they drag you and your sister off this farm. Have you thought about what you'll do to keep body and soul together when you lose the place? Life isn't easy for a woman alone. It isn't always kind, either. You remember that!"

Rachel reached the safety of the porch and let herself inside the house, closing the door on his angry threats. She eased back the edge of the curtain with her finger and watched Hiram stomp off to his buggy. With an angry crack of his whip, he lashed his horse and drove the buggy out onto the road to town.

And out of her life, she hoped, although she doubted her circumstances warranted such optimism. She leaned back against the door, fighting the urge to slide to the floor and bury her face in shaking hands. Hiram's rage had unsettled her more than she cared to admit.

Pitching the rotten egg at him had been the only way she knew to defend herself at the time, but it had also cut off any hope that Hiram might be swayed by pleas of leniency. If she couldn't raise the money for the loan payment in time, she knew he would show no mercy.

But she couldn't allow herself to dwell on that dismal prospect. Sinking into a mire of such gloomy thoughts would only send her spirits spiraling into despair. Wallowing in melancholy might be tempting, but it wouldn't get the work done. With a groan, she pushed herself upright and walked toward the kitchen, where she could hear the clanking of pots and pans. Violet must be starting supper.

Her sister looked up when she stopped in the doorway. "Was that Hiram Bradshaw?" she asked. "What got him all stirred up?" Her nose wrinkled, and her eyes grew round. "Rachel, what on earth is that awful stench? You didn't run into a skunk, did you?" Her gaze dropped to Rachel's hands and her lips formed an *O*. "Did you get hold of a bad egg?"

Rachel glanced down and saw she still held the basket. A basket only half full. She had lost more than the one she threw at Hiram in her dash for freedom.

Violet's forehead crinkled in concern. "You didn't have to do my chores, Rachel. I meant to tend to the chickens right after I fixed us something to eat."

"It's all right. I didn't think you'd neglected them. I just needed something to do right then, so I took care of them for you." She turned and hurried to her room before Violet could ask why she'd needed something more to occupy her on an already busy day. Violet didn't need to know the details of Hiram's visit . . . or hear any hint of his proposal.

In the privacy of her room, Rachel filled the bathtub with water she'd intended for the laundry, glad she didn't have to wait for it to heat. She started to unbutton her dress, then stopped in dismay. Until she finished the wash, she didn't have another clean garment to her name. What on earth could she do? All Violet's dresses soaked in the tub along with her own, and they were at least two sizes too small for her, anyway.

She tiptoed out to the cupboard where some of Pa's clothes were still kept. Silly, she guessed, but she hadn't had the heart to dispose of all of them yet. She pulled a shirt and a pair of overalls from a drawer and eyed them doubtfully. They would have to do, she decided. She only needed to wear them until her own clothes were clean and dry once more. Surely there wouldn't be any more visitors today.

With her mind made up, she carried them back to her room, pulled off her dress and underthings, and stepped into the tub.

Rachel closed her eyes, savoring the warmth of the steaming water. She reached for the soap and began to scrub, wishing she could scour away the memory of Hiram's nearness as easily as the smell of rotten egg. She pulled a strand of hair loose and sniffed. *Phew!* She would have to wash it too.

Even after her skin glowed pink and her hair hung over her shoulders in a damp cascade, Rachel stayed in the tub, longing to close her eyes again and relax just a few moments. It took all the force of will she possessed to get to her feet and begin toweling herself dry. Chores still awaited her, piled up even higher now that she'd lost so much time due to Hiram's visit and its aftermath. She squeezed the water out of her hair and thought bleakly of the days ahead.

Would the work ever ease up? She spent every waking moment tending to some aspect of the farm, whether working in the field or the garden, delivering vegetables and eggs to town, or totting up the latest figures in her ledger.

Even in her sleep, the constant worry never completely left her. More than once, she had awakened with a start after a series of nightmares. The worst one returned to haunt her again and again. In it, she and Violet stood on the porch in the dim light of a cold, gray dawn. Each of them held a small bag containing two dresses and a nightshirt. All their other belongings, even the photographs of Ma and Pa, had to stay behind. Weeping piteously, the girls clutched one another, knowing they were about to leave their home, never to return.

A grim-faced sheriff stood at the foot of the porch steps, ready to remove them by force if need be. Even their most heartrending appeals failed to move him. He never changed expression, only pointed toward the road with an unyielding arm. Feeling as though she were stepping off the edge of an abyss, Rachel put her arm around Violet's shoulders and led her off the porch. At the same moment, snow began to fall, huge flakes that tumbled from the sky and blotted out the distant landscape.

Blinking to see through the heavy flurry, Rachel could make out only one object: Hiram Bradshaw stood at the edge of their property, thumbs hooked behind his belt, and his mouth wide open in a triumphant laugh.

At that point she would sit bolt upright, chest heaving and covered with droplets of sweat despite the chill of the autumn night. Smoothing out the tangled sheets and blotting the tears from her face brought back some sense of normalcy, but she found it took longer each time to convince herself the unnerving experience had only been a dream.

Then there were the household duties. Using the hay box had freed both her and Violet from having to spend hours over the stove, but the remaining kitchen chores demanded attention, all the same. Violet took care of most of those as well as tending to the animals, but her gentle, dreamy sister was too easily diverted by any distraction that happened to catch her attention to always keep her mind on the task at hand. Thus, Rachel had to add keeping tabs on Violet to her other responsibilities.

She pulled Pa's shirt on over her head and stepped into the overalls, feeling burdened beyond her ability to cope. His clothes hung on her, and she leaned over to roll up the legs. Her fingers traced over a spot she'd mended for him just last spring. When Pa was alive, they'd worked plenty hard, but they still found time at the end of the day to visit and share with one another. Time to discuss the day's events, to reminisce about the past and plan for the future. Rachel worked her brush through the wet tangles in her hair and felt the hot sting of tears behind her eyelids.

What would she and Violet do if she didn't come up with the cash they needed by December 15? Hiram's dark allusions to the possible fate of penniless young women alone in the world haunted her. She had heard enough about other destitute girls forced to earn their keep in the saloons along Whiskey Row to know there was some truth to his assertions. Bad enough to think about letting Pa down by losing the farm; how could she bear it if she put Violet in peril of some hideous fate?

The sun moved further along its circuit through the sky, and still Rachel sat on the edge of her bed, staring into the prospects of a dismal future. How could they have reached such desperate straits in so short a time?

All she had ever wanted was to help Pa on the farm and someday to marry a hardworking farmer like him. Never had she faced the prospect of having to contemplate a different sort of existence. Farm life was all she cared about, all she ever wanted. She bent over and covered her face with her hands. Pa had admonished her about her stubborn streak more than' once. Had she been so bent on following her own desires that she had never considered the possibility that God might have something quite different in mind for her?

A new thought struck her with the force of a blow. Just how much did staying here mean to her? Would she ever be so desperate to cling to her beloved farm that she'd entertain the notion of accepting Hiram's offer, or one like it? She shuddered, not knowing whether she felt more repulsed by his contemptible proposition or herself for giving the idea even a fleeting consideration. She would find some way to keep body and soul together without compromising their honor. She had to.

She started to pull back her damp hair, then shrugged and decided to leave it hanging loose. With all the work still left to be done before dark, she couldn't spare even the few seconds it would take to twist it into a bun. Besides, it would dry more quickly that way. She picked up her reeking dress and carried it out her door at arm's length, so intent on getting back to her washing that she nearly crashed into Violet.

"Rachel, have you seen Molly?"

"Not lately," she said, debating whether to heat fresh water or use what she already had. She didn't know how clean the clothes would be if she didn't take the time to reheat it, but maybe soaking as long as they had already would be enough. She stepped onto the porch and glanced at the sun. The water they'd been sitting in would have to suffice, she decided. She just didn't have enough time to start over.

Violet touched her arm. "Rachel?"

"At least they'll be cleaner than they were, and that's a mercy."

"Rachel!" Violet's urgent tone finally claimed her attention.

"What is it?" she demanded.

Violet's lower lip quivered at the brusque question, but she continued. "I said I can't find Molly anywhere. Could you help me look?"

Giving her sister an exasperated glance, Rachel went down the steps and reached into the tepid water, grabbing the first garment her hands touched. She set the washboard into position and scrubbed the dress back and forth across its rough ridges.

Violet followed and took a challenging stance, hands on her hips. "You could at least answer me. I'm worried about her."

"I don't have time," Rachel replied, nettled by the new interruption. "With everything else that needs to be done, I really can't get too worked up about a cat." She clenched her teeth together before she could say more, not wanting to snap at her sister.

"She's not just any cat. She's Molly! I thought you cared about her." Violet whirled and went out to resume her search, but not before Rachel noted the crystal droplets shimmering on her lashes. She sighed in annoyance. How could Violet be concerned over something so foolish when real problems stared them in the face?

She worked her way through the clothes, fuming about her sister's behavior. If Violet would pay more attention to her responsibilities and spend less time fretting about nonsensical things like missing cats, maybe Rachel wouldn't have to shoulder the burden of their predicament alone.

Looking down at the water running from her elbows to the legs of Pa's overalls, a grimace of wry amusement twisted her lips. At least one good thing had come out of Violet's preoccupation with the cat's whereabouts. She'd been so worked up about Molly that she hadn't even noticed Rachel's unusual garb.

6

aniel shifted on the wagon seat and tipped his hat brim down to shield his eyes from the sun. He hadn't planned on getting back this late, but the long conversation over coffee in the supply sergeant's quarters had been a profitable one.

The sergeant's usually cheerful demeanor had been shadowed by worry over the low supply of fodder for the cavalry horses. When Daniel casually mentioned the enormous pile of cornstalks back at the farm, the soldier slapped his hand on the table and pledged to buy them all.

The extra money would be a welcome addition to their income. It had been time well spent.

Once he'd taken care of the horses, he'd be more than ready to tuck into a hot meal. He chuckled, wondering what Rachel and Violet had decided to fix for supper. He'd eaten better since he started working on the Canfield place than he had in months. No doubt about it, baching had its disadvantages, and one of them was having to put up with his own cooking.

The horses swung into the turnoff of their own accord and plodded toward the barn. Daniel squinted into the sun, trying to make out the forms in front of the house. A lone figure bent over the washtub. Daniel frowned. Rachel had told him she planned to use the day for household chores, but he would have thought the wash would have been finished long before this.

Had she hired someone to come in and help? He didn't recognize the overall-clad fellow. Wait. He slitted his eyes and stared in disbelief. A man with long brown hair? He blinked and took a second look, then let out a hearty guffaw when he identified the stranger as Rachel.

She raised her head and glared at him. Daniel wiped the smile from his face. What other woman did he know who would wear such outrageous garb? But then, he never quite knew what to expect from Rachel Canfield. She could work as hard outdoors as a man and still fix some of the lightest biscuits he'd ever tasted. The woman was a surprising blend of grit and femininity, and all the more captivating for her unpredictability.

"Looks like your pa's shirt fits you better than it did me," he said, unable to resist the urge to tease her. A rosy blush crept from below the shirt collar to tint her face and neck.

"It's about time you got back," she snapped. "What did you do, decide to take the long way home?"

Daniel only grinned. With that tinge of pink staining her cheeks and her hair hanging loose to her waist, she looked like a petulant little girl, but he wasn't about to tell her so. In her present testy mood, she'd probably heave a bucket of that wash water all over him.

"I got some good news at the fort," he told her, outlining his deal to sell cornstalks to the soldiers. "It will mean a few more trips over there, but it'll be more than worth it."

"Oh." Rachel's expression softened a trifle. She twisted the apron she held to wring out the rinse water and marched up the steps to hang it over the porch railing.

Daniel watched her hair swing behind her, his gaze following its rippling motion in fascination. *Almost looks like a mountain waterfall.* He'd seen shady forest pools just that color of oak-leaf brown.

He caught himself up with a start. Where had those thoughts come from? Calling himself all kinds of a fool, he clicked his tongue at the horses and urged them toward the barn once more.

Rachel shook out another of Violet's dresses and hung it up to dry. With such a late start, the clothes would probably have to stay out all night. She kept on draping the rest of the laundry over the porch rail and the rope Pa had strung at one side of the house, one part of her mind on the job at hand, the other intent on watching the barn door.

Funny how things never turned out quite the way you'd expect. She should have been mortified when Daniel came upon her wearing

Pa's clothes. But instead of being shocked, he'd sounded amused, and much to Rachel's surprise, his teasing comment had put her at ease.

Daniel's look had been nothing like Hiram's. She'd seen nothing improper in his gaze, only acceptance of an unexpected situation. Pa would have done much the same thing, she thought, a small smile curving her lips. He wouldn't have questioned why she had chosen such an outlandish getup, only assumed that she must have had a good reason.

It felt good to have that kind of unquestioning approval again. She hadn't realized just how much she'd missed it. Some of her weariness lifted, and her shoulders straightened as though a physical weight had been lifted.

Daniel emerged from the barn and started to swing the heavy doors closed. Good. If he'd agree to take over feeding the animals and shutting them up for the night, her chores could be finished before supper. Her smile faded when she saw Violet approach Daniel, laying a pleading hand on his arm.

Violet and her cat! Fortunately, Daniel understood the need to ignore such foolishness and focus on important matters. Her mouth fell open when he patted Violet on the shoulder and set off with her, apparently in search of Molly.

Rachel gritted her teeth. This was too much. She would have to take Violet to task about it later, after Daniel left. So much for any expectation of his help. She flung the last garment across the line and prepared to finish the chores herself.

Daniel walked into the barn just as she climbed down from the loft after forking down the last ration of hay for the day. "About ready for supper?" he asked.

"Did you find Molly?" she asked in a tone that rivaled a November frost.

"No. Violet's plenty worried about her too."

Rachel whirled on him. "Maybe Violet should try worrying about keeping this place going, instead of wasting her time on a fool cat. I could use more help around here."

"Whoa." Daniel held up his hand and regarded her thoughtfully. "Who are you really talking about here, Violet or me?"

Rachel drew in deep gulps of air. She knew if she opened her mouth again she couldn't control the tremor in her voice, knew she felt her frustration so keenly she might not be able to stop the flow of angry words once she got started. She pressed her lips together, but they tumbled out in spite of her efforts.

"How could you run off and spend the time on a fool's errand like that when there's so much work to be done? Violet should have better sense than to ask you to do something so trifling when you were late getting back in the first place . . . and you should have known better than to indulge her like that."

Daniel's sandy eyebrows drew together. "Have you looked at your sister lately? Really looked at her? She's hurting, Rachel. Remember, she lost her father too. Maybe she needs a bit more babying than she's been getting. Frankly, I'm a lot more concerned about Violet than the cat."

The truth of his words hit home like an arrow finding its mark. Rachel braced her feet and lifted her chin to keep him from seeing how his accusation had staggered her. "You'd better wash up," she told him through stiff lips. "It's time for supper."

He stared at his feet a moment, then lifted his gaze to meet hers. "Not tonight. I'll be heading on home. I have some chores of my own to do, and I don't want to be late in the morning."

He turned on his heel and left. Rachel stood rooted to the spot until he had ridden out and disappeared down the road. Even with both hands clamped across her mouth, she was unable to stifle the whimper that rose in her throat. How much would her stubborn pride cost her before she learned to control her tongue?

How could anyone so outwardly appealing manage to turn into a snarling wildcat at the least provocation? Daniel turned the question over in his mind on the way back to his diggings. The new source of income he'd discovered that day meant financial help not only for this season but for the years ahead. The Canfields' situation had taken a major turn for the better, yet Rachel seemed bent on finding something to raise a fuss about, no matter how much their outlook improved.

And what about that business of him being late? If he hadn't spent the extra time with the supply sergeant, he never would have learned of their need for stalks that would have otherwise gone to waste. It just went to show you could never tell about women. The way he felt right now, he'd be happy if he never saw Miss Rachel Canfield again. Still, there was his debt to Ike, and he didn't take his obligations lightly.

7

*A*fter a night's sleep, Daniel looked on the previous day's encounter from a new perspective. He'd been so elated by his business deal, then so troubled about Violet that he had failed to take into consideration the extreme pressure Rachel was under.

He knew how the nearing deadline weighed upon her, but instead of easing her burden, he had only added to it. Remorse for his short-sightedness gnawed at him. Hadn't he seen grown men snap with little more provocation than Rachel had experienced over the past months? She needed some relief and needed it fast.

Daniel mulled over the possibilities while he grabbed a quick breakfast and went about his morning chores. Washing up his dishes took only a few moments, and he didn't have much else to do around his temporary dwelling. Rachel had never inquired where he lived, and he wasn't about to tell her he'd thrown together this little hut just up the road from them in a matter of days once she agreed to let him stay and help out. Knowing her reluctance to accept his aid in the first place, he could just imagine what her reaction to that would have been.

There had to be some way to lighten the millstone around Rachel's neck, he thought while tossing a worn quilt over his cot. He couldn't guarantee it, but it looked to him like she should have enough to pay her debt to the bank on time. Rachel wouldn't rest, though, until she held the money in her hand.

He hung the washed pot back over the cold fire and prepared to leave for the day, chuckling at his quickly erected shelter. If Rachel got a glimpse of it, she would never believe he'd taken enough from his mining claim over the past two years to build up a sizable nest egg. More than enough to pay off her loan, in fact.

Why not do just that? He mounted his horse and set off, excitement rising in him at the thought. He could give Rachel the full amount, let her pay him off without a fixed deadline, and she could settle up with him whenever she had the funds to do so. It would solve everything. He tried to picture Rachel's reaction when he sprang the idea on her, and his enthusiasm crumbled into dust.

He knew full well what her reaction to such a gesture would be. Rachel, with her stubborn pride, would work until she dropped rather than take on another loan.

Scowling, he refused to admit his idea had run into a dead end. True, Rachel had a feisty, independent nature, but she was a hard worker, honest, and fiercely loyal. The type of woman a man could trust, if such a creature existed. Somehow Daniel knew he'd want to help Rachel out of this fix, even if he'd never met Ike Canfield.

He turned his horse into the corral and carried his tack into the barn. A flash of color caught his attention, and he spied Violet poking around in the dark recesses of an empty stall.

"Hasn't Molly turned up yet?"

The young girl turned at the sound of his voice, giving him the full effect of her startlingly blue eyes. With that lustrous dark hair and her heart-shaped face, she'd be downright beautiful one of these days, he thought. Rachel would have her hands full trying to keep hopeful suitors at bay once they noticed her.

"I don't know where else to look," she said. Her eyes brimmed with tears. "I can't find her anywhere. Do you think something's happened to her?"

A lot of things could have happened, but Daniel wasn't going to tell her that. Not right now, at least. Life in Arizona Territory wasn't easy for rugged men, let alone a small animal like Molly. She could easily have been picked off by an owl, or fallen prey to a pack of coyotes, or met one of any number of brutal ends. "Hard to say," he told her and left it at that.

Her frail shoulders slumped. "I guess I'd better get back to my chores. Rachel said she'll get me if she catches me lolly-gagging again."

Daniel stared after her. Something about Violet brought out a protective streak he hadn't known he possessed. *Would having a little sister or a daughter be anything like this?* He scoffed at his fancy, wondering where that errant thought had come from.

Turning to hang up his bridle, he stopped in midstride when a thought gripped him. When he first showed up with his offer of help, Rachel had turned him down flat. Not until he balanced out the proposition by adding some benefit to himself had she been willing to consent. He now faced the same sort of situation. Rachel would never accept an outright advance of money, but what if he made one modification to his bargain? What if he asked Rachel to marry him?

The more he thought about it, the more enthusiastic he became. He would present the plan as honestly as he knew how, letting Rachel know right up front that he offered it as a business proposition rather than a romantic proposal. She valued straight talk; she would appreciate his forthrightness.

He went over the advantages so they'd be straight in his mind when he talked to her. With him on the scene, Rachel would never need to worry again about having to run the farm on her own. And as his wife, she should have no objection to him making the land payment for her. For himself, he'd once again have a place to belong after years on his own and someone to talk to after a long day's work. Meeting Violet's needs as well would be almost like having a daughter, and with him around, he thought with a chuckle, Rachel would have much-needed help in dealing with her sister's would-be beaus.

Daniel slapped his hands on his knees, delighted with his plan. As a practical solution for them both, he didn't see how anyone could improve on it. He would be giving up some of his independence, true, but during the times the farm work slacked off he would still be able to spend time at his mining claim. Plenty of other men did that, and they got along just fine, so marriage shouldn't cramp his freedom too much.

Sometimes life called for a man to make a noble gesture for a good cause, and he felt pleased to be able to rise to the occasion. Now he only had to present the scheme to Rachel. He went off toward the cornfield, rehearsing what he would say in his mind to make sure he had the words right when he approached her.

Rachel shook the dirt from the bunch of carrots in her hand and stuffed them into her gunnysack. She could see Daniel swinging the corn knife, its blade flashing in the sun. *Thank goodness.* After yesterday's blowup, she couldn't have blamed him if he'd decided never to come around again.

She sat back on her heels and watched him wrap a length of twine around another shock. As far as she could see, he was putting as much energy into his work as ever, maybe even more. How nice to know he didn't hold a grudge!

She had prayed for forgiveness for her attitude the night before and made her peace with Violet over breakfast. She would have to make amends with Daniel at the first opportunity. After all, she had asked the Lord for help, and He'd sent it. She couldn't expect Him to shower her with further blessings if she didn't show appreciation for what He'd already given.

Some of her tension dropped away, and her mouth curved in a small smile. Daniel knew how to work hard, almost as if he loved the land as much as she did.

When the sun reached its zenith, she hurried back to the house to clean up before Daniel came in for lunch. She wanted to be presentable when she made her apology. To her surprise, he had already finished washing up before she arrived.

His freshly washed hands and face and slicked-back hair told her he'd taken some pains with his appearance. She hesitated, wondering if she should speak to him in her present grubby state, then decided to hurry to her room for a few quick moments with her washbasin and hairbrush. Then she would have the confidence to face him.

"Just a minute," Daniel called when she started to step through the doorway. "I'd like to talk to you, if you don't mind."

Rachel looked down at her dusty clothes and made a wry face. Did the Lord want to give her a lesson in humility as well as gratitude? "All right," she sighed.

Daniel led her a short distance away from the house. "I'd rather Violet didn't overhear us," he explained.

That suited Rachel. Admitting she'd been wrong didn't come easily for her. She would just as soon have no witnesses. She looked at Daniel, enjoying the way the sunlight glinted in his hair. His deep green eyes held only sincerity, and their frank expression twisted at her heart. The man had offered his aid to two strangers in their time of need. He had shown them nothing but decency and a willingness to help. How on earth could she have spoken to him the way she did?

"I needed to talk to you too," she began.

"All right. Just hear me out first," Daniel put in.

Rachel felt a twinge of impatience. Wasn't it just like a man to insist on getting his word in first when she was trying to apologize? "What I have to say won't take long."

"Neither will this."

"But listen—"

"I think we ought to get married."

Rachel froze, aware that her mouth hung wide open but powerless to do anything about it. Time seemed to stand still. She looked at Daniel as through a haze, saw his face alight with expectancy, and knew she ought to make some sort of response. "You—what?" she croaked.

"I know it's a bit sudden," Daniel began, "but when you think about it, it makes perfect sense."

Rachel stood motionless, waiting for him to explain how it could possibly make any sense at all.

"You've been knocking yourself out to keep things going and get the money you need to pay off the bank," he said. "You're working hard. Too hard. I have an idea that can help both of us. If you marry me, I can make the payment for you, and you can keep the farm."

Rachel's eyes narrowed. "You said it would help us both. What do you get out of it?"

Daniel stuck his hands in his pants pockets and swallowed. "Plenty. A home and a family and—"

"And my father's farm!" she shouted, hot tears spilling over to course down her cheeks. Decent and sincere she'd thought him. Had there never been an honorable man in the world save her father?

Daniel spread his hands, a look of bewilderment crossing his face. "Well, sure, I'd work the farm—"

"Leave me alone!" She bolted into the house, running past Violet to the sanctuary of her room and slamming the door behind her.

Lying across her bed, she let the tears flow unchecked. "Why?" she groaned aloud. "I thought he was different." All her earlier suspicions rose up to taunt her. Why hadn't she paid more attention to her initial misgivings? She had let Daniel sweet talk her, working hard and seeming trustworthy enough to make her think he only wanted to help. He had put on a good act, but it didn't make any difference now. No matter how upright Daniel had appeared, all the while he had only been out to get her land.

Rachel pushed herself to a sitting position, propping her elbows on her knees, and cradling her head in her hands. She should have known better. She could be honest in assessing her looks . . . or lack of them. Violet had turned out to be the beauty of the family. Rachel was the sturdy one.

She felt no shame in that; physical strength helped her get the work done. But she knew beyond a doubt she didn't possess the kind of allure that would make men flock after her. Certainly not enough to garner two proposals in as many days. Not for herself alone, at least.

To think she had felt chagrin at the way she had treated Daniel. Rachel writhed in mortification. What a fool she had been! What made her think she knew anything about men? Never mind. After Hiram's clumsy bid for her hand the day before and now this evidence of Daniel's perfidy, she now knew plenty about their scheming ways.

But he could have helped her save the farm. The thought teased at the corners of her mind and refused to go away. She rolled onto her side and curled her knees up under her chin. Had she made the worst blunder of her life in turning him down? In her heart, she knew marriage to be a sacred thing and not to be entered into lightly. But didn't love sometimes come later? Had she just bungled the one chance she and Violet might have to keep their home? Had her stubbornness and high ideals cost them everything?

"Rachel?" Violet's worried voice penetrated her awareness.

"Coming." She splashed water from her washbasin onto her face and blotted it dry. Violet didn't know about Hiram's proposal; maybe she wouldn't need to find out about Daniel's. If she hadn't acted like such a ninny, flying through the house that way, Violet wouldn't have had reason to suspect anything was wrong.

She opened the door, prepared to bluff it out. "Is lunch ready?" She tried to make her voice sound casual.

"Yes, but . . ." Violet paused. "I think something's wrong with Daniel. He saddled up and left without saying a word."

Rachel avoided her gaze. "He must have had some business to attend to."

"He didn't say anything about it earlier. And Rachel? He looked angry. Do you think he's coming back?"

"We'll just have to see, won't we?" Rachel sat down at the table and waited for Violet to join her before she asked the blessing.

Would Daniel return? Could she bring in the rest of the harvest alone if he didn't? Rachel pondered her dilemma while she ate. There wasn't much left to do, she assured herself. She could manage if she had to. She swallowed a spoonful of the soup Violet had made but tasted only the bitterness of Daniel's traitorous act.

Why should his leaving them to fend for themselves disappoint her so? She should feel glad his true motive had been revealed. What did it matter to her if he was no different than Hiram? The thought turned her stomach, and she left the rest of the soup uneaten.

8

*R*achel pulled her scarf close around her neck and pressed the tines of her digging fork into the garden soil. Giving the end of the handle a quick shove downward levered the tines back up, bringing a tangle of potatoes with them. She bent to knock off the dirt, then dropped them in her gunnysack and blew on her fingers to warm them.

The only thing certain about early fall weather in northern Arizona Territory, she thought wearily, was its unpredictability. Earlier that week she had enjoyed the warmth of the sun through her calico dress. Today, a biting wind stung her nose and fingers. She scanned the overcast sky, hoping the change in the wind didn't portend an early snowfall.

It had been two days since Daniel left. Two long, grueling days that made her doubt that she did have the stamina to make it through to the end of harvest. The warmth of the fireside tempted her, but this year above all years, she dared not leave one potato or carrot in the ground, one stalk of corn standing in the field. She shivered and bent to her task again, wondering which was harder to bear: the summer heat or autumn chill.

Violet had been pressed into resuming more of the simpler outdoor chores, leaving Rachel free to do the heavier work. After two days of silence, it seemed clear that Daniel had no intention of returning, and they simply couldn't fall behind. *Good riddance,* Rachel told herself, wishing her heart would join her head in celebrating his departure. He had shown his true colors at last, proving her instincts to be right all along. His absence shouldn't hurt so much.

She would get over it, she vowed, and be stronger for the experience. Next time she would trust her intuition and keep her distance from offers that sounded too good to be true. She couldn't risk losing her heart again, only to have it trampled underfoot another time.

With a sigh, she shouldered the digging fork and set off toward the barn, dragging the heavy sack behind her. Men like Hiram Bradshaw and Daniel Moore didn't merit the sorrow they caused. She used the back of her hand to dash away the tears that spilled from her eyes; she couldn't do a thing about the lump that clogged her throat.

Rachel dropped the sack inside the barn and gazed around the interior impatiently. Violet had been sent out earlier to tend to the milk cow, but the agitated lowing coming from the stall let Rachel know the animal hadn't been fed yet. And her sister was nowhere to be seen.

Probably off somewhere woolgathering, Rachel thought bitterly. Generally, she found Violet's dreamy nature entertaining, but seeing chores go neglected under the present circumstances made her fume.

"Psst." The soft hiss seemed to float out of the air over Rachel's head. She looked up to see Violet peering down from the hayloft.

"What are you doing up there?" Rachel demanded. If this was another of her sister's fanciful games . . .

"Shh. Not so loud. Come up here."

"Can't you come down?" Rachel softened her tone in spite of herself.

"Come on up, Rachel. Please."

She let out an irritated sigh. "Oh, very well." Why did she let Violet talk her into these things? She heaved herself over the edge of the loft and glared at her sister. "What now?"

Violet sat next to a mound of loose hay, watching a wriggling mound of fur with a rapt expression. "Look at them, Rachel. Aren't they precious?"

Rachel stepped closer and saw Molly stretched out on her side, licking a tiny kitten with maternal pride. Her shoulders sagged.

"There are eight of them," Violet whispered, oblivious to Rachel's weary posture. She reached out to stroke the nearest kit with one finger. "No wonder I couldn't find her; she'd gone off looking for the best place to have them. Isn't it exciting?" When Rachel didn't respond, she looked up. Her face clouded over when she saw her older sister's lack of enthusiasm.

"You're angry because I haven't fed yet, aren't you? I'm sorry, Rachel. I'll get to it in just a few minutes, really I will. I came up here to throw some hay down and found Molly, and . . . I guess I just got caught up in the excitement of it all. Please don't be mad."

Her plaintive tone cut straight to Rachel's heart. Daniel had been right about one thing: Violet had experienced loss too. No matter that Rachel now had eight more lives depending on her. How could she begrudge Violet this little bit of joy when their world had been turned upside down?

With an effort, she forced a smile. "I'm not mad, Honey. Just see to your chores before it gets too late, all right?" Violet's look of gratitude dispelled some of her gloom but didn't relieve her of her responsibilities. She descended the ladder and picked up the corn knife, feeling like she carried the weight of the world on her slim shoulders, and no one seemed to care, except to add to it.

All through cutting and stacking the stalks of corn, Rachel wrestled with the ache of loneliness. Even if they could get over this hump and hire some help next year, would she be able to go on shouldering the full load of responsibility?

How she longed for someone to share the burden with. Someone who could help her bear it. Violet loved her dearly, but they didn't have anything like the same kind of partnership she'd had with Pa. Not like she'd hoped to share with a husband someday.

A heavy knot settled in the pit of her stomach. After what she'd been through in the past week, thoughts of matrimony ought to be the farthest thing from her mind. But her wayward thoughts had a will of their own, and images of Daniel flashed through her mind like scenes from a magic-lantern show. Daniel, with his strong arms hefting a load of firewood as easily as she could pick up Molly. The broad back muscles rippling under the taut fabric of his shirt. The concern in his eyes when she'd struck her head against the door frame.

What would it be like if he had proposed for the right reasons? She dismissed the thought as quickly as it came, berating her traitorous heart for daring to harbor such thoughts.

She propped the shock she'd just tied upright, secured the barn for the night, and made her way to the house, hoping she'd be able to stay awake long enough to eat and undress before she tumbled into bed.

9

aniel rode onto the Canfield property just after daybreak, his mouth set in a determined line. How many ways could a man manage to make a fool of himself? He seemed bent on trying to figure them all out. If it hadn't been bad enough to insult Rachel with his bright idea of marriage, skedaddling like a scolded pup only made him look like a bigger idiot.

In the three days since his hasty departure, he'd had plenty of time to sort things out. At first, he'd headed straight for his claim, aiming to use his newfound time to catch up on all the work he'd let slide while helping Ike's daughters. He'd aired out his roomy cabin and set about repairing a leak in the flume to his sluice box. Try as he might, though, he couldn't escape the memory of Rachel's face. She'd looked tired, so tired, and he hadn't even given her a chance to freshen up before he launched into his brilliant plan.

She'd wiped the dampness from her brow, and her hand had left a streak of dirt across her forehead that showed when she lifted her face to his. He remembered that and the way her clear brown eyes had clouded over when he made his inept attempt at solving her dilemma.

" 'I think we should get married.' " The arrogance of the blunt statement made him squirm with embarrassment. Had he really thought her so desperate she'd jump at any lifeline thrown her way? What a way to spring a life-changing idea on a woman! Even coming as a strictly businesslike proposal, he should have given her some warning of what he intended to say.

These thoughts and more had eaten at him so over the past three days that the time he should have spent digging out a new pile of ore had been taken up with self-recrimination. As clearly as if she stood before him now, he could see the confusion written on her countenance, followed closely by disbelief, then anger. And he had put them there. As if she hadn't had enough to contend with, losing her pa, then working like a mule to make good on her loan payment.

She deserved a helping hand, and he had only added to her heartache.

Time alone with the Lord had given him a good opportunity to see his mistakes all too clearly. He'd learned something else during his absence. He missed Rachel. Missed her a lot, and that wasn't something he'd ever expected. Respect had turned into something far more tender, filtering into the background of his thoughts without him being aware of it.

His lack of experience in dealing with the fairer sex had never been more evident than when he spouted out his clever plan without ever thinking how it might sound to Rachel. If he had it to do all over again . . . but wishing wouldn't change a thing.

His biggest worry now—the one that drove away his appetite and kept him awake at night—was whether his colossal blunder had ruined any chance of ever regaining Rachel's trust. At this point, he hardly dared to hope for more.

Daniel unsaddled his horse and turned the gelding into the corral. Had he missed his one opportunity for happiness? He couldn't blame Rachel a bit if she never wanted to set eyes on him again. In her place, he'd probably want to pull that Henry rifle down from the wall and run him off the farm. On the other hand, the harvest still needed to be brought in.

A slow smile spread across his face. He liked having a strong bargaining point. She had to let him stay long enough to see it through. He wanted her to know that he followed through on his promises. Had she thought him a quitter the day he'd ridden off in a huff? The idea made him choke. It hadn't been like him to let his wounded feelings take over and goad him into deserting the sisters when they needed him.

Well, he was back to stay . . . at least until the harvest had ended.

After that, only the good Lord knew, and Daniel had been bombarding heaven with pleas for divine direction.

His practiced eye scanned the fields, assessing what had been done in his absence. Rachel had been busy, he noted. She must have cleared another two acres. But then, had he expected anything less? She had shown him time and time again that she knew the meaning of hard work. The thought of her having to tackle it alone because he'd gone off to lick his wounds strengthened his resolve to stay. He would pitch in and finish the job, whether Rachel liked the idea or not.

"Daniel!" Violet ran down the porch steps and hurried to meet him. "Where have you been? We missed you."

"I had to check on some things back at my claim," he told her, flinching at the half truth. "But I'm back now and rarin' to go. I need to make up for lost time."

"Come to the barn with me," she said, tugging on his sleeve. "I want to show you what Molly's been up to."

"Found her, did you?" He smiled and followed her into the shadowy interior. Violet, at least, didn't mind his coming back. He began to relax a fraction.

Rachel heard Violet's glad cry and pulled back the kitchen curtain. She saw her sister fly down the porch steps and run across the yard in the early morning gloom. Even in the dim light, Rachel recognized Daniel's form at first glance.

Violet pulled at his arm, then led him into the barn. "Those kittens!" Rachel muttered. Her sister was besotted with them. Daniel didn't put up much protest, but why should she expect him to? Violet, with her captivating personality, could persuade almost anyone to whatever she wanted.

Rachel twitched the curtain back again in time to see the two of them emerge from the barn, laughing and talking animatedly. Daniel had lost the set look she'd seen on his face the last time they talked. Or rather, the last time she'd shouted at him. A pang of remorse smote her at the memory. Today he seemed to be at ease, more like himself. At least one of the Canfield sisters knew how to treat a person decently, she thought moodily.

She started to drop the curtain but caught sight of her reflection in the window glass and paused to stare at her image. A solemn face framed by light brown hair returned her gaze. Nutmeg-colored eyes looked back at her with sad awareness.

Rachel turned impatiently and went back to kneading biscuits. No wonder she only received proposals when they were motivated by greed. Why would anyone take a second look at her with a beauty like Violet around? Violet, with her vivid blue eyes and glossy hair the color of an otter's sleek coat, would capture any man's attention . . . and his heart.

Rachel knew she possessed pluck and determination, important traits for survival in this rugged land and things her pa had valued. But strength didn't attract suitors. Violet would always be the belle of the family; Rachel would fill her role as the one born to the land. She might just as well accept that.

Daniel's mind churned while he started shocking corn. It struck him as odd that he could know Rachel's strength of character so well and still have so little insight into the way her mind worked. If only there were some way to understand the way she thought.

Over by the barn, Violet set out a pan of milk for Molly. A smile touched Daniel's lips, remembering her excitement at showing off the cat and her new family. An idea started out like a wisp of smoke, then took shape in his mind.

Who knew Rachel better than her sister? He'd always found Violet easy to talk to; maybe he should cultivate their friendship more diligently. A few well-placed questions ought to put him on the road to making some headway with Rachel.

Understanding her was essential to the success of his newly formed plan. He fully intended to propose to Rachel again. And this time he wouldn't be offering her a marriage of convenience.

10

*T*he *clop clop* of the horses' hooves beat a steady rhythm on the hard-packed road, playing a counterpoint to the squeak of the wagon wheels. Rachel swayed in the wagon seat, her eyes drifting closed, then open again. The horses knew the way home and didn't need her constant attention, she reminded herself, gathering the reins in her fist.

She braced her feet against the foot board, then rested her forearms on her knees and allowed her eyelids to fall once more. She'd catch a few minutes' rest before she got back to the farm and resumed the endless cycle of cutting and tying the cornstalks into bundles.

Her shoulders sagged, and her head nodded in time with the wagon's rocking progress, but a tiny smile lifted the corners of her lips. Despite her weariness, the knowledge they'd made significant progress in recent days gave her reason to rejoice.

Just an hour ago, she had sold the last of the garden vegetables to Jake Samson. Earlier that week, Daniel had added fodder to the items they could sell to Fort Whipple. Tonight, if she could stay awake long enough, she'd enter the latest sales figures in her ledger and see how much farther she had to go to reach her goal.

Rachel dozed, rousing only when the horses slowed their pace at the turnoff to her property. She transferred the heavy reins to the other hand, flexing her stiff fingers and rubbing the sleep from her bleary eyes. As soon as she unhitched the horses and put the harness away, she could start clearing the old potato vines off the garden plot.

She rolled her head from side to side to stretch the complaining muscles in her neck. If Violet had remembered to prepare supper instead of getting sidetracked by some flight of fancy, she could look forward to a hot meal in an hour or so. If only she could hold out that long, there would be a brief respite from her labor.

But the next day would come, and the next day, and the next, each bringing with it an interminable list of jobs to be done. Rachel groaned aloud. Her former hopes for a break once the harvest was in had evaporated when she realized that in bending all her efforts to the task at hand, she had let any number of other chores go undone.

Firewood needed to be cut. The fields and garden needed to be plowed. Food set aside for their own use had to be put up for the winter. All these tasks still waited for someone to do them. Waited for her.

Would there ever again be a time when she could relax for more than a moment? A time to sit and plan and dream? The enormity of the job she had undertaken overwhelmed her. If she ever got caught up, perhaps she could sit and rest for awhile. Maybe until spring, when the ground thawed and the fields and garden were ready for planting. Maybe forever. Once she sat down in the rocker in front of the fire, she might never want to get up again.

At the barn, she pulled off the collars and traces and turned the horses out into the corral, envying their freedom at having the rest of the day to themselves. She hung up the heavy harness and headed for the kitchen garden.

On her way, she glanced toward the house, wondering what Violet had decided to cook. A stew would be nice, she decided. A stew rich with savory broth and fluffy biscuits on the side. She looked off toward the edge of the cornfield where Daniel worked to repair the deer fence and blinked. Her steps slowed while she tried to focus her tired eyes, unwilling to believe what she saw.

Two figures, not one, stood at the fence line. Daniel leaned against a post and appeared to be listening intently while the second person spoke and fluttered her hands in lively gestures. Rachel's eyes narrowed. She recognized the coat the other person wore. Violet. When she finished talking, Daniel threw back his head and laughed, then squeezed her shoulder. Violet gave him a playful swat on the arm in return and ran back to the house.

Rachel stood motionless so long she thought she might take root, then forced her unwilling feet to move and resumed her walk to the garden, her emotions in turmoil. Didn't she spend every waking hour working herself into the ground? How could these two take time to indulge in chitchat when the sun still shone and work cried out to be done? She just hoped Violet hadn't let their supper scorch. That would be the final straw.

This wasn't the first time she had seen them together. More than once she'd spotted Violet tagging along behind Daniel when she had business of her own to attend to. Her frustration mounted until she thought she would explode. Didn't either of them care about the looming deadline? Didn't they care about her?

She couldn't expect Daniel to worry about anything but his debt to her father. After all, that was the reason he had come to them in the first place. Even after his proposal . . . but she wouldn't think about that. Violet, though, ought to show some concern for what Rachel was enduring, especially since she did it not only for the two of them but for their father's memory.

A tight knot of despair formed in her chest, growing until it threatened to choke her. All the while she gathered up the withered vines, bitter thoughts ate at her spirit like an acid. By the time she walked back to the barn to put her tools away, she knew she had to resolve her angry feelings or burst.

Perhaps she misread the scene she had witnessed earlier. Maybe Violet had a legitimate reason for going to the field. She would go to the house prepared to give them both the benefit of the doubt. But if she discovered her earlier assumptions had been correct . . .

Lamplight streamed from the windows by the time she mounted the porch steps. Through the kitchen door came the sounds of light-hearted laughter. Rachel clenched her teeth, reminding herself not to jump to conclusions, and pushed open the door.

Daniel leaned against the far wall, watching Violet pull a custard pie from the oven. "If that tastes as good as it smells, it'll melt in your mouth." He smiled. "But you probably put in salt instead of sugar or threw the eggshells in the pie by mistake."

"Ooh!" Violet set the pie on the windowsill to cool and threw the dish towel she'd used to pull it from the oven at Daniel in mock outrage. "You just sit down and mind your manners. If you behave yourself during supper, I *might* let you have a piece." She turned to Rachel as if noticing her presence for the first time. "Have a seat. I'm ready to dish it up."

Rachel went to her room to wash, then settled into her chair at the end of the table. Violet set a steaming plate before her. The meal she had so anticipated slid down her throat unnoticed while she eyed her sister and Daniel.

"Not bad." Daniel patted his mouth with his napkin. "Even if I do hate to admit it."

Violet wrinkled her nose at him, then turned to Rachel. "Are you all right?" she asked, concern tingeing her voice. "You're awfully quiet."

"I'm fine," Rachel told her. "Just a little tired." *Like you two would be if you'd been working as hard as I have.*

Violet threw her a hurt look. "You didn't even say anything about the chicken and dumplings. It's your favorite."

Rachel glanced down at her plate. Was that what she'd eaten? She had been so busy watching the two of them, she hadn't even noticed. A twinge of guilt pricked her conscience. How could she stand in judgment of their behavior when her own had been so thoughtless?

"I'm sorry. It's delicious." She took another bite, just to be sure. It *did* taste good. What a pity she had been so absorbed with her resentful thoughts that she had missed this wonderful meal.

"I agree." Daniel eyed the plate on the windowsill hungrily. "Now, that pie may be a whole different story. . . ."

Violet narrowed her eyes at him. "If you're so sure it's going to taste awful, I'd hate to inflict any of it on you."

Daniel held up his hands. "Chivalry demands that I taste it first to protect you ladies from possible discomfort."

Violet sniffed but cut a slice of pie for each of them. Despite his teasing, Rachel noticed that Daniel received the biggest of the lot.

After pronouncing the pie an unexpected success, Daniel moved to the chair he had claimed as his own and leaned back contentedly.

"I'll be there in a minute," Violet called. "Just as soon as I clean the kitchen." She looked at Rachel. "Didn't you say you were going to tote up the ledger tonight?"

Rachel hesitated, torn between the desire to know exactly where they stood financially and her body's cry for rest. The need for sleep won out. "Not tonight," she told her sister. The total wouldn't change overnight, but she wouldn't be able to function tomorrow if she didn't get to bed.

Her exhaustion notwithstanding, sleep eluded her. Moonlight washed through her window, casting strange shadows on the wall. She stared at the ceiling, thinking over the events that had so upset her. Had she overreacted to a friendly conversation? In her fatigued condition, it was possible; she had to admit that. Maybe she'd been wrought up over nothing.

"Let all bitterness, and wrath, and anger, and clamour, and evil speaking, be put away from you, with all malice." She could hear the words of the verse as clearly as when Pa had read them by the fireside. Had the seeds of bitterness sprouted and taken root in her heart? *Lord, I'm sorry. It's just so hard. Please forgive me and help me not to fall prey to the snare of the enemy.*

Her eyelids fluttered closed, then snapped open again when a new thought struck her. What if the byplay she had seen indicated not a lack of concern for herself but a burgeoning interest in Violet? She sat bolt upright in bed, her heart pounding.

The idea unnerved her, and she swung her legs over the side of the bed, wide awake now. What had she seen that put that notion in her head? Pressing her fingers to her temples, she reviewed the events of the last few days.

Just how many times had she seen similar behavior and written it off to Daniel's patience with Violet's constant pestering? Going over the last week in her mind, she realized there had been other instances like that. Why hadn't she paid more attention to it before now?

Alarm welled up inside her, and she rose to pace the room. She shivered when her bare feet met the cold wood floor, but she paid it no mind. Her thoughts tumbled over one another in rapid succession. Could it be possible? Did Daniel feel an attraction to Violet?

Or was it the farm that held his interest? "If at first you don't succeed, is that what you're thinking, Daniel Moore?" If that were the case, she would make sure he never succeeded, no matter how hard he tried. She would have a long talk with Violet, tell her about Daniel's attempt to gain control of the farm through his earlier proposal. She would make her see she couldn't get involved with him.

Violet had never had a suitor. With her innocent, trusting nature, she would be easy prey for any unscrupulous cad who showered her with attention. But Rachel wouldn't let it happen. If that was what Daniel Moore had in mind, he could think again.

She climbed back into bed and pulled the covers over her, shivering in earnest now that her thoughts had slowed and she realized how cold she felt. Her mind whirled with imagined scenes in which she broke the news to Violet.

It wouldn't be easy. Violet had gotten used to having Daniel around. His presence helped to fill the void in her life left by her father's passing. Rachel closed her eyes, planning how she would phrase her speech. She would have to be understanding yet firm, gentle but uncompromising.

And somehow she would have to do it without alienating Daniel. She realized full well what a tricky situation she faced. Not only did she have to save the farm, she had to save her sister as well. And the man she had to save her sister from was the only one who could help her save the farm.

Rachel groaned, feeling as though she were about to try to pick her way along a path riddled with pitfalls.

Since Daniel's arrival, Violet had seemed happier than she'd been in ages. How could she impart such shattering news without crushing her fragile spirit? It would be hard to convince her of Daniel's perfidy when he appeared so relaxed and content in her presence, not stilted as he'd been with Rachel lately. A picture of their easy camaraderie earlier that night floated through her memory. Daniel's friendly banter showed he felt right at home.

A new, unsettling notion flashed into her mind. What if Daniel truly cared for Violet? Could this be the best possible way for things to work out . . . for Violet, at least? That proposition added a new dimension to her dilemma and robbed her of the possibility of getting any sleep that night.

*D*aniel let himself into the shack he now called home and struck a match to light the lantern. He shucked off his clothes and climbed into his cot. *It's been a good day, Lord. Thank You for all the work I got done and for everything I learned from Violet.*

He blew out the light and smiled into the darkness. Taking Violet into his confidence had been one of his better ideas. He'd feared her reaction at first, but her delight at helping him win Rachel matched his own at discovering her willingness to lend a hand.

She would make a good partner. Her enthusiasm for their joint effort heartened him, made him feel that finding a place in Rachel's heart wouldn't turn out to be the unattainable goal he had feared.

He couldn't tell just when it had happened and sure couldn't explain why. Letting down his guard and allowing a woman to get under his skin went against his grain, but he knew the truth in his heart: Somehow, God had determined that Rachel Canfield would be his. And if he had learned one thing, it was not to turn down a gift, no matter how unexpected, from the Almighty.

With a peaceful sigh, he rolled over and went to sleep.

"You should have seen Molly carrying her babies down to the manger, one at a time. Maybe after two weeks with them up in the loft, she just wanted a change of scenery, do you think?" Violet lifted the tiny gray kitten from her lap and held him to her cheek. "Aren't they darling?"

Daniel unhooked the claws of its feisty black-and-white brother from his vest. The little animal batted his hand with its paw and hissed.

"Darling. Right." He grinned and tapped a forefinger on the kitten's nose. It leaped down off his lap, offended, and tottered off to find its mother.

Daniel leaned back against the manger and watched Violet play with the litter until one by one they wobbled away in search of their supper.

The last kitten scampered off to join its littermates. "Look at the way Molly takes care of them," Violet said. "There's something special about the relationship between a mother and her young, isn't there?"

Daniel's peaceful mood ebbed away in a flash. He merely grunted a response.

Violet shot a questioning look at him. "What's wrong? You look like someone just hit you over the head."

His stomach bunched into a knot, and he willed it to relax. He'd never talked to anyone about this before and didn't know why he'd chosen Violet as his confidante, but the time seemed right. He stretched out one leg and hooked an arm around the other knee. "Maybe my ma should have been more like Molly," he began, long-suppressed memories teasing at the fringes of his mind.

"I don't ever remember getting a lot of comfort from her. Plenty of that, though," he said when Molly swiped a paw at one of the kittens, sending it head over heels. He forced a chuckle and avoided Violet's curious gaze. "Seemed like none of us older kids ever did anything that suited her." He toyed with a sliver of wood hanging from the manger. "She took off with a two-bit gambler when I was thirteen."

"How awful for you!" Violet's eyes grew round with compassion. "What kind of mother would go off and leave her children?"

Daniel shrugged. "Hard to figure. She took my younger brother with her but left me and my older sister there with Pa." He swallowed hard, trying to banish the remembered pain of the past.

"And you never saw her again?" Violet's tremulous voice called him back to the present.

He shook his head, remembering the hard times that followed. "Pa started drinking pretty heavy after that. Sis was four years older than me, and she jumped at the first chance to get married. She told me I could come live with her, but that didn't last long. I'd only been with them for a few months when she decided she didn't need an extra mouth to feed and booted me out."

Violet gaped at him. "How old were you then?"

"Nearly fifteen. I decided it was time to see what I could make of myself. It turned out I was good with horses and made a fair teamster. I found work with a freighter hauling goods to Santa Fe and just kept working my way west." He broke the sliver into two pieces, then four. "And that's how I wound up with a mining claim next to your father's." He tossed the fragments of wood in the air, trying to lighten both the mood and his load of memories.

"No wonder it's hard for you to trust women."

Daniel froze. Violet's quiet statement drove the breath out of him as effectively as a punch to the stomach. She regarded him with solemn eyes. He opened his mouth to contradict her, but the words wouldn't come. How could someone so young cut straight through to a truth he'd tried to hide, even from himself?

Violet leaned over and laid a gentle hand on his arm. "Rachel isn't like that, you know," she said, coming straight to the point once again.

One look at her told him there was no point in trying to sidestep the issue with this girl. He patted her hand. "I know." A relieved smile spread across his face, and he felt the wall he'd built around himself begin to crumble. "I know."

From across the yard, Rachel watched the exchange, trying to get a grip on her tumultuous feelings.

Who would have imagined Daniel playing with a bunch of kittens? Not her. She'd seen him only as a heaven-sent solution to their problem, then a land-hungry scoundrel, then the man who'd decided to pursue her sister. If she wanted to be truthful, she'd also seen him in a far more tender light, but she wasn't about to go into that now.

She crossed her arms and continued to observe them. Daniel spoke at some length, a succession of emotions playing over his face. Then Violet placed her hand on his arm and gazed into his eyes. Rachel almost choked when Daniel clasped Violet's hand in return. She pivoted on her heel and stormed off.

A very pretty scene, she thought, trying to throw off the guilt she felt at spying on something not intended for her eyes. *Very sweet and tender.*

Almost as tender as her own feelings. She stopped short, waving a hand in front of her face as though by doing so she could sweep away the sensations that raged within her. She had to stop this emotional tumult, the overpowering feelings of . . .

Jealousy? Toward *Violet?* The unexpected revelation staggered her, and she fought to catch her breath. It couldn't be. She felt concern about her sister's well-being. She only had Violet's best interests at heart. Didn't she?

Shocked to the core at finding herself capable of such feelings toward her beloved sister, Rachel stumbled to the house and fled to her room. Chores could wait. The need to bring her bewildered state of mind before the Lord consumed her. Her relationship with Violet—and with the Lord—was more important even than the farm. She fell to her knees beside her bed.

Hands clasped and head bowed, she remained motionless for some time. The dreadful discovery had dredged up emotions so hateful, so ugly, she felt unable to voice them, even to her Savior.

"Father," she finally began in a faltering voice, "what is wrong with me? I thought I had done with thoughts of Daniel. I *shouldn't* think of him that way when I know he doesn't care for me." She drew a shuddering breath. "How can I—love Daniel," she uttered her admission with wonder and a tinge of shame, "when he's falling in love with Violet?" She covered her face with her hands, rendered speechless by her raw emotions.

"I love Violet, and I don't want to love Daniel. I don't want to—I *can't* be jealous of their feelings for each other. Oh, Father, help me!"

She cried out to heaven with inarticulate sobs wrung from the depths of her innermost being. Throughout the tumult, a still, small voice whispered one word to her spirit: *Surrender.* With a mighty effort of will, she forced out the words, "Lord, I give my feelings about Daniel to You. Help me to want what's truly best for Violet . . . no matter what it costs me." The act of submission, of relinquishing her will to whatever her Father might ask of her, brought the awareness of victory, and with it, peace.

She pulled her tear-soaked hands from her face, wiping them on the hem of her dress, then blotting her face with her apron. She kept to her room long after she would normally have been finished with her chores, knowing she didn't dare let Daniel or Violet see her swollen eyes and blotchy face.

The calm in her spirit assured her she had done the right thing. She just hoped she would be able to stay the course.

Daniel swung the axe high above his head, then brought it down with a loud *thunk* on the round of oak. He mopped his brow with his shirtsleeve. Nothing like splitting wood to work up a sweat, even at the end of October. Watching the mound of firewood grow filled him with satisfaction and pride.

He surveyed the pile of wood he'd already stacked in orderly rows. It would be enough to get the Canfield sisters through the next month or so, in his estimation. They'd need several cords more to see them through the winter. Daniel grinned. Plenty of reason for him to stick around awhile longer.

After that, he needed to hitch up the plow and turn the fields under before the ground froze solid. And after that, there would be plenty of other things a man could turn his hand to. He chuckled. Even with the crop finally harvested and delivered to market, there would be work enough to keep him there for months. He'd make sure of that, even if he had to create more jobs.

In his book, Violet deserved a prize for wisdom beyond her years. "Don't you dare leave once the crop is in," she'd admonished him, her eyes sparkling with excitement. "Spend as much time here as you can. If you're always around, she can't help but take notice of you."

Sound advice, he'd thought, and it seemed to be having an effect. He had noticed a definite softening in Rachel's attitude toward him over the past couple of weeks. If time would further his cause, he could stick it out however long it took.

He fetched the crosscut saw from its peg in the barn and set off to drop some more trees.

*R*achel took special pains to compliment Violet on her supper of venison and potatoes. Once the dishes had been cleared away, she sat at the table and spread open her ledger. Before she wrote down the first number, she closed her eyes and sent up a quick prayer. It had been some time since she'd last totaled up the figures. Surely after all their hard work, she must be near the three hundred dollar goal.

She opened her eyes and set pen to paper, copying the notes she'd jotted on scraps of paper to remind her how much she'd brought in and for what. The column of figures grew.

Daniel sat in his favorite chair, feeding an occasional stick of wood to the fire. Violet, curled up on the hearth rug, snuggled three kittens on her lap. Rachel envied the cozy domestic scene and wished she could be more a part of it. Suppressing a sigh of longing, she rubbed her eyes with her thumb and forefinger and returned to her list of numbers.

Violet handed Daniel their father's Bible with a wistful smile. "Would you mind? Pa used to read from it in the evenings. I miss it."

Another thing she'd failed to keep up with. Rachel fought off the whispers of guilt and strained to hear Daniel's voice read from God's Word. For several moments, silence reigned, broken only by the sounds of her pen moving down the column in her ledger and Daniel flipping through the well-worn pages.

At last he cleared his throat. " 'Therefore I say unto you, Take no thought for your life, what ye shall eat; neither for the body, what ye shall put on. The life is more than meat, and the body is more than raiment.' "

He paused a moment, then went on. " 'Consider the ravens; for they neither sow nor reap, which neither have storehouse nor barn, and God feedeth them; how much more are ye better than the fowls?' "

Rachel's heart rejoiced at the comforting words. Being reminded that God really did care for her renewed confidence that He would come to their aid.

" 'Your Father knoweth that ye have need of these things.' "

She jotted down the last figure, then went back to the top of the column and began adding. Her brow knitted, and her stomach tightened into a knot. Two hundred and thirty-seven dollars. How could that be? She went back again, marking each subtotal on a separate piece of paper to be sure she hadn't made an error in addition.

She hadn't. She stared at the inadequate total. It still came out to two hundred and thirty-seven dollars. Rachel dropped her pen to the table and cradled her forehead in her hands. With the income from their hard-won harvest, the vegetables, and the eggs, they still fell far short of the amount they needed.

It didn't seem possible, yet the figures didn't lie. They had worked like troopers and done their best. And even so, the goal eluded them. Now they had no prospect of anything to sell save eggs and only six weeks to go until they reached the fateful time limit. Despite her best efforts, she had failed.

A soft moan escaped her lips. Would she and Violet really be turned out into the world alone and penniless, and in the middle of winter? She rose and made her way to join the others and sank into her rocking chair. Right now, she only felt numb. How long would that blessed numbness last before bitter reality set in?

She pressed her lips together to mask her distress. Both Daniel and Violet had their laps full of kittens. The little four-week-old balls of fur cavorted in wild abandon.

Violet laughed, enchanted by their antics, and Daniel smiled indulgently. "Try this," Violet said, reaching into the sewing box for two lengths of yarn. She handed one to Daniel and kept the other for herself. They dangled the strands above the kittens' heads, chortling when the little animals leaped at their targets.

Rachel rocked steadily, trying to distance her emotions from the happy group. She couldn't afford to become attached to Molly's babies. They might grow to depend on her, and she would only let them down too.

"Do you want to hold one?"

Rachel glanced down to see Violet offering her a gray-and-white kitten. "No." She saw Violet's look of disappointment and forced a smile. "I think I'll just sit and rock for a bit."

Violet nodded and resumed her game. Daniel set his little playmates on the floor, then stood and stretched. "Time for me to leave," he said. "We've all put in a good day's work. I'll see you in the morning."

Rachel only nodded and let Violet see him out and pull the latch string in for the night. She watched her sister stow the kittens with their mother in the dynamite box, formerly the home of the injured squirrel, and stoke the fire.

"Coming to bed?" Violet inquired, reaching to turn down the wick on the last lamp.

Rachel shook her head. "Go ahead. I'll be along after awhile." She listened to the sound of Violet's footsteps going to her room and heard the door close. Minutes later, the faint rustle of her mattress carried down the hall. Then the streak of light under her sister's door vanished, leaving Rachel alone with her thoughts.

The kittens ate their fill and settled down for the night after mewing and fidgeting a bit. She rocked and watched the fire burn down, a thousand thoughts tumbling through her mind. What could she have done differently? Could she have worked harder, accomplished more? She shook her head, despair seeping into every fiber of her being. She had done all she could, but she hadn't raised enough to meet the loan amount, let alone pay Daniel for all his labor.

One kitten, as wakeful as she, stood on his sleeping siblings and clawed his way to the top of the box. Hanging precariously from its edge, he teetered a moment, then dropped to the floor. The kitten crouched and looked about warily, then began exploring his surroundings.

"Better not," Rachel said and scooped up the little mite. She bent to return him to his bed, then paused and sat back in her chair, settling the tiny creature in her lap.

"Can't you sleep, either?" She traced the length of his body with her index finger and was rewarded by a soft purr. The kitten looked at her with unblinking eyes.

Rachel resumed her stroking. "What's keeping you awake, young fellow? You don't have a load of problems weighing you down." She ruffled his silky fur. "It's a good thing your food is taken care of by your mother, you know. You and your brothers and sisters may be the only ones around here who'll be eating before long."

The truth of her words struck home, and she swallowed hard. "It's hopeless." She forced the words past the unshed tears that clogged her throat. "Absolutely hopeless."

One tear, then another traced a slow trail down her cheeks. Folding her arms across her stomach, she leaned over and wept, the tears flowing freely. The kitten patted at her face with his velvet paw.

"I'd better put you back before you get soaked," Rachel sniffled. She returned the kitten to his bed, where he immediately curled into a ball and closed his eyes, the picture of contentment.

Rachel watched his even breathing, her shoulders slumped with fatigue. All well and good for the cats and Violet to slumber peacefully. They could rest without worrying about what tomorrow might bring, as in the passage Daniel had read. They didn't carry the responsibility of meeting anyone's needs like she did.

She had to go on, but how? And how could she rely on God to provide when He hadn't supplied the money they needed?

What had gone wrong? She remembered a time when she felt as carefree as the kittens, trusting in her pa to meet all her needs. Now she was the one who had to provide, and she knew her inadequacy for the task. She caught her breath in a ragged sob. It seemed she had all of life's heartaches and none of its joys.

Icy wind whipped through the pines and stung Daniel's face. He hunched his shoulders inside his sheepskin coat, glad for its protection against the elements. November in the mountains didn't show compassion to anyone.

He passed through the valley of Lynx Creek. Only a few more miles to go. Then he could get inside his cabin and build a fire to warm himself before he ventured outside again.

After all the weeks of endless labor, it went against the grain to take a couple of days off to check things on his mining claim, but he had to do it. If he didn't keep showing significant improvements, he couldn't prove up on it, and he'd ignored it far too long already. All the same, taking the time to do something strictly for himself struck him as self-indulgent.

The look on Rachel's face when he told her about his plans let him know she shared his thoughts. That surprised expression of hurt, quickly replaced by a mask of indifference, told him she wanted to protest, but her pride wouldn't let her.

Daniel knew he had no reason to feel guilty. He tallied up the work he'd done. Fifty acres of land had already been turned under, and split wood lay stacked in neat piles, enough to last them through the next three months. He'd worked hard, he reminded himself, and planned to work even harder.

He just needed to take this day to make sure of his claim. The gold he'd taken from the waters of the creek had provided him with a tidy income, most of which he'd managed to save by virtue of frugal living. If things went as he hoped, a steady yield would assume even greater importance . . . if he could persuade Rachel to marry him.

Had he made any progress toward that goal? At times he thought he detected a tenderness in her attitude toward him, but he couldn't be sure. Even ever-optimistic Violet didn't know what to make of her sister's frequent changes in mood.

He knew Rachel hadn't expected him to stay on once they'd completed the harvest, but she hadn't voiced any objection yet. He listed the jobs he'd outlined for himself. When he had cut enough wood for this winter, he'd start on next year's supply. Another thirty acres remained to be plowed and prepared for spring. Maybe he would have won Rachel's heart by then.

Failing that, he'd already made note of a number of things around the house and barn that needed maintenance and repair, things that Ike would have busied himself doing throughout the winter months.

Rachel, though, might not have the time or the skills to take care of them. He had plenty of time to wear down her resistance, he assured himself smugly.

He topped a rise and looked down across the swale. Buckbrush and manzanita dotted the slope. In the spring, the whole meadow would be filled with lupine and Indian paintbrush. The scene never failed to fill him with a sense of wonder. The familiar feelings took hold now as he wended his way down through the trees. He glanced downstream. Abner and Seth Watson would be loading their sluice box, despite the bitter weather. He'd stop by their place first and see if they had any news to share.

Daniel pulled his gelding to a stop in front of the log-and-canvas shack, a crease forming between his eyebrows when he saw the sluice box sitting empty and no sign of activity. Normally, the two would have been hard at work since dawn. He scanned the area, a prickle of apprehension raising the hairs on the back of his neck.

It just didn't look right. Something had happened, he felt sure of it, but what? Unwilling to dismount and make himself vulnerable, he urged his horse forward and investigated more thoroughly. The only tracks he saw appeared to be days old and nothing gave any indication of foul play. Still, he couldn't shake the feeling that something had gone wrong.

"Abner?" he called softly. "Seth?"

Bushes rustled behind him, and he jerked his horse around, grabbing for his pistol.

"Daniel? That you?" Branches parted, and Abner Watson emerged from the brush, followed by his brother. Both looked as though they'd been holed up for days without sleep. "Man, I'm sure glad to see you and not some painted Yavapai warrior."

Daniel stiffened. "What are you talking about?"

Abner bit off a chew of tobacco and rolled it in his cheek. "Apaches. We've been sitting tight for three days now, ever since Bill Stevens rode over to tell us they were running wild. Don't know whether they'll head this way or not, but a body can't be too careful."

Daniel's eyes widened. "I can't believe they'd risk taking on Colonel Kautz."

Abner nodded and spat into the bushes. "Surprised us too. We didn't expect any trouble, leastways not until spring. Kautz and his troops went off on some foray to the east, though, and this bunch of renegades decided to stir up trouble while they were gone. They've been going after some of the farms and ranches. Raided Zeke Johnson's place over near the Dells, Bill said."

Daniel thought sure his heart had dropped into his stomach. Its wild beating the next instant assured him it hadn't. He dug his spurs into the gelding's ribs and headed him back the way they had come.

"Ain't you going to check your claim before you go running off?" Abner's voice faded away behind him.

The claim would have to take care of itself. Getting back to Rachel was the important thing.

13

Two hours later, he pulled his lathered horse to a stop in the Canfield yard. Rachel and Violet huddled over the washtub, scrubbing clothes vigorously.

Daniel turned his horse into the corral without bothering to unsaddle him and cupped his hands around his mouth. "Get to the house!" They looked at him, startled, and Rachel raised both hands in question. "*Now!*" he roared. His tone and actions would brook no argument, and they hurried to obey, dropping their laundry to the ground.

Daniel raced up the porch steps and slammed the door, dropping the heavy bar into place.

"What's this about?" Rachel bent double, panting after her headlong dash.

"Indians. What do you have in the way of guns besides the Henry? And where do you keep the ammunition?" He watched her lips form an *O* and saw Violet turn pale and press her hand to her chest. Given other circumstances, he would have broken the news more gently, but today he didn't have time to mince words.

Rachel didn't waste time asking questions but hurried to produce a shotgun and two pistols, along with boxes of shells. She lined them up on the table. "How long do we have, and what do you want us to do?"

Daniel felt a surge of pride at her matter-of-fact response. He couldn't spare a moment to tell her now, but when all of this was over . . .

"I'll take the front of the house. You keep watch out the kitchen window, and Violet can cover the back." He put action to his words, setting out weapons and piles of ammunition at each spot.

He turned to face the sisters, wanting to impress the seriousness of the situation on them without sending them into a panic. "Keep your eyes open for movement, shadows, anything at all out of the ordinary. Sing out the moment you notice anything unusual, whether you think it's important or not. I'd rather have a dozen false alarms than miss the real thing when it comes." He levered a shell into his rifle. "Thank God your pa cut down all the trees around the house when he built this place."

Rachel nodded solemnly. "I remember arguing with him when we first arrived, telling him I wanted at least some left near the house for shade." She flashed him a shaky smile. "I'm glad he didn't listen to me."

He sent them to their posts, repeating his instructions for good measure. They settled in, alert to the peril of their situation. Daniel filled them in on what he'd learned from Abner, as much to keep their minds occupied as to share information. Nerves stretched taut, they scrutinized every inch of ground within their view.

Hours dragged by and dusk settled like a fleecy blanket. From the bedroom Daniel heard a low rumble and Violet's embarrassed, "Rachel, I'm hungry."

"Why don't you put together something for us to eat," he called in a low voice. "Something light. We don't want the food to make us drowsy."

Rachel emerged from the kitchen long enough to hand each of them bread topped with a slab of venison. Daniel had just enough time to squeeze her hand and give her an encouraging wink before she hurried back to her post.

Daniel watched the shadows of the trees merge with the deeper darkness of night. "Might as well get some rest while you can," he told them. "I'll keep watch."

Rachel appeared in the kitchen doorway, hands on her hips. "We'll take turns," she stated, fixing him with a serious gaze.

He chuckled in spite of the tension. "Yes, Ma'am. But you go to sleep first. I'll wake you when it's time to take your shift."

The two women fumbled their way through the shadowy house and curled up side by side on a blanket near the cold hearth. Daniel made his rounds from window to window, thinking how much his life had changed in the past few months. He, who said he'd never wanted anything to do with another woman, now found himself responsible for two of them. And liking it.

Long after Daniel called her to stand watch and lay down to get what rest he could, Rachel recalled the touch of his hand on hers when she handed him his spartan meal. Even while she moved from room to room, the memory of their brief contact gave her courage.

She blinked heavily. Her eyes felt as though grains of sand had rubbed them raw, and she had to fight to stay upright. The sky lightened by degrees, the inky blackness fading to an ashen gray, then to a pearly hue as the first pink fingers of dawn crept over the horizon.

She rolled her shoulders and shook her head to clear her mind. Nothing less than wide-awake vigilance would do now. While her gaze probed for movement among the trees and grasses, her thoughts strayed to Daniel again.

She felt his presence, warm and comforting, although she couldn't see him from her position by the window and didn't dare risk turning to get a glimpse of him.

He didn't have to be here. The thought echoed through her mind. She marveled, thinking about the ride he'd had. Knowing what time he'd left the day before, she calculated the distance he'd had to cover to reach his claim, then return. He must have pushed his horse to its limit to make it back so quickly. And why? He must really care for them—for Violet—to ride so hard only to risk his life to stand watch with them. That spoke of a courage and integrity that awed her.

He would make Violet a good husband, she thought, telling the pang of envy that swept through her to leave her alone. With Daniel around, she would never have to worry about her sister's welfare. That would be one less responsibility on her shoulders. If she did lose the farm, she would only have to concern herself with her own survival.

She blinked and nearly dozed, then caught herself. A distant drumming came to her ears and she stood erect, her pulse pounding in her ears. "Daniel?" she whispered.

"I hear it." He stood beside her in a second. They listened, straining to determine its source. Hoofbeats clattered into the yard.

"Hello, the house!"

Rachel flinched, then sagged with relief at the sound of the stentorian voice. Behind her, she heard Daniel lift the bar and open the door. Then came the scraping of boots on the porch. The next moment, Daniel stood beside her, gripping her shoulder excitedly. "They're gone," he told her, relief flooding his voice. "Tell Violet, then we can get something to eat."

Rachel rushed to do as she was bidden. Exhaustion threatened to overwhelm her, but the release from the night's tension buoyed her. She and Violet returned to find Daniel talking to two men.

"How do," the older one said, bobbing his head first to Rachel, then Violet. "Just wanted to let you all know the danger's passed. Someone got the word to Kautz's men, and they hotfooted it back here."

"So we're safe?" Rachel asked. With the release came weakness; her knees buckled, and she sank into a chair.

"Yes'm. They're going to continue regular patrols until they're sure things are under control and will stay that way." The man lifted a hand to the three of them, and he and his companion galloped out of the yard.

Violet moaned softly and swayed. Fearing she would collapse, Rachel helped her to bed, then returned to the front of the house.

Nearly dead on her feet, she stumbled into the kitchen where Daniel sat cradling a mug in his hands.

"I made coffee," he said, reaching over to pour her a cup. "Figured we both needed it."

Rachel dropped into a chair and nodded her thanks. She sipped the rich brew and gasped.

Daniel chuckled. "I figured I ought to make it plenty strong," he said.

"You succeeded." Rachel caught her breath and took another drink. No fear that she'd keel over now. This stuff would keep her awake the rest of the day. She looked at Daniel over the rim of her mug. "Is it really over?"

Daniel stared into the bottom of his mug and didn't answer for a moment. Finally, he nodded. "I think so. We'll stay close to the house today. We can go out to the barn when we need to, but only to do what's necessary for the animals. If we don't hear anything more by tonight, I think we can rest easy. As easy as a body can rest at a time like this," he added.

Rachel shook her head slowly. "I've taken a rifle with me every time I've gone into town alone for years," she said. "But Colonel Kautz and his troops have kept things so quiet, I never really expected to have a need for it. Up to last night, that is."

She rose to fix a hearty breakfast of scrambled eggs with bread and jam, not bothering to ration the eggs after their harrowing night. They ate in companionable silence, with Rachel thinking how natural it seemed to be sitting across the table from Daniel.

He lifted his gaze to her face, concern clouding his eyes. "Do you think Violet's all right?"

Rachel brought her wayward thoughts up short. Natural or not, she'd better not get any ideas about Daniel as anything but a future brother-in-law.

In the week that followed, Daniel seldom left the property. After the threatened Indian raid, he'd spent a day putting up a crude shelter on the far side of the barn so he didn't have to be away, even at night.

Rachel felt grateful for his concern and slept better knowing he was never far away. She limited her visits to town to egg-selling trips only and kept the rifle close beside her all the way.

She found that Daniel's constant presence made for a mixed blessing. On one hand, it meant the opportunity to relax a bit, knowing she and Violet didn't have to defend their property alone. On the other, it made ignoring her feelings for him doubly difficult.

With winter coming on and fewer outdoor chores to do, Violet spent much of her time tagging along behind Daniel, talking to him nonstop. Rachel took over more of the cooking duties, resigned to her sister and Daniel forming a twosome.

She reached for the calendar hanging on the kitchen wall and marked off the day's date with an *X*. Another day. One day closer to the dreaded due date. Tears welled in her eyes.

Violet came through the front door, humming a lively tune. Rachel dashed the moisture from her eyes and busied herself cleaning the counter. She scrubbed the pine boards with an outward appearance of calm, but her thoughts continued to race. Twenty days remained until December 15 would be upon them. Less than three weeks, and she still fell nearly sixty dollars short of her goal.

Oh, Pa, if only I knew what to do! She looked around for something more to occupy herself. She had scoured every surface she could find, and still she needed some way to vent her pent-up anxiety.

"What are we going to do about tomorrow?" Violet queried.

Rachel blinked. "Tomorrow? What about it?" Her thoughts remained focused on a point three weeks away and the uncertain future that awaited them.

"It's Thanksgiving, you silly goose!" Violet fairly bubbled with excitement. "What are we going to do to celebrate? We've left off planning nearly too long as it is, but if we start now we can still do something nice. How many pies do we want, and what kind? I can start on the crusts—"

"We'll celebrate another time," Rachel interrupted before Violet got completely carried away. "Sometime when we have something to be thankful for." She watched the glow of anticipation fade from Violet's face and steeled herself for an angry outburst. When Violet walked away without so much as a word of protest, she heaved a sigh of relief.

Thank goodness she hadn't made a fuss. Rachel knew she couldn't have dealt with any bickering just then. She leaned back against the counter and tried to figure out ways to bring in sixty dollars within the next twenty days. As far as she could see, it looked utterly impossible. Concern for their future weighed too heavily for her to feel festive or make any pretense of it. Not with the inexorable approach of the bank's cutoff date.

14

en days later, the only thing that had changed was that the deadline loomed ten days nearer. Pellets of sleet peppered the windows, adding to the light skiff of snow that already layered the ground.

Rachel sat alone after supper, watching the fire and thinking over their situation. Violet had gone to bed early, giving her time to ponder her options. Ten more days remained until December 15. In just a week and a half, she would know whether the farm would belong to her or Hiram Bradshaw.

Her skin crawled at the very idea that man might ever look on her father's property as his. The memory of his face just after she'd pelted him with the rotten egg popped into her mind. A Christian young lady shouldn't enjoy the recollection so much, she supposed, but it might be the only satisfying remembrance she would carry with her in years to come.

She tallied the figures from the ledger in her mind. With the onset of winter, the hens quit laying as heavily. Mentally, she added up the number of eggs needed to make up the necessary difference, then shook her head. Even if they were laying at their peak, it still wouldn't be enough. A case of too little, too late.

A faint brush of sound on the wood floor caught her attention, and she turned. Violet stood in the doorway, looking like a little girl in her nightdress and robe.

"Are you sick?" Rachel asked, hearing the edgy tone in her voice and hating it. She didn't think she could handle one more setback.

Violet shook her head. "I just wanted to ask you something." She crept farther into the room and stared at Rachel with soulful eyes.

Rachel braced herself. That look on Violet's face usually signified the prelude to a request for a favor. A big one.

"I know it's still nearly three weeks away," Violet said timidly, "but I wanted to know ahead of time. Are we going to celebrate Christmas this year, or are we going to skip it too?"

Rachel pressed her lips together and blinked her eyes against the sting of tears.

"I know we don't have money for gifts," Violet went on, "and that's not the point. It isn't the trappings, or the food, or even the time together." She moved closer and knelt by Rachel's chair. "It's the blessing of God's love, Rachel. The celebration of the gift of Jesus and everything He's done for us."

Rachel's throat constricted. When had her sister been so hesitant to talk to her before? And did she truly think Rachel would ignore the birth of their Savior? Come to think of it, though, why would she have any reason to believe otherwise, given Rachel's moody behavior of late?

She reached out and stroked Violet's head lovingly, painfully aware that it was the first tender gesture she'd made toward her sister in weeks. "Go to bed, Honey," she told her in a gentle voice. "And don't worry. We won't skip Christmas this year . . . or any other." The light in Violet's eyes warmed her as her sister brushed her cheek with a kiss and scurried back to bed.

The fire burned low, but Rachel continued to sit, deep in thought. Blessings, Violet had said. When was the last time she had looked for blessings?

When had there last been any? a rebellious part of her mind queried. It didn't seem like God had done much of anything *for* them lately, although He'd allowed plenty to happen *to* them.

When did I become so bitter? Maybe that was a better question, the answer to which might prove revealing. Rachel covered her face with her hands. *What would Pa have done in these circumstances?*

I remember what it was like when he was alive, she mused. *I remember what it was like to feel happy.* Pa had always taken time to sit with her and Violet in the evening, reading to them from the Bible and talking to them about what had happened that day. A wistful smile curved Rachel's lips, remembering how he had listened patiently to their girlish questions and dreams.

How had he managed? Had times always been easy for him? She pondered the question with new insight. No, they hadn't. She could remember plenty of struggles without even trying.

What, then, made his response to life so different from her own? Her glance fell on the Bible on Violet's chair, and she reached for it with a tentative hand. Without question, she knew where Pa had found his strength. Hadn't he told her time and again that she could trust God no matter what?

She thumbed through the well-worn pages, trying to remember some of Pa's favorite passages. The pages opened of their own accord at the book of James. Rachel scooted her chair closer to the lamp and studied the words. "My brethren, count it all joy when ye fall into divers temptations. . . ."

She stared in disbelief. Joy? How could she count it joy when she felt so tired she could barely move, when she'd worked harder than she ever believed she could and yet saw nothing but destitution staring them in the face? What joy awaited them in knowing that unless a miracle occurred, Hiram Bradshaw would soon be the owner of Pa's farm? And was she supposed to find happiness in his vulgar treatment of her? Rachel cringed at the recollection of his leering face. Happiness? She thought not.

"Knowing this, that the trying of your faith worketh patience." Pa had penned a note in the margin, and she strained her eyes to see it in the lamplight. She turned the pages eagerly to 1 Thessalonians 5:18.

"In everything give thanks; for this is the will of God in Christ Jesus concerning you."

Rachel stared into the flames, seeing, not the dancing colors, but Pa's face. Pa, who must have been incredibly tired himself, yet found time to listen patiently to the chatter of two growing daughters. Pa, smiling even when he faced adversities as big as her own. Comprehension filtered into her awareness slowly. Pa hadn't found joy *because* of his circumstances but *in* every circumstance.

He didn't have it handed to him on a silver plate. He chose to take God at His word and be happy. *He chose that . . . and I can too.*

She closed the Bible and hugged it to her, turning this new idea over in her mind. She could choose to trust God no matter what— whether she and Violet lost the farm, whether Violet married the man who had won Rachel's heart. She could do all things through Christ, who gave her strength. With His help, she would weather any storm life sent her way.

She tightened her hold on the Bible and turned her eyes toward heaven. "Thank You, Lord," she whispered. "I choose joy."

The next morning dawned fine and clear. Rachel dressed warmly for her trip to town, knowing the drive would be cold, but grateful that yesterday's snow had already vanished. She packed the eggs carefully, layering them between towels in the basket, then wedging the basket between a pair of blankets to guard it against any bumps along the way.

"Do you want to come along?" she asked Violet, who had come out onto the porch to see her off. Violet blinked at her buoyant tone but declined. Rachel gave her a cheery wave and drove off, leaving Violet staring after her in amazement.

Moments after she reached the road, she pulled the rifle into the seat beside her instead of its customary spot in the back. The vigilant efforts of the troops at Fort Whipple seemed to be having an effect, but it wouldn't pay to be careless.

The crisp air nipped at her cheeks and nose. Rachel tipped her head back and inhaled its sweet freshness, wondering at her ability to enjoy the day when she knew this might be the last trip she made to town as the owner of the farm. It seemed the whole world had changed since last night, but she knew the biggest change had taken place within her.

Nearly an hour from home, a tiny cry caused Rachel to sit up straight, her mouth suddenly dry. Indians often imitated animal sounds. Had that been a signal? She tightened her grip on the reins, not sure whether to pull the horses to a stop or urge them into a run.

She heard the sound again and turned to the wagon bed behind her, feeling a mixture of relief and irritation.

One of the kittens reached out from its nest in the blankets and swatted a paw at her hand. Rachel sighed in exasperation. "How did you get in here? You must have jumped in just before I left." She scooped up the tiny creature and held it on her lap, considering. She'd gone too far to turn back now and return the baby to its mother. Little as she liked the idea, the kitten would have to travel to town with her.

She reached back to settle the stowaway again, pulling the blanket folds around it to form a warm nest. "Better stay put," she warned. "It's cold out here." She clucked to the horses and set off again.

Pulling the horses to a stop behind Samson's General Store, she jumped to the ground and brushed the wrinkles from her skirt. She would go in with her head held high. No one else needed to know how important every sale would be over the next few days.

Jake Samson looked up from the counter and beamed. "Pleasure to see you, Rachel. I was wonderin' whether you'd stop by soon. I've been out of your eggs for days, and I've had customer after customer pestering me about them."

Rachel fixed a smile on her face and set the basket on the counter. No need to tell Jake his egg supply might soon disappear.

"Fact is, the demand's been so high, I decided to raise my price." He gave her a conspiratorial wink. "I'm going to pass some of that along to you."

Her heart leaped, and she had to force herself to wait until she reached the privacy of Jake's back doorway to count the money he handed her. It wouldn't do to appear too eager.

She dropped the last coin into her hand and felt disappointment creep into her heart. The amount came to more than she'd hoped for, but it still didn't give her enough. *Trust in the Lord,* she reminded herself, trying to recapture her earlier gladness.

Rachel squared her shoulders and marched out the door to the wagon. She stopped abruptly at the sight of a grizzled miner standing next to the wagon box.

He started when he saw her, and a red flush suffused his face. "Beggin' your pardon, Ma'am." He ducked his head and scuffed his boots in the dust. "I didn't mean no harm. I was just lookin' at your kitten here." He held up the gray ball of fluff that Rachel had forgotten until that moment. "Cute little feller, isn't he?"

"I—I suppose he is." The kitten's charm had been lost on Rachel in the light of her present worries. Apparently the miner didn't share her lack of appreciation.

"Smart one too," the miner went on. "Watch this." He trailed his finger along the wagon bed and laughed out loud when the kitten pounced, swatting his hand fiercely. "See? He's a real feisty one."

A smile tugged at Rachel's lips. She had to admit he had a point. Nice to know that something could lighten her load of troubles, if only for a moment. She sent up a quick prayer of gratitude.

"Yes. Well, I need to be going now." She put one foot on the wheel hub and stepped up into the seat, hoping the man would take the hint.

He leaned over and placed the kitten in the wagon box with tender care but continued to stand with his hands on the side of the wagon. Rachel chafed, needing to be on her way but not wanting to appear rude.

The miner looked up at her with rheumy eyes and cleared his throat. "Beggin' your pardon, but I'm wondering if there's any way you could part with that little rascal."

He held up a hand to forestall any protest and continued. "I know you're probably real attached to him, and I'm asking a lot, but Ma'am, it gets mighty lonely out on the claim with only myself and my mule to talk to. If I could have this little feller with me, it would help a lot." He peered into Rachel's face like a child begging for candy.

She suppressed a laugh. Having one kitten less would lighten only a fraction of the load she bore, but even that would be an encouragement. She smiled. "Take him. I'd like for you to have him."

The man's face lit up in a snaggletoothed grin. He lifted the kitten from its nest of blankets and held it close to his chest. "You and I are gonna be pards," he crooned. "You like that idea?" The kitten responded by snuggling against his checkered shirt and purring loudly.

"You see that?" he asked triumphantly. "The little feller likes me already. Thank you, Ma'am. You've made me a happy man today."

Rachel smiled and nodded. She lifted the reins, preparing to leave, but the miner held up his hand again. "Wait a minute, Ma'am. I need to give you somethin' for him." He fumbled inside his coat, then pressed a lumpy object into her hand. "May the Lord bless you for your kindness." He dipped his head in farewell and walked away, cuddling the kitten against his scraggly beard.

Amused by the picture, Rachel opened her hand. A small leather bag rested in her palm. She tugged at the string tying the top together. The pouch fell open to reveal a small pile of glittering dust.

Rachel gasped. Gold? She glanced around to make sure no one else had seen, then tucked the poke inside her coat pocket before clicking her tongue and turning the horses toward home.

Once she'd gotten out of sight of Prescott, she pulled out the bag again and hefted it in her hand. Remembering similar pokes Pa had shown her, she estimated it to weigh about an ounce.

Quickly, she calculated its value. It put her nearly twenty dollars closer to her goal. It wouldn't make up the whole difference, but it would provide a little help for her and Violet while they looked for a place to stay and some means of support.

The income brought in from the harvest would go to the bank— she didn't intend to leave any more of Pa's debt unpaid than she could help. But this could be considered "found" money, something supplied by God to take care of their needs.

"Thank You, Lord," she whispered. Laughter welled up in her throat and burst from her lips in a joyful gurgle. "Thank You for Your provision and for letting me know I can trust You."

$$15$$

he next day found Rachel pitching hay down out of the loft, humming one of her favorite hymns. Violet appeared in the barn doorway. "There's someone here to see you," she said with a curious look. "He says Tom Dolan sent him."

"Dolan?" Rachel tried to recall anyone by that name but couldn't. Mystified, she followed Violet out to the yard, where the man awaited her. His tattered clothing and heavily laden mule gave away his occupation before he could speak.

"Morning, Ma'am," he said, removing his hat. "Tom Dolan told me to come see you, and Jake Samson told me how to find your place. Tom got a kitten from you yesterday, and I wondered if you might have more to sell." He wet his lips and stared at her, looking as eager as a schoolboy.

Rachel recovered from her surprise and shot a warning look at Violet. "They're in here," she told him calmly, leading the way into the barn.

The threadbare miner took his time inspecting the litter and finally selected the biggest kitten. "Looks like she'll make a good mouser." He grinned. "I surely do thank you," he told her and produced a bag identical to the one Tom Dolan had given her the day before. "Here. Tom said this was the going rate." He grabbed the mule's lead rope and started to walk off, then stopped. "Do you mind if I spread the word about them others?" he asked. "I know a bunch of fellers who'd be glad of a little company like that."

Rachel started, then rallied. "Go right ahead," she called, ignoring Violet's dumbstruck expression. "We'll be glad to see them." She gave her sister an exuberant hug. "God's in control, Violet. Isn't it wonderful?"

By the following afternoon, Rachel and Violet were once again the owners of only one cat, Molly. Rachel sat at the table, lining up their money in neat piles, then checking the total against the amount in her ledger. She blinked incredulously. Three hundred and eighty-one dollars. Far more than she needed to pay off her debts. Enough to give Daniel a share for all his hard work. Enough to see her and Violet through the next few months.

And enough to make this a special Christmas for her sister. Joyful tears sprang to her eyes and spilled down her cheeks. "Thank You, Lord, for what You've done," she prayed. "Forgive me for doubting You, and help me always to know that You're in charge of my life."

She might have missed the official holiday, but songs of thanksgiving rang in her heart. Reaching for her pencil, Rachel sorted the amounts from the various sources and added them up. She tapped the end of the pencil against her teeth and studied the paper. Everything they had done had played a part in their success—the corn, the kitchen vegetables, the unexpectedly lucrative eggs. They would be sure to continue all of them next year. But those kittens . . .

Rachel sprang to her feet, shoved her arms into her coat sleeves, and hurried out to the barn. Violet poked her head outside just as Rachel tucked the old sewing basket into the wagon. "What are you doing?" she called.

"I have an errand to run," Rachel replied and got the team moving. She had to do this before she changed her mind. If she took time to explain her mission to Violet, she might talk herself out of it.

She drove the team at a brisk trot along the frost-covered road, not slowing until they came to a shabby-looking place. Rachel stopped the horses in front of the run-down cabin. Hooking her arm through the basket handle, she marched to the door and rapped on it sharply. A moment later, a seamed face appeared in the doorway.

"Miss Rachel?" Jeb McCurdy's eyes widened ludicrously at the sight of his neighbor. He hurriedly smoothed his hair back with both hands and hitched his trousers a notch higher. "What can I do for you?"

Rachel lifted her chin and moistened her lips. "I've come to make you an offer on your tomcat, Mr. McCurdy."

"On my—" The old man's mouth dropped open. "Miss Rachel, are you joking?"

Rachel tapped her foot in irritation. "Of course not. I'm perfectly serious. I'm talking business here. Are you interested or not?"

Jeb McCurdy rubbed a gnarled hand over his grizzled beard and regarded her thoughtfully. "Seems to me, the last time you saw my cat, you called him some powerful unfriendly names. 'Wayward' and 'wanton' came into it, if I recall." His eyes narrowed. "And now you want to pay good money for him and take him home with you, is that it?"

Rachel felt a blush heat her face but held her ground. "That is correct. I wish to purchase your cat."

Minutes passed while her neighbor eyed her thoughtfully. "The thing is, I just have to wonder what on earth you want with him, you taking such a dislike to him earlier and all." A glint of suspicion sparked in his eyes. "Cats make good tamales, I hear. You ain't planning to eat him, are you?"

"Of course not." Rachel gagged at the revolting idea. "I simply feel that he might be of some value to me. . . ." She let her voice trail off, unable to find the words to explain her plan.

A moment of silence ensued, followed by a wheezing laugh. Jeb McCurdy's shoulders shook with glee. "So you decided there's something the old boy's good for, after all, eh?" His face contorted with suppressed mirth, then he leaned against the doorjamb and howled. "If that don't beat all!"

Rachel drew herself erect. "Are you willing to sell him or not?" she asked, her voice laced with impatience.

Jeb McCurdy caught his breath and wiped his watering eyes. "Oh, I'll sell him, all right. He doesn't stay around here half the time anyway, and now I won't have to worry about you coming after me every time he shows up on your place. What are you offering?"

Rachel held out a handful of silver, and the old man reached for it with a smile. "Just a minute," Rachel said, drawing her hand back. "The price includes the cat, caught and confined in this basket."

McCurdy looked as if he wanted to argue, then shrugged and pulled on his coat. "Come on, little lady. Let's go find your tom." He pocketed the money, then looked straight at her. "I want the pick of the first litter," he said with a knowing wink.

Thirty minutes later, she drove back into the yard, basking in her sense of accomplishment. Violet hurried out to greet her, pulling her shawl tight over her head and shoulders. "Where have you been?" she demanded. "And what's that noise?" She pointed to the wicker container, from whence an outraged yowling emanated. Her brow puckered in consternation. "Rachel, you haven't been doing anything to Molly, have you?"

"Help me fix up a place in the barn, and I'll explain." Rachel led the way into the barn, where she proceeded to fashion a sort of cage out of several old crates. When she felt satisfied, she held the mouth of the basket to the opening and released the catch on the lid. Out sprang the wide-eyed tom, his fur standing on end.

Violet gasped. "Rachel, what on earth—"

"He's a business investment," Rachel told her smugly.

Violet goggled at her. "Investment? You don't mean you spent good money on that creature, when you've been so worried about making ends meet?" She put her hand on Rachel's forehead.

Rachel laughed happily and brushed her hand away. "I'm learning, Violet, that God's provision comes in various forms, some of them quite unexpected."

The streets of Prescott bustled with activity. Rachel took her time stepping down from the wagon and meticulously straightened the lines of her best wool dress. Taking a firm grip on her reticule, she walked through the bank's doors and headed straight for Ben Murphy's office.

"Good morning, Ben," she called through the open door. "I need a moment of your time."

"Rachel, it's good to see you." The banker rose from his desk and hurried to greet her. His smile of greeting warmed her, but she could also see the worry in his eyes and realized he didn't expect her to make the payment. *He thinks I've come to beg for more time and doesn't know how he'll tell me no.* She smiled in return, planning to enjoy her moment to its fullest.

Ben pulled a leather-covered chair closer to his desk and seated her in it with a solicitous air. "How have you been, Rachel?"

"Pretty well," she replied. "We've been working hard, you know."

"Ah, yes." Ben's smile lost a fraction of its brightness, and he folded his hands together, tapping his thumbs nervously. "There's a lot to running a farm. Especially when you're trying to do it single-handed."

"That's true," Rachel agreed, maintaining her solemn expression. "Ben, it's almost Christmas. . . ." She allowed her voice to trail off.

He swallowed hard, his Adam's apple bobbing up and down behind his starched collar. "I know, Rachel, and don't think for a minute I don't sympathize with your plight. It's just that—"

"So I hope this will make your holiday a bit brighter." Rachel reached into her reticule and produced a thick envelope. She laid it in the center of Ben's desk with a flourish.

Ben's mouth dropped open, and he gawked at it in a most undignified manner. "What–what's this?"

Rachel stifled her inclination to laugh. "It's the money we owe you," she said in her most formal tone. "All of it. The amount of both notes, paid in full, and nearly a week ahead of schedule."

Ben closed his mouth and swallowed. He opened it again and tried to speak, but no words came out. He pulled a snowy handkerchief from his coat pocket and dabbed at his forehead. Finally he managed, "But how . . . ?"

"God's grace," Rachel replied softly. "It's His provision, pure and simple."

Ben nodded, still staring unbelievingly. After counting the money, he wrote out a receipt and handed her the cancelled note. "Congratulations. It's all yours now, free and clear."

Rachel left the bank, blinking back tears of joy. She stood on the boardwalk and surveyed the scene before her with heightened appreciation. The broad expanse of the plaza, the false-fronted buildings, and the wide, dusty streets held a beauty she'd never noticed before.

Even the gunmetal gray of the brooding winter sky couldn't dampen her euphoric mood.

She had done it. No, *God* had done it. She could hardly believe her ordeal had finally ended. The new sense of freedom seemed too good to be true. With a light step, she walked to the wagon and stepped up on the wheel hub.

"Trying to beg a little more time off Ben, are you?" Hiram Bradshaw's raspy voice came from directly behind her.

Rachel spun around and slipped off the wheel hub. She caught the side of the wagon to keep herself from toppling over and winced when splinters from its rough edge grazed her fingers. Pressing her hand against her dress, she ignored the hurt and glared straight at Hiram. Not for anything would she let him know she felt pain.

"As a matter of fact, you're wrong again. I've just paid off my loans. Both of them. The farm belongs to me, Hiram, and there's nothing you can do about it."

Hiram snorted. "Nice try, but I happen to know there's no way you could have come up with the money." He sneered and leaned against the wagon as though they were having a civil chat.

"There are ways higher than ours," Rachel told him, her joy overshadowing her distaste for his company. "Maybe this will convince you." She held the cancelled notes out for him to see.

With a look of disbelief, Hiram wheeled toward the bank. She could hear him bellowing Ben's name even after he entered the building.

16

*R*achel drove home in a blissful haze. Now that the load of responsibility had been lifted from her shoulders, she felt as though she might float right up to the top of Granite Mountain. Even her fingers had ceased to pain her. She threw back her head and laughed, causing the horses to prick their ears in her direction. "There's nothing to worry about," she called to them. "I'm just making a joyful noise."

While the team carried her home, she made plans for the coming year. With the extra money provided by the sale of Molly's kittens, she could buy additional seed and plant another twenty acres. That would cover the expense of hiring workers to help bring in next fall's harvest and still leave her and Violet with a tidy profit.

On top of that, she now knew her eggs could bring in enough to take care of most of their household expenses. And she had her newly acquired ace in the hole, Jeb McCurdy's tomcat. Any litters he and Molly produced would mean extra income they could put by for emergencies.

It meant freedom, she thought, reveling in the heady feeling of independence. No longer would she have to depend on Daniel and his sense of duty to her father. His debt had long since been discharged. He could pursue his mining interests, unhindered by any onus of responsibility toward them.

The thought of him leaving filled her with sorrow, but she knew God could take care of that part of her life too. She focused on her trust in Him and resolved to ignore the only dark cloud on her otherwise happy horizon.

* * *

Violet celebrated their release from debt by making a special supper of fried chicken, beans, mashed potatoes, and gravy. Conversation lagged at the table while the three of them savored the delicious meal.

Afterward, Rachel sat in her customary place by the fireside, wanting to enjoy an evening free from the hectic pace of the past months.

She glanced toward the table, where Daniel and Violet still sat engaged in an animated conversation. Rachel watched the glint of the firelight on their heads, one fair, one sable, and thought what a handsome pair they made.

She had to admit Daniel had been very good for Violet. Her sister had regained her vivacious spirit and had a sparkle in her eyes Rachel hadn't seen since before Pa's death. Rachel noticed a new lilt in her voice and spring in her step, as well.

Daniel too seemed different. Instead of the wary man Rachel saw when he first arrived, his eyes now held a flash of hope and determination. He looked like a man with a purpose, and Rachel knew full well what that purpose was.

How long would it be before he asked her permission to marry Violet? A sense of dread gnawed at her stomach, one she couldn't disregard.

Looking at it from a practical standpoint, it made perfect sense. The two of them could settle in Prescott, where Daniel could keep Violet in fine style as well as work his mining claim. It would give Violet the kind of home life Pa had wanted for her. And it would free Rachel from having to worry about more than just the farm and herself.

She could spend her days on the place she loved . . . alone. Rachel picked up some mending and concentrated on threading her needle, determined not to give in to the loneliness that beset her without warning.

After all her hard work to keep the farm, the prospect of having it all to herself seemed unaccountably bleak. What would her life be like without Violet around? It wouldn't be like she'd lost her sister, she admonished herself. Violet would still live nearby, close enough that they could visit frequently.

Rachel shot another glance at her sister, who listened to Daniel with rapt attention, then nodded eagerly. She seemed smitten enough with him, but then, who wouldn't? Rachel allowed her gaze to roam over his strong features, taking in the sandy hair bleached even lighter by the sun, the forest-green eyes, and the small cleft that softened the determined set of his chin.

How could any woman in her right mind not be attracted to him? If his physical appearance alone wasn't enough to capture attention, what about the character he had shown when he set himself to work unpaid for two young women he didn't even know?

Daniel patted Violet's hand, and Rachel smiled wistfully. He had only come to pay a debt. And she had only intended to let him. She'd never expected him to become such a permanent—and treasured—fixture in their lives.

Her mind flitted back to the day Daniel made his proposal. Looking back, she now believed he'd meant exactly what he said—he had only wanted to help them both. Her eyes grew misty. What would have happened if she had accepted his proposal and agreed to marry him? A shiver of delight ran up her spine.

No! She caught herself up sternly. She would not, would *not* dwell on idle dreams of what might have been. Not when his offer had been based on pity and not on a true desire to have her as his wife. Not when he was now the man Violet loved.

She stabbed the needle through the fabric with angry, jerky movements. These foolish fancies wouldn't do. She had determined before God to follow the right path and wish for her sister's good. She could only assume He had shown His will in providing a husband for Violet in this unexpected way.

At sixteen, Violet was undeniably young, but not so young she couldn't marry. Rachel had known plenty of girls who'd said their vows at that age. The surprise she felt that Violet would be getting married first rankled her. She'd always assumed it would be the other way around, with her being older and all, but who said it always had to happen that way?

She would endorse Violet's choice with a smile, giving her all the support she could muster. And somehow, she would get used to thinking of Daniel as her sister's husband.

* * *

The knife blade passed along the whetstone a final time. Daniel tested it with his thumb and smiled. Good and sharp. He had always had a knack for honing a tool to its keenest edge.

Careful of the razor-sharp blade, he carried the knife toward the house. Rachel had complained about its dullness only the night before. She should be pleasantly surprised by his good deed.

He had taken Violet's advice to heart and stayed around the place, making himself useful and keeping Rachel aware of his presence. Piling up firewood and mending tools and harness hadn't gone unnoticed by her, but he wanted to do something that would affect her more personally. A sharpened knife was a small thing, but it would be a start.

While the harvest was underway and they'd scrabbled to pull together every cent they could, he had held off on making major overtures to her. She'd had all she could handle then just trying to keep things going, and he saw no point in overburdening her. But now that she'd been freed from the pressure of the loan, Daniel felt the time had come to move forward.

He entered the kitchen and found Rachel, hands on her hips, staring at a loaf of freshly baked bread.

"Have you seen—" Her eyes widened when he held out the knife.

"Looking for this?" He grinned at her surprise. "Watch out for that blade," he cautioned when she reached for the handle. "It's sharp."

She tapped the edge with a cautious finger, and her face creased in a smile of delight. "Just what I needed!" She gave him a grateful look and began to slice the bread with easy strokes. "Just for that, how would you like some bread and jam?"

"Throw in a glass of milk, and you've got a deal." He watched her set a crock of butter on the table beside the bread, then reach for the jam jar. Even doing simple kitchen chores, her movements were smooth and graceful. *Easy on a man's eyes,* he thought. Something he could enjoy watching for a long time—like the rest of his life.

He tried to hide his pleasure when she poured two glasses of milk and sat down across from him. No point in scaring her away, not when he'd just started making progress. He searched for something to say.

"How does it feel to be half owner of the finest farm around?" The question seemed safe enough, given their recent celebration.

Rachel took a moment to spread jam evenly over her bread, then smiled. "Actually," she said, propping her elbows against the edge of the table and lacing her fingers together, "I'm the full owner. Pa left it all to me." Her smile broadened. "Violet isn't tied to the farm in any way." She popped a bite of bread in her mouth and chewed, a pleased expression spreading across her face.

Daniel pursed his lips and let out a low whistle. Why didn't it surprise him that Ike would leave his property in Rachel's capable hands? Her father had been well aware of her love for the land.

Rachel finished her bread and took a drink of milk. Daniel couldn't help but chuckle. She'd tilted the glass a little too high, and a thin white line decorated her upper lip.

He picked up a napkin and swiped at her lip. "Just wiping off your mustache," he said in answer to her startled look. He reached out to blot her mouth again. It felt good to be so close to her, to feel her breath brush across his hand. And she didn't need to know he'd gotten every bit of milk off her face the first time.

He polished off his milk with one long swallow and rose to leave. If he stayed there with her, he couldn't guarantee he wouldn't try to stroke her face again and again. No point in pushing things along too fast, not when it seemed he was finally making some headway.

Rachel watched the door close behind him and touched the knife with a tender smile. How kind of him to take note of her fussing last night and sharpen it without saying a word. One corner of her mouth tilted upward. It appeared that Daniel felt the same way she did—if they were going to spend the rest of their lives as part of the same family, they might as well make sure they would be on good terms.

She wondered what he would have done to get into Pa's good graces if he were still alive. It wouldn't have been anything like sharpening a knife, she thought, chuckling. More like helping him break a horse or mend a wagon wheel.

And Pa would have been just as impressed as she felt. It showed that Daniel planned ahead and wanted a good relationship with his family-to-be. It also showed that she had read his intentions correctly. He wouldn't be doing this if he didn't plan to ask for Violet's hand.

That night after Daniel had gone home, the sisters sat before the fire, Rachel with her mending and Violet struggling with yarn and a pair of knitting needles.

"It's no good," Violet said, tossing the needles aside in disgust. "I'll never get the hang of knitting. It's a good thing you learned from Mother. Maybe you can teach me someday when we're old and gray and have nothing else to do." She looked at Rachel from under lowered lashes. "We can sit and talk about our grandchildren and what all our husbands have been up to."

Rachel suppressed a smile with an effort. What a way to lead up to the subject of marriage! Did her sister really think she didn't know which way the wind blew between her and Daniel? Fine, then. She would let Violet break the news in her own way, and she would show suitable surprise and delight when the moment came. She finished reattaching a dangling apron string and reached for another piece from the mending basket.

Violet worked to untangle her yarn and roll it back into a ball. "What do you think about Daniel?" she asked, her gaze never leaving her busy fingers.

Rachel tried not to snicker. She'd never realized Violet had such a gift for acting. If she didn't know better, she'd think her sister had no interest in the man at all. She toyed with the idea of sounding unenthusiastic but dismissed it. No point in teasing when something as important as her sister's future hung in the balance.

"I think he's a fine man," she responded, keeping her tone casual. "He's a hard worker, and he loves the Lord. Pretty good qualities, if you ask me." She pulled her stitches tight, waiting for Violet's next remark.

"That's good. I mean, you're right," Violet said. She wound the last wrap of yarn and tossed the ball into the sewing basket. "Those are important qualities for a man to have, don't you think? Important qualities for a husband, I mean."

"Absolutely." Rachel had to bite her lips to keep from laughing out loud. Violet couldn't be any more transparent if she tried.

"I'm glad." Violet took a deep breath and licked her lips. "Because he has feelings for you."

The needle slipped and jabbed Rachel in the thigh. "What?" she yelped.

"Isn't it wonderful?" Violet seemed oblivious to her sister's pained cry. "Assuming, of course, that you like him too," she added cautiously. "You do, don't you, Rachel?"

"Do—I—like—"

"You said yourself he's a fine man. Hard worker and God-fearing." She closed her eyes and heaved a blissful sigh. "It sounds like a match made in heaven to me."

Rachel rubbed the sore spot on her leg and tried to concentrate. What had happened to the announcement of Violet's intention to marry Daniel? She would have thought it all a dream, had it not been for the tender spot where the needle poked her. What about all those private conversations? Had he been toying with her sister's affections?

"Violet, don't you think I know how you feel about him? I hope you know I would never try to come between you." She had spent enough time on bended knees to know she meant every word.

Violet raised her eyebrows quizzically.

"Look at all the time you've spent with him," Rachel told her, mildly irked that her sister would force her to explain. "I've seen the looks passing back and forth between the two of you, all the smiles and the whispering." She gave Violet a reproving look. "You haven't been as unobtrusive as you think. It's pretty obvious."

Violet sprang to her feet. "Rachel, you goose! It isn't me he cares for. It never has been. It's you."

Rachel studied her sister's face, her heart beginning a wild flutter. Could it be true? Did the possibility exist that Daniel cared for her, Rachel Canfield? For herself and not the farm?

She dropped her mending in her lap and leaned back in her chair, staring at the wall but seeing Daniel's face. He'd put in so much hard effort, taking over the heavy labor of harvest for her, then staying on to work even more without any apparent reason. Then there was the way he'd looked at her earlier that day, and the thrill she'd felt when his hand touched her face not once, but twice.

Her head grew light. What if it were true? What if all the thoughtful gestures were meant for her as the object of his love rather than a potential sister-in-law whose goodwill he wanted to win?

Rachel closed her eyes, the better to picture their time together in the kitchen. She could recall every moment—his words, his smile, the tingle that shot through her arm when he'd handed her the knife and his fingertips touched hers.

Her lips curved in a gentle smile. Maybe dreams did come true. Maybe God had decided to answer the deepest longings of her heart.

Without warning, another scene flashed before her eyes. She saw herself sitting at the table, explaining to Daniel that she was the sole owner of the property, that Violet had no legal interest in it whatsoever. Rachel jolted upright, the bitter taste of gall rising in her throat.

Of course he wanted her. She laughed in derision at her naivete, earning a puzzled look from Violet. He wanted her because she owned the land. She had been right about his intentions from the first. When he thought they both had rights to the property, pretty Violet had been the object of his attentions. Once he learned the truth, he switched his attention to Rachel without a moment's hesitation.

She pressed her hand to her mouth, fearing she might be sick. What made her think that Daniel, or any man, would want her? She wanted to howl out her anguish at her betrayal and even more at the realization that this new knowledge didn't change her feelings for Daniel in the least.

An idea took shape in her mind. Very well. If Daniel chose to play that game, she knew one way to find out his true motives, once and for all.

17

*H*e loved her. He loved her not. Rachel dropped the handful of straw to the ground, not having the heart to continue the childish game. Besides, loose straw made a poor substitute for the garden flowers she'd plucked petals from as a little girl in Missouri. But she had been hard-pressed to find any flowers blooming in the middle of December.

She stared across the yard, where the late afternoon had turned the snow into pools of slush. Dark gray clouds reappeared, and more snow drifted down into the puddles. It was a dismal day and a dismal scene. And Christmas was coming.

Her thoughts turned to Christmases past, times when her family didn't have a lot in the way of material goods but abounded in the richness of the joys of being together. This year the holiday looked as desolate as the landscape before her.

Pa had worked hard to keep the Christmas spirit alive even after their mother was gone, but now he too would be missing from the picture. It would be up to Rachel to carry on, and she didn't know if she could. Or whether she wanted to.

She shook herself, trying to cast off her downhearted mood. Hadn't she learned that God could be trusted, regardless of the circumstances? No matter what upheaval went on around them or within her emotions, she could experience joy, if she so chose, just in knowing His presence.

And He *was* there, she knew that for sure. Hadn't He given them help when they needed it most? Hadn't He blessed them with money over and above the amount she'd sought so desperately, even when she would have thought such a sum an utter impossibility? No matter what happened with Daniel, the Lord continued to be in control, she reminded herself, feeling a stirring of excitement. And she and Violet would celebrate His birth.

What could she do to make this Christmas especially nice for her sister? She felt compelled to make up for her surly attitude at Thanksgiving. A tree, she decided. Pa always sought out the perfect tree. Violet deserved some happiness, and she would provide it. She felt sure she could get Daniel to help cut one. She shrugged off a twinge of self-pity and set about making her plans.

What about gifts? Her pulse raced, realizing that with the money provided by the sale of the kittens, she would have a bit extra to buy something nice for Violet. With a light heart, she ran to hitch up the horses.

Rachel browsed through the selection of goods in the general store, feeling positively giddy. How long had it been since she'd been able to shop for anything but the barest necessities?

Today she had money to spend, and she intended to enjoy the sensation. She didn't plan to throw it away, but after their extended time of deprivation, the mere thought of being able to pay for a tiny bit of luxury made for a heady experience.

She had already spotted some possibilities at the dry goods counter at the mercantile. Once she finished here, she would go back to buy some fabric and bits of ribbon for Violet to use to trim their tree.

"Made up your mind yet, Rachel?" Jake Samson's friendly smile let her know there was no impatience behind his words.

"I think so." She set her purchase on the counter. "I'd like this one . . . and a bag of peppermints, please." Her gaze lit on a shelf behind the counter, and she paused. "I'll take three of those handkerchiefs too," she told him, hoping he wouldn't ask who they were for.

"Here you go." He wrapped her items without so much as a flicker of interest and added up the total. Rachel counted out the money, happy to have spent even less than she expected.

She picked up her parcel and strolled toward the mercantile, then paused, changed direction, and went into the bank.

Ben Murphy looked up with a smile that told her he felt as relieved as she did that she no longer owed him money. "What can I do for you, Rachel?"

"Do you have those papers ready?"

The banker pulled a file from his desk drawer and stood, his brows knitted. "They're right here." He tapped the thin sheaf of papers slowly against his hand. "I drew them up just like you asked me to, but I don't underst—"

"It doesn't matter whether you understand or not," Rachel said crisply. "Just so they're legal and in order." She gave them a quick glance and nodded. "Merry Christmas, Ben," she told the perplexed banker and proceeded to the mercantile.

Back at home, she secreted Violet's present in her cupboard and tucked the handkerchiefs in the bottom dresser drawer, wondering if she'd been a fool to buy even that small gift for Daniel.

She found Violet in the kitchen and handed her the fabric and ribbon. "You'd better get started on this," she said in answer to her sister's puzzled frown. "We'll need decorations for the tree soon."

"A tree? Oh, Rachel!" Violet hugged her ecstatically. "I'd been so afraid . . . well, you know. This will make it a real Christmas, after all!"

Rachel returned the hug. "I'm glad it makes you happy. I'll arrange for Daniel to take you out in the wagon, and you can make a day of picking out the prettiest tree you can find."

Daniel showed up the next morning, bundled up in his heaviest coat. His face barely showed above the scarves wrapped around his neck. He strode into the kitchen, clapping his hands together to warm them. "Ready to go find a tree?" He looked at Violet expectantly.

She paused, and Rachel glanced up from polishing the lamp chimney, surprised at her sister's hesitation. "Actually, I was hoping to spend some time alone. Why don't you go, Rachel?"

Rachel opened her mouth to protest, but Violet took the rag from her hand and replaced the shiny glass globe on the base of the lamp.

"If you must know," Violet said, pulling Rachel's heavy work coat from its hook and prodding her sister toward the door, "I need to work on your Christmas present . . . when you aren't around."

She stuffed Rachel's limp arms into the sleeves as though she were a small child and gave her a maternal pat on the shoulder. "Scat. Go with Daniel, and don't come back until you've found the perfect tree. Go!" She flapped her hands in a shooing gesture as Rachel hovered uncertainly in the doorway.

Rachel shot a quick glance at Daniel, who just stood smiling, a bemused expression on his face. He looked a question at Violet, and Rachel turned quickly enough to intercept her sister's quick wink. Daniel pushed the door open and swept his arm out in a courtly gesture. "Your coach awaits."

What had passed between them? Rachel glared at Violet, then shoved a pair of gloves in her coat pocket and wound a scarf around her head.

Daniel tucked a lap robe firmly around Rachel and made sure she was settled before he snapped the reins and sent the horses off at a lively trot. Their hooves crunched in quick rhythm through the light crust of snow.

Rachel sat upright and stared straight ahead, achingly aware of Daniel's proximity. The last time they'd been together alone, they'd sat on opposite sides of the table. Now, mere inches separated them physically, but a gulf of doubt lay between them. For once in her life, Rachel couldn't think of a thing to say.

Daniel seemed to suffer from the same malady. He held the reins casually enough, but a quick peek from under her lowered lashes showed her his wary posture and stiff facial features. When he finally broke the silence, the sound of his voice made her jump.

"I thought we'd go out by Spruce Mountain to look at the trees there." He looked at her as if seeking her approval, and Rachel met his gaze directly for the first time since their encounter in the kitchen.

The clear sky, the forest, the snow-covered hills all seemed to slip away. The only scenery worth looking at was what she found in Daniel's deep green eyes.

His gaze probed hers intently as if asking a question she didn't know how to answer. Despite the bitter cold, she felt as though unseen sparks shot back and forth in the narrow gap between them.

Rachel shrank farther into the protection of her coat and clasped her gloved fingers tightly together beneath the shelter of the lap robe. With all her heart, she longed to reach out to caress his face, to trace with trembling fingers the lines of his full lips. In that moment, she could almost believe he felt the same.

"Is that all right with you?" He barely murmured the words, but it was enough to break the tenuous spell that held them. Rachel felt as though she were awakening from a glorious dream.

"Is what all right?" She blinked her eyes, trying to recall what Daniel had asked.

A smile tugged at the corners of his mouth, causing Rachel's heart to race. "Going up to Spruce Mountain."

She nodded, then straightened her back, trying to pull herself together. Goodness! What had she been thinking? She'd never in her life gotten lost in someone's gaze like that. She must have looked like a lovesick calf. Blood rushed to her cheeks in a scalding blush. She'd better keep a tighter rein on her emotions and not let Daniel see how he affected her.

"Whoa." Daniel pulled the team to a halt at the edge of a clearing where stately pines towered over stands of oak and piñon and a scattering of spruce. "Here we are."

Rachel looked around dazedly. Had they reached the mountain already? If he said so. After five years of getting acquainted with this corner of the world, she had learned to tell her location at a glance. Today, she could have been plucked up by a giant hand and set down again in a foreign land, for all she knew. Her bearings had completely disappeared, swept away by the dizzying fact of Daniel's nearness.

He removed the lap robe, then jumped down from the seat and came around to assist Rachel. She stood on tottery legs and placed her hands on his shoulders. His broad hands encircled her waist, holding her in a grasp at once firm yet tender. He lifted her as easily as he would a shock of corn and swung her to the ground.

Had her perceptions been distorted by the wonder of this day, or did he really leave his hands clamped to her sides a moment longer than necessary? Rachel closed her eyes and breathed deeply to steady herself.

Daniel pulled an axe from the wagon bed and shouldered it, then reached for Rachel's hand. "Come on. Let's go find your tree."

The simple statement brought Rachel back to her senses. A gust of cold air nipped her cheeks and boosted her spirits. She had no idea what Daniel might be feeling at this moment or what the future might hold. In years to come, she might have only this one day to look back on with such fullness of delight. She would choose to enjoy it to its fullest. With that resolved in her mind, she clasped his proffered hand, and they set off together.

18

$\mathcal{A}$cross the meadow and along the mountainside they wandered, careful not to slip on patches of ice in shady spots or trip over fallen branches buried in the snow. They examined, then rejected, any number of trees for one reason or another.

Rachel thought briefly of the farm and the chores she could have been doing, then dismissed them. Violet could handle things until she got back. She found an excuse to turn down even more trees in order to draw out their time together as long as possible.

"What about this one?" She followed the sound of Daniel's voice over the top of a low rise and found him standing before a six-foot spruce, admiring the spread of its branches.

"What do you think?" he asked. "It's not too tall for the house, but it's nice and full."

Rachel circled the tree, trying to picture it in place. She could see it standing proudly in the corner, wearing the decorations Violet had been working on all week. Her lips curved in a smile. "Perfect."

Daniel answered her smile with a broad grin and set to work with his axe. Rachel could see the strength of his shoulders in each powerful blow. A woman would never feel unprotected in those arms. She felt the hot rush of blood to her face even as the thought crossed her mind.

She tilted her head back to stare at the tallest of the trees, hoping Daniel would be so occupied with felling the spruce he wouldn't notice her reddened cheeks. Or maybe he would think it due to the cold.

She tried to set her mind on the tree, the weather, anything but Daniel and her attraction to him, but all her efforts came to naught. She could no more keep her thoughts away from him than she could fly. But what would one afternoon's daydreaming hurt? If it turned out that Daniel didn't love her, the memory of this one lovely day might be all she had to carry with her in memory throughout the lonely years ahead.

What had prompted Violet to voice the idea that Daniel might care for her? Rachel hadn't thought to ask when she first made her astounding disclosure and hadn't had the nerve later to bring up the subject herself. Her sister and Daniel did spend a goodly amount of time talking, but would he confide such private matters of the heart to her sister?

Probably not. More than likely, Violet had sailed off into one of her fantasy worlds again and fabricated the wild conjecture from some offhand comment Daniel had made that didn't mean anything of the kind.

She thought back over the past weeks, trying to recall anything that would give credence to Violet's theory. There had been numerous little kindnesses, but how many of those could be chalked up to acts of compassion for two young women trying to pull their lives together?

What about today? Daniel hadn't come seeking out her company, she remembered with a pang. It had been Violet's doing that they had this time together. But what of the tender expression in his eyes when their gazes locked and she'd felt like she were drowning in a sea of green? Or the lingering touch of his hands around her waist? Surely she hadn't imagined that.

"There she goes!" The tree began to topple, and Rachel scrambled out of the way. While Daniel went back to get the team, she tried to gain some control over her turbulent emotions. For all she knew, whatever interest there might be existed only on her part. It wouldn't help her peace of mind to let Violet's capricious imagination spark a risky train of thought that could crush her as easily as a falling tree.

She sat quiet on the ride home after Daniel had lashed the tree to the wagon. He tucked her in as tenderly as before, but Rachel kept well to her side of the seat and fixed her gaze determinedly on the road ahead. She wouldn't risk the luxury—the danger—of looking into those forest-green eyes again.

She felt as though she stood on the brink of a deep precipice, ready to teeter right over the edge. What had happened to her level-headedness, the prudence that made her father willing to trust her with his property? All her reason seemed to vanish the moment she became vulnerable to Daniel's masculine appeal.

Her thoughts were interrupted when the wagon turned unexpectedly into the trees not far from Jeb McCurdy's land. Rachel blinked in confusion.

"I need to stop at home to pick something up," Daniel told her. "I hope you don't mind." He pulled up in a small clearing and leaped lightly from the seat. Rachel watched him hurry to a building that was nothing more than a glorified lean-to and duck into the doorway of the slapdash structure. Her lips parted in dismay. He called this place home? She stared around the property, looking for any sign of prosperity and finding none.

How could he have expected to redeem her from her money troubles? Cold fingers of misgiving clutched at her heart. If this run-down place gave any indication of his financial status, he was in a tighter fix than she and Violet.

"Got it." He returned to the wagon carrying a small bundle wrapped in burlap. Setting it behind the seat, he grinned and gave her a happy wink. "Ready?"

Rachel barely had time to nod before he shook the reins and headed out. She no longer wanted to believe he was only after the farm, but how could she think otherwise after the privation she'd just seen? The icy fingers squeezed her heart still harder.

Violet opened the door with a glad cry of greeting. "Let me see what you've brought!" She circled the tree, her hands clasped with delight, and exclaimed over its even shape.

They dragged it inside and set it up across the room from the fireplace. Violet produced her handmade ornaments, and they all helped adorn the tree. When the last bow had been hung, Rachel went to heat water for tea while Violet admired their handiwork.

Daniel excused himself and went out to the barn. He returned with a burlap-wrapped object in his hand. "This is what I stopped for," he told Rachel with unaccustomed diffidence. "I thought you might be able to use it."

She took the parcel from him, careful not to meet his gaze, and peeled off the protective layers. An angel, wings spread and face lifted in adoration, lay in her hands. "Wherever did you get this?" she asked wonderingly.

Daniel shrugged self-consciously. "Carved it from a piece of oak. A man's got to have something to do with his hands besides chop wood and push a plow." He pointed to a cavity whittled into the base. "You can set it on the top branch, if you like."

Rachel turned the wooden figure this way and that, admiring its delicate lines, then held it out to Daniel. "Would you put it up, please?" His fingers brushed hers when he took the angel back, and again she felt the familiar tingle run up her arms.

She steadied a chair for him to climb on to set the angel on the uppermost branch. He took his time positioning it just so, making sure the figure stood upright. Violet clapped her hands when he had finished, and Rachel felt a rush of admiration.

"Guess I'd better leave," Daniel said, picking up his hat.

Violet's brow crinkled. "Won't you stay for supper? After all, you spent a lot of time helping us get the tree."

Rachel's anxiety mounted while she waited for him to answer. After their splendid day together, she knew she would feel bereft if he decided to leave now.

"Better not," he said. "I have some things to do back at my place."

Rachel threw a shawl across her shoulders and followed him out to the porch, unwilling to let the connection she had felt be broken. "Thank you for all your help," she told him. "Getting that tree has made it a wonderful occasion for Violet. For both of us," she added, lowering her eyes.

"I enjoyed doing it," he told her, his voice husky in the clear evening air. "I enjoyed the company too." He raised his hand to her face, one finger trailing along her cheek to tuck a stray wisp of hair behind her ear.

Rachel caught her breath in a ragged gulp, conscious of his nearness, his warmth. She knew Violet was just inside the house, but it felt as though the two of them stood alone in the stillness of the eventide. She tilted her head back to search his face, hoping to find some hint of caring.

Daniel's hand cupped her face, and she pressed her cheek into the soft caress. He leaned so close his breath stirred the loose wisps of hair at her temples. "Rachel," he whispered.

She stared at him wordlessly, filled with a yearning beyond her powers to express.

He closed his eyes and shook his head, slowly withdrawing his hand. "Another time." He took two steps backward, not breaking their linked gazes until he turned and walked away.

Rachel stood gazing into the twilight long after the receding echo of his horse's hooves told her Daniel had gone. The evening chill permeated the scant protection of her shawl. She shivered and went into the house.

Later, she stared at her bedroom ceiling from her warm cocoon of blankets and wondered. What had he been about to say? His tone and abrupt departure made it seem like he'd interrupted a confession. But of what—love or deceit?

She twisted into a different position under the sheet, wishing she knew his heart. If only he cared for her. She moaned and pulled the pillow over her head. No use getting carried away by dreams of something that might not exist.

A log crackled and settled into the fire, sending a shower of sparks up the chimney. The burst of light illumined the lovingly decorated tree across the room. Rachel took a final stitch and bit off the end of the thread. The embroidered initials stood out clearly, even in the firelight: DWM. Daniel Webster Moore. She traced the letters, calling herself a lovesick fool.

When she had asked Jake Samson to add the handkerchiefs to her order, she'd told herself they were only to show Daniel some token of appreciation for all the hard work he had done. It was a good thing she'd decided to work on these after Violet had gone to bed, she thought, folding the handkerchiefs into neat squares. No matter what protestations of unconcern she might make, her sister would have seen right through her supposed indifference.

Handkerchiefs, to her mind, had been a safe choice. They showed she valued his hard months of labor but didn't give any indication of sentiment. The idea of giving Daniel a gift of thanks made perfect sense to her, even now. Spending the past two evenings embellishing them with her neatest stitches didn't.

She placed her needle and thread in the sewing basket and wrapped the kerchiefs in a scrap of calico, tying the parcel securely with string. After a moment's consideration, she bent to tuck the small package beneath the Christmas tree. It could wait for Daniel there until sometime after the holiday. Christmas Day would be just for her and Violet. After the way she had behaved over the past few months, a quiet day with just the two of them would help to make amends.

*H*ow can you not want to invite Daniel to dinner tomorrow?" Violet's eyes were wide blue pools of astonishment. "He's done so much for us!"

"Granted. But Christmas should be a family time. We've both worked hard, and I know I haven't always been easy to get along with. Tomorrow is *our* day, Violet."

"Where's your sense of fair play? You can't make him spend the day all alone. Please, Rachel, it's Christmas Eve!" Violet wrung her hands and danced from one foot to the other, looking for all the world like a child begging for a coveted treat.

"No, my mind's made up. I want time with just you."

Violet flung her hands in the air and stalked into the kitchen, muttering about ingratitude.

Rachel rolled her eyes. Why couldn't her sister enjoy the idea of the two of them having a relaxing day in each other's company? Sometimes she didn't understand Violet, didn't understand her at all. She opened her mouth to argue further, but a knock at the door interrupted her.

She swung it wide, to be greeted by a mass of dark feathers hanging at eye level. "What on earth—"

Daniel's grinning face peeked around the massive turkey. "I heard a bunch of gobblers out back of my place early this morning, so I grabbed my rifle and went looking. Quite a specimen, isn't he?" He hoisted the bird admiringly.

Violet hurried from the kitchen. "Goodness, what a huge bird!"

"I thought you might like to have him for Christmas dinner," Daniel said. "I'll pluck him and get him ready out back."

"What a lovely idea!" Violet gushed, darting a meaningful glance at Rachel. "How thoughtful of you to want to make our Christmas perfect." She dug an elbow into Rachel's ribs.

Rachel flinched and rubbed her side. "All right," she muttered between clenched teeth. "You win." Raising her voice, she called, "Would you like to have Christmas dinner with us? We'll eat about one o'clock." She managed a smile for Daniel, then turned to glare daggers at Violet. Honestly! Some people just didn't make it a bit easy to do anything nice for them.

Her annoyance melted away when she thought of a whole day in Daniel's company, with only minimal chores to claim her time.

Daniel tossed down the last handful of turkey feathers. Normally he hated everything about the messy job, but today he couldn't help but grin. Providing the main course for Christmas dinner had insured him of an invitation to join the Canfield sisters at their holiday meal, just as Violet predicted.

He shook his head in admiration. The girl knew her sister, all right. And she'd proved to be a quick thinker. Her idea of pushing Rachel into hunting for their tree at the last minute had taken him by surprise, but he'd caught her conspiratorial nod and played along with her strategy.

Good thing too. Look how well that had turned out. If he hadn't read the signs wrong, Rachel had been as sorry to end their day together as he'd been. He smiled, remembering the way she'd followed him outside. If he hadn't caught himself just in time, he might have jumped the gun and proposed out on the porch that night instead of following their strategy.

He only hoped the plans they'd laid for tomorrow ran as smoothly as Violet expected them to.

The earth wore a new coating of snow Christmas morning, giving the whole area a sparkling look of anticipation. Rachel felt that same sense of expectation mirrored in her heart all the while she set bread out to rise, prepared the dressing, and stuffed the turkey.

Daniel would be coming for dinner. The thought sent shivers of excitement along her arms, followed by a quick twinge of guilt. This was the very reason she'd wanted to have the day alone with Violet. If Daniel was anywhere nearby, her attention would be on him and not her sister.

Speaking of Violet . . . Rachel listened at her bedroom door, but the even breathing from under the blankets assured her that Violet still slept. Rachel tiptoed back to the kitchen. If nothing else, she could at least let her sleep late this morning.

She slid the bird into the oven and looked around, taking stock. Nothing remained to be done just now. Time enough later to wake Violet and let her help peel potatoes and roll out pie crusts. Until then, Rachel had a few precious moments to herself.

She exchanged her apron for her coat, then poured a cup of coffee and slipped outside, closing the door quietly behind her. Steam from the mug swirled before her eyes, then rose to join the dull gray clouds hanging overhead. Rachel sipped the fragrant brew and closed her eyes in pleasure. It had been far too long since she'd had time to savor a peaceful moment like this.

She opened her eyes again and surveyed the tranquil scene, determined to enjoy every bit of this blissful respite. To the north, Granite Mountain dominated the landscape, its frosty mantle flowing down its slopes and spreading out across the rugged land, stretching all the way to where she sat. The clean white blanket shimmered before her; only the tracks of tiny nocturnal wanderers marred its pristine surface.

She filled her lungs with the clear mountain air, refreshing as the purest spring water. Her heart overflowed with contentment, and a wellspring of gratitude for the breathtaking beauty of the place she called home flooded her soul.

Scuffing sounds from the kitchen alerted her to the fact that Violet had awakened. She hurried inside. Violet stood in the kitchen doorway in her white nightdress, tousled dark hair falling around her shoulders in unruly waves. She shifted from one bare foot to another, excited as a little girl. "It's Christmas!" she cried and ran to give Rachel a hug.

Rachel returned her embrace with fervor, breathing a quick prayer of thanks for God's grace in bringing them through the year's trials. Then she held Violet at arm's length and studied her. "You'd better go wash that sleep from your eyes and get dressed before Daniel comes, Lazybones."

Violet made a face but hurried to comply. "Do you want to exchange gifts now or later?" she called over her shoulder.

Thinking of the three wrapped handkerchiefs under the tree made Rachel's stomach lurch. "Let's wait until after dinner." Maybe by then she'd have worked up the nerve to give them to him.

Daniel dampened a cloth in his basin and used it to brush down his suit coat and pants. He stood back, checking it carefully for wrinkles. There. That should do it.

When Violet had questioned him about his wardrobe the week before, he'd told her he had some nice clothes back at his cabin at the claim without a second thought. He hadn't expected her order to make the long trip over in the snow to retrieve them, though. He'd grumbled all the way over and back, but he'd followed her directive, just the same. Hadn't she been right about everything so far? It wouldn't make sense to ignore her advice this close to achieving his goal.

He dressed, wishing he had a decent looking glass to check his appearance in. He didn't consider himself a vain man, but an occasion like this demanded he look his best.

"Lord, I'm really going to need Your help today." He wet his hands and slicked back his hair. "I believe this is what You want, what You've led me to, and I'll admit it sounds mighty good to me. Rachel may take some convincing, though. Soften her heart, Lord, and make her see Your will."

With a last glance in his cracked shaving mirror, he gathered his things together and walked out the door.

20

More potatoes?" Violet offered the heavy bowl to their guest with a sweet smile. Rachel cast a furtive glance at Daniel, trying to reconcile the sight of him today with the plain-dressed workingman she was used to.

What a picture he made today! She'd become so accustomed to seeing him in a flannel work shirt and canvas pants that when he showed up on their doorstep in a starched shirt with a wing collar, she almost didn't recognize him. She sneaked another look. Her heart hadn't resumed its normal pace since he walked in wearing a double-breasted Chesterfield and doffed his bowler hat.

Rachel reached to pass the gravy boat to Violet and saw Daniel watching her. Again. She took a deep breath to calm herself and hoped the gravy wouldn't slosh and betray her trembling hands. Much as she took pleasure in Daniel's company and lighthearted holiday conversation, the knowledge that his eyes seldom focused on anything but her had been unnerving.

She picked up her fork and speared her last bite of turkey. If she concentrated on eating, maybe no one would notice her lack of contribution to the dinner table conversation.

"You're awfully quiet." Violet's innocent comment dashed her hopes of going undetected.

She summoned up a smile. "Just enjoying this delicious bird, I guess." She rose to clear away the dishes, but Violet jumped to her feet.

"Let me do that, Rachel." She colored under her older sister's surprised scrutiny but didn't back down. "Sit still and relax for a change.

It *is* Christmas, after all." With a clanking of crockery that made Rachel shudder, she carted off an armload of dishes.

Rachel resumed her seat and tried to think of something to say to break the uneasy silence. She felt her face grow warm. They hadn't been given to doing much entertaining, but surely she ought to be able to do better than this. Violet returned for another load of dishes, but she didn't expect much help from that quarter. What would Pa have talked about if he were here today? Her mind fumbled around for likely topics.

"Did you get enough to eat?" The moment the words left her mouth, she knew how inane they probably sounded. Violet's eye-rolling grimace and the flicker of amusement in Daniel's eyes confirmed her fears, and she writhed in mortification. Violet left again, shaking her head.

"You ladies did yourselves proud with that meal. I can't remember when I've eaten as well."

Rachel gave Daniel an appreciative look, letting her gaze linger on his face.

Violet reentered the room. "Time to open our gifts," she said, clapping her hands like a schoolteacher calling her class to attention.

At the thought of the handkerchiefs she'd embroidered for Daniel, Rachel's mouth grew dry, and her stomach churned. She should never have bought them in the first place. Would he read into her gesture more than she intended? Worse, would he be able to read into it everything that *was* there—her hopes, her dreams, her longings?

She pressed her hands to her cheeks and commanded herself to calm down. How ridiculous to carry on like that over something that probably wouldn't matter to him in the least.

He would see the handkerchiefs as a gracious gesture provided by a thoughtful hostess, she assured herself, not a smitten woman's attempt to gain attention. They might even have been some of Pa's that she had pulled out at the last minute. Except that Pa's initials hadn't been DWM, she reminded herself, wiping her damp palms against her skirt.

Seating herself in the rocking chair, she lifted her chin and tried to appear unconcerned. What if he did realize she'd bought and monogrammed them just for him? He didn't have to know that all the longing of her heart had gone into every stitch.

"Who wants to go first?" Violet looked around with a bright smile. Rachel stirred uneasily, aware that at some point her younger sister had usurped her duties as hostess. "All right, Daniel, you start." She pulled a lumpy package from behind her chair and placed it in his hands.

Daniel turned the odd-shaped piece over in his hands, a bemused smile on his face. "I hope you aren't expecting me to guess what this is," he said.

Violet laughed delightedly. Rachel stared at the package, mystified. It bore no resemblance to anything she could imagine, with numerous protuberances angling up from a flat base.

Daniel pulled off the brown paper wrapping to reveal a horn mounted on a board. He held it aloft and squinted at it.

"It's a hat rack," Violet informed him proudly. "I made it from a shed deer antler I found." She grinned and added, "You're holding it upside down."

Daniel quickly reversed the contraption. "A hat rack, eh? And a fine one too." He leaned it up against the wall, where it tottered precariously. "Thank you, Violet. It was thoughtful of you to go to all that trouble."

Rachel closed her eyes in relief. *Thoughtful.* That's how he would see her gift too. A thoughtful remembrance, nothing more.

Violet scanned the small group of gifts under the tree and selected one wrapped in burlap. "I'll open this one." She unrolled the coarse fabric and squealed in delight. "Look, Rachel, it's Molly!" She held up a wooden carving for her inspection. "Oh, thank you, Daniel, it's adorable!"

"I don't know when you found the time to work on that and the tree angel," Rachel told him, examining the figure. "It's a wonderful likeness. You really do have a gift for this."

She handed the carved cat back to Violet, trying to hide her agitation. So Daniel had taken time to make presents for them? Then it was probably a good thing she had a gift for him. Embroidering his initials hadn't taken nearly as much time as carving a wooden figure, though. She just hoped her offering would be adequate.

Her imagination wandered while Violet sorted through the remaining presents. Daniel had obviously taken pains to come up with an idea that had special meaning for Violet. What could he have made for her? A voice penetrated her happy speculation, and she realized Violet was talking to her.

"Here." Her sister passed her a brown paper package. Her blue gaze held excitement and a bit of nervousness. "This one's from me."

Rachel fingered the flat square, trying to guess what it might be. Giving up, she tore off the paper wrapping and stared openmouthed at the intricate sampler within.

"Do you like it?" Violet asked doubtfully.

"Oh, Honey, it's wonderful." Rachel examined the delicate needlework. A vine wove its way through a border of dainty spring flowers surrounding the words "In everything give thanks." The words taken from Paul's second epistle to the Thessalonians spoke to her heart in a deeper way than ever before. Hadn't her heavenly Father been teaching her just that lesson through all her trials? Her eyes misted over, and she blinked back the tears. "I'll treasure it always."

Violet's smile was radiant. "We've gone around once," she announced, "so we'll let Daniel open his other gift. I think this is from Rachel."

She handed him the small package, and Rachel felt her heart begin a wild pounding. Would he think the gift foolish or overly sentimental? She barely breathed, watching him undo the string and pull open the calico wrapping.

Daniel spread the handkerchiefs open on his knee and traced the embroidered initials on each one with a work-calloused finger. He kept silent a long moment, then turned to Rachel with a solemn expression. "Thank you," he said simply. "You must have worked hard on these."

Rachel let her breath out in a whoosh. He hadn't seemed put off at all! Lightheaded with relief, she suddenly realized she was enjoying the day immensely.

She turned her attention back to Violet. While her sister studied her wood carving from Daniel more closely, Rachel did a mental inventory. Daniel had opened presents from both her and Violet.

Violet set down the little cat and prepared to open her second present, the one from Rachel. Rachel's stomach fluttered with excitement. Her gift from Daniel would be next. Giddy with anticipation, she could hardly wait to see what it would contain.

"Oh!" Violet had opened the box and withdrew a delicate gold chain supporting a heart-shaped locket.

"Open it," Rachel told her quietly. She watched her sister pry the locket apart and stare at the tiny photographs within. The tears welling in Violet's eyes told her she'd gone a long way toward atoning for her grumpy behavior by splurging on this gift.

"Ma's and Pa's pictures," Violet whispered, pressing the necklace to her chest. "I can't think of anything I'd like more than this."

Rachel basked in the warm glow of contentment that washed over her. Despite her earlier misgivings, this Christmas had turned out to be far more wonderful than she'd ever imagined. She looked at Violet expectantly, ready to open her last gift.

Violet gave her a blank look, then stared around the bottom of her chair and under the tree. "I guess that's all," she cried gaily. "Hasn't this been a lovely day?"

Disappointment wrenched at Rachel's heart. Just when she was ready to open herself to Daniel and dare to believe he might reciprocate her feelings, her expectations had toppled and fallen with a crash. The letdown made her feel as though she'd stepped off a cliff and would never hit bottom.

She stared unseeingly for a moment, then jumped to her feet, determined not to give the others any reason to suspect the bitterness of the blow she'd received. "Let's have our dessert now," she said, trying to inject a merry note into her quavering voice.

"Not just yet," Violet said. "I want to run out to the barn for a bit and take some scraps to Molly." She yanked her coat from its hook and answered Rachel's incredulous look with a cheery smile. "She deserves a treat too. It's Christmas." She grabbed a turkey wing, looked meaningfully at Daniel, and hurried out.

Rachel stared at the closed door in disbelief. Wishing a happy

Christmas to a cat? What had gotten into Violet? Being alone with Daniel just then was the last thing she wanted.

She cast about for some way to busy herself and went to fetch the pies. She would go ahead and dish up dessert while Violet was gone. It would give her something to do, something that didn't require looking at him and wondering what he could be thinking. Keeping active would help her hide her aching heart.

Moving to the sideboard, she selected three plates. She turned to carry them to the table . . . and bumped right into Daniel. The plates rattled in her unsteady grasp, and Daniel placed his hands on hers. Taking the dishes from her, he set them on the sideboard and recaptured her hands.

Rachel tried to pull them away but couldn't make herself move. Every muscle in her body seemed to have lost its ability to respond to her mind's commands. She stared into Daniel's face, drinking in his nearness and willing her feet to put some distance between them. She couldn't keep her guard up much longer, then he'd be able to read the truth in her eyes. If she didn't move now, right now, she was in fearful danger of making a terrible fool of herself.

Turn your head. Look away! her mind screamed, but she could no more tear her fingers from his gentle grasp than reclaim her heart.

Daniel's hands slid up past her wrists and over her sleeves, following the contours of her arms until they came to rest on her shoulders. The color of his eyes deepened, turning them almost to black. Rachel had to remind herself to breathe.

"We need to talk," he said, his voice barely above a whisper. His thumbs traced slow circles on her upper arms. "I once made you an offer. The right offer, it turns out, but for all the wrong reasons." He moistened his lips and leaned closer.

"Do you remember? I told you I wanted to marry you. Like a fool, I was so puffed up with grand ideas of chivalry that I only saw it as a means of simplifying things for us both. I didn't see until later that if I didn't have you in my life, I'd be missing out on the most wonderful gift God could ever give me."

She stood motionless, feeling the gentle pressure of his fingers on her shoulder blades and wondering how she should respond. Weren't these the very words she'd longed to hear? Why couldn't she give in to the cry of her heart and allow herself to trust him?

Her thoughts turned to the papers in the sideboard. Could she bear to produce them now? With all her being, she wanted nothing more than to proclaim her love for him, but she had to know the truth.

Shaky with emotion, she moved to the sideboard and drew the papers from their hiding place. "Before we go any further, I think you should look at these." Her voice shook, but she stood firm.

Daniel took the papers, his forehead creased in bewilderment. "What's this?"

Rachel cleared her throat, hating herself for admitting her doubts, but knowing she had to force herself to go through with it. "I had them drawn up at the bank. They give the house, the farm, everything to Violet. She'll have sole possession." She watched him scan the first page and waited for his reaction. If he wanted only the land, this would change his attitude in a hurry.

He tossed the papers aside and regarded her with an expression of infinite regret. She stiffened, preparing for the blow to come. "Oh, Rachel," he breathed and reached for her again. "You just had to make sure, didn't you?" A smile twisted the corners of his mouth, and he drew a deep breath.

"In a way, I'm glad you did this so there'll never be any uncertainty in your mind. I love you, Rachel. *You*, not this property. I'd have been glad to farm it and build it up, knowing what it means to you, but I'll be just as happy to start over anywhere you want . . . as long as I have you."

She repeated his words over and over in her mind before comprehension fully dawned on her. Then a joyful trembling began in her fingertips and spread through her whole body. He loved her. Her, Rachel Canfield, with all her foolishness and flaws! She roused from her daze to realize Daniel had taken hold of her shoulders once more.

"Now that you know what my true feelings are, let me try this again." He drew a solemn breath. "I love you and everything about you—your strength, your courage, your faith in God—all the things that make you the amazing woman you are. I couldn't ask for a better helpmate. Rachel, will you marry me?"

She opened her lips to answer but couldn't form the words. Instead she nodded her head, slowly at first, then more quickly as tears of joy spilled down her cheeks. "Yes," she breathed, the words bursting forth at last. "Yes, Daniel, I will marry you!"

One sun-bronzed hand slid behind her shoulders to caress her neck while the other moved to cradle her cheek. With infinite tenderness, Daniel pulled her to him, gazing intently into her eyes. "Know this, Rachel Canfield. I'm well aware of my faults, but one thing you can be certain of. No matter what may come our way, you can trust me, now and forever." Tightening his embrace, he lowered his face and covered her mouth with his.

Rachel closed her eyes and felt her arms creep up past his shoulders to twine themselves around his neck. Her fears crumbled and fell away, lost in the joy of the certainty of Daniel's love.

Long moments later he pulled away, still holding her close. "I have something for you." He reached into his pocket with one hand and produced a faded velvet box, opening it to reveal a gold band set with a small diamond.

"This belonged to my father's mother." He slipped it on her finger and sealed it in place with a kiss. "Merry Christmas, my love."

Rachel's gaze rested on the handkerchiefs. "I didn't get you much," she told him with a catch in her voice.

"You're wrong," he said, brushing his lips across her forehead. "You've just promised me the greatest gift I could imagine . . . yourself, for a lifetime."

She raised her face and lost herself in another lingering kiss.

Daniel cupped her face in both his hands and smiled at her tenderly. "So, where do you want to live once we're married?"

Rachel colored in embarrassment and dropped her gaze to the floor. A moment later, she looked up, shamefaced. "How about right here?" she asked sheepishly.

Daniel tilted his head and lifted one eyebrow.

She picked up the sheaf of papers and opened it to the last page. "I only had them drawn up . . . they've never been signed."

A look of incredulity flooded Daniel's face, then he threw back his head and laughed. "Rachel, Rachel. Life with you will never grow dull." He wrapped his arms around her and squeezed her tight. "I promise I'll do my best to make this the finest farm in the Territory and provide a good home for you and Violet . . . and our children," he added softly, stroking her cheek with his knuckles.

Rachel pressed her head against his chest and melted into his warm embrace. A tap on the door roused her, and she turned to see Violet poke her head inside.

"Are you two about finished?" she asked through chattering teeth. "I've done everything I can possibly think of to do outside, and it's freezing out here."

21

$\mathcal{I}$s everything in place?" Rachel pressed her hands to her face. "My mind is in such a whirl I can't think straight."

"You're doing just fine," Violet assured her, spreading a white cloth across the table and smoothing out its snowy folds. "And yes, we're nearly ready." She stepped back, eyed the cloth critically, and reached out to straighten one corner. "There." She smiled in satisfaction. "Doesn't that look nice?"

Rachel nodded distractedly. "The food—is it ready? I can't remember if I took the bread out of the oven or not. And what about the decorations?"

With a patient sigh, Violet took her by the shoulder and turned her around to face the room. "Just look at it, Rachel. The house is lovely. Don't worry, everything is going to be fine."

"Fine," Rachel repeated, trying to absorb her sister's words. She forced herself to concentrate and scanned the room. Richly colored bows, fashioned by Violet from pieces of fabric she'd discovered in an old trunk, festooned the walls. An arrangement of pinecones and evergreen boughs held a place of honor atop the mantel. And over in the corner stood the Christmas tree, lending its air of regal beauty to the scene.

"Fine," she said again. It did look nice. She relaxed a fraction, then she thought of the kitchen. "The bread!" she cried, whirling to run check the oven.

Violet caught her arm and held her in a firm grasp. "I took the bread out twenty minutes ago. It looks wonderful." She held up a hand to cut off further protests. "The venison is roasting now, and I've put the potatoes and carrots on to boil. The whole meal will be done to perfection, and you don't need to worry about a thing." She emphasized the last words with a jab of her finger.

"Trust me, Rachel. Everything will be ready well before the guests arrive. I've even made a cake," she said smugly.

Rachel stared at her sister through eyes that didn't want to focus. When had they traded places, with Violet taking over the role of the down-to-earth counselor? She shook her head to clear it but only succeeded in making it throb.

"Relax," Violet told her, wrapping her arms around her in a comforting hug. "You're just tired. It's a lot of work putting a wedding together in a week."

Rachel returned the hug, appreciating the emotional lifeline. Had it been a week since Daniel proposed for the second time, the time that took her breath away and sent her into this state of rapturous confusion? Sometimes it seemed like only a moment had passed, other times she felt as though he'd been woven into the fabric of her life forever.

And maybe he had, she mused. Maybe the sense of completeness she now felt came as the result of finally finding a part of herself she hadn't realized was missing.

She pulled away and turned to survey their preparations one more time, unable to believe they'd been able to pull everything together in a mere matter of days. Try as she might, she couldn't find a thing out of place. Violet was right; she needed to relax and enjoy this day of days.

The image of Daniel's dear face formed in her mind. She remembered the feeling of his strong arms around her as he took his leave the night before. "I know a week hasn't given you much time to get ready," he whispered, his lips grazing her ear. "But without a lot of family to plan for, there just didn't seem to be much point in waiting any longer."

He tilted her face up to meet his smiling gaze. "Besides, I like the idea of starting out a brand-new year as man and wife."

"Rachel?" Violet's insistent tap on her shoulder interrupted her reverie. "I said to relax, not fall asleep. You'd better start thinking about getting dressed."

With a startled glance at the mantel clock, Rachel hurried to her room. There on her bed lay the treasure Violet had found while digging through trunks for more decorations. The yellowed satin of their mother's wedding dress spread across her comforter in flowing lines.

A lump formed in her throat, and she blinked back sudden tears. "I wish you could have been here on this day, Ma. You and Pa both. It would have been good to have you with me." But maybe they knew of her newfound happiness; maybe they were watching from the portals of heaven even now. The thought cheered her, and she raised her hands to undo the buttons on her dress.

"Need any help?" Violet slipped into the room and lent a hand with the buttons, then lifted the wedding dress reverently. It slid over Rachel's head and shoulders in a rush of satiny smoothness. Violet fastened each tiny button up the back, then stood back and looked at her sister with awe.

"You're beautiful," she whispered. She hurried to tilt the looking glass so Rachel could see her reflection.

Violet was right, she thought in stunned wonder. Love for Daniel shone in her face, giving her a radiance she had never dreamed possible. A knock at the front door jarred her back to the present.

"Fix your hair." Violet thrust a hairbrush in her hand and hurried from the room. "I'll let you know when it's time."

The scuffle of boots in the front of the house told her their guests had arrived. Through the commotion, she heard the voice of the minister from town. Thank goodness. They could manage a wedding without guests, but the preacher was a necessity. In another moment, Daniel's deep baritone filtered into the room. Rachel closed her eyes and sighed. The minister was there; Daniel was there. Everything would be all right.

Her door opened and closed again, and Violet stood before her, eyes sparkling with excitement. "Ready?"

"I think so." Rachel drew a shaky breath and smiled at her sister. "Someday you'll be wearing this dress."

Violet returned her smile and squeezed her hands. "That someday may be a long way off. Right now, you have a very handsome man waiting for you out there. Let's go."

Rachel nodded and followed her sister from the room. She searched the happy faces that turned to greet her: Ben Murphy, Jake Samson and his wife, two unfamiliar men she assumed must be Abner and Seth Watson. Not a large number of onlookers, but people who were dear to her and Daniel.

Beyond them, a lone figure stood silhouetted in the doorway. Rachel strained to make out who it was, then felt a quick flush rise to her cheeks when she recognized the grinning face of Jeb McCurdy.

She moved past their guests, her step hesitating when she finally glimpsed the one person her eyes had sought. Daniel stood before the fireplace, waiting. Waiting for her. The next moment, she clasped his fingers in her own, standing at his side before the little group as she would from this day forward.

The minister cleared his throat. "We are gathered here today in the sight of God and these witnesses," he began, "to join this couple in holy matrimony."

Over Daniel's shoulder, she could see the angel atop the tree, seeming to assure her that heaven saw and blessed their union.

"Daniel, do you take this woman to be your lawfully wedded wife?"

The forest-green gaze drew her into its depths. "I do."

"Rachel, do you take this man to be your lawfully wedded husband?"

She tightened her fingers around the hands of the man she loved. Strong hands, good hands. "I do," she whispered.

"Then repeat after me . . ." His words and Daniel's reply faded into the distance as she thought about God's unsearchable goodness, the unbelievable blessings He had bestowed on her. Daniel gave her hands a squeeze, and she realized the minister looked at her expectantly.

"I, Rachel, take thee, Daniel," she repeated obediently. *My wonderful Daniel, my other half.*

"To be my husband . . ." *I'll be the best wife I know how.*

"To have and to hold from this day forward, for better for worse, for richer for poorer, in sickness and in health . . ." *The Lord has seen us through this time of testing. He'll be with us in whatever comes our way.*

"To love, honor, and obey, until death do us part." She spoke the final words, almost certain that somewhere her parents wept for joy.

"You may kiss the bride."

Daniel raised his hands, placing one on each side of her face. Slowly, he bent toward her, and she raised her lips to his, melting into his kiss and floating away on a cloud of pure joy.

When they parted at last, Rachel smiled at the sound of the guests' applause but didn't remove her gaze from Daniel's face. The face of her husband. She marveled at the thought.

Her spirit sent a joyful shout of praise to heaven. God had not only seen her through her darkest hour but added in the unexpected gift of Daniel's love.

The time of sorrow had passed, giving way to a season of hope.

Sleigh Bells

by Judith McCoy Miller

To Sondra Boyer—friend, confidante, and genuine seeker. Isn't He wonderful!

Special Thanks to Raymond Dunn for his time, energy, and assistance in curing my computers of their many ills; and to Gaylynn Childs, Geary County historian, for her valuable assistance, knowledge, and information regarding Junction City, Fort Riley, and Geary County.

Fort Riley, Kansas—October 1870

heodora Yorke stared out across the parade field, where her father was leading his unit through the rigors of cavalry tactical training. The soldiers, in their blue, wool uniforms and buffalo coats, appeared unaffected by the light snow that had been falling for several hours and now dusted the ground. Plumes of cold air fanned out from the horses' nostrils, and steam rose off the animals' glistening bodies as they snorted and raced back and forth across the field, the soldiers drawing their sabers in mock battle.

"How much longer is Father going to keep those poor men out there? At this rate, they'll all be admitted to the hospital by nightfall," Teddi complained.

"You seem a bit agitated, my dear. Your father isn't drilling the men any longer than normal, and they're not going to freeze. It's more likely they are overly warm in those heavy buffalo coats. Do move away from the window and come have some tea," her mother replied as the maid carried a flowered porcelain teapot and cups into the parlor and, with a practiced ease, placed each piece of the tea service on the cloth-covered table. "Sitting there with your nose pressed to that frosty windowpane isn't going to hurry him along."

Teddi rose from the chair and absently moved about the room. She straightened the tatted edge of a doily, then moved a vase from the small, marble-top table beside the sofa to one end of the thick wood mantle before returning it to its original position. Moving back toward the mantle, she ran her finger along the metal stripping on the edge of the fire screen standing in front of the fireplace. Startled by the heat, she hastily stuck the finger in her mouth.

"A bit warmer than you anticipated?" her mother asked with a chuckle.

"What? Oh, my finger . . . Yes, I didn't think about the metal being so hot," Teddi replied as she walked back toward the window.

"Teddi, *please* come over here and sit down," Isabelle urged. "Let's have our tea; perhaps your father will complete his training exercises, and the two of you can be off to the train station by the time we've finished."

Isabelle Yorke smiled at her youngest child. After giving birth to four sons, Isabelle had given up on the idea of ever having a daughter. During her final pregnancy, Isabelle had been determined she would not be disappointed with another son. In fact, she had done everything in her power to avoid thinking the possibility even existed that she might give birth to a daughter. In keeping with that decision, she chose a suitable name for the yet unborn child—Theodore Edward. When the midwife announced that she'd had a daughter, Isabelle held fast to the name she had chosen for the baby. Clayton had briefly suggested that they name their daughter Lydia, after an old family friend, but Isabelle said they would merely alter the name to Theodora Edwina. It hadn't taken long for the baby girl's four older brothers to nickname their little sister Teddi. And that moniker had remained.

Jonathan, their youngest son, had just turned four, and William, the eldest, had been twelve when Isabelle gave birth to the long-awaited baby girl. Smiling as she recalled those fond memories, Isabelle once again beckoned her daughter to the tea table. That darling baby girl had grown into the independent-thinking, twenty-two-year-old woman who now walked toward her.

Because Teddi was the only girl among four boys, Isabelle and Clayton had understandably taken great pleasure in indulging their daughter. Fortunately for all of them, Teddi was not a demanding child, and, through no effort of her parents', their little girl had not become the spoiled, petulant child that one would have expected. She was bright and well mannered, although she was more of a tomboy than Isabelle would have preferred. But, as Clayton was always quick to point out, what could one expect with four older brothers and a father who enjoyed boisterous play? Isabelle was pleased that Teddi had acquired her stylish taste in clothing and home decor, but it was evident to even the casual observer that Teddi Yorke's physical appearance was not inherited from her stunning mother.

Teddi stood at the window and pulled back the heavy, burgundy drape for one final glance. With a long, deep sigh, she allowed the curtain to fall back into place as she walked to the table, sat down, and began stirring her cup of tea with a vengeance.

"You certainly are out of sorts today. Is your grumpy behavior due to the fact that your father wouldn't share his secret?" Isabelle inquired as she poured a splash of cream into her steaming cup of tea.

"I don't think he has a secret. I think he just wants company when he goes to the train station. Now that I've agreed to go, he's bound and determined to keep me waiting. At this rate, I won't get anything accomplished this morning. I really should be at the hospital checking on patients. You *know* those two orderlies won't take care of things properly."

"I'm sure the hospital will be just fine without you for one morning. Besides, those few patients should be ready to return to duty soon, shouldn't they?"

"Well, yes," Teddi admitted begrudgingly. "But they are still entitled to decent care until their release. After all, they've had only the most rudimentary medical treatment as it is."

"I wouldn't say that! You're an *excellent* nurse, and the hospital is very fortunate to have you—especially during these past few months."

"Having me available is not the same as having a qualified doctor on hand," Teddi argued.

"Perhaps. But I'd wager those young men would much rather have you caring for them than all the doctors the military has to offer."

Teddi smiled. "Only because I spend more time listening to their complaints. But thank you, Mother. You always seem to cheer me. I'm sorry I've been acting like such a bore."

"Here's your father now," Isabelle said as she rose from the table and greeted her husband with a warm embrace. "Ohhh, your face feels like a chunk of ice!" she exclaimed, pulling away and shaking her finger at him when he persisted and buried his freezing face in her neck.

Teddi laughed at her parents' antics but fled when Clayton headed in her direction. "Afraid of a little cold?" her father called after her when she took refuge in the dining room. "Better get your warmest cloak, and then let's get going. The train should be arriving soon."

Teddi shook her head as she walked into the parlor. "I've been waiting for an hour; he's home for one minute and tells me *I* should hurry," Teddi said to her mother, feigning indignation.

"Oh, you know how he is. Just because he's a general, he thinks everyone should jump to his command," Isabelle replied, giving her husband a mock salute.

"What is this? The two of you carrying on a conversation about me as though I'm not even in the room?" Clayton asked, unable to keep the sparkle out of his eyes. "You continue with *that* behavior and you'll never know my secret," he teased.

"I don't think you *have* a secret. I think you just want company going to the train station," Teddi countered as she fastened her fur-trimmed, red, wool cloak. Pulling the matching fur-trimmed hat down on her head, she peeked up at her father. "I'm right, aren't I?"

"No, you're *not* right. But if you'd rather stay home . . ."

"I didn't say I wanted to stay home. I'm coming. See?" Teddi asked, holding out her hands to emphasize the fact that she was pulling on her gloves. "We'll be back soon, Mother. Are we bringing the surprise home for Mother to see?"

"Yes, as a matter-of-fact, I believe we'll do just that," Clayton replied while he winked at Isabelle.

"I saw that! Do you know what the surprise is, Mother? You do, don't you? And you've let me stew and fret all morning, acting like you didn't know a thing!"

"Go along with your father, Teddi; don't concern yourselves if the train is late. I'll have Florence hold the noonday meal until your return," Isabelle replied, ignoring her daughter's question and walking off toward the kitchen at the rear of the house.

A gust of wind whipped across the open expanse of the parade grounds, and Teddi snuggled more deeply under the heavy, wool lap robe. Her father gave her a grin as he flicked the reins and the team of horses pulled the sleigh into motion. "First sleigh ride of the winter. Are you warm enough?" he cheerily inquired.

Teddi nodded. "You *do* love winter, don't you, Father?" she asked, giving him a broad smile.

"Best season of the year, as far as I'm concerned. I've always loved the snow and cold weather—and then there's Christmas, of course," he replied with a wink.

She shivered as the unrelenting wind whipped the blanket and a gush of cold air rushed down her neck. "Christmas is two months away. I think we could agree that winter has arrived, even if the snow holds off a little while longer."

"Perhaps. But the more snow, the better, as far as I'm concerned," he replied, puffs of frosty air billowing forth with each word he spoke. "Pull my buffalo robe over you if you're cold," he offered, pointing toward the furry animal hide lying on the opposite seat. "We'll be in Junction City soon."

It was too cold to carry on a conversation, Teddi decided. Besides, the only thing she really wanted to know, her father wouldn't tell her. He'd been teasing and dropping hints about his surprise for the last three weeks, much as he did as Christmas approached each year. Her father loved keeping secrets even more than he loved wintertime! And this secret was particularly annoying because she hadn't been able to figure out even one of the clues her father had given.

At first she had thought her brother Jonathan was coming home for a visit before he began his military assignment at Washington Barracks in Washington City, D.C. When her father had told her that she was wrong, Teddi had been extremely disappointed. General Yorke was devout in his Christian convictions, and his daughter knew he wouldn't lie. It had always been a strict rule in the Yorke household that lying would not be tolerated. The children grew up memorizing Bible verses, but Clayton and Isabelle were in agreement that it was most important that the children also put those memory verses into practice. Never ones to believe that their children should look elsewhere for a good example, the Yorkes practiced what they preached.

Even on the few occasions when one of the children would correctly guess a Christmas surprise, Clayton would readily admit to the truth. This, of course, caused no end of difficulty for Isabelle. Knowing the disappointment her children would experience if they had no surprise on Christmas morning, Isabelle would scurry about, attempting to find some other exciting yet inexpensive Christmas gift. On each such occasion, Isabelle had been successful, serving to reinforce Clayton's stance that no matter what the circumstances, telling the truth was the best policy.

Hearing that Jonathan would not be on the train seemed to suddenly deepen Teddi's longing to see him. She had formed a close relationship with her youngest brother as they were growing up. Her other brothers had been gone from home by the time she was old enough to become a pesky little sister. She was sure there was no one quite as wonderful as Jonathan, and when he left for college, she was sure she would die of loneliness. Then, after three years of school, he came home and announced he was planning to attend the United States Military Academy at West Point. Although Clayton had been sure that the boy would change his mind when they received word he would be required to enter the academy as a freshman, Jonathan had been undeterred, and Teddi had been distraught that he would once again be leaving.

Since his departure to the academy over four years ago, he had come home for only one visit. Teddi had fervently hoped he would return after graduation last spring, but once again she had been disappointed. They had received a letter shortly before his graduation, advising that he had received orders to report to Washington City, D.C., and there would be no time for him to return home for a visit. Her parents had taken it in stride, saying it was a part of military life, but not Teddi. *Likely, we'll never see each other again,* Teddi thought, knowing her father would chuckle and call her melodramatic if she voiced her opinion. Smiling, she waved at a couple of young boys with ice skates slung over their shoulders as they headed toward the river.

"That ice isn't thick enough for skating," her father called out to the boys as their sleigh continued onward across the Republican River Bridge.

Perhaps she could visit Jonathan in Washington next spring after he had an opportunity to settle into his new command. After all, Aunt

Nina and Uncle Frederick lived in the nation's capital, and she could stay with them during her visit. She would discuss the idea with her mother when they returned home. Just thinking of the prospective visit warmed Teddi's spirits.

"Here we are," her father announced as he pulled back on the reins, drawing the team to a halt. The horses perked their ears at the sound of a train's shrill whistle in the distance. "Won't be long now." He gave Teddi a broad grin as he tied the reins to a rough wooden hitching rail and then returned to assist her out of the sleigh. "Let's go into the station and wait. I'm sure Harold has a fire burning that will warm you."

Teddi didn't hesitate. Stepping down, she quickly grabbed her father's arm and rushed toward the depot. An iron, potbellied stove stuffed with wood sat in the center of the room, the firebox glowing a bright reddish orange.

"Better get the lid off that pail," Clayton hollered in greeting to the stationmaster. Teddi looked toward the stove and spotted a syrup bucket sitting on top of the heating device.

"Thanks, Clayton. I meant to take the lid off that bucket, but then I got busy," Harold replied, stepping quickly toward the bucket and carefully removing the lid. He peered into the container and then gave them a smile. "Good thing you came in. My soup's already boiling. A minute or two more and we'd have had us one fine explosion! I'd be cleaning up soup for days to come."

Teddi took a deep whiff of what smelled like a savory beef and barley concoction. The pleasurable aroma and her growling stomach served as a reminder that it was past noon, and, except for a few bites of leftover cornbread that she'd grabbed while passing through the kitchen much earlier in the day, she'd not yet eaten.

"What brings you into town in this cold weather?" Harold asked while Teddi moved closer to the heating stove and held her hands out toward its warmth.

"Meeting the train," Clayton replied. "Can't tell you any more than that, or I'd spoil Teddi's surprise."

Harold nodded and motioned Clayton to come nearer. Teddi watched as the two men leaned closely together and spoke in hushed tones. A few moments later, Harold slapped Clayton on the back, and the two men shared a deep belly laugh. Teddi shook her head at the men and turned away. She was determined not to ask any more questions about her father's surprise.

"Won't have to wait much longer," Harold chortled as the train slowly chugged closer to the depot. "I'd better get out there," he said, pulling his heavy coat from a peg and then shoving his arms into the sleeves of the woolen jacket.

A gush of cold air and featherlight snow surged into the room, causing Teddi once again to retreat toward the black iron stove. "Don't you want to go out to the platform and wait? The train's coming to a stop," her father urged, obviously anxious for her to catch an immediate glimpse of the secret.

"Too cold out there—you go ahead," she smugly replied. She wasn't about to let her father have any more satisfaction than he'd already enjoyed with his mysterious surprise!

C aptain Phillip Hamilton leaned forward and peered out the dirty train window that was now frosted from the cold. He felt as though he'd been traveling for months, although his journey had taken only a week and had even permitted him the luxury of a relaxing overnight stay in St. Louis. Now his dark blue uniform was rumpled, and his calf-high, black boots had lost their luster. Nothing a good spit-shine wouldn't fix, but there would be no time for such last-minute repairs before his arrival in Junction City.

He leaned back against the hard, wooden seat, ran his fingers through his thick, chocolate-brown hair, and once again told himself that he'd made a sound decision. Fort Riley would be a new beginning, his first assignment as a military chaplain. A new beginning with a few old friends to assist him with his adjustment to army life on the prairie.

How long had it been? At least seven or eight years since he and Jonathan Yorke had become best friends at Fort McHenry, where their fathers had both been serving as army officers. They had attended high school together, and when Phillip's parents were required to leave for their new military assignment two weeks before graduation, Phillip had remained behind with the Yorkes. They had been his surrogate parents that summer before both boys left for college.

The boys had formed a rare friendship that had not dimmed through the years. They had remained in contact and enjoyed occasional visits, although their fathers had never again been stationed at the same military post. In fact, Phillip had managed a visit to West Point for Jonathan's graduation ceremonies in the spring. Each of them was still amazed that the other had chosen a military career. Unhappy with the separations that the military had caused in their lives, both boys had vowed never to choose such a career. Now, however, they were both officers in the United States Army. Phillip smiled at the thought.

The train slowed and then lurched to a stop a short time later. *Well, here goes,* he thought, *the start of my life in the vast, open spaces of the West.* Picking his way down the narrow aisle of the train, he slung a canvas bag over his shoulder and grabbed his black leather satchel before disembarking.

"Phillip!" a resonant bass voice called out. "Over here."

Phillip turned and caught sight of General Yorke. It didn't appear that the general had changed a bit. Perhaps the laugh lines around his mouth and eyes had grown a little deeper, and a few gray strands were woven into his dark hair, but Phillip would have recognized Clayton Yorke anywhere.

"Good to see you, sir," Phillip said, raising his arm in a smart salute.

"Plenty of time for the formalities of military protocol later. Come here, boy," he said, pulling Phillip into a bear hug. "It's good to see you. I can't tell you how pleased I was when I heard that you had requested to serve at Fort Riley."

"Thank you, sir. I'm sure it will be one of my most pleasurable assignments. Although I must admit I hadn't expected the cold temperature—not at the end of October."

"This is Kansas, my boy. The weather changes here more often than most of us change our underwear," Clayton replied, giving a hearty laugh. "Don't tell the missus I said that. She'd have my hide," he continued, emitting another deep belly laugh. "Come on inside. Got someone in there you're probably going to enjoy seeing again."

Teddi's head snapped upward as the depot door swung open, permitting entry to a cold gust of wind, along with her father and another army officer. She glanced toward her father's hands. He wasn't carrying anything. Perhaps his surprise hadn't arrived after all.

"Look familiar?" General Yorke inquired, nodding toward his daughter, then looking back at Phillip.

Phillip looked more closely at the young woman, attempting to discern who she was, and hopeful he could give General Yorke the answer he was seeking. She wasn't overly attractive. In fact, her nose was rather large, and she was somewhat thick-waisted. He forced himself to concentrate. She reminded him of someone. Just then, she turned and looked him square in the eyes. Jonathan! She looked like Jonathan.

"Teddi?" he questioned the general.

"Yes indeed, our little Teddi—all grown up. Come here and take a good look at this fellow," Clayton urged his daughter.

Teddi rose from the bench near the warm stove and hesitantly moved toward the two men as she narrowed her eyes and surveyed the visitor. She was only inches away when she looked deep into the velvet-brown eyes and then quickly turned toward her father. "Phillip?" she inquired.

"None other," her father proudly replied. "Now how's that for a surprise?"

Phillip gave her a weak smile. *He* was the surprise for Teddi Yorke? Somehow he didn't quite understand what kind of surprise he could possibly be, and he wasn't sure he wanted an explanation—at least not until he was alone with the general.

Not sure what else to do, Phillip proffered his hand. "Good to see you again, Teddi. You were just a young girl the last time I saw you. In fact, you probably hardly remember me at all," he said, continuing to pump her arm up and down until she finally pulled her hand from his.

"I remember you, Phillip," she replied, giving him a feeble smile and then turned to look at her father in what appeared to be utter confusion.

"Really? You would have only been twelve or thirteen years old when I last saw you," he said, grappling to make polite conversation.

"Is this another matchmaking attempt that you merely decided to call a surprise?" Teddi whispered to her father.

Clayton gave her a warning look. "In addition to Phillip's arrival being a surprise, he has news that will certainly be of interest to you. Tell her, Phillip," the general commanded, ignoring his daughter's question.

"Tell her what?" Phillip inquired, clearly confused by the conversation.

"Oh, never mind. I'll tell her. Phillip is our new doctor and chaplain. He's been assigned to Fort Riley. There . . . now isn't that a fine surprise?"

"*You're* going to be the post surgeon?" Teddi asked.

Phillip thought she sounded as though that were an incredible idea. He glanced back and forth between father and daughter. Something had gone amiss, but he wasn't quite sure just why his being a doctor would cause Teddi such surprise.

"Physician *and* chaplain. At least that's what my orders state. Beginning Monday morning," Phillip answered.

"And none too soon, I might add. We've been without a doctor for nearly three months. Isn't that correct, my dear?" Clayton inquired.

"Four months. But we already have an excellent chaplain. Are we ready to go home now? I'm sure Mother is anxious for our return," Teddi urged.

"Have I done something to offend you?" Phillip asked once they had climbed into the sleigh and were headed back toward the post. He wasn't an expert in matters concerning women, but he certainly realized that the chill in the air was caused by more than the unseemly Kansas weather.

"Since your arrival a few moments ago? Of course not. I'm merely anxious to get home and have lunch," Teddi answered.

He gazed at her, certain that something was amiss. But surely she would have told him so. There would be no reason to keep him in the dark. Besides, what could he possibly have done to vex anyone? He'd been off the train for only a few minutes. There must be some plausible answer. Maybe Jonathan had spoken ill of him to Teddi, or perhaps it was some childhood prank he and Jonathan had played years ago that she hadn't forgotten. But that didn't make any sense. She would have been a gangly, twelve or thirteen year old and surely would have forgotten a childhood prank by now. His forehead creased into a frown as he continued to stare at her profile; all the while, she ignored him, gazing at the passing countryside.

"You look as though you're deep in thought, Phillip," Clayton called over his shoulder as he urged the horses toward home. "You two should be busy talking—getting caught up on old times."

Teddi turned, gave Phillip a perfunctory half-smile, and then glared at her father. "Phillip is Jonathan's friend. They would be the ones needing to catch up on old times, not the two of us," Teddi explained, sounding like an exasperated schoolteacher attempting to teach the class dunce a rudimentary lesson.

Clayton ignored his daughter's arresting glance and continued as though she'd not spoken. "If you don't want to talk about old times, Teddi, the least you could do is tell Phillip about the hospital and his waiting patients."

"I'm sure Phillip would rather make his own assessments once he's arrived at the hospital."

"You mentioned there is already a chaplain at the post?" Phillip questioned. He certainly didn't want his arrival to cause an argument between Teddi and her father.

"Yes, Colonel Lane has been chaplain for the past five years. And a very fine one, I might add."

"Oh, I thought he was slated for retirement."

"You'll have to ask Father about that. I've heard nothing about his leaving. How is it that the army has assigned you as post surgeon *and* chaplain?"

"Guess they decided to make use of all my education. I applied for a transfer, hoping to become the chaplain, but the post surgeon position is the one that seemed to attract the most interest from my superiors. I was told that I would be able to fill both vacancies here," he replied. "But there are few other places outside of a church where one can minister as well as in a hospital."

"I don't see how you can possibly handle both positions. Not only does Chaplain Lane take care of his ministerial duties, but he also serves as librarian, and manager of House of Blazes No. 2."

"House of Blazes?"

"The post bakery," Teddi replied, obviously amazed he didn't know what she was talking about.

"There for a minute I thought you were referring to the afterlife.

You know—those who don't get into heaven find themselves in the House of Blazes," he joked.

She merely gave him a weak smile and turned her attention back toward the passing scenery.

"Here we are, Officers' Row," Clayton announced as they came to a halt in front of a row of limestone officers' quarters.

Phillip spotted Mrs. Yorke watching from the parlor window as he offered his hand to assist Teddi out of the sleigh. He wondered if Mrs. Yorke knew why Teddi seemed so distant. The general obviously had no idea! Perhaps he would have an opportunity to speak privately with Mrs. Yorke before the afternoon was over.

"Here is my surprise," Teddi announced, quickly nodding her head toward Phillip as the three of them walked through the front door. "You remember Phillip Hamilton, don't you, Mother?"

"Of course I do. It is absolutely wonderful to see you, Phillip. How are your parents? Doing well, I hope. Get out of those wraps and come into the dining room. Florence makes the best chicken and dumplings I've ever tasted, and she'll not soon forgive me if we let them get cold," she rattled without taking a breath.

"Do I take that to mean we are to join you in the dining room for our noonday meal, my dear?" the general asked with a glint in his eye.

"Well, of course," she replied, laughing at herself.

"My parents are doing very well and send their regards to all of you," Phillip answered, once they were seated in the dining room. "They were delighted that I would be serving under your command, General Yorke."

"I hope that one day Jonathan will have the privilege of serving under *your* father's command," Clayton replied. "You have fine parents. I've often wished that your father and I would be assigned to the same post once again."

"My father said the same thing when I told him of my assignment to Fort Riley," Phillip replied.

"How did you ever end up with this dual role as physician and chaplain?" Mrs. Yorke inquired after they'd given thanks for their meal. "I don't believe that I've ever heard of such a thing. Have *you*, my dear?" she asked as she offered Phillip a large tureen of fatback-seasoned green beans.

"Can't say as I have," Clayton replied, ladling a serving of the steaming chicken and dumplings onto his plate. "Smells wonderful, Florence," he complimented the maid, who was heading off toward the kitchen.

"Serving the Lord is *now* my first love. While attending medical school, I received God's call upon my life and knew that He wanted me to serve Him. I find that the two professions complement each other."

"So you feel the Lord wanted you to minister to our families and young men in the army! Well, I'm glad He's sent you to us. It's going to spread you a bit thin, having to serve in two positions, but you'll have Teddi to help you at the hospital. You couldn't ask for any better help than our Teddi. She's a fine nurse. You just ask any of those patients over in the hospital," General Yorke stated, nodding his head for emphasis.

"I don't doubt that. I'm looking forward to a close relationship with your daughter—*working* relationship, that is," he quickly added.

"If you'll excuse me, I've finished my meal and have some matters that need my attention upstairs," Teddi stated as she pushed away from the table.

"Teddi . . . ," Isabelle began.

"I'm sure you don't need me sitting here. You go ahead and catch up on old times," Teddi replied as she exited the room before anything further could be said.

Moments later, Florence scurried to the front door in answer to a resounding knock.

"General Yorke, you're needed back at headquarters for a staff meeting," the maid announced as she entered the dining room.

"Well, at least they waited until we had finished our meal. My apologies for running off, my boy, but I'm sure you understand. I'll be back at around three o'clock and show you to your quarters. I think you'll find the house more than adequate. If Teddi comes back downstairs, you might ask her to give you a tour of the hospital and chapel. I've left the sleigh tied outside," he suggested while he threw his military cloak around his shoulders and began walking toward the front door.

"Let's move to the parlor and have our coffee in there," Mrs. Yorke, ever the perfect hostess, suggested.

Phillip nodded in agreement, carried the tray and cups into the parlor, and then seated himself opposite the general's wife. "Mrs. Yorke, I believe I may have offended Teddi in some way. She seemed very displeased by my arrival. Can you tell me if there's something I've done—something she may have mentioned to you? We're going to be working together, and I certainly don't want us starting off on the wrong foot," Phillip explained.

"Perhaps you should ask Teddi," Isabelle tactfully suggested.

"I did, but she merely stated I'd done nothing to offend her since my arrival. If she's concerned about working with me, I want her to be assured that I'll do nothing to risk losing a fine nurse. What I mean to say is, I wouldn't be pursuing a romantic relationship with her."

Isabelle merely nodded at the last remark. She was relieved Teddi was upstairs, out of earshot. Phillip's quick assessment that he found Teddi undesirable as a romantic interest would only reinforce her daughter's belief that appearances were all that mattered to the opposite sex.

"Then I thought it might be something that occurred when we were youngsters. Perhaps some childhood prank? Can you help me?"

"What did you say? Some childish prank?" Isabelle questioned, obviously embarrassed that she hadn't been following Phillip's conversation.

"I wondered if Teddi might be upset about some childhood prank," Phillip repeated.

Isabelle leaned over and patted his hand. "I'm not sure exactly what is bothering Teddi, but I'm certain that when the time is right, she'll take you into her confidence."

3

eddi sat staring at her reflection in the oval mirror that topped an oak chest in her bedroom. *It was just an insignificant childhood event that he doesn't even remember.* Yet that incident had been the cause of a great deal of pain throughout her growing years—it still caused her pain, or perhaps it was embarrassment. But if Phillip didn't even remember, there was no need to be embarrassed. And he *had* appeared truly baffled by the whole situation. Perhaps he couldn't recollect, or perhaps seeing that she had grown into what her mother called a somewhat *plain* young woman, he had no desire to remember her childish infatuation with him.

"Teddi, dear," her mother called from the bottom of the stairway. Teddi wanted to ignore the pleading tone in her mother's voice, but she couldn't. After all, her mother had nothing to do with Phillip Hamilton's reappearance in their lives.

"Yes, Mother?" Teddi responded, walking to face her mother from the top of the steps.

"Your father suggested that you take Phillip on a tour of the hospital and chapel. Do you feel up to doing that?"

"I'm not ill, Mother." The *last* thing Teddi wanted Phillip Hamilton to think was that his presence could so unnerve her that she would become physically ill. He would think her one of those fainthearted women who couldn't possibly be trusted to help run a hospital.

"Well, no, I realize you're not *ill*. But I didn't know if you wanted to go outdoors in this chilly weather," Isabelle replied, obviously wanting to give her daughter an excuse to remain at home if she so desired.

"I'll be down in just a moment. Tell Captain Hamilton that I'll escort him if *he* feels up to braving the snow and wind." Turning on her heel, she returned to the bedroom, ran a brush through her reddish brown hair, and then pulled the unruly locks into a cascade at the back of her head. Leaning in close to the mirror, she carefully checked her reflection. Puffy eyes would be a certain giveaway that she had been crying, and she wouldn't want Phillip Hamilton to think she would cry over some silly childhood occurrence. After patting her face with a cool cloth, she carefully applied a light dusting of powder under each eye. Checking the mirror one last time, she shook her head in disgust. Why did she even bother? No amount of powder was going to hide the size of her nose or cause her imperfect features to appear beautiful.

"Are you ready for your tour?" she asked as she entered the parlor a few minutes later.

"Absolutely! Whenever you are," Phillip answered as he bounded out of the collapsible Huntzinger chair in which he'd been seated. The piece of furniture folded and went crashing to the floor. "I'm sorry," he stammered as he sat the chair aright and then fumbled to replace the fringed tapestry cushion upon the seat.

Teddi grinned as she watched his attempts to rearrange the cushion. He had the fringe turned to the back of the chair instead of the front but hadn't yet discovered his error. When he turned toward her, she pointed to the chair. "I think that you need to turn the cushion— the fringe should be facing the front," she instructed.

"It's all right. I can fix that after you two have gone," Isabelle stated. "It happens to folks all the time, Phillip. Don't look so concerned."

"Mother! I don't remember that *ever* happening before," Teddi chastised. "You wouldn't be telling a fib to make the chaplain feel better, would you?"

"I most certainly would not!" her mother replied haughtily. "It's happened to your father several times, and you may feel free to inquire if that's not the truth. In fact, he now refuses to sit on a Huntzinger chair."

"I'm sorry, Mother. I should have known you wouldn't tell a lie— especially to someone as upstanding as Phillip," she said.

Seeing Phillip in a disconcerting situation seemed to relieve her anxiety. In fact, he appeared almost as uncomfortable as she was, and that thought gave her satisfaction.

"You want to drive the team or shall I?" Teddi asked as they reached the sleigh. The snow was no longer light and feathery but had turned to damp, heavy flakes that had accumulated to well over three inches of new snow.

"I will. You snuggle down under the blankets," he replied.

"It will be a little difficult to direct you if I'm in back under the blankets," Teddi responded. "I'll sit up front with you."

Phillip merely shrugged his shoulders. "Suit yourself—merely trying to be accommodating."

"No need. I'm capable of being out and about in the cold weather," Teddi replied.

"I'm sure you are," Phillip replied, a look of confusion crossing his face.

"Turn the horses to the right up here," she instructed, settling back on the seat.

Teddi loved Fort Riley and knew almost every inch of the grounds. Whenever they had visitors, Clayton was sure to take Teddi along on tours of the military post. She had become an accomplished guide, quick to point out every object of interest to anyone who would listen—but not on this trip. The sleigh coursed along down Soapsuds Row, the runners making a swooshing sound as they cut through the snow and carried them toward the post hospital.

"Is that it?" Phillip inquired, gesturing toward the sprawling, stone structure.

Teddi nodded. "That's it. There's a place out back where we can shelter the team and sleigh."

Phillip directed the horses toward the back of the two-story, limestone building. "It's larger than I expected," he commented as they walked under the covered porch that ran across the front and down the east side of the structure. To the west were the physician's quarters and the smaller quarters of the hospital steward. Beyond the porch, to the east, was what appeared to be a large, fenced garden. "Vegetable garden?"

"Yes, although the productivity this year was rather low. I didn't have enough time to tend to the garden and the patients. Sergeant Feighney offered to put some of the soldiers to work hoeing and pulling weeds, but reassigning the men from their regular duties to raise vegetables didn't seem proper—especially since Mr. and Mrs. Sawyer provide such excellent produce," Teddi replied as they entered the largest ward.

Several of the men pulled themselves to attention and saluted the captain as he walked toward them. "No need for that," Phillip said to one of the men as he struggled to salute. "This is a hospital, not the training field. I hear Miss Yorke has been giving you men fine care. You'll be sorry to hear that I've been assigned as the new post surgeon here at the fort, and I'll be relieving Miss Yorke of the extra duties she's been required to endure for the past four months."

Phillip was right. The men did appear sorry to hear the news. "You'll still be working here, won't you?" one of the young privates asked Teddi.

"Yes, I'll be assisting Dr. Hamilton and performing my nursing duties, although I doubt that I'll be seeing *you* much longer. Upon examination, I believe Dr. Hamilton will find you fit to return to duty," she replied, giving the soldier a broad smile.

"I'll miss seeing you, Miss Yorke, and that's a fact. But I can't say I'll miss being cooped up in this hospital. You just say the word, Captain, and I'll be on my way," the private replied.

"I don't officially begin my duties until Monday. Think you can stand being hospitalized a few more days, or shall I have the hospital steward check you over?" Phillip inquired.

"I'll wait. I guess there's always the domino tournament to keep me busy."

"Interested in seeing the operating room?" Teddi asked when they left the ward and walked down a narrow hallway lined with wood-framed pictures of military officers in full-dress uniform.

"Absolutely," he replied, following her into a large room. A solitary, wooden operating table stood in the center of the stark-white, rectangular room. Oak cabinets and shelves containing instruments, medical supplies, and a variety of medical books lined the walls. "Instant reference for those operations that go awry?" he asked, nodding toward the books and giving her a chuckle.

She returned the laugh—with a soft, melodious intonation that appeared to stop him in his tracks. "Is something wrong?" she asked when he stood transfixed, staring at her.

"No, nothing—your laughter," he stammered.

"There's something wrong with my laugh?" she asked. He was tongue-tied, and she wasn't sure why. All she had done was laugh.

"No, you have a beautiful laugh. The sound reminds me of my mother's wind chimes—you know, that light, tinkling music they play when a soft breeze passes through on a summer day."

"I see. And it surprises you that someone that looks like me could have a pleasant laugh," Teddi responded as she nodded her head in understanding. "I shall consider your answer a compliment. Please accept my thanks, Phillip. Or do you prefer to be called 'Captain'?" she asked, adroitly changing the subject.

Phillip gave her a faint smile. "There was a time in my life when I would have *insisted* upon 'Captain.' Nowadays, military rank is of little importance to me. It's my position with the Lord that counts."

"Really? Perhaps that's an opinion you'd best keep to yourself when among some of the young officers who are busy working for those bars you're wearing."

"Quite the contrary, Teddi. I think they need to know that, ultimately, God is our commander in chief. Don't misunderstand—I feel that every soldier has an obligation to do his duty to the very best of his ability and serve his country proudly. But I also think we all need to keep God first in our lives—and that includes soldiers."

"Well put, Phillip. I stand corrected. Perhaps you *should* voice that opinion. It may not please some of the officers, but I'm sure your attitude pleases God," she replied, impressed with his remarks.

Teddi rode in silence as they traveled from the hospital to the old limestone chapel. She was thinking of Phillip's words. He had changed dramatically from the boy of seventeen that she remembered. Now, some ten years later, he was a man who had given his heart to the Lord. She was beginning to feel foolish for holding a grudge against him for something he'd done when he was still a schoolboy—something he obviously didn't even remember.

"That's the chapel up ahead," Teddi said, pointing toward the structure.

"Not many buildings made of wood on this post, are there?" Phillip asked as he drew the horses to a stop in front of the arched door of the stone building.

"A few. But limestone is prevalent in this area, and it can withstand just about anything. When the winds come whipping across the plains, I'd much rather be inside one of these stone buildings than in a frame house," she explained. "I don't know if Chaplain Lane is here. I didn't see his horse, but sometimes he walks. He lives in those quarters," she explained, pointing to a house at the end of a row not far from the church.

"Why don't you stay here, and I'll see if he's in the chapel. If not, we can get you back home. From the looks of the sky, it doesn't appear as if this snow will be letting up anytime soon. Can I assume this is the beginning of a long, hard winter in Kansas?"

"Not yet. We usually get one snowstorm at the end of October or early November. Then it lets up for a while, and we often don't see any more snow until December or January. But we do have bitterly cold winters in this part of the country, snow or no snow. When you stop at the sutler's store to purchase your supplies, you may want to consider investing in a buffalo coat. Most of the men living here find the warmth of a buffalo coat a necessity," she advised.

"I'll remember that," he said as he jumped down from the seat and ran up the steps to the chapel. "Door's locked," he called back to her.

She motioned him back to the sleigh. "Let's head home. Father is probably back at the house by now. I'm sure he'll want to introduce you to some of the other officers and give you a tour of your quarters. The surgeon's quarters are quite nice, although you may find them a bit large for only one person," she added.

"I hope I will have a wife and children to help fill my quarters one day," he replied.

"So you're engaged?" she ventured. *Why did I ask such a personal question? That will give him leave to do the same,* Teddi scolded herself.

"No, I'm not. I was engaged to a young lady once, but we've long since parted company. And you?"

I knew it! I left the door wide open for his questions, and he's walking right in, she thought. Giving him a smile, she folded her hands and placed them on her lap. "No, I have no plans for marriage. What happened to your young woman?" she inquired. *Oh, no! I've inquired into his personal life again,* she immediately thought. *I don't want to answer personal questions, but here I am barraging him with inquiries.* "I'm sorry; your past is *none* of my business. Please don't answer that question," she added quickly.

"I don't mind answering. After all, we're old friends, aren't we? I was engaged to a young lady whom I met while attending medical school. She was born into a Baltimore high-society family and was pleased with the idea of being married to a doctor and living in a large eastern city. She also thought that she could convince me to leave the army. Then when I decided to seek a position as a chaplain, she became furious—not enough prestige. That caused the final breach in our relationship. And I don't think she could picture herself living on military posts and never having a permanent home."

"Many women find the idea of military life unappealing, but once they've been subjected to the lifestyle, they make an admirable adjustment. I'm sure that your mother could have convinced her of the benefits."

"You're probably right—my mother has always enjoyed military life. But I decided that if Caroline was going to base her decision to marry me upon where we lived, perhaps she was more in love with the idea of marriage than with me. The last I heard, she was happily married to a bank president. I'm sure she's very content. And what of yourself? Surely you've had opportunity to tie the knot or break some fellow's heart."

"I tend to shy away from discussing my personal life," she replied as they reached home. "There's Father," she continued while pointing toward the general, who was sitting atop a chestnut mare and heading in their direction.

4

*T*eddi's answer was so serious. She obviously felt that he had crossed the boundaries of etiquette with his brazen questions about marriage proposals. Phillip certainly didn't want to frighten her off. If there was one thing he knew, it was that he needed Teddi's capable assistance at the hospital.

"I'm sorry, sir. What did you say?" Phillip stammered. The general was standing beside him with a look of amusement on his face.

"Finding your new duty assignment a bit overwhelming?" General Yorke inquired as he slapped Phillip on the back and gave him a hearty laugh, which caused a frosty white puff of vapor to hang in the freezing afternoon air. "I merely asked if Teddi had given you the grand tour of Fort Riley."

"No, just the hospital and chapel. She seemed a bit chilled," Phillip replied as the two men entered the house.

"Never thought I'd see the day Teddi Yorke would give up a chance to talk about the marvels of this military post. She usually bridles visitors and forces them to listen to every minute detail," the general stated while stomping the remaining snow off his boots.

"Careful with the mess you're making in that hallway, Clayton. I don't think you're ever going to remember to come in the back entrance when you're covered with snow or mud," Isabelle chastised her husband as she bustled toward the front door.

"You mean we have a back door to these quarters?" Clayton asked, placing a hand alongside his cheek and feigning surprise.

"Oh, Clayton! That's not the least bit funny," Isabelle remarked, her eyes cast downward toward the snow that was beginning to puddle around her husband's feet.

"I thought that's why you put this old piece of carpet on top of the good one," the general continued, oblivious to his wife's exasperated glance.

"I put that ugly, old rug down because you won't follow instructions," Isabelle replied, though unable to suppress a smile.

"Phillip and I thought we'd join you ladies for some hot tea or cocoa, whichever you prefer," Clayton stated as he hung his cloak on one of the wooden pegs.

"Where's Teddi?" Phillip asked, surveying the room.

"I believe she's gone upstairs to her room," Isabelle answered, a slight blush coloring her cheeks. "I'll see to some refreshments and be back in just a few moments."

Phillip's gaze rested upon the box-style grand piano sitting along the west wall of the parlor. He could recall Teddi sitting on the velvet-cushioned stool as a young girl, her fingers running over the ivory keys as she practiced to the rhythm of the clicking metronome.

"I don't know what's gotten into that girl today. She's not acting like herself," General Yorke mused as he joined Phillip.

"Perhaps she doesn't find my company very appealing," Phillip ventured. "I fear I'm the cause of her unusual behavior. I'm sure that it has something to do with our younger days at Fort McHenry, but for the life of me, I can't remember what I did, *or didn't do*, that has offended her. Do you have any idea what the problem may be?"

"How could you be a problem? Teddi was a mere child when the two of you last saw each other—she would have been only twelve or thirteen, at most. No, I think her mood has more to do with Captain Albright than with you, Phillip."

Before Phillip had an opportunity to explore who Captain Albright was and what that man might have to do with Teddi's behavior, Isabelle returned with a tray bearing her etched silver teapot, cups, saucers, and a plate heaped with buttery, fresh-baked cookies.

"So that's why it smells so good in here! Florence has been baking again. I do enjoy that woman's culinary abilities—not that you can't put her to shame, my dear," Clayton quickly added.

"Ever the diplomat," Isabelle replied, giving him a broad smile as she poured the steaming liquid into three cups. "Sugar?" she asked, meeting Phillip's gaze.

"No, plain is fine," he replied. "Perhaps Teddi would care to join us?" he optimistically inquired.

"Oh, I don't think . . ."

"Phillip fears he's done something to offend our Teddi," the general explained, interrupting his wife, "but I told him I was sure that her mood had more to do with Herbert Albright's antics than anything Phillip might have done years ago."

"Clayton!"

"What? Did I say something wrong?" he asked, a bewildered look crossing his face.

"I don't think Teddi would appreciate your discussing her broken engagement to Captain Albright," Isabelle chided.

"I didn't discuss it. In fact, I didn't even tell him she had been engaged. All I said was . . ."

"Goodness! Now look what I've done with my jabbering. Teddi will never forgive me."

"Forgive you for what, Mother?" Teddi asked as she gracefully entered the room and seated herself in a wicker chair opposite her father.

"How about one of Florence's famous butter cookies?" the general asked, extending the plate toward his daughter.

Teddi shook her head. "No, I don't care for anything to eat right now. What were . . ."

"Tea then?" the general interrupted. "Pour her a cup of tea, Isabelle. I'm sure she'd like that."

"Yes, of course," Isabelle replied while quickly turning her attention toward the tray.

"Tell me, Phillip, what did you think of our hospital?" the general inquired, obviously intent on ignoring Teddi's earlier question.

"I was *very* impressed. And the patients reacted much as you'd anticipated—none of them wanted a replacement for Teddi. As far as I could tell, the men are more than pleased with the care they've been receiving. And I'm sure their assessment is warranted. I doubt that any of them could have received better care anywhere."

He turned toward Teddi with a smile on his face. But she didn't smile in return. Instead, there was a look he couldn't quite comprehend. Not anger, but that look certainly couldn't be mistaken for joy, either. Irritation. That was it! She had a distinct look of irritation—and that look was aimed directly toward him. But why? He hadn't done or said anything inappropriate. It was her parents who were dropping hints about some past affair of the heart and a Captain Albright. So why didn't she aim her looks of disdain toward them instead of him?

"Yes, she's gained quite an excellent reputation among the medical community as well," Isabelle chimed in. "When Dr. Jeffries was the post surgeon, he couldn't say enough good things about Teddi. In fact, Dr. Jeffries is now out of the military and has a flourishing medical practice in Junction City. Would you believe that rascal tried to convince Teddi to quit her work at the hospital and come to work for him?"

"I wouldn't have *any* problem believing that, Mrs. Yorke," Phillip replied. He didn't turn to look toward Teddi, fearful he'd be met by another one of her frowning stares. "Perhaps I should think about getting settled into my quarters," Phillip continued as he handed his cup and saucer to Mrs. Yorke.

"There's no need to hurry. In fact, why don't you spend the night with us? We have plenty of room, and it's already beginning to turn dark outside. These fall days are so short. Besides, you'll have ample time to get settled over the next few days, won't he, Clayton?" Isabelle asked. "Don't you think it's best if Phillip spends the night with us?"

"Yes, of course! We'll not hear of you leaving us so soon. If I weren't concerned that a few eyebrows might be raised, I'd insist on your living with us while you're stationed here. Having you in the house would almost be like having Jonathan home again," Clayton replied.

"Father! Having a stranger in the house is *nothing* like having Jonathan with us," Teddi retorted.

"Phillip isn't a stranger, Teddi. With this nomadic life we lead, he's about as close to family as we could hope for," the general replied, his voice tinged with displeasure.

"I'm sorry, Father," Teddi replied with a note of contrition in her voice.

"I don't want to be any trouble . . ."

"You'll be no trouble at all, and tomorrow we can get you settled in your own place, Phillip," Isabelle interrupted as she gave her daughter a sidelong glance.

"Take your bags and follow Isabelle upstairs. She'll show you to your room," Clayton said as he rose from his chair and gave Phillip a smile. "Teddi, why don't you join me in the kitchen?"

At the very least, Teddi knew that she owed her father respect and obedience—and she was sure that she was going to be told those very words once she was alone with him. Clayton Yorke wouldn't consider the fact that Teddi disliked the comparison of Phillip Hamilton and her brother Jonathan. There were certain behaviors the Yorkes would not tolerate, and one of them was rudeness—especially from one of their children. It was obvious that she had provoked her parents, and the meager apology she had offered would do little to salve her father's displeasure. She should apologize to Phillip, but she wasn't up to making amends just now. Besides, any excuse she could make would ring false. *No apology is better than a contrived one, isn't that true?* she rationalized.

Her father wasn't about to waste time dealing with her boorish behavior. His jaw was firmly set and his shoulders squared as he led the way through the parlor and back toward the kitchen. Teddi had barely set foot in the room when her father pivoted on his heel and faced her. His normally ruddy complexion had turned the purplish red shade of a freshly picked beet, and his dark brown eyes shone with anger.

"Would you like to explain what has gotten into you? I can't believe that a child of mine would treat another human being so impolitely. *Well?* What do you have to say for yourself?"

"I'm sorry, Father. You're right, of course, but your comparison of Phillip and Jonathan caught me off guard—I lost my sense of good judgment. My behavior was terribly rude. I'm sorry; I totally forgot my manners. *Please* accept my apology," she implored.

"It's Phillip to whom you owe an apology. Can you imagine how embarrassing that whole scene must have been for him? Just put yourself in his place for a moment. And it's not merely that insult you threw in his direction—you've been ungracious to him ever since he set foot in the train station. He asked me earlier what he'd done to offend you."

"What did you tell him?" Teddi pleaded.

"I told him that I didn't see how he could have done anything—especially since he hasn't seen you for all these years."

"Is that *all* you said?"

"No," Clayton hesitated a moment. "I told him that I thought your attitude had more to do with Captain Albright than with him."

"You didn't!"

"I did. At that particular moment, I thought I was making a true statement. Now I'm not so sure."

"How *could* you, Father?"

"How could I *what*? Tell him that I thought he was blameless? Because that's what I believe," Clayton replied.

"No! How could you tell a complete stranger that Herbert had broken our engagement? It's none of Phillip's business. It's nobody's business."

"I didn't tell him about your broken engagement. Your mother did that!"

Teddi fell onto one of the wooden kitchen chairs with a plop. Everything was swirling about. None of this made any sense. She felt her cheeks grow warm and glanced toward the hearth, where flames licked upward and radiated heat throughout the room. It took a moment for Teddi to gain her composure. But then the full impact of her father's words struck home.

"What? Mother wouldn't—she *couldn't* have done anything as thoughtless and cruel as to tell that, that . . ."

"Old friend?"

"That *stranger* . . ."

"Thou doth protest too much, my dear. I think there's more here than meets the eye."

175

"I don't care to discuss anything except why Mother felt inclined to betray my confidence."

"She felt no such inclination. She thought that I had already told Phillip about your broken engagement. Your mother was in the process of reprimanding me for what she considered a violation of your privacy. Little did she realize that she was providing Phillip with information he'd not heard from my lips. Unfortunately, we made a mistake. Quite frankly, I don't think Phillip is going to use the information to do you any harm," her father replied in an obvious attempt to make light of the situation.

"This *isn't* amusing. My personal life is none of Phillip Hamilton's business. He's the last person I would *ever* trust."

"Why don't you tell me what this is *really* about, Teddi?"

Her voice was no more than a whisper as she croaked out a tearful reply. "It's about betrayal, Father. Now, if you'll excuse me, I have nothing further to say." She turned and ran up the back stairway that led from the kitchen to the rear hallway of the second floor.

She knew that she was overreacting, allowing her behavior to be clouded by the anger and frustration of her broken engagement to Herbert. But the wound was still fresh, an embarrassment inflicted upon her in front of both the military and civilian communities. Tongues had wagged incessantly when her engagement to Herbert had been announced. Herbert Albright, the strikingly handsome, young captain, interested in marrying the homely Teddi Yorke? She knew the stories that had circulated soon after the announcement—tales of Herbert's desire to enhance his chances of being promoted through the ranks of the military by marrying the general's daughter. After all, they surmised, why else would he be interested in marrying unattractive Teddi?

Only months later, the rumormongers had new grist for their gossip mill. Herbert had broken his engagement to Teddi, pledged his undying love to a young debutante in Junction City, and planned to marry her in December. The marriage, however, had been hastened when Herbert received military orders sending him to Fort Brown. It had given Teddi some sense of relief to know that she wouldn't be forced to socialize with Herbert and his fiancée. And although Herbert's departure had helped to subdue the gossip, Teddi still received more than a few pitying looks as she entered a room or walked about town.

Reaching the top of the stairway in record time, she rounded the corner and, with a resounding thud, collided headlong into Phillip Hamilton's broad chest. Teddi watched the satchels drop from his hands and hit the floor. In one fluid movement, his arms raised and he grasped her by the shoulders.

"I can't seem to stay out of your way," he whispered, their eyes only inches apart.

"It's my fault. I wasn't watching where I was going. I'm sorry for my rude behavior. Please accept my apology."

"Apology accepted," Phillip replied.

His voice was barely audible, and Teddi leaned closer as he spoke. She heard him accept her apology, but it sounded as though he had added something else. She looked at his mouth, but it wasn't moving. Perhaps she was hearing things. Allowing herself another glimpse, she stared at his unmoving lips and then permitted her eyes to travel upward until she met Phillip's questioning gaze. Startled, she jumped back, freeing herself from his grasp.

"Any chance that we could start over and become friends again?" Phillip ventured.

"I don't know. I really don't know, Phillip," she stammered.

Making her way around him, she hastily proceeded down the hall and into her bedroom. Closing the door behind her, she clutched the doorknob in her hand and leaned her forehead against the dark, cool wood. What was happening to her? She had vowed never to have feelings for another man, especially a handsome man who was bound to cause her nothing but heartache.

5

December 1870

*H*urry, Mother! They're here."

Isabelle Yorke pulled off the muslin apron that had carefully protected her green, lace-trimmed dress throughout the last-minute preparations for her children. Her face was flushed with excitement, and the rigors of assuring that the house was in perfect order had added a becoming blush to her already pink cheeks. Rushing to the front door, she came to a halt just as Jonathan and George, the youngest of her four sons, bounded onto the front porch, immediately followed by their father.

"Stomp that snow off your feet before you come in here," she ordered.

"Listen to *her*, George! We haven't even received a welcoming hug, and she's reminding us about the house rules." Jonathan stomped his feet wildly and watched as his mother shook her finger in mock indignation. "Come here, Mother," he ordered, playfully grabbing Isabelle and twirling her around before setting her back on her feet. "You look grand! And *you*," he said while pulling his sister into an embrace, "look magnificent. Doesn't she, George?"

"You both need to get inside so I can close the front door, or I'm going to be in your mother's bad graces for the rest of the day," Clayton said as he pushed the boys forward. "Surely you both remember . . ."

"We don't live in a barn," they both chimed in unison.

"I can see this is going to be one of those make-fun-of-Mother's-rules days. That's perfectly fine with me. It's those rules that have turned both of you into fine, upstanding young men who will one day be commendable husbands. And, I might add, I would like to think

178

that a marriage might occur within the near future? Grandchildren would be lovely," she merrily gibed in return.

"You can't make us feel guilty about our bachelorhood, Mother. You already have four grandchildren. William and Martin have taken care of that request," George quickly replied.

"That's true, but one can never have enough grandchildren. Besides, I seldom get to see any of them."

"It would seem that if you want grandchildren close at hand, you should be pushing Teddi toward the altar, not us," Jonathan retorted while giving his sister a wink.

Teddi cringed at the remark, but said nothing.

"Speaking of which, I can't understand how you've escaped marriage while living among all the lonely men on a military post," George added.

"Remaining single hasn't been so difficult. Men can be afflicted by a wandering eye, even when there's a shortage of women," Teddi responded with a weak smile. "Anyway, things aren't as bleak as you might suspect. We have more social activities than you might expect, and there are quite a number of single, young ladies in Junction City who are included in our gatherings. So, you see, these men aren't overly deprived."

"No single young men live in Junction City?" Jonathan inquired.

"Of course. And they're included also, but I didn't want George thinking that there were no women to be found in Kansas. In fact, I'd be pleased to introduce both of you to several young ladies. I'm sure the holiday festivities will be greatly enhanced with a suitable lady on your arm."

"That's most kind of you, Teddi. I may take you up on the offer," George replied. "Speaking of festivities, I was hoping for some of your delicious molasses cookies before waiting much longer, Mother."

"Only the *molasses* cookies?" Isabelle called from the kitchen. "As I recall, you never had a preference, as long as they were sweet and piled high on the plate."

George laughed as he rose from the velvet-cushioned rocking chair. "That would be correct, Mother. Would you like me to help you? I can fix a plate for myself out there in the kitchen. That would save you from running back and forth to replenish the supply for everyone else."

"Some things never change," Isabelle remarked as she entered the dining room carrying a two-tiered silver serving tray laden with an appealing array of cookies. Florence followed close behind, balancing the tea service and a platter heaped with thick slices of fruitcake, while George rubbed his hands together and circled the table for a better view.

"Now *this* is what I call hospitality," George announced after completing his inspection of the pastries. "I do miss home cooking. Perhaps Florence would like to come live back East and become *my* housekeeper?"

"You know better than that, Mister George. I like working for your mama and papa just fine. You single boys are just too messy," Florence joked as she scurried back to the kitchen.

Wagging her finger at George, Isabelle furrowed her eyebrows and gave him a frown.

"What? It was worth a try, wasn't it?" George questioned.

"I've worked my fingers to the bone, baking and cleaning for you boys, hoping for the best holiday in years. And what are my thanks? You come into the house and try to steal away the best cook this side of the Mississippi!" Isabelle replied, feigning indignation.

"Now, Mother, you know I would never take Florence away from you," George answered as he continued piling cookies on his plate.

"You can go back for seconds, George. You don't need to pile those so high that they end up on the floor. We're going to think you haven't had anything to eat since you left Washington," Clayton said with a laugh.

"We've eaten, Father. It's just that growing boys are hard to keep full," George answered.

"Speak for yourself, George. I consider myself a man," Jonathan called out, his comment causing the room to fill with laughter.

"You folks sit still; I'll get it," Florence instructed as she rushed through the dining room in response to a sharp knock at the front door.

"I hope that's not Sergeant Luckert wanting to pull me away from my family," Clayton commented while carefully choosing several cookies.

"Look what the wind blew in," Florence announced. She was holding onto Phillip's arm while pulling him forward into the dining room. Meanwhile, Phillip was glancing back behind himself, obviously unsure whether he was tracking snow into the house.

The entire family rose to greet Phillip, with each voice attempting to rise above the other in a hearty welcome to their newly arrived guest. The entire family with the exception of Teddi, that is. She alone remained seated and mute, observing the familial scene as though she were no longer a member of the group. However, no one seemed to notice. No one except Phillip, who met her glance and gave her what appeared to be a questioning expression in return.

"Sit down, sit down," Jonathan urged his friend, pulling a chair up beside his own and patting the seat. "I must tell you, Phillip, the fact that you're here at Fort Riley made it impossible for me to stay away this Christmas. The opportunity to see both my family and my closest friend all at the same time—how could I possibly turn down such an occasion? How have you been? Is Father making your life unbearable? No, I'd wager it's my sister who's truly making life unbearable. I can't imagine how you put up with our little Teddi all day long at the hospital. Tell me, what's your secret for getting along with our little sister?"

Phillip squirmed in his chair for a moment as all eyes rested upon him, mischievous smiles lurking upon their lips in anticipation of his forthcoming answer. Teddi merely stared at him, her eyes void of expression. There wasn't a hint of amusement on her face as she waited along with the others to hear what he might say.

"Actually, she makes it quite easy. Whenever I enter a room, she finds an excuse to leave," Phillip finally replied.

"But that can't work for long. How do you take care of patients without talking to her?" Jonathan persisted.

"Your sister prefers written instructions rather than verbal," Phillip answered. "So tell me, Jonathan, how are you enjoying your assignment?"

"He's trying to change the subject and thinks I won't notice," Jonathan told his family. "I'm enjoying it immensely, though probably not as much as you're enjoying Fort Riley. Teddi tells me there are flocks of beautiful young women in these parts and numerous social activities. Have you found yourself someone special—aside from our Teddi, that is?"

"No, no one. Aside from Teddi, as you put it."

"And what of the social happenings? Are they as exciting as our sister boasts?"

"I couldn't answer that. I've attended only a few," Phillip responded.

"But he's taking part in the theater production, which will debut next week," Isabelle offered.

"So you're putting your thespian abilities to good use. I'm glad to hear that. He was quite the actor while we were in school. Several of the instructors encouraged him to consider studying abroad and make acting his career choice," Jonathan told his family.

"Well, I, for one, am glad he didn't. He's a remarkable asset to the army," Clayton replied.

"I never gave acting any serious consideration. My father would have throttled me," Phillip remarked.

"I must say I'm surprised to hear there's a theater out here in the Wild West. Are you hoping to completely civilize your troops, Father?" George joked.

"Now, don't you start looking down your nose at the military, young man. We're every bit as cultured as you Easterners," Isabelle warned.

"Watch out, George. You're going to get Mother on her soapbox if you keep it up," Jonathan teased.

"I'll have you both know that we have a grand theatrical hall. It's been completed only this past year, and you two will be privileged to see the first major production," Isabelle replied as she began clearing dishes from the table. "Why don't you go into the parlor, and I'll join you shortly."

"I'll help, Mother," Teddi offered, but Isabelle shook her head and waved the group away from the table and into the adjoining room.

Teddi remained at the table a few moments, hoping that perhaps she could escape up the back stairway to her room. After spending the past month anticipating her brothers' arrival, she now disliked the idea of sharing them with Phillip. It was obvious her mother had invited him, and just as obvious that her mother had intentionally failed to include Teddi in that decision. As far as Teddi was concerned, Isabelle had been Phillip's strongest supporter since his arrival. She included him for Sunday dinners, seated him beside Teddi at the military ball, assured his name was included on invitation lists for the Junction City social gatherings, and even took warm meals to him when she knew he was working late at the hospital. However, when Teddi complained to her father, he laughed and said Isabelle was merely enjoying having a boy around to take care of once again.

"Come on, Teddi," Jonathan called, breaking into her thoughts. "Fill us in on this theater and the play that will be presented. I'm sure you have a starring role."

Teddi stood in the doorway to the parlor, glanced around the room, and then shrunk back. The only remaining seats were her mother's rocker, which Teddi wouldn't dare occupy, and the sofa, where Phillip was already seated.

"Come have a seat," Phillip urged, nodding toward the empty space beside him.

"Better yet, why don't we go see the theatrical hall?" Teddi suggested. "They just finished hanging the new drop curtain last night after we completed practice. I haven't even had an opportunity to see it."

The four men glanced at each other, obviously content to stay and enjoy their full stomachs and the warmth exuding from the glowing fireplace.

"Why don't you young people go? I'll stay here and keep Isabelle company," Clayton suggested as he wriggled down into his chair a little farther.

"Come on. Don't be so lazy, you two," Teddi urged as she poked her finger first in one brother's chest and then the other's.

"I don't suppose she'll give us a moment's peace unless we accompany her," George said, eyeing Jonathan and Phillip.

"Guess we might as well give in," Jonathan agreed while rising from his chair. "Come on, Phillip. I'm not going to let you stay here and keep warm while we go traipsing about the post."

"He doesn't *have* to come," Teddi responded just as Phillip stood up.

The room fell silent, and nobody moved for a moment.

"Unless he truly wants to," Teddi quickly added.

It was a halfhearted attempt to restore a bit of decorum to the uncomfortable situation she'd created, but it was the best she could muster at the moment. Phillip wasn't *really* welcome, at least not where she was concerned. These were her brothers, and she didn't want to share them, especially with someone as disquieting as Phillip Hamilton.

"Of course he wants to. And *I* want him to," Jonathan responded, giving his sister a surprised look.

The group was unusually quiet as the foursome made their way to the building, but the silence was soon broken when Phillip announced their arrival. "There it is," he said, pointing toward the long frame building.

"Well, I must admit, I'm surprised. The building must be at least 120 feet long," George commented.

"One hundred and thirty-five," Phillip answered.

"And sixty-eight feet wide," Teddi added. "Wait until you see the stage. It's huge. And the auditorium will seat eight hundred people," she exclaimed as they entered the building.

"And would you look at that curtain," Jonathan remarked, walking toward the stage.

"It's beautiful," Teddi replied as she gazed at the skillful touch the artist had rendered upon the curtain. "Even the folds of the drapery can't be seen."

"Looks like the Bay of Naples with Mt. Vesuvius in the distance," George replied.

"Who's the artist?" Jonathan inquired.

"One of the soldiers," Phillip answered.

"I'd say he's missed his true calling. And speaking of callings, Phillip, how is your ministry going? Are you able to spend time gathering a flock, or are you too busy taking care of their medical maladies?"

"I haven't been able to spend as much time as I'd like, but it's working out. The previous post chaplain, Colonel Lane, retired only a few weeks ago, giving me adequate time in which to acquaint myself with the medical part of my position before beginning my work with the spiritual side. I'm hoping to implement a few new ideas, but mostly I'll follow Colonel Lane's lead."

"What new ideas?" Teddi questioned. "You think there are things you can add that would make the chapel better than when Colonel Lane was in charge?"

Phillip hesitated for a moment. "No, not better," he cautiously answered. "Just add a little more variety. Change is good for the soul, don't you think?"

"Absolutely," Jonathan enthusiastically responded, while slapping his friend on the back.

"I see no need for change when things are going as well as they are," Teddi countered.

"I'm not really changing much, Teddi. I thought it might be nice to have a candlelight Christmas Eve service. Colonel Lane said he had never done that. I also thought it might be nice to have a Sunday school class for married couples to attend together instead of going to a men's or women's class. These are merely ideas; nothing's been decided. Colonel Lane suggested I change things a bit, breathe fresh life into the body of believers. You know, stir things up a little," Phillip added.

Teddi remained silent. How could she argue if Colonel Lane had given Phillip the go-ahead to promote change? To make matters more difficult, his ideas sounded quite innovative and exciting, but that didn't mean she had to like them. Since he had assumed his new duties, there'd been nothing but change going on in her life. In particular, Captain Hamilton had managed to stir up emotions and feelings that Teddi wasn't ready to deal with.

6

$\mathscr{A}$s he sat in one of the leather-upholstered chairs in Phillip's office the next morning, Jonathan was puzzled about why Phillip had insisted they meet so early in the day. After all, he was on leave and enjoyed sleeping a little later than usual, and he was certain his mother had invited Phillip to dinner that evening. Consequently, there seemed to be no logical reason for this meeting. Jonathan couldn't think of anything Phillip might want to discuss that couldn't have been better said as they relaxed with coffee in the parlor after a satisfying evening meal. But Phillip had been insistent, and Jonathan had relented.

Now, after waiting for fifteen minutes, he was becoming irritable and even more certain that this meeting could have waited until a civil time of day. Jumping up from his chair, he paced the length of the room several times and then wandered to a bookshelf that lined the west wall of the room. Running his fingers across the leather-bound volumes, he finally pulled one of the books from the shelf, flipped back the cover, glanced through several pages, and shoved it back onto the shelf with a grunt of disgust.

"Looks like Greek to me," he mumbled, looking at another one of the volumes.

"Actually, it's Hebrew," Phillip replied, striding into the office. "Sorry to keep you waiting. Had an unexpected patient show up."

"You should have left the patient to Teddi. She loves taking care of emergencies," Jonathan said with a chuckle.

"I give Teddi only those duties she's been accustomed to handling or the ones she volunteers to complete. Besides, it's a bit early, and she hasn't yet arrived at the hospital. In fact, that's why I asked you to come here for our talk. I wanted it to be private—just the two of us. We could have met at my quarters, but it would have appeared rude for me to invite you and not include George."

"Believe me, George wouldn't have even considered getting out at this time of day when he's on holiday. What's so private that you can't mention it in front of anyone else?" Jonathan asked, his interest obviously piqued.

"Teddi," Phillip simply stated.

"Teddi? What about her?"

"I've done something that has angered her. Unfortunately, I can't get her to tell me what it is, so I don't know how to make amends."

"You've been here only a couple of months, Phillip. How could you possibly have managed to mess things up so badly in that short a time?" Jonathan joked.

"No, it's not since I've been here. Something in the past, before I ever arrived," Phillip replied.

"How can that be?"

"I'm hoping you can tell me," Phillip answered.

For the next hour, Phillip related the events that had transpired since his arrival: Teddi's obvious disapproval of him because of something he'd supposedly done to hurt her in the past; her anger that Isabelle had mentioned Teddi's broken engagement; and her obvious distrust of men, particularly him.

"I even went so far as to ask your mother what I'd done. But she wasn't of any assistance. Can you give me any help with this, Jonathan? I'm at a complete loss."

"You haven't seen Teddi since you moved from Fort McHenry, have you?" Jonathan quizzed.

"No, that's not possible."

Jonathan eyed his friend. "Do you have feelings for Teddi?"

"I have the highest regard for her. She's an excellent nurse, has a quick wit, and is intelligent, capable, compassionate, and devout in her religious beliefs . . . ," Phillip hedged.

"But she doesn't possess the beauty necessary to make you a good wife," Jonathan interrupted.

"That's unfair, Jonathan. I recall that *you* always look for the most attractive young lady with a comely figure when you're seeking out prospective love interests," Phillip countered.

"I suppose that *is* true enough. It's just that, to me, Teddi is beautiful. She's the most engaging woman I know. She can discuss almost any subject with as much authority and intelligence as a man, while at the same time, she finds pleasure in decorating a home or teaching small children. And how could I think her anything but handsome? People say we look like twins," Jonathan added.

Phillip shifted in his chair. He knew that Jonathan's statements were true. A person's outer appearance was not a true measure of who that person was. And he genuinely liked Teddi's company, working side by side with her in the hospital, especially on those occasions when she let down her guard and didn't measure every word that she said. But his feelings for her stopped short of romance.

"For now, I want to be Teddi's friend, but there is something that's preventing her from trusting me. I need to find out what that is, and I'm hoping you can help," Phillip finally replied.

"Let's think back to when you left Fort McHenry," Jonathan suggested, falling silent for a moment. "Teddi was infatuated with you— remember? In fact, she gave you that silver sleigh bell that my father had special-ordered for her charm bracelet. Oh, boy, did she ever get into trouble for that," Jonathan recalled, putting his hand alongside his face and letting out a howl. "Father was furious. Teddi was in trouble the rest of the summer."

"She can't still be angry about that," Phillip protested. "I told her that I didn't want to take her sleigh bell, but she insisted. Besides, I gave it to you to return to her. You *did* return it to her, didn't you?" Phillip persisted.

Jonathan's face turned ashen. He looked as though he were going to be sick.

"Are you all right?" Phillip asked, moving toward his friend.

Jonathan nodded his head. "I think so, but you may never speak to me again."

"Why?"

"I completely forgot about the sleigh bell. I never gave it back to Teddi. After you gave it to me, I put it in a small wooden box in the bottom of my bureau drawer for safekeeping until I returned home from college. I've never taken it out of the bureau," Jonathan admitted.

Phillip folded his hands and sat on the edge of the desk across from his friend. "I see. I suppose she has a right to be angry with me," Phillip murmured.

"Perhaps. But I think this has more to do with her broken engagement than the return of that charm," Jonathan argued.

"Perhaps it's a combination of things. She felt betrayed by me when she was young because I never answered her letters and didn't return her valuable gift. Then, only weeks before I reenter her life, she's betrayed by her fiancé. My presence serves only to reaffirm those feelings of betrayal. The problem is now compounded by the fact that if you return the sleigh bell, she'll never believe I gave it back to you years ago. I'm certain that she'll think I've put you up to it," Phillip finished with a sigh.

"If I try to talk to her about what's going on in her life, ask her why she's behaving so rudely toward you, it will present an opening. If she mentions the sleigh bell, I can tell her I have it and explain that you asked me to return it long ago. The truth is, I *have* wondered why she is so inhospitable to you. I thought perhaps she was romantically interested in you but you had rebuffed her," Jonathan remarked discreetly.

"She's given no indication that she has any interest in me. In fact, I think she wishes I'd never arrived at Fort Riley. Attempting to figure out why has just about driven me mad," Phillip emphatically replied.

Jonathan laughed. "My sister has a knack for driving even the soundest mind into turmoil, it seems."

"I've not given into it quite yet," Phillip replied. "But if I don't figure out how to win her trust and become her friend in the foreseeable future, you may have to commit me to the nearest asylum," he said, joining Jonathan's laughter.

"I'll talk to her and see if I can somehow help untangle this mess that I'm afraid I've helped to create," Jonathan promised as the two of them left the chapel. "You are coming over for dinner tonight?"

"Yes, but we have dress rehearsal this evening. Why don't you come along? I'm merely an understudy. We can sit in the audience and watch the performance," Phillip suggested.

"I'll see what mother has planned. I've promised to haul boxes of Christmas decorations from the storage room. She wants to go through the old ornaments and discard the ragged things. Of course, she'll end up keeping it all. She can't ever bring herself to throw away those ugly little decorations we've all made for her throughout the years."

Phillip nodded and laughed. "I know. My mother is the same way."

Teddi sat in the meager dressing room while rehearsing her lines one last time. Above all else, she needed to remain calm. The last thing she wanted to do was go on stage and deliver her lines in a warbling voice. There was still an hour before the curtain would go up, but she could already hear the excited voices of theater patrons as they arrived. Last night's dress rehearsal had gone smoothly. Corporal Wigand had forgotten his line in one place, but she'd been able to prompt him without anyone noticing. Even the director hadn't caught on, and the play had continued without further mishap. She hoped things would go as well this evening.

The orchestra was beginning to warm up, and the tentative sounds of violins strumming and horns tooting in preparation for the overture sifted through the door. Teddi relaxed, knowing that soon the conglomeration of sounds would blend together in beautiful harmony.

"Change in cast, Miss Yorke," Private Mosier announced after lightly tapping on her door.

"Who? Why?" Teddi asked, yanking open the door and meeting the young private eye to eye.

"Corporal Wigand is ill. Terrible case of laryngitis—nothing but croaking noises," the private explained while pointing to his own throat. "Captain Hamilton, his understudy, will play the part."

"Phillip Hamilton is going to play the lead opposite me?" Teddi asked, her mouth gaping open in surprise.

"He's the only understudy we have for that part," the private replied with a quizzical expression.

"Of course. Captain Hamilton will be playing the part. Thank you, private," Teddi replied as she closed the door, made her way back across the room, and fell into the straight-backed wooden chair. *Phillip is playing the lead. We haven't even practiced together. How could this happen?* she wondered. The director had been so certain there would be no need for understudies, he'd never even bothered to check and see if any of them knew their lines.

Quickly she made her way down the hall and stopped in front of Corporal Wigand's dressing room. She hesitated only a moment and then lightly tapped on the door. "Phillip, it's Teddi. Are you in there?"

"Yes," he replied from the other side. "I've not finished dressing, so I don't think I'd better open the door."

"Of course not! I just wanted to ask if you've memorized your part. Since the understudies have never practiced, I just wanted to assure myself . . ."

"I'll do my best to keep from embarrassing you," he interrupted.

"It's not me that I'm worried about," she began.

"Oh, really? You were worried about *me?*" he asked, pulling open the door and meeting her gaze.

"Well, yes," she stammered. "You and the others in the play. We've worked so hard, and . . ."

"I know that you've worked hard, Teddi. But this is only a few hours of entertainment, a means of amusing those in attendance. If we forget a word or two and give them cause for laughter, that's all right, too, don't you think?"

"No, at least not for me. We've all worked too hard to be laughed at. This isn't a comedy. Furthermore, it will be yet another embarrassment for me to endure. Now, do you know the lines or don't you?" Teddi insisted.

"Yes, Teddi, I know the lines," Phillip replied and promptly closed the door, leaving her staring at the wobbling cardboard placard that had been stenciled with Gardner Wigand's name.

Turning on her heel, she marched down the hall, entered her dressing room, and slammed the door. Minutes later, a light tapping sounded at the door.

"Five minutes until curtain," Private Mosier called out before proceeding down the hallway.

Teddi's palms moistened and her heart began to pound in her chest. She gave herself one final glance in the mirror and opened the door. Phillip was moving toward the opposite side of the stage for his entry. She gave him a faint smile, but if he returned the greeting, it was hidden in the shadows of the darkened stage. She shouldn't have been so brusque. After all, he was probably a bundle of nerves, trying to remember his lines as well as stage directions and costume changes. An apology was in order and she'd see to it—unless he caused her no end of embarrassment during the performance!

The orchestra was positioned in front of the large stage and was just completing the overture when the director gazed about, apparently assuring himself that the actors were properly aligned to step onto the stage at his prompting. On the other side of the curtain, the chattering of small children mingled with the murmuring of adults in the nearly full auditorium. An occasional cough could be heard; then, finally, all was silent except for the whirring of the curtain as it rose toward the ceiling.

Up, up the giant mural began to roll until, without warning, the whirring sound momentarily ceased, causing one side of the curtain to hoist higher than the other. Suddenly, the painted scene of the Bay of Naples and Mt. Vesuvius began to roll up askew. Muffled laughter finally gave way to joyful merriment before General Yorke finally called out from the audience, "Steady there! Dress to the left, men!" With renewed vigor, the curtain began to rise, this time lifting the painted drapery to the ceiling in proper fashion.

The director waited until the crowd had settled, and then the actors began their first scene in earnest. However, Teddi's attempts to remain calm were falling short of perfection. She was rushing through her opening lines, and her voice was warbling so violently that the words she was speaking were barely distinguishable. The director's wild motioning for her to slow down seemed only to make her speak more rapidly. She couldn't seem to gain control of herself and gave momentary consideration to rushing offstage. Instead, she turned on cue, watched, and listened as Phillip made his entrance and recited his lines in a calm, self-assured voice.

With a practiced ease, he moved to where Teddi stood, took her hand in his, and whispered into her ear, "Relax, Teddi. The audience has come to have fun—there's no need to be nervous." He squeezed her hand and gave her a wink as he moved to his proper mark on the stage. Taking a deep breath, she forced herself to calmly recite her next lines. With each word, the recitation of her part and moving about the stage became more comfortable. By the second act, she felt certain that she was having every bit as much fun as Phillip.

When the final farewell scene arrived, Phillip swept her into his arms, captured her lips with his own, and kissed her soundly. It took her breath away, and she hadn't fully recovered by the time the curtain began its ascent for their bows. A roar of applause thundered through the auditorium as the actors joined hands, stepped forward, and all of them bent in unison for a final ovation.

"What were you thinking?" she asked as they continued bowing.

"I can't hear you," Phillip replied while pointing toward his ear.

"I said, what were you thinking?" she shrieked into his ear.

"I was thinking about making the play as realistic as possible. It would have been obvious to the audience if I had only pretended to kiss you," he said while giving her a broad smile.

"It's not the way we rehearsed it," she retorted.

"Well, of course not. Gardner's a married man. It wouldn't be seemly for you to be kissing a married man. I, on the other hand, am not married, not even betrothed, so it seemed the proper thing to do. You know, in the interest of giving the audience our very best performance. It was, after all, merely a performance," he hastily added.

"Well, of course I realize that," she replied a little too quickly.

"Then why are you making such a fuss?" he inquired, moving back as the curtain made its final descent.

She remained silent, knowing she dare not speak the truth.

He would surely be appalled to hear that his kiss had sent ripples of excitement coursing through her body, that she had enjoyed the excitement of his lips against her own, and that she was still taking pleasure in the warmth of his kiss that lingered on her lips. Or would he be so horrified? The kiss had seemed genuine; yet, when questioned, he had been swift to say that he was merely acting his part.

Why was she even entertaining such silly thoughts? A man was interested in having only a pretty woman on his arm, one that caused heads to turn, and she, with her plain face and imperfect figure, could never be such a woman.

7

re you by yourself?" Teddi questioned, attempting to peer around Jonathan as he entered her dressing room.

"Mother and Father said they would join us at the party, and George found several young ladies to keep him busy," Jonathan answered. "Were you expecting anyone else?"

"No, I don't suppose I was. Thank you for waiting, Jonathan."

"It's an honor to escort the star of the play," he joked. "You were very good, do you know that?"

"I was frightened senseless, until . . ."

"Until Phillip came on stage. You were rushing your lines a bit before then, but he seemed to have a calming effect upon you. He does that to me, too. Good man, don't you think?"

"I don't know him well enough to know if he's a good man or not. We'd better get going," Teddi replied, fastening her woolen cape.

"Don't know him well enough? You were in love with him when you were ten," Jonathan retorted.

"Thirteen!" Teddi quickly corrected.

"Okay, thirteen, but you *do* remember."

"Remember what? That my big brother's friend rebuffed me? Of course I remember. It's a painful memory."

"Even after all these years?"

"You wouldn't understand; men think differently than women. You'll come closer to understanding the concept once you finally decide to settle down and have a serious relationship," Teddi retorted.

"But *that* wasn't a serious relationship, Teddi. You were thirteen, just a kid. And it was, after all, one-sided. Phillip didn't even know about your feelings until—"

"I made a fool of myself?"

"I didn't say that, Teddi. You didn't make a fool of yourself. You were a young girl infatuated with your big brother's best friend. You told him that you cared for him. That's not making a fool of yourself," Jonathan countered.

"I don't want to discuss this any longer. Besides, I'm already late for the cast party," she replied, gently pushing him aside and moving out the door.

"Teddi, Mother told me about Herbert Albright. I'm truly sorry, but if he was so shallow as to be drawn away by the first pretty woman that passed his way, you're better off without him. But you shouldn't use his unchivalrous behavior as a measurement of all men. Phillip and Herbert are two entirely different people," Jonathan argued as he rushed to catch up with her.

"Oh, for goodness' sake, Jonathan, will you please quit defending Phillip? Let's just go to the party," she insisted.

The enlisted men's dining hall was ablaze with light. A mixture of laughter and chatter filled the night air as Jonathan pulled open the door for his sister. A sea of men in dark blue dress uniforms and women in brightly colored gowns parted as they made their way through the room.

"May I have the first dance?" General Yorke inquired, handing Teddi's cape and bonnet to her brother. "Jonathan will see to your wraps."

Teddi giggled as she watched her brother feign indignation. "I thought that surely I would have the privilege of the first dance. After all, I escorted her, Father," Jonathan argued.

"Perhaps, but age does have its advantages, my boy. Now, do as you're told," he said, genially dismissing his son with a wave of his arm. "Come, my dear. I'll show these young fellows how it's supposed to be done," he said, leading her onto the gleaming hardwood floor.

In keeping with the season, the large room was festooned with green cedar branches adorned with red berries and tied with wide red-and-white ribbons. The dining tables had been moved along the walls and were now draped with crisp white tablecloths and laden with holiday delicacies of every variety. Centerpieces crafted from dried flowers and greenery were flanked on either side by tall, flickering candles; the festive combination graced each of the serving tables. Isabelle's cherished sterling punch bowl was centered on a table at the rear of the room, its highly polished silver reflecting a rainbow's array of colors as the dancers whirled by.

"Wonderful performance, my dear. Watching you up on that stage made me very proud. It was like old times, seeing you and Phillip having fun together," Clayton commented.

"Old times? I don't remember ever having much fun with Phillip. But I do remember chasing after him and Jonathan, begging them to let me join in their fun," Teddi replied. First her brother, and now her father. Why did everyone have to keep bringing Phillip into the conversation?

"Ah, but isn't that the way of all children? Half of their time spent playing is making it look as though they're having so much fun that others want to join in?" Clayton asked.

"Perhaps. But if you're the one chasing after them and begging to be a part of their games, it isn't such fun. Besides, that was years ago. Phillip and I are both adults now, and the drama we performed tonight wasn't a child's game."

"Well, it certainly appeared that Phillip was having a grand time—especially that last scene. But now that I think about it, he looked as though he was taking that kiss pretty seriously," Clayton replied, giving her a boisterous chuckle just as the music ceased.

"You're letting your imagination and propensity toward matchmaking get the best of you, Father. It was nothing but acting," Teddi replied defensively.

"I'm not so sure," he argued. "I'd better get you back to your brother, or he'll be complaining that I've stolen you away for the whole evening," Clayton continued as he began to direct Teddi toward her brother.

Helen Hanson was clinging to Phillip's arm, obviously mesmerized by his charms as the two of them stood chatting with Jonathan. Teddi attempted to guide her father in another direction, but his bulk proved more difficult to maneuver than she had anticipated, causing them to end up directly in the midst of the threesome that she had hoped to avoid.

"Well, here she is, fit as a fiddle and ready to dance the night away," the general announced as he deposited Teddi between her brother and Phillip and walked off toward his wife.

"Oh, Teddi, I was just telling Phillip what a simply divine performance the two of you gave us this evening. If I had known that *Phillip* was going to play the lead, I would have auditioned for the part," Helen purred.

"Perhaps next time, Helen. You do seem to have a flair for the dramatic," Teddi responded as she watched Helen tighten her hold on Phillip's arm.

The band director lifted his arms to signal the next dance, and Jonathan quickly reached out and grasped Helen's free hand. "Come along, Helen. Let's permit the stars of the show to have this dance," he said, deftly moving her onto the dance floor before she could protest.

"Shall we?" Phillip asked, holding out his hand toward Teddi.

She nodded her agreement, and soon they were circling the floor, his hand resting lightly at her waist. Her palms were damp. She could feel Phillip's eyes upon her, and she longed for some sensible thought to enter her mind, some coy or amusing anecdote that might serve to fill the silence between them.

"You have quite a talent on the stage, Teddi. I was wondering if I could convince you to direct the children in the church pageant this year?"

"I believe Colonel Lane asked Mrs. Bennett to perform that duty several months ago—before his retirement," Teddi replied. "But should she decide she needs assistance, I'll be more than pleased to help. However, Mrs. Bennett is accustomed to working with the children, so you need not worry. She'll do an excellent job."

"I see. And who's in charge of the oyster supper? I hear that's one of the major events of the holiday season," Phillip inquired.

"My mother, although I wish that she hadn't agreed to do it again this year. It becomes a family event, with plenty of work for all of us.

Of course with Jonathan and George here, it may not be as difficult this year. I'll suggest she keep them busy."

"So both of your brothers will be here for Christmas?"

"They'll leave after New Year's Day. It's going to be great fun having them here to enjoy the holidays. I know my parents are delighted that Jonathan and George could both manage to remain throughout the holidays."

Phillip nodded. "That is good news."

"Aren't you going home for the holidays? To see your parents, I mean," Teddi quickly added.

"No. I don't think the army would consider a request for leave so soon after my arrival. Besides, being with your family is almost the same as being with mine," Phillip remarked, giving her a broad smile. "Would you like some punch?" he offered as the music ended and they left the dance floor.

"That would be nice," Teddi agreed, watching as he strode toward the rear of the hall.

"Put in a good word for me, would you?" Helen whispered, grasping Teddi by the arm and pulling her close.

"With my brother?" Teddi asked, now giving Helen her full attention.

"No, silly, with Phillip. Tell him that I'd make a perfect military wife. Isn't he just the most handsome man in the room?" she asked as Phillip walked toward them with two silver punch cups filled to the brim.

"Why, thank you," Helen cooed as she extended her hand toward one of the cups. "How very thoughtful of you, Phillip."

Phillip handed the other cup to Teddi, glancing first at Teddi before allowing his sight to rest upon Helen.

"This *was* for me, wasn't it?" Helen asked, in her most charming voice.

"If you are in need of a cool drink, it is most certainly for you. I'm pleased that I could be of assistance," Phillip gallantly added.

"Well, dear me, when you came in my direction, I just naturally assumed you were bringing the punch for me, rather for us—for you and me to share," she continued explaining as she determinedly moved closer to his side.

"Actually, I had gotten the punch for Teddi and me. I assumed you were busy on the dance floor. But, as I said, I don't mind coming to your aid," he answered.

"Let me thank you properly by permitting you the privilege of the next dance," Helen crooned. "I'm sure that one of Teddi's brothers will be more than happy to escort her onto the dance floor."

"I would love to, Helen, but I've already signed Teddi's dance card for the next dance and Mrs. Yorke's for the one following Teddi's. But if you're free after that, I'll be back," Phillip replied.

"I'll be waiting right here," Helen cooed as Phillip and Teddi returned to the dance floor.

The band seemed to play on indeterminately and Helen paced along the edge of the floor until Phillip finally returned Teddi to the punch table.

"What did you say to him?" Helen whispered as she sidled up to Teddi.

"About what?" Teddi absentmindedly inquired as she watched Phillip and her mother take to the dance floor.

"Me, of course," Helen tersely replied as she tucked a ringlet of dark hair back into place. Her large, bow-shaped lips were formed into a pout that reminded Teddi of a two year old.

"Your name didn't come up," Teddi replied.

"*You* were supposed to bring it up, remember? I specifically asked you to put in a good word for me. I should have realized that you were eyeing him for yourself, now that Herbert's walked out on you," Helen rebutted, her razor-sharp words meeting their mark.

Teddi shrunk back from the attack, her eyes darting about the room in hope of finding some point of refuge. *Jonathan!* He was making his way across the dance floor toward where she stood. Without a word, she shoved her punch cup into Helen's free hand and walked onto the floor, meeting Jonathan midway.

"I presume you'd like to dance?" Jonathan said with a laugh.

"We don't have to dance. Just get me away from Helen Hanson and her vicious tongue," Teddi answered.

"What's Helen's problem? Not enough beaux, or no special beau?"

"She wanted me to tell Phillip what a catch she'd make for him. When I didn't take the first opportunity available to pass along the information, she became insulting."

"You should have just told her that when the right moment presented itself, you'd talk to him," Jonathan instructed.

"Why should I be Helen Hanson's matchmaker? She's never had the time of day for me unless she wanted some favor. Furthermore, I don't think that I'd be doing Phillip any favor by telling him that Helen is considering him as her next beau," Teddi told him.

"Hmmm. You wouldn't be jealous that other women find Phillip desirable, would you?"

"Of course not. Why should I be? He's nothing to me."

"You sound a bit defensive, dear sister. Sure you're not still carrying a torch for our old family friend after all these years?"

"I'm not carrying a torch for anyone. If Helen had asked me to act as a go-between with you or George, I wouldn't have done that, either. My refusal to help has nothing to do with Phillip. It's Helen. I'd have to see some dramatic changes in her behavior before I'd ever speak on her behalf," Teddi explained.

"I see," Jonathan replied, nodding his head.

"You don't believe me, do you?"

"It doesn't matter what I think, Teddi. You know what's in your heart. I do know that Phillip is a good man and would make a fine husband and father. And I think he's reached a point in his life at which he's ready to settle down—with the right woman, of course. Not with someone as shallow and devious as Helen Hanson. Perhaps you can think of someone who might qualify?" Jonathan asked, his voice filled with seriousness.

"Tell me, Jonathan, is that truly your assessment or Phillip's? Because from my point of view, he seems much more interested in attracting beauty than avoiding shallow or devious behavior," Teddi replied.

"Well, I'm sure that he wouldn't hold beauty against a woman," Jonathan said, giving her a laugh. "Ouch!"

"Oh, I'm so sorry. Did I hurt your foot, big brother?" she asked as they continued to move around the dance floor.

"You intentionally stepped on my foot, Teddi," Jonathan accused.

"You're right—I did," she admitted with a sweet smile curving her lips. "And you're intentionally trying to get me to admit I have feelings for Phillip. But I don't. At least not the kind you're talking about."

"Well, what kind *do* you have, then?" he doggedly insisted.

"The bad kind. As I told you earlier, Phillip treated me shabbily when I was a little girl, and I haven't forgotten that."

"What did you expect? That he would write long love letters pledging his undying devotion to my pudgy little sister? Come on, Teddi."

"He could have at least acknowledged the letters. Even a short note telling me I was a nice little girl, but I was too young for him would have sufficed. Something—anything. He could have returned my gift. I certainly suffered Father's wrath for giving away my sleigh bell," Teddi answered, her voice filled with remorse.

"*Sleigh bell?*" Jonathan stopped dancing in the middle of the floor. The other couples were swirling about them as he stood there looking dumbstruck. "He *did* return your sleigh bell, Teddi. He gave your charm back to me years ago. You remember that little, carved wooden box of mine? I put your sleigh bell in there for safekeeping, and the charm has remained there ever since. I'm telling you the truth, I promise. I'll send it to you as soon as I return to Washington," Jonathan continued.

They were standing in the middle of the dance floor. The music had ceased playing, and the floor had emptied. Now the other couples stood watching the brother and sister who were so engrossed in their own conversation that they seemed unaware of their surroundings.

"Jonathan Yorke, how *could* you?" Teddi responded.

"I told you—I forgot. Don't make it sound like I intentionally set out to hurt you," Jonathan replied.

"Do you remember the punishment I suffered because I gave away that charm?"

"You spent most of the summer indoors helping Mother, as I recall," he said with a sheepish grin.

"Not *that* punishment. Don't you remember that Father had always given me a charm every year on my birthday? When I gave away the sleigh bell, he told me there would be no more charms. He said that if I didn't value his gift enough to keep it, he wouldn't purchase any more charms for my bracelet. And I've never received another since then," Teddi said in an anguish-filled voice. "And to think you've had my sleigh bell hidden away. . . ."

"It wasn't hidden, Teddi. I put it away for safekeeping. You make it sound as though I was purposely trying to hurt you."

"Perhaps it wasn't intentional, Jonathan, but that didn't change the outcome, did it?"

"No, and I'm not shirking my responsibility. But, if you're going to direct your wrath at me, I hope you'll let Phillip know that I've set the record straight," Jonathan replied. "And I'll explain to Father," he quickly added.

"Are you two going to spend the remainder of the evening entertaining us?" General Yorke called out from where he stood by one of the serving tables. "The rest of us are going to eat some of this sumptuous-looking food."

Teddi looked at her father, feeling as though she'd been pulled from a trance, and then glanced about the room. Everyone was staring at them, and she could feel the heat rising to her cheeks. Jonathan, on the other hand, seemed to be enjoying the unsolicited attention, as he gazed about and gave the crowd a winsome smile.

"Oh, Jonathan, quit making a further spectacle of yourself," Teddi chided as she pulled her brother off the dance floor. The *last* thing she wanted was more embarrassment and another story for the local gossips.

"Come along, my dear. You and Phillip are supposed to begin the serving line," Isabelle instructed her daughter.

"You and Jonathan certainly appeared to be engrossed in your conversation," Phillip commented after they had filled their plates.

"Part of that conversation was about you."

"Really?" he asked, his gaze immediately drawn to her eyes.

"Do you remember the silver sleigh bell charm that I gave you years ago? When you were moving away to Fort MacKinac?"

Phillip nodded his head. "I remember."

"Jonathan just now told me that you returned my charm years ago. Unfortunately, he failed to give it back to me. So I owe you an apology. All these years I thought you'd probably discarded it or, worse yet, given it to someone else," she said, looking down at her plate as she murmured the last few words.

"My dear Teddi, I would never have given your silver charm to another girl. Besides, I had already returned it to your brother before I started buying gifts for girls," he said with a chuckle. "Does this mean that perhaps you've forgiven me, and we can be friends?"

"Yes, Phillip, you're forgiven, and I apologize for behaving so boorishly since your arrival," Teddi replied.

"Your apology is accepted. Why don't we seal our new friendship by doing something special together? What about the skating party tomorrow—may I be your escort?"

She thought for only a moment. "Yes, Phillip, I'd love to go to the skating party with you. Provided you don't mind Jonathan and George tagging along. They're not about to stay home when there's a party to be enjoyed."

"The more the merrier. It will be a good time, I'm sure of it," he said. "You can't imagine how relieved I am that we've finally settled our differences," he said, giving her a broad smile.

8

he morning dawned crisp, the pale blue sky laden with heavy white clouds. Teddi's father referred to them as "snow clouds," more out of his desire for snow than any weather-predicting ability, she suspected. The bedroom window was frosted both inside and out, evidence of a significant drop in the temperature during the night. Teddi burrowed a little more deeply under the covers. The embers in the bedroom fireplace had grown cold hours ago, and the only thing that would now warm the chilled bedroom was heat rising from the kitchen below. She could hear Florence downstairs. It wouldn't be long until a fire was blazing in the kitchen and breakfast was cooking. Teddi decided she would venture out from the warmth of her nest once the smell of frying bacon wafted up the stairway and drifted into her room.

She rolled over and relished the idea of the day that lay ahead. After breakfast she would need to check several patients at the hospital and study her Sunday school lesson; after lunch, she'd go off to the skating party. Phillip hadn't mentioned if he'd be at the hospital this morning, but surely he would be there to see to his patients' progress. The thought of seeing Phillip almost made her want to get out of bed. Almost, but not quite, she decided.

"Teddi! We're going to start breakfast without you if you don't come downstairs this minute," General Yorke called.

"Coming, Father," she replied as she quickly set about buttoning her white percale shirtwaist.

Teddi was fashioning a bow of dark red silk under the collar when she finally entered the dining room several minutes later.

"Were you planning on having Florence fix you a separate breakfast today?" her father asked as Teddi settled into one of the straight-backed dining-room chairs and then waited for Jonathan to pass the tureen of scrambled eggs.

"No, I would never expect special favors from Florence—unlike some other people seated at this table. If I'm late for a meal, I'm perfectly capable of heating up leftovers or finding something to fix for myself—also unlike some others seated at this table," Teddi replied with a note of satisfaction in her voice. "Isn't that right, Florence?" she asked as the maid carried a pot of fresh coffee into the room.

"Yes, indeed. I don't think I've ever been asked to perform any extra duties for you, Miss Yorke, except maybe to press a special shirt-waist, or soak and wash bandages for the hospital patients, or air out your bedding and pillows every day, or . . ."

"Guess she got you on that one, Teddi," the general chortled.

"You do enjoy getting the best of a situation, Father. But I'm not going to let it ruin my good spirits."

"Are you in good spirits because you're off to work at the hospital while George and I relax here at home?" Jonathan gibed.

"No, I'm in good spirits because there's an ice-skating party this afternoon, and Phillip offered to escort me."

"Is that a fact? Nobody mentioned the skating party to me," George sulked. "Surely you planned on inviting Jonathan and me along."

"As if I could stop the two of you from going to a party, invited or not," Teddi replied, giving her brother a smile. "I told Phillip that I was sure the two of you would be tagging along."

"Ah, we'd best get some extra rest this morning so we'll be well rested for a busy afternoon of skating with the gorgeous young ladies from Junction City. They *will* be attending, won't they?" Jonathan inquired.

"I'm sure the young ladies *and* the young men from Junction City will be in attendance," Teddi teased as she rose from the table. "Well, I'm off to the hospital. I should be back by eleven o'clock."

"Wait, Teddi. I'll take you in the sleigh," Jonathan offered.

"That's not necessary. I go to the hospital by myself every day. Besides, you'll just have to come back later, and you may be busy helping Mother with her chores by then!"

"But I *want* to take you," he insisted.

They had hardly gotten into the sleigh when Teddi realized just why Jonathan was so determined to accompany her. He questioned her incessantly, desiring every detail of what had occurred between Phillip and her. He wanted to know why she had suddenly accepted an invitation to attend a social function with Phillip, if he had explained the mishap regarding the missing charm, and if she had been gracious in her acceptance of his explanation. Jonathan absolutely insisted upon knowing if she had apologized for her rude behavior. By the time they arrived at the hospital, Teddi had fielded more questions than would a soldier being interrogated at his own court-martial.

"For the first time, Jonathan, I must say that I'm glad to get away from you," Teddi said with a sigh of relief as he offered his hand to assist her out of the sleigh.

"Too many questions for you?" he asked with a laugh.

"Far too many, and no means of escape. I'm going to remember this device the next time I want to wheedle information from you or George," she promised.

"It won't be necessary. We have no secrets," he answered, taking the reins into his gloved hands. "I'll be back at eleven, and I'll spend the next several hours making up a list of additional questions I forgot to ask."

She started to respond, but he laughed, slapped the reins, and waved over his shoulder as the horses jerked the sleigh into motion. Teddi stood listening as the jingling of the sleigh bells grew faint in the distance.

"Good morning," Phillip greeted Teddi as she walked into the hospital. "It's a good day for ice-skating, don't you think?"

"Good morning to you. And, yes, it's a perfect day for ice-skating. By the way, at breakfast this morning I mentioned that there was an ice-skating party this afternoon. Jonathan and George didn't surprise me. They immediately sought an invitation," she told Phillip while hanging her cloak on a wooden hook in the vestibule.

"Did you tell them I didn't need any more competition for the pretty, young women?" he asked, giving her a laugh. "They are more than welcome, and I'm sure you told them so," he added.

"Yes, but knowing my brothers, I imagine they would come along anyway, welcome or not. I'd better get busy. Jonathan said he would come back for me at eleven. I want to finish my Bible study before going skating this afternoon," she told him.

"Well, that's certainly a praiseworthy endeavor. Fortunately, my sermon has been prepared for several days, or I would need to give up the party this afternoon. I'll be in my office if you need me. There are some medical records I want to review. Just in case I don't see you again before you leave the hospital, I'll plan to come by your quarters at two o'clock."

"That will be fine," she replied as she exited the room and walked down the hallway.

Teddi quickly made her way through the ward, checking each patient, making notations on the charts that hung on their beds, and moving on to the next patient. She attempted to make small talk with the men, but her mind kept wandering back to Phillip's remark about her brothers providing him with competition for the pretty, young ladies. Since he was escorting her to the skating party, why was he concerned about the other girls who would be attending? After all, if he wanted to keep company with one of the other girls, why hadn't he invited one of them? Or had he merely been jesting—making a casual remark that meant nothing at all. Most likely she was spending the morning worrying about something that was of absolutely no consequence. What was that verse in the Bible? *"Take therefore no thought for the morrow: for the morrow shall take thought for the things of itself. Sufficient unto the day is the evil thereof."* Yes, that was it—she was borrowing trouble. Trouble that would only spoil the good time that she intended to have later today!

Phillip leaned back in the leather-upholstered chair that sat behind his desk and, with a deliberate snap, closed the medical book he had been reading for the past hour. If he hurried, he would have time to get back to his quarters, change out of his uniform, and arrive at the Yorkes' on time. Good sense dictated that he should have gone directly to his quarters after having lunch in the dining hall, but during the noon meal he had decided there was sufficient time to catch up on some long overdue reading. Now, he wished he'd taken the book instead. Muttering to himself, he locked the office door and strode out of the hospital, anxious to be on his way.

An afternoon of skating would provide additional opportunity for him to socialize with some of the young adults from Junction City. And perhaps he would be fortunate enough to spark some interest in the Bible study and social activities he hoped the parishioners of the chapel would sponsor throughout the winter. Fortunately, he was now back in Teddi's good graces. She could provide valuable information about the folks living in and around the military reservation and might even agree to make arrangements for some of the activities.

His mind was filled with ideas as he bounded up the steps to the Yorkes' quarters a short time later, knocked on the front door, and was met by George, who was already wearing his coat and heavy gloves.

"Teddi and Jonathan were sure you had stood us up, but I assured them you wouldn't do such a thing," George said as he held open the door.

"Don't believe a thing he tells you. I thought you might have an ill patient at the hospital," Teddi quickly defended. "It was Jonathan who commented that you'd probably found better company!"

"How could I possibly find better company?" he asked with a broad smile. "Let me help you with your coat," he offered, his hand brushing against hers as he took the coat.

"We're leaving, Mother," Jonathan called out as he bounded out of the kitchen with several of Florence's freshly baked sugar cookies in his hand, his coat flapping about as he made his way out the door and down the front steps.

"I think you may want to fasten your coat and make sure you have some gloves," Teddi instructed as Jonathan piled into the sleigh.

They all laughed as he stuffed the remaining cookie in his mouth and retrieved a pair of gloves from deep inside his coat pockets, waving them in the air.

"I have gloves," he announced when he'd finally swallowed the mouthful of cookies.

"Good! Then we're on our way," Phillip announced, flicking the reins. The horses snorted and shook their heads, as if to ward off the icy chill, before beginning their journey.

The runners of the sleigh cut through the ice-crusted layer of snow, which broke the serenity that blanketed the vast expanse of rolling hills and prairie. The group's laughter echoed through the quiet countryside as a light snow began to fall. However, the flurries only added to the excitement of the day and somehow seemed appropriate for the first skating party of the season.

"You know what's wrong with this sleigh?" Teddi asked as they were nearing the creek.

"Nothing!" the three men called out and then laughed cheerfully at their unified response.

"Yes, there is something wrong with it," Teddi insisted.

"Please tell me, and I'll see that it's remedied," Phillip replied with a glint in his eye.

"This sleigh doesn't have any bells. It *needs* sleigh bells!"

"Well, of course. We all know that sleigh bells are a necessity. Otherwise, a sleigh just won't operate properly, Phillip. How could you possibly own a sleigh without bells?" Jonathan bantered.

"Teddi has a valid point. I rather like the sound of sleigh bells myself," Phillip agreed. "I'll have to see if I can rectify the problem. Thank you for bringing it to my attention," he added.

"I'm sure that Teddi would be happy to help you find just the right sleigh bells," George offered.

"Oh, stop it, George, or I'll tell all the girls that you're not worth their time," Teddi retorted.

"Looks like quite a crowd has already gathered," Jonathan said as they approached the creek. "Give me your hand, Teddi. I'll help you out of the sleigh."

A small group of men and women were already on the ice as the foursome walked down to the edge of the creek. Several skaters were warming themselves at a crackling fire that was being fueled with branches from a nearby dead tree. The women, with brightly colored knitted scarves tied tightly around their heads, were discussing whether to move away from the fire while the men were devising a plan to pull a sled onto the ice with a heavy piece of rope.

"Let's go over to the fire, and you can make some introductions," Phillip suggested while her brothers quickly nodded their heads in agreement.

"Good idea, Phillip," Jonathan chimed in. "I'm hoping I can find an agreeable young lady I can escort to all the Christmas parties I've been hearing about."

"Only one? I would think you'd want to find several. That way you'd have a bit of variety," Phillip said with a chuckle.

"Is that what *you* prefer—variety?" Teddi inquired.

There was an edge to her voice that took Phillip by surprise.

"Well, I wouldn't put it quite that way. I'm looking for a woman who has the same beliefs and values. Someone who loves the Lord . . ."

"And the army," George chimed in, laughing at his own remark.

"That too," Phillip agreed.

"Sounds like you've just described our Teddi," Jonathan remarked while giving his sister an exaggerated wink.

Jonathan's statement caught Phillip off guard and was obviously embarrassing to Teddi. The chilly December weather had caused Teddi's cheeks to turn pink, but her brother's casual remark had now intensified the color to flaming red.

"Of course, a woman of beauty is always agreeable," George observed.

"Not necessarily," Phillip countered. "Sometimes beautiful women rely solely on their physical attributes to get them through life. I've met some lovely women who were shallow."

"Well, I would love to continue this discussion, but I feel it's my duty to escort one of these young ladies onto the ice," Jonathan bantered. "That is, if you're ever going to make those promised introductions, dear sister."

Teddi poked him in the side and began to lead him toward a young woman not far from the group, with Phillip and George following along behind.

"No, *that* one," Jonathan instructed, pointing toward a girl with unruly golden locks peeking out from beneath a cream-colored, woolen scarf.

Teddi smiled. "You don't agree with Phillip, I take it. You want beauty rather than—"

"Some women have both," Jonathan asserted.

"I really think you'd find Ruth Ann much more to your liking," Teddi argued.

"No, I want to meet *her*," Jonathan insisted while pulling Teddi in the young woman's direction.

"Fine, but I don't think . . ."

"Just introduce me," Jonathan insisted. "You can introduce George to Ruth Ann, can't she, George?"

George merely nodded his head as Phillip watched the scene in amusement. It was obvious that things weren't going as Teddi had planned, and he was finding her mounting frustration with Jonathan entertaining.

"Good afternoon, Margaret. I would like to introduce you to my brother, Jonathan Yorke. Jonathan is visiting us at Fort Riley for the holidays. Jonathan, this is Margaret Willoughby," Teddi said in her most formal voice.

The girl looked back and forth between Teddi and Jonathan and appeared somewhat confused, but finally gave Jonathan a tentative smile. "Nice to meet you. Would you mind helping me with my skates?" Margaret asked, dangling the pair of skates from her gloved hand.

"I'd be delighted. Why don't you sit on that stump over there, and I'll get them clamped," Jonathan suggested as the twosome walked away.

"Are *you* interested in meeting Ruth Ann?" Teddi asked, turning to stare at George.

George compliantly nodded his head in agreement, while Phillip laughed aloud. "What are you laughing at?" Teddi asked, obviously irritated with both of the men.

"I think George knows better than to say he doesn't want to meet Ruth Ann. If he values his life, that is," Phillip replied, still laughing.

"All three of you are beginning to wear on my patience," Teddi responded as she marched off toward where Ruth Ann was standing.

Phillip walked alongside George, both of them following closely behind Teddi as she approached the dark-haired, young woman and quickly made introductions. George and Ruth Ann were soon making their way toward the ice when Teddi turned toward Phillip.

"And which of the young women do *you* wish to meet?" Teddi asked.

"I've already met her. Would *you* skate with me?" he asked, extending his hand.

"Well, yes, I'd love to," Teddi replied, obviously pleased by the invitation.

They joined several other couples on the ice, gliding down the creek's frozen path and then back toward the widest part where most of the skating crowd was congregated. The skaters were moving gracefully on the ice, a canopy of frozen branches extending overhead as a light snow continued to fall. Suddenly, waving arms and a woman's voice calling from the creek's edge broke the beautiful winter scene.

"Phillip! Over here!" A woman's shrill voice screamed from the distance, her arms raised high above her head and a red scarf swinging from her hand as she waved her arms back and forth.

"Is that . . . ?"

"Helen? Absolutely," Teddi replied.

"Perhaps we should go over. If she keeps screaming like that, she's liable to cause a crack in the ice," Phillip joked.

"I don't think she's quite *that* loud, but she probably won't stop until you go over there," Teddi agreed.

He really didn't want to leave the ice. He and Teddi were having a wonderful conversation, discussing everything from operating procedures to Scripture interpretation, and Phillip had been thoroughly enjoying himself. Teddi seemed to have an opinion about everything, yet she was willing to listen to his viewpoint and even change her beliefs if given valid reasons for doing so. She was indeed refreshing— a woman with spirit and substance, he decided, just as they approached the lovely Helen Hanson.

9

*T*eddi stood by the bonfire, forcing herself to concentrate on the conversation taking place around her. She couldn't do it. Her gaze continued to follow the handsome-appearing couple skating arm in arm, now gliding down the creek and slowly leaving her field of vision. Moving around the edge of the fire, she repositioned herself and hoped to gain a better view, but they were now out of sight.

"Helen certainly has her cap set for the new doctor, doesn't she?" Mattie Fielding stated while shaking her head.

"He's a preacher, too, not just a doctor," Teddi countered.

"Doctor, preacher, lawyer, store clerk—makes no difference. There's no stopping that girl once she sets her sights on someone."

"Did she tell you that she's interested in Captain Hamilton?"

"Yes, but she wouldn't have to *tell* me. Just watching her is evidence enough," Mattie replied with a giggle.

"But what did she say?"

"That he was the best-looking single man to be stationed at Fort Riley in ages and that she planned to make him her very own. She did mention that she thought your brother Jonathan might interest her even more, but he'd soon be leaving. So she decided not to waste valuable time with Jonathan. I think she was fearful that someone else might snag Captain Hamilton if she decided to spend time with your brother."

"I see," was all Teddi could manage, suddenly thankful to see George and Ruth Ann approaching.

"We've decided to leave. Ruth Ann needs to be home soon, and I've agreed to escort her," George informed his sister.

"How?" Teddi inquired. "You don't have a sleigh."

"She came with several other couples. The men said they would take me back to the post once we've escorted the girls home," he replied, obviously anxious to be on his way.

Teddi stared after her brother, wishing that he and Ruth Ann had remained to keep her company. But at least they seemed to enjoy being with each other, and *that* was satisfying, she decided as she watched the sleigh move off toward town.

The silence after their departure was soon broken by Mattie's shrill voice cutting through the crisp air. "He is rather handsome, don't you agree?" she asked, looking out across the ice just as Helen and Phillip made their reappearance.

"What? Oh, yes, extremely handsome. She'd be a fool to let my brother slip away," Teddi responded.

"Not your brother, Captain Hamilton," Mattie corrected, giving Teddi an exasperated look. "I told Helen there was nobody who could turn the captain's head if *she* took an interest in him. There's no one who can hold a candle to Helen, except Margaret Willoughby. And who's going to be interested in Margaret? Except your brother," she added, noting Jonathan coming toward them with Margaret in tow.

"So you think it's only beauty that matters to men?" Teddi asked.

"Well, of course, silly. They all make those perfunctory statements about wanting a woman who's a good cook, can keep a spotless house, is devout in her Christian beliefs, and is intelligent, but when it comes down to actually choosing a wife, they pick the most comely one that will have them. You, of all people, should know that!" Mattie added.

The words stung like salt in an open wound, causing Teddi to flinch. Yes, she knew what people thought. After all, she believed the same thing. When given the choice of a beautiful, young woman, Herbert Albright had succumbed, leaving plain, thick-waisted, intelligent Teddi at the altar. Well, not really at the altar, she told herself. She and Herbert had set their wedding date for May 23, but he had betrayed her many months before the arranged day. Besides, she reasoned, it was better to suffer the humiliation now as his former fiancée than as his wife. But Mattie's comments served as a reminder that gossip was not soon forgotten, nor people soon forgiven. Why, even

Margaret Willoughby's name had come up in Mattie's comments, and how long had it been since *that* consequential day?

The thought caught her by surprise. She was just as guilty as Mattie. Perhaps she hadn't put words to her thoughts, but she had certainly discouraged her brother from meeting Margaret. Hadn't Margaret come before the body of believers confessing her sin, repenting, and seeking forgiveness a long time ago?

The congregation had listened; the preacher had told Margaret that she had been correct in coming forward to confess her sin. He had gone a step further and assured her that not only had God forgiven her, but the body of believers had done the same. Unfortunately, it hadn't been altogether true. Oh, people had spoken to her when it was absolutely necessary, and she was usually included in activities for which a general invitation was extended. But nobody had befriended her; nobody had *truly* accepted her; nobody had ever extended a special invitation to Margaret Willoughby. Not after hearing that Sunday morning confession a year ago.

Teddi's shoulders slumped, and her head dropped as she acknowledged her own participation in such disappointing behavior. Certainly her actions didn't exemplify Christ's teachings. Who was she to treat another human being with such contempt? Especially one who had been so brave, one who had followed the Bible's teachings, one who had done what was required of God to assure forgiveness. The shame of Teddi's behavior welled up inside her until she thought it would cut off her breath and choke her.

"You seem deep in thought," Jonathan remarked as he moved alongside Teddi.

She startled at his voice, glanced around, and was eye to eye with Margaret. "I told Jonathan not to disturb you. I thought you appeared to be praying," Margaret said, her voice barely a whisper.

It was obvious Margaret was unsure how she would be received. There was a tentativeness about her, a wounded look that Teddi had never before noticed.

"You're right, Margaret. I was praying. Asking for God's forgiveness. And now I need to ask for yours," Teddi replied. "I've treated you unkindly, not shown you the friendship you deserve. I've shunned you when what you did was courageous and true to God's Word. I'm afraid I've been guilty of not truly forgiving you of your past mistakes and, worse yet, being judgmental. I don't know what I would have done in your situation, but I do want you to know that I'm very sorry and ask that you accept my apology. If you could find it in your heart, I'd be honored if you would accept my offer of friendship."

"Of course I accept your apology, Teddi. I knew that when I went in front of the church to announce I'd had a baby out of wedlock, it would probably end any hope I might have of forming friendships, and that it would certainly limit my opportunities for marriage to a good man. But I did it out of submission to God, and I knew He would be faithful to honor my obedience. Perhaps not in the way I would choose, but in ways that would even go beyond my expectations."

"And has He done that?" Teddi asked.

Margaret smiled a beautiful, broad smile that turned her already pretty face into a glorious work of beauty. "He just did," she said. "I almost stayed at home today, not wanting to sit on the sidelines watching while others enjoyed the pleasures of a winter afternoon skating. But something nudged me to quit feeling sorry for myself. And look what has happened! I've made a new friend and also enjoyed a good portion of the afternoon skating with the most handsome young man in attendance."

"Thank you for your generous forgiveness," Teddi said, leaning forward and giving Margaret a hug. "One thing, however—my brother is *not* the most handsome man in attendance."

"I heard that," Jonathan retorted.

"You'd have to be deaf not to have heard it, brother. It was intended for your ears, also," Teddi replied. "It appears as though you've managed to convince Margaret, but I don't want you getting yourself all puffed up and proud, thinking that everybody agrees with her on that point."

The three of them were enjoying a good laugh when Phillip and Helen returned from skating and joined them, with Helen clinging to Phillip's arm and appearing surprised to see Margaret in their company.

"You three seem to be having a good time. I needed to warm up," he said, nearing the fire. "After I've gotten my circulation going again, would you care to join me on the ice, Teddi?" he asked.

"But I thought *we* were going to skate once you had warmed your hands," Helen complained to Phillip while giving Teddi a loathsome glare.

"I don't think we've been formally introduced," Phillip said, turning to Margaret.

Helen's irritation that she was being ignored was evident to all of them, yet she refused to loosen her hold on Phillip.

"I'm sorry. Phillip, this is Margaret Willoughby. Margaret, may I introduce you to Captain Phillip Hamilton, who is our new chaplain at Fort Riley," Teddi graciously replied.

"I'm pleased to meet you, Margaret," Phillip said, extending his right arm to shake Margaret's hand.

Unfortunately, Phillip's act of courtesy proved disastrous for Helen, who was still resolutely clinging to his arm and refused to let go when he extended his hand. The motion caused Helen to lose her balance, her arms and legs flying about pell-mell until she finally landed in a heap on the snow-covered ground in front of them.

"Look what you've done!" she screeched while looking directly at Margaret. "This is all *your* fault. Who invited you anyway?"

Phillip and Teddi gazed down at Helen, their faces etched with disbelief, while Jonathan rushed to Margaret's side.

"Phillip, help me up!" Helen commanded as she continued to glare at Margaret, who was now talking quietly to Jonathan.

"I'll help you to your feet, Helen, but that's all I intend to do," Phillip replied as he leaned down to help her up. "I'm shocked by your contemptuous attitude toward Margaret."

"You don't know anything about that woman. She's a harlot. In fact, she's even had a baby out of wedlock. You think that such a woman deserves to have her honor protected?" Helen spat.

"I don't know anything about her past, but I do know rude behavior when I see it. Good-bye, Helen," Phillip replied as he aided her and then turned away.

"Why don't we go skate for a while," Phillip said to the others. "Unless you'd rather leave?"

"We could skate a bit longer and then go back to our house for hot chocolate," Teddi suggested.

"That sounds like an excellent plan. What do you think, Margaret?"

"Me? Oh, I couldn't go to your home," she said in a throaty whisper.

"Why can't you? Are you expected home early?" Jonathan inquired.

"No, but perhaps you should discuss it with your parents, and then if they agree that it's all right, I'll come another time," she ventured.

"No need for that. Our friends are always welcome in our home," Teddi answered. "It will be fine, Margaret. You'll see. Please say you'll come with us," she encouraged.

Margaret nodded her agreement, and the four of them made their way onto the ice, the two couples skating off in opposite directions.

"I have a feeling there's more to this story than I've heard," Phillip remarked as he and Teddi glided toward the narrow portion of the creek where they had skated earlier in the afternoon.

"You're right, Phillip. And much of what I'm going to tell you may cause you to think that I'm not very different from Helen Hanson," she sadly related.

They moved up and down the ice, Teddi quietly telling Phillip of Margaret's confession and the brutal treatment she'd received since that time. At one point, Teddi noticed him wince at the words she was speaking, obviously pained by the shunning that Margaret had received from fellow Christians.

"I'm sure you find my behavior abhorrent," Teddi said as she concluded the ugly tale.

Phillip nodded his head in agreement. "Yes, I'm afraid I do. I'm sad that such a thing can happen, but I'm afraid that all too often, that's how we Christians treat one another. However, the difference between you and Helen is that you now realize the error of your ways and have asked God's forgiveness—and Margaret's," he added. "Perhaps your actions will begin to get things started down the right path with others. You've done a good thing today, Teddi," he said while squeezing her hand.

"Today I set things right, but when I think of all that Margaret has endured when I could have helped put an end to her suffering, I don't deserve her forgiveness," Teddi replied remorsefully.

"That may be true, but there's nothing you can do to change the past. Instead of using valuable time worrying about the past, let's concentrate on what we can do to help Margaret in the future," Phillip suggested.

"You're right, of course," she said.

"It appears that Jonathan and Margaret are ready to leave," he said, pointing toward her brother and Margaret, who were now standing beside the sleigh.

By the time they had piled into the sleigh and were ready to head back home, only a few couples remained on the ice, and several of the men who had gathered around the fire were discussing how soon they should depart. Jonathan suggested that Teddi sit up front with Phillip and keep him company while he and Margaret sat in back. Giving her brother a knowing smile, she held out her hand and allowed Phillip to help her up beside him. The sun was beginning to set as Phillip pulled on the reins and a half-hour later brought the horses to a halt in front of the Yorke residence.

"Everybody out," he ordered as he jumped down, came around the sleigh, and assisted Teddi down.

"I told your father that you children would be home in time for supper," Isabelle announced as she pulled open the front door. "Didn't I, Clayton?" she asked, turning toward her husband.

"That you did, my dear. But, more importantly, you told Florence. Had you told only me of your belief, they would all go without supper since I've not yet learned to cook," he announced with a laugh.

"Where's George?" Isabelle asked while pointing at Jonathan's feet and motioning him toward the rug in front of the door.

"He went with Ruth Ann and some others that were heading into Junction City. They promised to bring him home. I thought he might already be here," Teddi replied.

"Well, if he went to Ruth Ann Langely's house, I'm sure he's sitting down to supper right now. Kathryn Langely never misses an opportunity to have a guest for dinner. You children get your coats off and come in the parlor and warm up," Isabelle encouraged.

"I think you and Kathryn have a lot in common," General Yorke surmised as he gave his wife a broad grin.

Teddi noticed Isabelle's eyebrows rise after realizing it was Margaret Willoughby whom Jonathan had escorted home. Signaling her mother toward the kitchen, Teddi quickly recounted the day's events, told her mother she would answer any questions later, and graciously returned to the parlor with the report that dinner would soon be served.

Florence was at her culinary best, serving fried pork chops, mashed potatoes swimming in butter, and warm, flaky biscuits accompanied by her famous apple butter. After General Yorke gave thanks for the meal in his customary fashion, it became abundantly clear that the afternoon of skating had stimulated the appetites of the younger set, and, much to her delight, Florence was soon scurrying back to the kitchen to replenish the bowls and platters. Once their initial hunger had been appeased, their eating slowed to a normal pace, and the sounds of congenial conversation began to fill the room. Jonathan proudly announced that Margaret had mastered several new ice-skating maneuvers, and he was especially pleased to announce that she could now skate backwards.

Margaret soon joined in, acknowledging that she had been somewhat successful but confessing that her talents weren't nearly as admirable as Jonathan was boasting.

"After all, I did fall down four times and never did triumph totally unassisted. You *were* holding onto me," she admitted, giving Jonathan a sidelong glance.

"Success comes with patience and lots of practice, my dear," the general encouraged. "Jonathan will have to get you back on the ice soon. You'll be able to skate backwards unassisted in no time."

"Perhaps it's better that she doesn't learn *too* well, Father. I enjoy holding onto beautiful young ladies," Jonathan replied.

With the exception of Isabelle, who, Teddi decided, seemed somewhat distracted, their voices rose in laughter at Jonathan's comment. None of the others seemed to notice her mother's rather odd behavior until Isabelle, without warning, rose from the table and requested Teddi's assistance in the kitchen.

"Ring for Florence. You don't need to be running off to the kitchen when we have guests," the general stated as he motioned toward the small bell sitting by Isabelle's plate.

Isabelle complied and gave the bell a gentle shake, which caused Florence to hastily reappear.

"Yes, ma'am?" Florence questioned, wiping her wet hands on a cloth napkin.

"I was going to go to the kitchen and prepare coffee, but the general insisted that I remain at the table," she explained.

"But you always take your coffee in the parlor after dessert," Florence replied, her confusion evident.

"Well, I thought I'd do things differently this evening," Isabelle answered.

"So you want coffee now? Before I serve dessert?" Florence questioned.

"Oh, never mind. We'll have our coffee in the parlor after dessert, as usual. Well, I am permitted the privilege of changing my mind, aren't I?" she asked, obviously noticing the baffled look on Clayton's face.

"Of course, my dear. I'd never tell a woman she didn't have that privilege," he replied. "Now, then, what were we discussing? I believe you were telling me that you moved here when your father opened the dry goods store a year ago," the general continued, turning his attention back to Margaret.

"That's what *you* were talking about, Father. I was going to ask Teddi to give me a list of dates and times for the holiday social activities in order to gain Margaret's assurance that she'll attend them all with me," Jonathan jovially interrupted.

"Well, I suppose that should take center stage," Clayton agreed. "Let's test your memory, Teddi. What's the social calendar look like for the next few weeks?"

"I'm not sure I can remember everything, but it's all written down in my journal. The next thing is the Hornbys' whist party on Tuesday, and then on Friday the party at Bert and Hannah's."

"Have the Mahoneys returned? That party may be canceled if they don't get back soon," Isabelle interjected while fidgeting with a small cameo brooch fastened to the collar of her dress.

"They got back yesterday," Clayton advised. "Bert said they had a good time, visited with relatives, and got some much-needed rest. Oh, he's brought another hunting dog back with him."

"And of course, there's the masked ball on Saturday," Teddi continued.

"Are you spoken for on those nights? I'd be proud to escort you to each of those parties. Please say yes," Jonathan implored a bewildered-appearing Margaret.

"She probably can't give you an answer right now, Jonathan. Besides, I thought you'd be escorting Teddi to the Christmas festivities," Isabelle replied before Margaret could speak.

"Why would Teddi want me as an escort when she can have Phillip?" Jonathan inquired, turning his full attention toward the beautiful, young woman at his side. "Have you agreed to attend with someone else?" he once again quizzed.

"No," Margaret answered softly.

"Then you'll allow me to escort you," he confidently remarked.

"I suppose, if you really want to, and if your family doesn't mind," she murmured.

"Well, if we're going to take care of these matters right now, I suppose I'd better do the same. Teddi, may I have the honor of escorting *you*?" Phillip inquired.

"Why don't we discuss our arrangements later?" Teddi responded, sure that Phillip now felt required to invite her. But she wouldn't be anyone's obligatory date. She'd been attending social functions with her parents since Herbert's departure, and if her brother George wasn't available, she would continue to do so.

The logs in the dining-room fireplace had begun to turn an ashen white by the time Florence announced that coffee would be served in the parlor, *as usual.*

"I'm afraid my parents may begin to worry if I don't get home soon. Perhaps I could forego coffee?" Margaret inquired meekly.

"Of course! Clayton, why don't you see if one of your soldiers can take Margaret back to Junction City," Isabelle suggested to her husband.

As soon as the words had been spoken, a host of confused looks were once again cast in Isabelle's direction. A deafening silence filled the room until Jonathan gained his composure and spoke.

"Why would Father need to do that? Margaret is my guest, so I'll be escorting her home. Mind if I use your sleigh, Phillip?"

"Not at all. I'll walk back to my quarters, and you can have the privilege of caring for the horses upon your return," Phillip replied in a lighthearted voice as the group rose from the table.

$\mathcal{W}$ hat *were* you thinking, Mother?" Teddi inquired after Phillip had bid them good night, and Clayton had excused himself to go over some paperwork upstairs.

Isabelle didn't lift her eyes from the piece of embroidery work upon which she was carefully stitching. "I thought that Margaret should probably ask her parents before accepting Jonathan's invitations," Isabelle replied.

"No, mother, I'm inquiring about *everything*. Why did you treat Margaret so rudely, suggesting that one of the soldiers take her home and making it obvious you didn't want her to accept Jonathan's invitations? Why, you didn't have one kind thing to say to her all evening. I'm shocked at your behavior, especially after what I told you in the kitchen," Teddi angrily replied.

"It's one thing to forgive her past mistakes, Teddi. But I don't want your brother keeping company with her. What if he should fall in love with Margaret and want to marry her?" Isabelle asked, putting her sewing aside to give Teddi her full attention. "It could have a lasting impact on his personal life as well as his career. Right or wrong, I want the very best spouses for my children, and I don't think Margaret falls into that category."

"You thought Herbert Albright was an excellent choice for me, and look what happened there," Teddi countered. "And is it truly forgiveness when there are exceptions such as those you're imposing, Mother? What if Jesus had placed such limitations on His forgiveness?"

"I want to discuss this with Jonathan as well as your father. I'm sure neither of them knows anything about—"

"Knows anything about what?" Jonathan asked as he walked in

the front door. Stomping the snow off his feet with great bravado, he pulled off his overcoat and walked into the parlor, immediately making his way to stand in front of the fireplace.

"We were having a private conversation," Isabelle replied.

"Well, I heard you say that you wanted to discuss something with me. Here I am," he said, giving her a winsome smile. "So let's discuss!"

Isabelle looked as though she wanted to flee from the room, but there appeared to be no escape. Jonathan was wide awake after being out in the cold, late-night air, and Teddi had settled back into her chair with her hands folded in her lap, awaiting her mother's opening remarks.

Isabelle absently picked up her sewing and began making tiny satin stitches, the needle moving in and out of the piece of fabric at breakneck speed. She cleared her throat several times and then, while keeping her gaze focused on the sewing, began to question her son's earlier decisions.

Teddi watched her brother stiffen as Isabelle began recounting the events of Margaret's past, his irritation growing more and more evident as Isabelle continued her speech while never once raising her eyes. Finally, Jonathan took three long steps to where his mother was sitting and stood directly in front of her.

"Why won't you look at me, Mother? Do you find what you're saying so embarrassing that you can't meet my eyes, or is it that you know you're wrong, and I would see the deceit if you met my gaze?"

Isabelle's head snapped upward at his remark, her face now filled with anger. "Can't you see that I'm trying to protect you from a future of misery and shame? I don't dislike Margaret. I suppose making her confession in front of the congregation was commendable, although I'm not convinced it showed good judgment. And I'm certain her parents would have preferred that she remain silent about her past. All of that happened before she moved to Junction City, so I'm not sure why she felt it was necessary to make it known. It's almost as though she's proud of having had a child and giving it up."

Jonathan dropped onto the sofa across the room from the two women. "I can't believe this is my mother speaking. Margaret was very honest with me. We hadn't even circled the ice when she told me all the things you've recounted. Perhaps she wouldn't have felt it necessary to do that if people around here had truly forgiven her. I knew all of those things before I invited her to be my guest, and I'll be proud to escort her.

"There are things in my past that I'm not proud of either. But I didn't have Margaret's courage. I merely confessed my sins to God and asked His forgiveness, rather than that of my fellow man. We're a strange lot, we humans, feeling rather smug with our deep, dark secrets privately tucked away from the world. But let one brave soul come forward, making public a past failure and begging our forgiveness, and what do we do? We pay lip service to their courage, tell them all is forgiven, and then politely ignore the fact that they exist. Quite noble, don't you think?"

"I know my feelings are unjustified, but . . ."

"But what, Mother? Your statements are in total opposition to the Bible's teachings. There is no justification for that, and I've never known you to defy the Word of God. Is the opinion of other people so important to you?"

Isabelle rose, placed her sewing in the basket near her chair, and turned her tear-filled gaze upon Jonathan. "I need to pray about this," she said as she turned to leave the room. Her shoulders were slumped and her gait slow and measured as she walked to the staircase and made her way up the steps.

"*You* don't agree with her, do you?" Jonathan asked, quickly turning his attention toward his sister.

"No. In fact, I had been questioning her behavior toward Margaret before you returned home. She's trying to protect you, Jonathan. I know, I know," she said, holding up her hand to stave off his interruption. "You don't need protection. But parents don't quit doing that just because their children reach a certain age or leave home. Trust her when she says she'll pray about it, Jonathan. She will! And I am certain she'll receive clarity on the issue. I can't completely condemn her because I haven't treated Margaret any more civilly than the rest of the community," Teddi replied. "Come on—we'd better get to bed."

"I'm not tired. I think I'll wait for George," he answered. "Any of Florence's pie left in the kitchen?"

"Of course, and I'm sure you'll be able to find it without much difficulty. Good night, Jonathan," she said, rising up on her toes to kiss him on the cheek.

"Thanks for your support with this whole thing. Margaret is a wonderful girl, and I don't intend to lose her," Jonathan replied.

"And beautiful, too," Teddi added.

"*Very* beautiful," he responded.

"And that's the most important thing," she muttered to herself while walking up the stairway to her bedroom.

Phillip had been at the hospital only a short time when he heard the front door open. Jumping from his chair, he turned for a moment as the anatomy book he'd been reading went tumbling to the floor with a resolute thud. Leaning down, he grabbed the book, threw it back onto his desk, and rushed to the vestibule. Teddi had just arrived, the bottom of her long, woolen coat covered with a dusting of snow that was beginning to melt and drip onto the small rug at the entryway.

Moving with a long, determined stride, he reached out to assist her as she removed her coat.

"Thank you, Phillip," she said with a look of amusement on her face as she hung the coat, careful to ensure that the melting snow would fall upon the small, braided rug.

"You're smiling. Did I miss something amusing?" he inquired.

"No. I'm just not used to having help with my coat. I'm sure you have much more important things to do."

"Not at the moment. I wanted to have our discussion this morning before we got too busy. Why don't you come into my office?" he offered.

"Our discussion?"

"Yes. Last night you said we would discuss our arrangements later—about my escorting you to the upcoming social events. Several of the parties are only a few days off, so I thought we should proba-bly—"

"Have our chat so you have time to make other arrangements once I've freed you from your obligation to escort me," Teddi interrupted.

"What? I *don't* feel obligated, as you so ineptly put it. I would consider it a privilege to have you on my arm. I thought we would be making arrangements about the times and dates, not about whether we were actually going to attend the parties as a couple."

"You expect me to believe that you intended to invite me before my brother made his ill-spoken remark at dinner last night?" she asked, giving him an incredulous look.

"Yes. Why would you find that so hard to believe?"

"Let's see. Perhaps it's because you couldn't keep your eyes off Helen Hanson at the cast party. Or perhaps it's because you were completely infatuated by her beauty and charm at the skating party, until she offended you with her treatment of Margaret. I think you'd be happier with someone whose appearance you find more pleasing, and wearing a gown isn't going to change me into a beauty," she candidly answered.

"I'll not deny that initially my head was turned by her beauty. But it didn't take long for me to realize that she's a shallow, vain, young lady and that we have nothing in common. I apologize for my behavior and promise that it won't happen again if you'll agree to accompany me. Don't I get a second chance?" he asked, giving her a doleful look.

"I suppose we all deserve at least a second chance," she agreed, giving him a halfhearted smile. "You can call for me at eight o'clock on Thursday evening."

"What about Friday and Saturday?" he quickly interjected.

"Let's see how Thursday goes."

"But if everything goes well and you have a pleasant evening, you'll accompany me on Friday and Saturday?" he pursued.

Teddi leaned forward in the chair and gave him a grin. "If we have an agreeable evening, and if you still want to escort me on Friday and Saturday, then the answer would be yes," she conceded.

"Wonderful!" he whooped, bounding out of his chair. "Now that we've gotten that settled, let's get to the ward and begin seeing our patients."

As they worked side by side during the succeeding days, Phillip determined Teddi was beginning to trust him a little more. She appeared more relaxed in his company, and she didn't hesitate to ask for his assistance when a problem arose with one of the patients. There were more patients in the hospital than Phillip had anticipated, but with all of the men garrisoned at the post for the winter, he assumed the increased number of patients was to be expected. It would have been impossible to care for all of them without Teddi's capable assistance. She ensured that the soldiers working in the hospital were trained and skilled in their duties, and if they didn't meet her standards, she asked that they be reassigned outside the hospital. There was no doubt that Teddi's first concern was the care and well-being of the patients. She had even mentioned planting a vegetable garden outside the hospital again this year, and Phillip took that as a favorable sign. At least she was planning to continue working at the hospital.

And yesterday she had completely surprised him by asking when he planned on beginning the Bible study, suggesting several topics she thought might interest the young adults. Her ideas had been sound, and it pleased him that she was giving positive consideration to some of his suggestions for the chapel.

By Thursday, Phillip was looking forward to spending the evening with Teddi. "I'll be at your quarters by eight o'clock," he said as they were leaving the hospital.

"We should probably leave a little earlier. Jonathan will need to stop at Margaret's home in Junction City before going on to the Hornbys'. Will that be a problem?" she asked.

"No, not at all. I'll be there at seven-thirty. The more time together, the better, as far as I'm concerned," he replied with a broad smile.

He watched until Teddi was out of sight and then walked back to his quarters. Phillip had decided to wear one of his two civilian suits to the party. Both were quite stylish, and since he was required to wear his uniform to all military galas, it seemed the party in Junction City would provide him with an opportunity to blend in with the rest of the town's residents. Besides, he reasoned, being out of his military uniform might cause Teddi to view him as more of an admirer than the doctor or chaplain she worked with at the hospital.

Straightening his tie, Phillip rushed up the front stairs to the Yorke residence and knocked on the door. General Yorke pulled open the door but appeared startled when he saw Phillip standing before him in a black greatcoat, which remained unbuttoned and permitted a view of his gray double-breasted jacket, waistcoat, and trousers. A gray silk tie was neatly fastened around his starched, white collar, and a pair of shiny leather oxfords had replaced his black military boots. He quickly removed the black, silk top hat when the general motioned him inside.

"Surprised to see you in that getup," the general remarked as he gave Phillip a slap on the back. "Tired of the uniform already?"

"No, sir. Just thought it might be a nice change," Phillip replied.

"Women prefer men in uniforms, you know," he said with a boisterous laugh.

"Well, I'm not looking to impress anyone but Teddi, so I hope she doesn't mind," he said just as Teddi descended the stairs.

"He looks very handsome in civilian clothing, Father. Besides, I think that it was probably a soldier who decided women prefer men in uniform," she said with a smile.

"Possibly. But there are a lot of military wives who agree with me. Where's your brother?"

"Right here, Father," Jonathan replied as he came down the steps two at a time. "You're going to put me to shame," he said to Phillip, pulling back the overcoat to gain a better view of Phillip's suit.

"I doubt anyone is going to be interested in what we're wearing. It's always the ladies' dresses that everyone's interested in. Speaking of which, that's a lovely gown you're wearing," he said to Teddi.

"Thank you, Phillip. We'd better be going or they'll start without us. Don't wait up, Father," she instructed, leaning over to place a kiss on his cheek.

"Have a good time, but don't forget that tomorrow's a working day, and there's a party tomorrow night, too. Best not stay out too late."

Ella Hornby was beginning to arrange people at the tables just as the foursome arrived. Mrs. Hornby greeted them, took their wraps, and instructed them to join the others in the parlor. They each dropped a calling card in the silver tray that was placed in the center of a claw-footed oak table in the entryway. Phillip breathed a sigh of relief when Mrs. Hornby didn't appear disturbed by Margaret's appearance at the party.

"Hurry up—I've already placed your names in the drawing," Ella told them as they entered the room.

"Drawing for what?" Jonathan inquired.

"To see where we'll be seated to play whist. I've divided the ladies' and gentlemen's names into separate bowls. I'll draw two from each bowl, and those four people will play at the first table, and so on," Ella explained.

"I want to sit with Margaret," Jonathan whispered at Teddi.

"It's not my party. You'll have to go along with it."

Phillip was pleased when Ella drew Margaret's name and she was seated at the same table as Jonathan. But when the drawing was completed, Teddi was seated across the room with Ella and two fellows who had attended the skating party, while Phillip ended up with Helen Hanson, Mattie Fielding, and William Hornby.

Phillip saw Teddi glance in his direction just as Helen placed her hand over his and gave it a squeeze.

"I need to talk with you. It's very important," Helen whispered with a note of urgency, her breath tickling his ear as she spoke.

"Talk away. You have my undivided attention," he replied, beginning to shuffle the cards.

"Not here. It's a private matter. When we change tables, we always mingle and have refreshments. We'll talk then," she quietly replied.

It had been several years since Phillip had played whist, but the game soon came back to him. In fact, he and Mattie managed to soundly defeat Helen and William. However, Helen was playing so poorly that it gave him cause to wonder if she didn't understand the game or if she was intentionally misplaying her cards. Poor William seemed totally unnerved by her lack of skill, and when the game was finally over, he vaulted out of his chair to the refreshment table without saying a word.

"Could you give us a few minutes alone, Mattie?" Helen purred.

Mattie jumped at her cue and rushed off to join William at the refreshment table. None of the others had completed their game, and Helen took the opportunity to move her chair closer to Phillip. Once again she leaned over and began whispering, occasionally leaning back to emit a soft giggle or murmur some remark loud enough for the others to hear. Her performance didn't go unnoticed.

Finally, when the last group had completed their game, Ella announced they would adjourn to the dining room for refreshment before beginning the next game. Phillip immediately rose from the table, only to feel Helen's fingers winding around his arm, digging into his flesh with a viselike grip. As he attempted to free his arm, Teddi turned toward them, watching as Helen giggled. When Phillip asked her to release his arm, instead she shrewdly placed her head on his shoulder for a moment and gave him an engaging smile.

"Teddi," he called out, finally wresting his arm out of Helen's grip and crossing the room.

"Feel free to join Helen at the refreshment table. I can find my own way," Teddi snapped.

"I don't want to join Helen. I didn't ask to sit with her and I can't control her behavior. She said she had something she needed to discuss with me as soon as I was seated at the table," he explained.

"I see. And the only way she could talk to you was by putting her lips up against your ear? Quite frankly, Phillip, I didn't see you objecting to her attention," Teddi stated. "If you'll excuse me, I'm going to get a cup of cocoa and something to eat."

Phillip stood in stunned silence as Teddi marched off, leaving him to his own devices. Before he could decide how to handle the situation, Helen was back from the refreshment table carrying two plates laden with tasty treats.

"I brought you a plate, and I have something else I want to tell you," Helen said as she settled in beside him. "I apologized to Margaret for my bad behavior the other day." There was a look of pride on her face, and she stared at Phillip as if she expected some sort of enthusiastic reply.

"That's wonderful, Helen, if your apology was genuine and not given to serve some ulterior purpose," Phillip said.

"Well, of course it was genuine, Phillip. Why would you doubt my intentions?" she asked while giving him an exaggerated pout.

"If you'll excuse me, I see someone I want to speak to," Phillip said in an attempt to get away from her. "Jonathan!" he called, quickly moving toward his friend.

Jonathan turned and gave him a smile. He and Margaret seemed to be enjoying themselves, and as far as he could tell, the other guests were including Margaret in their conversation.

"Where's Teddi?" Jonathan inquired, looking about the room.

"It appears I've offended her—again," Phillip answered. "Do you think you could speak to her and help me straighten this out?"

"I can try. What happened?"

Phillip gave his friend a quick explanation and sent him off in search of Teddi while he remained close by Margaret's side. He wanted to protect Margaret from any ungracious behavior that might occur in Jonathan's absence, but he also hoped that her presence would keep Helen at arm's length.

"I understand Helen apologized," Phillip quietly remarked as they stood at the far end of the dining room.

Margaret gave him a faint smile and nodded her head ever so slightly. "I suppose you could call it that."

"Was she unkind?"

"Helen's apology is of little consequence to me. She's not someone I would choose as a friend, so it makes no difference. I'd rather talk about something more pleasant," she answered.

Phillip honored her wishes and quickly changed the subject, but he was now sure that Helen had merely added insult to injury with her so-called apology. They were discussing the upcoming masquerade ball when Teddi and Jonathan approached. Phillip breathed a sigh of relief when Teddi smiled and moved next to him.

"Have you had refreshments?" she asked.

"Yes, Helen . . ." He wanted to choke back her name, but he couldn't. It was hanging in midair, separating them, just as immovably as if she'd physically walked between them.

Teddi finally broke the thick silence. "You and Helen ate together?"

"Not exactly. She went and filled a plate and brought it to me. I certainly didn't ask her to do such a thing, and I never expected it. She just appeared with two plates of food and sat down beside me.

Teddi, I don't want to spend the evening with that woman. I don't know how to make you believe me. Surely you realize that I had no control over the seating arrangements."

"Yes, Phillip, I do understand what occurred. Let's go back into the parlor."

When Ella announced that the guests could choose the partner of their choice for the remainder of the games, Phillip quickly asked Teddi. He hoped that her agreement was a sign that the earlier events of the evening had been forgotten.

11

*A*t her mother's insistence, Teddi had been working on her costume for the masquerade ball for several months. Now, she was pleased that it had been completed and was hanging in the closet awaiting the party. There were a number of guests who had failed to appear at the Mahoneys' due to last-minute stitching on costumes, among them Helen Hanson.

Helen's failure to appear at that get-together had permitted Teddi to relax and enjoy the evening's festivities. The game of charades had been great fun, and she'd been amazed by Phillip's clever performances. He had proved to be good at both acting out his clues as well as guessing the actions of others who were performing. In fact, their team had been in total agreement that, without Phillip, they would never have won.

Although she had all but begged him to tell, Phillip had steadfastly refused to divulge what he would be wearing when he came to call on her this evening. Many of the married couples wore outfits that complemented each other, but those who were single most often decided upon a costume without consulting their escorts.

Phillip had agreed to help Jonathan and George find costumes among the wardrobe stored for use by the theater troupe. Isabelle had been delighted to have that task removed from her list of worries and promised Phillip Sunday dinner for the rest of the year. She had, however, been somewhat embarrassed when Phillip pointed out the fact that there were only two Sundays left until the beginning of the new year and that he hoped she would consider an extension.

"Are you absolutely positive that you don't want to tell me what you'll be wearing this evening?" Teddi asked as she was leaving the hospital for the day.

"Of course not! That's half the fun. I want to see if you'll be able to find me in the crowd."

As was the custom, Teddi would go to the ball with her family. Then, after everyone had arrived, the partygoers would begin to seek out their escorts. Inevitably there were occasions when couples would go through most of the evening thinking they'd found their escort, only to be surprised when the masks came off. Although the use of accents to disguise voices was commonplace on masquerade night, Teddi was certain she'd have no difficulty detecting Phillip.

Jonathan insisted he was not going to attend with the family and had already left for Junction City to get Margaret. Teddi wasn't sure if it was because he feared the possibility Margaret might suffer insult from someone attending the party, or if he was unwilling to spend any part of the evening with other girls while he attempted to find her. Either way, Margaret had agreed to the arrangement. And surprisingly, Isabelle had remained silent on the issue.

"Do you need any help with your costume, Teddi?" Isabelle asked as she tapped on Teddi's bedroom door.

"No, I think I'm ready. Come in and see what you think."

"It's lovely, and such a unique idea. I don't think you need worry about anyone else duplicating your costume. Come along. I believe your father is waiting impatiently at the bottom of the stairs."

"You look beautiful, Mother," Teddi remarked as they walked down the hallway. "Do you feel like you're getting married all over again?"

"Not quite, but it does please me that I can still wear my wedding dress. Especially since I had to let out all the seams in your father's suit," she said, causing both women to laugh.

"What's so funny?" Clayton asked as mother and daughter walked down the steps.

"Just reminiscing, dear," was all that Isabelle said.

"Well, now, that certainly takes me back," Clayton said as he twirled Isabelle around in the parlor. "My bride has returned after all these years, looking even more beautiful, if that's possible," he complimented. "And, you, Teddi, aren't you just gorgeous? I would have never known it was you. What a remarkable costume!"

"Where's George?" Isabelle inquired. "We need to be on our way."

"He decided to ride along with Jonathan, so it's just the three of us."

"Don't forget, we're going to the theater building, not the mess hall," Isabelle instructed as Clayton helped them into the sleigh.

Clayton gave her one of his uncontrolled laughs, his beefy cheeks puffing the cold night air. "I think I can remember where we're going. My mind isn't quite that bad yet, my dear."

"I wasn't insulting your memory, Clayton, but the masquerade ball has been at the dining hall ever since we've been at Fort Riley. With all the important things you have to remember, I didn't know if you might overlook something so trivial."

"That was an excellent piece of diplomacy," he said, kissing his wife on the cheek.

"We're off," he called out into the cold night air. "To the theater," he added, and then he graced them with another hearty laugh.

The theater was ablaze with light when they arrived amid guests alighting from sleighs that in many cases sat some distance away from the front door.

"I'll let you ladies out here and go put the sleigh in back," Clayton instructed. "Go on inside, and I'll be with you momentarily."

"I've never seen so many people at this ball," Teddi said to her mother.

"The Junction City newspaper printed several excellent articles about the event and encouraged everyone to attend. And the theater has enough room for them all," Isabelle replied.

The stage curtain had been raised, and the stage would be their dance floor for the evening. Barry's Band from Junction City was in the pit providing music, and many of the theater chairs had been removed to allow the guests extra room to mingle. Large banquet tables were covered with linen cloths and decorated with greenery and candles, and festive, red bows festooned the rough-hewn support beams throughout the building.

"Oh, look, there's Jonathan. He must have told Margaret what he would be wearing. Their costumes match. Folks will think they're a married couple," Teddi remarked as she moved toward them. "Jonathan!" she called, waving her arm.

"Don't you look quite stunning," Jonathan remarked. "Where did you ever come up with the idea of dressing like a rainbow?"

"I don't know. I think they're beautiful and decided I could make a dress and accessories that would resemble a rainbow."

"And so you have. It is truly beautiful," Margaret replied. "Here we are dressed as hobos, looking quite destitute while you look stunning."

"I don't think I could ever look stunning, Margaret, but thank you for your kind words. I haven't spotted Phillip. What is he wearing, Jonathan?"

"I don't know. He wouldn't tell me—said he was sure you could wheedle it out of me if he told. He's probably right!"

"He truly didn't tell you? But I was depending on you, Jonathan. Look how many people are in this place! How am I ever going to find him?"

"I suppose like everyone else. Accept dance invitations and talk to everyone you can. You'd best get started mingling; we're off to the dance floor. Now you see why I didn't want to come without Margaret on my arm," he said with a laugh.

In the past, attending with her family had never been a problem. Their first year at Fort Riley, she didn't have an escort; after that, Herbert had always told her in advance what he would be wearing. If she had known there would be so many guests, she would have insisted Phillip divulge his costume.

"May I have this dance, lassie?"

Teddi looked at a man attired in a gray-and-red-plaid Irish kilt, a white shirt, gray wool waistcoat, and red kneesocks. She didn't think it was Phillip, yet there was something strangely familiar about him. He was disguising his voice with a pronounced Irish accent. Perhaps once they were on the dance floor, she'd be able to tell for sure.

"My, but you're lookin' lovely tonight, lassie," he said as they twirled across the wooden boards. "And you feel just right in my arms, I might add."

"Phillip?" she asked.

"You can call me by any name you like, so long as you promise to spend your time with me," he replied.

His hands! That would let her know for sure. But as soon as the thought raced through her mind, she felt the cloth of his gloved hand. He'd even thought to cover his hands. It must be Phillip, for he'd expect her to look at his hands. Yet something wasn't quite right.

"Do I have the promise of all your dances, lassie?" he asked as the music ceased playing.

"Not yet. I'm not sure you're Phillip," she replied. "I'd better wait until I've danced with some other gentlemen."

"I'll be here waitin' for you, lassie. You're the one I came for, and you're the one I'll have," he said while escorting her off the stage.

Before she had time to give further consideration to the Irishman, a pirate was walking her back to the stage. However, they had taken only a few dance steps when she was sure the pirate wasn't Phillip. She giggled when the pirate kept forgetting his pirate jargon and slipped back into using his own voice.

She moved through dance after dance while the Irishman continued to stand by the stage and watch her, never leaving his post.

"Have time for a dance with your father?" Clayton asked.

"Of course," Teddi replied, taking his hand and walking onto the makeshift dance floor. "Have you seen Phillip?" she asked once the music had begun.

"No, can't say as I have. Of course, I haven't figured out who much of anybody is. I take it you're having trouble finding him."

"I'm not sure. The first person who asked me to dance is that man dressed like an Irishman standing by the stage. He seems so familiar, yet I'm not positive it's Phillip. When I asked him if he was Phillip, he said I could call him by any name I liked as long as I spent my time with him," she explained.

"If you don't know of another gentleman who might want to spend the evening with you, I'd say it's probably Phillip. That man looks to be the same size and height as Phillip. Did you ask Jonathan?"

"Phillip wouldn't even tell him what he was wearing. He said I could probably wheedle it out of Jonathan."

The general gave an uproarious laugh. "I'd say Phillip knows you pretty well! Why don't you dance a couple more dances with the Irishman? Then maybe you'll be sure," he suggested as they left the floor.

She nodded her head, and General Yorke led her off the floor toward where the man stood watching them.

"Good evening, General Yorke. I hope you're bringing your lovely lassie to dance with me," the Irishman said with his thick accent.

"I think perhaps I am," Clayton said, handing Teddi over.

"I've decided I need to dance with you again in order to be sure you're the man I want to spend my evening with," she told him.

"Ah, Lassie, not only am I the man you want to spend the evening with, but I'm also the man you'll be spending your life with," he confidently replied.

Teddi was surprised by the comment. Obviously Phillip felt much more assured of their relationship when hidden behind a mask and Irish brogue.

Phillip surveyed the crowd. He knew Teddi wouldn't stay close by her parents, but he had felt an assurance he'd be able to find her. Jonathan had even volunteered to ask what she'd be wearing, but Phillip had declined the offer. Just as he was becoming a bit concerned, he was certain that he now spotted her. There was no doubt it was Teddi, although he was surprised she hadn't taken greater pains to hide her identity.

"So you did recognize me. I told Jonathan I was sure I'd be able to fool you," Phillip said as he approached her. "I could have picked you out anywhere. That's a beautiful costume," he added, relishing her portrayal of a Southern belle as she twirled a fancy parasol above her head.

"Why, thank you, kind sir," she replied, giving him a deep curtsy while feigning a Southern accent.

"You don't need to use that accent, Teddi; I know it's you," Phillip replied, lifting the side of his mask and allowing her a peek. "I told you I'd reveal myself if you found me," he continued.

"I've decided I rather like my Southern drawl. By the way, how did you know it was me? Now, that was a silly question, wasn't it? All these tiny-waisted girls, and then there's me."

"Don't talk about yourself in such a manner, Teddi. You are a lovely, young woman, and I admire you very much. It hurts me when you speak poorly of yourself. If it were only appearances that interested me, I'd be searching out someone like Helen Hanson. I thought you understood that what I'm seeking in a wife is someone with your attributes. Beauty isn't merely someone's outer appearance; it's who that person is inside," Phillip replied.

"Let's don't talk anymore, Phillip. Let's enjoy the music and dance."

They finished the set without so much as a word passing between them, although he was pleased when she squeezed his hand several times and placed her head on his shoulder.

"Why don't we get some punch?" Phillip asked as the music stopped.

"I'm quite warm. Could we go outside?"

"It's freezing out there. You'd catch your death of cold," Phillip warned.

"We could sit under the buffalo robe in your sleigh and talk for awhile. There are some things I want to discuss with you, and it's noisy in here. I'm sure I'd be able to keep warm there," she said, the words dripping with her Southern drawl.

"I suppose, if you really want to," he hesitantly agreed, though surprised by her request.

"Teddi, my love, you've brought me such joy this fine evening. I have a very important question I want to ask you before the night has ended," the Irishman whispered in her ear.

A tingling sensation coursed down her spine with each word that he spoke, and his lips lightly brushed her neck in the slightest hint of a kiss as he pulled her closer. She squeezed his hand in her own, unable to restrain the love that had begun to well up inside her weeks ago. Not that she wanted this to happen so quickly. After Herbert, she had never wanted to love again. But Phillip's kindness and concern, his gentle acceptance of her, and his sweet words whispered in her ear dissolved all her defenses. Phillip was an honorable man who would be a good husband to her and a good father to her children. There was no reason why she shouldn't love him.

"Would you like something cool to drink?"

"Yes, thank you," she replied, following him to the refreshment table.

He filled two cups and handed her one. "Follow me. There's a quiet place where we can talk back here."

"In one of the dressing rooms? I don't know if we should," she stammered.

"Trust me, Lassie," he said, pulling her along beside him until they reached the hallway.

The hallway behind the stage was narrow, causing Teddi to follow along behind. The man held her hand tightly as he opened the door and pulled her inside. The door closed behind them and the room was dark and silent. She felt his hands touch her face as he slowly lifted her mask and ran his finger ever so lightly across her lips. She could hear his shallow breathing as his face lowered toward hers, his mouth seeking and then covering her own in a lingering kiss.

"Phillip, we need to go back to the party," Teddi urged as their lips parted.

"Say that you'll marry me," he demanded, still using his Irish accent as he pulled her tightly against him. "Give me your promise, or I'll keep you here until you do, lassie."

His lips once again found hers, and she yielded to the tenderness of his kiss. "Yes, I'll marry you," she whispered. "I promise."

12

*G*eneral Yorke pulled off his shoes and leaned back in his favorite chair, wishing he'd have pulled the seat a bit closer to the fireplace, yet too weary to get up and move it. Isabelle came fluttering in from the kitchen, still wearing her wedding dress, carrying a pan filled with warm water.

"Give me a pair of leather cavalry boots over these fandangled gentlemen's slippers any day of the week," the general complained as he rolled up his trousers, pulled off his socks, and tentatively placed his big toe in the water.

"It's not hot. You act as though I'm going to scald you," Isabelle remarked.

"Just checking. It's bad enough having these blisters; I don't want burns on my feet, too. I wouldn't be able to walk at all," he complained.

"Good heavens, Clayton, what are you going to do if you ever have a serious medical problem?" Isabelle retorted. "I'm going upstairs to get out of this dress. I'll be down and see how you're doing in a few minutes."

She had made it to the first landing when the front door burst open and Teddi rushed into the house, the Irishman following close on her heels.

"Why did you leave without me?" she asked in an accusatory tone.

"Your father said you'd come home with Phillip. Oh, oh," Isabelle gasped. "Where did *you* come from?"

"What's going on out there?" General Yorke called from the parlor.

"Good evening, General. I wanted to come in with Teddi to tell you the good news. She's given her promise to marry me!"

"What? She would never give her promise to marry you, Albright. Teddi, what's he talking about, and what is he doing in this house?"

"Herbert is the Irishman, Father. He pretended to be Phillip and asked me to marry him," Teddi answered, tears streaming down her face. "After the two of you left, he went about telling all the guests that we were going to be married. I denied it, but he kept telling people I was only jesting, that we were truly to be married, and that I had forgiven his outrageous behavior."

The sight of Herbert Albright had caused Isabelle to visibly pale, but her faintness soon gave way to anger. "How dare you humiliate our daughter again! What are you up to? You're already a married man. Why would you do such a thing?"

"Alas, my wife succumbed to cholera out on the prairie," he replied with theatrical flair. "Had she lived, the marriage wouldn't have lasted. She knew my heart remained with Teddi."

"You unfeeling cad! I want you out of this house and out of my life," Teddi cried.

"I'll leave for now, but I'm sure you'll come around. I'll be staying in Junction City for the next month, so we'll be seeing each other at all the socials. In fact, I'll just plan on being your escort."

"Get out of here! I would rather *die* than be seen with you," she screeched.

"You may change your mind, so let's keep the option available. After all, you don't know where Phillip was spending his time this evening, do you?" he asked as he left the house.

"Oh, Mother, what if someone told Phillip that I've pledged myself to Herbert again? How could this happen?"

"We need to remain calm and keep our wits, or none of us will be able to think," Isabelle replied. "Did you ever see Phillip?"

"No, I thought Herbert was Phillip. He used that foolish accent all evening. I kept sensing a familiarity about him and thought it must be Phillip. I asked both Jonathan and George throughout the evening, but both of them denied ever seeing him. Maybe he's ill and didn't go at all. Oh, I hope that's what happened," Teddi said, the thought giving her a glimmer of hope. If Phillip hadn't attended the party, she could explain everything before he heard the lies from others.

"Nothing's going to be settled by sitting up all night. Besides, this water is getting cold," the general stated as he pulled his feet out of the water.

Teddi went upstairs and readied herself for bed, but instead of crawling beneath the covers, she paced back and forth until her father finally knocked on the wall and told her to get in bed. Later, when she heard Jonathan come home, she considered running downstairs to talk with him. But she would have awakened at least one of her parents and suffered their wrath, so she reluctantly turned over and stared at the wall, finally falling asleep shortly before dawn.

A tapping at her bedroom door awakened her only a few hours after she had fallen asleep. "You need to get up, Teddi, or we'll be late for church."

Church! She'd see Phillip at church, but in all likelihood he'd already have heard about last night's happenings before she arrived. The thought of seeing all those people, having them stare and whisper behind their hands, watching them give each other knowing smiles, made her want to plow back under the covers and remain there for the rest of her life.

"I'm not sure I can go to church this morning, Mother."

"Are you ill?" her mother questioned.

"Not exactly. But I will be if I'm forced to face all those gossips," Teddi replied.

"The longer you hide behind closed doors, the harder it will be to face the world. Get out of bed and get ready. We're going to church!" Isabelle responded firmly.

Teddi pulled out a dark brown dress with pleated sleeves and tan decorative lapels. Both the skirt and lapels were adorned with matching, gold buttons. Looking into the mirror, she donned her dark brown hat that sported tan and brown feathers, and snugly tied it under her chin.

"Come have some breakfast before we leave," her mother urged.

"Where are Jonathan and George?" Teddi asked, surveying the room. She wanted them close at hand in case she felt the need to make a quick getaway.

"I'm not sure. They were up early and have already left," Isabelle said. "Hurry now!"

Untying her hat and placing it on a table in the living room, Teddi hesitantly filled her plate and sat down at the table; however, eating proved impossible. She chased her scrambled eggs around the plate and nibbled on one of Florence's muffins, but her stomach rebelled, so she finally quit trying.

"You ladies ready?" Clayton asked as he came in the front door. "I've got the sleigh waiting."

"We'll get our coats and be with you in just a moment," Isabelle replied.

"I'd really prefer to stay home," Teddi said, remaining in her chair.

"You're not staying home. Don't forget we'll have extra guests for dinner, Florence," Isabelle called out toward the kitchen.

"Oh, that's right. You invited Phillip to dinner."

"And Margaret, plus both of your brothers, and I believe George invited Ruth Ann. We should have quite a roomful."

"Wonderful," Teddi replied dejectedly.

"That didn't sound very enthusiastic. Don't borrow trouble, Teddi—everything may turn out just fine."

"I know, Mother. 'Do not worry about tomorrow, for tomorrow will worry about itself. Each day has enough trouble of its own.' I've been repeating that verse quite a bit lately," Teddi replied as they walked out the door.

The ride to church came to a halt much too soon for Teddi, but she gathered her courage and stepped into the limestone chapel, with her parents following close behind. Jonathan, Margaret, Ruth Ann, and George were already seated in the Yorkes' regular pew. Teddi slid in beside Ruth Ann and turned her attention to the front of the church. Phillip was busy leafing through his Bible, and if he ever attempted to look in her direction, she missed it when someone tapped her on the shoulder.

Glancing to the row behind her, Teddi found herself eye to eye with Herbert, who was looking far too smug to suit her. Ignoring his grin, she turned around and faced forward. She wanted to tell her mother Herbert was seated behind them, but she knew he would be delighted if she did anything that indicated he was making her uncomfortable. She was surprised to see Helen Hanson and her friend Mattie seated across the aisle. They were both members of a church in Junction City, and Teddi couldn't remember ever seeing them at the post chapel before. Obviously Helen was not going to give up on Phillip, she surmised. But then she saw Helen looking in Herbert's direction and wondered if perhaps she might be interested in him instead.

Those two would make a perfect couple. Not only did both of their names begin with the letter "H," but they also had a multitude of traits in common, none of which Teddi admired. However, she decided that they probably deserved each other.

Before the service officially began, Phillip stood up and announced that a young adults' Bible study would begin on Wednesday nights after the first of the year. Enthusiastically extending an invitation to all those young people, he then asked them to spread the word among their friends in Junction City and Fort Riley. Once the announcements were completed, Sergeant Little went forward to lead the singing. His rich baritone voice boomed through the small chapel, encouraging those in attendance to join him in praising the Lord.

When the singing had ended, Phillip walked to the podium and began his sermon. He spoke about deceit and broken relationships among humans, comparing those to man breaking his relationship with God. His words were eloquent, but as Teddi listened to the words, she wondered if the sermon was aimed at her and the occurrences of the previous night. Surely he couldn't have written and delivered so powerful a sermon with only a few hours of preparation. Or could he? If the sermon dealt with personal events and feelings, he may not have needed much time at all. Her mind was racing by the time the service ended, and when they finally reached the back of the church, she noticed Phillip looking her way as he was shaking hands with one of the soldiers.

"I'm not going to make it for dinner today. There's something I must attend to immediately," he hurriedly explained.

Teddi noticed him looking at someone behind her as he spoke, but didn't turn to look. It might be Herbert, and she didn't want a scene before she spoke privately with Phillip.

"I truly need to talk to you, Phillip. Isn't it something that could wait just a couple of hours?" she asked. She didn't want to keep him from his pastoral duties, although she couldn't keep the sound of urgency out of her voice.

"Are you ill? Your color doesn't look good," he said while taking her hand.

"I didn't get much sleep last night. Were you at the ball? I never did see you," she continued as the line formed behind her.

"Yes, I was there. If I don't have time to stop by your house today, we can talk at work tomorrow," he said, nodding toward the crowd that was gathering to shake his hand.

"Yes, of course," she quietly replied.

What else could she do but agree? It was obvious he wasn't going to change his mind. Turning to leave, Teddi permitted herself a quick look over her shoulder. Helen Hanson stood directly in Phillip's line of vision, her hand raised to cover her mouth as she whispered something to Mattie. Teddi watched the twosome as she stood waiting for her parents in the vestibule of the church. Their whispering was continual, as was Helen's obvious admiration of Phillip. Her stare remained fixed on him until Teddi and her parents left the church.

"I'd be pleased to take Phillip's place at your dinner table," Herbert said when General Yorke had gone to fetch the sleigh.

Isabelle turned on her heel and pointed her finger in Herbert's face. "You are not welcome at our dinner table or in our house. Leave Teddi alone, or you'll have my husband and sons to contend with, Herbert, and I know you don't want that. Since you've already shown what you're made of, I'm sure you'll want to avoid a confrontation with the Yorke men!"

Herbert merely nodded and gave them an evil grin. "Remember, Teddi, things aren't always what they seem. I'm going to look very appealing to you in a short time."

"What does he mean by that?" Isabelle asked as Clayton arrived with the sleigh.

"I don't know, Mother. He's said several strange things about the future."

"Was that Albright I saw?" Clayton asked as he assisted the women.

"Yes, Father, but I hope Mother has made it abundantly clear he should stay away."

They rode home in silence, except for the sound of the jingling sleigh bells. But even the bells didn't improve Teddi's mood. What was so important that Phillip couldn't spare her a few hours? Helen Hanson? She *was* standing there and waiting after church.

Her brothers and their dates came alongside them in another sleigh and immediately challenged Clayton to a race.

"To the Republican River Bridge and back. How does that sound?" Clayton called out.

"Sounds good," Jonathan yelled as he slapped the reins and moved ahead before Clayton could say anything further.

"Turn this sleigh around, Clayton. I need to get home. We're having guests for dinner," Isabelle ordered.

"Your guests are all in that sleigh we're racing, Isabelle, so sit back and enjoy the ride," Clayton replied with a boisterous laugh, obviously delighted with the competition.

Teddi was as disgruntled as her mother with the lighthearted race that her brothers and their girlfriends seemed to be enjoying. She wanted to go home and spend time in her room thinking, and perhaps talk to her brothers and see if they had heard anything or could help solve this riddle. But they were too busy enjoying themselves to be concerned about her problems, she decided.

By the time they reached the bridge, Clayton had gained and the horses were neck and neck as they began their turn. Clayton brought his team around, keeping them in a tighter turn, and when they were back on the straightaway, he was in the lead. Teddi pulled the buffalo robe up around her mother and noticed a familiar sleigh coming toward them, headed toward Junction City. The sun was shining brightly, causing a blinding glare as it hit the whiteness of the snow. Cupping her palm above her eyes, she stared off in the direction of the sleigh. She was right; it was Phillip. Phillip, Helen Hanson, Mattie, and *Herbert?* She turned around and stared after them, unable to believe her eyes. However, just when she was sure it couldn't possibly be true, Herbert stood up in the back of the sleigh and waved.

What was going on? What reason would Phillip have to be in the company of those three people? And why would he want to be with them rather than her? He had said there was something he had to attend to, but what business could he possibly have with them?

"Was that Phillip?" her mother asked, a look of astonishment crossing her face.

Teddi nodded her head, but remained silent. Her stomach began to roll, and she felt bile rising in the back of her throat.

"It looked like Helen and Herbert in the sleigh with him," Isabelle continued without noticing that Teddi had grown unusually quiet. "That couldn't be, could it?" she asked, now looking at her daughter.

"You really are ill. I should have permitted you to stay home from church this morning. Hurry up, Clayton. We need to get Teddi home," Isabelle shouted to her husband.

"In case you hadn't noticed, I'm in a race, Isabelle. These horses won't go any faster, or they'd already be doing it," he hollered back over his shoulder.

"Well, find the quickest route home," she commanded, unwilling to allow him the final word. "Not much longer, dear," she said to Teddi in a soothing voice. "We're almost back to the fort."

Within a few minutes, Clayton pulled the team to a halt and jumped down to help Teddi out of the sleigh. "Let me help you upstairs," he said, placing his arm around her waist as they walked into the house and up the stairs.

Isabelle stopped in the kitchen to issue a few orders to Florence; then she secured a pitcher of fresh water and a cloth. That accomplished, she scurried up the steps, nearly spilling the water on Clayton as he was leaving the bedroom.

"Let's get you out of that dress," Isabelle said as she entered the room.

"I can't move right now, Mother. I'll take off my dress as soon as I feel a little better," Teddi groaned. "Go take care of your guests. I'll be fine."

"I'm going to have Jonathan bring up a bell so that you can ring if you want me. There's a fresh pitcher of water right here if you need it. When you're ready to get out of your dress or if you want something to eat, just ring the bell."

"Fine, Mother, but I really don't think I'll need you."

Arguing would serve no purpose. If her mother decided a bell was needed, there would be a bell in the room! Teddi rolled over and watched the door. No matter how awful she felt, she wanted to speak to Jonathan. Moments later her brother appeared at the door dangling a bell between his index finger and thumb.

"You rang?" he asked while jingling the bell. "How are you feeling?"

"I'll be all right. I think it's more a lack of sleep and a series of unsettling circumstances that have me upset. Have you talked to Phillip?"

Jonathan shook his head. "Just for a minute at church, but he seemed preoccupied with the crowd, so I said we'd see him for dinner later. That's all. I didn't see him at the party last night. You did find him, didn't you?"

"No. I thought he was the Irishman, but it turned out to be Herbert. It's a long story, and I'm sure Mother will share all the gruesome details at dinner. When I'm feeling better, I'd like to talk with you."

"Just let me know when you're ready. Now get some rest, and maybe you'll feel strong enough to come down later and join us," he instructed as he left the room.

The sounds of laughter and clanging china floated up the stairway as Teddi relaxed and fell into a deep sleep.

13

hillip squinted his eyes against the brilliance of the sun glistening on the expanse of chalky-white snow that stretched before him. He could feel his heartbeat increasing as blood pulsed through his veins. His head was pounding. Taking both reins in his left hand, he massaged his right temple, then switched hands and began rubbing the left side of his head. It was at that moment that he noticed two sleighs racing toward him, and one of them was strikingly familiar.

Straining, he kept his gaze fixed upon the sleigh on the left. Surely it couldn't be. But as the two teams raced alongside each other, he knew his eyesight hadn't betrayed him; it was the Yorkes, and Teddi was looking in his direction. He turned his head, hoping she wouldn't recognize the sleigh—or him, for that matter. But he knew it was unlikely that they would go unnoticed, especially when he turned and saw Herbert standing up and wildly waving his arms at Teddi.

"Sit down before I knock you down," Phillip shouted over his shoulder.

"Just wanted to be sure Teddi saw that you were in such fine company," Herbert shouted back.

His words and the evil laugh that followed reinforced what Phillip already knew. This whole group was up to no good, and he was going to find himself smack in the middle of their depravity. He had fallen prey to Helen's conniving plot at every turn, from following her outdoors the previous night, to having Herbert Albright in his sleigh at this very moment.

Mattie seemed somewhat distressed with the situation, but Phillip realized that Mattie would do whatever Helen ordered. The poor girl was obviously afraid of losing the only friend she had, but too shallow to realize that Helen didn't even know the true meaning of friendship. He didn't know if there was any way Mattie could help, but even if she could, he doubted his ability to win her allegiance.

"Where are we going?" Phillip finally asked when they had arrived in Junction City.

"Mattie's house. There's nobody home, and we can talk privately," Herbert replied, pointing for Phillip to turn east on First Street and then motioning him to turn in beside a small frame house.

Helen and Mattie jumped down from the sleigh as Phillip tied the horses and followed Herbert onto the front porch of the modest home.

"My parents will be home by five o'clock. You've got to be out of here by then," Mattie warned as she opened the front door and permitted them entry.

"This won't take long. I'm sure Phillip is going to be *very* cooperative," Herbert sneered, leading them into the parlor.

Herbert and both of the girls removed their coats, but Phillip remained encased in his heavy, wool greatcoat, removing only his gloves and hat.

"Sit down, sit down, my good man. We're not going to torture you, merely have a civil little chat," Herbert said in a cunning voice.

Phillip obeyed the command by perching himself on the edge of a padded wicker chair, certain that he wanted to take flight and even more certain that nothing good was going to come from this meeting. Absently twirling a lock of hair around her finger, Helen was poised on the sofa with Herbert flanking her on one side and Mattie on the other. All three of them turned and focused their attention upon him.

"It seems you've caused a bit of a problem in my life, and, fortunately for all of us, I've found a reasonable solution. I think it will make all of us happy, perhaps with the exception of you, Phillip. But since you're a man of God, I'm sure you'll learn to adjust, and in time you may even be thankful for what is going to occur. And when that time comes, please remember that you have me to thank for your good fortune, not God," Herbert said.

"There's no need to blaspheme," Mattie whispered.

"Poor, dear Mattie. She's afraid God is going to strike her dead for her part in this little charade. I can't seem to convince her otherwise. Why don't you give her your assurance that she's not going to burn in hell for merely corroborating Helen's statements?" Herbert said, his tone condescending.

"Mattie knows the real truth and also knows how to avoid burning in hell, don't you, Mattie?" Phillip asked.

Mattie nodded her head. "Reverend Lewis says you have to accept Jesus into your heart as your very own personal Savior and repent of all your sins, and if you do that, you'll go to heaven," Mattie replied.

"And have you done that, Mattie?" Phillip asked in a kind voice.

"Oh, shut up," Herbert angrily interrupted. "This isn't some tent revival, and you're not going to save her soul while I have more important things to take care of. You have something that I want, *and* you have something that our sweet, little Helen wants. Now, this can be a very simple thing if you'll cooperate, or it can be very ugly if you don't."

"How could I possibly have anything that either one of you wants?" Phillip asked.

"If you'll let me finish, I'll tell you. Unfortunately, my poor wife of only a few months met with an untimely death, leaving me once again a single man. Since your arrival at Fort Riley, you've been pursuing the woman I intend to marry."

"What kind of a man are you? You've just buried your wife, and now you come here telling me you intend to marry Teddi Yorke. Well, sir, she'll never have you!" Phillip exclaimed.

"There you go, interrupting again. I have this all worked out, Phillip, and if you'll just listen, you'll soon see that she *will* have me. In fact, I dare say she'll be thrilled that *anyone* would consider marrying her after the humiliation you've caused her."

Helen looked at Herbert as though he were a genius ready to solve all the mysteries of life, while poor Mattie nervously fidgeted about, jumping up and down to peek out the heavily layered, emerald green draperies and then returning to her appointed position beside Helen on the settee.

"What are you talking about? I've done nothing to cause her shame or embarrassment," Phillip defended.

"Do you hear that, Helen?" Herbert asked, giving Helen a look of amazement. "Why, he's already forgotten what he did to you last night. The scoundrel!" Herbert sarcastically exclaimed.

"Phillip, don't you remember last night in your sleigh? Although I protested violently, you took advantage of me—a poor, defenseless, young woman. You've stolen that which is most prized among all unmarried women. What man would want me now that I've been defiled? You have an obligation to marry me!"

"That's a lie, and you know it. I never laid a hand on you, although you used your wiles to try to entice me to do so. I'll deny it. Nobody will believe such a story."

"Won't they? Mattie, get back over here and tell Reverend Hamilton what you saw," Herbert commanded.

Mattie once again moved away from the window and back to the sofa. Sitting down beside Helen, she lowered her eyes and spoke. "I came outside looking for Helen when the two of you had been gone from the party for such a long time. When I got close to your sleigh, I heard Helen crying, saying that you had ruined her and begging you to marry her since you had stolen her virtue."

"You heard *what*? And what did *I* say, Mattie?" Phillip asked.

"You? Oh, you said that you couldn't marry her even though you truly wanted to, because she's the most beautiful woman in the world."

After she had spoken the words, Mattie stopped for a moment and looked at Helen, her eyes seeming to seek out the other woman's approval.

"Go on, Mattie. You're doing a wonderful job. Tell him the rest," Helen encouraged.

Mattie nodded her head and gave Helen a smile. "You said you found Teddi Yorke completely undesirable, but you were going to marry her because you knew her father had inherited a lot of money, and one day you'd get your share of it. Then you said that marrying Teddi would probably help your military career, too, and that Helen had nothing but her beauty to offer. And then," Mattie continued dramatically, "you said that you would keep Helen as your *mistress*."

The last words were barely audible, and Phillip strained to hear her declaration. He could feel the blood rush to his face as he jumped up from his chair, his anger barely under control as he moved in front of the trio of conspirators.

"How dare you! Who do you think is going to give credence to this host of lies? I can't believe that the three of you have collaborated to manipulate and ruin the reputations and lives of others in such a callous, unfeeling manner. What is wrong with you? Are you all so insecure and pitiful that you can't build a relationship with another person except by deceit and lies? You're a pathetic group of human beings."

Only Mattie looked uncomfortable with the words he'd spoken. Helen and Herbert merely glanced at each other, as if they had expected such a reaction and were quite willing to take it in stride.

"I will not be a party to any of this. I won't marry you, Helen. I won't permit you to seduce Teddi under the pretense of lies, Herbert. And I won't allow you to denigrate my name with your lies, Mattie. Now if that's all you have to say, I'm leaving," Phillip proclaimed.

"You may want to give this a little thought. A court-martial could be an ugly smear on your good name. I'm sure Teddi Yorke wouldn't consider marrying someone who left the military with less than an honorable discharge. And then there's your reputation, *Reverend*. Whatever are your parishioners going to think of a preacher who would ruthlessly frolic about underneath the blankets of his sleigh while a party was going on only a short distance away? I don't think they'd be very pleased. Shame, shame," Herbert replied, shaking his finger at Phillip and giving him a depraved laugh.

"People will believe me," Phillip avowed.

"Perhaps if it were only your word against sweet, little Helen's. But with Mattie to take an oath and swear the story is gospel—well, I don't think you have much of a chance. As I said, give it some thought. I'll come by the hospital tomorrow afternoon, say about four-thirty. Or would you prefer that I come to the church instead, since the object of our affections may be at the hospital?" he asked, a smirk twisting the corners of his mouth.

"I'm not concerned about Teddi seeing you. I'll be at the hospital at four-thirty, just as I am every weekday. Suit yourself as to whether you come or not," Phillip replied as he pulled on his gloves and donned his black beaver hat.

Mattie was standing guard at the front door as Phillip entered the small foyer. "I'm sorry, Reverend Hamilton. But Helen's my friend, and she needs my help," the girl whispered.

"And do you think that makes what you're doing right in the eyes of God, Mattie?" Phillip whispered back.

"No," she replied, shaking her head back and forth, her lower lip trembling. "But perhaps someday God will forgive me my sin. Helen would *never* forgive me if I betrayed her."

"Did you listen to my sermon today, Mattie? About how we humans break our relationship with God?" he asked, still keeping his voice low.

The girl nodded her head up and down. "I know, but—"

"What are you two whispering about out there?" Herbert hollered, jumping up from the settee and coming toward them.

"Nothing you'd be interested in, I'm sure," Phillip replied as he pulled open the door and hastened down the steps toward his sleigh.

A loud rapping on the front door awakened Teddi from a restless sleep. She could hear Ruth Ann's laughter and then Jonathan's voice as he opened the front door and shouted a greeting to Phillip. Jumping up from the bed, Teddi rushed to the bureau, grabbed her comb, and began to straighten her disheveled hair with one hand while using the other to straighten the wrinkles from her rumpled dress.

She heard Jonathan racing up the steps, taking them two at a time until he reached the hallway. "You awake, Teddi? Phillip is downstairs wanting to talk to you."

"Yes. Tell him I'll be down in a moment," she replied, glancing in the mirror and pinching each of her cheeks, which she hoped would add a tint to her colorless complexion. Pressing her fingers down the front of her dress one last time, she decided there was nothing more that could be done to straighten the dress without the aid of a flatiron, and made her way downstairs.

Phillip rushed to the bottom of the staircase as soon as she turned at the landing and stepped onto the lower flight of stairs. At least he was anxious to see her. Perhaps that was a good sign.

"We need to talk," Phillip said in a hushed tone. "Is there somewhere we can speak privately?"

Teddi glanced toward the parlor where her parents, brothers, Ruth Ann, and Margaret were engaged in conversation. "I suppose we could go out to the kitchen. I don't think Florence will be in there right now."

He nodded his head and followed behind, seating himself opposite her on a wooden stool. His face was etched with concern, and perhaps a bit of anger. He must have heard the rumors about her agreeing to marry Herbert, Teddi decided.

When he opened his mouth to speak, she immediately interrupted him. "Phillip, let me say my piece; then I'll listen to whatever it is you want to tell me," she pleaded. "There is no way I could give my full attention to what you're about to say unless you've heard me out beforehand."

He seemed confused by her statement but didn't argue, and for that she was grateful. It would take all the courage she could muster to speak of last night's events, and if he argued with her, she knew that she would lose her boldness.

"I saw you in the sleigh with Herbert and Helen, and I'm sure that Herbert has already told you what occurred last night," she began. He visibly winced at her words, but he didn't speak, so she continued. "It is true that I agreed to marry Herbert," she said, watching the disbelief that crossed his face at her pronouncement.

"What? You say you agreed to marry that immoral rogue? I don't believe it!" he exclaimed, leaping up from the stool and causing it to hurl backward to the floor in a riotous crash.

"Didn't he tell you?" she asked, stunned by his seeming lack of knowledge.

"No, he *didn't* give me that bit of information. If you've agreed to marry him, then why is he coercing me?"

"I agreed only because I thought it was you," she whispered. "He was dressed in costume and used an Irish accent. I truly believed it was you. He took me back into one of the dressing rooms. It was dark, and he kissed me and asked that I pledge my love and promise to marry him. I'm sorry, Phillip. I've embarrassed myself *and* you. After he revealed his identity, I told him I would *never* consider marriage. But my refusal didn't stop him from going about the room telling the other guests that I had agreed to marry him. Can you ever forgive me?" she asked, gasping to take a breath.

"There is nothing for me to forgive. You're blameless. But when I've finished my tale, you may feel otherwise," he said.

She sat with her back straight and a stoic expression on her face as Phillip then recounted how he had taken the woman, whom he soon discovered was actually Helen, out to his sleigh. He related how Helen had used the same trickery as Herbert, luring him to the sleigh by pretending to be Teddi—how she'd worn a costume that padded her figure and had effected a Southern drawl.

Teddi wasn't sure she cared to hear the details of Helen being required to pad her figure in order to pass herself off as Teddi. But, no matter how hard it might have been to hear, she knew that padding would have been a necessary part of Helen's clever costume. By the time Phillip had completed the details of his trip into Junction City, Teddi was aghast at the malicious scheme Herbert and Helen had devised.

"Now, I must ask if you can forgive me and believe that what I have told you is true?" Phillip somberly inquired.

She nodded her agreement, and, after a brief conversation with her father, Teddi returned to the kitchen. Moments later she heard Ruth Ann and Margaret bidding her parents farewell and the sound of sleigh bells jingling as her brothers hitched the team and drove the sleigh around to the front of the house.

*P*hillip spent a restless night and rose the next morning feeling as though he'd never gone to bed. It would be a long day, and the four thirty appointment with Herbert loomed over him like a thundercloud on a spring day. Teddi arrived at her appointed time and appeared well rested, greeting him with a cheery "good morning" as she waved and headed off toward the ward to care for the patients.

He was astounded. She hadn't even stopped to tell him what had happened after he had left their quarters last night. When Jonathan and George hadn't returned by nine o'clock, the general had instructed his wife to leave a note for them to waken him when they got home; then he announced that he was off to bed and suggested that Phillip do the same.

Teddi had shrugged her shoulders at his questioning glance and advised him that if her father suggested that he go home and get some rest, he'd best do so. She had bid him good night, seeming assured that their problem was under control. Unfortunately, Phillip didn't share her optimism. After returning home, he had spent several hours on his knees seeking God's direction, and, although he hadn't received an answer, he had experienced a bit of pain in his knees when he attempted to stand up and get into bed.

And now, without any form of explanation, Teddi had just marched into the hospital and had left him totally in the dark. Phillip now found himself in a quandary. What if Clayton, George, and Jonathan had never met to devise a plan to thwart Herbert? What if Herbert showed up at four thirty and Phillip had absolutely no plan of action? If the three Yorke men hadn't gotten together, perhaps Phillip could meet with them now. He needed answers, and he needed them soon! Rising from his chair, he purposefully marched off toward the hospital ward.

"We need to talk," Phillip whispered to Teddi as she stood near a patient's bed, checking his bandage.

"I'll be through here in about an hour. I can stop by your office then," she said, giving him a smile.

"No, you don't understand. We need to talk *now*," he said, his teeth gritted together and his blood pressure steadily increasing as they spoke.

She nodded. "Everything is fine, Phillip. I'll come to your office shortly," she said, continuing to wrap the soldier's bandage.

There was no need to continue the conversation. He could hardly argue with her in front of a ward filled with sick soldiers. Not knowing what else to do, he breathed a deep sigh, turned on his heel, and stalked off to his office.

During the next hour, he pulled his pocket watch out of his trousers at least every fifteen minutes, rose from his desk, paced to the doorway, and peered down the long, narrow hallway. Teddi was never there. After an hour had passed, his concern turned to fear; his fear turned to concern; and his concern finally turned to anger. Why didn't she come and talk to him? Was this some sort of torture? Just when he had determined to drag her back to his office if she wouldn't voluntarily return, the front door of the hospital opened. Phillip felt himself relax when Clayton, Jonathan, and George entered the building.

"I'm certainly glad to see the three of you. I can't get your daughter to talk to me," he said, looking at Clayton.

"I told her we'd be coming by to explain things. There were a few details we needed to work out. No need to have Teddi give you a plan of action that we might be required to change. Simpler that way," he said, obviously unconcerned about the fact that Phillip was now at his wit's end.

"Well, it may have seemed that way, but I was about to go in and demand that Teddi speak with me. It may be difficult for you to imagine, General, but I'm a bit on edge," Phillip replied while attempting to keep his temper in check.

"Have a little faith, son—in God . . . and in me. I told you that I'd develop a plan. We're going to go over it, and when Albright arrives, you'll put it into action," he said, pulling up a chair. "Sit down, boys," he ordered as he leaned back, unbuttoned his coat, and began to lay out his strategy.

"So what do you think? Can you carry it off?" the general inquired once he'd finished.

Phillip nodded his head. "Sure, I should be able to do it. Now all we have to do is wait until four-thirty arrives. I'm afraid it's going to be a long afternoon."

Teddi entered Phillip's office a short time later, greeting the general and her brothers with enthusiasm. Although Teddi didn't win her debate with Clayton wherein she attempted to remain at the hospital, they all agreed that she had waged a laudable argument. Their praise didn't seem to appease her, but she did as she had been ordered, bidding Phillip good-bye at four o'clock, after he promised to come to their quarters immediately after Herbert left.

Herbert arrived at the appointed time, neither a minute early nor a minute late. He walked into the hospital as if he owned the place, his pompous attitude causing Phillip to bridle. However, he knew he *had* to control himself. Anger would not serve him well if their plan was to go as intended. Steeling himself, he held out his hand to Herbert, giving him a gratuitous smile, all the while wishing he could ball his hand into a fist and shove it down the deadbeat's throat.

"Well, here we are," Herbert said as he pulled off his overcoat and threw it onto one of the chairs. "I assume I'm welcome to have a seat?" he acerbically questioned.

"Sit, stand—it makes no difference to me. You're the one who arranged this meeting," Phillip replied tersely.

"Well, at least it should be a short meeting. What's your answer?"

"Before I give you my answer, I want to be sure that I completely understand the ground rules," Phillip replied, easing himself back in his chair.

"Oh, I think you understand," Herbert replied.

"This is a lifelong commitment you're forcing upon me. I think

I'm entitled to be sure I have a thorough understanding of the facts," Phillip countered.

"What is it you want to review?" Herbert asked, clearly annoyed.

"As I understand it, you and Helen have both decided that rather than Teddi and I exploring the possibility of marriage to each other, you intend to marry Teddi in the hope of achieving higher military rank and possibly gaining a sizable inheritance. Helen, on the other hand, has declared that she will lie under oath in order to have me court-martialed, claiming that I took advantage of her the night of the masquerade ball. Unless, of course, I agree to marry her. In that case, she will suddenly forget all of those alleged facts, and we will enter into wedded bliss," Phillip recounted.

"That's about it. Of course, you've left out a few minor points, such as the fact that Mattie is willing to corroborate Helen's testimony. Oh, I think I may have forgotten to mention that Teddi *has* agreed to marry me. Naturally, I was sure to spread that information last Saturday night—promoting public acceptance in advance, you might say," Herbert stated smugly.

"And now you expect me to roll over and accept this deceitful contrivance?"

"I think doing so probably outweighs the alternatives," Herbert chuckled.

"Well, I don't!" General Yorke announced, walking through an adjacent doorway with Jonathan and George following close behind.

"What are—what are *they* doing here?" Herbert stammered.

"We're listening to your lies so that *we* may act as Phillip's corroborating witnesses at the court-martial you and your accomplices are proposing. This whole situation is repugnant. If anyone is court-martialed, it won't be Phillip. It will be *you*," the general snarled.

With only a moment to regain his composure, Herbert was once again on the offensive. "Ah, but General, don't you think that when I bring to the board's attention the fact that you and your sons are merely seeking to protect your daughter's interests, the board members may look upon your testimony with a jaundiced eye? The fact that you are the commander of this military reservation may cause the board to scrutinize your testimony very closely. After all, the military and civilians, as well as the press, would be quick to point out the fact that you might unduly influence the members sitting on the court-martial board. In fact, I think your testimony could very well work in our favor."

"Don't you count on that," General Yorke replied, his face turning bright red.

"I'm not concerned that you've overheard this conversation, gentlemen—not in the least," Herbert replied as he picked up his coat. "Since I've given you additional food for thought, Phillip, I'll give you a little longer to come to a final decision. I will expect your answer by Wednesday—right after the church service would be a good time, don't you think? It will give you that final opportunity to pray for a miracle," he snickered as he gave the general an irreverent salute and confidently strode out of the room.

"He's not the least bit concerned. And, unfortunately, he did make a valid point. The court-martial board would weigh your testimony against your connection to Teddi and me," Phillip remarked.

"We need to think this through. It's almost time for supper, and crisis or not, my stomach is growling to be fed. Let's get home and have some dinner. We'll think better once we've eaten. At least I will," Clayton exclaimed.

"Come along, my friend. I'm sure Teddi is champing at the bit to hear what's happened," Jonathan said as he pulled Phillip a few steps ahead of his father and George. "We'll get the sleigh. The two of you can wait here and keep warm."

The general nodded his acceptance of the offer, and George was more than willing to wait with his father in the warmth of the hospital while the two other men trudged off to retrieve the sleigh. They had descended the final porch step, when Jonathan threw his arm across Phillip's shoulder.

"Would you like to hear some good news in the midst of all this turmoil that's swirling about?" Jonathan asked as they rounded the corner of the building.

"Certainly," Phillip halfheartedly replied.

"That didn't sound very enthusiastic!"

"Sorry, but it's a little difficult for me to get excited about much of anything right now," Phillip said.

"I understand, but keep your faith, Phillip. I agree with my father—this will work out. Now for my news: I've asked Margaret to marry me—and she's accepted!"

"You hardly know Margaret! Don't you think this is a little sudden, Jonathan? Besides, you'll be leaving in a couple of weeks, and then what?"

"How long does it take to fall in love when you meet the right woman? Aren't *you* the one who was telling me you were going to settle down as soon as you found a good woman?"

"Yes, but what about your family? Do they know? Do you think they'll be pleased with your choice? Don't misunderstand what I'm saying, Jonathan; I think Margaret is a lovely, young lady and a good woman. However, it can make for a rocky beginning to your life together if your families aren't in agreement," Phillip cautioned.

"I'm well beyond the age of needing my parents' approval, although I would prefer that all parties be in agreement. Margaret said she was certain her parents wouldn't have any objection. I think my mother is the only one who may disapprove. Unlike my father, she tends to worry about gossip. However, Teddi tells me that she and Mother have had several conversations lately concerning the topic of genuine forgiveness, and Mother's attitude has changed a great deal."

"Teddi's wisdom never ceases to amaze me!"

"Our Teddi may not be a raving beauty, but she's a very special woman, and that's a fact," Jonathan concluded as he drove the sleigh toward the front of the hospital.

"Well, whatever you and Margaret decide, I'm rooting for you. Just remember that I expect to be the one presiding over your vows," Phillip said while giving Jonathan a slap on the back.

"The cold air seems to have enlivened your spirits," the general said as he approached the sleigh. "It always does the same for me. Nothing better than cold weather and an invigorating snowfall."

Phillip attempted to give Teddi an encouraging smile as he entered the house, encircled by her father and brothers. She was searching his face, obviously looking for a clue, but he followed the general's advice and waited until after dinner. Isabelle and Florence were nowhere in sight, but the mouthwatering smells that permeated the house sent all four of the men searching after food. They had the scent and were like dogs to the hunt, unwilling to stop until they located their quarry.

Isabelle appeared from the kitchen, an apron tied around her waist and her cheeks flushed from the oven's heat. She carried loaves of freshly baked, crusty bread and placed them on cutting boards at either end of the table. A sharp knife and small crock of churned butter sat beside each loaf. A large tureen of beef stew was centered on the table.

"I thought we'd have a simple meal this evening. Thinking we may have some private matters to discuss, I told Florence she could have the evening to herself," Isabelle explained as she removed her apron before seating herself.

"That was an excellent idea, my dear. But if it's all the same to you, I'd rather wait to talk until after dinner," Clayton replied.

"After dinner Teddi and I will be busy serving coffee and clearing the table. Since we're the only ones who don't know what happened this afternoon, I'd prefer that we talk during dinner—if it won't upset your digestion," Isabelle added with a grin.

"There's not much that upsets my appetite or my digestion, but I'm hungry and would rather eat than talk. However, you're right. It's not fair to keep you two in the dark. I'll eat and you can tell them about this afternoon's happenings, Phillip," he said with one of his boisterous laughs.

Her father's upbeat conversation and jovial laughter seemed to relax Teddi, and Phillip now worried that she would consider the general's buoyant spirits a signal that things had gone well. Both women turned their gaze upon Phillip, but their looks of expectation were more than he cared to deal with at the moment. The general had cleverly sidestepped discussing the issue himself, and Phillip couldn't blame him. It was, after all, his own foolishness that had caused this predicament, and thus far, his prayers for a quick, quiet resolution to the situation had gone unanswered.

General Yorke was well into his second bowl of stew by the time Phillip had finished divulging the brutal details of the meeting with

Herbert. His words had managed to erase any visible trace of joy from Teddi's demeanor, her face now etched with concern and dismay. His attempts to keep the mood lighthearted had fallen flat, and Teddi now looked at him as though he had utterly and completely failed her.

"I know it's of little consequence since the damage is already done, but how has Herbert managed to be so long absent from his military assignment, Clayton?" Isabelle asked, breaking the silence that had hung in the room.

"My guess would be that his commanding officer allowed him to come back to Junction City to spend time with his deceased wife's family—advise them of her death. I doubt his company would be leaving on a campaign until spring, so it's probable that he was given leave. I don't think he's a deserter, since one of his reasons for marrying Teddi is to help advance his military career."

Isabelle nodded her head, gave Teddi an encouraging smile, and began clearing the table. "I'll bring coffee to the parlor when you're ready," she said as the men began moving away from the table.

"Let the dishes go, Isabelle. I want you and Teddi to join us. We need all the help we can get if we're going to devise a plan that will set things aright," the general stated.

They talked, they prayed, and then they talked some more until finally the general announced it was time they get to bed. His decision was met with unanimous approval, although none of them was sure that anything had been solved, or for that matter, that anyone had even come up with one good idea.

When Teddi didn't arrive at the hospital the next morning, Phillip was certain she had washed her hands of him, most likely deciding that the only way to make a clean break was to quit working with him. And why should he blame her? She would once again be subjected to ridicule, her name spilling off the wagging tongues of local gossips. It saddened him to realize how foolhardy and reckless he had been. When all was said and done, he'd be lucky if there would be any church that would have him, and his military career would certainly be in ruins. Perhaps, if he were lucky, he would be able to skulk away and practice medicine in some small community needing a doctor. It was a foregone conclusion that he could forget his plans for preaching the Word and winning souls for Christ. No church would desire a man who lacked the ability to keep himself free of such personal adversity.

It was sometime after one o'clock when he heard the door to the hospital open. He certainly could have used Teddi's assistance today. It seemed that every child living on the post had been dragged into the dispensary with varying complaints throughout the morning, and now it sounded as though it was going to continue through the afternoon hours.

"I'm sorry I didn't get word to you that I wouldn't make it in this morning," Teddi said as she greeted him in the hallway. "Have you been busy?"

Just seeing her caused his heart to lighten. "I'm so happy to see you," he exclaimed, a smile spreading across his face. "Let me take your coat," he offered as he rushed to assist her. "I *was* worried when you didn't arrive, thinking perhaps you'd decided it better to stay away from the likes of me."

"Do you think I have so little character that I would actually desert you, Phillip?" she asked in a pain-filled voice.

He took her hands in his own and met her intense gaze. He was certain her eyes were filled with as much love and concern as his own. Turning over each of her hands, he bent his head down and tenderly kissed the palms of her hands, his lips trailing up each hand until he reached her fingertips.

"I am so very sorry," he murmured, his head still bowed. "Can you ever forgive me for being such a fool?"

"Is your memory so short that you don't remember I've already forgiven you, Phillip?"

"You forgave me, but that was before we knew all of this was going to turn into a public spectacle. The court-martial will turn into a feeding frenzy for the gossips, and I know how much you detest being at the center of such idle chatter."

"My forgiveness wasn't conditional. If there's one lesson that God has recently taught me, it's forgiveness. I don't want to make the same mistake with others that I made with Margaret. Public humiliation is a small price to pay for doing what is just, and only God knows what will eventually happen. We both know that He is at work in every situation, and I feel an assurance that no matter how all of this turns out, we're going to be fine," she said.

"I should be ashamed of myself. I'm a preacher, supposedly a man of God, yet I need you to keep me grounded in my faith. You are, in every way, the woman I have prayed I would find. Now I pray that I won't lose you," he whispered.

"Oh, Phillip, you won't lose me. We're going to stand our ground, declare the truth, and rely upon the hand of God to see us through," she replied confidently.

$$\left(\widehat{15}\right)$$

*T*eddi sat beside her brother on the settee while Isabelle perched on the edge of her rocking chair, staring at them in disbelief. No one spoke for several minutes, and the crackling fire was the only sound that broke the deafening silence that hung in the room.

"You need to give this more time, Jonathan. We'll discuss it with your father and get his opinion," Isabelle asserted, her chin jutting forward as she spoke.

"I didn't tell you in order to secure your permission or your opinion, Mother, although I would be pleased to have your blessing. However, whether you and Father agree has nothing to do with my decision. I plan to marry Margaret. You and Father may be as involved in, or detached from, the process as you wish."

"Oh, good, here's your father now," Isabelle stated, projecting herself from the edge of the rocker and rushing toward Clayton. "I'm so glad you've come home. We have another crisis."

"I don't have time for another crisis, Isabelle. I merely came home to gather some papers and a map I need at my office. I'm sure you can capably handle any household crisis that has arisen with more expertise than I could muster," Clayton replied.

"This *isn't* a household matter. Jonathan is getting married," she announced without further fanfare.

"Well, that's good news. I was beginning to think you would never take a wife," Clayton stated as he walked into the parlor and embraced Jonathan. "So what's the crisis, Isabelle? You can't find a new dress in time?" Clayton asked, emitting a loud guffaw.

"Oh, stop it, Clayton—this isn't funny. And before you go any further with your congratulations, I think you need to know who it is your son is planning to marry," Isabelle chastised.

"If I were a betting man, which I'm not, I'd put my money on Margaret," Clayton said. "Am I right?"

"Yes, you're right," Jonathan replied.

"Well, congratulations to you. I doubt that you could do better. She's bright, pretty, and devout in her Christian beliefs. Couldn't ask for much more than that. Can she cook?" Clayton asked, once again laughing at his own question.

Isabelle dropped into her rocker with a thud. "Is that *all* you have to say?" she asked.

"What else is there to say?" Clayton asked as he gathered up papers from the dining room. He waved his paperwork in the air as he hastened toward the front door, leaving as quickly as he'd entered. Jonathan had settled back onto the settee beside Teddi, while Isabelle vigorously rocked in her chair. Except for a faint squeak from one of the rockers on Isabelle's chair, silence reigned.

Finally Isabelle ceased her rocking and rose from the chair. "I'd like to talk to Margaret. Go into town and fetch her. She can eat lunch with us, and then we'll talk—alone," Isabelle instructed her son.

Jonathan didn't argue or comment. After donning his coat and gloves, he bid them good-bye, stating that he and Margaret would be back in time for lunch.

"See to preparations for lunch, Teddi. Florence can help you. I need to go upstairs," Isabelle commanded.

"Mother, Phillip is expecting me at the hospital. I'm already late," Teddi replied.

"This is more important. I'm sure that if there's an emergency, he'll send one of the soldiers over to advise you," Isabelle absently replied as she marched up the stairs.

As if on cue, her mother descended the stairs at the exact moment Jonathan and Margaret entered the front door. Teddi watched as her mother greeted Margaret with a seemingly genuine hug and exchanged pleasantries about the weather and the approaching holiday festivities.

Isabelle had changed her dress, and although her eyes seemed slightly red and puffy, she appeared in good spirits as she presided over lunch.

Jonathan appeared somewhat edgy when Florence was serving her warm bread pudding for dessert, and by the time the meal was finally completed, his complexion had paled, and he looked as though he would grab Margaret and bolt from the room. Margaret, however, seemed relaxed as she chatted about the new arrival of goods at her father's store, including some special items that he had received just in time to delight Christmas shoppers.

"Teddi, you'd better hurry on over to the hospital. Jonathan can take you in the sleigh. Do stay and visit with Phillip for a while, Jonathan. Margaret and I are going to have a little chat of our own," Isabelle stated.

"I think I'll remain here. You don't mind taking the sleigh by yourself, do you, Teddi?" Jonathan inquired.

Before Teddi had an opportunity to reply, Isabelle was rising from her chair. "Don't be difficult, Jonathan. It's an excellent opportunity for you to spend a little free time with your friend. Once you return to Washington, you don't know when you'll be back to Kansas. Oh, and ask Phillip if he'd like to join us for supper. You *will* stay for dinner, too, won't you?" Isabelle asked as she turned toward Margaret.

Margaret looked toward Jonathan, obviously unsure how she should answer. "You may plan on our being here for dinner," he began, "unless—"

"Good," Isabelle said, interrupting her son. "Now get along to the hospital," she ordered, waving her arms at them as though she were shooing chickens out of the barnyard.

"If necessary, I think Margaret can hold her own with Mother," Teddi said as she and Jonathan left in the sleigh. "Not that she would ever be disrespectful, but Margaret is a strong woman who has a great deal of courage. Don't worry."

"I don't feel quite so confident, but when Mother asked Margaret to stay for dinner, I took that as a good sign. Either that, or Mother has totally convinced herself that she can dissuade Margaret from accepting my proposal. Do you think that's possible?" Jonathan asked with a note of alarm in his voice.

Teddi giggled and threaded her arm through her brother's. "Oh, Jonathan, I don't think *anyone* could convince Margaret that you weren't created by God for the sole purpose of becoming her husband."

"I think that I would have to agree with that statement. Except, perhaps, that God may have had one or two other things for me to accomplish in addition to my marriage. But I won't tell Margaret that," he replied, giving his sister a broad smile. "Speaking of marriage, how are things with you and Phillip?" he asked with a grin.

"When I was late to work yesterday, he was convinced that I hadn't been able to forgive him and wouldn't be returning to work at the hospital. It took a bit of persuasion to convince him that my days of only paying lip service to forgiveness ended when God convicted me of my behavior toward Margaret. I think I've convinced him that my forgiveness wasn't based upon whether it would be easy or difficult to face the eventual consequences of his actions—or my own conduct, for that matter," she added. "I should never have left the party and gone off to the dressing room with Herbert, even if I *did* think he was Phillip. It wasn't appropriate behavior, and now I'll suffer the consequences. I'm sure Herbert will leave no stone unturned in his attempts to prevail, but I wouldn't marry him if he were the last man left standing," Teddi vowed.

"Well, I hope that your late appearance today hasn't caused Phillip additional worry," Jonathan said as they arrived. "Let me help you out. Tell Phillip that I'll be in as soon as I've taken care of the horses. If he's busy, I'll just wait in his office."

Teddi nodded and rushed up the steps and into the hospital. After hanging her cloak in the vestibule, she peeked into Phillip's office, but when she noticed he was nowhere to be seen, she walked down the hallway and into the ward. Phillip was sitting beside the bed of a young soldier and was deep in conversation, so Teddi began checking charts and giving necessary medication to several of the men.

"I'm glad to see you," Phillip murmured as she stood by one of the soldiers who was suffering from a severe case of tonsillitis.

"Private Lowry seems to be responding to treatment and will be ready for discharge," Teddi commented.

"Private Lowry and I have agreed that perhaps he's enjoying the pleasure of extra rest and attention just a bit too much. We've agreed he'll be moving back to the barracks and assuming his regular duties tomorrow," Phillip advised with a slow, easy grin.

Teddi nodded her head. "That sounds like an excellent decision, gentlemen. By the way, my brother is in your office. He thought that the two of you might have a visit if you weren't too busy. I can finish up in here if you'd like to join him."

"Are you sure you don't mind?"

"Of course I don't. You two need to have some time to visit. Besides, I've been gone all morning, but Jonathan can explain that," she told him. "Oh, Mother invited you for dinner this evening if you're free," she added after he had turned to leave.

"I wouldn't miss it," he called back over his shoulder.

Phillip made his way down the hall, trying to assume his usual jaunty step. He believed that Teddi had truly forgiven him, but the fact that he would be forced to meet with Herbert tomorrow after church loomed in his thoughts, a veritable thundercloud floating overhead, just waiting to deluge him.

"Jonathan, good to see you," Phillip cheerfully greeted him as he entered the office, his hand outstretched in welcome.

"Is that an act, or are you really feeling lighthearted?" Jonathan asked with a smile.

"You know me, my friend. I'm attempting to fight the good fight, but it hasn't been easy the past few days. It appears that Herbert isn't going to back down. I'll advise him that he and Helen can go ahead and file whatever charges they care to conjure up. Your father tells me we can push to have the board convene quickly. However, I'm concerned that you and George will be gone before the court-martial begins. And I'd guess that Herbert is counting on that fact. Barring a miracle, this may prove to be the darkest hour of my life. We'll all need to continue to pray that some good will come from all of this," Phillip replied.

"I wouldn't worry about the board not being able to convene before George and I leave. Father knows it's important for us to testify, and he knows when we'll be leaving the post. Personally, I hope it can take place before Christmas so that we can relax and enjoy the remainder of the holiday. And speaking of good coming from this incident, it appears my sister is quite smitten by your charms. And she tells me she wouldn't marry Herbert Albright if he were the last man left standing," Jonathan stated.

"Still, it's no way to begin a relationship."

"It can only make you stronger. Besides, it sounds to me as though this relationship has more than merely *just begun*," Jonathan gibed.

"I'd ask her to be my wife this very minute if it weren't for this pending difficulty," Phillip admitted. "And why aren't you visiting the lovely Margaret on this crisp December afternoon? I'm sure her company would be much more pleasant that my dour attitude."

"I would have to agree with that statement. However, Margaret is currently embroiled in conversation with my mother over at our quarters. I broke the news of our engagement to Mother early this morning. After quite a discussion, she ordered me to invite Margaret to lunch, stating that she intended to have a private talk with her. I went to town and told Margaret that I thought we should ignore Mother's command, but Margaret insisted, saying she didn't want to begin our marriage by showing disrespect toward either of my parents. Poor girl, she thinks that Mother will cave in and bless our union. Of course, Teddi seems to think Margaret can hold her own against Mother. We'll know by this evening. You *are* joining us for dinner, aren't you?"

Phillip nodded his head. "Teddi extended your mother's invitation. I'm not sure I'll be good company, but I always enjoy being with your family."

"Don't concern yourself with the need to be good company. I'm sure that hearing the outcome of my mother's conversation with Margaret will provide ample entertainment," Jonathan remarked.

Their afternoon of conversation was interrupted on several occasions by soldiers with varying ailments, along with a laundress who had severed her small finger while helping to butcher a hog. The bleeding had been intense, and Jonathan had fled the room in search of Teddi as soon as the woman entered Phillip's office. After Phillip and Teddi had managed to stop the bleeding and stitch the woman's hand, they turned her over to Jonathan, who agreed to take her home in the sleigh.

"We'll be ready to leave for home by the time you return," Teddi called after her brother as he helped the woman into the sleigh.

"Think he'll be all right?" Phillip asked with a grin.

"I'm not positive. He never could tolerate the sight of blood. I didn't think I was going to convince him that the sleigh ride wouldn't cause her to begin bleeding again. Sometimes it's hard to believe we're related," Teddi responded, returning his smile.

"Not so hard," Phillip said. "You are both genuinely kindhearted people with a loving concern for your fellowman. Jonathan just has a little difficulty if his fellowman is bleeding."

It felt good to laugh. He hadn't laughed since all of this mess began at the masquerade ball. Somehow the holiday festivities had lost their luster. There had been no mention of the oyster dinner at the Mc-Calebs' last night, and he was certain that none of the Yorkes had attended, although it was one of the most highly anticipated events of the year. Folks loved the oyster supper at the church, but the dinner at McCalebs' was an invitation-only affair that was served in their luxurious home, with no expense spared. Teddi had told him that once you were invited, it was something you didn't want to miss. But they had missed the anticipated affair without giving it as much as a single thought.

"Jonathan's here," Teddi announced, breaking into his thoughts.

"Then we'd best be off," he replied, giving her a smile as he held out her cloak.

Jonathan took the lead as they entered the house, obviously anxious to seek out Margaret and assure himself that she had survived an afternoon of his mother's incessant questions and prying. He looked back at Teddi in surprise when he didn't see either his mother or Margaret in the parlor or dining room. Teddi followed behind him, but they both stopped in their tracks when they heard the sound of laughter coming from the kitchen. It was Isabelle and Margaret, and they certainly seemed to be enjoying themselves.

"What are you two doing in the kitchen?" Jonathan inquired while shooting Margaret an inquisitive glance.

"I saw that look, Jonathan. Your bride-to-be is just fine. In fact, she's more than fine; she's wonderful. We were just discussing how many children you two were hoping to have," Isabelle proclaimed.

Jonathan moved back from the kitchen door, obviously stunned by the turn of events. "Do I get any say-so in this matter, or is it solely up to you and my mother?" Jonathan inquired, the look of surprise still etched on his face.

All of them were enjoying a laugh at Jonathan's expense when Clayton entered the house. "What's going on in here? You folks having a party, and I wasn't invited?" he asked.

"I wouldn't call it a party. It seems that Mother and Margaret have spent the afternoon making decisions regarding how many children we should have. For some reason I thought Margaret might want to consult with *me* about the subject of children rather than Mother," Jonathan explained facetiously.

"We discussed much more than that. Why don't we all go into the parlor," Isabelle suggested, pulling off her apron and bidding Margaret do the same. Once the group was seated, Isabelle shifted in her seat so that she could face all of them. "I don't plan to go into all the details of our discussion, but I do want my family to know that I'm ashamed of my behavior. I asked Margaret's forgiveness, and although I'm not sure I would have been so kindhearted, she has accepted my apology.

"Teddi, I'm sorry that I didn't take your advice and teaching to heart when you first talked to me about forgiveness. It would have saved Margaret from once again being mistreated by an insensitive Christian—namely, me! I hope I've learned my lesson. And although Jonathan has already been very clear that he planned to marry Margaret no matter what my objection, I want you both to know that I will be exceedingly proud to have Margaret as a member of our family. Now that I've admitted my shortcomings to Margaret and asked her forgiveness, I feel I must also ask you to do the same, Jona—"

"No, no, that's not necessary, Mother," Jonathan interrupted, obviously quite moved by his mother's sincere comments.

"Then at least let me say that I am very proud of you. Your father and I always prayed that our children would grow into adults who actually lived what Christ taught. You children do it much better than I ever have, and I am exceedingly blessed to have all of you.

"I'm finished with all this serious talk. Margaret and I have been hard at work in the kitchen, and I think it's time we all partake," Isabelle said, rising from her chair with a flourish.

"Let's hope that things go this smoothly for us tomorrow night," Phillip murmured to Teddi as they walked into the dining room.

16

ll day Wednesday, Phillip attempted to keep himself composed, wondering how he could possibly preach a sermon in a few hours. Teddi had struggled to help him focus on the message he would deliver, but maintaining his concentration had been difficult. Finally, she had joined him in his office at the hospital, making several suggestions as she pointed out Scripture verses to reinforce her ideas.

The singing during the church service was particularly inspiring, and Phillip was pleased to see that there were more people at the Wednesday night meeting than generally attended. It was probably due to the holiday season—folks always seemed to remember the importance of church attendance at Christmas and Easter, he realized.

Stepping up to the podium, Phillip placed his Bible in front of him, cleared his throat, and stared out into the sea of faces; all eyes were focused on him.

"I want to talk to you about leading more Christlike lives. For those of you who call yourselves Christians, I thought tonight might be an excellent opportunity to take personal inventory of how your life compares to that of Jesus Christ. For example, do you compromise Christ's teachings in your day-to-day life? Do you think that if nobody sees you cheat or steal, it doesn't matter? Do you think that when you mistreat another member of the human race, you're following Christ's example? Do you think your idle gossip doesn't constitute sin? Do you think your unforgiving attitudes go unnoticed? Do you think that when you covet another man's possessions, it's all right because you deserve more than you have?"

Phillip continued with the list of questions, watching as members of the congregation squirmed and looked away, unable to meet his eyes when the arrow of truth pierced their hearts. When he had finished the questions, he placed his written list in front of him on a metal plate. Taking a burning candle from its holder, he touched the flame to the pages and watched until the fire had consumed them, leaving nothing but ashes on the plate.

"For those of you who are Christians, your sins are like those sheets of paper. Once you've asked God's forgiveness and have truly repented, your sin is gone, forgotten, wiped away. That's a difficult concept for us to understand because we humans have a great deal of difficulty forgiving others and forgetting what they've done to us; but aren't we thankful for a God who will do that for us? Now, for anyone here who hasn't accepted Christ, this gift can be yours—it's a free gift from your Creator. All you must do is accept it. But listen carefully: If you don't take that step and actually accept God's gift of salvation, your sins remain *your personal baggage*. They aren't erased or turned into ash like those sheets of paper on the plate; no, they are yours to carry with you to the grave and beyond."

He had the attention of the congregation, although he wasn't sure they were happy with his message. Most of them had probably come to church expecting to hear a sermon relating to the birth of Christ, something more in keeping with the season. But Teddi had been right; he needed to preach what was in his heart, and that's what he had done.

At the end of the sermon Phillip was astounded by the number of his parishioners who came forward and prayed for forgiveness, wanting to clear the slate and make a fresh attempt at leading a Christian life. Even more wonderful was the fact that three people made their way to him and asked how they could have Christ as their personal Savior, sure there must be more they must do in order to receive such an extraordinary gift.

"This has been quite a night," Phillip said to Teddi shortly after the service. "No matter what Herbert has to say, I know that God has been at work in this matter."

"Isn't it wonderful? I'm thrilled at what happened here tonight.

Please don't let your meeting with Herbert spoil the amazing things that just occurred."

"I won't," he promised. "I'll talk to you in the morning," he added before walking off toward his office.

"I think I'll join you for that meeting with Herbert," Clayton said as Phillip neared the small antechamber at the back of the church. The general placed his arm across Phillip's shoulder as the two of them entered the room.

"Well, aren't you two a sight," Herbert sneered from the doorway. "Have you come to your senses, Hamilton?"

"I have indeed," Phillip replied. "I'll not be coerced by your bullying tactics, and if you're hoping to stick to your plan and marry Teddi, you'd better move quickly. Otherwise, she and I may be married before you have time to file your charges. That's my answer. I have nothing further to say."

"You're going to be sorry. You'll be thrown out of the army, and I'll make it my mission to destroy you," Herbert snarled as he pushed by both men and left the church with the sound of the slamming door reverberating through the sanctuary.

It was shortly before noon the next day when Clayton entered the hospital and advised Phillip that Helen and Herbert had submitted sworn statements. After reviewing the documents, Colonel Cartwright determined that charges should be filed against Phillip. However, General Yorke had already received assurance that the process would move forward as quickly as possible.

"Colonel Cartwright is in charge of the proceedings. He has given his word that the board will convene on Friday. I told him I would be surprised if it took more than a few hours. Captain Pauley will act as your counsel; he'll come here to meet with you at two o'clock this afternoon. Jonathan, George, and I plan to arrive at two-thirty to meet with both of you and go over our testimony."

"You've been busy this morning. I can't believe all you've accomplished in such a short time. Do you think there's a possibility that Herbert will object to the trial taking place so rapidly?" Phillip asked. "I do want to get this over with."

"The paperwork he signed contains a waiver declaring that he will agree to the time and date of the hearing. It also contains a clause stating that at the time the complaint was signed, the complainant who brought the charges possessed sufficient evidence to immediately go to hearing. If he objects, his complaint will be dismissed. Fortunately, this decreases the amount of time he'll have to spread the word about town, which is all the better for us. I'd like to avoid having this thing turn into a spectacle. When you meet with Captain Pauley, you might want to suggest that he talk with Mattie—about her testimony," the general suggested.

"No. I think I'll just leave that in God's hands," Phillip replied.

The room was hushed, Herbert and Helen sitting side by side at a wooden table only a few feet from where Phillip now sat beside Captain Pauley. General Yorke's desire that the hearing be a quiet affair had fallen flat. Every chair was occupied, while additional spectators stood crowded at the rear of the room; they all appeared anxious to hear the offensive details. The board members were seated at a long, narrow table facing the crowded room, each of them appearing uncomfortable with the size of the crowd assembled before them.

Colonel Cartwright cleared his throat, struck his wooden gavel on the table, and advised all in attendance that the matter would proceed henceforth. Looking toward Herbert, he instructed him to commence with his case against Captain Hamilton.

At Herbert's instruction, Helen moved to the witness chair and, after being sworn to tell the truth, began answering Herbert's questions. A murmuring of voices erupted as Helen staunchly proclaimed that her life had been left in ruins the night of the masquerade ball. Obviously anxious to hear all of the details, the crowd hushed when she once again began to speak. A tear slid down her cheek as she declared that Captain Hamilton had forced her into his sleigh. Herbert gallantly rushed to offer his handkerchief as she continued with her story, stating that Phillip had taken advantage of her inability to fight him off. A small sob erupted as Helen wiped her eyes and then asserted to the board that Phillip had spoken harsh words to her.

"Captain Hamilton said that he would *never* give up his plan to marry Teddi Yorke. He told me that marrying into the Yorke family would help his military career while I had nothing of value to bring to a marriage. He did say, however, that he would enjoy having me as his mistress once he married Teddi," Helen averred.

Once again, gasps of surprise and murmuring voices filled the courtroom. Colonel Cartwright's gavel rapped on the oak table as he called for silence in the room.

"You may continue, Miss Hanson," Herbert sympathetically encouraged.

Helen nodded her head, wiped her nose, and looked out at the crowd. "*Now* Captain Hamilton denies all of the horrid things he did to me. But I have a witness who will tell you that I speak the truth," Helen purred, having now turned her full attention to the members of the board. "That's all I have to tell you, gentlemen. I know you'll do the right thing." She batted her eyelashes, gave them a seductive smile, and stepped down from the witness chair.

"Let's hear from your corroborating witness, Mr. Albright," Colonel Cartwright directed.

Herbert turned toward the roomful of spectators. "Mattie Fielding, step forward."

All eyes scanned the room waiting, anticipating, eager to hear what little Mattie Fielding would tell them. The rustling of feet and scraping of chairs were finally rewarded as Mattie moved from among the onlookers at the rear of the room and walked toward the witness chair. Once seated, she quickly scanned the spectators and then allowed her gaze to rest upon Phillip for a brief moment.

Herbert vaulted out of his chair, obviously anxious to complete his unconscionable prosecution so he could bask in the glory of his unjustified victory. After casting a depraved look in Phillip's direction, he turned his attention toward Mattie, who sat facing him, her fingers gripping the arms of the wooden chair with such intensity that her knuckles had turned white.

"Good morning, Mattie," he greeted in a soft and amiable voice.

She nodded but remained silent as he padded about the room in front of her—a cat cornering his prey, relishing the moment before moving in for the kill. She squirmed in her seat and then hunched down as if succumbing to a predator.

"Now then, Mattie, since you appear somewhat disconcerted, why don't I help you along? I'll ask you questions that you can simply answer yes or no to make this easier for you. Would you like that?"

Mattie nodded her bowed head in agreement.

"Did you attend the masquerade ball at the theater last Saturday night?"

"Yes," came her whispered reply.

"Just so the board is certain you can identify Captain Phillip Hamilton, would you please point to him?"

Mattie raised her head and quickly pointed toward Phillip.

"Thank you, Mattie. You attended the ball in the company of Helen Hanson. Is that correct?"

Mattie shook her head affirmatively. "Helen and you," she added.

"Yes, and we quickly separated company, didn't we? You and Helen went off in search of Captain Hamilton because he told Helen that he would meet her at the party, isn't that correct?"

"We went to search for Captain Hamilton, but—"

"Objection. She can't testify as to what Captain Hamilton and Miss Hanson may have discussed. Both parties are present in court. If Mr. Albright wants that information before the board, let him ask one of them," Captain Pauley interjected.

"Oh, never mind. You do agree that you and Helen parted company with me," he angrily continued before Colonel Cartwright could rule on the objection.

"Did you see Helen Hanson and Phillip Hamilton leave the party and go outside that night?"

"Yes."

"And did you see them get into Captain Hamilton's sleigh?"

"Yes," she quietly replied.

"And where were you when you observed this?"

"His sleigh was sitting beside the shed in back of the theater. I was inside the shed," she meekly replied.

"But the door was open, and you could hear everything that was said?"

"Oh, yes," she replied, her voice now growing stronger. "Every single word."

"That is all. You may step down," Herbert said.

"Not so fast, Mr. Albright. I want to cross-examine this witness," Captain Pauley stated while rising from his chair.

"Go right ahead. You'll only be helping to dig your client's grave," he whispered as Captain Pauley walked forward.

Captain Pauley ignored Herbert's remark and approached the witness stand, giving Mattie an encouraging smile. "You know that you are under oath and sworn to tell the truth, Miss Fielding?" he asked as he stood at one side of her chair.

"Yes, sir, and I've spoken nothing but the truth," Mattie avowed.

Herbert nodded his head, a smile spreading across his face. He turned toward the crowd, obviously hoping that Mattie's declaration had impressed them.

"Good. Now, you said you could hear everything that was said between Captain Hamilton and Miss Hanson while they were in the sleigh, and from where you were positioned, I don't doubt that. But could you tell me, Mattie, *why* you followed Helen and Captain Hamilton outdoors on that cold night?"

Mattie shifted in the chair. "Because Helen told me to," she replied.

"I see. And did she tell you why she wanted you to hide outside and listen?"

"So I could be a witness to the fact that she and Captain Hamilton actually were outside in the sleigh for a long time."

Captain Pauley nodded his head. "And now I'd like you to tell this board exactly what you heard that night."

Mattie gazed toward Helen and then toward Phillip. She took a deep breath, and in a calm, steady voice, she told the board of Helen's plan of blackmail, slander, and seduction, as well as her subsequent lack of success. Step by step, she disclosed the plot contrived by Herbert and Helen and how she, as Helen's friend, had been pressured into assisting with the plan.

"Herbert wants to marry Teddi Yorke, and Helen wants to marry Captain Hamilton. They thought this plan would succeed in getting both of them what they wanted," Mattie stated, keeping her gaze upon Captain Pauley.

"She's a liar!" Herbert retorted.

"I'm not lying, sir. And had it not been for the fact that on Wednesday night I accepted the Lord Jesus Christ as my Savior, I *would* be sitting here telling you exactly what Herbert and Helen told me to say. But I can't do that now, Helen," she said, turning toward her old friend. "It's wrong, don't you see?"

A scarlet-faced Helen jumped from her chair and ran out of the room as Herbert stared after her in disbelief.

"I'll dismiss the charges," Herbert announced as he jumped out of his chair.

"In that case I'll release this board from further duty. . . . Not so fast, Captain Albright," Colonel Cartwright called out as Herbert began to turn and leave the courtroom. "Until such time as a board can be convened to investigate your conduct in this matter, you are immediately confined to officers' quarters on this military post. Your commanding officer at Fort Brown will be notified of these proceedings and the probability that you will not be returning to his command. On a personal note, Captain Albright, I might suggest that you and Miss Hanson would make a lovely couple. In all likelihood, you'll soon be relieved of your military obligations, and I, for one, certainly think you deserve each other," Colonel Cartwright remarked dryly as members of the community slowly filed out of the room, nodding their heads in agreement.

*G*eneral Yorke smiled as he walked to the parlor windows and pulled back the curtain. "Looks like we're going to get us a good snow. It's flurrying already, and those are some mighty big snow clouds looming overhead."

"Clayton! You've been saying that for days now. Every time we get a few flurries, you predict a major snowstorm. It's wishful thinking on your part. You can come help me with these boxes. Staring out the window isn't going to make it snow," Isabelle said with authority.

"I thought Jonathan was going to help you sort through these decorations weeks ago," Clayton replied as he carried the boxes into the parlor.

"He seemed to lose interest once he met Margaret," his wife said with a smile. "I still wish they would wait so that there would be time to plan for a formal wedding. A Christmas wedding would be such fun compared to the small ceremony they've planned," Isabelle stated.

"Now, Isabelle, I think you can find more than enough to keep you busy during the holiday season without planning a wedding," Clayton replied. "Of course, you may be able to convince Teddi to have a Christmas wedding."

"What's this about convincing me of something?" Teddi asked as she and Phillip walked into the house.

"Your mother is lamenting the fact that there wasn't enough time to plan a large wedding for Jonathan and Margaret. She thinks making arrangements for a big Christmas wedding would give her great enjoyment, so I told her she might take it up with you. Perhaps the two of you would like to plan on a large Christmas wedding next year?" Clayton asked.

"Father! You weren't supposed to tell. We wanted our wedding announcement to be a surprise," Teddi scolded.

"Phillip has asked you to marry him?" Isabelle asked with a look of amazement on her face. "Why didn't you tell me? How long have you known, Clayton?"

"You see, Teddi? I didn't betray your confidence. Seems I remember something like this happening not so long ago. Remember when your mother thought I had betrayed your confidence by telling Phillip about your broken engagement? You both seem to think I can't keep a secret, when really it's the two of you who jump to conclusions and tell everything you know," he replied as his boisterous laughter filled the room.

Phillip put his arm around Teddi's shoulder. "We can still make the announcement after we've finished decorating the tree this evening. George, Jonathan, and Margaret don't yet know of our plans. It will still be a celebration," he promised.

"Well, I suppose you know that I couldn't be more delighted that you're going to become a member of our family, Phillip. Just think— your wedding will be a grand opportunity for us to see your parents again. They *will* be coming for the wedding, won't they? Have you already agreed on a date? A Christmas wedding is always so beautiful, Teddi, but if you think you'd prefer to marry in the spring or summer, I can certainly have everything ready in time," Isabelle rattled on.

"We haven't actually settled on a date, Isabelle, but if you're going to hold out for a Christmas wedding, it will have to be this year. I'm not about to wait a year before making your daughter my wife," Phillip staunchly replied as he squeezed Teddi's hand.

"You could have a double wedding with Margaret and Jonathan. . . ."

"No, mother, we are *not* getting married next week. That's much too soon. I understand why Jonathan and Margaret are hurrying their plans. They have good reason, but I think Phillip and I would prefer to take a little time to enjoy preparing for our wedding."

"Hrmmph! Let me interpret that for you, Phillip," Clayton offered. "Taking time to enjoy preparing for the wedding means your fiancée wants time enough to plan the *perfect* wedding, one that she believes will provide her with enough memories to last a lifetime. You, my boy, will have very little to say about the matter, and *I* will have even less. In fact, my input will consist of providing adequate funds to cover the costs of what will likely turn into an extravaganza."

"You're exaggerating, Clayton," Isabelle chastised. "It may turn into a gala event, but I doubt Teddi would go so far as to create an extravaganza."

"Just wait!" Clayton warned as Jonathan and Margaret walked in the front door, covered with snow.

"It's no longer flurries falling out there," Jonathan announced, stomping his feet while brushing snowflakes from Margaret's coat.

"Where's George?" Clayton asked. "I haven't seen him since the noon meal."

"He said he was going down to the river with some of the soldiers. They were going to cut ice for the icehouse," Teddi replied. "I told him to check with you, that I didn't think the ice would be thick enough yet."

"He knows better. That river won't be frozen thick enough to cut ice blocks until the end of January. My guess is he's down there ice-skating," Clayton replied.

It was only minutes later when George returned, his ice skates tied together and thrown over his shoulder. "Look who I brought along," he announced, pulling Mattie forward. "The ice wasn't thick enough to cut, so I went into town for a couple of Christmas presents. There was Mattie at one of the stores, and I asked her to join us," George announced.

"We're delighted to have you, Mattie. Your parents don't mind if you spend Christmas Eve with us?" Isabelle kindly inquired.

"No. Since my pa died, my mother isn't interested in much of anything, especially celebrating holidays. She doesn't care that I'm here," Mattie answered docilely.

"Well, we're pleased to have you here to help us celebrate Christ's birth, Mattie," Clayton said with a welcoming smile. "You just dig in there and help with those ornaments. I'm sure that George will be glad to let you do his share of the work."

"Yep, sure will. Is supper about ready?" George asked, rubbing his stomach as though he were starving.

"Dinner will be ready by the time you've finished sorting through the ornaments. It's got to be done before we decorate the tree. By the time you finish, we'll be ready to eat," Isabelle replied, shooing him toward the boxes while the rest of them laughed at her antics. "There may be some of Jonathan's old homemade ornaments you'd like to take for your tree next Christmas, Margaret," Isabelle offered as she hurried off toward the kitchen.

"I doubt that," Jonathan replied, pulling out a box that had been carefully labeled with his name. There were ornaments made of pinecones, milk pods, and other sundry reflections of nature, most of them now falling apart. Teddi held up one of her prized creations, which had been reduced to shriveled berries inside half a walnut shell. They laughed and reminisced while digging through the boxes, each of them quick to tell the others the history of a particular ornament before it was carefully tucked back into the box.

"I think we're ready for dinner," Isabelle announced. "You should be finished by now, I would think. Give me the trash, and I'll ask Florence to toss it in the fireplace."

Each of them looked at the other and began to laugh. "There is no trash, Mother. After spending the last hour telling the wonderful stories that go with these ornaments, we couldn't throw any of them away."

"You see, Clayton, it isn't such an easy thing to do. Your father's after me all the time to get rid of things. He says that if you're in the military, you need to travel light, but I say that a family needs its memories!"

"And after listening to our children this afternoon, I'd have to agree. I think it would make for a special tree if you used those old ornaments one last time this year," Clayton suggested.

Teddi laughed at the suggestion. "I don't think Mother would want her majestic tree covered with these dilapidated decorations."

"You're wrong about that, dear. I think it would make for a beautiful tree," Isabelle replied.

Once they had finished dinner, the group of young people decorated the tree while Isabelle and Clayton directed the proceedings. There was just enough time to light the candles for one glimpse of the tree before leaving for church services.

Sleighs were gathering around the chapel by the time they arrived, and Christmas greetings were being exchanged as people entered the church and were seated. The pews were almost full when the worshipers began to sing Christmas carols and to celebrate Christ's birth. Then, as midnight edged closer, each person walked down the aisle carrying a small, lighted candle, received communion, and left the church, with the trail of flickering light providing a festive illumination for the congregation as they bid each other Merry Christmas before heading home.

"It was a beautiful way to celebrate Christmas Eve," Teddi said as she and Phillip arrived back at the Yorkes' quarters. "Mother said I was to invite you in for coffee and cookies."

"It's not too late?"

"Not on Christmas Eve. Everyone else is already inside!"

The snow had ceased falling, and a full moon surrounded by a myriad of stars shone down on the fresh blanket of glistening snow. Phillip tugged on the reins, and the horses snorted and shook their heads as they came to a halt.

As they reached the porch and Phillip opened the door, a grin spread across his face. "I have a special gift I want to give you—a surprise. Could we go into the parlor by ourselves for just a few moments?" he asked while reaching into his pocket and retrieving a small box wrapped in brown paper and adorned with a sprig of holly.

"My ring?" she asked, leading the way into the parlor.

The rest of the family was gathered around the dining-room table, seemingly unaware of the newly arrived couple now standing by the Christmas tree.

"No. That wouldn't be a surprise—you already know about your ring," he replied.

Teddi carefully removed the sprig of holly, untied the thin red ribbon, and lifted off the lid. Tucked into a small piece of red satin was a tiny ice-skate charm. "Oh, Phillip!" was all that she could manage as she lifted the charm from its snug resting place.

"It's wonderful! How did you ever—?" She could say nothing else, a lump rising in her throat.

"Margaret's father found a jeweler in Kansas City who said he could craft the charm and have it delivered by Christmas. I briefly considered a sleigh bell, but Jonathan has given me his word that yours will be returned. I decided upon an ice-skate because the day of the ice-skating party is the day I knew that I truly loved you."

"It is? I didn't know that."

"That's the day I knew that you were a woman of virtue, the woman with whom I wanted to share my life," he said, his eyes filled with adoration.

"Thank you, Phillip. You couldn't have given me a more perfect gift. And I have something for you. Wait here," she said, leaving the room and returning a few moments later. She carried a large, wooden box without a lid. Inside the box was a lumpy, folded sleigh blanket, tied with a thin cord.

He gave the odd-looking package a questioning look, and then glanced back at Teddi.

"Go ahead—open it," she instructed merrily.

Phillip tentatively unknotted the twine and pulled back the gray, wool blanket. "Sleigh bells!" he shouted joyfully. Each of the two leather straps sported at least thirty bells, all jingling noisily as Phillip pulled them out of the blanket. "You got me sleigh bells! Come on— let's go outside and put them on the horses," he said, pulling her to her feet.

"We'll be right back," Teddi called over her shoulder toward the dining room as the two of them rushed out the door, oblivious to the cold night air.

"They're wonderful, just like you," Phillip delightedly stated as he finished attaching the jingling leather straps to the team of horses.

Pulling her close, he stood back and gave the sleigh one final look of appraisal before nodding his head in satisfaction. Wrapping his arms around her, he leaned forward and gently kissed her lips. "Merry Christmas, my love. The sleigh bells are grand, but *you* are truly God's splendid gift to me," he whispered.

Candy Cane Calaboose

by Janet Spaeth

To M.E. Froelich
Friends 4Ever

"This is the day which the LORD hath made;
we will rejoice and be glad in it."
Psalm 118:24

1

"No, no, stop!" Abbey Jensen yelled futilely at the package that slithered off the towering pile of decorated Christmas socks. But the package continued on its wayward course, sliding through the slots of the grating that blocked the front entrance of Trends and landing on the highly polished floor of the empty mall just outside the store.

She looked around her as if a solution beyond the only obvious one would suddenly appear. But nothing materialized.

She was going to have to open the security gate and retrieve the package from the mall floor.

She just wanted to go home. She'd been at the store since shortly after seven that morning, and it was now—she glanced at her watch and nearly gasped—almost eleven at night. At this rate, she might as well just go ahead and set up a cot in the store—if she could find a spot that wasn't covered with racks or shelves. Her store was getting crowded with the holiday displays that arrived daily.

Abbey turned her key in the grid work's lock and winced as it groaned open. The sound echoed through the empty mall. The gate raised itself no more than a yard above the floor and stuck.

It wasn't the first time. She ducked under the gate and snatched up the socks from the gleaming tile of the outer mall. Glaring at the recalcitrant grid work, she kicked the bars angrily. "Piece of junk—"

As if in reply, the gate slammed shut.

Her keys were still dangling in the lock on the other side of the gate, tantalizingly just out of reach. Abbey tried to reach the keys, but her hand wouldn't fit through the grating. She was stuck inside the cavernous Cedar Mall.

What should she do? The mall doors were set up so that she could leave through any of them without setting off an alarm, but then what? The keys to her car and her house were on the same ring as the store's keys—on the other side of the grating.

Frustration rose in her like an angry fountain. She could see the keys, but they might as well be in Timbuktu.

She set off through the mall in search of a security guard.

That meant she had to run the gauntlet that the mall management had placed in her way. Cedar Mall looked more like it was situated at the North Pole than in Northern Mills, Minnesota. The numerous Christmas decorations, normally so festive, now looked merely stupid. At Santa's workshop, an elf held a little silver hammer that was minus its tip. Santa himself, lit only from the faint glow of security lights, appeared old and tired. Only the plastic reindeer seemed to have any personality. One of them faced her as if ready to take a bite out of her.

The expression on the reindeer's face reminded her that she was hungry. If she didn't get something to eat pretty soon, she'd take a bite out of the reindeer. She hurried past the display.

It was just one of many ahead of her. The mall owners had decided that this year they would go all out. Games and kiosks, exhibitions and artwork, all jostled each other for room. She ignored them and headed toward the mall office. Security was usually there at night.

It wasn't that she had anything against Christmas. Christmas was, in fact, one of her favorite holidays. At least it had been when she was a little girl. Now that her family was scattered across the continent, she had to spend Christmas alone. As a store manager, she no longer had the luxury of leaving Minnesota to spend the holidays with her parents in their home in Connecticut.

And the specter of spending Christmas alone was enough to put a damper on even the most fervid Yule fan. The solution was easy: She didn't think about it.

What she needed to think about now was getting in touch with mall security.

A light in another store a bit further down gave her an idea. *Tuck's Toys*, Mike's store . . . she breathed a sigh of relief.

She and Mike Tucker had been friends since they were children.

Not good friends, and certainly not as close as their parents would have liked, but friends nevertheless. He'd let her in to use his phone.

As she peered through the grating of Tuck's Toys, she saw a head moving behind a display and she called out, "Excuse me? Is someone there? Mike?"

A familiar face popped up. "Abbey!"

Abbey breathed a sigh of relief. Never before had Mike's round brown eyes and dark blond hair seemed so welcoming.

"I'm locked out of the store, Mike," she said. "Can I use your phone to call Security?"

"No problem." He turned the key in the grid work of his store.

His gate, she noticed, didn't groan and screech the way hers did. And it didn't catch part way up. She was going to have to talk to the mall management about hers.

She ducked in under the opening grid and followed him to the phone as he asked, "Are you working late tonight too?"

Abbey nodded. "I wanted to rearrange the entrance displays. What about you?"

"Oh, I took a break earlier. I ran out to Golden Meadows to see Grandma, and I had dinner with her out there."

Her stomach growled in response to the word "dinner." "How's she doing?" Abbey had never met his grandmother, but she knew that Mike was devoted to her.

"Pretty good. She's a cool lady. You should come with me someday and meet her. I think you'd like her."

Not a chance, Abbey thought. Maybe Mike liked going to Golden Meadows—after all, his grandmother lived there—but for her it would just be a visit to a place where old people went to die. No, thank you.

"And then," Mike continued, as if he hadn't noticed her chill, "it was back to work." He motioned toward an open box. "More Wag-A-Muffins."

"Wag-A-Muffins?" She stopped and stared at him.

"Have you been living on another planet, or what?" He grinned and reached into the box. "This is a Wag-A-Muffin, the hottest toy in the universe. By noon tomorrow, we'll be sold out."

He held up a small brown stuffed dog. "Watch this." He stroked the toy animal's back, and the tail curled. "Neat, huh? There are about thirty-five different animals, although I doubt that I have all of them here."

She touched it, and the tail lifted into a curlicue. "It's really cute."

Silence met her statement, and she raised her eyes to see him leaning against a display of computer games, a contemplative soft smile on his face.

"What's the matter?" she said and immediately regretted the belligerent tone.

He shook his head and smiled brightly at her. "Nothing. It's just that for a moment I thought I saw a streak of humanity in you."

She glared at him. The old familiar taunt he'd leveled at her since they were children still hurt, although she'd never let him know it.

"The only warmth that flows through my bloodstream comes in at a steady 98.6, thank you very much," she shot back.

"What about when you get a fever? Oh, I know," he interrupted himself as she tried to speak. "You don't get sick. That's for wimps."

"I don't have time for it." Abbey shrugged off the argument. "Actually, I don't have time for anything right now except to head back to my store and get my keys. I want to go home. I'm hungry, and I'm tired. It's been a long day."

"And they're not going to get any shorter now that the Christmas season is gaining on us," he agreed amiably.

He handed her the phone, and within minutes the two of them were walking back toward Trends.

"What do you think of this Christmas Village idea?" Mike asked as they walked by Center Court, where an entire town was set up. Each tiny building was in fact a kiosk with a seasonal specialty. Stuff Your Stockings sold leg wear of all kinds, Lollipop Time sold candy, and Piñata Pete's sold piñatas in imaginative shapes.

"It's, well, a bit much." Abbey wrinkled her nose at the display. "I can understand why they're doing it, and it's already bringing in lots of foot traffic just to see it, but it's too busy for me."

"You know, it's not all that the mall management has planned," he said, but Abbey had lost interest.

She spied the security guard ahead and sprinted toward the gate.

She was dimly aware of the fact that Mike had dropped back, but all she could think of was what awaited her: a hot dinner, a warm bath, and a cozy bed.

Mike watched her head for the guard as if the man held the keys to heaven itself.

Mike knew he was frowning, but he couldn't help himself. He'd always cared for Abbey, but her aloofness had kept him at a distance.

Still, she had a talent for fashion. With her sleek black hair, clear gray eyes, and willowy figure, she could be a fashion model. She also had an instinctive feel for business that he envied. When he'd heard that she was taking over Trends, he was delighted. The fashionable store had suffered under poor management and was near closing, but she had brought it back to life.

But she'd accomplished it at great expense. He'd seen the lines of exhaustion etched around her eyes. He wanted to take her in his arms and hold her, let her rest her head against his shoulder, while he breathed in the fresh scent of her perfume.

But that would never happen. She'd made that clear. No relationships, no ties. She was building her résumé, she'd told him, and she had no time for anything that would swerve her off that course.

He watched as she stumbled slightly. She was fatigued beyond even her capability. She was definitely too tired to drive, but he knew she'd never admit it, and she'd certainly never accept a ride from him. Abbey would insist on driving herself home.

Mike shut his eyes and offered a quick prayer. *Father, take care of her. See her home safely. She is so worn out.*

His gaze stayed on her as the guard opened the gate and she reentered the store. It took him less than a second to know what to do. As quickly as he could, he hurried back to his store, switched off the lights, and closed the gate. Then he retraced his steps, looping around Christmas Village, and left through the door of the mall that was closest to Trends.

His breath froze in his nostrils as he stood outside, scanning the expanse before him. The parking lot was empty. Or almost empty.

His instincts had been right. He could see her car pulling out of one of the far-off slots where mall employees were supposed to park, and from the pause before she switched gears, he could tell how deep her exhaustion was.

He followed her home, staying a discreet distance behind, and left only as he saw her put the key in the door of her house. She would be safe. He smiled and let out a sigh of relief.

Abbey leaned against the storm door, letting the cool metal refresh her tired forehead. Tomorrow she'd have to find some time to shovel the steps. The snow was so drifted, even this early in the season, that the door wouldn't fully open.

But the snow was more compacted than she'd figured. She dug into the drift with her toe to clear it.

It wasn't all snow. There was something there.

She reached down and burrowed through the snow until her fingers closed around a squarish form. It was a package, she realized, as she dusted the snow off. And, from the emerald green writing on the address, she knew immediately whom it was from.

Aunt Luellen. Loopy Aunt Luellen.

She opened the door and dropped the package inside the entryway as she shrugged out of her coat. She was so tired. But first she'd have to take care of this soggy package on her floor. It was already dripping into a rapidly spreading puddle.

Microwavable meatloaf was just moments away. Flannel pajamas were waiting for her. A nice comfortable bed was around the corner. A quick face wash—she was just too exhausted for a bath—a few moments to brush her teeth, and she'd be asleep.

It was a lovely thought.

But Aunt Luellen was, well, Aunt Luellen.

And the package was wet. Whatever was in it needed to be rescued. She sighed and opened the sodden package.

She blinked once. Twice. Three times. But the image remained.

Yellow fuzzy slippers with a grinning frog on the toe of each— that's what Aunt Luellen had given her. And the eyes on the frogs were bright blue plastic gems. Aunt Luellen was even loopier than ever.

A note fell from the toe of one of the slippers and Abbey unfolded it. Maybe this would give her a clue as to why on earth her aunt thought that this was an appropriate gift for a woman who owned only one pair of jeans, for whom comfortable shoes were two-inch heels.

"Claire: Every time that you wear these slippers, look at the toes and tell yourself that this day is a jewel, perfect, and ideal. If life at Golden Meadows is getting you down, look at where the jewels are— and smile! Wishing you great hoppy-ness always, today, and many tomorrows, Luellen."

Claire? Her name wasn't Claire. Aunt Luellen had gone from loopy to lunatic. Suddenly, through the fog of exhaustion, she realized what was going on. The slippers weren't meant for her. She had no idea who "Claire" was, although she was obviously one of Aunt Luellen's cronies if she lived at Golden Meadows.

Abbey sighed. She'd have to get the slippers to whoever this Claire woman was. But she didn't have the time to do that—she hadn't even had time to eat dinner. How could she fit in a trip to a retirement home? Besides, she told herself grumpily, she did not want to go to Golden Meadows. If her head weren't so clogged with a desperate need for sleep, she'd be able to figure it out.

She laid the slippers aside, planning to deal with them in the morning, and another bit of paper fell out of the other toe. "This is the day which the Lord hath made; we will rejoice and be glad in it."

The Bible. That sounded like Aunt Luellen. The woman had the whole book memorized, or so it had always seemed to Abbey. Aunt Luellen could quote Scripture with an astonishing ease. Of course, she was a missionary, so she lived and breathed religion, but nevertheless, her ability was uncanny.

Religion. That was where Abbey and Aunt Luellen parted ways. Sometime, when Abbey was established in her career and had gotten her MBA, she'd look into it again. Clearly, religion took a lot of time, and that was one thing she didn't have.

Time—and sleep. "And food," she said to the frogs, whose bright blue eyes sparkled back at her. Meatloaf would take too long. She reached into a box of sugar cookies and held one out toward the slippers. "Froggy want a cookie?"

Abbey shook her head. Any longer with the slippers and she'd be as loopy as Aunt Luellen.

But a moment of clarity came right before sleep claimed her.

Mike.

His grandmother lived at Golden Meadows. He went there all the time. She'd give the slippers to him tomorrow, and he could take them out there to their rightful owner—whoever "Claire" was—and she'd be finished with the whole messy thing.

Abbey smiled happily. Mike would take care of everything. She just knew it.

2

"No."

"What do you mean, 'No'?" Abbey asked as they stood outside Tuck's Toys where she'd come to visit Mike.

"Simply that. No. I won't take the present for you."

"But why not?" She could not believe what she was hearing. Why wouldn't he do this one little favor for her? "You're going out there anyway, right?"

He nodded.

"Then why not take it with you?"

"Nope."

His refusal had her flabbergasted. It didn't make any sense at all.

"You should take it out to her. For one thing," he said, "this Claire probably has your present. And besides, it just would be the Christian thing to do for your aunt Luellen."

Abbey barely restrained herself from snorting. Christian, indeed. Just because Aunt Luellen had turned her life over to the church didn't mean that she, Abbey Jensen, should act all holy. Religion wasn't one of those things that ran in the family, like red hair or big ear lobes.

"I'm going out there tonight, and I can give you a ride if you like," he offered.

"You're going out there? Just take the stupid slippers with you and be done with it, then. I can't understand why you won't." She knew she sounded like a petulant child, but she couldn't help herself. "It's no big deal."

"And I can't understand why you won't go," he parried. " 'It's no big deal.' "

His words, slung back at her like that, sounded terrible.

But the fact was, she did not want to go to Golden Meadows. The thought of being surrounded, even for a minute or two, by old people was awful. That's why she liked the mall; it was young and very much alive.

"I'm going at five-thirty," Mike continued, as if he hadn't noticed anything wrong.

Abbey breathed a sigh of relief. She absolutely couldn't go. "I'm the only one in the store then."

Mike shrugged. "You deal with this on your own schedule. I go at five-thirty so I can have dinner with my grandmother. It means a lot to her."

He turned to leave, but he paused and faced her again. "It really wouldn't take you long. For about fifteen minutes of your time— which I know is precious—you could make two women very happy."

Abbey could feel herself frowning. "Two women? Oh, you mean Aunt Luellen and this Claire woman."

He smiled at her. "That's right. I know that most of the people at Golden Meadows love visitors, but even if Claire is a total recluse who hates everybody and doesn't want to see anyone for the rest of her natural days, you do have her Christmas present from your aunt. Give it to her. Not only is it hers and not yours, but Abbey, it's Christmas!"

He was making this difficult, she thought as he walked away. What he didn't know about her, what he couldn't know about her, was that her heart was made of marshmallow fluff. She just had it cased inside steel.

She'd work on it. She'd figure out some way to get the slippers to Claire.

Abbey walked back to Trends, scowling at the mechanized group of carolers that sang outside the music store. Noise. Just what this world needed. More noise.

Once, just once, she was going to say it, and she did so at the Dickens village: "Bah, humbug."

Christmas didn't have to be all this complicated. And it certainly didn't have to be this loud!

*   *   *

The evening shift crew arrived on time, and Abbey found herself with an hour and a half free. She had wandered back to the evening dresses and began unnecessarily straightening the already-neat rack, when she heard two teenaged girls giggling together.

"Look at these! Aren't these a hoot?"

One of the girls, Abbey saw, was showing the other one something in a bag.

Then, to Abbey's astonishment, the girl pulled out a pair of yellow fuzzy slippers, complete with frog faces on the toes.

"Those are like the coolest slippers ever!" the other girl gushed. "Where did you get them? I don't care if I am supposed to be shopping for my mutant brother, I've got to get some for myself!"

The two girls briefly examined a display of jewelry before ambling out of the store.

Abbey didn't believe in signs, not really, but she had to admit it: This was clearly a sign.

"Okay, that does it!" she said to the heavily-beaded green gown she was holding.

"Excuse me?" A woman browsing through the evening jackets on the other side of the aisle looked at her curiously and pulled her purse a bit closer to her side.

Abbey tried to disguise her embarrassment with a laugh. "Sorry! Talking to myself!"

The woman smiled. "I understand. I've got five kids and sometimes I talk to myself just to have an adult conversation. Honey, whatever it is that you've just decided to do, you go for it!"

Abbey laughed, but she watched thoughtfully as the woman moved on. Go for it. That's exactly what she was going to do.

Mike smiled as the elderly woman next to him tugged on his sleeve. "Mike, dear, could you please play 'Red Sails in the Sunset'?"

"Sure, Grandma."

He was sharing a piano bench with her. His grandmother had lost her ability to walk, and her sight wasn't very good any longer, but her hearing was as sharp as ever.

She loved music, and soon after she had moved into Golden

Meadows, she had enlisted him to play some old favorites on the shiny piano in the fireside lobby of the retirement home.

Usually he loved playing for her, but tonight his fingers were clumsy and found the wrong keys.

"Something bothering you, Sweet?" she asked him.

He grinned at her nickname for him. "Nothing really."

"There is something," she insisted. "I can tell. You know, I can almost smell it. You've got a guilty conscience."

"You can smell a guilty conscience?" He laughed.

"Yes, a bit. It's a kind of fear, you know, and you might not be able to notice it, but when you're like me and the only things you've really got left are your hearing and sense of smell, they get stronger." She touched his shoulder. "Want to talk about it?"

"Oh," he said, his fingers running lightly across the keyboard, "I committed a sin of omission."

"You didn't tell someone something?"

"That's right, and I should have. It wasn't fair to her either. But my intentions were good."

"Well, you know what my Arthur used to say. The road to you-know-where is paved with good intentions."

"I have no intentions of going to you-know-where," he said, unable to keep the amusement from his voice. "Guess that means I'd better take care of it, right?"

"Well, Sweet," his grandmother said, her thin papery cheeks dimpling with impish delight, "if this involves a woman, I'd say you'd better race to it and get this straightened out."

"If it were a man, I could take my time fixing my mistake, huh?" He couldn't resist teasing her.

"Sweet, there's no doubt in my mind that I have the world's best grandson. I couldn't ask for better than you. But I also want great-grandbabies one of these days. I'm not getting any younger, and neither are you." Her eyes, their brightness only partially dimmed behind thick glasses, followed him as he stood up and got his coat from the rack.

"I'll walk you to your room if you'd like," he offered.

"I'll be okay here. But you've got work to do. Go get her!" She shook a bony fist in the air. "Go now!"

"Yes, Ma'am!"

He was still chuckling as he drove away from Golden Meadows and toward the mall.

Abbey had driven by the sign for Golden Meadows countless times, but she'd never turned down the lane that led to it.

It was, like many retirement communities, near the hospital, but this was tucked back in a grove of trees. What seemed like several buildings were, she realized as she drove up, in fact one large building with connecting halls made primarily of tall, polished windows. On the front door hung a large wreath, its green boughs interwoven with twinkling lights. All in all, it was a bright and cheerful place, not at all like she had imagined it.

The true test would be what the interior was like, she told herself as she parked her car. Inside, it might be the dreadful place she'd imagined it to be.

But as she entered the door, she had to admit that she had been wrong. The front door opened into a great-room, the high arched ceiling allowing the biggest Christmas tree she'd ever seen. And it was real. The clean aroma of the large pine tree permeated the air.

"May I help you?" A young woman behind the desk to her right beamed at her.

"It's somewhat hard to explain," Abbey began, suddenly nervous as she put the present on the counter beside her. "You see, I received this gift from my aunt Luellen, who is a dear but a bit on the, well, loopy side. And no big surprise to anyone who knows her, but the present wasn't for me. I don't know who it is for, but maybe you can help me."

"Your aunt Luellen lives here? Are you sure?" the woman asked her, turning toward her computer.

"No, no. Aunt Luellen lives in Brazil right now. She's a missionary."

"How very interesting." The glaze over the young woman's eyes told Abbey that she was perilously close to turning away.

"Let me start again. I have a gift for a woman named Claire. It came from my aunt Luellen. I don't know anyone named Claire, but apparently she lives here, and I'd like to give it to her." Inspiration struck. "Or, I could leave it here, and you could give it to her."

The woman behind the desk pulled back a bit, and her eyes narrowed with faint suspicion. "You want to leave a wrapped parcel for someone you don't know? Oh, I don't think so. It's not our policy to do that."

"Okay, then can you let me know who Claire is, or where she is? I'd like to make sure she gets it, and I do have to get back to work." Abbey glanced at her watch as if to confirm that.

Never taking her eyes off Abbey, the woman dialed a number. "Claire? This is Nadine at the front desk. I have someone here. Her name is—excuse me, what is your name?"

"Abbey Jensen. Tell her I'm Luellen Gregg's niece."

The woman repeated the information into the phone. Her eyebrows rose as she listened to the response. "Are you sure?" she asked.

She paused, then shrugged. "Fine. I'll send her down to your room."

She turned to Abbey. "Room 108. Take the hall on your right, and it's the fourth door down."

Abbey fled the desk and the woman's wary eyes and walked as quickly as she could to the door of room 108. She took a deep breath and knocked.

The door opened to reveal an elderly woman in a wheelchair. Her china blue eyes sparkled behind thick lenses, and she leaned forward a bit, as if to bring Abbey into focus.

"Abbey Jensen? Luellen has talked so much about you, I feel as if I know you! Come in, come in!" She wheeled herself back into her room, motioning Abbey to follow her. "What's Luellen been up to lately?"

"She's still a missionary in Brazil," Abbey said as her eyes took in her surroundings. The room was lovely, done in clean white and bluebonnet blue, and as neat as the proverbial pin. A white porcelain cross hung over a small table on which a Bible was neatly centered. It was bigger than any Bible Abbey had seen, and she realized that it was undoubtedly a large-print edition.

"Brazil? Last I heard it was Chile."

"It probably was Chile, then. I'm pretty bad with keeping up with her."

"Isn't it exciting, though? Traveling through the world, spreading the Word." The old woman's face appeared almost transfixed. "She and I are total opposites of each other. She's the world traveler, and the most I do is go down the hall for dinner."

But rather than sounding sorry for herself, she seemed quite happy.

"By the way, I'm Claire Thorson. Luellen and I have known each other since we were girls. I have a scrapbook I'd love to show you if you have time."

"Actually, I'd love to look at it," Abbey said, amazed that she really would, "but I have to get back to work. I brought your Christmas present from Aunt Luellen. She sent it to me by mistake."

Claire laughed. "Somehow that doesn't surprise me. Luellen was always the one with her head in the clouds, just to be closer to heaven, we used to tease her. I suppose that means I have your gift, then."

She wheeled over to the small tree that was set up by the window and picked up one of the many packages under it. She held it close to her face, trying to read the name.

"Don't worry about it," Abbey reassured her. "It's not that important."

"A Christmas present 'not that important'? My goodness, Abbey Jensen! Yes, it is!"

Abbey grinned at the elderly woman's honesty. Her eagerness about Christmas reminded her of Mike's comment. Christmas mattered quite a bit to Claire. "You're right. It is important, and here is yours." She held out the slippers, now completely rewrapped in bright red foil with a shiny gold bow on the top. "But now I've got to get back to work."

"Where do you work?"

"At the Cedar Mall. I manage Trends."

"Cedar Mall? My grandson works there. Maybe you know him."

"Maybe." Abbey impulsively dropped a kiss on the top of Claire's head. "But I've got to go now."

She opened the door to leave and there, in the hallway, still out of breath from running, stood Mike Tucker.

They all managed to speak at once, and for a moment, chaos reigned supreme. It ended with a sudden blanket of silence as their words settled on them.

"You've met Grandma, I see," Mike said at last.

Before Abbey could say a word, Mike took her by the arm. "Let's go have some coffee," he suggested as he steered her out of Claire's room. "We need to talk."

As they left, Abbey saw Claire lift her hand ever so slightly in a fisted salute. And perhaps her ears were playing tricks on her, but she was sure she heard the older woman whisper, "Wahoo!"

3

$\mathcal{M}$ ike led Abbey into a small room that opened off the lobby. Several small round tables were clustered near a cozy fireplace, where a hearty fire burned. He poured them each a cup of coffee from the pot on the counter and dropped some change in the pottery piggy bank beside the coffee pot, moving with the easy grace of someone who knew the ropes of Golden Meadows.

A few surprised residents lifted surreptitiously interested glances at them. When he nodded at some of them, smiling and greeting them, Abbey said through closed teeth and a tight smile, "Why don't you introduce me to your friends?"

He nodded at a table of three gentlemen, then sat beside her, sliding a cup toward her. "Because this way you'll be the hit of the rumor mill. They'll all be speculating who Sweet's new girlfriend is."

"Who's Sweet?" she asked, momentarily diverted.

A stain flushed his cheeks with dark color.

"Mike, are you blushing? Well, will you look at that? You are!" She grinned. "Are you Sweet?"

"Yup," he said, ducking his head. "Grandma always said I was the sweetest grandbaby boy in the world, and that soon became Sweet."

"I like it," Abbey said truthfully. "It fits you, in a way. Plus, it's, well, sweet."

Their laughter broke the uneasiness only for a moment. They had serious matters to work out, and Abbey went right to the point. "Mike, why didn't you tell me that your grandmother was Claire?"

His dark eyes were serious when he studied her face. "Would it have mattered?"

"Yes," she replied. "Yes, I think it would have."

"How?"

She thought about her answer before speaking. "Well, I think I would have come out here right away."

"Really?"

Annoyance tinged her response. "Really. I would have at least given it stronger consideration."

He shook his head. "I'm not so sure about that."

"Michael Tucker, I would too have come out here!" she protested, her back straightening. "How can you say such a mean thing about me?"

Mike shifted in his chair. "Let's face it, Abbey. You and I have known each other since we were kids. We never were buddies even when we were children, and the years didn't draw us together; they emphasized our separateness. Your life has been focused on your career."

She tried to interrupt him, but he held up his hand. "Wait. Let me finish. I might as well be hung for a sheep as a lamb, and after all I've said, I'm well on my way to the sheep gallows."

Abbey settled back in her chair, but every nerve in her body tingled with anxious worry. She felt exactly the same way she did during performance evaluations at Trends, knowing that she was about to hear something she didn't want to and that it was unavoidable. The riot in her stomach turned and churned, and she had a fleeting thought that she shouldn't have had the evening special at Pizza Fair.

"We're friends, Mike." She congratulated herself on how even and calm her voice sounded.

"Are we?"

Abbey had heard people say that it felt like their world had been pulled out from under them, but it was a phrase she'd never really understood. But now she did.

"Yes, Mike, we are."

"And who else are your friends?" His words were deadly quiet.

"Well, let's see. There's Brianna and Selma at the store, of course, and, um, then there's Terri. Terri and I have been pals since we were in diapers."

"When did you last see Terri? Talk to her? Write to her?"

"Write to her?" She looked at him blankly.

"Terri moved to Rochester in August," he said gently.

She put her face in her hands. She hadn't known that. She'd been too busy to call Terri, too busy to drop by, just too busy.

This was terrible, absolutely terrible. The pain was almost too intense to feel. It was as if she were having major surgery—without anesthesia.

A touch on her shoulder startled her. "Is this young man acting like a cad?"

Beside her a thin elderly man balanced on a cane. His hands shook with palsy, and his eyes were murky with cataracts. But his voice was strong, and his meaning was clear as he glared at Mike.

"No, he's fine." She shot a furtive glance at Mike, then looked back at her defender. "He's just offering me some suggestions on how I might improve myself."

Abbey thought the elderly fellow was going to raise his cane and shake it at Mike. But instead, older eyes glared at younger eyes, and the gentleman said, "If there's one thing you should learn, young man, it's that you can't tell a woman anything."

She tried to protest, but he continued, apparently unaware of her interruption. "You can't tell them anything because they know every-thing. My Eleanor, may she rest in peace, may not have gone past the twelfth grade, but she had a doctorate in Life. Good Christian woman too." The man nodded. "Actually, you can't tell men anything either," he said to Abbey. "It's not because they know everything—they don't—but they've got this problem with their ears."

Abbey was fascinated by this man. "Their ears?"

"Yup. And the fanciest hearing aids in the world can't help with their problem. You can't tell a person anything they don't want to hear, whether they're male or female." He leaned on his cane thought-fully. "So here I am telling you this, and you probably don't want to hear me either. Go figure. Just because you're old, don't mean you're smart."

"I think that you are extremely smart," Mike declared, "and I'm glad you stopped to talk to us. Right, Abbey?"

"It seems to me that Eleanor got a pretty good deal when she married you," Abbey said softly, suppressing the urge to give the man a hug.

She noticed Mike's quick glance at her as the gentleman walked away. "What?" she snapped.

"You sounded almost like a romantic for a minute there," he said, nearly laughing.

"Yeah, right. Your hearing is pitiful."

"Well, he did say that you only hear what you want to hear," he reminded her.

"And you wanted to hear that I'm a romantic?" She meant it lightly, as a quick and witty response, but as she said it, the meaning struck her.

Mike didn't know it, but his offhand comment—and it was an offhand comment, she was sure—had struck pay dirt. The problem was that this gushy romantic, which she had efficiently buried under the lacquered coat of her career, tended to surface at the most inopportune time, like whenever she watched *Miracle on 34th Street* or when she attended weddings or even when a certain greeting card commercial appeared on television. It was really quite inconvenient.

Hastily, she tried to cover the glimpse of her inner self that had escaped. She changed the subject to something she was more comfortable with: "I've got to get back to work," she announced. "It's late."

Mike glanced at his watch and nodded. "You're right. I'm supposed to meet a friend at Tuck's Toys in fifteen minutes, so I'd better hustle."

She couldn't resist it. "A friend?"

"Yes, Miss Snooper," he answered. "A friend."

"Big friend? Little friend?"

He laughed. "Are you trying to find out if I'm seeing someone? Well, not in that sense, no."

She stood up and busied herself with clearing away her coffee cup. "It's just that you work almost as many hours as I do. I don't even see my mailman, let alone get out to meet people. What do you do? Do you go to the bars after work?"

His expression was half shocked, half amused. "The bars? No, I don't go to the bars. They're not my scene at all. No, my dear, I find my friends at the best place in the world. I find them at church."

"Oh, that," she said dismissively. "They don't count."

He stopped midaction. "Why not?"

"Well, for one thing, they've got to love you. Kind of like parents."

He chuckled. "Not exactly. But in a way you're right. They do have to love you, because Christ told them to."

Abbey responded with a very unladylike snort.

"It's true. Oh, admittedly there are moments when we disagree, but that's just part of it all. That's how we grow."

He was so serious. Mike must take this religion stuff pretty seriously. Of course, his grandmother did too, judging from her room décor.

He took her by the hand. "Abbey, want to come with me to church on Sunday, give it a try?"

"Nah. I need to be at the store early. We're starting our big Christmas promotion that day." For once, she was grateful for the signs and displays that had arrived earlier in the day. She had a ready-made excuse for not going with him.

"There's an early service. You could be out by ten o'clock."

She shook her head. "No, Mike. Thanks for inviting me, but I just don't go for this organized religion stuff."

He grinned. "Well, sometimes we're not so organized at the early service."

"You know what I mean. I believe in God and all that, but this church business is, well, not for me. If I want to say hello to God, I can go to the lake and do it."

"And do you?" His question was quiet and unnerving.

"I've got to get going, Mike." Abbey turned on her heel and left the room before he could say another word.

She fumed all the way back to the mall. Religion was one of those things that people were supposed to keep to themselves.

It was true that Mike had never proselytized. As a matter of fact, this was the first time he'd even mentioned anything having to do with church. But his invitation made her uneasy. And she had to admit that part of the feeling was born of the fact that this opened up another area of Mike that she didn't know existed.

For some reason, she wanted to know more about Mike.

A lot more.

The evening mall traffic had picked up, and Abbey grimaced at the new booths that had gone up since she'd left. The latest one was a peppermint-striped building. Instead of a wall facing the mall corridors, the space was lined with black metal bars.

She edged closer. A large heart-shaped black lock hung on the door.

Abbey couldn't believe her eyes. It looked almost like a jail, but what on earth did a jail have to do with Christmas?

As if in answer to her unspoken question, a workman wearing a Cedar Mall uniform hauled a ladder up to the front of the building. Curiously, she watched as he set up the ladder and climbed it, balancing a large wooden sign. After a few quick taps of his hammer, she had her answer. The sign was lettered in Old West style: "The Candy Cane Calaboose."

"Well," Abbey said to no one in particular, "that explains it." She shook her head. "Or not."

As she started to walk toward Trends, another worker joined the first. The second man carried a sign that was also immediately nailed to the building. She retraced her footsteps and read the new sign: "The mall merchants invite you to watch this spot for holiday fun!"

"Oh, right," she muttered to herself. "Well, not this mall merchant. I wonder what on earth they've decided we're going to have to do now."

She walked back to Trends, mumbling and grumbling about past mall endeavors, such as the potluck when everybody brought desserts and potato salad, and nobody brought a main dish. The mall office had been forced to buy meat and cheese trays from a neighboring grocery store. Then there was the picnic, scheduled for mid-July, prime mosquito season. Even the toughest repellent hadn't been able to repel the hordes of hungry buzzing insects. Next time, Abbey thought, they probably wouldn't have the picnic next to the river.

Another one of their grand plans had been a talent show to raise money for a local charity. It soon became apparent that few, if any, of the mall merchants had any talent at all. The talent show had never been repeated, and she thought it was possibly at the charity's request.

No, whatever this Candy Cane Calaboose was, it was going to prove to be an awful idea.

But Abbey hadn't gone to the potluck or the picnic or the talent show anyway. And she had no intention of having anything to do with this latest brainstorm of the mall's management.

She shrugged. This Candy Cane Calaboose nonsense wouldn't bother her one way or the other.

he alarm went off, and Abbey realized it was aptly named. The little torture device was truly alarming. Every morning its persistent buzz startled her into wakefulness.

She slammed her hand on the snooze button, hoping for a few more precious moments of sleep, but that was a luxury she'd never been able to manage. Once she woke up, she was awake, and there was no going back to sleep for her. Her parents had teased her about her hidden "on" switch.

She missed her parents, especially during the holiday season. But she was a realist. Connecticut might as well be on the other side of the moon this time of year. And they had their own lives, their own friends, and although she knew they'd have been delighted to see her, she also accepted that they were comfortable with their annual summer visits.

It was one of the sacrifices she made for her career, and they understood. The other sacrifice she made for her career was never having a leisurely morning . . . at least not at Christmas.

As she hurried through her morning routine at a pace that surprised her, she tried not to think about families, the night before, or her visit with Claire. But her thoughts kept returning to Mike and his grandmother.

Somehow it all fit together perfectly, with Aunt Luellen at the center. When things got crazy, her aunt was often the precipitator, with her well-meant actions and her impulsive engineering of situations. She was a kook, that one. Abbey smiled as she thought of what her aunt must be like as a missionary. What on earth did the people of Brazil—or wherever she was—think of her version of the gospel?

She could only imagine how it would come out through the filter of Aunt Luellen's nutty brain.

Abbey gasped with surprise as her feet touched the linoleum of her kitchen. It was icy cold. Slippers. She needed to get some slippers. She was on the verge of making a mental note to buy some at the mall when the irony of it all struck her.

She could have had slippers—goofy frog slippers. At least Claire's toes should be toasty warm after Christmas.

That reminded her. She had to get out to see Claire and retrieve the package that Aunt Luellen had sent. That is, she corrected herself, if it were for her. Knowing Aunt Luellen, she might have her entire Christmas gift list scrambled beyond repair. The gift that Claire had could easily be a fishing rod meant for Uncle Kirby in Oregon.

But the sooner she got out there and straightened this whole mish-mash out, the sooner she could get back to her own life again and shrug off this crazy business. Her conversation with Mike was still making her uncomfortable, and she didn't like to be uncomfortable.

She snatched her purse from the hook by the door and headed out into the cold. Yes, if she was ever going to have peace of mind, she was going to have to get this thing taken care of once and for all.

Her car groaned into life, and Abbey shivered as she sat in her driveway, waiting for the engine to warm up. There wasn't any new snow, and the sky was a bright, clear blue, but that didn't mean any-thing when it came to the temperature. It had to be below zero.

She glanced at the spot where an indoor/outdoor thermometer had been attached to her house, but it had fallen off during a late autumn windstorm, and she just hadn't had the chance to put it back up. Then she remembered: The thermometer had fallen off during the autumn of last year. She was really letting things slide.

Well, she countered as she continued her discussion with herself, it wasn't as if she had time. She was busy at the store . . . and looking into maybe going back to school . . . and life was just generally hectic. It was something she'd come to live with.

She rubbed her hands together. Even through her thick mittens— on sale at Trends, two pairs for eight dollars—the icy air pierced right to her bones. The defroster had cleared only a small section of her frosty windshield, and she impatiently turned on the wipers, hoping to hurry the process along. She did not want to get out and scrape the window off. It was just too cold.

But the windshield began to film up on the inside from the warmth of her body, so she knew she was in for a wait, and she was too edgy to sit in her car and wait patiently. She fidgeted with the wipers, monkeyed with the defroster, and tried to rub the frost off with her mittened hand, succeeding only in smearing the fog. At last the windshield was clear enough, and she headed off.

This was going to be quick, she promised herself. She'd run in, pick up the present from Claire, say a few bland and polite words, and be on her way. Five minutes, tops. And she'd be through with this whole bizarre slippers thing and able to get on with her life.

Whatever that might be, a nagging little voice whispered in her heart.

Mike? Surely, Mike didn't have anything to do with her life. He was just a friend—or not a friend, she thought as she remembered their conversation. It made her stomach hurt.

She pulled into a spot near the door of Golden Meadows. The tall windows sparkled in the morning light. From the parking lot, she could see the mammoth Christmas tree through the largest windows in the entryway. The lights were on, catching the sunlit crystals of ice on the edges of the windows. With the early morning frost lit by the tree lights' multicolored array, the building looked incredibly picturesque.

She briefly considered leaving the car running but decided against it. She was already low on fuel and about the last thing she needed now was to run out of gas in the parking lot of a retirement community. So she switched off the ignition, telling herself she'd be inside such a short time that the car would still be warm—or warmish—when she came out again.

Resolutely, she marched into the high arched lobby of Golden Meadows and approached the desk. Just her luck. The same woman who'd been there earlier was there again. Nadine, that was her name.

"Yes?" It was remarkable, truly remarkable, how much iciness the woman could pack into the single word.

"I'd like to see Claire. Claire Thorson."

"Is she expecting you?"

"Yes. No. She is, but probably not right this minute. I mean, she knows I'm coming, but not necessarily today. Well, really, she's not expecting me at all right now, since it's opening time at the mall and it's Christmas."

The woman behind the desk stared at her, her expression never wavering. What was it about her that made Abbey splutter and blither like this?

"You're the lady with the package," Nadine said at last.

Abbey nodded, unsure of what the woman was going to do.

She certainly didn't expect this: Nadine burst into a huge smile and leaned across the desk to capture Abbey's hands. "Thank you so much for bringing the gift to her. You know, Mike's pretty much the only family she's got here anymore, and while he is here daily, bless his heart, having a new young face in her life has meant so much. She's really perked up."

Abbey could feel the smile freezing on her face as the woman continued to gush. "I hope you'll be back more often. This is just doing her a world of good." Then the woman delivered the *coup de grace*. "Plus you're almost family."

"Almost family?" Abbey gulped.

"You and her grandson, Mike. You're, well, you know." Nadine stopped just short of a conspiratorial wink.

"We're what?" Abbey asked through nearly numb lips. "No, never mind. I have the feeling this is something I don't want to hear." She shot a wild smile at the receptionist. "So, is Claire in her room?"

"No, Honey. She's with the others, down in the Fireside Lounge. You can go ahead. It's just down this hall, take a left, then a quick right. You can't miss it. There's a fireplace the size of a Buick in there. And they're all in there singing their dear hearts out, so follow the music."

Abbey felt her face relax. Maybe she could make it through this after all. She started down the hall, and she could just make out the sound of voices raised in song. They finished the last triumphant notes of a hymn Abbey somewhat recognized and, after some murmured discussion, a series of chords led them into another song.

What the group lacked in talent, they made up for in enthusiasm. Some voices were quavering with age; others were strong and true, undiminished by the years. One clear tenor led them all. She knew even before she peeked around the corner who the voice belonged to. He motioned her in as he kept on leading the group in singing.

If only the song hadn't been a rather rousing rendition of "When the Saints Come Marchin' In." Abbey's face flooded with red when the audience's singing lagged as they turned around to stare at her with open curiosity. The voices faded out as the residents studied the newcomer.

She tried to cover her embarrassment by whispering loudly to an elderly gentleman in the back row: "I'm not a saint, and I'm not marching."

To her chagrin, he leaned back and said, just as loudly, "Could have been worse. The song before last was 'How Great Thou Art.' "

She knew she shouldn't, that she would be doomed if she did. But she couldn't help it. She looked at Mike.

His face was as red as hers but with suppressed amusement. As their eyes met, Abbey and Mike dissolved into laughter. It wasn't the genteel, tee-hee, hymn-sing kind of laughter either. Oh, no. It was the can't-catch-your-breath, clutch-your-sides, gulp-and-snort brand of laughter that takes over and won't let go.

Tears ran down her face, and she collapsed onto the nearest folding chair and wiped her eyes as she tried to control herself. The harder she tried, the worse she laughed.

Just when she thought she had mastered her laugh attack, she looked at Mike. His attempt to look as sober failed as their glances locked again, and once more they both gave way to the laughter.

"Hmmph!" A man in a plaid shirt settled himself into a posture of righteous indignation. "Such behavior! Have you ever witnessed such a scene in your life? This is a hymn sing, not a vaudeville show. They ought to—"

"Get married," a tiny lady with a lace scarf finished for him. She sighed happily. "Get married and have lots of little Sweets."

Abbey stopped midgulp. The woman's voice carried clearly through the room, and from the way that Mike froze in place, bent at a nearly impossible angle, she knew he had heard her. His hand was motionless on the strings of his guitar, and if she didn't know better, she'd think he was a wax figure from Madame Tussaud's.

Lots of little Sweets?

Mike was staring at her, looking at her with a strangled pain she knew mirrored her own shock. She knew she should get up and leave, but her muscles were apparently cemented into place. Dimly she heard sounds behind her, and a familiar tinkling giggle broke the silence. "Speaking of Sweet, how about 'Sweet Hour of Prayer'? Come on, everybody! I love that hymn. I'll start." Claire's wavering but true soprano started the hymn, and the others soon joined in.

Abbey could have kissed her as the crowd faced forward again. Mike, after a split-second pause to collect himself, joined in with his guitar.

As soon as the attention had turned from her, Abbey decided, she'd leave. She'd creep out, hoping no one would notice. She'd deal with the wayward Christmas gift later. She had to get back to the mall. Her fingers pushed back her sleeve, and she grimaced. She'd forgotten to put on her watch.

Surreptitiously she glanced around the room, trying to find a clock. Surely there'd be one on the fireplace. But nothing. There were no clocks in the room at all. Maybe, she thought, when you got to this point in life, time didn't matter. You just moved from Activity A to Activity B to lunch, then rested, then Activity C, Activity D, dinner, television, and to bed. She resisted the urge to shudder. This was definitely not the life for her.

The woman with the lace collar leaned over to her. "Need the time?" she asked as she held her thin wrist over toward Abbey.

Abbey realized she was the only person in the room without a watch on. That might explain the dearth of clocks. Golden Meadows supplied the activities, but each resident was responsible for his or her own time.

Maybe that was what Aunt Luellen was talking about. Maybe this was what rejoicing in the day meant.

She smiled at the woman with the watch. The group had begun another song, a Christmas carol. She should leave, but this was "Joy to the World." It had been her favorite when she was a child, and she couldn't resist joining in as the words came back easily to her mind.

She'd stay for this one song, and that was it. How long could a song take? A minute, two tops, right? She'd allow herself the luxury of one song, then she had to get to work.

But the lure of the familiar carols soon wrapped their magic around her, and she stayed for "He Is Born" and "Hark, the Herald Angels Sing." As the last note drifted into silence, she glanced at her neighbor's watch.

It was a few minutes after ten!

Trends was already open! She scooped up her purse and made a hasty, muted farewell to the members of the hymn sing and raced out the door, down the hall, past a surprised Nadine, and into the cold clear air of a Minnesota morning.

It wasn't as if no one was at Trends to open it. Selma was scheduled to be there at eight-thirty, and she was so reliable that Abbey knew she was there by eight-fifteen. But Abbey needed to be at the mall, at Trends.

Actually, what she needed was to be away from here, away from Golden Meadows and this whole bizarre scene with Mike. And away from all those hymns. Her mind swam with the memories of long-neglected melodies, and the words came back to haunt her. It was amazing how easily they sprang back into her mind, although it had been years since she'd set foot inside a church.

The carols, of course, she'd heard every minute of every hour of every day since November fifth, the official start of the holiday season at the mall. She could sing them in her sleep. Abbey snorted. She probably did sing them in her sleep.

She snapped her attention back to the road as a patch of ice nearly sent her car spinning off the paved parking lot. Now there was a metaphor she could understand: Be in control. Hold the steering wheel tightly and never take your eyes off the road ahead, and you will stay directed. For her, that meant staying on track, straight toward her MBA and a real career with mega-bucks in her bank account. If she kept her target in sight, as she had been, she'd stay on the path to her heart's treasure.

Somewhere in the back of her mind, she could hear Aunt Luellen saying something about heart's treasure. Abbey shrugged. If it was Aunt Luellen, it was undoubtedly something from the Bible.

She'd had her dose of religion for the day. A couple of rousing Christmas carols, and look at her. She was wrapped in that soft-focus, greeting-card kind of glow that retailers relied on to pull them through the Christmas season.

There were Christian retailers, she was sure, who looked upon the season as a time to celebrate Jesus' birth. But there were just as many, if not more, who saw this as a season of profits, and a tiny baby born in a stable played only a minor part in it. The thought saddened her, even though she wasn't a dyed-in-the-wool Christian like Aunt Luellen.

Christmas was the base of the retailer's year. It was what carried them though the lean times in other months and kept them going. Without Christmas to boost their sales, many stores would not be able to stay in business. And now that she was a store manager, she was part of the feeding frenzy when it came to Christmas. She had to be. She had a responsibility to the storeowners and the other employees. Abbey sighed and pushed away the thoughts that jostled around in her mind, arguing with each other. Why did Christmas have to be so complicated?

She pulled out of the Golden Meadows parking area and into the stream of traffic, trying to squish the not-so-tiny voice that insisted she didn't believe a word she was thinking—that Christmas was a time of holiness and joy, and that stores like Trends played only the most minor of roles in its celebration.

The wise men may have bought the newborn Jesus gifts of incomparable value, but somehow she didn't think they would have shopped at the Cedar Mall, with "forty-two individual stores offering the region's widest assortment of shopping pleasure," as the television commercial boasted.

As if on cue, she could hear Aunt Luellen's voice from many childhood Christmases: "The greatest gift of all was not what they brought Him but what He brought us."

Abbey sighed. That was true. What was a television set compared to everlasting life?

Or a pair of goofily grinning frog slippers?

5

he mall was already filling with customers, even though it had been open less than an hour. Selma was busily refreshing the stock from one of the cartons that seemed to arrive every hour, although Abbey knew deliveries were only twice a day.

"Hey, Stranger, good to see you! Don't tell me you overslept!" Her clerk grinned at her.

"Ha. I don't even sleep, so oversleeping is too much to ask for." Abbey said it lightly, but the weariness that seeped into her bones told her that her words weren't that far from the truth.

"No kidding. One of these days you'll have to try sleeping. It's vastly underrated, at least in your world," Selma commented wryly.

"After Christmas. Then I'll have time."

Selma snorted inelegantly. "After Christmas come the returns, then it's Valentine's Day, then . . ."

"Okay, I'll take a Wednesday off sometime and try sleeping."

"Wednesdays are Senior Citizens days here, remember?"

Abbey made a face at her salesclerk. "Whatever. I'm too tired to argue." Their eyes met, and both women laughed.

"Okay, lecture ended. Now, where do you want these?" Selma handed Abbey a box of brightly colored slipper socks, and Abbey gasped.

She'd gone all the way out to Golden Meadows to pick up the gift, but she'd left without it. She slammed her fist down on the counter.

"Okay," Selma said, drawing the two syllables out. "What just took you from mellow to mad?"

"These slippers."

In one smooth movement, Selma reached out, took the box, and tossed it under the counter, then smiled innocently at her boss. "What slippers?"

"No, no," Abbey responded with a frustrated sigh. "They just reminded me that I was supposed to pick something up, and I forgot. Now I have to go back, and I don't really want to."

Selma knelt to get the box again. "Anything I can do to help?" Her voice was muffled from under the counter.

Now there was an idea! Selma could go to Golden Meadows. . . . But before the thought took full root, Abbey dismissed it. She had to see this through to the end.

"No, I'm just busily berating myself. For some reason I can't seem to remember to pick up the gift my aunt Luellen sent to Golden Meadows."

"She sent your Christmas present to Golden Meadows? Isn't that a retirement home?" Selma threw back her head and roared with laughter. "Honey, I think your auntie is trying to tell you something!"

"You are not even a little bit funny," Abbey responded, although she had to smile. "All I need is a simple brain transplant, and I'll be fine."

"Would that be out-patient surgery?" Selma ducked the teasing swipe Abbey gave her.

The two spent the rest of the day companionably unpacking new arrivals and setting up the merchandise. As soon as they emptied one box, another arrived to take its place, or so it seemed. Between the two of them, they barely made a dent in the towering stacks of cardboard boxes, all marked "URGENT: OPEN FIRST."

"I'm here!" The voice of the college student who worked part-time called to them from the front of the store.

"Hi, Brianna." Abbey groaned as she rose from the crouched position where she'd been retrieving an entire boxed shipment of rings that had broken open a few moments ago. Rings had rolled all over the store, coming to rest in the most difficult-to-reach positions. "What are you doing here so early?"

"Early?" Brianna looked confused. "I'm here to work. I'm supposed to be here at five, aren't I?"

Abbey and Selma exchanged glances. Selma said affectionately,

"Yes, Dear, but it's only—" She consulted her watch and gasped. "It's nearly five!"

"No wonder I'm so hungry. Selma, you can go on home, and Brianna, if you'll straighten that holiday sweatshirt display, I'll—"

"Get something to eat." Selma pushed Abbey toward the front of the store. "You haven't even had lunch, and I suspect you skipped breakfast too. I'm on for another hour anyway, and Brianna and I can certainly cover long enough for you to get a decent meal."

Abbey opened her mouth to object when a familiar voice spoke from behind her.

"I'll take care of it, Selma. Come on, Abbey, let's go get some grub." Mike grinned at her.

"Some grub?" Brianna laughed out loud. "Man, you've got to do something about your romantic style."

It seemed to Abbey that everyone began to speak at once, and the mayhem ended only when she was unceremoniously shoved outside the open gate of Trends, her coat in her hands, with Mike laughing at her side.

"I think we're going out to dinner," he said at last.

"I don't need my coat for that. Actually, I don't need dinner at all but—" As if on cue, her stomach rumbled loudly.

"The case of the tattletale tummy," Mike said. "Let's go."

"Just let me put my coat back. We can run down to the pretzel place and grab a stuffed pretzel and a soda."

He put his hand on her arm. "No pretzels. We're going to go out for a real dinner."

"A real meal?" A terrible thought struck her. He had said that he often ate with his grandmother. "Oh, no, Mike. We're not going to eat at Golden Meadows."

He shook his head. "No, but I do go out there sometimes to eat with Grandma. I like to do that."

She shuddered. "I don't mean to be horrid, but I can't imagine that being anything you'd want to do."

"Well, I like it. But that's not where we're going tonight. We're going to a real restaurant, the kind where you sit down, they hand you a menu, you get a salad and a meal with vegetables. And maybe a dessert that doesn't come wrapped in plastic."

It did sound good. So Abbey allowed herself to be ushered through the icy-cold parking lot, then driven to a nearby family restaurant, Ginger's. The restaurant's brick and glass exterior was softened by chintz curtains and tablecloths, and Abbey detected the warm inviting scent of meatloaf. She had to admit it; this was a great idea. She was starving.

"This must be new. I've never been in here before," she said as she sipped the water the waitress handed her.

Mike shot her a curious look. "It's been here about a year and a half. I'd ask where you've been, but I know—working."

"That's not really fair," Abbey protested. "It's not like I don't have any life at all outside Trends."

Mike smiled ruefully. "I'm sorry. It came out sounding harsher by far than I intended. It's just that it's been true of me. I realized that my whole life was revolving around work. I'm trying to cut back a bit."

Abbey couldn't help it. She laughed. "You're cutting back? That's ludicrous."

He seemed surprised. "Why do you say that? I don't work nearly as many hours as you do."

"Who was the only person besides me at the mall at eleven o'clock at night when I got locked out of the store? You. Mike Tucker. Workaholic."

He had the grace to look abashed. "That's true. But I am trying to do better. Like not grabbing a hot dog or a pretzel in the evening and calling it dinner."

"We're busy, Mike," she said in her own defense—their own defense. "It's not like we have the time to do full-course meals."

"We don't? I don't know about you, but I've been neglecting myself lately."

"Neglecting yourself?"

"I know. Sounds kind of selfish, doesn't it? But I'm starting to realize that I've got to take care of my body. And that includes eating right as well as getting some exercise."

Abbey glanced at him suspiciously. "Are you one of those exercise fanatics?"

He struck an exaggerated muscle-man pose. "I'm in the running for Mr. America, hadn't you noticed?" He laughed, and for the first time she noticed that he had dimples. Actually, very cute dimples. The kind that made his eyes light up like—She broke off that train of thought before it could go further.

He was still talking, and she pulled her attention back to his words. "So I promised myself that one day I'll join a gym, and I will, but right now if I can make a turn around the mall with the other mall walkers, I consider it my exercise for the day. No, right now I'm aiming for some sleep and some veggies. Baby steps first."

The waitress appeared with their coffee. "You ready to order?"

Her words took Abbey by surprise. She hadn't even looked at the menu. "What do you recommend?" she asked mike.

"They have really good soup," he said.

Soup sounded wonderful. Nice and warm and filling, the perfect food for a cold December evening.

"I'll be right out with the bread," the server said as she collected their menus and left.

"We get a loaf of homemade bread with flavored butter. It comes with our meal," Mike said. "It's just this side of heaven."

"I haven't had homemade bread in years," Abbey commented. "Not since Mom made it, and that has to be, wow, four years ago? They've been gone that long?"

Mike's forehead wrinkled with concern, and it took Abbey a moment to realize why. "Oh, I didn't mean that kind of gone, I meant gone as in gone from Minnesota. They live in Connecticut now. Dad was transferred just shortly after I graduated from high school. I guess that's something you wouldn't have known."

He nodded. "Probably. Are you going to go out there for Christmas?"

"No." For the first time since she and her parents had been separated, she felt a twinge at being apart from them at the holidays, but she quickly suppressed it. "That's okay. We've only got Christmas Day off anyway. It's not worth it. What about you?"

"Well, Dad passed on last year."

Abbey felt herself flush. "Oh, I'm sorry. I didn't know. What a horrible thing to bring up at this time of year."

"It's certainly true I miss him, but I miss him every day of the year. It's still raw, and it hurts, but I know he's celebrating Christmas in heaven." He smiled contemplatively. "To be honest, that's what gets me through. I know you might not believe it, but it's enough."

His words took her by surprise, and her expression must have mirrored her feelings, because he continued, "I'm not saying that those first days didn't hurt with a pain as if someone had cut my heart right out of my chest, but my faith is strong, and his faith was stronger. He taught me that this life is great . . . and the next life is going to be even greater."

"How about your mother?" Abbey wanted to change the subject. She was in no mood for the turn the conversation was taking. She didn't want to think about things like religion, at least not now. She wanted to relax.

It wasn't that she didn't believe, not really. She did. She just didn't have the time to reason it all out. One of these days she would, when she had time.

Mike didn't seem to be bothered by her lack of interest in his family's faith. "Mom moved to Arizona, and she lives with her sister in a mobile home where she can reach out her bedroom window and pick an orange for breakfast. She says she doesn't care if she never sees another snowflake."

"So she's not coming up here for Christmas?"

He shook his head. "No. I won't get to see her at all this Christmas, sad to say. I have to stay here because of the store. This is the worst time of year for a toy store owner to take a vacation."

Abbey smiled. "I suppose you're right. It's the price you pay for owning your own store."

"Keep that in mind, Abbey, in case you decide to trade in managing for ownership. But I'll pop down there in February and visit. Right about then I figure I'll really need a blast of warmth. It'll be interesting to see what she thinks about celebrating Christmas in the desert."

"Arizona is a real change from Minnesota," Abbey commented. "I don't know if I could do it. I need snow and sweaters and mittens for it to be Christmas."

"I know what you mean," he agreed. "But there are times when I think I'd really like to try a Christmas without snow." He shivered. "Like last night. Did you hear how cold it got? Can you imagine what it must have been like to live here before electricity?"

"I remember reading about how people used to live in sod houses," Abbey said. "First off, I can't for a minute imagine what that was like." She shuddered. "Living in a house made of dirt? And what was it like to heat it by a stove? I'm glad to have my house, that's for sure."

"And my coffeemaker," Mike added, with a wry grin. "These cold mornings, I think I take all that for granted."

Their food arrived, but they barely noticed it, chatting companionably about the blessings of modern appliances, especially furnaces. All too soon, the soup was gone, the coffee cups drained, and Mike leaned back and rubbed his stomach. "I don't know about you, but I'm stuffed. We'd better get back."

They'd talked about nothing, but at the same time they'd talked about everything. Abbey thought that over as they rode in the comfortable dark cocoon of Mike's car. Somehow she felt she knew Mike better, but how on earth had that happened? The most personal their conversation had gotten was about their parents and where they lived now. Hardly the kind of thing that would qualify as an innermost secret. But now she felt closer to him.

And, she realized with surprise, she liked him. She really liked him.

He pulled into the snowy stretches of the mall's parking lot. As she opened the door on her side of the car, he pulled on the handle from the outside. Suddenly their faces were only inches from each other, and the strangest thing happened. Her mouth poised for his kiss, and she felt herself leaning in toward him, as if it were the most natural thing in the world.

Abbey hadn't had much experience with romance. Her knowledge was pretty much limited to some clandestine smooching behind the school with Edwin Carlson when she was fourteen. But she'd heard that a really good fellow and a really good kiss would sweep her off her feet.

Apparently it was true. She felt her feet leave the ground, as though she were floating, while Mike's arms grasped her shoulders, then her waist with a fervent intensity. The world spun around in a dizzying whirl, and the stars arched overhead.

"Aaaaaaabbey!" His voice echoed in her ears as they ascended quickly and just as rapidly descended.

Whomp!

With a very definite thump, she landed on the ground in an inelegant sprawl, with Mike nearby. Her long skirt was tangled in the heel of her boots, and her hat had slipped over one eye. Her bright yellow mittens were now smudged with black where she'd tried to stop her fall. The contents of her purse had escaped, and a lipstick was still skittering across the pavement.

"Are you okay, Abbey?" Mike said. "Wow, this parking lot is icy."

Her hip ached, and her arm, she knew, was going to sport a livid bruise in the morning. But it was nothing compared to her crushed ego.

This was why she had never been a ballerina, why she had never been chosen as a cheerleader. She had all the grace of a lumbering orangutan. She looked as if she should be a dancer, with her slender build, but somewhere between her brain and her feet, the message got scrambled. She was such a klutz. Mike undoubtedly thought she was clumsy, to the point of being dangerous to those standing near her, but what worried her most was something else.

Had she really wanted Mike to kiss her? What on earth had she been thinking of? And worse, what if she hadn't slipped? What if she had actually leaned in too far and kissed him?

He probably would have pulled away, and that would have been the end of their rapidly developing friendship.

Did he know she had been leaning in for his kiss? And if he did, did he think that she was forward, that she did this with anybody who took her to dinner? Being a recluse floating on an iceberg in the middle of the Atlantic Ocean was looking better by the minute.

* * *

Mike cradled his head in his hands. He'd never been the most graceful gazelle in the herd, that was a given, but tonight he'd really blown it. He'd been about to kiss her and had lost his bearings completely.

He had wanted to kiss her so badly that he'd lost whatever moral compass he had. He wasn't the kind of fellow to just kiss a woman because she was pretty, or because he'd had a good time being with her, or anything like that. No, for him a kiss was serious business.

That is, it was until his fancy footwork took them both down in a mall parking lot. The memory made him cringe. She must think he was a total idiot, or at least a complete clumsy Charlie. The next time he was going to get carried away by the moonlight, he'd make sure he wasn't standing on a patch of ice.

6

bbey woke up the next morning feeling a mixture of contentment and annoyance. She had enjoyed dinner far beyond what she'd expected. It was the kind of thing she could get used to . . . as long as she had someone to eat with.

Someone like Mike? a little voice nagged.

She'd known Mike since they were children. All through their teen years, when everybody of the opposite gender was a potential love interest, she had never thought of him in that sense, and she was sure the thought of going out with her had never crossed his mind either.

Not that it mattered. Even if she were attracted to him—which she wasn't—last night certainly made it clear that he saw her as a friend. A klutzy friend.

She mulled it over as she waited for her curling iron to heat. Although Mike had been ever-the-gentleman and helped her up, even retrieved her wayward lipstick from under a car where it had rolled and at last come to rest, he had to be wondering about her. What kind of woman would try to kiss somebody in a parking lot, then lose her balance in the process?

Could she be any more out of practice?

She hastily dismissed the thought. For one thing, she was perfectly capable of doing anything she wanted to do. If she'd wanted to make their dinner date an evening to remember, she certainly could have done so. She stood straighter and glared at her mirrored reflection. Yes, she could have knocked his proverbial socks right off.

The truth was, she had come really close. She'd knocked his hat off.

The image in the mirror glared back at her and reminded her of one important element that she was overlooking in this conversation with herself: this developing romance that she sometimes felt and sometimes didn't was completely one-sided. Mike was only trying to be her friend.

That brought her back to the second part of her morning thoughts. It hadn't been a date. Not even close. It had simply been two friends having dinner together.

Friends. The conversation at Golden Meadows sprang back into her mind, and for a moment Abbey felt uneasy. Maybe she—

She shook her head. No. She was fine. Just fine. All she had to do was quit mooning at the mirror like a lunatic and get going, or she was going to be an unemployed lunatic.

A light snow had fallen during the night, and while it made the main road to the mall a pleasant seasonal white, it also made it a crazy ride. The slicked roads forced her to drive slowly, because the fairly simple act of braking to a stop took at least half a block.

A blue four-wheel drive vehicle passed her, able to go faster because it had greater traction than her small car had. She glanced at it, then did a double take.

It was Mike's car, and by the way he was tapping his fingers on the steering wheel and moving his lips, she figured he must be singing along with the radio.

She didn't have time to react emotionally. She'd taken her eyes off the road just long enough to lose control. With a sick sensation in the base of her stomach, she tried futilely to bring her car out of its slide and back into the line of traffic.

"Don't let me hit someone," she said, and she didn't worry about who she was talking to. The message was more important.

The sensation of having her car skid, the steering wheel useless in her hands, was horrible. Then she saw a child walking on the sidewalk, completely absorbed in sliding on the slick pavement, gliding along as if he were ice-skating. The scream that rose in her throat died as her car slid sideways and launched itself, neatly and totally, into a snow bank, a few yards from the little boy.

She popped open the door of her car. As completely wedged in as she was, she could get it ajar just a few inches. "Are you okay?" she called to the boy, but he continued to skate on, the muffler and hat that covered his ears apparently preventing him from hearing her.

"Thank God," she breathed. That had been entirely too close.

The boy was all right. Now she had to get to the business of getting her car out of the snow. She drove into the snowdrift, she told herself, so logically she should be able to drive out again.

After futilely switching gears between reverse and drive, she gave up. She had two options. One, she could call the neighboring gas station to come and get her out. But who knew when they'd get there, and she could guess at how much that call would cost her. Or she could go directly to the second option. It was free. It was the shovel in her trunk.

The first challenge was getting the door open. It would only open about six inches before the snowdrift stopped it. She was thin, but not that thin.

How could she dig herself out when she was trapped inside the car?

Finally she settled on a successful combination of digging with her hand for awhile, then slamming the door open, and repeating the motion. Dig, slam. Dig, slam. Dig, slam. At last it worked, and she was able to escape from her car.

Her success was limited, however. She was still in the snow bank.

Abbey clambered across the snowdrift, wincing as a soft patch of it gave way, and her foot slid up to her knee in the icy crystals. The sharp pain from her hip as her leg turned reminded her of her elegant fall in the parking lot the night before. She opened the trunk, taking care not to drop her keys in the snow, and got the shovel.

She began digging the compressed snow from under her car. Her long scarf, which she'd purchased for its color rather than its utility, was much too short and slid down from the bottom of her face and hung loosely. After the fourth time that it got caught in the shovel and nearly decapitated her, she yanked it off and threw it aside in disgust.

Her nose was running, and she was sure that her hair looked like elves lived in it. Somehow, she knew, Mike Tucker was to blame for this.

*   *   *

Mike whistled as he raised the grating that covered the entrance to Tuck's. He ducked under it, and as he turned the key to lower it again, he smiled to himself.

You've given me a good year, Lord, he prayed silently as he always did while he went about the opening process. He was in the store by himself, and it was a good time to visit with God. It wasn't his only time of prayer, but even though it was informal, he found it to be valuable preparation for the day—and he was able to focus more clearly for evening prayers.

He continued to talk to God as he restocked the displays, started up the tills, and dusted off the countertop. *The store is doing well, Grandma is settling in just fine at Golden Meadows, and my mother is adjusting to living without Dad in Arizona. Thank You for the blessings You've given me.*

Two thoughts popped into his prayers simultaneously. The first was simple: *How can I repay You?* The second was complex: *Watch over Abbey Jensen and touch her heart to open it for You. She needs You so much.*

Even as he prayed the words, he knew what was being asked of him. The second thought was the answer to the first.

Aw, God. I meant for You to watch over her. Not me. I'm not good at that. He paused and straightened an already straight display. Here's a suggestion: How about if I serve on another committee at church instead?

Silence. Not that he had expected God to answer him aloud. He could always feel the response in his soul. God wasn't a bargainer, he knew that, but maybe he just hadn't offered the right bait.

No, huh? Okay, I'll increase my giving at church. Surely You can't argue with that.

God didn't argue, but that resounding emptiness stayed hollow, and Mike had to accept the truth: God wanted him to do what he could to point Abbey toward God.

He thought about it as he went through his workday. He didn't want to get involved romantically with Abbey. It wasn't that he didn't like her—he did. Oh, as a friend, he hastily told himself. And he'd enjoyed their time together.

But he certainly didn't want to get involved with her as deeply as he thought God was asking him to.

Besides, he could imagine what Abbey would say if he started hanging around her, watching over her both physically and spiritually. He laughed. *Are you sure about this, God?*

Well, he'd give it a try. The warm, loving glow that came over him told him that this was the right thing to do.

Caring for Abbey . . . He had to admit, the thought had its appeal.

Thanks to having stuck her car in the snow pile, Abbey had pulled into the parking lot with only moments to spare before Trends opened.

Usually, her lateness would have made her tense—even more so after her unfortunate experience with her car—but today she welcomed the diversion. The morning scurry to have the tills ready by the time the front gate came up was intensified, and she was glad to see an early morning crowd already window-shopping in preparation for the stores to open.

"Honey, you look like you've been at hard labor," Selma said as Abbey rushed to have the store in perfect condition by opening time.

"That's not far from the truth," Abbey said. "A snow bank and I had a disagreement."

Selma clucked sympathetically. " 'Tis the season, that's for sure. The roads were in pitiful shape this morning, weren't they? I almost got to meet the fella down the street. You know I've been wanting to run into him sometime to introduce myself. Well, this morning I almost got my chance. In fact, I nearly ran him down when my car went out of control on an ice patch."

They chuckled. Selma's romantic life was a constant trial to her. She had more boyfriends than Abbey had been able to keep track of, but none of them seemed to materialize into husband material.

Selma got a sly look in her eye and asked with clearly faked casualness, "So how did it go last night?"

Abbey diverted her eyes and attentively arranged the Christmas jewelry display. "Last night? Oh, that's right. It was fine."

"Fine? That's all you have to say? Fine?"

"Okay, 'fine' may not be the best word to describe it. It was great."

Selma smiled happily and settled back onto the chair behind the cash register. "Now we're talking! Did anything exciting happen?"

"As a matter of fact, it did. Something totally unexpected, and I was soooo glad." Abbey couldn't resist baiting Selma.

Selma's eyes got huge. "What? What?"

Abbey took a deep breath, then said melodramatically, "We went to Ginger's. I'd never been there before. They have good soup."

For a moment, she thought Selma might explode. "Never mind the soup. I want details. Give me details."

"You want details? What kind of details?"

"Boy details. Girl details."

"There are no details," Abbey said, bringing the conversation to an end. "The best part of the evening was the soup."

As she walked to the front of the store, she was sure she heard Selma mutter something under her breath that sounded not very nice.

Abbey raised the gate to the store, and a handful of customers wandered in. Those early customers got her total attention, and soon the conversation with Selma was ancient history in her mind. After all, the last thing she wanted to think about today was dinner last night with Mike.

"Want me to get the mail?" Selma asked awhile later. "It's almost noon. It should be here by now."

"Why don't I do it, then you can take the first lunch shift," Abbey suggested. "I could use a break, and so could you."

"I'd argue," Selma said, "but I wonder if part of the reason for your decision is the chance that you might meet a certain toy store owner at the mailboxes."

Abbey didn't answer, partially because she knew Selma was teasing, but also because her assistant was right on the mark.

The mall mailboxes were clustered at the end of a service entrance on the opposite side of the mall, and all shop owners and managers watched for the mail arrival carefully, especially this time of year, when the pace of sales picked up in the afternoon. If she didn't get the mail now, it would be early evening before she'd have a chance to do so.

It was something all the managers knew, so between eleven-thirty and noon, they tended to cluster down there and spend a few minutes sharing quick updates—and extensive gossip.

She could hear them laughing even before turning the corner to the service entrance. From the words that floated free of the general chaotic noise, she realized that the topic of conversation had something to do with a recent decision of mall management.

She slipped through the cluster of kiosks that broke the traffic pattern—when had that fireplace mini-store gone in?—and made her way to the mailboxes. The trip usually took her under five minutes, but now, thanks to the displays the mall management had put up, she had to run an obstacle course.

The managers motioned her into their group, and one of the women handed her a flyer. "Get this," she said to Abbey. "Honestly, what this new executive outfit won't do!"

"I've heard of stupid ideas, but this takes the cake!" added another.

"What's going on?" Abbey asked the woman who had handed her the flyer. "What have they done now?"

The woman just shook her head and threw her copy of the flyer into the nearby recycling bin. "You don't want to know. Oh, you've got one of their notices. Read it for yourself. I, for one, don't have time for this kind of nonsense. If they want to help the retailers, they could hire some extra help. But not this. The last thing I need is to be taken off the floor at Christmas!"

"Those people who come up with these ideas must have fruitcake for brains," another woman chimed in.

"Or reindeer tap-dancing on their heads," someone else agreed. "This idea is downright idiotic."

"Careful what you say," a man in a three-piece suit added. "Or you might end up in the slammer, er, calaboose."

The entire group burst into raucous laughter.

Abbey looked at the flyer to see what was causing this wild reaction on the part of the other store managers.

The flyer was the traditional mall office notice, with a candy-cane striped border around the edge, and on it red letters proclaimed: "The Candy Cane Calaboose is on its way!"

Candy Cane Calaboose? What on earth was that? She remembered seeing the construction going on down the mall corridor from her store, but she hadn't bothered to investigate further. She certainly didn't have the time to keep up with all the little "enhancements" the mall management had added this season.

Abbey shrugged, and her flyer joined the others in the recycling bin by the mailboxes. The Candy Cane Calaboose sounded like another one of the half thought-out ideas of the mall management, and certainly nothing she had the time or energy to deal with.

It was just silly, and it certainly had nothing to do with her.

⑦

he pace of Christmas sales had picked up tremendously, and Abbey felt her spirits rising to meet the challenge of the increased traffic. The weather had been cooperative—except for the snowfall that had resulted in the brief skirmish she'd had with that snow bank—and the crowds in the mall had increased as Christmas approached.

The nice part about it was that she had a reason to stay at the mall from early in the morning until late at night, and when she went home she dropped into bed, exhausted, and slept. For others, that might be a nightmare, but for her, it was great. She was in her element at the store. She knew the rules, she knew the way things went, and she felt good about her abilities.

It's not the kind of life that most people dream of, she acknowledged to herself the next day as she waited for her car to warm up before leaving her house, *but it's perfect for me. Everything now is building toward a good future in business, and all the stress, all the struggle, is going to pay off, and pay off well.*

Still, a part of her argued back, *wouldn't you like to have someone to be there for you, someone to say, "Poor baby," when you complain about the shipment that didn't arrive or the salesclerk who forgets her shift? Wouldn't it be nice to have someone to talk to in the morning while your car warms up . . . instead of having to talk to yourself?*

She was clearly losing her mind. Sitting in her car, having a full-fledged conversation with herself about talking to herself—this was definitely not a sign of strong mental health.

She sent the wipers across the windshield in one last angry sweep. The glass wasn't entirely clear of frost, but there was a small window

348

of visibility that she decided to take advantage of, and she backed out of the driveway.

As she crept along the road to the mall, the radio played Christmas carol after Christmas carol. She wanted to change the station, but she didn't dare take her hands off the steering wheel; she didn't want a repeat of yesterday's encounter with the snow bank.

"Joy to the World" began to play, and she recalled the hymn sing at Golden Meadows.

Golden Meadows!

She started to slap her head but remembered just in time not to let go of the steering wheel. In the bustle of the Christmas trade and the emotional chaos Mike had thrown her into, she'd forgotten to get the gift from Claire and get the mess straightened out once and for all.

For a moment, she considered writing the whole thing off as a loss, and if loopy Aunt Luellen inquired about her present, she could lie and say it had gotten lost in the mail. It was only a teeny white lie, Abbey reasoned, since Aunt Luellen had sent the gifts to the wrong address, and it was only through a momentary lapse on her part that the slippers had gotten to Claire.

Why, oh why, hadn't she simply tossed those dreadful slippers in the trash that evening?

Abbey tried to imagine how her life would have been different had she done just that. She wouldn't have met Mike's grandmother, and she probably wouldn't have gotten to know Mike better. Life would be calmer. More orderly. Peaceful.

And boring.

Mike smiled as he listened to the voice on the phone. The store was packed with people bearing lists of Christmas wishes, some carefully detailed by organized parents, others crayoned haphazardly by anxious children. Nick, his assistant, was making frantic signs at him that his help was needed with customers.

Mike waved him away, but Nick was persistent.

"Not now," Mike wrote on a piece of paper and shoved it to Nick. "In a minute."

"Who are you talking to?" his assistant asked him.

"No one," Mike mouthed at him.

"Whaaaat?"

Mike put his hand over the mouthpiece and whispered, "It's my grandmother."

"Your grandmother is not 'no one.' Honestly, Mike, I thought more of you than that!" Nick told him indignantly.

Mike grinned. "I meant I wasn't talking. She talks. I just listen."

He returned his attention to the voice on the telephone. "Yes, Grandma," he said at last. "I'll be there. And yes, I'll do my best to do that. Yes, Grandma. I understand. Okay."

At last he hung the phone up. "I do love my grandmother," he told Nick, "but when she's got something on her mind, heaven and earth must stop until it's done."

"What's up?" Nick asked.

"The story I just heard was a long, convoluted saga about a plugged drain and a handyman shortage at Golden Meadows. I didn't follow it all, but I'll run over tonight during the supper lull and see what's up."

Any further discussion was stopped by a harried-looking woman bearing five wrinkled lists. "How does Santa do it?" she asked, juggling the packages she already carried while trying not to drop the stack of games and action toys she had picked up. "I've only got five kids, and I can't keep their lists straight."

"Volume," Mike answered. "He buys in volume."

She grinned at him. "I think that's what I'm doing today. At least, that's what my checkbook is telling me."

"Want some help? I could put those smaller packages into some larger ones with handles," he offered. "That would make them easier to carry."

"Oh, bless you. I love Christmas, even though it is a financial crunch." She heaved the packages and the toys onto the counter. "It reminds me to take another look at my children and see what miracles they are, what a fount of possibilities they are, what a gift they are. God trusted me with them—me! It humbles me every time I think about it."

"I like that," Mike commented. It was a refreshing change from the complaints he heard so often from parents who had overspent their budget to buy toys that their children wanted at the moment but might very well forget about in a week or two.

She blushed. "I know I should do this every moment of my life, but sometimes life gets in its own way, if you know what I mean. Christmas is a nudge in the side to look at those children. Okay, look at them when they're asleep, which is about the only time they're not fighting, but that's kids for you. Anyway, even with the wildest of the bunch—that'd be my Richie—I know I see the face of an angel in training."

She frowned as she looked at the pile of toys. "Could you do me a favor and add these things up? I have the dreadful feeling my Christmas Club account has run dry."

Mike totaled the items up. She sighed with relief as he told her the sum. "Just under the wire." She handed him the money. "Thank you so much for the bags—and for listening to me. Have a Merry Christmas!"

It was interesting, Mike thought as she left, how someone so unexpected could give you a gift . . . one you couldn't buy at any mall.

The thought of a gift reminded him that his grandmother had mentioned that Abbey hadn't picked up her gift from her aunt Luellen yet. This might be the perfect chance for her to do so. He'd stop by Trends on the way to Golden Meadows. That way Abbey wouldn't have time to think of reasons why she shouldn't go.

For some reason, there was a special lilt in his step that carried him through the rest of the day.

Abbey put away the last of the new shipment of holiday earrings and stretched. The day had gone on endlessly. Maybe she should take a walk down the mall and get a cranberry Italian ice. It was one of the seasonal offerings the mall had that she actually liked.

"Abbey!" Mike's voiced hailed her from the front of the store. "You about ready to take a break?"

"I don't know when you started mind reading," she said, her voice only somewhat grumpy, "but I was just getting ready to go down to Italian N'Ice. Want to walk with me?"

"Sounds good, but I'm headed out to see Grandma. Would you like to join me? We can go through some hamburger joint drive-in on the way back if that's okay with you. I usually don't go for fast food, but tonight that's all I can manage—Nick is leaving early since he has a final exam at seven."

She paused, and Mike added, "Grandma isn't going to leave you alone until you go get your gift, you know. You might as well accept that. When she gets a project—and right now straightening out the confusion with the gifts is her project—she doesn't stop until it's resolved. She did mention that she has your present out there, and she suggested, as only my grandmother can suggest, that you could come out there and pick it up."

Abbey opened her mouth to object, but then thought better of it. This might be the perfect chance for her. If they weren't going to stay long out there, she could get the package, wish Claire a Merry Christmas, and be on her way, back on track, within an hour.

It was the ideal situation.

"I'll go," she announced. The expression on his face made her add hastily, "But only to put an end to this maniac mix-up."

The evening was warmer than it had been during the day, and Mike commented on the mild temperature.

"It'll snow soon, then," Abbey said. "Didn't you pay attention to Mr. Lloyd's science class in high school, when he talked about weather?"

"He talked about weather?" Mike laughed. "Oh, that was the class that Eileen Jamison was in. No wonder I don't know anything about weather. There was no way I could concentrate on anything when she was in the room. I had such a major crush on her. Then she married some football player, like the day after graduation. My teenaged heart was broken."

"I didn't know you and Eileen were a couple," Abbey said with some surprise. Eileen had been the class president, a cheerleader, and a soloist in the chorus. Mike had always been in the background of activities.

"We were a pair in my adolescent dreams only." Mike sighed dramatically. "I don't think she even knew I was alive. Well, maybe she did. Remember that showcase that had all those dusty old trophies dating back to the turn of the century—the nineteenth century, that is?"

Abbey nodded. "I don't remember seeing it after my junior year. Didn't they finally get rid of it?"

"They had some help. I was watching Eileen in the hall one day, being the googly-eyed lovesick teenaged boy that I was, and I wasn't watching where I was going. A staircase just appeared out of nowhere, and suddenly I was going head over heels down it. As if that weren't bad enough, as I started down the stairs, I grabbed her arm—why, I don't know—and she went with me. That showcase broke our fall. Or maybe I should just say that the showcase broke."

"What did she do?" Abbey asked, laughing over the image of them tumbling down the stairs together.

"She was very polite about it. She got up, helped me up since my long gangly legs were tied into a knot, or so it seemed, and asked me if I was okay. Then she grinned and said that she had never taken that particular set of stairs so quickly or so noticeably—and that once was quite enough. So if was all right with me, she'd be taking another set of stairs for awhile—and she was doing so without my help. And that was it."

"Didn't you just about die?"

"I asked my parents to move so I could go to another school. They said no. I thought maybe I could go live on a mountaintop like those hermits but realized I would have trouble finding a mountain in this part of Minnesota. One of the troubles with being a teenager is that your range of movement is limited. So I stayed on and lived with the utter humiliation."

They discussed the trials and tribulations of being a teenager until Mike pulled into the parking lot of Golden Meadows. True to Abbey's earlier prediction, thick white flakes had begun their lazy drift from the sky. Residents were lined up at the large glass windows watching the snowfall.

It was pretty, Abbey had to admit that. The air was quiet, free from sound, and the evergreen garlands and wreath were frosted with the new snow. For this one moment, away from the bustle of the holiday mall, she could almost like Christmas.

Mike took a deep breath. He needed to talk to Abbey about the other night and apologize for his clumsiness. Hopefully he could do it without taking a header on the parking lot of Golden Meadows.

Maybe he should wait until he was inside, he told himself ruefully. He seemed to have better luck staying upright when he was inside. But he knew that once he was inside, the residents wouldn't let him have a minute alone with Abbey. Toss in the fact that the retirement home was one of Abbey's least favorite places on earth, and he realized that this wasn't the place.

He'd try the parking lot, but he just wouldn't touch her arm when he talked to her. Maybe that would help him keep his equilibrium.

It would also help if he didn't try to kiss her, he reminded himself. There was nothing wrong with being head over heels in love, but not in an icy parking lot.

8

ike paused a moment before entering the oversized entrance of Golden Meadows. "I want you to know that—"
He wasn't able to finish the sentence. The door was flung open, and a crowd of elderly laughing women yelled, "Surprise!" One of them held a bough of something over his head, then stood on her tiptoes and kissed him soundly on the cheek.

"Marlys, do you have mistletoe?" he teased.

She blushed and nodded. "Yes, I do."

"Can I borrow it?" he asked with a wink.

Abbey's stomach twisted with anticipation and anxiety. Surely he wouldn't . . . surely he would.

Which did she want?

"Sweet's going to smooch his sugarplum," someone in the group crowed.

"That's right," he said, his eyes twinkling as he turned to look at Abbey.

Her heart and her mind waged war. She wanted him to take advantage of the mistletoe, and yet she didn't. For a moment, time held its breath.

Then he announced, his warm brown eyes twinkling, "The first kiss goes to my favorite girl."

All heads swiveled with one accord to look at Abbey. She knew she was blushing, but there wasn't a thing she could do but stand stock-still and wait for her fate.

Mike raised the mistletoe and turned to the woman who was watching from the corner. "Grandma, pucker up!"

Disappointment caught Abbey off-guard. Of all the emotions she might have expected, this was not one of them. What had she been thinking? That they'd share their first kiss in front of a group of senior citizens—when they hadn't even really dated yet?

And besides, it wasn't as if she cared about him one way or the other. He was simply a friend, a fellow retailer, and no more.

Nevertheless, the image in front of her blurred, and the carols that were piped into the great-room faded into the background. She blinked her eyes rapidly and willed her emotions back into line. This was just silly. He didn't matter to her, not at all.

Mike was bent over, talking to his grandmother, an attentive expression on his face, and she was reminded that he was a good, caring man. Then he stood up and walked away.

She realized that Claire was watching her, and she forced a smile. "Claire, it's good to see you again."

Claire reached out a gnarled hand. "How nice of you to come see me! At least, I'm assuming you've come to see me."

"Of course I'm here to visit you. Shall we go to your room to visit, or is there another place you'd rather go?"

"Let's go to the Fireside Lounge and sit beside the fire. There's a big picture window there, and we can watch the snow falling. Mike will be tied up for awhile finding that reprobate handyman to unplug my drain. Can you stay?"

"Not for long. This is my dinner break."

"Have you eaten?"

"Mike and I will stop on the way back."

Claire made a face. "Not that dreadful fast food stuff, I hope."

"I'm afraid so, but just for tonight. I think we'll live through it."

The Fireside Lounge looked different than it had before. The folding chairs that had been set up for the hymn sing had been taken down, and now small tables and comfortable chairs were scattered in conversational groups throughout the room.

Abbey helped Claire settle near the fire. It was a cozy setting, with upholstered wingback chairs positioned on either side of the native stone fireplace. A large picture window looked out on the rolling back lawn of the home, and in the starlight the pines that ringed the clearing enclosed the peaceful world.

"How are you doing, Claire?" Abbey asked, and she was amazed at how much she really did care.

"Pretty good. Oh, there are days when I'd like to complain, and maybe I do, but for the most part I'm doing well. How are things with you?" Claire's china blue eyes fixed on Abbey from behind the thick lenses of her eyeglasses.

"The store is doing well, but of course much of that right now is the Christmas trade. It'll drop off in January, after the returns are done, of course."

"Sweet says the same thing about his store." Claire leaned back contentedly. "I'd have never thought that a grown man could make a decent living selling toys, of all things, but that boy sure did prove me wrong."

"Especially this time of year," Abbey agreed. "I think everybody buys toys at Christmas."

"He's going to make a fine husband for some lucky woman," Claire said with studied casualness. "He'll be a good provider, he's not bad to look at, and he's a Christian, which counts for everything in this world."

Abbey could feel a flush rising up her neck. Had Claire seen her get flustered when Mike was fooling with the mistletoe? "He's a nice person," she said, noncommittally.

Those bright blue eyes sharpened behind the thick lenses. "He's the best, and I'm not just saying that because we're related so I have to. He really is. And it appears to me that he thinks highly of you."

Claire was clearly matchmaking. In her mind, she already had Abbey and Mike paired off, probably with 2.5 children in a house surrounded by a white picket fence and morning glories that bloomed in the morning sun. Abbey knew she had to put that idea to rest. And the best approach was the direct one.

"I'm going back to school to get my business degree," she said gently. "First my undergraduate degree in business, then my MBA. I can't do that here. I'll have to move."

Claire's lips curved a bit in a secret smile. "There are plans, and there are plans," she said enigmatically.

"My plans are real," Abbey said. "I have a ten-year strategy all worked out. I know exactly where I'll be and what I'll be doing."

Claire's smiled deepened. "The certainty of youth. Oh, I'm not going to argue with you," she said as Abbey started to interrupt. "It's always good to have a plan, but it's like the good book says: God has His own set of plans for us. Just when you think you've got it under control, God comes along and shouts, 'Surprise!' right into your heart."

"You speak like someone who's experienced that firsthand." Abbey knew that the best way to derail Claire was to change the focus of the conversation.

"God's given me many a surprise in these years He's had me on this planet. Some are good, and some . . . well, some weren't."

Claire paused, and Abbey watched the wave of memories wash over the elderly woman's face—twinges of pain mixed with uplifting joy.

"I've had a good life, you know—not that I'm writing the last chapter to it yet, don't get me wrong on that! But I'm happy with what the Lord has given me."

"Did you always feel that way?" Abbey asked. "I don't know how to ask this, but did you have a career outside the house?"

Claire patted Abbey's hand. "You're a dear. Yes, Honey, I was a teacher until I got married and had my children, then I took some time off. I went back for awhile after they grew up and started their own lives."

"Did you have a plan?"

Mike's grandmother laughed. "A plan? I don't think they'd been invented yet! But I did have an idea of what I wanted to do and why. It's not quite the same as the life plans people do now, but it worked at the time."

Abbey stirred uncomfortably. She lived so tightly by her ten-year plan that she couldn't imagine life without it. But apparently Claire had done fine without one as detailed as hers. On the other hand, Abbey told herself, life had been simpler for Claire. Her life couldn't have been as complicated as the one Abbey led.

"We didn't have money for much of anything," Claire reminisced, "but we had lots of love. You hear that all the time, and sometimes it seems like they're just so many words. But with us it was true."

"What was your husband like?" Abbey asked.

"My Arthur was a God-fearing man—although he used to insist that he was also a Claire-fearing man. We had good times together. Lean times, sorrowful times, stressful times—they were all made better by the fact that we had each other. Abbey, don't get so caught up in your career that you overlook the importance of having someone to love—and to love you," Claire implored her with earnestness.

"I'm not overlooking that," Abbey answered stiffly. "I'll get to it when I have time. I just don't have time right now."

"Make time. Don't build walls around your heart. Your career is important, but don't let it become a prison. You have your whole life ahead of you, and I'm serious when I tell you that it's a whole lot easier when you have someone to share the burdens and the joys with."

"Claire—"

"Don't interrupt your elders, Dear. I'm not through yet. Let yourself be open to love. Promise me you will."

"I will," Abbey said, but mentally she added, *In my dreams.* What Claire said had the flavor of truth, but it left a sour taste in her mouth.

"What are you ladies discussing so seriously?" Mike asked behind her.

"We're just talking about what to do with young men who sneak up and listen in on women's conversations," Claire said half-jokingly.

"I didn't hear a word," Mike said seriously, but the sparkle in his eyes made Abbey wonder if he was being completely honest. "Abbey, I don't want to hurry you, but we'd better get going."

"I'll go with you to the front," Claire said. "Mike, why don't you go ahead and start the car so it'll be at least a little bit warm for Abbey?"

Mike grinned at Abbey. "She's still trying to make me a gentleman. Okay, Grandma, I'll go." He dropped a kiss on her head. "I'll try to get over here tomorrow. Abbey, I'll pull up in front."

He left quickly, and Abbey and Claire proceeded at a more leisurely pace with Claire wheeling herself out of the room and down the corridor.

As they started down the hall back to the great-room, a gentleman leaning on a cane turned toward them. "Is that Sweet's lady friend?"

Abbey recognized him from her first visit to Golden Meadows. He had been her champion when Mike had lectured her about friendship. She looked at Claire and grinned. "Yup, she's right here, Sir. Claire's his grandmother."

He waved a hand twisted with arthritis. "That's not what I mean, and you know it, young woman. I mean you. Is that fellow treating you better or do I need to give him a piece of my mind?" He shook his cane. "I'd be glad to do it too. These young chaps have no sense of chivalry at all."

Claire grasped Abbey's arm. "Did Sweet treat you badly? What did he do?"

Laughter bubbled out of Abbey. These two darling senior citizens were ready to defend her honor, even at Mike's expense. It was utterly charming.

She leaned over and kissed Claire's furrowed forehead. "Don't worry. Mike has been a perfect gentleman."

Claire said something that sounded suspiciously like, "Rats!"

The busy evening left Mike few minutes of quiet to reflect upon the evening's events. His grandmother had called him out there on some obviously trumped-up excuse. She'd given him some line about the sink in her room being plugged up, but by the time he'd gotten ahold of the Golden Meadows handyman and they'd gone to her room, the clog had miraculously taken care of itself.

It was almost, he thought, as if she'd been maneuvering to get some time alone with Abbey. And considering how things had been going lately, that was probably exactly the reason she'd engineered the whole thing.

And there was only one reason for her to want to have time alone with Abbey.

He probably should tell her that her efforts were futile, that Abbey was the ultimate businesswoman, focused on her career only. Although, he mused, lately she had seemed to be friendlier. Perhaps his talk—no, his lecture—about friendship had gotten through to her. He still felt a bit guilty about how heavy-handed he'd been that day.

Nevertheless, she'd needed to hear every word of what he'd said. He knew what it was like to feel so tired that exhaustion swirled through your body like a living thing. He'd been there himself, and he had to admit, there were times when he still overworked himself.

But friendship was the glue that held humanity together. Abbey needed a friend, and he was willing to be that friend. Just a friend, he told himself for the thousandth time that night. That was all. A friend.

He had the same uneasy feeling he used to get when, as a child, he tried to lie to his parents.

His mind leaped back to the moment with the mistletoe. He'd truly wanted to hold it over her head, but he knew he didn't dare. Friends didn't kiss under the mistletoe, the contrary voice in his head pointed out to him. And even if he had tried, she probably would have decked him on the spot.

But hadn't he, maybe, seen hope spring into her eyes like a flash of light?

9

*T*don't have time to do it," Abbey said, staring at Mike as if he'd lost his mind. "You know perfectly well that I'm working eighty hours a week. And now you want me to do something like this? And in three days?"

He was out of his mind. That was the only reasonable explanation. He'd taken total leave of his senses. Asking her to give a presentation on career guidance, and during the busiest time of the year at Trends!

"It'd be fun," he countered. "A nice change of pace."

"Sleep would be a nice change of pace. Mike, really, I'm sure—"

"You'd reach so many lives," he interrupted. "The Jeremiah Group is a great program. We got the name from the Bible verse, Jeremiah 29:11–14."

When she didn't respond, he prompted, "The one where God says that He has plans for us."

"I'm familiar with the verse," Abbey answered, with a mental addendum: *Sort of.*

"The Jeremiah Group is made up of young women who need to hear what you have to say."

"Oh, yeah, right." She snorted. "I don't know anything special. What do I have to talk to them about?"

"A lot. They don't have guidance from the outside, so I know they'd be interested in how you decided to go into retail, and how this job you have now is a steppingstone to your career goals."

"Mike, it's Christmas. You know what that means. We never have a minute to ourselves." She motioned around the interior of Trends and realized, too late, that they were the only ones in there. "Okay, so at this particular moment no one else is here. Come back in an hour or so. Then this place will be jumping with shoppers."

He didn't say anything, and she added defensively, "It's not like I could simply show up and give a talk. I'd need time to prepare. Three days isn't enough lead-time. What happened to whoever was supposed to talk to them originally?"

"She went into labor."

"Some people will do anything to get out of a commitment, won't they?" Abbey said wryly. "I'm sorry. I just can't. Not now. Maybe next spring." She turned to refolding a table display of brightly striped sweaters.

"If you don't do it, the meeting will have to be cancelled."

"So? They probably have better things to do . . . like Christmas shopping." She smiled at him, but he didn't return her smile.

"Abbey," he said seriously, "these girls don't have money to shop with. That's the point of the whole thing. It's a career guidance group."

She couldn't do it, she reasoned. She kept coming back to the one irrefutable fact: She didn't have time. When would she squeeze something like this into her already overpacked day?

And besides that, she had no expertise when it came to guiding young women, especially those who were considered at risk. What would she say to them? She'd never addressed a group at all, let alone a selection of teenagers who were bound to be a reluctant and captive audience.

She knew how it would go. She'd bumble her way through, and they'd laugh at her. Maybe openly, but most certainly behind her back.

Actually, that was a best-case scenario. What if she said something terribly wrong . . . and messed up someone's life?

No, it was too much to ask of her. She couldn't do it.

"Plus I don't go to your church." She clutched at that straw. "I couldn't talk about religion. All I know about religion is what I got from Aunt Luellen, and loopy as she is, I wouldn't be surprised if she didn't mix up Jeremiah with Niemeier."

"Nehemiah. That doesn't matter. We'll do that part. All you have to do is come in, tell the girls a bit about how you decided what you wanted to do for a living, and talk to them about goal-setting and career-planning."

"That's all, huh?"

"Yup." He smiled at her winningly.

"How long would I have to be there?"

"An hour, hour and a half tops."

An hour? It loomed like a lifetime. She couldn't do it. She wouldn't do it. But her traitorous mouth opened, and she heard herself saying, "All right. I'll do it. Let's hope they're not expecting too much."

"You'll be great!" Mike said with enthusiasm. "I'll talk to you more about it tomorrow and see how you're doing, okay?"

"Okay." Abbey was sure she was making a monstrous mistake, but it couldn't be that bad, could it?

Mike turned at the entrance to Trends. "Oh, one more thing, Abbey."

"What's that?"

"Don't quote from the book of Niemeier."

Abbey laid out her presentation as she worked. While she was arranging a shimmering display of vests, she organized her biography. As she positioned another rack of evening gowns in an impossibly tight corner, she prepared the steps of effective goal-setting. She shifted sale purses to a table near the front of the store while she created questions sure to provoke vital and intelligent discussion.

As she drove home, she thought of the young women. She would have benefited from such a group, she knew that. Whether she would have listened when she was that age was another matter entirely. Well, all she could do was go and share what she had, and if something took root in even one girl's mind, it was a good thing.

For the first time in months, Abbey felt really good. She was energized. She was excited. She tried to ignore the fact that she was undoubtedly nuts.

Mike picked her up at Trends an hour before the Jeremiah Group was to meet. "You look nice," he commented. "I meant to tell you not to wear a suit, so what you have on is perfect."

This was the seventh outfit she'd put on. Her bed was piled with discarded dresses, slacks, and skirts. She'd finally chosen a long denim skirt and fleece vest with a turtleneck. She hoped she exuded a sense of confidence she didn't truly feel.

"Thank you," she said.

There. She was in trouble. If her voice was going to waver and wobble like that, and she hadn't even left her store, she could only imagine what a nightmare her presentation was going to be.

Mike put his hand on her arm. "Abbey, these are girls who are starting from ground zero. Some of them may even be below that. Don't be afraid of them."

"I'm not afraid of them," she said defensively, lifting her chin just a bit. "What I'm scared of is myself. What if I blow it?"

"You'll be fine."

"I hope you're right." Abbey's hands were sweating as she pulled on her yellow mittens. Their bright wool reflected a cheerfulness she didn't feel.

Mike talked about everything except the presentation as they drove to his church, Word of Faith Community Church. She'd seen it before, but she'd never gone in. It was a simple pale brown brick building with a white-painted steeple and cross.

Every muscle in her body urged her to turn back as she and Mike entered the building. But the window of opportunity closed quickly, and she was soon enveloped with warm greetings of others who were waiting inside.

"It's so nice of you to do this," one woman said. "I have everything ready for you, even a laptop and a projector."

The woman took Abbey's coat and introduced herself as Mrs. Robbins. "I'm one of the counselors for the Jeremiah Group," she explained. "There are many people involved with the program. Mike, for example, coordinates the speakers. My specialty is helping the young women with filling out job applications and going to interviews."

"It sounds interesting," Abbey commented, realizing it was a bland statement that didn't really focus in on what Mrs. Robbins was saying.

"The girls in this group—and they are rather young this time—

need this kind of assistance. Whatever we can offer them is beneficial. In some cases, their parents don't work, or they rely on seasonal or part-time employment. Two of them have been shuttled around in foster homes so much that they don't have a clear picture of what a career even is. That's why what you're saying to them today is so important."

Mrs. Robbins motioned to a nearby room. A green and gold plaid curtain hid the interior from view, but from the way the drape moved a bit, Abbey knew she was being observed. She was only faintly aware of the curious gazes studying her covertly. She was using all her energies to keep from passing out from stage fright.

Mrs. Robbins saw Abbey's glance and smiled. "They'll be very distant, almost detached, but don't let that bother you. That's their defense against a world that often makes them into outsiders. Being aloof is their way of turning the tables."

Abbey could understand that. She had been through a rebellious stage herself, although what she'd been rebelling against was still a mystery to her. It was probably just teenaged angst.

"Shall we go in?" Mrs. Robbins asked, leading her toward the curtained room. Abbey was sure that mortal embarrassment waited for her.

They had done all that they could to fill the requests she made and to make her feel welcome, and with fearful feet she went in to meet the Jeremiah Group.

A flurry of activity greeted their entrance as the young women scurried away from the window that looked out on the narthex. They made a great show of not being at all interested in the guest as they gathered in the far corner and talked lazily to each other.

"Don't let them deter you," Mrs. Robbins whispered. "They're dying to meet you."

I'm the one who's dying, Abbey thought. This was the modern day equivalent of being thrown to the lions. Didn't that happen in the Bible? She remembered seeing a vivid picture in her children's Bible of a man sitting amidst a group of ferocious lions.

Scrap that. Insert a picture of a completely terrified store manager surrounded by a small group of bored young women. Truly a horrific scenario.

She looked at her tormentors. There were fourteen of them in attendance that day, most of them in their mid to late teens. Some viewed her with hostility, some with smiles, some with suspicion.

Her mouth was suddenly very dry, and the first words she had formulated to speak wouldn't come out at all. The teens watched her with increasing interest, inquisitiveness edging into their expressions as she continued to stand in front of them, mute.

It was just as she had feared. It was like one of those dreams she used to have in which she was addressing Congress in her pajamas, the fuzzy white ones with the chickens printed in bright yellow. The women's faces faded in and out again, and for a moment she thought she was going to be sick. That might not be such a bad thing, she reflected, because then she could leave.

She turned pleadingly at last to Mike. He'd have to take over and save her.

Sure enough, Mike stepped into the breach. He introduced her, then said, "Let's open in prayer. Blessed Father, guide Abbey's words as she speaks to the members of this group. Guide our ears that we might learn from her. And guide our feet as we go forth with today's message. Amen."

Abbey shot him a look of surprise. "That was short," she whispered.

"Cool, huh?" Mike grinned at her and turned his attention back to the assemblage. One woman chewed on the edge of her fingernail while another curled a lock of her hair around her finger. They could not have looked less interested.

Yet Mike persisted. "You all know that this group got its name from Jeremiah 29:11-14, right? God has plans for you, but there's absolutely nothing wrong with helping Him along and making the most of the talents He gave you. That's what Abbey is here to talk to you about—maximizing your time and your talents. Let's welcome her."

Some lackluster applause accompanied Abbey as she faced the group again. She knew her first instincts had been right. She shouldn't be here. What on earth had she been thinking of? What kind of insanity had overtaken her when she agreed to do it?

I need some help here. If there was ever a good time for prayer, this was it.

The sea of faces swam into focus. One by one, she looked directly at each young woman and saw them as individuals, not a homogenous group of blasé girls. Their eyes met hers, and in that moment of contact, each teenager let Abbey see past the artifice. She saw the fear of rejection behind the bravado, the hurt behind the mask of boredom.

The words she had so carefully prepared vanished from her mind, and suddenly they were replaced by words from her heart. The group quit shifting in their seats and focused their attention on her. The young women watched her, transfixed, and her speech gained power. She talked about finding her talent and making the most of it, and the satisfaction of knowing that she was doing what she was meant to do, and doing it well.

The teenagers rarely looked away as she talked. And finally, she realized she was through. Her energy reservoirs were totally depleted, and she felt as limp as cooked spaghetti.

Mike stood and shook her hand. "That was wonderful. Thank you so much for coming today and sharing your expertise with us. Abbey will stay for a few minutes if you want to talk to her some more. I'm sure she won't mind answering any extra questions you might have."

There was a moment of silence before the worldly cloaks fell back over their eyes and they retreated to their façade of coolness. Yet as soon as Mike left the podium and the session was clearly over, in one wave of movement, the young women stood and came forward to surround Abbey.

Mike sighed with relief. Abbey had done extremely well to get this kind of reaction from them. He offered up a quick prayer of thanksgiving for the success of her talk. Not only did the girls need it, he sensed, but Abbey did too.

Finally the last teenager drifted away, and Mike moved over to where she was standing. "You must have been quite the success," he said. "These girls may be anywhere from fourteen to eighteen in chronological age, but in street years, they're much older. They're usually so blasé that we're lucky they're not doing their nails during the presentation. And you were worried!"

To his amazement, she sat down and put her head in her hands. "What's the matter?" he asked.

"Are you ready for this? They all had the same question." Abbey shook her head in amazement, but she didn't look up.

"Really? What was it? Did they want details on how to find career counseling or something like that?"

"No." Her shoulders began to shake.

Mike ran his fingers through his hair. Why was she crying? He never knew what to do when adults cried.

"Did they have educational concerns, like where to find a school?"

"Not exactly."

"They were intrigued by a career in retail?"

"Um, sort of," she hedged. She raised her eyes, and he realized that she had not been crying. She was laughing. "They wanted to know where I got my vest."

They looked at each other, and together they howled with laughter. It was getting to be a habit with them, this roaring into uncontrollable laughter over the most inane things. But it was a nice habit.

"It's so absurd," Abbey said at last. "All of that emotion, that worry, that preparation, and all they wanted to know is where I got my stupid vest."

"It's good advertising for Trends," Mike said.

"No, it isn't." Abbey couldn't avoid the absurdity of the situation. "I got it at the discount store at the other mall about four years ago. I had no idea what to tell them, so I just said I'd had it for ages."

"Do you feel bad that you put so much work into the presentation only to have it turn out this way?" Mike asked gently.

It was a legitimate question, and Abbey's response was a bit surprising to her. "I've got to admit it would have been a lot simpler if I could have had them come over to my house and go through my closet, if that's what you mean. But yes, it's a bit distressing. All that planning, only to find out I'd been preparing for the wrong thing. Go figure."

"You know," Mike said, standing and reaching for their coats, "the verse in Jeremiah applies to you too. We don't know what God's plans are for us. We can only trust that He won't do anything too rash to set things in motion. Maybe one of these teenagers has had her life changed today by that woman in the dynamite vest. It could be that's why you wore it today."

She remembered the many changes of clothes before she'd decided on this particular outfit, how often she'd tossed aside an outfit simply because it didn't "feel right." Could he be onto something? She'd heard that there were no true accidents.

Mike continued as they left the little church, "And who knows, you may very well have touched someone's heart here today in a way you can't know."

She'd touched a heart, all right, he acknowledged, *but God, did it have to be mine?*

10

*A*bbey was still chuckling over the incident the next day. She was telling Selma about it when suddenly a man dressed in a Keystone Kops outfit, complete with a rounded helmet and a billy club, invaded her store.

"Officer Oliver P. Torkelson here. I have a warrant for Abbey Jensen," he said loudly. "I've come to arrest you!" His handlebar moustache tilted forward dangerously, and he shoved it back into place.

"What on earth?" Abbey asked. She'd never seen anything like this. "You must have the wrong place, or at least the wrong person."

"You're under arrest, young lady. The charge is—wait a second, let me check." He pulled a folded sheet of paper from his shirt pocket with great ceremony and proceeded to read: "Abbey Jensen is hereby placed under arrest for being a Holiday Hooligan."

"A Holiday Hooligan? What is that? This is crazy!"

"Got the warrant right here. All written out proper-like. You'd better come with me."

"I'm not coming with you," Abbey protested. "I have no idea what this is all about."

"Sorry, Ma'am." Torkelson produced gigantic red plastic handcuffs. "Resisting arrest means I'll have to use these."

A strangled sound from behind her made Abbey turn her head. Selma was overcome with giggles. "Do you know anything about this?" Abbey asked her employee warily. "You do, don't you?"

Selma shook her head wordlessly.

"Mike. Mike had something to do with it," Abbey accused. "And from that grin on your face, you do too know what's going on."

Officer Torkelson cleared his throat loudly. "Enough chitchat. You'd better come with me to the Candy Cane Calaboose."

"The Candy Cane Calaboose?" Abbey repeated. "What is that?"

The policeman tsked and wrote something on the warrant. "I'm going to have to add Failure to Read Merry Mall Mail to the complaint."

"Merry Mall Mail?" Abbey couldn't believe her ears. "I've never heard of such a thing."

"That's because you never read your Merry Mall Mail," Officer Torkelson said logically. "If you'd have read it, you'd know what it was."

Abbey covered her face with her hands. "This is unreal. I never heard of Merry Mall Mail. I don't know what the Candy Cane Calabash is."

"Calaboose," Selma corrected. "A calaboose is a jail. A calabash is a gourd."

"Calabash, calaboose. This is insane."

Officer Torkelson stroked his moustache reflectively. "Trying to cop an insanity plea, eh? Are you insane? Do I need to get a straightjacket?"

"No, I'm not insane. They're insane, whoever 'they' are. And I certainly don't need a straightjacket." She paused as she realized what was transpiring. "Oh, for crying out loud. This is what the other managers were talking about down at the mailboxes, isn't it? Please tell me this isn't the brainchild of the mall management."

The policeman's moustache twitched dangerously.

She knew she had no choice except to go. Selma would watch the store, and besides, it would probably be just a few minutes. Even the mall administration wouldn't be as silly as to take people off the selling floor during the busiest season of the year for any extended period of time.

"This won't take long," she told Selma grimly as she left in the custody of Officer Torkelson. "And if it gets busy, call the mall office. This is their idea, so they might as well reap the results of it."

She'd walked by the Candy Cane Calaboose, but she hadn't paid much attention to it other than to note that it was another way of making use of every inch of the mall's space. The wooden structure was clearly modeled after an old-fashioned jail but with one crucial exception: the bars on the cells were painted in red and white spirals.

"Here, put this on." A woman dressed in a skirt and blouse printed with tiny candy canes handed her a bundle. "These are your jail coveralls."

Abbey shook them out. They were striped, like the prisoner outfits of the old movies, but instead of black and white, these were red and white, like candy canes.

"I can't put these on," Abbey objected. "I'm wearing a skirt, in case you hadn't noticed."

"Just pull them on top," the woman instructed her. "By the way, I'm the warden here, so don't get snippy with me." She shook the large key that hung around her neck, which was apparently used with the oversized heart-shaped lock on the cell door. The twinkle in her eyes softened her words, and she added in a whisper, "It could have been a lot worse. They started out with this being a dunking tank, so count your blessings."

Abbey shuddered at the thought of what havoc that idea would have wrought. "The mall management has had some nutso ideas," she muttered as she pulled the coveralls over her clothes, "but this takes the cake."

Her skirt bunched up around her hips under the coverall, and she was sure she looked as if she had the world's biggest caboose. The Candy Cane Caboose, she told herself.

"Did you see that you have company?" the woman added, pointing to a second chair in the cell.

Abbey had almost missed him, but how, she couldn't have said. Mike was also garbed in the candy-striped coverall.

"You look ridiculous," she said, plopping into the vacant chair. "Kind of like an oversized after-dinner mint."

"They don't call me Sweet for nothing," he quipped.

"Fill me in on this, please," she said. "Apparently I didn't read my Merry Mall Mail—whatever that is—but I have no idea who ratted on me. And I was certainly never aware that it was an offense that was going to get me arrested."

He chuckled. "Here's the scoop. Anybody at the mall—employees, customers, competitors, whatever—can pay to have you put in the slammer, er, calaboose. And there you stay until someone bails you out. All the money goes to charity."

"A noble goal," she grumbled. "So what you're saying is that somebody, some rat fink, paid to have me put here?" She glowered at him suspiciously.

"First of all, I don't believe I've heard someone actually say 'rat fink' in the past decade, and secondly, don't glare at me. I thought you were responsible for me being here, but since you are clueless about this whole Candy Cane Calaboose thing, I guess I have to blame one of my employees."

She recalled Selma's bout with hysterics when Abbey was "arrested." "I think I know who the culprit is . . . at least for me being stuck in here. Selma."

A sudden thought struck her. Selma was a one-person fan club for romance; it wouldn't be too hard to imagine her putting both Abbey and Mike in the Candy Cane Calaboose at the same time.

Mike leaned back and hummed along with the public address system, which boomed non-stop Christmas carols at top volume. Abbey craned her neck and noticed that they were positioned directly under a circular speaker embedded in the wall.

"I used to love those songs," she mused. "But somewhere around November tenth, they lost their appeal."

"You're kidding!" Mike seemed genuinely surprised. "I love the whole Christmas scene. Carols, trees, presents, the whole nine yards."

Abbey motioned at the mall outside their cell. "But look at this. 'Gaudy' doesn't even begin to describe it. They've added another scene. A purple plaster seal wearing a wreath around its neck. Isn't that charming?"

"The seal is inexplicable. I don't know what that's doing here." Mike cocked his head and studied the statue. "No, I can't say as I see any reason for it to be here. It's ludicrous at best."

"Well, that's my point. What does it have to do with Christmas?"

He leaned forward earnestly. "That isn't Christmas. That's profit margins, pure and simple—if there is anything pure or simple about profit margins. The seal has more to do with the mall manager and his exquisite artistic taste than the future of a major world religion. Christmas is about the birth of hope. It's the first day of our salvation."

"You sound like my aunt Luellen." The conversation made Abbey uneasy, but at the same time she craved talking about her confused feelings. And oddly, having this discussion about Jesus in the midst of this crazy Candy Cane Calaboose made it easier.

"Your aunt Luellen is pretty smart."

"My aunt Luellen is a kook. She's the reason we're even having this talk. If it weren't for her getting those packages mixed up, we'd still be going on with our lives . . . separately. And I wouldn't even be thinking about Jesus or God or anything except my own profit margins."

"Like I said," Mike said, so softly she had to crane to hear his words, "your aunt Luellen is a very smart person."

Abbey snorted in derision. "How can you say that? That would mean that Aunt Luellen would have done this . . . on purpose," she ended slowly as the realization of what he was saying dawned on her.

There comes a moment in love when time stands still—or wishes it could. And just as frequently, that instant is pushed away in the flurry of life.

She liked him, she told herself. That was all. He was a nice guy. Okay, he was a nice guy with very nice eyes and a very nice smile and a very nice way of approaching life. But she didn't love him. Love meant—well, she couldn't define it, not here in a makeshift jail in the midst of a busy mall filled with curious shoppers. She'd have to think about it. But the fact was that she was pretty sure she'd know if she was in love. At least there would be—or should be—fireworks and volcanoes and shooting stars. She didn't feel any of that when she saw Mike. What she felt was a pleasant warmth, like the good basic meal they had at Ginger's the other night. Nothing fancy. Plain home cooking didn't equal love.

The food analogy made her hungry.

She looked at him covertly. He was a bit pinker than usual. Was it possible? Was Mike Tucker blushing? Or was it only the reflection of his candy-striped jail coveralls?

She had to change the subject, and fast. "I wonder if they feed us in this Candy Cane Calaboose," she said. "I'm starving."

Mike seemed as equally grateful for the switch in the direction their conversation was taking. "Even a candy cane would be welcome. I think that woman who's supposed to be our warden probably has some. Want me to get one for you?"

Abbey shook her head. "I don't know if I'll ever be able to look a candy cane in the eye again."

Mike hooted with laughter. "I didn't know candy canes had eyes, but I get your point."

"How can you be so cheerful about this shenanigan?" she asked crossly, but before he could answer, a voice hailed them from the mall corridor.

"Yoo-hoo, Candy Cane captives!" Selma was approaching them, and obviously enjoying their predicament entirely too much. "Ready to get out?" She waved a ten-dollar bill at them.

"Am I ever!" Abbey stood up. "Pay my bail, and let's go. Say, if you're here, who's watching the store?"

"I closed it."

"You what?" Abbey thundered.

"Oh, I'm just kidding. Brianna came in." Selma walked around and studied the jail from the outside. "This isn't too bad. I've lived in worse places."

Mike grinned. "It's about the size of my apartment, now that you mention it. Are you springing both of us, or just Abbey?"

"Both of you. You two ready to go?"

As Abbey sprang to her feet, Mike touched her arm. "It hasn't been that bad, has it?"

The sharp retort that sprang to her lips died, and the truth—in a single word—replaced it. "No."

That evening, as Mike said his nightly prayers, he asked for reassurance. It wasn't something he often did, usually choosing instead to trust in his Father's leadership.

I'm trying, Lord. Every time I think I've taken a step closer, though, she steps back. This would be a lot easier if she'd just stay still. Am I doing this right? And, by the way, God, am I supposed to be falling in love with her?

And across town, a young woman found herself in an unusual position, her head bent and her heart open. "Tell me what to do about the way I feel," she said quietly, although who she was speaking to, she couldn't have said.

11

bbey leaped out of bed, horrified at the bright light that shone in through her window. Clearly she had overslept. A quick glance at the clock beside her bed verified it. It was nearly eight. She pulled back the curtain and peeked outside. Already the first round of rush hour was underway, with the late-to-work drivers stretching the speed limit.

Usually she was up early, quick to get ready for her busy day and always the first one at the mall. What was happening to her? She hadn't overslept in a couple of years. Crazy dreams had haunted her sleep, dreams filled with dancing candy canes and prisons made of sweets.

And Mike. He'd been in all of her dreams, all night long.

Once when she was in high school, studying French, her teacher had told her that when she dreamed in French, she could be assured that she had total command of the language, that she totally understood it. What did that mean when she dreamed about Mike?

She'd never dreamed in French anyway, she told herself as she slurped down a gulp of too-hot coffee, so she'd never had the chance to test the hypothesis. She needed to wake up and quit worrying about such inane stuff.

Customers were already browsing through the sales racks as she slipped into her spot behind the cash register at Trends.

Selma glanced at her curiously. "Oversleep?"

Abbey nodded. "I couldn't believe it myself." She busied herself with rearranging the display of glittery necklaces and earrings. "I guess there's something about winter that makes me want to hibernate."

Her associate snorted inelegantly. "There's something about working sixteen-hour days that makes you want to hibernate." Selma put her hand over Abbey's and stilled her active fingers. "Quit dinking around with that stuff and look at me. You need to take a break. You're working too hard and too long—"

"It's Christmas," Abbey replied, as if that explained it all.

"So go have a Christmas. Even a couple of hours. Go shopping. Drive around and look at the lights. Sit at home and watch that Christmas special with Charlie Brown and Snoopy."

As Selma spoke, Abbey felt a hunger rise in her, almost palpably. She wanted to shop, to look at lights, to watch Charlie Brown with his pitiful little tree.

She nodded. "I will. I promise. Tonight I'll take a break."

Selma looked at her with unsure eyes. "You'd better. A promise is a promise, and I'm holding you to it. You're missing the best part of Christmas, hanging out inside this mall day in and day out."

"Okay, okay, you've made your point!" Abbey cried with exasperation. "I'll do it, I promise!"

"It's four o'clock," Selma said pointedly when the afternoon rush had tapered off.

"I know. Did you want a break?" Abbey began sizing the sale blouses.

"Yes, I do, but not for me. For you. You promised."

"And I will." Abbey stooped to pick up a blouse whose hanger had broken. "Selma, can you get another hanger for this?"

"I'm going to keep after you until you go," Selma warned. "Brianna will be here in less than an hour, and then you have no excuses, M'lady."

"But who—"

"I don't know because I'm not going to listen to your question so I can't answer it. But you are going to go. How do I know? Because I can be the world's biggest pain in the neck when I need to."

Abbey grumbled under her breath.

"I heard that," Selma snapped. "I'm not sure what you said, but I can't think it was nice. Now go."

"All right." Abbey gave in grudgingly. "But first I'm off to grab a bite to eat. I'm just running down to that pretzel place, then I'll be back to do those markdowns."

Selma barred her way. "You will not. You promised me you were going to take the evening off, and I'm holding you to it. Brianna will be in to cover tonight, and there's that high school student backing her up. The store will be fine tonight. Go get some R & R."

Abbey couldn't summon the strength to argue. "You win. I'll be back tomorrow morning."

"Good. Now, at the very least, I want you to promise me you'll get in your jammies with some popcorn and veg out in front of the tube. Either the Peanuts special or *It's a Wonderful Life*." Selma almost pushed her into her coat.

"They might not be on tonight," Abbey protested lightly.

"Ha. It's December. They'll be on." Selma's laughter followed Abbey as she left the store.

Mike smiled as he stopped at the door to Trends. He'd come to see if Abbey wanted to go back to Golden Meadows, but Selma's voice had stopped him. He was glad he hadn't barged on in.

Abbey didn't even see him as she swept out with her coat on. That was good. She needed to get away for awhile, and it didn't matter where she was going: home, grocery store, Laundromat. Just as long as she wasn't living her life here in the mall.

He'd seen the little lines that were beginning to etch themselves around her eyes. She was far too young for that hard-worn look. Exhaustion radiated from her like an aura. Abbey clearly needed someone to make her leave the mall once in awhile, someone to insist that she take some time to herself.

That's why he wanted her to go with him to Golden Meadows. That's why he was going to ask her to go to dinner with him tomorrow night. She was a child of the heavenly Father, and she deserved time to relax. That's why he was taking her away.

And it had nothing, nothing at all to do with the way her gray eyes made him feel suddenly warm and protective.

* * *

Her car sputtered and bucked. Abbey's eyes darted to the dial on the dashboard. Gas. She'd forgotten gas.

Luckily the station by the mall was open, and she basically coasted into the bay.

"Fill 'er up?" the attendant asked.

"Oh, no, I can—" she stammered in confusion. Then she realized she had driven into the full-service bay. A slow smile crossed her face. "No, go ahead. Fill it up."

It felt nice to let someone do this simple task for her. She leaned against the headrest and felt the tension try to leave her body. And she felt the resistance of habit. Go. Do. Get busy.

They were hard habits to let go of.

"Don't forget to plug in tonight."

The voice of the station attendant startled her. "What?"

"Plug in tonight. Supposed to be eighteen below." He clasped his hands together and rubbed them briskly. "Already twelve below."

She thanked him for the reminder. Minnesota winter evenings were sometimes so cold that cars needed block heaters so they'd start in the morning. Born and bred Minnesotan, Abbey thought briefly that any car without the plug hanging out of the front grillwork looked odd.

She paid for her gas and headed home. Popcorn and a television movie did sound heavenly. If she tried really hard, she might be able to get into this relaxing stuff.

But success isn't measured by how much you're relaxed, a nasty little voice whined inside her head. *It's measured by how much you've achieved, and you're not going to achieve anything by lolling around the house.*

One night, she told herself, *just this one night*. It was an experiment to see what it was like.

The wind whistled around her ears as she dug the plug-in out of the snow bank. The fellow at the gas station was right: it was already cold enough tonight to plug in her car. She hurried through the task and was glad to get inside to the warmth of her small house.

One of these days she'd actually do something to decorate the inside. The house was still painted the same bland off-white it had been when she'd bought it. The furniture was, to put it bluntly, practical, and that was all. It was the same couch, chair, bed, and table that she'd had when she was in college.

But before she committed herself to anything, she would think about what kind of furniture she wanted. And that took time. She didn't have time.

She shed her suit and wrapped a thick terrycloth robe around her. Popcorn, then the television.

Abbey pulled open first one cabinet, then another. They seemed to gape at her. Where was the popcorn? Didn't she just buy some? She shook her head as she realized that she had last bought popcorn nearly a year ago.

"Okay, no popcorn." She shut the last cabinet door, perhaps a little harder than necessary, and opened the freezer. It was well-stocked with frozen dinners. "And this, my friends," she intoned to an imaginary group of visitors, "is what the larder of the busy career woman is like. Cabinets are empty while the freezer is stocked."

She'd make a list, she decided, and put everything she needed on it. She returned to the bare cupboard shelves. It was amazing how empty, how totally empty her shelves were.

"Okay," she continued aloud, "first item: everything."

She microwaved a macaroni and cheese dinner, figuring that was as close to popcorn as she was going to get, and sat down in front of the television with the remote control.

Click.

The screen lit up with fuzzy static. She tried another channel. It was no better. And on through all the channels, still no picture.

"Stupid cable company," she muttered, getting up to shuffle to the phone and call them.

Abbey punched in the numbers with a vengeance. "Hello, this is Abbey Jensen. My cable isn't working."

She gave them the pertinent information, then paused, aghast, at what she heard. "I haven't had cable since when? No, I guess I haven't turned on my television since then. Oh, no, no need to come out. No, I don't want the service started again. Thanks, though."

She hung up the phone and stood motionless, staring at the mute television screen.

She hadn't had cable in five months. She'd been disconnected when she hadn't responded to a switch in service. And she'd never realized it.

Abbey sank to the kitchen chair beside her. She didn't know she was out of popcorn, and she didn't even know she didn't have cable TV. Could it be worse?

How had her life gotten so far away from her? No wonder she spent so much time at Trends. She didn't have a life at all.

That wasn't true, she argued with herself. She had a VCR, and she could rent a movie and watch it. The more she thought about it, the better the idea sounded. There was a video store just around the corner. Actually, she could even walk there.

She quickly changed from her robe to a pair of woolen pants and her thickest sweater and piled on a coat, boots, mittens, and hat. She stuck her Video Video card in her pocket and headed out.

The crisp air froze the inside of her nostrils. That, she told herself as she strode enthusiastically through the December night, was one of the best things about living in the north. Where else could you experience that?

The cloudless sky sparkled with a few random stars that were powerful enough to overcome the lights of the city. Abbey stood still and tried to pick out Orion's belt and the Big Dipper.

A sudden memory shot into her mind, like a long-forgotten message. She had been tiny, two or three perhaps, and on such a winter night as this, her parents had bundled her up and driven her out of town, far away from the streetlamps and house lights, to the absolute darkness of the countryside where her father pulled the car over.

Abbey could still remember the rush of cold air invading the heated car as they took her out. And there, as her mother held her, still wrapped in too many layers of quilts, her father pointed out the constellations in a sky that seemed to have too many stars.

"This is Cassiopeia. See her throne? Orion the Hunter: that's his belt, those three stars in a row. The Pleiades, the Seven Sisters. The

North Star is at the end of the Big Dipper's handle. Sailors used it to navigate by, and it's still the first star our eyes see in the heavens."

On and on he talked, naming the magical constellations, most of which her young eyes could not take in, but even now she remembered her mother's warm breath on her cold cheek and her father's calming voice. She was cocooned in their love.

She missed them.

A tear threatened to slide down her face but began to freeze. Abbey swiped at it with her gloved hand. There was no time for this foolishness. And it would never do to step into Video Video teary.

The video rental store was so bright her eyes hurt after being in the dark night. A teenager, so tall and thin that his long-sleeved Video Video shirt could cover only part of his arms, approached her. "Can I help you find something?"

Abbey sniffled. The problem with that marvelous feeling of breathing in icy air is that when she got into a warm room, her nose began to run. "Yes. I'm looking for *It's a Wonderful Life.*"

"Right here." The boy stretched one long arm and snagged a video from the Christmas display at the register. "Can I see your card?"

She pulled the card from her pocket and handed it to him. The clerk frowned. "This expired three years ago."

"You're kidding me!" Abbey snatched it from his hand with more gusto than she intended. "How can that be? Why, I just—" She sighed. It had been that long. "Fine. I'll get a new one."

"Okay. I need a picture ID." The teenager handed her a clipboard with a pencil dangling from a grimy string.

"ID?" she asked blankly. "I don't have my ID with me. Can't you just reactivate my old card?"

"Not after three years. Sorry, but it's—"

"Company policy," she finished for him. "I know, I know."

"You know, you could buy it for only $4 more. There's a special right now, it being Christmas and all."

"Oh, I don't need to—" she began, then stopped. *Four dollars,* she told herself. *Four dollars. Bend, Abbey. Bend and breathe.*

"That sounds like a deal," she said brightly.

What's wrong with me? she asked herself as she hurried home, the video tucked under arm. She'd forgotten the present at Golden Meadows, she'd neglected to put gas in her car, she was out of popcorn and just about everything else to eat, her cable TV bill wasn't paid, and now her video card had expired.

What else could happen?

She stared at the VCR. A tangle of cords emerged from the back of it, and somehow they were supposed to be hooked up to her television and who knew what else. Abbey sank to the floor and put her head in her hands as she remembered. She'd bought it, and as she was trying to put it together, she had been called back to Trends.

And she'd never gotten back to finishing it.

Well, she told herself, *it can't be brain surgery.* She bravely took a cord and studied the back of the television. There was no place that it fit. She checked the other end of the cord. Nope.

If she had the directions, she could figure this out. But she had no idea where they might be.

Call Mike. She knew she could do that. He undoubtedly knew how to put one of these monstrosities together, just like he probably put gas in his car, paid his bills, stocked his cupboards, and never let his memberships lapse.

Or, she told herself, she could do it herself. Not that she had any idea how to do it, but she could certainly sit down and give it a shot.

Surrounded by mysterious wires and cords, the VCR on her lap and her television turned out so that the back faced the living room, she put it together. It would have been easier with the directions, but it was possible.

Soon, *It's a Wonderful Life*—her own copy—was playing as she curled on the couch, snuggly wrapped in pajamas and robe, a bowl of freshly popped popcorn—purchased at the video store—in her lap. But Abbey was completely unaware of George Bailey's plight.

She was sound asleep, snoring lightly, with the remnants of a satisfied smile on her face.

$$\textbf{12}$$

bbey awoke from her exhausted sleep with the instinctive feeling something was wrong. Had she overslept again? She'd been doing that a lot lately, it seemed, even if only for fifteen minutes. She had her morning regime down perfectly, and the slightest variation threw her off. She glanced at the alarm clock.

It was still early. The alarm wasn't set to go off for another half hour.

She knew she couldn't go back to sleep, but she didn't want to get up. It was too cold. The only reason it would be this cold was because the power was out, and the way the window shook told her why.

Blizzard.

She sighed and resisted the urge to tunnel deeper into the covers. Instead, she threw back the blankets and shivered as her feet touched the frigid floor. She pulled her thick robe on and tied it tightly, a faint defense against the chilly bedroom.

The hall, usually brightly sunlit, was shrouded in grayish-white, the color reserved for an intense snowstorm. Abbey padded into the living room and peered at the thermostat. Sixty-four degrees. Not bad. There had been days in August when sixty-four degrees would have seemed like a blessing, she reminded herself.

A gust of wind made the windows chatter in their frames. This was a major blizzard indeed. It must have just started, because the wind was picking up speed even as she listened.

She was a good Minnesotan. She knew what to do. The first thing was to determine if it was just her house that was suffering from the power outage, or if it was everyone. She crossed to the window and drew back the curtain.

The houses on her street could have been lit up like Las Vegas, and she wouldn't have been able to tell, the storm was that intense. She couldn't see anything except a wall of white.

White-out. She hated this part of winter storms, when she couldn't see more than an inch or two in front of her face.

As if angry, the wind rattled the panes of glass even more. White snow, once so fluffy and Christmassy, had become suddenly granular and menacing. She couldn't see past the curtain of white that blew sideways, obscuring even her car.

Almost idly she thought that she should have put it in the garage last night. Now she'd have to dig it out.

Then Abbey laughed out loud. At the rate this storm was raging, she'd be shoveling one way or the other.

One thing was clear: She couldn't tell if it was just her house or if the entire block was powerless. She checked the phone. It was dead too.

What she needed now was light and some way to make coffee. She rummaged through her closet until she found what she was looking for. It was a centerpiece she'd gotten as a housewarming gift—from Aunt Luellen, now that she thought about it—and had never used. In the midst of a fuchsia raffia circle studded with oversized fake roses was a huge glaringly pink monstrosity of a candle, with three wicks and a definite strawberry scent. Right now it seemed lovely.

Abbey had a plan. All she had to do was find something to light the thing with, and she'd be in business.

She dug in the utensil drawer fruitlessly until she had an idea. Bracing herself against the cold, she zipped into the garage, grabbed the barbecue lighter off the hook on the wall, and tore back inside.

Abbey clicked it, and a flame sprang into life. She felt ridiculously happy to see it.

"And now, my strawberry-pink eyesore, you are about to make yourself useful."

She spent the next few minutes rigging up a metal measuring cup and a coat hanger. She did some quick pouring, measuring, and stirring, and after waiting somewhat patiently, was rewarded with a warmish cup of coffee. It was not Starbucks by any means, but she said to herself as she cradled the precious cup in her hands, it was coffee.

The next matter of business was getting warm.

She had a fireplace, but she hadn't gotten around to getting firewood. Her only option was to put on more clothes. Abbey pulled on another sweatshirt and wrapped the throw from the couch around her shoulders.

The batteries in her transistor radio were dead, so she shook one out of her alarm clock and commandeered another from the miniature flashlight the bank had given her and finally tuned in a local radio station. The reception was uneven at best. Static cut through the announcer's words, but she hung on every syllable.

"Lines are down . . . neighborhoods south of . . . plows are waiting out the storm . . ."

The sporadic news was her link with the outside world. There was nothing quite like being in a blizzard to make a person feel isolated. The swirling snow shut out everyone and everything.

". . . Senior citizens . . . residents are urged to use caution . . . hypothermia . . . and small children. . . ."

Claire. She hoped Claire was all right. Certainly Golden Meadows had a back-up plan—at least a better plan than she had. She grimaced at the gaudy pink candle and the rig she'd designed to make coffee. She was pitiful.

Anyone would have a better severe weather plan than she had. Mike, for example, was the kind who'd have flashlights with batteries. She didn't even know where hers was, and if she did find it, she was sure the batteries would be too old. No, she had to rely on a grotesquely pink candle for her light and heat.

Actually, knowing Mike, he probably had all the residents of his apartment building gathered in one room, singing "Kumbaya."

That was mean-spirited, she knew. It was just that she had let everything slide. Everything, except her career. That she had firmly in her grip. She needed to take comfort from that.

"Closed . . . Also the schools, the mall, the post . . ."
That was what she was listening for. The mall was closed.

Mike pulled the drapes shut on the window of his apartment. He'd seen enough. This wasn't going to be one of those blizzards that blew through quickly. No, this blizzard was settling in for awhile.

It was hard to concentrate when the walls of the apartment shook with every windy blast. That was one of the problems of living on the fourth floor. It seemed as if his floor took the brunt of the storms.

If the electricity were on, he could watch television, or maybe a videotaped movie. He told himself he could read a book, but the fact was he didn't want to. He couldn't concentrate on it.

He was glad he'd chosen this apartment. It had a fireplace, so he was warm. But despite the comfort of the fireplace, he couldn't shake a feeling of worry. He knew that his grandmother would be safe at Golden Meadows. The generator would keep the heating system going, and there were round-the-clock aides to reassure the residents. But he wished the phones were working so he could call Abbey. Something told him that this storm had caught her unaware. She didn't watch television and rarely listened to the radio. He knew that. The blizzard warning had come late too. Had she prepared for it? Was she all right?

This was the first blizzard of the season. That wasn't too bad for Minnesota. He remembered years when the snows started coming in October. Maybe it signaled an easy winter.

He couldn't shake this worry about Abbey. He opened the curtain once again and looked out. The storm wasn't breaking, and it didn't seem to have reached its full fury yet.

He checked the clock. Six A.M. Abbey was probably asleep.
God, could You please watch over her?

He felt better after asking for God's protection, but he remembered something from his childhood. A burden shared in prayer was halved. That's what his mother used to tell him. Any load was lightened by prayer, she'd explained, but that didn't let you off the hook. You still had to do what you could. It was a partnership.

Now he had to figure out what he should do. Blizzards limited his alternatives to, well, zero. But he'd figure something out. He had to.

The announcer's voice continued with his broadcast, which arrived in intermittent sputters.

Abbey peered outside. The storm whirled on, pausing occasionally, then increasing its intensity. She couldn't tell if it was growing worse or not.

She shivered—and only partially from the cold. There was something elementally terrifying about a blizzard, although she'd lived through enough of them to know that the safest place for her to be was inside. The problems happened when someone went outside and got stuck in the snow, or perhaps got turned around and lost.

It had happened to her once. She had been in college, walking home from the part-time job she had at a restaurant. She'd lived only a few blocks away, but the wind-borne snow was so intense that she'd had to walk with her head down and somehow had turned mistakenly. She'd ended up in an unfamiliar alley and had wandered for over half an hour before stumbling upon her apartment. She'd managed to escape frostbite, although her face had been swollen for a day from the icy blast of the snow.

This forced seclusion was going to drive her crazy. She cooked herself another cup of coffee, but it tasted terrible. She walked through her house, picking up the newspapers from the past week that had piled up. Then she straightened the towels in the bathroom.

What she really wanted to do was go to the store. The weekly sales figures were due, and there was the box of sweaters that had arrived late the day before. If they weren't unpacked soon, they'd be irretrievably wrinkled.

Of course, the power was probably off at the mall, so the computers were down, and the steamer would be useless, but she could do some of the work by hand, and if she took the sweaters out of the box and laid them out on the workroom table . . .

There was a break in the wind, and she could see her driveway. The area behind her car was blown clear, and an idea began to form in her mind. She could back out.

"No travel is advised . . . snow gates on the interstate are closed . . . extremely slippery . . . finger drifts . . ." The radio crackled back into life.

The snow gates were huge metal gates that blocked the ramps to the interstate during a snowstorm, but they wouldn't affect her. She didn't use the interstate to get to the mall. And slippery? She'd go slowly. As for finger drifts, the long, narrow heaps of snow that stretched across a lane or two of traffic, they were no problem. She'd accelerate through them.

And besides, she reasoned, she'd stay just long enough to do the weekly report and take the sweaters out of the box.

She got dressed as quickly as she could, pulling on several layers. The temperature in her house was dropping, and according to the thermostat, it was already four degrees colder inside than it had been when she got up.

A blast of icy wind threw snow in her face as she opened the front door, and instinctively she tucked her head down as she scurried to her car. The man on the radio had been right. It was very slick, and she had trouble keeping her balance with the force of the wind.

She hurried around the back of her car and stopped. What she hadn't been able to see from the kitchen window was a huge drift that wrapped around the driver's side of the car, just out of her view. It was almost as high as the side mirror. It would take her forever to shovel it out, especially with this wind. She gave up and crept back inside, abandoning her plan.

The house, although there was a definite chilly edge to the air, was much warmer than outside. She kicked off her snowy boots and dropped her coat unceremoniously on the entryway floor. She was stuck here, and she might as well make the best of it.

Abbey wrapped herself in the throw from the couch and curled up. Maybe she could just sleep through it.

At first sleep seemed impossible, but the pound of the blizzard eventually lured her eyes to close and her breathing to even out.

Then the blizzard began pounding harder.

She sat up, groggily, and realized that the sound was coming from outside. Someone was knocking at her front door.

13

*W*ho could be at her door during a full-fledged blizzard?

Abbey paused for only a moment. On one hand, her visitor could be an ax-murderer, but on the other hand, this was a blizzard and no one should be out in it, not even an ax-murderer.

She peeked through the window in her kitchen. Another vehicle was parked beside hers. The snow was swirling so thickly that she couldn't tell what color the car was, just that it looked to be something with four-wheel-drive. Ax-murderers didn't drive four-wheel-drive vehicles, she was pretty sure of that.

She opened the front door a crack and saw a rather tall, huddled shape. It certainly didn't look like an ax-murderer.

He looked like Mike. A very cold Mike.

She threw open her door. "Come in!"

He stepped inside her entryway, and an eddy of snowflakes accompanied him. "Do you need firewood?" he asked without preamble.

"It's good to see you too, and yes, I do," she answered. Her heart was ridiculously elated to see him.

"Wait a second, then."

He vanished back into the storm and went to his car. Within moments he was back, carrying an armload of firewood.

She took it from him. As he kicked off his boots and shed his coat and muffler, she arranged the logs in the fireplace and started the kindling.

"I'm impressed." He spoke behind her.

"Why?"

"It's not easy to lay a fire and have it start that quickly. At least

I've never been able to do it. I have a fireplace in my apartment, but I go through a lot of matches getting it started, and even then it doesn't always work out right."

Abbey rocked back on her heels. "It'll take a couple of minutes to catch. The trick is where to put the kindling, and to remember to put the logs in bark side down. My dad taught me how to do it. We used to camp out a lot."

"Really? You don't strike me as a camping kind of gal."

"I'm not. I never was. My parents were, though, so I got dragged along. I never did figure out the charm of cooking over a campfire. I always ended up with everything charred on the outside and raw on the inside. Plus sleeping in the woods is an open invitation to any biting, creeping thing to come along and bite and creep on you. What's the point?"

Mike stood behind her, rubbing his hands together, and she realized he must be frozen.

"Where are my manners?" she asked. "I have a visitor, and I haven't even offered him something to wrap up in."

He chuckled. "I wonder if Emily Post dealt with blizzard etiquette."

She gave him the throw from the couch. "Here, use this. I'm plenty warm here by the fire . . . er, the single little flame that will soon catch."

As if on cue, one of the smaller logs sparked into life. Abbey smiled. "Good. Now it's only a matter of time before the other logs catch too, and we'll have a real rip-roaring fire."

Mike draped the woven throw around his shoulders. "Great. That wind is fierce."

Abbey looked out the window. "Is it really bad?" An idea was formulating in her mind. If he could get to her house, then he could take her to the mall. It wasn't that much further.

"The roads are awful. It took me forever to get here. I had to go five to ten miles an hour the whole time."

"But you got here," she pointed out, smiling brightly.

"I hope you're not thinking what I think you're thinking," he said, "because the answer is No."

"How do you know what I'm thinking?" she asked somewhat peevishly.

"Let me guess. You'd like a lift to the mall."

"Okay, you do know what I'm thinking. Please, Mike. I have so much to do." She felt like a child wheedling for a toy instead of an adult asking to be taken to work.

"No. The streets are dreadful." His voice was adamant, and he sat down squarely on the couch.

"But you got here," she repeated.

"And it was stupid, but I was worried about you."

"Which was stupid, driving here, or worrying about me?" The words were out before she thought about them.

His lips curved in a slow smile. "In this world, worrying about other people is not stupid, at least in my experience—well, I need to clarify. Maybe we're mixing up worrying and caring. Worrying is out of control, whereas caring is in control. When I start to worry, I know I need to take it to God. It's an alert to me that I'm not handling something well, but I know that God can."

She sat on the sofa beside him. "Only you would see worry as a call to prayer. The rest of the world worries about worry. Just check the cover of any magazine. 'Fifteen Ways to Worry Less.' 'Worried about What's Worrying You?' And I'm sure it's just a matter of time before someone comes up with 'Worry Your Way to a Slimmer, Trimmer You!' "

"Worry is a signal," Mike said, wrapping the blanket around him tightly. "Whenever you worry about someone, it's because you have a concern for them, usually for their welfare. Worry by itself is futile, but if you turn it into action and prayer, then it becomes helpful."

"I don't know about that," she said slowly. "I worry about a lot of things, like the store, for example. I was even worried about Claire when I saw the blizzard."

"You're sweet to think of her. They do have an emergency generator out there, by the way, so they're nice and warm at Golden Meadows."

Abbey felt her muscles relax. She'd been more apprehensive about the elderly woman's situation than she'd allowed herself to recognize.

"No, worry isn't good at all. It consumes you and does nothing for the person you're worrying about," Mike continued, as if knowing where her thoughts had led her. "What we do when we feel worried is up to us. If there's something we can do to ease our concern, then of course we should do it."

"That's the hardest part," she confessed. "What if we can't do any-thing—like today, when the storm prevented me from getting out."

"That's when prayer comes in. We give it back to God, tell Him that we recognize our anxiety, and we trust Him. That's the sticky part—letting God do His work, having faith that He is at work, even when it isn't readily apparent to us. The problem is when we don't handle our concern well and let it take over our minds. That's worry."

The radio, which had been silent for some time, suddenly sput-tered with static. "Situation improving . . . northern Minnesota . . . back to regularly . . ."

Abbey and Mike looked at each other and laughed. "Well," said Mike, "thanks for the update, huh? Sort of sums it all up."

She rose from the couch and looked out the window. "I think they may have been a bit optimistic about the storm. It looks as bad as ever."

She hugged her arms as she sat back down. "I don't know if I ever thanked you for bringing the firewood—I was so glad to see it . . . and you."

His warm brown eyes twinkled with a soft reflection of the fire-place's cheerful blaze. "My pleasure. See, this blizzard's not all that bad. You've got a fire burning; you've got a friend with you. What more could you ask for?"

"A cup of coffee."

He stood up and went back to the front door. She could hear him pulling on his boots and coat. Was he leaving? She stood up and joined him in the entryway.

"Was it something I said? Look, I can live without the coffee if that's what the problem is, although I personally don't see . . ." Her voice trailed off as she realized that under the muffler and pulled-up coat collar, he was smiling.

"I'll be right back."

"It's not that important—" she began, but he brushed away her concerns.

He vanished from the warmth of her house and was soon lost in the swirl of white. But within seconds he was back, and he held out a large blue vacuum bottle. "I made this before I left the house. The power did flicker back on for awhile early this morning, and I made a pot just in case. I can't believe I forgot to bring it inside with me."

Within minutes, they were both seated again in the living room, cups of coffee in their hands. As the fire warmed their faces, she felt her tension ease.

"This is the life," she said, a bit surprised at how relaxed she felt. Her usual reaction to being housebound would have been restless energy, and she had to admit, if she had been here alone, by now she would have been a nervous wreck. "I suppose I could get used to it, but I'd really have to try."

"You should. God didn't mean for us to spend our lives at work."

She studied him covertly. He talked so easily about God. His life must center around his faith. It was something she couldn't quite understand.

"Everything with you is God, isn't it?" she asked.

He had his head back and his eyes closed, and for a minute he didn't answer. She couldn't tell if he was sleeping or praying or just resting his eyes.

At last he opened his eyes and looked at her with his clear amber gaze. "Yes, it pretty much is. He is my life. Make that a capital L: Life."

"How did you come to that?" she pressed, finding that she really did want to know. "I mean, was it always like that, or did you have some kind of experience, or what? And please tell me if I'm being too snoopy."

"I'm always glad to share my story. I was raised Christian. I went to Sunday school and to church. I'd accepted Jesus as in I accepted Him without thinking, the same way you accept a bit of snow in the winter or a pleasant day in June. But when I really accepted Him in my heart and my mind and my soul was in church one Sunday. Are you sure you want to hear this?"

Abbey nodded. "Please."

"I must have been growingly aware of the lack of something in my life, but I couldn't put my finger on it. And then, one day in church, the gospel reading was the story of Jesus and the lame man. You know, where Jesus says, essentially, throw away your cane, your crutch, your mat, and get up and walk."

"That did it?"

"I realized at that moment that it was very simple. I had to put aside the 'canes' I used in my everyday life—for me, that meant the whole slew of excuses I'd use to get out of anything that would require me to lay my heart on the line, like I didn't have the time, or it was someone else's turn to do the work—and get up and walk on my own, with Him."

"And that's what you did."

"That's what I'm doing," he corrected. "It's all a process, which is why so many people refer to it as a path. I'm still walking and stumbling."

"I can't believe that little Bible story did all that," Abbey said. "I'd always thought it would a big knock-you-off-your-feet experience."

"I was sitting down when it happened, so I can't speak to that," he answered, his eyes gleaming. "But even the little things are what make the big things happen. Like the fire. You started by lighting the kindling, little bits of wood that burn out quickly. But the kindling sparked the twigs, which lit the small sticks, which lit the logs."

"The Parable of the Fireplace."

He laughed. "Well, you get the idea. We now have a wonderful fire keeping us warm, and that's my point. From that one thin match came this great blaze."

"I don't know," Abbey said doubtfully. "I need to think about it."

"I'll pray for you," he said. "I can do it right now if you'd like."

The radio chose that moment to burst forth with renewed life and issue an updated weather bulletin: ". . . Storm has diminished . . . plows are out now . . . tomorrow . . ."

The lights flickered on, and the furnace clicked into operation.

"You don't need to," she said. "I think my prayers have just been answered."

*   *   *

Mike concentrated as he drove along. He knew he shouldn't be out yet, but with his vehicle in four-wheel drive, he'd be all right. And Golden Meadows wasn't that far away.

He'd had to leave. He knew now that more than anything he wanted Abbey to know the Lord the way he did. *That's asking a lot, isn't it?* he questioned God. He knew what the answer was.

She'd have to do it on her own terms, in her own way. For everybody it was different. He could feel her hunger for faith, her thirst for salvation. All he could do was give her the kindling and hope the fire caught.

His vehicle still hadn't warmed up, and at the first stoplight he rubbed his hands together. Now that the storm was over, the sun was out, making the late morning seem warmer than it was. Once the snowplows got out and did their job, the only evidence of the morning's blizzard would be the deep piles of snow scooped aside by the plow blades.

God had asked him to watch over Abbey, and it was a burden he had accepted. Was what he had shared this morning too much—or not enough?

His advice to Abbey about worry came back to him. He could continue to worry, turning his thoughts over and over in his mind in the futile hope that he'd see something new there, or he could do what he should do. He could examine the reason for his concern and give it back to the Lord in prayer.

But the questions in her eyes did something strange to his heart, and for once it was very hard to take his own advice.

14

A small snowplow was already clearing the lot at Golden Meadows. Mike pulled into a parking space and gave the snowplow driver a jaunty wave before dashing into the retirement home.

The snow had drifted against the west side of the doorway, and over the top of the pile he could just make out the curious faces of some residents who were checking the aftermath of the storm.

When he came through the door, they surrounded him, chattering about the excitement of the blizzard. One woman pushed her walker closer. "Wasn't that something, Sweet? We couldn't see past the edge of the parking lot!"

The fellow standing beside her frowned. "Snow is snow, Marlys. Don't tell me you haven't seen snow before."

The woman beamed at him happily. "Actually, I've never seen a blizzard before at all! I came here from Florida."

The grumpy man seemed somewhat abashed. "Well, a blizzard is just snow with some oomph, that's all."

Another woman, who stood behind him, rolled her eyes expressively. "It was exciting. They had to use the generator since the power went off. Did it go off where you were?"

Mike nodded. "But it's back on now."

He'd been scanning the group, but he hadn't seen his grandmother, which was unusual since something this exciting should have sent her down to watch the storm and its aftermath. Maybe she had gone to visit someone or to pick up an item at the small store here at Golden Meadows.

He asked about her, and the group discussed her absence with enthusiasm and concern. "I didn't see her at breakfast," the first woman said, "but a lot of people chose to stay in their rooms this morning. Storms do that to some folks. They just hole up."

"We had oatmeal with raisins for breakfast," the grouchy man offered. "There's some as what don't like that. Maybe that's it. I didn't come down because I can't abide raisins. Nasty little things. Stick in your teeth. Not a fan of oatmeal either. Horrid glop that tastes like somebody forgot to finish cooking it."

"Oh, John, you are such an old crank. Can't you lighten up?" Marlys said.

The man who had talked to Abbey and Mike about relationships joined the group. His long-sleeved shirt was neatly pressed, and he leaned on his cane. "Is Mrs. Thorson under the weather?"

"I hope not," Mike said, but he didn't like the sinking feeling in his stomach. Claire adored breakfast, especially oatmeal with raisins. If anything happened to her . . . It was too painful to even think about.

"I'm sure she's okay," Mike told them reassuringly, "but I'd better go up and see her."

"You do that," the man said, turning to leave. "She's a good woman, almost as good as my Eleanor, may she rest in peace. Tell her Albert Caldwell asked about her."

The group resumed their watch of the man on the snowplow as he continued to scrape the snow out of the parking lot.

Abbey attacked the snowdrift that locked her car in. She really needed to get a better shovel than the one she'd inherited with the house. This one was ungainly, and as much snow slid back onto its original spot as was left on the blade of the shovel.

She probably should have insisted that Mike take her along to Golden Meadows. Then she could have easily asked him to give her a ride to Cedar Mall.

Her back protested as a sudden realization brought her upright. She had never picked up the present from Aunt Luellen.

This was getting ridiculous. How hard would it be to go out there and pick it up? She made a mental note to go out there and get the gift later in the day, once the snowplows had cleared the roads . . . and she'd gotten out of her driveway.

She jammed the shovel into the snow and looked at her handiwork. All she'd succeeded in doing was demolishing the drift from a smooth pile of snow into a ragged heap. But it was not a bit smaller.

Maybe if she backed out as quickly as she could, she'd clear it. It was worth a try.

She headed back inside to get dressed for work. There might even be enough hot water by now for her to take a shower.

The red light on her answering machine was blinking. She pushed the button and heard the voice of the manager of Cedar Mall, clearly reading a prepared message: "The lots are being cleared by snowplows, but to ensure the safety of the drivers as well as our employees, we are requesting that you do not come into work until the parking areas are done. The mall will reopen at five P.M. today."

She was tempted to ignore the dictum. Those reports were waiting, and she could get so much done before the mall opened. But she knew that mall management was serious when they made these policies, and she did not want to tangle with them. So she resigned herself to spending the rest of the day inside. There was a book on the end table that she had started reading in the summer that she could start in on again.

Abbey got the book and sat down with it. She opened it to the spot that was bookmarked and read for a few lines. It made no sense. She'd have to start it again.

Well, that was okay, she told herself. She could do that. She turned to the front of the book and began to read.

Coffee. Another cup of coffee would be nice. She made a pot and sat down once more with the book. Two pages later she was up again, looking for something to eat.

"Oh, give it up, Abbey," she scolded herself out loud. "You're more antsy than an August picnic." She paced through the house until she finally sank down onto the couch.

It wasn't just the forced house arrest that bothered her. It was Mike . . . and what he'd said.

What exactly was it about him? She'd known him, somewhat, for many years, but lately their lives had become conjoined, primarily because of those goofy frog slippers that Aunt Luellen had sent to her instead of Claire.

Abbey had long ago taken the idea of loving someone and shelved it in the back of her mind, right next to religion. She had always intended that one day, when she was settled in her career, her MBA in hand, she would look into love and faith. But with Mike, they came perilously close to arriving hand in hand.

This wasn't the way she had planned it, not at all. She had plans for her life, a career plan. It was what she had talked to the young women at his church about.

What made her life work for her, what gave her days shape and meaning, was her career. She was good at what she did. She'd brought Trends back from being on the brink of closing to one of the most financially stable businesses in the mall. She had done it because she was focused. She'd started young, identified her strengths, and built on them.

What was wrong with that?

Aunt Luellen used to talk about the parable of the talents. It was everyone's responsibility, Aunt Luellen had told her, to make the most of the gifts God had given them. Wasn't that exactly what Abbey was doing? And rather than running ahead, helter-skelter into the future, she'd laid out a path to follow.

The problem was that people kept stepping onto her path. People like Mike. And what had become painfully clear to her since her growing friendship with Mike was what she hadn't included in her plan: fun.

That Bible verse that was tucked into the toe of one of the slippers sprang to her mind: "This is the day which the Lord hath made; we will rejoice and be glad in it." That was Mike. He certainly was having a good time with God. Was that his secret?

The phone rang, and she leaped to answer it. It was probably mall management, telling her that the parking lots were cleared, so she could go to work . . . assuming she'd be able back out.

But it wasn't the monotone voice of the mall manager. It was Mike, and he began without preamble: "Claire is ill. Very ill."

*A*bbey paused in midmotion, the scarf she was knotting around her neck hanging from her numb fingers. She must have heard him wrong. "Ill? What do you mean? How ill?"

"She's feeling dizzy, and she says she has pains." Mike's voice was calm, but Abbey could hear the worry behind the words.

"What kind of pains? Chest pains?"

"No, stomach pains. Probably something she ate."

Abbey realized that the scarf was now trailing in her coffee cup, and she pulled it out and swabbed at it as she spoke. "Is she in the hospital?"

Mike hesitated a moment before answering. "She refuses to go."

"Refuses to go?" Abbey realized she was nearly shouting and forced herself to moderate her speech. "Why on earth won't she go?"

Mike's pause was even longer, and when he spoke, Abbey could hear his stark fear. "She says she wants to die at home in her own bed."

Abbey's world collapsed. "Die?"

He spoke so softly she had to struggle to hear him. "She always said that when she died, she wanted to do it in her own bed, and preferably around Christmas. She wants to spend Christmas in heaven . . . where there's bound to be a birthday party the likes of which earth has never seen."

"No, no. She's not going to die, is she? She's not going to die! Please tell me she isn't." This was not the way things were supposed to happen. Abbey had just gotten attached to Claire. She couldn't let her go.

He became reassuring. "It's probably not that major—at least that's

404

the sense I got from the nursing staff. A doctor did come in and check on her. Praise God that he had been on ER duty at the hospital and had walked over to visit his own father at Golden Meadows. It's just a short trip, but I guess it took him quite awhile since he waded through snow. The plows hadn't been out yet."

"Well, if a doctor has seen her . . ."

"But I have to be realistic."

"I don't like realistic." She was aware that she sounded like a little child, but that was exactly how she felt—small and powerless. Realistic was sickness and pain and parting. It wasn't good, especially now.

"She's not young. Every illness is a stress for her. All we can do is pray for her." The words hung in the air. "Please pray for her, Abbey." Then he hung up the phone.

Pray for her!

Didn't you have to be a Christian to do that? She didn't know how to pray, not really. She'd learned as a child that it wasn't right to pray for a bicycle—her aunt had straightened her out on that one— but that was about the extent of her knowledge on the subject.

She didn't want Claire to be sick, and she particularly didn't want her to die. *Please, please, make her all right.*

Well, she'd just have to leave the praying to Mike.

Abbey poured herself another cup of coffee and carried it into the living room. She sank onto the couch and didn't even bother with the pretense of trying to read one of the magazines piled on the end table.

Make her better.

She couldn't abide sitting here a minute longer. She had to do something. Abbey put her cooling coffee on the kitchen counter and pulled on her boots. She was going to go to Golden Meadows.

The sky was a bright, clear blue now that the storm had passed, and the sun hurt her eyes. The world looked sculpted in snow. *A single storm can change everything,* she mused. *One storm blows through and another takes its place,* she thought. *First snow, and now this. Her emotions were battered.*

The demolished snowdrift was still behind her car, and she studied it briefly. At just the right angle, she could make it through.

But then she saw the impediment that she could not cross.

The snowplows had been by, and the end of her driveway was blocked with the snow the plows had pushed in. Heavy chunks of compacted snow and ice lay in a thick, impenetrable ridge. There was absolutely no way to get through that with her car. It had to be shoveled out, or preferably taken out with a plow or a strong snowblower. All she had was this insufficient shovel.

Once again, she was ill-prepared for the storm. Abbey sighed. Was everything a metaphor?

She mounded her hands over the end of the shovel and rested her chin on her knuckles as she surveyed her predicament. She was really locked in now. It would take her all afternoon to break through . . . if she were lucky. Experience had told her that she was not getting out any time soon.

Thwarted by a snowstorm.

Hot tears pressed against her eyelids. Why did she even care about this old woman? And what did she hope to accomplish by going to Golden Meadows, anyway? It wasn't as if she could help Claire. She was a store manager, not a miracle worker.

Why did Claire have to get sick? And why couldn't she just go to the hospital? That's what most people did. They got sick, and they went to the hospital to get better. Why wouldn't she do it? This wasn't fair!

Abbey slammed her fist onto the side of her car. It was all wrong. Claire needed to be well.

She abandoned the effort to dig herself out and put the inadequate little shovel back into its spot in her garage and went back inside. She poured herself a fresh cup of coffee, but it was bitter on her tongue.

The coffee at Golden Meadows was good. She remembered the conversation with the man who had spoken to them on her first visit. His Eleanor was lucky indeed. Would Abbey ever find a love as real as theirs?

God, save Claire.

She paced through her small house. All she could think of was a single phrase: *God, save Claire. God, save Claire. God, save Claire.*

Suddenly her feet stopped their mindless steps. She was praying.

She, Abbey Jensen, was praying! For the first time in years, she was praying for someone else. And it felt terrific.

She continued: *God, save Claire.* The words were simple, but they said it all. In her mind, she could picture the elderly woman, her nearly sightless eyes still alert behind the substantial lenses. The Bible, such a sign of her faith, centered in her room—as it must have centered in her life.

And those slippers. Those goofy frog slippers with the fake gemstone eyes. Claire hadn't even opened them yet.

What had Aunt Luellen written on the note? "Wishing you great hoppy-ness always." That's what Abbey wanted for her too. Great hoppy-ness.

"Don't spend Christmas with God," she whispered to Claire. "Spend it with me."

Mike held the gnarled hand and gazed into his grandmother's eyes, which opened and closed irregularly. "Grandma, go to the hospital."

Claire shook her head. "I'm staying here. I'm around the people I know. Sweet, for us here at Golden Meadows, death isn't quite the scary ogre it is for you young folks. It's not wearing a big black cape and reeking of the grave. It's simply how we get from this life to the next. Kind of like a bus."

He laughed. "Only you, Grandma, would come up with that. Death is like a bus. But this bus isn't yours. Yours is waaaaaay across town."

She patted his arm. "When my bus comes, Honey, I'm hopping on. Destination: Promised Land!"

"Plus it's almost Christmas," he reminded her. "You know how much you love Christmas. You wouldn't want to miss that, now would you?"

"Christmas! That reminds me. Help me sit up, Sweet."

"Oh, Grandma, do you think you should—"

"Hush your mouth and help me. I'd hope by now you'd know enough to listen to your elders. I'm not going to run a marathon. I just want to sit up." Her china-blue eyes twinkled weakly.

He gently lifted her thin shoulders and helped her edge up to a sitting position. "Good?"

"Super. Now, you have to get Abbey out here. I've got her present, you see. She never did pick it up." Claire leaned forward and whispered conspiratorially, "She's a bit absent-minded, I'm afraid."

Mike smiled at that. "I suspect she likes coming out here to see you more than she lets on, and that present is just an excuse."

"Do you think so?" Claire seemed very pleased.

"By the way, a gentleman named Albert Caldwell asked me to relay his concern."

His grandmother sat up straighter and patted her puff of white hair. "He did? Did he say anything else?"

"We—"

A knock at the door interrupted them. It was the doctor who had checked on Claire earlier.

"Sweet, do you mind for just one minute?" Claire asked. "I'd like to talk to Dr. James for a moment alone."

Mike hesitated, but the doctor nodded and said, "Go ahead and wait in the lobby. I'll stop by before I leave and give you an update."

"Then you can come back up and see me. But if you can find me a piece of chocolate, that'd be nice," Claire said. Then, as if suddenly tired, she sighed. It was the sigh that worried Mike. His grandmother wasn't a sigher.

He did the only thing he knew to do: he prayed. *God, make her all right. If she needs to go, I'll try to understand. But I love her, and I want her with me a little while longer. I need her.*

This prayer came with a postscript that totally surprised him: *And Abbey needs her too.*

Dr. James joined him in the lobby and, after updating the other residents on Claire's condition, invited Mike into the Fireside Lounge. Most of the chairs were filled, and their arrival created a curious stir, but the two men managed to find a fairly secluded spot.

"I'll tell you what I know," the doctor began, "which is that I don't know. She seems to be as healthy as a horse, although, of course, the horse is eighty-two years old. She seems to have good moments and bad moments, but her mind is sharp."

"That's true," Mike agreed. "What concerns me is that she seems to be willing to let go so easily. She's not fighting any of it."

"In most patients, that would be a worry," the doctor said, "but with Claire, I see it more as a natural acceptance. She's certainly not hurrying toward death."

"Not racing to catch her bus," Mike murmured.

"Excuse me?" Dr. James was clearly confused.

"Just vintage Claire," Mike said.

Abbey's pacing had slowed down, simply because her legs were getting tired. She hadn't heard anything more from either the mall or from Mike. How could all her worries come together like this on one single day . . . and just before Christmas too?

She stared at the phone, her arms clutched across her chest. If only she could will the phone to ring!

As if by telepathy, it did just that.

She lifted the receiver, dreading the mall manager's drone. But instead it was Mike.

"The doctor checked on her again, and they're going to keep her here at Golden Meadows tonight. If her condition worsens, they'll move her to the hospital pretty much whether she wants them to or not. The hospital is less than a block away, and for now she's comfortable in her own room. They can monitor her there for the time being."

Abbey breathed a grateful sigh. "It sounds like she's going to be fine."

"I'm still being cautious. She can still use our prayers."

She paused. "I prayed for her."

There was a long silence. Abbey wished she could see his face to know how he was reacting. Then he said, simply, "Thank you. By the way, she wants to see you. She still has your present."

"Oh, I forgot! I'm getting as loopy as Aunt Luellen. But I'm not going to be able to get out until I get ahold of someone to plow me out. The snow fairies didn't come in and dig out my car or my drive-way."

Mike promised to come by the next day and either get her car out or give her a ride to Golden Meadows, then to work.

"Tomorrow's Christmas Eve," he reminded her.

16

bbey awoke to the sound of a snowplow outside her window. She leaped off the couch where she'd fallen asleep and stumbled to the front door. She opened it a crack. Mike was out there, a blade attached to the front of his four-wheel drive vehicle. He waved at her, and she wiggled her fingers back at him before retreating into the bathroom to pull herself together.

One look in the mirror confirmed her worst suspicions. She looked horrible. One side of her face was wrinkled where she'd slept on it, and her eyes were puffy and swollen. She hoped that Mike wouldn't hurry with his plowing outside. Maybe he'd go slowly and give her the necessary time to make herself presentable. Nobody, she reasoned as she splashed water on her face, deserved to see her looking the way she did when she first woke up. It was enough to scare a bear back into hibernation.

One side of her hair bent straight up, and no amount of combing would make it settle down. In desperation, she clipped a barrette in it. It didn't look very good, but this was no time for vanity. She wanted to get to Golden Meadows and see how Claire was doing.

She'd caught only a glimpse of Mike's face, but it had been enough to know that the news from the retirement home must have been good. Plus, he wouldn't have stopped to plow out her driveway if his grandmother was still gravely ill.

She had just pulled on a red sweater when he knocked on the door.

"Thank you so much," she said as she let him in. "How's Claire?"

He smiled. "Much better but still weak. She's holding her own, and I think we'll have her around to tell us how to live our lives for quite awhile."

Our lives. The words had a glorious ring to them.

"Are you ready to go?" Mike was wrapping his muffler around his neck.

She gulped down a final splash of coffee. "Ready."

It was odd, she thought as she rode to Golden Meadows with him, how much everything about her had changed. Just a month ago she would have done anything to avoid going to the retirement home. Now she couldn't wait to get out there.

And Mike. He had changed her in ways she wasn't yet ready to explore. What was especially strange, she mused, was that she was still changing, and it was a wonderful sensation, like a butterfly must feel when it finally emerges from its long cocooned sleep.

Perhaps she was just caught up in a generally good mood. It was the day after a storm, the sun was shining, it was Christmas Eve morning, and Claire was doing better.

Mike's car was already warm, and Abbey's lack of sleep began to catch up with her on the drive to Golden Meadows.

He glanced over and grinned as she yawned. "Big night?"

"I couldn't sleep, worrying about Claire, so I decided to watch *It's a Wonderful Life*. I just bought it the other day, and I still hadn't seen it all the way through."

"So what did you think?"

"A bit predictable."

"Really?" His eyebrows arched in surprise.

"But sometimes predictable is good, very good." Her smile threatened to wobble out of control as she added, "Last night I would have taken predictable."

"No kidding. I was so scared about Grandma. I must have talked God's ear off. I couldn't stop praying." He pulled into the parking lot of the retirement home. "Well, here we are."

He turned off the car engine and sat, his hands still on the steering wheel. "Can you give me a minute here? I need to get a little strength before I go in."

Abbey reached over and touched his arm. "Please, pray aloud."

"Dearest Father, thank You for another morning, for a blessed morning, as we approach Your Son's birth. Abbey and I ask that You keep Grandma in Your healing hands. We love this woman." He paused. "Amen."

"I'm not very good at praying out loud," he confessed as he helped Abbey out of the vehicle. "I know what I'm saying in my heart, but when I say the words out loud, it sometimes seems too little."

"I'm sure God listens to both your heart and your lips," Abbey said.

Mike's quick smile told her how much he appreciated her comment.

They were mobbed as soon as they opened the front door of Golden Meadows.

"How's she doing, Sweet?"

"Tell her I've been praying!"

"She'll pull through. She's a strong one."

"A good Christian woman."

"That Norwegian blood, it's going to keep her going, that's for sure."

Mike laughed as their voices assailed him. "I'm going to go up and see her, and I'll tell her you're all thinking of her and praying for her."

Claire's eyes were shut when they entered her room, but they flew open as if spring-loaded. "Sweet! Abbey!"

"Merry Christmas, Grandma," Mike said, dropping a kiss on her forehead. "How are you feeling?"

"Better. A little on the woozy side, so I'm afraid I'll have to pass on the ice-skating. Remember, Sweet, how we used to go ice-skating on Christmas Eve? The moonlight on the pond made it look like we were skating on a huge diamond."

Mike laughed. "I'd almost forgotten about that! We'd pretend that the diamond belonged to us, and we'd decide what we were going to buy with the money we'd get when we sold it."

Claire turned her bright blue eyes toward Abbey. "What would you buy?"

"Skating lessons, to start with. I'm afraid I'm probably the only Minnesotan who's a total klutz on the ice."

The elderly woman beamed happily at her. "When I met Arthur, I could have skated circles around any Olympic ice-skater, but I pretended I didn't know how, just so I could hold his hand. Silly fool, he fell for it. He couldn't skate for beans, but I sure did like to hold his hand."

A beeper sounded. Both women looked at Mike, who had the grace to be abashed about the interruption. "Sorry. I got this pager, but I never thought anybody would ever page me on it. Grandma, can I borrow your phone? It's the store."

After a quick conversation, he hung up the phone and turned to them. "I've got to run. The cash register won't start up. Abbey . . . ?"

"Oh, no." Claire looked as disappointed as a child who'd just lost out on candy. "I wanted to watch Abbey open her present from Luellen."

Abbey looked at Claire, at the forlorn expression on her face, and made a decision: "I'll stay. I can take a cab back."

Claire beamed happily. "Good."

Mike hugged his grandmother and promised to be back later. Then he left them alone together.

"Abbey, Dear, I know you need to get to work, especially with this being Christmas Eve and all, so I won't keep you long. It's just that I'm so anxious to find out what Luellen gave you." Claire wiggled with barely-subdued enthusiasm.

At that moment, a health-care aide knocked on the door and entered, pushing a metal cart covered with a white linen napkin. "Claire, I have some breakfast for you. It's your favorite—French toast. I knew you had guests, so I brought some extra."

Claire's eyes lit up at the sight of the French toast, but she glanced at the Christmas present. She was clearly torn between finding out what was in the package from Aunt Luellen and having the French toast, so Abbey resolved the issue for her. "I'd be glad to join you for breakfast. We can open the package when we've eaten."

Abbey was amazed at how hungry she was, and she mentioned it to Claire, apologizing for gulping down her meal.

"Young people don't eat enough anyway," Claire said. "Everybody worries about being thin, although I don't know why. What's the point of dieting all the time? Especially when you can't have chocolate. I love chocolate."

Abbey smiled. Claire was really a dear.

"I know you have to get back to your store; Abbey, but I really do want to see what Luellen sent you. She always sends such interesting gifts." Claire motioned toward the tiny tree. "It's over there. Could you get it for me, please?"

The package was wrapped in gaudy green foil sprinkled with golden stars. "I wonder if this paper came from Brazil."

"Chile, Dear. Luellen's in Chile. Open it so I can see what it is!"

Abbey pulled the paper off the box. Inside was an elegant leather-bound pocket calendar. "It's beautiful!" she exclaimed as she examined the burgundy, tooled leather. "Look, Claire, there's even a spot for one of those teeny electronic gizmo things that does everything but park your car!"

As she handed it to Claire, a piece of paper fell out. "Of course! It just wouldn't be a gift from Aunt Luellen without a note."

"What does it say?" Claire asked expectantly.

"Wow. This is short for Aunt Luellen. It just says, 'As you plan your days ahead,' and then 'This is the day which the Lord hath made; we will rejoice and be glad in it.' "

"Ah." Claire nodded her head as if that explained it all. "From the Psalms."

"That's the same one that was in—" Abbey said, stopping before she could spoil the surprise of Claire's slippers, which remained unopened under the Christmas tree. "But why—" And before she could finish the question, she answered it.

Because Claire, whose days were limited, looked forward, while she, who had her whole life ahead of her, planned only by an hourly schedule at work. The Lord, the one that Mike spoke of so easily, existed for her too, and He gave her each day as fresh and new and bright as each day that He gave to Claire.

The same God made them all. The same God. This was why Mike and Claire were so happy—they were rejoicing in each day that the Lord had given them. It didn't matter if she had a thousand days . . . or one. They were all gifts.

The iron bars that had held her heart imprisoned fell away. She was free, totally free now to love . . . and to be loved. An aura of happiness and well-being surrounded her, too new and fragile to be analyzed or explained. She knew what she had to do. She had to tell Mike.

"Can I borrow your phone, Claire?"

Just exactly what she was going to say to him, she had no idea. She just knew she wanted him to be with her right now, to be at her side as she explored this wonderful sense of freedom.

But Mike wasn't at his store. The employee who answered the phone said that after Mike unjammed the cash register, he had run over to the church to drop off some toys he was donating for the Christmas Eve service. So Abbey kissed Claire goodbye with a promise to come back later and fairly flew down the hall to the lobby.

Too bad she didn't have her car with her. She could have zipped right over there, but instead she was forced to wait for a taxi.

And wait she did. She watched the clock over the door of the lobby as the minutes slowly ticked by. Selma assured her, when Abbey called every five minutes, that the store was doing fine. Both Selma and Brianna were on duty and wouldn't need Abbey there until noon.

Nadine, the desk clerk, emerged from the office with a young woman at her side. "Miss Jensen!" the teenager exclaimed.

Her face was familiar, but it took Abbey a minute to realize where she'd seen her before.

"I'm with the Jeremiah Group. Remember, you came out and talked to us?" She stuck out her hand awkwardly and said, "I'm Mona, by the way."

"Mona, it's good to see you again," Abbey said. "Do you work here?"

"I do now," the young woman declared. "Something you said got to me, and I had a talk with the career counselor with the Jeremiah Group, and bingo. Here I am. I want to be a nurse, I think."

"That's great! Nursing is a wonderful, noble career."

"I have you to thank for it too," Mona added shyly, her eyes darting down to study her shoes.

Warmth surrounded Abbey's heart. "That's so sweet," she said.

"Thank you for saying that. You know, I wasn't too sure that anything I said that evening had an impact at all."

"It wasn't anything you said. It was what you wore."

"Excuse me?" Abbey couldn't believe what she was hearing.

"Oh, not that it was gross or anything. It just made me realize that I didn't want a job where I had to dress up everyday like that. So when I thought about what I did want to wear, I always saw myself in a nurse's uniform. I figured, hey, nobody's going to come to my door and hand me one. So I decided to go out and get it myself. And this is where I'm starting. I've even signed up at the university to start on my degree."

Abbey was overwhelmed. She remembered Mike's words: "Who knows, you may very well have touched someone's heart here today in a way you can't know." And in turn, today, that someone had touched her heart.

"Mona, good luck on your new career. I know you'll be an outstanding nurse." She couldn't resist adding, "And you'll look smashing in a nurse's uniform."

Mona left with Nadine, and Abbey was left alone to wait for the cab. What a day this had been! Truly it was one to rejoice in!

While she waited, she prayed and rejoiced and turned her newfound knowledge over and over in her mind. At last the cab arrived, and Abbey decided to have the driver take her directly to the Word of Faith Community Church to save time.

The small church looked like Christmas itself, with glistening white snow drifted around the brick walls. The steeple sparkled in the morning sunlight, and the cross at the top of the spire pointed straight to heaven.

Mike was arranging gift-wrapped packages around a small tree in the narthex. He smiled when he saw Abbey. "How does it look?" he asked, stepping back to look at his handiwork.

"A pile of Christmas presents could never look bad," she said.

"You've definitely been with Grandma," he said. "Her Christmas spirit has been rubbing off on you! What happened to your humbug disposition, Scrooge?"

"It's gone. There's . . . something else there instead."

"Wow, that's a change. Cool!"

"That's not the only thing that's changed," she said, suddenly shy.

He stopped and stared at her, a gaily-wrapped package dangling from his fingers, forgotten for the moment. "What do you mean?"

"I mean I'm different. I mean that all the pieces fell into place. They've been there, bit by bit, but this morning it all came together. This is the day that the Lord has made, you know? Every day is the day. Every day is, all by itself, the most tremendous gift we have." She rubbed her forehead. "Am I making any sense?"

"Oh, yes," he said softly. "You're making a lot of sense."

"Good, because I want to talk about it, but I don't know exactly what to say. This Christianity thing needs some kind of manual."

"It has one. It's called the Bible."

"I don't know why I'm telling you this."

"I think I do," he said softly. "At least I hope I do."

He took her hand and looked into her eyes. "I have prayed for this moment for a long time, almost hoped against hope that this would be the one prayer that God would grant. And He has blessed me beyond belief. This is my Christmas gift from Him, knowing that you are His."

For a moment, neither of them spoke, until Mike broke the silence. "Would you like to go into the sanctuary with me?"

She nodded, and he guided her into the darkened sanctuary, with only the light from the stained glass windows to illuminate it. "I love that this room is called the sanctuary. I think of all it means—a haven, a safe place, a refuge—and I know that I'm in His presence."

They stood together, absorbing the atmosphere. "When I'm here," Mike continued, "the rest of the world falls into the background. I can focus on Him. It's a special place, beyond explanation. God is very real to me, Abbey, very real. I can't imagine trying to live without Him—or wanting to."

There, with the scent of the Christmas tree in the narthex, the wreaths by the coat racks, and the candles on the altar, Abbey thought of the little Baby who was born so long ago and yet had been born again two thousand years later in her own heart. She thought of His death and resurrection and knew, in that moment, that He lived in her heart. She gave her life to God, and her heart sang the wonders of the first birth long ago . . . and of the birth that had just happened in her.

Mike watched her face as she was transformed. He had prayed for this. He knew that this was God's plan, and he was but a part of the plan.

I don't ask for much, God, he began, then almost laughed. That wasn't true. He'd already asked for Claire's recovery only slightly more than an hour ago. *Okay, I usually don't ask for much,* he revised his prayer. *But if I could have one more thing. Just one more . . .*

He paused before proceeding. Was he asking too much? Would God reject his plea outright?

Abbey looked at him, her eyes glowing, and he knew he had to continue.

Please, God, let her love me.

17

bbey stared at Mike. Could it be true? Was what she was seeing in his eyes real—or was it just a mirror of her own? Without the prison walls around her heart, she could see so much more. Had she always loved him, or had it just happened? As she put out her hand, she realized it didn't matter. Either way, she loved him.

The words were extraordinarily simple. She loved him. And, possibly, just possibly, he loved her too.

She felt absolutely liberated by the thought.

"Excuse me." A voice echoed in the empty sanctuary from behind them. "Mike, the store just called. The cash register is jammed up again."

The magic hovered around them a moment longer, until they both smiled.

"Tell them I'm on my way," Mike called back. Then his glance returned to Abbey, and so did the magic. "Can you come to the Christmas Eve service with me tonight?"

"I'd be delighted to." And she meant it.

Christmas was full of presents.

The day flew by. Selma and Brianna barely had time to tease their boss about her new attitude. Abbey sang with the mall's Christmas carols. She bought a cinnamon flavored sucker at Lollipop Time, and by the time lunch rolled around, it was already gone. She got polka-dotted socks with individual toes in them for Selma. She stopped at Piñata Pete's and purchased a piñata shaped like a cow for Brianna.

It was Christmas!

But at last the mall closed. The recalcitrant metal grating slid down to close Trends.

"Whew!" Selma said. "I think we managed twice the sales that we did last year. At least that's what my aching dogs are telling me." She leaned over and massaged her swollen feet.

"We did do better. I haven't run the sales record yet, but—"

"What?" Selma said, in mock horror. "You, Miss Retail-Is-My-Life, you can't quote me our receipts? You're slipping, Gal!"

Brianna pushed her coworker toward the door. "Leave her alone, Selma. Can't you tell our boss is in love?"

"You two!" Abbey protested, but she couldn't dispute it. They were right.

"There's something else going on," Selma said thoughtfully. "Something else has made Abbey different. Softer."

"Love will do that," Brianna told her.

"Well, sure, but this is something else. What's up, Boss Lady?"

Abbey reached for her purse. "It's very simple. A Baby born in a stable touched me. A star over a small town on the other side of the world touched me. A flock of angels singing in the heavens touched me. Christmas touched me."

Selma and Brianna stopped. Then, they looked at each other and smiled. "All right!" Brianna said, hugging her.

"Hallelujah!" Selma echoed. "That's wonderful news!"

"It is," Abbey agreed. "It is."

"We'd better get going," Selma pointed out, "or we'll still be here when people start rolling in with returns on the twenty-sixth. Eight A.M., right, Boss?"

Abbey groaned. "Unfortunately."

The two women picked up their packages and purses and prepared to leave by the delivery door in the back of the store.

"See you two the day after tomorrow," Abbey said. "Have a very Merry Christmas!"

"And a Merry Christmas to you too!" Selma called. Brianna waved a cheery farewell.

Abbey hurried down to Tuck's Toys. She walked through the gamut of the deserted kiosks, most of which would be gone after the returns and sales had ended in a week or two. She'd miss them when the mall went back to its normal schedule and appearance.

Unless, of course, the mall management decided to go with a King of Hearts theme or something equally as bizarre for Valentine's Day. She could see it now; Kiss Me Kandies next to Love in Bloom Florists.

But somehow it wasn't as dreadful as it had first seemed. Maybe falling in love had softened her.

She paused at the now-abandoned Candy Cane Calaboose and remembered the time she and Mike were locked in there together. Well, she mused, even the Candy Cane Calaboose wasn't bad if you could fall in love with your cellmate.

A horrible realization struck her. She didn't have a present for Mike.

On the wall, a poster for the Candy Cane Calaboose fluttered by a single staple. An idea struck her, but she'd have to hurry. She tore down the poster and ran back to Trends. One of the last shipments had been picture frames, and she held her breath as she looked through the display, searching for one in particular.

She breathed a sigh of relief. It was there.

The frame itself was a series of interlocking candy canes, and the poster fit perfectly inside it. She wound some tissue paper around it and stuck it into one of their gift bags. She dug through the remaining stock of complimentary small gift cards until she found one with a candy cane on it.

Abbey chewed on the end of her pen. She couldn't think of a thing to say on a card. "You're very sweet" was very dumb. "I CANEn't live without you"? "We were MINT for each other"?

It was always difficult to be clever. Sometimes it was downright impossible, and this was one of those moments.

She opted for no card at all. After all, she'd be handing him the gift in person.

Her eyes scanned the shop for a gift for Claire. Then she remembered something that had come in that morning's delivery. She had opened the box, but she had gotten so busy that she hadn't had the chance to unpack it and put the contents out. She dashed into the storage room and dug in the box until she found it.

It was a blue and white china jewelry box. The blue exactly matched Claire's eyes. Impulsively she tucked a gaily-striped candy cane pin inside it.

She tied it up in bright red paper, then wrote a sales receipt for the items so she could pay for them the day after Christmas.

"Ready to go?"

Abbey jumped as Mike's voice echoed throughout the cavernous mall. "You startled me!"

She shoved the hastily wrapped packages into a bag. "I'm going out the side. I don't trust this rusty old gate to work right tonight, and I sure don't want to be late."

He handed her a take-out bag as she met him in the mall corridor. "Not too fancy—just a burger and fries from Boomtown Burger. I've got two cans of soda in my coat pocket too. We'll have to eat on the run, or I'm afraid we'll be late."

The church service was wonderful, Abbey thought. The carols had a meaning far beyond what they had portrayed while they'd played on an endless loop at the mall, and she sang along with heartfelt gusto.

At the end of the service, ushers passed out small candles with circular cardboard drip-stoppers. The lamps dimmed, and the minister began: "I am the light of the world . . ." One by one the church members lit their candles from their neighbor's as the light was passed from the minister to the last guest, until the entire sanctuary was lit only by the glow of a hundred candles. And one by one they blew out their candles after the benediction while singing "Silent Night."

Abbey could not bear to speak until they had left the church and were standing outside, the cold air turning their breath into clouds. A light snow had fallen, making everything freshly white.

Her heart had opened honestly, and she needed to face life—all of it—honestly. She turned to Mike, her emotions overflowing, and started to speak, but he put his finger over her lips.

"Sssh," he said. "Listen."

From inside the emptying church, the faintest sounds of the last notes of "Silent Night" drifted out. "It's the Christmas prayer, the search for silence," he whispered.

She held his hand until the last notes faded away. "Thank you for giving me this Christmas Eve," she told him. "There's something else I wanted to tell you."

She had to open up, she simply had to, or she would burst with the joy of it. "Mike, I—"

He bent toward her, and time stood completely still. They were the only ones in the world. They were everyone. Then, he kissed her.

It was true. She heard bells. Big loud bells that played "Joy to the World."

He laughed as their mouths separated. "Perfect timing," he said, motioning toward the spire where the bells rang out the Christmas carol.

If it were possible to save time, to press it between the pages of the calendar so that she could take it out and look at it again and again, this would be the moment she would save, Abbey thought. It was perfect, completely and totally perfect.

"Abbey, I think I'm falling in love with you." His words carried across the wintry night, and two of the people leaving the church heard and bent their own heads together.

There was so much she wanted to say, but the words stuck in her heart. Instead, she stood on her tiptoes and kissed him gently, reverently, in answer.

"I'd love to stay here and kiss you in the moonlight," he said at last, "but there's another woman in my life, and I've promised her I'd go out to Golden Meadows to play Christmas carols for a sing-along. Want to come?"

But Claire didn't join them in the Fireside Lounge. She was asleep, the aide told them. It was a calm, healing sleep, though, not the fretful tossing and turning that had signaled her illness initially.

The sing-along was attended by a majority of the residents, many with holiday sweaters and ties on. It was the perfect way to end the perfect Christmas Eve, like a bow on the present of life.

The next morning, Mike picked Abbey up early. "Grandma's waiting, anxiously I'm sure, to open her presents. She likes to dig in before breakfast, but I've told her she'd have to wait a bit later today."

"She's like a kid about Christmas, isn't she?" Abbey asked. "It's wonderful to see that enthusiasm."

Claire was sitting up, looking much better than she had, when they arrived. "I've got the presents ready," she announced. "Let's go!"

At her insistence, Mike helped her out of the bed and into the overstuffed blue chair. Abbey suppressed a grin at the yellow frog slippers that she slid her feet into. Clearly Claire hadn't waited for her and Mike before starting to open gifts.

With a flurry of paper and ribbons flying, Claire unwrapped her presents. She oohed over the Wag-A-Muffin and the sweater that Mike gave her and aahed when she opened the jewelry box from Abbey.

"This has been a wonderful Christmas," Claire said. "And these are terrific presents. Thank you both."

"The best Christmas gift of all," Abbey said, giving Claire's hand a squeeze, "is seeing you healthy again." Then she looked at Mike. "Slight correction. It's one of the best presents."

"What? What?" Claire asked, her eyes glowing with excitement.

"This may be a bit premature, Grandma, since I haven't checked it out with Abbey, but I think there might be a wedding in the future." He dropped a kiss on Claire's forehead. "That is, of course, if we have your blessing."

Claire wriggled even straighter. "I have a problem with this, Michael James Tucker."

"You do?" Mike's face flushed. "Grandma—"

"I can't believe that you didn't ask her first!" Claire scolded. "Now, get down on your knees and do it properly."

"Yes, Ma'am!"

Mike gave her a jaunty salute and dropped to one knee. Taking Abbey's hand in his, he said, "Abbey, we've known each other since we were kids. We've been through many changes, some good, some bad, that have taken us apart from each other—and brought us back together again."

His voice caught in his throat, and he had to stop and take a deep breath to keep his words even. "I want to spend the rest of our lives together."

Abbey could only hold onto his hand as if it meant life itself. Her lips opened and closed, but no sound came out. Perhaps it didn't need to.

"Abbey?" His forehead wrinkled in concern. "Are you all right?"

"Yes," she said, her voice somewhere between tears and laughter. "Yes, yes, yes!"

"Kiss her," Claire commanded from her chair. "That's the next step. Sweet, do I have to think of everything?"

Mike playfully shushed his grandmother. "I know what I'm doing."

Claire gave a good-natured snort. "Ha. Well, it's a good thing I'm here in case you mess something up. Go ahead."

"Thanks," Mike said, grinning at her. Then he fished in his coat pocket and pulled out a box that was about the size of a small popcorn bag. "Okay, let me explain. See, when you've got two lovely women in your life, what are you going to do on Christmas? Clearly, get them the same thing. Abbey, here's your Wag-A-Muffin."

She opened the box and pulled out a pure white dove, embossed with a golden cross on the wing, a golden collar around its neck. "It's beautiful!" she said, running her hand down its back and watching the dove's tail move.

"I'm glad you like it. But now here's my dilemma. I got Grandma a sweater, and it just didn't seem right to get you one too."

"It's improper," Claire interjected. "The first gift you give someone shouldn't be clothing."

"See what I put up with?" Mike said teasingly. "But then I realized that these old rules are for the birds, so I went ahead and got you something to wear."

Then he continued to stand there, his hands in his pockets, smiling at her.

"Where is it?" Claire asked impatiently. "I want to see!"

He didn't say anything for a moment, until at last he said, "Abbey has it already."

"I do?" she asked in surprise. "What?"

"Look closer at the dove. It's got a collar on . . ."

Abbey gasped as she realized what the collar was. It was a simple gold band set with a single clear diamond.

"If you don't like it, we can go pick out another one."

"I love it," Abbey managed to gasp, once her heart had returned to beating in a fairly normal pattern. "It's beautiful!"

He slipped it on her finger, and for a moment they stood together, their gazes locked in a timeless embrace. "Now do I kiss her?" he asked over his shoulder to his grandmother.

"Now would be a good time," Claire said, and before her eyes shut, Abbey caught a glimpse of Claire's satisfied smile.

"I have a present for you too," Abbey said at last. She handed her gift to Mike. "I was going to wait, but now I think this is the right time."

Mike opened the framed picture and grinned. "I love it!" Then his eyes met hers. "Does this mean what I think it does?"

"I think I knew that you were my destiny when we were locked up together in that silly *Candy Cane Calaboose*. I thought I'd hate it, but deep inside me, I wanted it to go on and on." Abbey gave him a tremulous smile. "Isn't that funny? When I was locked up with you, I found my freedom."

Her heart was no longer imprisoned in its cage of defiance. She was free now, in so many ways. The walls were down; the door was unlocked and open, ready to welcome love.

"Grandma," Mike said at last, "you need to get healthy and stay that way. I think we have a wedding in our future!"

Claire wiggled her toes happily, and Abbey was sure she saw the frogs on the yellow fuzzy slippers smiling.

ℰPILOGUE

℘he Word of Faith Community Church was packed. A gentle snow had fallen, but it did nothing to diminish the happiness of those gathered within. It was December twenty-fifth, and this was a wedding. There was little that people liked more than a Christmas wedding.

It had been a year since Abbey had accepted Mike's proposal, and the days since then had flown by as if winged. The only change was that as the days passed, she loved him more.

The blessings in her life had grown and intensified since that amazing Christmas Eve. God continued to touch her life daily. She saw it in her work as well as her love. God did care for His own.

She'd gone back to college, preparing for the MBA she'd always wanted. Mike had come home one day with a brochure about distance education classes, and she'd signed up right away. They were perfect for her schedule.

After a period of relatively ineffective resistance, she'd answered the call to work with the Jeremiah Group. Her focus area was appearance, and she now advised the young women on the proper clothing to wear to work and how to find appropriate yet inexpensive apparel.

Mona had easily established herself as one of Abbey's favorites. Her natural affinity for the elderly served her well at Golden Meadows. Mona had even started college with a nursing degree as her goal, and Abbey was as proud as a mother peacock. As matter of fact, the young woman was presiding over the cake table at the wedding reception.

"Your veil's crooked." Selma's voice caught, and although Abbey saw the glimmer of tears in her friend's eyes, she knew they were tears of happiness.

"I can't go in with my veil crooked," Abbey teased her gently. "People will talk."

Selma sniffed back the threatening sobs. "They will anyway."

"Honey?" Her mother's hand caressed Abbey's cheek. "The usher says it's time to seat me, so I have to go. Abbey, I love you. Mike will be a good husband, I can tell."

"Any last words of motherly advice?" Abbey asked shakily.

"Just love him. That's it. Just love him."

Her mother started to go, then turned back. "I think I need to modify that a bit. Love him simply. Don't get carried away over-analyzing him. But also don't forget that you are a child of God too. Be careful not to lose yourself." She paused. "I didn't know that when I first got married—or maybe I did, and I just ignored it—but it kept both Ed and me from having the best relationship we could, and that wasn't fair to any of us, including you."

Abbey saw tears pool in her mother's eyes. "Mom, I understand. And it's all right. Even when I was a teenager and fighting back against anything and everything, I still knew, in my heart, that there was love in our house."

"And one more thing, Abbey. Always, always trust God. Again, your dad and I didn't have that trust, and it made marriage just that much harder. But now we know, and life is better. I'm so happy to know you're starting your married life with God as the head of your household."

"Oh, Mom." It was all that Abbey could manage.

Her mother laughed shakily. "Look at me. The wedding hasn't even started, and already I'm a sodden mess. I need a handkerchief."

"So do I." Abbey confessed, feeling her emotions starting to crescendo. "We'd better get this show on the road," she told her mother. "If I start crying now, I'll have a drippy nose and swollen, red eyes by the time I get to the altar. Mike will turn and run."

Her mother smiled mistily, gave her a quick kiss, and left to be seated in the sanctuary.

"Ready?" Brianna spoke to them from the door of the room where

Selma and Abbey had dressed. "We've got a church full of people anxious to see you. Some of them are worried about getting back to Golden Meadows in time for the Christmas party there, so I think you'd better get moving before they mutiny."

"All right. I'm ready. Nervous as a cat, but I'm ready." An entire flock of butterflies seemed to have made their home in her stomach.

Selma smoothed her red velvet bridesmaid's dress. "Next time, I get to be the bride, okay?"

"Okay. You've got to find your own fellow, though."

Selma made a face. "I knew there was going to be a catch somewhere."

Abbey enveloped Selma in one last hug. "I'm so happy," she confided. "I think I could burst."

"Well, don't," Selma said practically. "That's a new dress you've got on, you know, and white stains like nobody's business."

Abbey left the room with Selma and joined the rest of the bridal party in the small area behind the sanctuary, which was decorated in red and white. She adjusted her bouquet, which, like those of the others in the bridal party, included tiny candy canes sprinkled among the red and white carnations.

She leaned down and kissed her matron of honor, whose wheelchair was festooned with garlands of red and white tinsel.

The music started, and the four women proceeded down the aisle.

I should remember this, Abbey thought as she passed through the wedding guests. Their faces blurred, but she knew they were all smiling at her. *I need to remember this always.*

The minister was waiting for her at the altar . . . and so was Mike. He had never looked so tall, so capable, so trusting.

The minister began to speak the familiar words: "Dearly beloved, we are gathered . . . ."

Her mind wandered back to the day the socks dropped through the grating, to the time of the blizzard, to the afternoon in the Candy Cane Calaboose.

"I do."

She looked at Mike, and the world got smaller, the congregation vanished, and there were only the two of them.

"I now pronounce you husband and wife. You may kiss the bride."

The world exploded with joy. The minister turned them to face the congregation. "I'd like to introduce to you Mr. and Mrs. Michael Tucker."

The organ burst into glorious song, a collection of Christmas carols, and hand in hand, Mike and Abbey rushed back down the aisle and into the narthex.

"We're married, Honey," he said to her as he took her in his arms. "Now and forever."

He bent to kiss her, and as she lifted her lips to meet his, the guests began to file out.

Claire was the first to get to them. Abbey leaned down to hug her, and the older woman beamed at her. "Weddings are so romantic, aren't they?" she cooed. She blinked her eyelashes flirtatiously at her companion. "Albert, do we have something to tell them?"

The gentleman whom Abbey had met in the coffee shop during her first visit to Golden Meadows looked fondly at Claire. "Would that be advising them to keep Valentine's Day open?"

"What are you two planning?" Abbey asked. "A party?"

Albert and Claire's eyes sparkled with a shared secret. "Perhaps," Albert said.

"You could call it a party," Claire said, "except that we prefer to call it a wedding."

Abbey reached for both of them and enveloped them simultaneously in a bear hug. "I'm so glad for you!" She knew she was gushing, but she couldn't stop.

"And don't think you can just recycle the gifts from this shindig that you don't want," Claire said with an impish grin. "I'll be watching."

Abbey turned to Mike. "Did you know anything about this?"

He shook his head. "Nope. I'm as surprised—and as pleased—as you are. Grandma kept this locked tighter than the closet where she used to hide our Christmas presents."

"Well," Claire explained, "I had to get you two together first."

Mike grinned. "I don't know what to say, except thanks and congratulations!"

"By the way," Claire continued, "I do have another surprise. Want a hint?"

"Sure!" Abbey said.

"Okay, here it is: Great hoppy-ness always." The elderly woman motioned toward the entry to the church.

Abbey turned startled eyes to the door. "Aunt Luellen! You came all the way from Brazil?"

"Chile, Honey, and of course I did. I couldn't miss seeing my favorite niece get married!" The woman was tanned and fit and didn't look half of her eighty-something years. "And I can't wait for you to see what I got you!"

"If it turns out to be half as good as what you got me last Christmas," Abbey said, "I'm going to love it!"

Aunt Luellen looked confused. "I can't remember what I got you last year."

Abbey looked up at her handsome new husband. "Love," she said. "That's what you gave me."

FOR A FATHER'S LOVE

BY JOANN A. GROTE

For my brother-in-law, Mark Falvey, because he's a wonderful father and because he keeps my computer running. And for my dear friend Patricia Thomas—thanks for your medical expertise. (Any mistakes related to medical situations in this story are mine.)

$\mathcal{J}$ ason punched the speakerphone button, irritated by the incessant buzz. His secretary wouldn't put through a call this afternoon unless it was important, but he still resented the intrusion. He faced a mountain of information to wade through before the corporate takeover meeting the next morning.

"J. P. Garth, here," he barked, scowling at the financial statement on his desk.

"Jason, it's—"

"Mandy." He dropped into the high-backed leather chair. His heart plunged to his stomach. The eight years since he'd heard her voice rolled away in a millisecond.

"I-it's your grandfather, Jason. He's had a heart attack."

"Heart attack? But he's strong as an ox." Jason's mind immediately built a foundation for his denial. Years of working on the mountainside Christmas tree farm kept Gramps in great shape. Besides, if he'd a heart attack, why would Mandy be the one to call? Last he knew, she lived more than an hour's drive from his grandparents.

He heard her take a shaky breath. "Your Grandma Tillie and I are at the hospital. She asked me to call you."

Fear surged through him. It must be true if Gram couldn't make the call herself. She was one tough lady. "Is he . . . is he dying?"

"No, but Dr. Monroe said it's an acute attack. They took an EKG and put Grandpa Seth on an IV with a drug to dissolve the clot in his heart. He started feeling better almost immediately."

"But he's still in danger?"

"Not after the clot dissolves. Not immediate danger. They'll have to do tests to see whether he needs angioplasty or bypass surgery."

"Bypass surgery?"

"Jason, I—"

"Tell Gramps and Gram I'll catch the next plane home."

He heard her sigh of relief. "Good. They need you."

Guilt pushed at his fear. He hadn't seen his grandparents since Christmas, ten months earlier. "Mandy . . ." Even with the arrangements to make and his fear for his grandfather, Jason hated to break the only connection he'd had with her since graduating from college.

"Yes?"

"Thanks."

"Good-bye, Jason."

He hung up, then took a deep breath and punched the button connecting him with his secretary. "Ida, get me on the next flight to Greensboro or Charlotte, North Carolina."

"What about the meeting tomorrow?"

"Neal will tell you what arrangements to make for it. First, get me on a flight."

"Yes, Sir."

Moments later Jason entered the senior partner's office through huge paneled doors and succinctly explained the situation to Neal.

After a few words of sympathy, Neal scowled. "Sounds like there's nothing you can do for him at the moment. Meetings on the Sullivan takeover begin tomorrow. We both know they're going to be rough. Can't you wait a few days?"

"No."

"He's your grandfather, J. P., not your father."

Jason leaned both hands on the senior partner's desk. "My parents died when I was a teenager. My grandparents took me in. They're as close to parents as it gets. I'm going home."

"I didn't realize," Neal blustered. "Of course, under the circumstances, a few days is understandable."

"I might be gone for more than a few days."

"What can you do for him if he's lying around recuperating?"

"He may be a grandfather, but his age doesn't keep him from running his own Christmas tree farm."

"It's only the end of October. Surely he doesn't need you yet."

"Just starting the busiest time of year."

"But the takeover—"

"Timmins has been working with me on it. I know he's a junior partner and hasn't handled any negotiations alone, but he's a good man. He knows the facts in this case and my strategy. Every man jumps out on his own sometime. Guess this is Timmins's time."

Neal's face paled. "This is the largest case we've handled in three years. We can't entrust it to a tenderfoot."

"He can call me if he needs advice. You'll sit in on the meetings. Teamed with your prestige and experience, Timmins can pull it off. You hired him, Man. Put a little faith in him."

"I hired him for his potential. It takes more experience than he's had, even with your excellent tutoring, to pull off a coup like the one we plan." Neal tapped his fingertips on the mahogany desktop. "Let's postpone."

"If you postpone, our opponents will think we're waffling. You and Timmins can pull the meeting off. I need to catch a flight. I'll call you from North Carolina." Jason turned on his heel and left Neal protesting to empty space.

It had been dark for hours when Jason's flight left New York. He leaned back in the wide, first-class seat, slowly removed his tie, and pulled his shoulders down, trying to stretch. Would his muscles never relax? He should sleep—he'd need his strength tomorrow—but his body wouldn't cooperate.

He glanced toward the window and saw his pale reflection there. His short brown hair looked crisply neat as always, the style chosen to present a dignified, self-confident business image, the same as his clothing. His eyes stared back at him from beneath almost straight, dark brows in a lean face. The ghostly image didn't show the lines that at thirty-two were already making inroads. All hints of the boy who grew up in North Carolina's Blue Ridge Mountains had long since left his face. *And left my heart,* he thought, turning away from the window.

What would he find at his grandparents' mountain home? Would Gramps be better or worse? *Or might he? . . .*

Jason couldn't finish the thought.

A vision of his grandfather slid through Jason's mind: thick white hair, a trim white beard bordering a broad, tanned face with a permanent smile. His chest tightened. In many ways, Gramps had been more of a father to Jason than his own father. Sam Garth's position as professor of finance at the local university had supplied the family's material needs. He'd stressed to Jason the importance of responsibility and had groomed Jason for a successful career. But it was Gramps who had loved Jason unconditionally.

Jason lost his father when he was sixteen, half a lifetime ago. Now he might be losing Gramps. The tightness in his chest grew tauter.

He turned his thoughts deliberately from his fears. *Mandy.* Closing his eyes and leaning his head back against the seat, he let her voice drift through his memory. Had she been visiting Gram and Gramps at the time of the heart attack? She'd always liked them. He smiled, recalling how she called them Grandma Tillie and Grandpa Seth. He'd often suspected in the four years they dated that she loved his grandparents almost as much as she loved him.

As much as I thought she loved me.

Wouldn't he ever get over her refusal to marry and move to New York with him? He remembered everything about the day he'd proposed: the way the sunlight shone through the trees, adding copper lights to her brown hair, the determination in her wonderful, fir-green eyes, and the words that ripped his world apart: "I'll never leave the mountains, not for you, not for anyone."

He loved the mountains too, but when his parents died, he'd abandoned his dream of owning a tree farm like his grandfather's and embraced the career his father had wanted for him—a career in finance in New York City, the nation's financial hub.

Wasn't that what love did—sacrifice its own desires for the loved one? He'd trusted Mandy's love completely, but she hadn't loved him enough to sacrifice her precious mountains for a life with him.

"Mandy," he whispered. He rubbed a hand down his face. Turning his thoughts from his grandfather to Mandy had only replaced one kind of pain with another, more familiar one.

O oh, aren't you beautiful." Mandy Wells lifted the fragile angel from its protective wrappings. The morning sun streamed through the large window behind her, its rays resting on the tiny porcelain head, bringing to life the pink cheeks, blue eyes, and blond hair.

Mandy smoothed the angel's flowing gown of ivory satin and hand-spun lace, which was in striking contrast to her own faded blue jeans and oversized topaz sweater. "You'll be perfect for the top of the tree beside the door." Stepping quickly over cardboard packing boxes, Mandy made her way through the layer of crushed newspaper and Styrofoam beads covering the wooden floor.

She touched a switch, and the Christmas shop burst into life. Dozens of trees sparkled with every type of ornament. Spicy cinnamon and orange odors from Christmas potpourri and pine scent from swags hanging from wooden beams filled the air.

She stopped beside a tree decorated with Victorian nose-gays, miniature dolls, wide ribbons of cream and pink, and sprays of baby's breath. Dragging a decorated wooden stool over, Mandy climbed up to remove a lace-backed nosegay of rose and cream buds from the treetop. Holding her breath, she stretched to attach the angel to the treetop.

Brass bells above the door jangled merrily. Mandy gasped as the door crashed into her stool.

"O-oh!" Mandy clutched the precious angel in one hand and grasped for the bedecked tree with the other. The tree tumbled to the floor. The stool slipped from beneath her. Mandy shut her eyes in anticipation of a hard landing.

There was a loud masculine grunt. Muscular arms closed about her, crushing her against a hard chest with the delicate angel between her and her rescuer. The man lurched back with the sudden force of her weight. The door thudded shut when he crashed against it, the bells once again tinkling merrily.

She opened her eyes slowly. Finely cut light brown hair topped the ruggedly handsome face above her. The lips were colorless, the square jaw tensed, the green eyes wide with shock.

She knew those eyes. "Jason." The name came out in a hoarse whisper. Every nerve ending tingled to life. She thought she'd braced herself for the moment they'd meet. *Obviously I deluded myself.*

The shock in his eyes shifted to anger. Their fury brought Mandy back to her senses. She squirmed slightly. "If you'll let me go," she suggested, congratulating herself silently on her calm tone.

He set her roughly on her feet, steadying her with strong hands on her waist.

Instantly she regretted the lack of his arms about her. She'd longed to be back in those arms for years. *Idiot,* she reprimanded herself. She brushed the angel's golden hair into place, searching for time to compose herself. "You're certainly the man for the moment."

"Are you all right?"

He didn't look as though he cared. "I'm fine." She set the angel on the counter behind her, then turned to survey the scattered nosegays and broken miniature Victorian dolls. "Unfortunately, my tree didn't have as soft a landing."

Jason scowled at the rubble he'd created, then scanned the shop. "What is this place?"

She clasped her hands behind her back and surveyed the large room with its decorated Christmas trees, satin angels, and glittering snowflakes dangling from the wooden beams. Red-and-green stockings stuffed with toys hung from the oak mantel above the stone fireplace in the middle of the former barn, and brightly wrapped packages were piled everywhere. "It's a Christmas store. I thought so, but since you didn't recognize it as such, I thought I'd better give it another look."

He took a deep breath. "What are you and this store doing in

Gramps's barn?" The question came slowly, each word forced between clenched teeth.

She took a couple steps back and stared at him in surprise. "Your grandparents never told you? They leased it to me last January."

"Why?"

She couldn't pretend she didn't know what he meant by that one-word question. "The short answer is that last year when I bought my Christmas tree from them, I told them my dream of opening a Christmas store in a barn like this. They'd just built that long warehouse-type building for their tree business, so they offered me this barn. I accepted, and"—she spread her arms toward the store—"here I am with my Christmas store."

"You know what I meant."

You meant why would they let me use the barn only a few hundred yards from their house when they know how much you and I meant to each other once; why would I want to be so close to the only family you have left. "Can't a more complete explanation wait? You must be eager to see your grandfather. Or have you just come from the hospital?"

"No, I haven't seen him yet. I thought Gram would be at the house and we could go to the hospital together."

She noticed the circles beneath his eyes. She'd been avoiding his eyes, avoiding looking at that face she saw all too often in her dreams. Stubble shadowed his cheeks. His finely tailored gray suit was wrinkled; the white shirt with its monogrammed pocket was rumpled and open at the neck. The tip of a navy-and-gray-striped tie poked from a suit pocket. Obviously he hadn't slept all night.

The realization softened her tone. "I took Grandma Tillie in to the hospital this morning."

"Already? The sun's barely up."

"She couldn't sleep last night. She wants to be with your grandfather every minute."

"I guess that's no surprise. She and Gramps have spent almost sixty years together."

His green-eyed gaze gentled, holding her own. Her throat tightened, remembering they'd promised to love each other as long and as fully as Grandma Tillie and Grandpa Seth. Was Jason remembering too? She shifted her gaze to the floor to break the spell, but the taut feeling in her chest stayed.

Jason cleared his throat. "You say Gramps is doing okay?"

She glanced back at him, ashamed at daydreaming about the two of them when Grandpa Seth was so ill. "He's doing as well as can be expected."

Jason's lips thinned. "I haven't stopped imagining the worst since you called."

She reached toward him, longing to ease his pain. When her hand was a fraction of an inch away, she snatched it back. *I haven't the right to comfort him with more than words anymore.* The old sense of loss stabbed through her.

He rubbed a hand down his face in a gesture so familiar it caught at her heart. "I'm sorry I snapped at you. Chalk it up to shock and exhaustion, though it's no excuse."

"It's okay." The words came out in a cracked whisper. She pressed her lips together hard, unable to tear her gaze from his, wishing she could talk with him without remembering the way it felt to laugh with him and be in his arms.

"Mandy, we're back."

She whirled around at her sister Ellen's voice, swallowing hard and pasting on a smile. The back door slammed. A moment later, two girls raced across the room, dodging trees and gift items.

Six-year-old, chestnut-haired Bonnie threw her arms around Mandy's legs in her usual exuberant greeting. Mandy lifted the girl and gave her a hug. "Hello, Precious."

Bonnie's round arms tightened about Mandy's neck, and the gentle scent of baby shampoo filled Mandy's senses.

Eight-year-old Beth smiled, tilting her head, straight blond hair sliding over the shoulder of her red sweater. "Hi, Aunt Mandy."

Mandy slid her palm along the child's silky hair. "Hello, Sweetheart. What's for breakfast?"

Beth held up a white bag which emitted fast-food odors. "Sausage biscuits." A frown puckered her brow. "What happened to the tree?"

"A small accident. Nothing that can't be fixed."

"Sorry it took us so long." Ellen's voice preceded her as she crossed the room, expertly dodging Christmas trappings while tugging off her leather gloves. "The place was packed, and—" She caught sight of the tree with its broken and smashed decorations. "What happened to—"

She stopped, gloves dangling from one hand, and stared at Jason with her mouth open.

Jason nodded brusquely. "Ellen."

"J. P."

Ellen sounds as breathless as I was when I first saw him, Mandy thought in amusement.

Ellen closed the few feet between herself and J. P., her shoulder-length, straight brown hair swinging. She reached to shake hands. "Hello, J. P. I'm sorry about your grandfather. All my hopes and prayers are for his recovery."

"Thanks."

His gaze shifted from Ellen and rested on Bonnie, who still clung to Mandy's neck. Mandy noticed his puzzled look and remembered he wouldn't recognize the girls. Resting a hand on Beth's shoulder, she said, "You remember Ellen's daughter, Beth, don't you?"

He smiled at the shy, slender girl. "I remember. You were only a few months old when I last saw you."

Beth blushed and stared at him soberly.

"This is J. P.," Ellen told her. "Seth and Tillie's grandson."

Beth kept staring, not smiling.

His glance slid to the girl in Mandy's arms.

"This is Bonnie," Mandy said.

"Hello, Bonnie."

The girl burrowed her face into Mandy's neck at Jason's intense gaze. Why had his voice cracked when he greeted Bonnie? Mandy wondered. Was he thinking of the children they'd talked of having one day? Her stomach tightened painfully at the memory of the once-shared dream.

Ellen settled onto a backless stool beside the counter. "Is someone going to tell me why that Christmas tree looks like it belongs to Scrooge?"

Mandy shifted Bonnie to her other hip. "In a minute. We mustn't keep Jason. He hasn't seen his grandfather yet."

Mandy cringed inwardly at the look Ellen shot her. She could tell Ellen wasn't fooled by her polite dismissal of Jason.

"Of course," Ellen said smoothly. "Do give Seth our love, J. P. Tell him we'll bring the girls around to see him as soon as the hospital allows."

"I'll do that." He opened the door, then looked back, his gaze shifting between Mandy and Bonnie. "I'll talk to you later, Mandy."

She nodded. The tone beneath his simple statement raised havoc inside her. Would he demand a more complete explanation of why she'd leased this barn? Would he want her to give it up? Wait until he heard she lived above the shop.

Ellen pulled a biscuit from the bag. "All right, tell all."

Mandy set Bonnie down and knelt to pick up the crushed ornaments. "There's nothing to tell. Jason arrived at the farmhouse expecting to find Grandma Tillie. When he didn't, he stopped here, looking for her or some news about Grandpa Seth."

"That's all you two talked about? Grandpa Seth? After all these years? There were no sparks? No arguments? No kisses?"

"Kisses?" Beth was suddenly all eyes and ears.

"No kisses," Mandy told Ellen and Beth firmly. "Beth, will you and Bonnie help me pick up these nosegays? Watch out for broken pieces from the dolls' heads."

The girls joined her.

"You're avoiding me, Mandy Wells," Ellen charged.

"There's nothing to tell. Besides, I thought you'd given up on men."

"For me, not for you."

Mandy looked pointedly at the old schoolhouse clock on the wall above the counter. "You'll be late for work if you don't leave this minute, and I've got to feed the girls and get this mess cleaned up before I open for business."

Ellen slid off the stool. "All right, but you can't avoid me forever. I'll be back for your story at five-thirty. If the girls are too much trouble, make them take a nap—or pretend to take a nap."

"Mo-o-om," the girls chorused in indignation.

"Bye." Ellen headed toward the back door.

I won't be urging naps on the girls today, Mandy thought. Watching them, cleaning up the mess, and waiting on customers should keep her mind off Jason. Sunny October Saturdays always brought lots of people to the mountains and customers to the Christmas store.

She should be an expert at keeping her mind off Jason by now. It had taken years to get over him. *No, that's not accurate. It's taken years to get used to the pain of living without him in my life.* Still, she knew they couldn't make a marriage work, not as long as he insisted on living his father's dream instead of his own.

"Aunt Mandy." Bonnie tugged at the sleeve of Mandy's sweater. "Aren't you goin' to help us clean up?"

"Of course, Precious. I was just thinking about all we must do today."

"Looked like you were daydreaming." Beth glanced up from the floor with a crushed nosegay in her hand. "Mom says daydreaming is a waste of time."

Mandy didn't agree, but she didn't believe in going against her sister's parenting. Besides, this time, maybe Ellen was right. Instead of daydreaming, she should be praying for Jason.

She knew what was ahead for him. She'd seen Grandpa Seth only an hour ago when she'd dropped off Grandma Tillie. A monitor and IVs were attached to the dear, rugged, usually blustery old man lying in the hospital bed. Her heart ached, wishing she could spare Jason the shock of seeing his grandfather that way.

But all she could do was pray for Jason—and hurt with him for what he was going through.

3

*J*ason headed up the hill toward the car, his shiny black wing tips crunching through fallen leaves on the gravel drive. The sharp scent of dying leaves and earthy scent of loam in the nearby woodlands filled his senses. Songs of birds greeting the morning were a sharp contrast to the traffic sounds that usually surrounded him this time of day.

His grandparents' two-story white frame house with its dark green shutters nestled against the mountain and rose above the black rental car. High-backed oak rocking chairs sat on the porch that ran the width of the house, inviting him to "set a spell."

Jason scanned the view the house had looked out upon for 130 years. The mountains rolled away, ridge after ridge of rich autumn color with lazy fog drifting between them. Orderly rows of blue spruce and Fraser firs, the best Christmas trees grown, covered most of his grandfather's mountain. He loved those trees. Fear gnawed at him despite Mandy's assurances. Would his grandfather ever return to this place?

He turned his back on the tranquil scene and slid into the rental car. *The mountain's peace is an illusion,* he thought as he started down the mountain road toward town.

On top of his fear for his grandfather, he had to face his feelings for Mandy: beautiful, sweet, delightful, maddening Mandy. "Meddlin' Mandy," he'd teasingly called her, for her habit of involving herself in others' lives. Why hadn't his grandparents told him they'd leased the barn to her?

Bonnie was the spitting image of Mandy. The same unusually dark green eyes wide with permanent wonder beneath a spray of ridiculously long lashes, the same round face with the smallest sprinkling of freckles across her nose and beneath her eyes, the same silky hair the cinnamon color of acorns that fell from the tree in his grandparents' yard in autumn.

Pain coiled inside him. When had Mandy married? With other women, Bonnie might have been the result of a relationship outside marriage, but not with Mandy. Mandy believed in intimacy only within marriage. He believed the same, but it had been mighty hard to keep his hands from roaming during the years they'd dated.

He'd felt like he'd been hit in the gut with a sledgehammer when he saw Bonnie and realized Mandy was married. *What did you expect— that Mandy would sit around the mountains growing old, waiting for you to return?*

Deep in his heart, that's exactly what he'd expected, he grudgingly realized. He hadn't admitted it to himself before, but the surety that she could no more love another man enough to marry him than Jason could another woman had lived in his heart.

The child looked about six years old. Mandy couldn't have waited long after they broke up to marry. The pain in his chest twisted tighter.

She'd given her heart to someone else, and Gramps lay in a hospital bed trying to recover from a heart attack, he thought, turning into the hospital parking lot. Life couldn't get much bleaker. The takeover negotiations would have been a picnic compared to this.

Jason asked at the desk for his grandfather's room. A nurse directed him to ICU. The halls seemed hushed, filled with smells of disinfectants and medicines that spoke loudly of this being a place of death and healing.

His grandmother wasn't in the waiting area. Another nurse, middle-aged with red hair, directed him to the room. "Even family is allowed only a few minutes with the patient every couple hours," she warned.

Jason stopped with his palm against the door, closed his eyes, and pressed his lips tightly together. *Help me, Lord.* He was accustomed to facing wealthy, powerful men, helping them win in takeovers or mergers of mind-boggling dollar amounts—or helping them lose, depending on which side of the table they were seated. He'd never experienced the cold chills and dread he did now, facing his grandfather gravely ill, facing the fear in his grandmother's eyes, and knowing he couldn't make things better for either of them.

Jason took a deep breath and pushed the door open.

Only one bed stood in the room. On it lay an old man, his white hair and trim beard blending in with the pillowcase.

Jason shoved down the panic that swept through his chest at the sight of the tubes attached to his grandfather. Several IVs dripped drugs into his body. A steady *beep, beep* brought Jason's gaze to electrodes attached to Gramps's chest, connecting him to the monitor that watched his heart to catch any irregular beats. At least at the moment, the monitor wasn't off to the races or showing a flat line.

Gramps lay with his eyes closed. Gram held one of his hands in both her own, her gaze not leaving his face. Her long, thin frame was tensed, as though she was willing her own strength to become part of her husband. Neither noticed Jason's arrival.

He tried to say hello. His throat might as well have been glued shut. He swallowed. "Hello, Gram."

She whirled in her chair, still holding her husband's hand. Jason's heart clenched. Wrinkles had covered her face for as many years as he could remember, but until now she hadn't looked old and beaten. "Thank God, you made it."

The barely suppressed panic in her voice sent terror spiraling through him. Did she mean thank God he'd made it before Gramps died?

"You came." Gramps's voice was stronger than Jason expected, still a deep friendly growl. But the old man's smile was weak, and his pale blue eyes shrouded in pain—or fright.

Jason smiled, trying to ignore the fear inside. "Where else would I be, Gramps?"

"S'pose Tillie here went and called you. Made it sound like I was halfway to the other side."

Gram's backbone straightened beneath her dark green sweat suit. "Course I called him. And you were more than halfway to the other side, Seth Kramer. If it weren't for Mandy helping me get you here, and for our prayers and Doctor Monroe—" She choked up.

Mandy had helped save his grandfather's life, Jason realized. Gratitude and guilt fought for supremacy. He should have been the one there for Gramps. Jason struggled to focus. Time for self-pity later. He shook his head, still smiling. "Womenfolk. Take credit for everything."

Gramps chuckled weakly. The chuckle turned into a cough, and pain creased his face.

Jason leaned forward. "Are you all right?"

He nodded. "Have a little pain in my chest, but Doc says that's not unusual."

Jason glanced at the monitor. It bleeped away, steady as a metronome. He breathed a sigh of relief.

The red-haired nurse entered. "You need to let the patient rest now." She held the door open while Gram kissed Gramps's cheek.

Jason slipped an arm around her shoulders. They felt as bony as always, but unlike normal, they trembled. He squeezed her reassuringly, then patted his grandfather's hand. "See you later."

"I'm glad you're here, Jason."

Gramps became a blur through Jason's sudden unshed tears. "Me too. I love you, Gramps."

Jason's thoughts raced as he and Gram stepped into the hall. He wanted to ask so many questions: What was Gramps's prognosis? Had he had any more attacks? Had the attack been mild or massive? Had the doctor performed any tests? Was the doctor still considering surgery or angioplasty?

He didn't know whether he dared ask Gram any of the questions racing through his mind. In spite of her tender heart, she'd always faced life's troubles with the sturdiness of a mountain. Now she seemed about to collapse. She paced the hall, her arms clutched tightly over her chest. Was she trying to keep from screaming with the pain and fear?

At least Mandy had been there for Gram and Gramps until he arrived. Warmth flooded his chest in bittersweet gratitude. If Mandy had married him and moved to New York like he'd wanted her to do, she wouldn't have been there yesterday afternoon.

When Dr. Monroe—a middle-aged man with pepper-and-salt hair and a calm, competent manner custom-made for reassuring patients and kin—came by, Jason questioned him with a thoroughness learned from tenaciously tracking down every pertinent fact in his business dealings. After fifteen minutes, Jason felt convinced of his grandfather's relative safety for the moment, and the doctor moved on.

Gram said, "They won't let us see Seth again for almost an hour. He needs his rest, they say. I think he needs the people he loves more, but the doctor and nurses are firm about the rule."

"They want him to recover too, Gram, and they've a lot more experience with heart attacks than we do. Let's go to the cafeteria. You probably haven't eaten yet today."

Gram insisted she wasn't hungry, but Jason plied her with cinnamon rolls and decaffeinated coffee. Not the best nutrition, but good for calming the nerves, and they needed that.

"If you stopped by the farm, I guess you saw the Christmas barn." Gram looked down at her coffee cup, appearing a tad ashamed.

"Yes, and Mandy." Jason felt a sliver of satisfaction at her discomfort.

"You talked to her?"

"For a few minutes."

She sighed. "S'pose we should have told you 'bout Mandy's store months ago."

"Would have been nice." He kept his voice even. This was no time for the full-scale bawling out he'd like to give her and Gramps.

She stirred her cold coffee. "We kept waiting for the right time. We convinced ourselves to wait until you came home for a visit. Then this happened." One bony shoulder lifted the sweatshirt in a shrug as if to say, "and you know the rest."

Guilt swamped him—again. Her voice held no hint of reproach, but he couldn't pretend she and Gramps weren't aware his last visit home was last Christmas. He'd told his prickling conscience the demands of building a career justified his absence, but he knew better.

"How is your job going?"

He was glad for the change of subject. To try to keep their minds away from their fears, he chatted on about his work and life in New York while they walked back to the visitors' lounge on the ICU floor.

Finally the red-haired nurse told them they could visit Gramps for a few more minutes.

"Heart surgery?" Gramps was asking Dr. Monroe when they entered the room. "Are you sure I need that? I mean, the heart attack didn't kill me."

"The next one might. The valves at the back of your heart are blocked. Without the bypass surgery, if the next attack doesn't take you out, the following one will. It's only a matter of time."

"Can't it wait, Doc? Our busiest season is just starting."

Gram hurried to the bedside. "Seth Kramer, how dare you talk about business when your life is at stake."

"If I'm going to live, I need to support us, don't I? With Ted gone, there isn't another man I trust to take us through the Christmas season. If we miss this season, we don't make any money until this time next year."

Ted had worked with Gramps all Jason's life until just a few months ago when Ted had died of cancer. Eight other men worked full-time at the farm, but Gramps didn't trust any of them the way he had Ted. Jason knew if Ted were still alive, Gramps would have followed the doctor's advice. Without Ted . . .

Gram's pointed chin jutted out. "I can run things this one year."

"You handle the paperwork side of the business fine, Tillie. And the wreaths and roping too. Better than fine. But you don't know diddly-squat about the rest of the business."

"Foolish old man."

"Hold it." Dr. Monroe lifted both hands. "Arguing about business isn't going to help your heart, Seth."

Jason spoke up. "Nothing to argue about anyway. I'm taking a leave of absence from the firm. I'll run the Christmas tree farm through the busy season."

Gramps's frown deepened. "You can't do a thing like that, Boy. You've got your own career to think about. What would happen to that important takeover you're working on?"

"Others in the firm can handle it. I'll keep in touch by phone and E-mail."

"You haven't worked at the farm since your college days. Things have changed."

Jason saw the hope growing in the older man's face in spite of his protests. "You can explain the changes to me. I'll talk with the other growers. We'll work it out together."

Gramps closed his eyes. "It's too much to ask of you."

"You're not asking. I'm offering. I want to do it."

Gramps studied Jason's face. Jason met his gaze evenly. He'd do anything in his power to increase his grandfather's chances of recovery. Neal wouldn't be happy about the leave of absence, but he'd go along with it. Jason knew his worth to the company.

"You're sure about this, Boy?"

"I'm sure."

"Welcome aboard." Gramps lifted his hand a short way above the mattress. Jason met it with his own.

Dr. Monroe breathed an exaggerated sigh of relief, bringing nervous laughter from them all. "Now that that's resolved, I suggest you two let Seth rest awhile."

Back at the visitors' area, Gram grasped one of Jason's hands in both her own. "Thank you."

She looked more relaxed than when he'd arrived, and her shoulders no longer trembled. *At least my offer to help with the farm gave her a measure of peace,* Jason thought. He pulled her close in a hug and planted a kiss on her wrinkled cheek. She wasn't a woman who ordinarily inspired protective gestures. She was almost as tall as he and slender. Rangy, Gramps affectionately described her.

The large round clock on the wall read eleven o'clock. Only nineteen hours since he'd received the call about his grandfather's heart attack. Nineteen hours in which his whole life had changed. Nineteen hours in which his own heart hadn't stopped hurting, fearing, or praying.

God willing, Gramps would come through the bypass surgery with flying colors, but how long before Jason and Gram could look at Gramps without wondering when another attack might come?

Gram pushed herself out of his arms and went to stare out the window.

Jason pulled his cell phone from his suit-coat pocket and punched the power button. The battery was dead. He grimaced. "I'd better call New York and tell them my plans, Gram. I'll be back in a few minutes."

"All right, Jason."

He started down the hall toward the public phones he'd noticed earlier. He was growing accustomed to hearing himself called Jason again. At work, everyone called him J. P., for Jason Peter. His father had given him the nickname years ago, saying with a grin that the initials were good for a man in finance, the same initials as J. P. Morgan and J. P. Getty. Only his grandparents and Mandy never called him J. P.

Mandy. A shiver reverberated through him at the memory of his name on her lips this morning. He'd hungered to hear her whisper his name for so long, but in love, not shock.

For the foreseeable future he was back in the mountains he loved, the mountains he'd forced himself to leave, doing the work he'd loved and left as well, watching and worrying over Gramps.

And living on the same farm as Mandy and her Christmas barn. The same Mandy who'd lived in his dreams for eight years, preventing him from giving his heart to another woman—not that he hadn't tried.

The picture of Mandy holding Bonnie flashed through his mind, and pain tore sharply through him. Mandy wasn't the same person after all. She was a mother. And that meant she was a wife.

Nineteen hours ago he'd thought himself in control of his life. He was good at his profession. He'd learned to live without the mountains and Mandy and was used to the dull pain those losses left inside him.

The toughest months of his life were just ahead. "I never needed Your help more, Lord," he whispered, lifting the pay phone from its cradle.

(4)

was sure right about that phone call to Neal, Jason thought a few days later as he walked from the groves to the farmhouse. Neal's anger and frustration had heated the phone lines but hadn't changed Jason's mind.

He'd been too busy to worry about Neal while working the trees, but he'd need to make his daily check-in call before too long. Maybe he could work it in during the supper break.

Half an hour wasn't nearly enough time to eat and renew himself for another round of work that evening. Jason had thought his daily jog and workout kept him in shape, but only determination not to be shown up by the locals and migrant workers had kept him going through the long days of physical labor, cutting trees and loading them into the binder and then onto trucks.

Mouthwatering odors met him when he entered the old kitchen. He sniffed appreciatively. Roast beef. "I'm home, Gram," he called. "Supper sure smells good."

"She isn't here."

"Mandy." He whirled toward the dining room door. Mandy wore one of Gram's old terry-cloth aprons over a white shirt and jeans. His insides tightened with the pain of knowing she was unattainable. He felt too tired to fight his attraction for her. The knowledge sharpened his voice. "Where's Gram?"

Mandy pushed her hands into the apron pockets. He saw her make fists, bunching the material. "Grandma Tillie is still at the hospital. She asked me to make you dinner." She waved a hand toward an orange slow cooker on the wooden counter. "Roast beef, browned potatoes, and carrots. I hope you're hungry."

"Hungry like a bear, but you don't need to look after me. I'm quite accustomed to taking care of myself. Gram forgets that sometimes."

"She doesn't forget. She cares about you. She knows how long the days are working the trees and wants to make things easier for you."

He hated the hurt-animal look his attitude had put in her eyes. "Sorry. Guess I've lived so long by myself that I've forgotten what family is like."

She removed an ironstone platter from the white, wooden standing cupboard, then forked the roast and vegetables onto the platter. "The gravy should be ready about the time you finish washing up."

He looked down at his pine-tar-covered hands and grimaced. Leaving his heavy boots beside the door and hanging his jacket on a peg above them, he walked to the sink. While washing up, he watched Mandy stir gravy in a cast-iron skillet. She didn't look much older than when they'd dated. She'd spent lots of time at the farm with him then. It seemed natural to see her here. "Will you join me for dinner, Mandy?"

Her startled gaze darted to him.

No wonder his suggestion surprised her, considering the way he'd snapped at her earlier. Before he could let himself change his mind he wheedled, "You're the one who made the meal. You deserve the pleasure of eating it."

Her cheeks dimpled. "Assuming it is a pleasure. You haven't tasted it yet."

He grinned. "I'll take my chances."

She continued stirring the gravy while she bit her bottom lip and looked as if she were debating his invitation. It rankled him that she hesitated. He whipped a blue-checked towel from the wooden towel rack above the sink. "Look, don't think you need to stay."

"I don't. I was thinking about Grandma Tillie. I promised to pick her up."

"Gram won't leave the hospital for hours yet, even though Gramps is out of ICU now."

"There's the store too. I need to check on things before going to the hospital."

Was it his imagination, or did she sound panicky? Did she find his company so unpleasant she couldn't share a few minutes with him over dinner? "I need to be back in the fields in twenty-five minutes. You wouldn't have to endure my company long." He threw the towel down on the counter.

"I didn't say—"

"You didn't have to." He heaved a sigh and ran a hand over his face. "Look, you have every right to leave. You've done more than enough making the meal." He forced a smile. "I plan to enjoy every bite."

"Jason . . ."

He yanked out a chair. Its legs scraped across the black-and-white linoleum. "You've given more time than our family could expect already."

"I was glad to make supper." She set the platter down on the table, followed by two plates.

His heart skipped a beat, then raced on. She'd decided to join him.

"I'm not talking only about the meal." He tried to keep his voice casual. "You've spent a lot of time chauffeuring Gram back and forth to the hospital and visiting Gramps."

"They're friends." Mandy's eyes flashed. She settled her fists on her too-round-for-fashion, apron-clad hips. "People might not help friends in New York, but here it's still considered the proper thing to do."

Laughter rumbled in his chest. He leaned back, balancing the chair on its hind legs. "I haven't seen you spit fire like that since I sneaked the black snake into English lit class."

"And scared poor Professor Potts out of her wits."

"It was just a little black snake. Couldn't hurt her any."

"Especially since she was standing on her desk, screaming bloody murder."

He shrugged. "Class needed some excitement."

"English lit was an elective. If you didn't like it, why did you take it?"

"You were in the class."

Her eyes widened. She glanced away from him and sat down. As she bowed her head, he did the same and said a silent grace.

When he looked back up, she was lifting her fork. "A snake, Jason. Honestly." A smile teased at the edge of her full lips, then grew. "You were impossible back then." Her voice dropped to a soft level that set his pulse racing.

He shrugged and picked up his own fork, hoping she couldn't see how much she'd affected him. "I wasn't impossible. I was just a typical college boy who didn't know whether a certain girl liked him and wasn't very sophisticated in his attempts to get her attention."

"You were never typical."

Her grin turned his insides to Jell-O.

"Besides," she continued, her attention, focused on cutting her meat, "you had nothing to worry about concerning that girl's affections."

He rested his forearms on the table and stared at her. "If that's true, why are you living in the mountains when I'm living in New York?"

Her gaze jerked to his. He saw disbelief and pain in her eyes.

His question hadn't been a question at all. He saw she recognized it for the accusation he'd meant it.

"You know the answer to that." Her voice held no hint of the defense he'd expected. "I—"

"You're right." He lifted one palm to stop her. His voice rose in anger. "Forget it." He didn't truly want to hear again that she hadn't loved him enough to marry him and leave the mountains.

Mandy pushed her chair back and stood. "I need to get back to the store."

"Mandy, I'm sorry. I—"

She hurried to the door, grabbed a brown corduroy coat from the peg beside his jacket, and left. The door slammed behind her.

Jason sighed and rubbed his eyes with a thumb and index finger.

"Don't know how to handle women any better than I did when I was a college kid."

Loneliness twisted through him. He shoved away his still-full plate.

5

he brass bells over the Christmas shop door announced another customer. The spicy scent of autumn leaves wafted inside on the October wind, reminding Mandy of the world outside the shop's constant holiday environment.

I should have put the closed sign on the door after the last customer left, Mandy thought. She glanced at the ornately carved cuckoo clock on the wall above the counter. Almost seven o'clock. At this rate she'd never get to the hospital to see Grandpa Seth and pick up Grandma Tillie.

Her gaze shifted to the man who'd entered. Jason. Her heart missed a beat. She hadn't seen him since the roast beef meal two evenings earlier.

She knew from Grandma Tillie that Jason divided his time between visits to the hospital, work in the Christmas tree groves, and phone calls to his New York office. Mandy had left hot meals in the slow cooker the last couple days, but she'd carefully stayed away from the house when she expected him there.

Why was he here? He wore a cautious look. Likely he wondered what kind of welcome she'd give him after the other night. She wished he hadn't brought up the subject of their breakup. Obviously he planned to live in New York permanently. Neither of their goals had changed. So why bring up a subject that could only open old wounds?

Jason nodded a greeting, jammed his hands into the pockets of his stone-colored twill slacks, and began wandering around the shop.

Smothering a sigh of relief, she turned her attention back to the middle-aged woman with the gray-streaked black hair seated in the wheelchair, and the burly, brown-bearded man standing beside her.

A dozen Christmas cards with the look of hand-painted water-colors stretched across the counter. At one end lay a large painting of Seth and Tillie's mountainside home in winter.

"The cards are exquisite, Alma." Mandy touched the deckled edge of one. "My customers will love them."

A grin wreathed Alma's face. "I never thought I'd see my paintings outside my own home." She glanced up at the large man beside her. "Or my boy's home. I'd never have dared try sell them if not for you, Mandy."

"Thank your son." Mandy smiled at the man. He smiled shyly back. "He's the one who showed me your paintings. How could you keep such a talent secret?"

"Not hard when you're an invalid. People don't expect much from invalids." The words were said matter-of-factly, without self-pity.

"People will know they've been wrong when they see your cards and paintings."

"That they will," Tom Berry agreed.

"Tom's convinced other shops to carry my cards," Alma said proudly, "but not around here. I want your store to be the only place to offer them in this area."

"I take samples along on my selling trips," Tom explained. "Leaving next week on another. Last chance to get things into shops before Christmas. Most of the stores placed their orders six months ago."

"Tom?"

Mandy jumped at the sound of Jason's voice beside her.

Jason reached out a hand. "Tom Berry? I didn't recognize you until I heard your voice. Guess we've both changed a bit since we graduated from high school."

Tom shook Jason's hand. "Good to see you, J. P."

Although Jason was a good-sized man and as tall as Tom, he looked slender and small beside him, Mandy thought.

"How is your grandfather?" Alma asked.

Jason filled them in, accepted their best wishes for his grandfather, then turned his attention to the greeting cards. "These are great. Your work, Tom?"

"My work," Alma corrected.

Shock registered in Jason's eyes. His glance fell to the hands lying useless in Alma's lap. "I didn't realize you painted."

Mandy wished she'd had a chance to tell Jason about Alma Berry's talent. She knew he hadn't meant to be rude.

"I hold the brush in my mouth." Alma's voice was as stiff as her chair. "It takes awhile, but I get the work done."

"And beautifully." Jason held one of the cards where the light could strike it better.

"For an invalid?" There was a quiet challenge in her question.

Jason met her gaze evenly. "For anyone. You have a true talent for catching the mountain's beauty."

"Thank you." Alma's voice relaxed.

His gaze slipped to the large painting. "My grandparents' farm."

The woman laughed. "I'm glad you recognize it."

"It's perfect." He turned to Tom. "So if you're not an artist, what do you do?"

"I'm an artist of sorts—a potter. Didn't take it up until after high school. Started out small, just doing local craft shows, but I'm doing pretty well at it now, thanks to this little lady." He nodded his massive head in Mandy's direction. "She managed a shop in Asheville. When she saw my work at a local craft show, she bought a few pieces for her shop. I never would have had the courage to try to sell to an upscale shop like that."

Mandy grinned at him. "I know talent when I see it, even if I can't create masterpieces myself. Now his work is in demand throughout the surrounding states," she told Jason.

"Haven't had the kind of success you've had, J. P." Tom's beard-surrounded grin showed he wasn't jealous.

Mandy thought Jason looked uncomfortable at Tom's comment. Jason's shoulders lifted his brown sweater in a shrug. "Everyone has their own definition of success."

Tom nodded. "Isn't that the truth."

Mandy studied Jason's face. Wasn't he happy with the life he'd worked so hard to build in New York, making his father's dream his own?

The brass bells jangled as Beth and Bonnie burst into the room, followed by Ellen. The girls saw the Berrys and dashed over, throwing themselves against Tom's trunklike legs. After he'd greeted them to their satisfaction, they turned to Alma, each standing on tiptoe to kiss the older woman's cheek.

They ignored Mandy and Jason. Mandy smiled. She knew the girls would greet her later. She was a fixture in their lives.

Beth grabbed one of Tom's arms with both hands. "Lift us up."

Bonnie grabbed the other arm. "Yes, lift us up."

"You two have grown so much, I might not be strong enough to lift you anymore."

Usually sober Beth giggled. "You're strong enough."

"Yes," Bonnie encouraged. "Lift us up."

"I'll try. Beth first. Hang on tight." He lifted his arm slowly. Beth swung from it, giggling so hard her face turned red. His own face showed the strain of her weight, but he lifted her until his arm reached shoulder height.

Mandy chanced a glance at Jason's face. Shock, then humor and admiration for Tom's strength showed plainly.

"Beth!" Ellen's cry brought Mandy's gaze to her. She'd forgotten Ellen hadn't seen the girls and Tom pull this stunt.

Ellen's exclamation caught Tom's attention too. He lowered Beth carefully to the floor.

Ellen grabbed Beth's shoulders. "That's no way to behave."

"But Tom always lifts us."

"That's right." Tom intervened.

"It's my turn." Bonnie tugged at Tom's hand.

Tom glanced at Ellen and lifted thick brown eyebrows in question.

Ellen grinned. "If you want to, go ahead, but don't blame me for the veins bulging in your neck and forehead."

His eyes twinkled. "Fair enough. Ready, Bonnie?"

Ellen watched Tom easily lift Bonnie, then turned to Mandy and asked whether the carpenter had shown up that day. He hadn't. "I'm about ready to repair that chest myself," Ellen said in disgust. "That's the fourth time he's promised to come and not shown."

"I'm pretty good at carpentry, Miss Ellen," Tom offered. "I'd be glad to help you out."

"We couldn't ask you to do that," Mandy protested. "Especially at this time of year. You're busy with your own work."

"I like doing something other than pottery. Relaxes me."

"Well, if you're sure . . . ," Ellen said, hesitating for his answer.

"Then it's settled." Tom nodded at Ellen. "If you'll show me what needs to be repaired, I'll know what tools to bring."

She led him to the loft, the girls following at Tom's heels.

Mandy was relieved to see Jason start about the room again, examining the trees and other decorations. Alma began a conversation again, but Mandy had difficulty following it. Instead her mind followed Jason.

Why had he come today? Did he have the same desire to talk with her that she had to talk with him? She'd heard a great deal about him through his grandparents over the last eight years, but she wanted to find out for herself if he was happy, if he'd found what he'd sought when he left her and the mountains for New York—whether it had been worth the cost of their love.

He stopped briefly at a teddy bear tree, at another tree covered with Scandinavian woven-wheat and red wooden ornaments, and yet at another with delicate, handblown glass balls.

He lingered longest at her favorite, a copy of the famous angel tree set up each year at the Metropolitan Museum of Art in New York. The tree was covered with copies of eighteenth-century angels and cherubs. A large crèche stood beneath the tree. Shepherds, kings on camels, and animals spread out among the rocks and moss surrounding the crèche. She watched Jason run a finger lightly along an angel's stiff, rose-colored gown.

Alma was eagerly explaining some detail of her paintings, but Mandy couldn't drag her attention back from Jason. Did he recall when they saw the original tree at the Met? The way they'd stood before it in hushed awe, holding hands, and afterward admitting they felt as though they'd been blessed with witnessing the closest thing possible to the actual night of Christ's birth? Her chest ached, suddenly too small to hold the emotion-charged memory.

Jason turned, his finger still on the angel's gown. His gaze met hers across the room. A bond bridged the distance between them. To

Mandy it seemed tinged with regret for what they'd lost, filled with hope for forgiveness.

Abruptly, he turned his back to her, and the delicate bridge collapsed. Mandy blinked and took a shaky breath. Had she imagined it all? Or had he pulled back when he sensed what was happening between them, not ready even after eight years to forgive her for not marrying him?

She'd desperately wanted to marry him, but she'd always known she wanted to live in the mountains. Living in the city would be like a living death for her, the same as her beloved mountains would be a prison to a true city lover. It made no sense to begin a marriage with such a wall between them, but she hadn't been able to convince Jason of that.

She forced her attention back to Alma. Mandy lifted Alma's painting, admiring again the winter mountain scene. "I'd like to put this above the fireplace. What do you think?"

Alma's dark eyes sparkled. "Do you honestly believe it's worthy of such a prominent placement?"

"Quit begging for compliments," Mandy teased.

Alma shifted in her chair, a pleased smile on her face. "J. P., can you help Mandy with this painting?"

"I can hang it myself." Mandy wondered whether she actually paled at Alma's call. She didn't need Jason any closer to her. She was all too aware of his presence as it was.

Jason's glance met hers above the painting. "Where do you want it?"

"Over the fireplace." She started for the center of the room, carrying the painting.

Before following Mandy, Jason took time to turn Alma's chair so she could see the fireplace. "You let us know when we have it positioned just right, Alma," he said. "A painting should always be hung to please the artist."

Where did he come upon that bit of wisdom? He hadn't known much about art when they were dating. No telling how much he'd changed since they'd been together. It surprised Mandy to find how much it hurt to realize she no longer knew him inside and out.

But if she'd really known him inside and out back then, she'd have known he'd eventually leave her for a career in New York, instead of fooling herself into believing that deep inside, he wanted to stay in the mountains she loved—with her.

She set the picture down and pulled the overstuffed, red plaid footstool over to the hearth. Jason stepped on the stool and reached for the huge grapevine wreath above the mantel. Handing it to her, he said, "Give me the painting."

She steadied the painting as he took hold of it. Much of the painting's weight stayed in her hands, and she looked up at him. Why wasn't he taking it?

His gaze was riveted on her left hand. Had the grapevine scratched it without her noticing? She glanced down but saw nothing unusual and looked back, puzzled.

His questioning gaze shifted to hers. "You aren't wearing a wedding ring."

The accusation in his tone sent a warm wave up her neck. She was glad he hadn't spoken loud enough for Alma to hear over the Christmas music. "There's no law that a thirty-year-old woman has to be married."

"Is something wrong with the painting?" Alma called.

Jason lifted the painting from Mandy's hands. "Nothing at all," he assured the artist. "Just wanted to be sure I didn't snag Mandy's hands with the wire."

Mandy wished she and Jason were alone so she could ask him why he'd thought she was married. His question intensified her already-overactive awareness of him. They were so close she could hear his breathing.

By the time Jason had the picture hung to Alma's satisfaction, Tom, Ellen, and the girls were down from the loft. Tom showed Jason a tree decorated with Tom's slender pottery ornaments, and then the Berrys prepared to leave. Ellen and the girls went out to the car with them.

When Jason and Mandy were alone, Jason said, "The girls certainly like Tom."

"Tom and Grandpa Seth are the only two men those girls trust anymore." It felt safer talking about them than herself, Mandy thought, but safe wasn't always the best. She took a deep breath and plunged in. "Who told you I was married?"

Deep red color crept up his neck. He lifted his shoulders in a shrug. "I . . . assumed. Are you divorced?"

"No." Her answer came out louder than she'd intended. With an effort, she lowered her voice. "I never married. What made you think . . . ?"

His gaze darted away. His face scrunched into a wince. "Bonnie. She's the spitting image of you, and I didn't think you would . . . not without being married." His voice dropped significantly on the last words.

Did he think she'd abandoned her values after they broke up? "Bonnie is Ellen's daughter."

Jason's eyes widened, then begged forgiveness. "I'm afraid I've put my foot in it."

She turned her back and fiddled with a Victorian ornament on a tree to prevent his seeing the hurt in her eyes.

He rested a hand on her arm. His touch sent a charge blazing through her. She heard his breath catch. Had he been as affected by their touch as she was?

"Mandy, I'm sorry. I didn't think you'd abandoned your values or your faith. I thought you were married because Bonnie looks so much like you, and I knew you wouldn't sleep with anyone outside marriage."

The huskiness in his voice assured her of his sincerity, but his voice combined with his touch caused dangerous warnings of desire to dance along her nerve endings. She stepped back, and his hand fell away.

The only sound in the room was a harpsichord rendition of "Hark, the Herald Angels Sing." It didn't hide the tension between them. Jason cleared his throat. "I didn't put much hope in Ellen and Zach's marriage lasting, but I guess Beth and Bonnie are proof that it has."

Mandy shook her head, glad for a topic less personal than her own choices about marriage and sex. "Zach left her and the girls last year. The divorce was final last month. He believes he's meant for better things than managing a small-town clothing store. He's in California. He's written a screenplay and feels he can sell it better face-to-face than through the mail."

"Couldn't he let an agent handle the selling? He could support himself here, living here with his family, while someone else hawks the script."

"That's too sensible. You know Zach. Besides, he evidently feels a family is a liability to his dreams."

He scowled. "I always felt guilty for introducing him to Ellen."

"You hadn't much choice, as I recall. Zach crashed the pizza party that night and demanded an introduction to Ellen. Besides, you couldn't have kept them apart. Remember how the air between them sizzled?"

"I remember. They were married only . . . what . . . three months later?"

His intense gaze and strained voice made her wonder if he was recalling that he'd told her how, in spite of his doubts about Ellen and Zach's marriage, he was jealous of them and wished it were he and Mandy marrying instead. The memory made it difficult for her to concentrate.

"Uh, yes, three months. Look, did you come here for something special? I told Grandma Tillie I'd stop at the hospital to see Grandpa Seth tonight and bring her home."

"Actually, Gram asked me to come down."

Irrationally, his comment sent disappointment burning through her. In spite of telling herself for years that it was for the best that they hadn't married, and even though they'd parted angry the other evening, part of her had hoped he'd come tonight because he couldn't stay away from her.

"I brought Gram home," he went on. "She's already asleep. She wanted to stay at the hospital all night. She hasn't said so, but I know she's frightened about Gramps's bypass surgery tomorrow. Gramps told her he's tired and will rest more easily knowing she's at home getting some sleep. Besides." He grinned almost conspiratorially. "He says he'll go into surgery more positive tomorrow if he knows she's at the hospital praying for him, not asleep because she's been up all night worrying about him."

Mandy couldn't help smiling back. "That sounds like Grandpa Seth. I wish I'd made it up there to talk with him tonight."

"You can talk with him after the surgery."

His voice trembled only slightly, but enough for her to recognize his words were a defense against his own fear.

She nodded. "Of course."

Her heart smarted. He looked so tired. She wanted to draw his head against her shoulder, caress his hair, and whisper words of comfort. Instead she sat down, folding one leg beneath her in the wing chair, putting further distance between them.

Jason cleared his throat. "I also wanted to apologize for the other night." He dug his hands into his slacks' pockets, then pulled his hands out and sat on the edge of the wing chair opposite her. "I spoke out of turn. The past is past. Since I'm going to be around for the next couple months, I'm hoping we can be friends."

She nodded. "Sure." On the surface they could be friends, but the past wasn't behind them, not when he hadn't forgiven her for not marrying him, not when she still longed to share life with him.

He must want to put it behind him, she thought with a sinking feeling in her stomach. *Even though during our disagreement he'd sounded as though he wished we hadn't broken up. He found out tonight I'm not married, and instead of saying he'd like to try again, he's telling me he wants to put the past behind us.* She bit back the regret burning within her.

The door flew open. Beth's and Bonnie's giggles interrupted them. The girls raced each other across the room and threw themselves against the arms of Mandy's chair.

"I won," Beth called.

Bonnie shook her head until her curls swirled against her round, flushed cheeks. "No, I won."

"No, you didn't."

"Yes, I did, didn't I, Aunt Mandy?"

Both were giggling so hard they could barely challenge each other. Mandy gave each a quick one-armed hug. "I declare the race an official tie."

"Anyone for hot chocolate?" Ellen asked, taking up last place in the newcomers' race. "I need something to settle these two down before they go to bed."

"Bed?"

"We're not ready for bed."

Jason stood. "I should be going."

"Don't leave on our account," Ellen protested. "Mandy and I can talk whenever we want. I'll take the girls up to get their pajamas on, and then we'll be back down for hot chocolate."

Mandy and Jason watched the three climb the open wooden staircase to the loft.

Jason's gaze wandered to the fireplace with its mountain river rocks reaching to the beamed roof. "I don't remember the fireplace."

"I had it built."

"Nice." Jason walked to the hearth, staring into the embers.

Mandy listened to the embers crackling and bursting and felt the pain of the thick, uncomfortable silence between herself and Jason.

It was a relief when Bonnie came bounding down the stairs, a huge brown teddy bear in her arms. Leaning her head against Mandy's knees, she studied Jason with her wide-eyed gaze.

He smiled at the girl, and Mandy thought his face truly relaxed for the first time that night. She'd always loved watching him with children; he so thoroughly enjoyed them.

"Great Barbie doll nightgown," Jason said.

"Thank you," Bonnie answered primly.

"Why do you keep your pajamas upstairs here? Are you and your sister going to have a sleepover under the Christmas trees?"

Bonnie shook her head, her brown curls bouncing. "No. We're goin' to sleep upstairs in our bed."

Jason frowned, looking puzzled. "Your bed is upstairs?"

"Of course, Silly. We live here."

Jason's eyebrows shot up. "You live here?"

Mandy touched the tip of her tongue to suddenly dry lips.

"Who lives here with you, Bonnie?" Jason's voice held a cautious note, as though afraid he already knew the answer.

"Mommy, Beth." Bonnie nodded once for each name. Mandy held her breath as the girl nodded a third time. "And Aunt Mandy."

Jason's gaze darted to Mandy's.

She spread her arms and grinned, hoping he couldn't see how her courage wavered. "Surprise."

6

surprise, indeed," Jason agreed with what he congratulated himself was a good degree of calm considering the jolt he'd just received. "Amazing that you, Gram, and Gramps all forgot to mention that little detail. From the mouths of babes."

Bonnie frowned. "What's that mean? 'From the mouth of babes.'"

"That one is all yours," Mandy challenged Jason.

He knew what she meant. No six year old wanted to be called a baby. "It's a very old saying," he explained. "It means children say wise things."

Bonnie's eyes sparkled. "Children like me?"

"Just like you," Jason assured her. He sat down with his elbows on his knees and his fingers linked.

Bonnie studied him soberly, crushing her beige teddy bear against the pink-clad blond Barbie on her nightgown. "Would you like to see my teddy bear?"

"Sure."

She stepped cautiously to the coffee table and handed the bear across.

Jason examined it soberly. Its curly tan fur was well worn, and the red-and-green ribbon around its neck looked like it had been chewed, most likely by Bonnie's tiny white teeth. "A very handsome bear. What's his name?"

"Teddy."

"Very appropriate."

"What's 'propie . . . , 'propie . . . ?"

"Appropriate," he repeated slowly. "It means it's just right."

Her grin widened, and she stuck out her stomach in pride.

A movement caught his eye, and he looked up to see Ellen sit down in the wing chair opposite Mandy. Beth leaned against her mother's knees, her hair, as blond as her negligent father's, brushed behind her ears in a smooth sweep. Her nightgown featured the dark-haired princess from *Aladdin*.

When Beth noticed him looking at her, she slipped the tip of her little finger between her lips and turned her head partially away, as if wanting to hide. *Shy thing,* he thought. He winked at her and felt pleasantly rewarded he'd surprised her into a smile, even though she instantly retreated behind her sober face and measuring eyes.

"Ready for your hot chocolate, girls?" Mandy asked, rising. At the girls' assurance that they were indeed ready, she went to fill their cups.

Jason absently bounced the bear up and down on one knee.

"Teddy likes 'to market, to market,' " Bonnie informed him.

"What's that?"

"You know. Teddy rides to market on your leg, only he's really riding a horse, of course."

"Give me a hint how it starts."

She heaved such a huge sigh of disgust that he bit back a laugh. " 'To market, to market,' " she began, waving her hands like a phil-harmonic conductor, " 'to fetch a skein of wool.' "

"I remember. 'Uphill, downhill, fall in a hole,' " he finished with her, bouncing the bear high on his knee, then plunging the bear almost to the floor.

Bonnie clapped, laughing. "Do it again."

"We don't want to get Teddy too excited so close to bedtime."

Bonnie accepted the bear without further quibbling. But it was Mandy's chuckle at Jason's diplomatic argument that was music to his ears as she returned with cups of chocolate with bobbing marshmal-low clouds for the girls. When he glanced at Ellen and Beth, Beth was smiling too, until she saw him looking at her.

Bonnie leaned against the coffee table, concentrating heavily on Teddy's face, where her tiny fingers tugged at one black button eye. "Mr. J. P., are you a daddy?"

"No."

"Why not?"

"I was never blessed with nice girls like you and your sister."

Bonnie looked at him, her smiling glance almost shy, obviously pleased with his answer.

Beth wasn't pleased. "Our daddy doesn't feel blessed to be a daddy. He left us."

Ellen's arms circled Beth's waist, but the girl stood stiff, watching for Jason's reaction.

He felt Bonnie watching him too, as well as Mandy. What could he say that wouldn't be dishonest or cruel to the little girls? Anger built inside him, sweeping up through his chest. How could any man leave his children? "It's hard to learn to live without your dad, isn't it? I had to learn to live without mine too."

"Did he divorce you and your mom?" Beth asked. Curiosity and caution mingled in her blue eyes.

His heart caught at her belief her father had divorced not only Ellen but the girls. "No. When I was a teenager, my dad died in an automobile accident."

Beth and Bonnie stared at him, wide-eyed. The fire spit and crackled from tree sap while the girls absorbed what he'd said.

"I know lots of kids at school whose dads left them like ours," Beth said slowly, "but I don't know anyone whose dad is dead."

"Did it hurt you when he died?" Bonnie rubbed her Barbie-covered chest. "In here?"

He nodded. "Yes, it hurt me a lot in there."

"Does it hurt still?"

"Sometimes, but not as bad as it used to."

Bonnie's chubby fingers pulled at the bear's black button eye. "I still hurt lots when I think about my daddy."

Beth pushed at her hair and lifted her pointed chin defiantly. "I don't hurt. I hate him."

"Honey," Ellen protested, "you know you don't hate your father." She tried to pull the girl closer, but Beth pushed free. "Yes, I do."

"I think it's time for bed," Ellen said softly. Jason saw tears glittering in her eyes.

"I haven't finished my hot chocolate," Bonnie protested. "Take it upstairs with you."

"I'm sorry, Ellen." Jason spoke quietly. "I didn't mean to disturb the girls."

Her eyes looked old and tired. "You didn't say anything wrong. The fault lies elsewhere."

He noticed she didn't say where. Was she one of those gallant mothers who never said anything negative about her ex-husband in front of his children? Difficult task, to put it mildly, but he admired her for it.

Ellen stood. "Come on, girls, let's get going."

Mandy leaned forward to give Bonnie a hug that was strenuously returned. Jason's heart constricted at the sight, at the thought of what it would be like if Mandy was saying good night to their child, his and Mandy's. If they'd had a little girl, would she look like Bonnie, like a miniature Mandy?

"Good night, Mr. J. P." Bonnie's round brown eyes gleamed in a smile repeated on her lips, but she didn't offer to hug him.

"Good night, Bonnie. And you don't need to call me mister, since we're friends."

She grinned.

Beth hugged Mandy with only slightly less reserve than her sister. Standing safely by Mandy's chair, Beth gave Jason a small wave and a smaller smile. He smiled and waved back. "Night, Beth."

She bit her bottom lip, studying him. He waited, meeting her gaze. Finally she walked over to him, resolve in every step. She rested her hands on the arm of the chair and whispered, "I'm sorry your dad died."

"Thank you, Beth. I'm sorry your dad isn't here too. Maybe sometime you can tell me about your dad, and I'll tell you about mine."

She nodded, then ran across the room to the stairs.

"Thank you," Mandy said softly to him as the girls and Ellen reached the loft.

He turned to her in surprise. "For what?"

"For telling the girls about your loss. It's good for them to know there are adults who lost parents as children and survived. It's been awful for those girls since Zach left."

Jason's nails bit into the palms of his hands. "When I think of him abandoning those girls, I'd like to take him out behind a barn and teach him a lesson." He glanced at the pine-covered rafters and gave a short laugh. "No pun intended."

"Before Zach left I didn't know I was capable of almost hating someone. I keep asking God to help me forgive him."

Jason couldn't imagine sweet, patient Mandy hating anyone, even Zach. "I grieved when I lost my parents, but I knew they hadn't wanted to leave me. Beth and Bonnie know their father chose to leave them." He slammed his fist on the arm of the chair. "They're too young to experience that loss of trust."

"Yes, yet they're only two of millions of children experiencing it. All we can do is show them every day that there are still people in their lives who won't leave no matter how tough things get."

She was right, of course, but it didn't stop the girls' pain at the moment. Still, knowing the children had Mandy and Ellen in their lives calmed him somewhat. They'd never let the girls down.

Losing Mandy had hurt him almost more than losing his parents. He'd given her all his love, all his trust, and she'd chosen to leave him. On a much larger scale, that was the kind of rejection Beth and Bonnie must feel because of Zach's selfishness.

He forced his mind from the painful memory. "How did all of you end up living upstairs?"

Mandy curled deeper into the wing chair. "I turned your grandparents down when they first offered me the use of the barn. Ellen kept after me to rent it. I was living in Asheville. Ellen and the girls lived here near Boone. After Zach left, Ellen didn't want to disrupt the girls' lives further by moving, but she needed someone close by for support." Mandy shrugged. "So I decided to rent the barn."

"And live in it."

"I only meant to live here until I found an apartment. Grandma Tillie and Grandpa Seth offered to let me stay with them, but . . ." Another shrug. This time her gaze wandered away from his. He knew it was because of him that she'd chosen not to stay with his grandparents.

She moved to the fireplace, opened the brass screen, and used a cast-iron poker to break a log into embers. "Things were tough for

Ellen financially. Finally I realized it would be cheaper for all of us to live together here. Ellen and the girls loved the idea."

He walked to the hearth. Leaning his elbows against the massive oak beam mantel, he fingered a colorful wooden gnome sitting on a pine branch. "So now instead of just running a store, you help raise the girls."

She glanced at him sharply. "I like having the girls around. Ellen too."

"It wasn't an insult. It's like you to be generous with your home and time."

She poked especially hard at the log, and a chunk broke off with a sputter. "You make me sound like a saint."

"Hardly that. I remember a few faults." *Like not loving me enough to marry me.* His conscience immediately kicked in. That wasn't a fault, just the reality with which he'd had to learn to live.

"Only a few?" A teasing smile lit her eyes before she abandoned the topic. "Ellen and I expected to stay here for just a few months, but it's worked out well. In addition to helping me in the store, she's working as a bookkeeper for a clothing store, but it doesn't pay well. Living here gives her the time and money—barely—to take classes toward her accounting degree."

It probably never occurred to Mandy that most people don't consider themselves their sister's keeper, Jason thought. "Good for her. Sounds like she's got guts."

Mandy nodded, and he watched lights dance in her hair. "She has." She closed the grate and replaced the cast-iron poker in its stand. "So does Grandpa Seth. I'm sorry I missed visiting with him tonight. How is he doing?"

The weight of the world seemed to drop back onto his shoulders. "He's still scheduled for surgery first thing tomorrow."

She rested her hand on Jason's, but almost before his mind could register her hand's softness or his heart skip a beat at the joy from her once-familiar touch, she withdrew it. He pretended not to notice. Isn't that what she'd want? "Dr. Monroe says Gramps's chance of coming through well are good," he said, "but there's always a possibility . . ."

"The operation is so standard now. It's not as risky as it once was."

He nodded and wondered whether she could tell how forced his smile was. "Thanks for the reminder."

"You look so tired."

The huskiness in her voice drew his gaze to hers. The concern he saw there for himself warmed his heart. "I guess I am." He rested his forehead on the back of his hand. He'd thought himself strong enough to support his grandparents, but after only five days, weariness engulfed him. "When my parents died, Gram and Gramps were the strong ones, always there for me even though they'd lost a daughter. Now Gram leans on me. For the first time, I can see how vulnerable she is beneath the image she's worn all these years."

"Her strength has always rested in her faith in God, but I think the love between her and Grandpa Seth is another part of her strength."

He nodded. "And now she's afraid she might lose that." He sighed deeply and closed his eyes. "So am I."

"I'm so sorry this has happened, Jason."

Her soft voice and gentle touch on his arm brought sudden tears to his eyes. He squeezed his lids tightly. He reached for her. Sliding his arms around her waist, he buried his face in her neck beneath a silky wave of hair to hide his tears from her. She stirred, and thinking she was going to pull away, he tightened his hold.

He felt her stiffen. Heard her gasp softly as if in surprise. Then she rested her palms on his shoulders. She barely touched him at first. Slowly she slipped her arms around his neck and hugged him tightly.

The strength he'd demanded of himself—forcing himself to stuff his emotions into hiding—collapsed. He felt it break, felt the emotions he'd struggled to dam up flood through him. With a shudder, a sob wrenched from him.

7

$\mathcal{M}$ andy felt Jason's chest jerk in his attempt to stifle a sob. The force of the buried cry seemed to rip through his body. *I love you, Jason.* The words repeated in Mandy's mind while she held him. Her chest ached with her desire to heal the pain caused by the fear his grandfather might die, but she knew only God had that capability.

Besides, she had no reason to believe Jason wanted to hear her words of love. No reason to believe the words would give him even a modicum of comfort. No reason to believe he'd want the kiss she longed to press to his temple.

So she simply continued to hold him, her cheek against his hair, stroking the back of his head lightly, her heart crimped in empathy. Wonder at the familiarity of him filtered through her concern. Her hands and arms remembered the way he felt beneath her touch.

Soon his chest stopped heaving with the sobs he held within himself. His cheek remained on her shoulder where a warm dampness seeped through her sweater. She knew it was his tears. The knowledge brought tears to her own eyes.

They stood that way a long time. Finally his hold loosened, though his arms remained around her waist. He straightened, and Mandy loosened her hold also, resting her hands on his shoulders.

When his gaze met hers, she saw no tears in his eyes. Apprehension looked out from them, but he only said, "I'm sorry."

"You're entitled to worry about your grandfather."

"Yeah." He released his hold and stepped back. "I'd better get going. Need to get up early tomorrow. Gramps's surgery is scheduled for seven. Gram and I want to be there."

Mandy clasped her hands behind her back, trying to act as though her heart wasn't slamming against her ribs from recently holding Jason in her arms. "I'll stop at the hospital too, if that's okay."

"Sure. Gram and Gramps would want you there."

But you don't? Mandy's heart asked the question she didn't dare voice.

Jason took a couple more steps back toward the door. "Want to ride to the hospital with us?"

"I'd better not. I may need to get back to the store before you're ready to return home."

"Then I'll see you at the hospital. Night."

"Good night." She spoke to his back as he hurried across the room. A moment later the bells above the door tinkled merrily as he left.

Mandy took a deep, shaky breath and lowered herself into the wing chair. She drew her legs up, wrapped her arms around her knees, closed her eyes, and allowed herself to relive the minutes holding Jason.

She'd spent years trying to forget how she'd felt in his arms, trying to forget how it felt to hold him.

"I haven't forgotten, Jason," she whispered, pain tightening her chest. "I haven't forgotten anything. And I've never stopped loving you, not for a moment."

Jason slouched down, rested the back of his head against the top of the blue sofa, and let his gaze slowly scan the ivory-white waiting room walls. A picture of roses hung on each wall, adding color and impersonal cheer. A basket of pink-and-blue silk flowers—he didn't know what kind—rested amid stacks of magazines on the oval, oak coffee table in front of him. *A pity,* he thought, *that the flowers aren't real.* If they were, their fragrance might mask the hospital smells.

It had already been a long morning, and Gramps was still in surgery. Family of other patients had drifted in and out of the waiting room. Right now, Jason and Gram were alone. *No, not alone. God is here.*

The thought brought a bit of refreshment to Jason's spirit, though it didn't quiet all his fears. He silently repeated the petitions he'd made a number of times already: *Please, God, bring Gramps through this. Guide the surgical team. Give Gram and me strength.*

Jason wondered why Mandy hadn't shown up yet. It wasn't like her not to keep her word. Besides, she loved Gram and Gramps as much as her own kin.

The intensity with which he wanted her there surprised him. Beneath her vivacious energy lay a serenity and confidence in God's love which he longed for now.

Even so, embarrassment squirmed through his chest at the remembrance of the previous night. As an "enlightened male" he knew intellectually that it was okay for a man to cry, regardless of the messages a boy received growing up. But it didn't feel right. It was downright scary, his emotions getting away from him that way. Not that Mandy would think a man's tears a weakness.

The compassion he'd felt in her arms swept over him. He hadn't hung onto anyone during life's storms for a long time.

His glance slid to Gram, who sat beside him wearing a rose jogging suit. Was she wondering whether she and Gramps would ever hold each other again?

Rays of sunlight slipped through the window blinds behind them and laid pale yellow light on her gray hair. An open devotional book rested on top of the black leather-bound Bible in her lap. With the fingers of one hand, she played with the simple gold cross on the chain about her neck. Gramps had given her the cross on her sixtieth birthday, Jason remembered. She always wore it.

She looked small, sad, scared, and incredibly vulnerable—everything he wasn't accustomed to seeing in her spirit. Love and a desire to protect her rushed through him. He reached out, laid his arm across her shoulders, and gave her a squeeze.

She looked up, and his heart contracted at the fear he saw in her eyes.

"I keep asking God to bring Seth through this," she admitted. "I want to believe God will do just that. But I can't forget that we all die. That's the plan. Makes it hard to know what God's will is now."

He squeezed her shoulder again. "I have those same thoughts every time I pray."

She gave a little sigh and shifted until she leaned against him.

A movement caught Jason's attention. His spirits lifted at the sight of Mandy entering the waiting area at a quick pace. He shoved away the temptation to retreat behind a wall of embarrassment at his actions the night before and smiled a welcome.

Gram reached both hands toward Mandy. "You made it. I knew you would."

Jason felt the chill of the cold air Mandy brought with her from the outdoors as she grasped Gram's hands and kissed her cheek. "Sorry I couldn't get here sooner. The girl scheduled to work this morning called in sick. Ellen promised to drive for a class trip today, so she couldn't help out."

Gram continued to cling to Mandy's gloved hands. "You didn't close the store, did you?"

"No. A wife of one of your farm workers agreed to help out."

"That's good." Gram released Mandy's hands.

Mandy removed her gloves and gray winter jacket. Jason noticed that the cold wind had left her cheeks almost as bright as her red sweater.

She sat down near Gram on the edge of a blue club chair which stood at a right angle to the sofa. "Is Grandpa Seth still in surgery?"

Jason and Gram both nodded.

"Has anyone told you how it's going?" Mandy looked from Gram to Jason.

Jason shook his head. "No. We're hoping that's a good sign."

Mandy glanced at the round, oak-rimmed clock that hung above the small desk in one corner of the room. "Is it normal for the surgery to last this long?"

"According to Dr. Monroe, it is," he assured her. "It's a pretty complicated surgery. They strip arteries from his legs to replace the clogged arteries around his heart. Have to admit, though, I didn't know time could move this slow."

Gram leaned forward. "Which of the girls is on the class trip?"

Glad to think about anything other than the operation, Jason thought. *Can't blame her.*

"Bonnie. Her class is visiting a log cabin where women still spin wool and weave the old-fashioned way."

Gram's eyes brightened with interest. "The children will like that. My grandma had a loom. Grandpa built it for her when they were newlyweds. My, she made that shuttle fly. She wove beautiful rugs. Remind me to show you next time you're up to the house."

"I will." Mandy looked from Gram to Jason and back again. "Did Beth's teacher, Miss Lewis, get in touch with either of you? She wants the class to visit a Christmas tree farm."

"I thought the school didn't allow Christmas celebrations any-more," Gram said, "what with students from religions other than Christianity and that separation of church and school law."

"You're right, but the school does allow studies of different traditions. Beth's class is studying Christmas, Hanukkah, and Kwanza. Since Christmas trees are one of our state's largest businesses, no one should object to the class visiting a farm. Miss Lewis would like it to be yours, but Beth told her about Grandpa Seth's surgery, and Miss Lewis didn't want to impose on you."

"We'll be glad to have the class visit," Jason assured Mandy. "Right, Gram?"

Gram nodded. "We can give them a hayride. And hot apple cider and cookies afterward."

"I'll arrange the ride and a tour if you ladies take care of the eats," Jason agreed. It meant additional work at an already busy time, but it would be good public relations and give Gram something to look forward to. Besides, he wanted to do it. "It will be fun."

Mandy smiled at him. "I'll tell Miss Lewis to call you."

The conversation dried up. After a couple minutes, Mandy leaned forward and patted Gram's hand. "Are you doing all right?"

Gram gave her a thin smile. "As all right as a body can be at a time like this, I reckon. I'm trying to keep the faith, as they say, but . . . but it's his heart, you know?" Her voice faltered on the last words. "I mean, hearts are . . . vital."

Mandy patted Gram's hand again. "The doctors know what they're doing. There's no denying there's risk involved, but it's Grandpa Seth's best chance to stay here with us."

Gram nodded.

"I won't pretend I know how God's going to answer our prayers." Mandy's tone was gentle. "But remember what He said in Jeremiah: 'I know the plans I have for you, plans to prosper you and not to harm you, plans to give you a hope and a future.' He only has good in mind for Grandpa Seth and you and Jason."

Jason felt Gram's shoulders rise beneath his arm as she took a deep breath. "Thanks for reminding me," she said, her voice firmer than he'd heard all morning. "I'm glad you're here, Mandy. You're family, and our family didn't feel complete until you arrived."

"Thank you. This is exactly where I want to be right now."

Jason caught the glitter of tears in Mandy's eyes before she blinked them away.

It does feel right that Mandy's here, Jason thought. He didn't let himself explore the fact that she'd refused to formally join the family by marrying him. He hadn't enough emotional energy to deal with that now. *I'm just glad she's here, Lord. Thank You for bringing her back into my life.*

Mandy pulled two folded papers from her purse. "Beth and Bonnie made get-well cards for Grandpa Seth."

"How sweet." Gram accepted the papers.

Jason glanced down. Both homemade cards were addressed to "Grandpa Seth." Jason smiled. It touched and amused him that the girls had adopted Mandy's name for his grandfather.

Beth's card showed a girl hugging a man with a beard. Beneath the picture she'd written in blue crayon, "This is me giving you a bear hug." Bonnie had drawn a girl sitting on a bearded man's lap and written in red, "I miss you. Come home soon."

Jason chuckled. "Gramps looks like Santa Claus in their pictures."

Mandy and Gram agreed, laughing.

Their conversation dwindled to a few comments and words of encouragement. They passed the Bible and devotional book back and forth among themselves until Dr. Monroe walked in with an infectious grin. "Seth held his own in there. The operation couldn't have gone better."

"Does that mean he'll be all right?" Hope filled Gram's face.

"There are no guarantees, but he has a great chance of recovering."

Gram's face relaxed somewhat. "Thank the Lord." She gave a mischievous grin. "And you, of course."

Dr. Monroe chuckled. "I don't mind not receiving top billing."

"Can we see him?" Gram's voice trembled.

"He's not awake yet. They're moving him back to ICU. He'll be there a couple days. Just standard procedure."

"When can we see him?" Gram asked.

"When he wakes up. Let me give you an idea of what to expect during the next couple months."

The next couple months. The words brought relief to Jason. They sounded so positive. Not the next couple hours or days—but months.

"Seth will be on a ventilator for a day and a half," Dr. Monroe continued. "That's normal, so don't let it worry you. Looks a little scary, but it's a good thing. After he wakes up, we'll get him out of bed and into a chair."

Jason started. "So soon?"

"He won't be staying there long, I assure you. A short while and then back to bed. After a couple days, if there are no complications, he'll be moved out of ICU. We'll keep him here four or five days longer, monitoring him until we're sure he's recovered sufficiently to go home."

Gram's grin widened. "Home."

Jason caught Mandy's glance and smiled. She smiled back, her eyes sparkling with the same joy he knew she saw in his eyes.

"I didn't think he'd be home before Thanksgiving," Gram admitted.

"Definitely by Thanksgiving, barring complications."

"Will he need medications?" Jason asked.

"Only aspirin. I don't want him doing anything too physically demanding for the first few weeks," the doctor warned.

"I suppose Seth needs to change his diet," Gram speculated dryly.

"Low fat, low cholesterol is the way to go. I'll talk with you about it in more detail before Seth is discharged. I've some brochures that might help you out." The doctor drew his pepper-and-salt eyebrows together. "Along with the physical issues, there are other important changes to watch for."

Unease slithered through Jason's chest. "What changes?"

"Depression is common after this kind of surgery. A lot of heart attack survivors become reflective, almost have a change in personality. They look back over their lives—see what they've done, what they wanted to do and didn't, what they may never have a chance to do now. Let me know if he gets depressed, but don't be surprised by it. It's normal. Seth's life has changed forever."

Jason nodded. *This has changed all of our lives forever.*

8

*J*ason leaned against an old, white wooden pillar on his grandparents' back porch, removed his billed hat, and rubbed his red-plaid-flannel-covered forearm across his forehead. He glanced at his watch. Only time for a quick break before Beth's class arrived.

He breathed the crisp mountain air in deeply, relishing the pleasure of spending a day outdoors in the mountains instead of inside his Wall Street office. Looking at his hat, he grinned. ASU for his alma mater—Appalachian State University—stood proudly in gold against the black background. The cap was worn, the colors faded. Gram had found it in the attic yesterday.

The hat brought back memories—some fun, some fond, some not so pleasant. Fun memories of the companionship he'd found as part of the college baseball team. Fond memories of meeting Mandy and the relationship that grew quickly to love. Not-so-pleasant memories of Mandy refusing to marry him.

He wrenched his thoughts from the past and forced them to the scene before him. Mountain ridges spread into the distance like stilled waves. They were covered with Christmas trees, which looked like green pyramids standing in orderly rows. The scene, as always, filled him with awe and quiet joy. In spite of the fourteen- to sixteen-hour days he and the other men put in, he loved this work and this place. If it weren't for Gramps's heart condition and Jason's knowledge that Neal and the other partners back in New York were overworked because of his absence, Jason would have felt completely content.

"Mandy's presence would still have played havoc with that contentment," he admitted with a wry shake of his head to a scarlet cardinal in a nearby holly bush.

Moving color in the form of people and trucks filled the Christmas groves: men cutting trees, carrying trees, stuffing trees into binders and pulling them out, piling the trees on trucks. Besides Ted, who'd helped Gramps manage the farm, eight men worked on the farm year-round. That number neared thirty with the locals and college students hired this time of year.

Business was going well. All the overseas orders had been shipped, as well as orders to retailers in distant states, along with most of the live trees, which were shipped with ball and burlap around their roots. This coming week—the week before Thanksgiving—would be a challenge. Gramps had retail lots in Atlanta, Charlotte, Winston-Salem, Raleigh, and other large cities. It took two truckloads of trees a day just to keep the lots in Atlanta stocked. No rest for the weary here.

He stretched his arms over his head and winced. He thought he'd have worked out all the creaks and crimps in his joints and muscles by now.

"Hi, Jason."

"Hey, Mandy." He lowered his arms as she stopped at the bottom of the steps. She looked great in a red-and-black-checked wool coat. She looked good in anything, for that matter, but he especially liked to see her in bright, cheerful colors. "What are you doing out of the store? It's only one o'clock; a lot of hours left before quitting time."

"Beth's teacher asked if I'd act as a chaperon for the tour this afternoon. The school requires one adult for every seven children on field trips. One of the class mothers who'd pledged her time for today called in sick. You won't mind if I tag along, will you?"

"The more the merrier." He glanced at his watch again. "The kids should arrive anytime now."

"They're already here. Grandma Tillie was leaving the store when they arrived. She asked me to find you."

He took the four wooden stairs in two steps. "I'd better get a move on."

"It's okay." Mandy fell into step beside him. "She's taken the class to the nursery. She said she'd start the tour there, and you can take over when you catch up with the group."

"I'm surprised she left Gramps alone."

"He's napping, so she took advantage of the time to bring her frosted sugar cookies down to the store. That's where we'll serve the kids cider and cookies after your tour and the hayride. I don't think she'd leave him for a moment except for the cell phones you bought them." Mandy gave a bright laugh. "She keeps her phone in a carrier attached to her belt. She said she feels like a cowboy wearing a six-shooter."

He chuckled.

"It was a great idea you had," Mandy continued, "that Grandpa Seth, Grandma Tillie, you, and I carry phones with us and then programming all our numbers in so Grandma Tillie or Grandpa Seth can reach any of us in an emergency with just the touch of a button."

"The phones are worth the cost in peace of mind."

"Here's my phone." Mandy held it up. "I've decided to get a holder like Grandma Tillie's. That way there'll be no chance I'll set the phone down and forget it someplace."

"Your dedication to them means a lot to me."

"They're special people. I've loved them since we first met."

He remembered that meeting. He'd introduced them, confident he'd found the girl of his dreams, confident she'd one day be part of their family.

Mandy stuck her phone in her pocket. "Grandpa Seth is certainly glad to be home."

"That he is. In the two days he's been back, he's given Gram more than her share of headaches. I don't remember Gramps showing much temper down through the years, but he sure is ornery now. Doesn't like being dependent on Gram, I suppose." Jason reached to open the door to the nursery. "Guess I wouldn't like depending on someone else either."

Mandy's eyes flashed with teasing laughter as she moved past him. "Ah, yes, you independent mountain men."

Her friendly, fun manner bordered on flirtatious. Jason caught himself just in time from kissing the lips smiling up at him. The realization jolted him and roughened his voice when he replied, "You mountain women hold your own with us."

"We do our best."

Mandy's response was almost lost in Gram's greeting. "You're just in time, Jason. I've told the children all about how Christmas trees start as tiny seeds in the crevices of pine cones, then are grown in here until they're strong enough to survive outside. I'll let you tell them about the rest of the Christmas tree business."

"Thank you, Gram." He raised one hand high in greeting. "Welcome to the Always Christmas Farm."

As he smiled at the children returning his greeting, he thought, *Those third-grade mountain boys have no idea what's in store for them in a few years from those future sixth-grade mountain girls.*

Mandy stood, hands in her jacket pockets, behind the children at the edge of a grove of Fraser firs.

"It smells like Christmas out here," one little girl said.

The adults laughed, but the other children chimed in to agree with their classmate.

"It always smells like Christmas here," Beth said. Her dry tone spoke volumes of the sense of ownership she felt for the farm that had in such an unexpected manner become her home. Beth stood right in front of Jason. *As if claiming ownership of him too*, Mandy thought. She wished Beth dared let her guard down and allow herself to like Jason, but she realized that might make it more difficult for Beth when Jason returned to New York.

Mandy looked over the children to where Jason stood. It felt luxurious, this opportunity to openly watch Jason without worrying he or anyone else would think her indiscreet.

His looks hadn't changed much in the eight years since they'd stopped seeing each other. He was still trim, and his hair hadn't started graying, but his skin had lost the fresh look of youth and gained a tougher texture. The laugh lines at the corner of his eyes had deepened and now stayed visible whatever his expression.

The largest difference was the sense of maturity. Anyone meeting him would immediately recognize him as a man who carried responsibilities well. She felt a twinge in her chest. He'd grown into a fine man. Any woman would be honored to be loved by such a man. And she'd turned his love down. She'd make the same decision today given the same circumstances. But there was a difference—today she'd make that decision knowing she'd never stop missing him.

"There are many kinds of Christmas trees," Jason was saying. "The trees in this grove are Fraser firs. Some people call Frasers the Cadillac of Christmas trees. Frasers have strong branches with short needles, so it's easy to hang ornaments on them. Come close and look at the needles on these trees." The group shifted closer to the trees on either side of him. Some of the children reached out to feel the needles. "As we go through the farm, I'll show you how to tell the different kinds of Christmas trees apart. Notice that the needles on these Fraser firs are flat, a rich, dark green on top, and silvery underneath."

His words opened a memory in Mandy's heart. The night they met, they'd gone with a group of friends to a pizza parlor. Long after the others went home, Jason and Mandy had stayed, talking into the night, learning pieces of each other's lives and hearts. He'd looked across the table, playing with the straw in his empty soda glass, and said, "Your eyes are the same shade of green as Fraser fir needles in the sunlight."

She'd laughed, truly amused to hear her eyes compared to the needles of a tree, but secretly she'd felt a deep joy at his comment. Already she'd learned how he loved trees, especially the royal Fraser fir.

Two tractors pulling large, hay-filled wagons chugged to a stop nearby, jolting her back to the Christmas farm. At Jason's command, the group climbed into the wagons and selected places to sit in the scratchy, sweet-smelling hay.

The children sang Christmas songs as tractors pulled the wagons between groves of different kinds of trees. At each stop Jason explained more about the trees and business. He described the care that went into a tree for the seven to ten years it took for a tree to grow from a seedling to a treasured part of someone's Christmas: keeping weeds and grass mowed, fertilizing the trees, shearing them to keep the near-perfect triangular shape people like. "We spray the trees for pests too.

That's important. The wrong pests can wipe out an entire crop of trees."

He invited the children to gently touch the trees, study the shape and feel of the needles, and smell the trees. "Not all Christmas trees smell the same. Rub the needles of this Douglas fir. They smell a bit lemony, don't you think?"

Mandy watched Jason introduce the children to the trees, watched the excitement that radiated from him the tenderness in the way his large fingers touched the needles. A strange combination of quiet joy and sadness filled her. He seemed made for this world. The man who'd burst into her store the day after Grandpa Seth's heart attack, the man whose picture accompanied articles in business magazines wasn't the Jason Garth she knew. In spite of the years he'd worked in New York, she couldn't imagine this man in the billed black-and-gold college cap and tan corduroy jacket living the life of a high-powered executive in one of the world's most powerful cities.

The children's delighted laughter broke into her thoughts. Jason had spread the branches of a fir to reveal a bird's nest. He led the children to a nearby tree and showed them where a deer had nibbled at the tender growth. At another spot he pointed out where he'd found a wild turkey nest. For the rest of the ride, the children kept a lookout for wildlife, not even disappointed that they saw only small birds, squirrels, and one rabbit.

A boy with thick brown hair that reached his eyebrows shifted to his knees in the crackling hay. "I bet there's bears around here too, aren't there, Mr. J. P.? And wolves and panthers."

The relish with which the boy envisioned dangerous wild creatures running free on the farm amused Mandy.

Beth groaned. "You're just trying to scare us girls, Andy. There's no dangerous animals around here, are there, J. P.?"

Mandy saw Jason's hesitation and knew he was searching for an honest answer that wouldn't frighten the children. "It's true there are dangerous animals in the mountains, Beth, but they seldom stray out of the deep forests into civilized areas like this."

Beth and Andy exchanged I-told-you-so looks.

When the wagons returned to the nursery, Jason led the children into the one-story, warehouse-looking building where workers boxed trees to send to individuals and made wreaths and roping at long tables.

"You send Christmas trees in the mail?" A red-haired, freckled, skinny boy looked skeptical.

"Yes. We ship trees to some faraway places: Canada, the Virgin Islands, Chicago, Phoenix, Hawaii, Miami—"

"My grandparents live in Miami," the boy interrupted. "Did you send a tree to them?"

Mandy grinned as she watched Jason struggle to keep from laughing.

"I'm not sure. I don't personally address all the packages we ship out. Maybe you should write your grandparents and ask them."

The boy nodded, his expression sober. "I'm going to e-mail them and tell them they should buy one from you 'cause you have the best trees."

"We sent my grandparents a Christmas tree from here," Beth announced. "They live in Texas."

"That's right," Mandy agreed. "And now it's time for us to head to the Christmas store for cookies and hot apple cider."

The children cheered and headed for the door.

"Do you have time to join us for a snack?" Mandy asked Jason.

He hesitated. "I should get back to work."

"Will your conscience allow you to stay a few minutes if you tell it hot cider will warm you up and give you extra energy?"

Jason grinned. "Hot cider does sound good. Okay to invite the guys who drove the tractors?"

"Absolutely."

When Mandy and Jason entered the store, the children were following Beth and Miss Lewis to the local crafters' display room at the back. The group moved slowly, the boys' and girls' eyes wide as they viewed the trees, the limbs heavy with ornaments. Heads tilted back, necks stretched, the children looked at the pine roping, strings of plastic cranberries and popcorn, dolls, gnomes, and wooden cars that hung from the rafters.

"Wow!"

"Look at that—a Christmas tree covered in teddy bears."

"I never saw one of those before."

"I never saw so many Christmas trees at one time before."

"Yes, you did. We just saw thousands of Christmas trees outside."

"Not decorated ones."

"Santa's workshop must look like this."

"There is no Santa Claus."

"Is so. You just think there isn't because you're such a bully that Santa doesn't bring you anything for Christmas."

"Does so. Hey, look at the train beneath that tree. Boy, I'd sure like one of those."

Mandy and Jason shared laughing glances, and in doing so almost bumped into three girls exclaiming in rapturous terms over three child-sized angels dressed in ivory silk overlaid with gold-starred gauze. The couple carefully worked their way past the girls to follow another girl who danced down the narrow aisle between trees, singing along with the Charlotte Church rendition of "Mary's Boy Child" which played over the store's sound system.

Andy pushed past his singing classmate and stopped short in front of Jason and Mandy. "Mr. J. P., why aren't there any real Christmas trees in here? These are all fake."

Mandy swallowed a groan. Artificial Christmas trees weren't popular with Christmas tree farmers. She'd heard all the they-aren't-good-for-business-and-our-local-economy arguments.

Jason folded his arms across his chest and smiled an overly sweet smile at her. "Maybe we should ask Miss Wells since she's the store's owner."

Andy turned to Mandy. "How come?"

Mandy smiled back at Jason, thinking, *I can smile sweet too, Mister.* "Real trees would die, so we'd need to replace them every few weeks. That would make a lot of work and take a lot of time. Real trees might also cause a fire hazard. We use lights on every tree and leave the lights turned on much longer than most people do on their Christmas trees at home."

"Oh." Andy considered her explanation for a minute. "I see. But I still like real trees better."

"So do I," Mandy agreed.

The boy turned away, his attention caught by a large wooden truck beneath the artificial fir standing beside them.

"I guess it does seem strange to have a store filled with artificial trees on a Christmas tree farm," Mandy admitted as she and Jason continued walking.

"You don't sell the trees, do you? Just decorations?"

Incredulous, she stared at him. "Of course we don't sell these trees. Do you think we'd compete with Grandpa Seth's business?"

His lips twitched, and she realized he'd been teasing.

"We don't sell wreaths or roping either," she informed him. As they passed a tree covered with colorful old-fashioned ornaments from Germany, she added, "Did you notice the wreaths on the door and behind the counter are real?"

"Yes. And Gram says you'll be displaying our wreaths outside near the front door, where tourists who aren't in a position to buy a tree from us might be tempted to purchase a wreath they can easily carry in their cars. Thanks."

Mandy noted a bit of a grudging tone to his words but chose to ignore it. "Two live trees with their roots bundled standing on either side of the door might be nice too. We could decorate them with red ribbons, carved birds, and real pine cones."

"Great idea. I'll tell one of the men to bring them down. I suppose you're expecting a rush over the Thanksgiving weekend?"

"Yes." Now that she'd started thinking about using real trees, ideas sprouted. "I suppose it wouldn't be too terribly dangerous to have one live tree inside. Maybe next to the door, where the visitors will catch the fragrance when they enter. I could use the coolest lights available on it and not keep them on all day and evening. Of course, I'd need to remember to check the water every day."

When he didn't respond, she glanced up at him.

He looked straight ahead, his expression sober. "You don't need to do that, Mandy. I know real trees in a place like this are a fire hazard, just like you said. Even Christmas tree farmers like me know that."

"I know you do. But it might be nice, just one real tree. I'll think about it." Then it struck her. He'd said, "Even Christmas tree farmers like me." Did he realize he'd identified himself as a tree farmer, not just a financial expert substituting for a tree farmer? She chose not to comment on it. Likely he'd only become defensive, say it was a slip of the tongue. She happened to believe there were no slips in the words people spoke, but a logical Wall Street man wasn't apt to agree.

At the entrance to the local crafters' room, Mandy smiled at Miss Lewis, who returned the smile with a shake of her head. "The children love your store, Mandy."

"Maybe while the kids eat, Jason can give them some safety tips for their Christmas trees at home."

"That's a great idea," Miss Lewis agreed. "I'll round up the children and get them settled while you get ready, Mandy."

"Ready for what?" Jason's brows met in a curious glance at Mandy.

Mandy darted him a mischievous grin. "You'll see."

9

*J*ason looked at the group of whispering and giggling children seated on the wide, wooden floor planks and marveled at Miss Lewis's ability to so quickly draw the children from the Christmas wonders in the larger room and bring order to the group. Now they sat while Miss Lewis and the chaperons passed out frosted sugar cookies and Styrofoam cups filled with fragrant, warm apple cider.

Of course, Christmas items for children and the adult chaperons to drool over filled this room too. His gaze wandered the wooden walls. A quilt hanging held a place of honor, dark green squares framing a picture of Mary, Joseph, and baby Jesus beneath a lean-to style manger. Quilted and embroidered stockings hung from the deep window ledge. A tree covered with patchwork ornaments, straw figures, and popcorn strings stood on one side of the window. On the other, white crocheted snowflakes, stars, and angels danced on tree limbs.

Carved wooden toys—some painted, some not—sat about the room. Rag dolls and dolls with china faces and homemade dresses silently tempted little girls and mothers and grandmothers. Tin candle holders and cookie cutters sparkled from the top of a twig table. Pottery dishes and ornaments sat on a log table. Jason wondered whether Tom Berry had made that pottery. Handmade baskets—some woven of pine needles, some of oak—hung from the rafters. Other baskets filled with ornaments were scattered about the room.

A cane-seated oak rocking chair with a fir-green throw tossed over the back sat invitingly near the window, where handblown glass ornaments captured the sunlight. On the floor beside the chair, a baby doll in a hand-embroidered white gown lay in a small wooden cradle.

When all the children had received their cookies and drinks, Jason gave them pointers on how to care for their Christmas trees to reduce the chances of fire. He headed to the back of the room when he finished.

Mandy's sister, Ellen, handed him a cup of cider.

"Thanks. Where did you come from?"

"I just got home from my classes. What do you think of this room? It's Mandy's pride and joy."

"She told me it's the local crafters' room. Does that mean everything in here is made by local people?"

"Yes."

"I had no idea this area held so much talent." Jason's gaze swept the room again, this time with a new sense of respect. As a businessperson, he realized what it meant to devote an entire room to local work. But maybe it was a wise move. The room certainly embodied a homey, family-Christmas atmosphere.

Ellen nudged him with her elbow. "Here comes Mandy. Did I make it back in time for her show?"

"Uh, yes, I think so." Jason's curiosity stirred again. What was this show?

Mandy's dress only increased his curiosity. A huge old-fashioned bib apron of rough, off-white material covered her clothes. The apron touched the tops of her shoes and completely hid her slacks. She'd wrapped a white knit shawl over her shoulders.

Jason shifted his weight from one foot to the other as Mandy stopped in front of the window. He should get back to work. The men who drove the tractors had already finished their cider and headed out to the trees. Maybe he'd just stay a couple minutes and see what Mandy was up to.

Miss Lewis introduced Mandy's program. "Miss Wells prepared a special surprise. She's going to tell you a Christmas story from long ago. The story took place in a section of the Appalachians farther north than these mountains. In 1752, before the American Revolution and before the United States became a country, the French and some Native American tribes were battling with the British and other North American tribes over who would control America. Two hundred years later, Paul Gallico wrote this story down. He called it 'Miracle in the Wilderness.' " She brought her index finger to her lips in the universal "quiet" sign. "Listen while Miss Wells tells us what happened on Christmas all those years ago."

Jason noticed the ever-present music had changed to Christmas hymns played on a harpsichord. No words conflicted with the story. The instrumental music seemed appropriate for a story from the 1700s.

Mandy drew her shawl close about her shoulders and shivered visibly. "It was cold on Christmas Eve in 1752 as Jasper Adams and his wife Dorcas stumbled through the snow-covered forest with their Algonquian captors." She knelt and lifted the baby doll from the small wooden cradle beside the rocking chair. "Colder than the air was the fear in Jasper's and Dorcas's hearts for their eight-month-old son, whom one of the Algonquian carried on his shoulder."

Mandy explained how the little family had become captured. So skillful was Mandy's telling of the tale, she drew Jason completely into the story until he felt the cold and the fear and later the wonder. When the first miracle was revealed, it seemed to Jason that he could see the buck, doe, and fawn kneeling in the midst of the forest in honor of Christ's birth. Jason felt the courage it took for Jasper Adams to tell, at the fierce Algonquian leader's insistence, of the Child who caused the animals to pay Him homage. He felt the Algonquian leader's awe at the miracle in the wilderness, his respect for Jasper's God—the respect that caused him to release Jasper and his family in a second miracle.

Jason was so enraptured by the story that when it ended, he discovered his cider had grown cold. He'd planned to stay only a few minutes before returning to work. Half an hour had passed during the storytelling.

For a full minute after the story ended, the children sat transfixed, leaning forward, their gazes riveted on Mandy. Then the children gave a common sigh and sat back.

Customers who'd wandered close enough to hear Mandy's voice had stayed to hear the entire story. Now they too stirred and drifted back to their shopping, murmuring to each other, "Wasn't that a beautiful story?" and "Lovely, just lovely."

Beside him, Ellen took a deep breath. "Guess I'd best get out front and help with the customers."

Jason lifted his shoulders in a stretch. Time for him to go too. A question stopped him.

Andy raised his hand. "Miss Wells, is that story true?"

"I don't know. The author wrote that his great-grandmother told him the story."

"I like the story, even if it's not true," Beth asserted.

A chorus of agreements rose from the class.

Jason smiled, amused and touched by Beth's attempt to protect Mandy's reputation with her fellow students.

"But deer don't know about Jesus," Andy persisted.

How is she going to field that? Jason wondered. He didn't envy her this predicament.

"I guess," Mandy started slowly. "I don't know what deer do and don't know. But I believe in miracles."

Miss Lewis stood. "Thank you for the story, Miss Wells. Class, put on your coats. It's time to go back to school."

Jason frowned slightly. Was she wondering if inadvertently she'd allowed Mandy to creep over the boundary between church and state? He didn't believe the story crossed that well-watched line, but another might interpret it differently.

"Do I have to go back to school too, Miss Lewis?" Beth asked.

"No, you can stay here since the school day is almost over."

"Yeah!" Beth skipped over to Mandy. "I liked that story."

Andy turned back to Mandy while zipping up his red jacket. "I'm part Cherokee." A challenge underlaid his tone.

Jason tensed, watching for Mandy's reaction. Amazing that the simple story brought up so many issues.

"That's a fine heritage." Mandy smiled at Andy. "Your people lived in these mountains a long time before America became the United States."

"The Cherokee were like the Algonquian in your story. They didn't believe Jesus is the Son of God. I don't either, but I like your story

503

anyway." Andy spun about and pushed past a red-haired boy, apparently eager to leave before Mandy could reply.

Jason nodded to the students as they passed him on their way out. Most thanked him for the tour. Their enjoyment of the day left a smile in his heart.

Over the last of the students' thanks, Jason heard Beth's troubled question to Mandy.

"God punishes people who don't believe in Jesus, doesn't He?"

Jason glanced over at the girl. Mandy slipped her arms about Beth's shoulders and dropped a kiss on the top of the girl's head. "God is love, and I think God loves your classmate, don't you?"

Beth nodded, still frowning.

"Since God is love, I think we can trust Him to do what's best for people whether or not they believe in Jesus."

"I guess so." Beth didn't look convinced.

"There are some cookies left. Will you do me a favor and take the plate around to customers and offer them cookies?"

Beth brightened immediately at the prospect of such an important duty. She lifted the green-and-blue pottery plate from the table near the entrance, gave Jason a blinding smile, and moved into the large room, stepping slowly so as not to drop the plate.

Jason walked over to Mandy. "When did you become such a great storyteller?"

She furrowed her brow as if puzzled, but her eyes sparkled with fun. "Is that a compliment or a question?"

"Both."

"Then I thank you for the compliment, kind sir. As for the question, anyone can tell stories."

"Not everyone stirs their audience's emotions the way you did today."

She looked down and played with the shawl's fringe. "It was the story that touched people, not me."

"It was both." *So like her to be humble about her talent,* he thought. "Andy sure came up with some challenging questions. Beth too."

"Whew. I'll say."

He started the oak chair rocking with a push from his foot. "So you don't believe God punishes people?"

"I didn't say that. I said I believe He loves people. I believe we can trust that love to do what's best for every person." She slipped off the shawl and began folding it. "Besides, I'm concerned about Beth. I think she's angry with God. If that's true, she's likely also worried He will punish her for that anger. I believe trusting in His love for her will help her get over her anger faster than worrying He might punish her."

"She's only—eight? Why would she be angry at God?"

"Because—"

"Oh, of course," he interrupted. "Because her dad left."

Mandy nodded. "She's really hurting." She glanced past his shoulder. "Here she comes." She lifted her voice. "The plate's empty. The customers must have liked the cookies. Thanks for doing that, Honey."

"You're welcome. Mom says can you please help with the customers 'cause it's busy."

"Sure." Mandy dropped the shawl on the chair and reached behind her back to untie the enveloping apron. "Will you take the plate up to the loft kitchen, Beth? Thanks." She slipped the apron off, grabbed the shawl, and started to the outer room.

"Bye," Jason called out.

She looked back over her shoulder and smiled, continuing her hurried steps. "Bye. Thanks for all you did for Beth's class today."

"Yes, thanks, J. P." Beth smiled. "It was fun riding through the trees in the wagon."

"Glad you enjoyed it. I'd better get back to work before I'm fired."

She giggled, walking alongside him, carrying the plate. "Grandpa Seth wouldn't fire you."

"Don't think so?" He gave a strand of her blond hair a playful yank. "If he gives me a hard time, I'll send you to stand up for me. How's that?"

"All right." Her giggles continued as she headed for the loft.

Once outside, Jason's steps quickened into a jog. His thoughts stayed back at the Christmas barn while he ran. Was Mandy right, was Beth angry at God as well as Zach? Jason hated to think of all the hurt that sweet kid carried inside her because of her selfish father.

Zach has a lot to answer for.

10

*M*andy hummed along to Bing Crosby's "White Christmas" while gently tucking a handblown purple-and-gold tree topper surrounded in bubble wrap into a box. A steady stream of customers had filled the store all day. Even now at two-fifty-something, women in the middle of the room were trying to decide on which buildings to add to their Snow Village collections. Mandy was accustomed to taking advantage of "spare" minutes such as this to work on small tasks like this mailing. Beside her, Ellen stuck price tags on pieces of pottery dinnerware Tom Berry had just brought in.

We're a good team. The thought added pleasure to Mandy's already-happy day. She felt blessed, doing work she loved with someone she loved.

Mandy scooped Styrofoam beads up with an old plastic measuring cup from the large plastic bag stored behind the counter and filled the remaining space in the cardboard box.

"Did you notice how he watched you yesterday?" Ellen studied the Christmas design on one of the plates, but her attention was obviously elsewhere.

"Who watched me?" Mandy's brows met in puzzlement. "What are you talking about?"

"J. P. He watched you while you told that story."

"Everyone in the room watched me. I was the only person talking."

Ellen set the plate down on the counter. "I mean he really watched you, the way a man watches a woman he really likes."

Mandy's heart rate picked up speed at Ellen's words, but she shook her head. "You saw what you wanted to see. Jason isn't interested in me that way. Not anymore." *Not that I'd mind if he were.*

"You're not going to try to convince me there's still been no kisses between you?"

Mandy reached for the wide roll of postal tape. "Definitely no kisses."

"Right." Ellen's dry tone clearly announced that she didn't believe such nonsense.

The two customers approached the counter with their Snow Village purchases, preventing further discussion even if Ellen had been inclined to force the issue. While Mandy rang up the orders and Ellen bagged the purchases, the customers chatted happily about their Snow Village collections.

Beth, Bonnie, and Tom Berry came out from the local crafters' room as the customers left. The girls were only halfway between the back room and the front counter when Jason entered carrying a stack of plastic food containers.

"Hi, J. P." Beth and Bonnie raced toward him, each flinging their arms around him when they reached him. "I got here first," Bonnie announced.

Beth lifted her chin. "Who cares?" Her haughty tone made it clear she cared.

Jason grinned. "Whoa. A professional football team could use you two."

Watching the girls giggling at his teasing, Mandy felt her heart soften. Jason seemed so at ease with the girls. He and Tom were good for Beth and Bonnie. Perhaps the girls didn't find the men threatening since neither of them were in the position of a father figure.

Chuckling, Jason freed himself from the girls and set the plastic cartons down on the counter between Mandy and Ellen. "I come bearing gifts. Gram is afraid you two are working too hard and not eating properly, so she sent dinner. Grilled chicken and steamed vegetables." He nodded at Tom. "Hi."

"Mmm." Mandy opened the chicken container, leaned down to smell, and closed her eyes. "Wonderful."

Ellen grabbed the container. "Hey, share it. I'm starved."

Tom grinned and closed the cover. "Plates and silverware might be a good idea."

Ellen waved her hand. "What, you've never heard of picnics and finger foods?"

"Fingers might work for the chicken, but for steamed veggies?" Tom shook his head. "You'd end up with mushed vegetables."

His description set the girls on another giggling spree.

Ellen heaved an exaggerated sigh. "Okay, if you insist, we'll use plates and silverware. Beth, would you run upstairs and get some dishes for us?"

"Okay." She skipped between glittering trees to the loft staircase.

Ellen picked up one of the pottery plates she'd priced earlier. "This dinnerware you made is almost too beautiful to eat off, Tom."

"I suppose that's a compliment, but I hope your customers don't feel it's too pretty to use. I'll sell a lot more if they buy it to put on their tables than if they buy an odd piece to display."

Bonnie climbed up onto a stool. Beside her, Jason leaned against the counter. "I had the trees you wanted for beside the front door brought down about an hour ago, Mandy."

Mandy straightened. "Thanks. Now I can decorate them in time for the Thanksgiving weekend shopping rush. Will you help me decorate them, Bonnie?"

"Sure."

"I've decided to use a real tree inside too," Mandy told Jason. "I think it will be perfect for the Mitten Tree."

Jason's brow furrowed. "Mitten Tree?"

"Pastor talked about it in church Sunday. Don't you remember?" Bonnie reproached.

" 'Fraid not. Suppose you tell me about it."

"Well." Bonnie took a deep breath. "People bring mittens and hang them on the mitten tree, and Mandy gives them a free Christmas tree ornament."

Jason nodded. "I see. And why does Mandy want a tree full of mittens?"

"They aren't for her." Bonnie cast her gaze at the ceiling. "They're Christmas presents for kids whose parents can't afford to buy them mittens."

"Sounds like a great idea."

Mandy thanked him with a smile.

"If you pick out a tree, I'll see it's brought down here and set up," he told her. "Consider it the Garth donation to the mitten cause."

"Thank you."

"Planning to take time off from the Christmas tree business to celebrate Thanksgiving, J. P.?" Tom asked.

"Part of the day. After Gramps's heart attack, I'd hate to completely miss spending the holiday with them. We're trying to get all our retail lots set up before the Thanksgiving weekend rush begins, and that usually means our people work Thanksgiving. Hate to take the whole day off when our people can't do the same."

Tom nodded. "I see your point, but if you can spare half an hour or so, I'd like your help. I have a large nativity to set up. An outdoor one. The pieces are pretty heavy."

"I'll work it in. Speaking of work, I'd better get back to it."

"Aren't you going to eat with us?" Bonnie asked.

"I ate with Gram and Gramps."

From beside the cash register, Mandy picked up an envelope from the pile of mail that had arrived that day. It was the first chance she'd had to open it. "Thanks for bringing us the leftovers, Jason. And the trees."

Jason waved and started toward the door.

As Mandy slit the envelope with a silver letter opener, the phone rang.

"I'll get it." Bonnie grabbed for the phone. "Always Christmas Shop. This is Bonnie. How can I help you?"

Mandy listened to Bonnie's prim phone voice with half her attention, the other half on her mail. She and Ellen preferred the girls not answer the store phone, but knowing it was inevitable the girls would sometimes do so, they had taught them to answer in a professional manner.

"Daddy!"

Bonnie's squeal of delight caused Mandy's stomach to turn over in a nauseous sense of foreboding. Out of the corner of her eye, she saw Jason stop and turn around just inside the door.

Her glance darted to Ellen. Her eyes filled with apprehension, Ellen watched her happy daughter.

Tom's gaze also rested on Ellen, his lips pressed tightly together.

Bonnie continued her conversation, blissfully unaware of the tension with which her father's call had flooded the usually cheery store. "I miss you, Daddy. Where are you? What are you doing?" The child's eyes were large with excitement.

None of the adults spoke.

Beth's quick footsteps sounded as she descended the stairs and came across the room, carrying a stack of plates, forks, and knives. Tom took them from her and set them on the counter.

Bonnie held out the phone to Beth. "Here."

Beth reached for the receiver. "Who is it?"

"Daddy."

Surprise and joy filled Beth's eyes. Then red color surged across her face. Her eyes shuttered. She handed the receiver back. "I don't want to talk to him." She turned and ran back across the room toward the stairs.

11

$\mathcal{F}$or a moment the only sound in the room was Beth's retreating footsteps thudding against the wooden floor and stairs. Mandy, her heart crimped in pain for the girl, stared after her.

"Give me that." Ellen grabbed the phone, breaking the illusion of a frozen setting. She turned her back to Bonnie in what Mandy guessed was an attempt to hide her anger. But Mandy saw the fury flash in her sister's eyes, and Ellen's voice held little restraint when she spoke. "Why are you calling, Zach?"

Jason moved quickly to Bonnie and slipped an arm around her shoulders. "Why don't you come outside with me and check out the trees I brought for your aunt Mandy? See if you think they're all right or if we need to select some other ones."

"Okay." Bonnie slid off the stool, her gaze still on her mother.

Mandy mouthed a silent "thank you" to Jason, warmth filling her chest at his desire to spare Bonnie from witnessing anger between her parents. Especially when the gesture took him away from his work.

Mandy started around the counter. She wanted to get out of earshot of Ellen and Zach's conversation too. Should she go with Jason and Bonnie or go after Beth? She wavered a moment. Would Beth want someone to talk with right away, or did she need some time alone? Rather than barging in, maybe it would be wiser to let Ellen talk with Beth.

Mandy's decision made, she addressed Bonnie brightly. "Is it all right if I come too? I haven't seen the trees yet either."

"Sure, the more the merrier." Jason's voice was more jovial than the simple event normally justified. "What do you say, Bonnie?"

512

"Yeah, sure."

Mandy doubted Bonnie realized what she was agreeing to. Though she followed Jason, she looked over her shoulder, her troubled gaze on Ellen.

Tom followed them out the door. "Think someone should check on Beth?" he whispered in Mandy's ear.

His concern for Beth increased Mandy's admiration of him. "Let's give Beth a few minutes alone. If she doesn't come downstairs soon, I'm sure Ellen will check on her."

Brass carriage lamps on either side of the door lit the entrance area, in addition to the lighted icicles which decorated the roof. Together they supplied enough light to see the Fraser firs in their burlap bags.

Jason engaged Bonnie in a serious consideration of the trees. Did she like the kind he'd chosen? The height? The shape? Did she think they matched each other well?

Bonnie took time to think through each question before answering, walking around the trees, standing back to view them. In the end, she complimented Jason. "These are perfect."

Mandy stood near the heavy wooden red door, rubbing her sweatered arms and shivering, wishing she'd grabbed a coat. "Will you help me decorate the trees, Bonnie? I thought I'd use red ribbons and wooden birds."

"The little painted birds?" Bonnie's face brightened. "The cardinals and blue jays?"

"Those are the ones."

"Oh, they'll be just right. Let's get them now."

Mandy hesitated, not ready to go back within hearing distance of Ellen and Zach's conversation.

Bells jangled as the door opened. Sweet strains of "O, Little Town of Bethlehem" with its message of peace floated onto the night air as Ellen stepped outside.

Everyone looked at her, but no one asked the question in all their minds.

Ellen crossed her arms over her chest, warming her hands beneath her arms. She looked at Mandy. "Zach's coming here for Thanksgiving."

"Daddy's coming home! Yeah!" Bonnie jumped up and down, clapping, her face wreathed with joy.

Doubt darkened Mandy's anticipation of the holiday. Would it end up the wonderful experience Bonnie expected?

Tension filled the Christmas barn the next two days. Zach's news tarnished the joy with which Mandy had looked forward to her only day off until Christmas.

Beth declared firmly she wouldn't see her father. She continued that assertion all the way through to Thanksgiving, but Mandy felt certain she saw a sense of excitement and hope in the girl's eyes that wasn't due to anticipation of a turkey dinner.

Grandma Tillie invited Mandy, Ellen, and the girls to join her, Grandpa Seth, and Jason for Thanksgiving. Ellen tried to decline, explaining Zach's uninvited presence. "We'll go to a restaurant," Ellen said, wrinkling her nose. "Less chance for him to make a scene and less excuse for him to hang around too long. I haven't said anything negative about his visit to the girls, but from past experience I don't expect him to get through an entire day in a pleasant mood."

Grandma Tillie brushed aside Ellen's excuses. "He won't dare act up in front of Seth and Jason. Seth and I want you to spend the day with us. We won't take no for an answer."

In the end, Ellen agreed. "Actually, it's a relief knowing we won't be alone with him," she admitted to Mandy after Grandma Tillie left. "It's not that I'm afraid of him. He's not a violent man. But he does have a talent for knowing just the right thing to say to cut a person's heart. He seems to enjoy hurting people with words."

As a writer, Zach should understand the power of words, Mandy thought. Perhaps he did. Perhaps he realized words could maim and kill as effectively as guns or knives. How had life wounded him that he felt the need to use words against the woman he'd once loved and against his own children? She doubted Ellen had any desire to extend the man sympathy at the moment, so she only said, "How sad that he chooses to use words to harm instead of to heal and encourage."

*   *   *

"Mommy."

The bed shook.

"Mommy."

Mandy fought to stay in her dream, to stay in the warm though unreal shelter of Jason's arms, the wonderful world of his kiss.

The bed shook again. Mandy groaned and forced her eyelids open. Bonnie, wearing her Barbie nightgown, stood beside the bed Mandy and Ellen shared. A frown furrowed the girl's usually smooth forehead as she stared at her mother. "Wake up, Mommy." Bonnie pushed both hands against the mattress, trying to make it bounce.

Ellen rolled onto her back, her eyes still closed. "What's the matter? Are you or your sister sick?"

"No, but—"

"Then go back to bed."

Mandy agreed wholeheartedly though silently.

"It's Thanksgiving, Mommy."

"I know." Ellen's murmur grew fainter. "That's why we can sleep in."

"But Daddy's coming. We need to get dressed."

"He won't be here for hours and hours, Pumpkin."

"Are you sure?"

"I'm sure." Ellen opened her eyes to narrow slits and glanced at Mandy. "He hates morning. He thinks dawn is synonymous with noon."

"Maybe Daddy will get up early this morning 'cause he's excited to see us."

Ellen groaned and pulled her pillow over her face.

Mandy chuckled. "I think your daughter inherited her persistent streak from our mother. Remember how she woke us up when we were kids?"

Ellen groaned again. "Don't remind me."

"How? Tell me how," Bonnie demanded, leaning against the bed.

Mandy stretched her arms toward the ceiling. "She'd sing to us. A good-morning song. Something about dancing all night."

Bonnie climbed onto the bed, a mischievous gleam in her eyes.

Pushing herself to her feet, she started jumping. Her hair, mussed from a night's sleep, bounced in brown curls on her flannel-covered shoulders. "Good morning. Good morning. Good morning."

No melody tied her song together, but it obtained the desired effect. Ellen pushed her pillow off her face and grabbed Bonnie's legs. The girl dropped giggling to the mattress between Ellen and Mandy.

Ellen gave Bonnie a hug. "I give up. Go pour us some orange juice. I'll be out in a minute."

"Okay." Bonnie climbed over Ellen and slid off the bed. The girl started toward the door, then rushed back and planted a kiss on Ellen's cheek. "I love you, Mommy."

"I love you too, Pumpkin."

Bonnie skipped away with a wide grin.

Mandy pushed back her covers and got up, still reluctant to leave the warmth and comfort of bed behind for the day. Ellen climbed out of bed too. They straightened the top sheet of lavender-colored flannel, then pulled up the violet-spattered eyelet comforter.

As they plumped the pillows, Ellen said, "This is one Thanksgiving Day I'm not looking forward to."

"I know." The thought of Zach's expected appearance made Mandy's stomach queasy. It must be worse for Ellen. "But a day can't be all bad that starts with a wonderful little girl like Bonnie saying she loves you."

Ellen's smile chased away the tension in her face, softening her features. "I guess it can't at that. I'm pretty blessed, aren't I?"

Mandy nodded. She felt blessed herself with Ellen and the girls such an integral part of her life.

As Mandy showered, she hummed her mother's good-morning song and turned her thoughts to the day ahead. In spite of Zach, she looked forward to the day. After all, she was spending it surrounded by people she loved: Ellen, the girls, Grandpa Seth, and Grandma Tillie.

And Jason. She and Jason hadn't celebrated a holiday together in more than eight years.

"Okay, so Jason and I aren't actually celebrating Thanksgiving together," she admitted, lathering the shampoo in her hair. "Not like a couple. But we'll be in the same place with people we both care about."

Definitely something to be thankful for. Her heart expanded in sweet anticipation.

12

*G*randpa Seth and Grandma Tillie's home had stood watch on the mountainside for 130 years. It wasn't the old-fashioned architecture or comfortable furniture passed down through the generations which struck Mandy most each time she entered the house. Rather, it was the warmth and love that filled the large, square rooms and settled about her spirit like a soft, well-loved shawl.

Mouthwatering aromas of roasting turkey and baking pumpkin pies greeted Mandy, Ellen, and the girls when they arrived in late morning. The girls carried the toys they'd brought into the living room to play with beneath Grandpa Seth's watchful eyes while the women finished preparing the meal.

The large country kitchen with its cheery-yellow walls allowed Grandma Tillie, Mandy, and Ellen to work without crowding each other. Pots and pans filled with potatoes, carrots, green beans, and cranberries covered all four stove burners.

Grandpa Seth's great-great-grandmother's woodburning stove still stood against one wall, but it was only used in emergencies when electricity fell victim to mountain storms. Grandma Tillie kept the stove's cast iron gleaming. A huge old graniteware coffeepot sat on a burner like a proud watchman.

Mandy, still humming the morning song, stood at the white rectangular table in the middle of the room and sliced celery for the relish tray. The fresh smell of soap and water and the enticing scent of aftershave warned her of Jason's presence before she heard him. The sense of his nearness sent delightful tingles along her nerves.

He reached around her and picked an olive from the crystal tray in front of her. "Happy Thanksgiving, Mandy."

The simple action provoked a sweet memory of the way her father loved to come up behind her mother when she worked in the kitchen, give her a hug with one arm to divert her attention while with the other he stole a tidbit from whatever she was preparing.

"Happy Thanksgiving, Jason." She turned to smile at him and caught her breath softly. He'd changed from his usual jeans and flannel shirt into gray chinos and a black polo sweater.

Ellen, holding a jar of spiced apple rings, stopped beside them. "You clean up good, J. P."

He certainly does, Mandy thought.

"You ladies don't look so bad yourselves."

"Why is it compliments are so hard to recognize coming from you? 'Don't look so bad.' You couldn't say we look movie-star gorgeous?" Ellen held out the jar of apple rings toward him. "Here. Make yourself useful."

He took the jar. "What am I supposed to do with this?"

"Take the rings out of the jar and put them on the relish dish." Ellen explained slowly and distinctly as if speaking to a young child. "And use a fork, not your fingers."

Mandy grinned. Ellen and Jason had always teased each other this way. Mandy retrieved the jar from Jason. "You know better than to put him in charge of any kind of food, Ellen. There won't be any apple rings left for the rest of us if he gets a chance at these." She slapped lightly in the direction of Jason's fingers as he reached for another olive. "See what I mean?"

Jason shook his hand in pretend pain. "You are two tough ladies in a kitchen."

"Someone needs to guard the food," Mandy retorted, "and make sure others get to eat today." She enjoyed the everyday ordinariness of simple exchanges like this with him.

Beth and Bonnie wandered into the kitchen. Bonnie held up a folded piece of white typing paper. "Look what I made for my daddy, J. P."

Jason looked at the paper. "Hey, it's a turkey."

"It's a Thanksgiving card," she explained.

Beth shook her head. "He can tell that, Silly."

Bonnie ignored her. "I made it myself. I held my hand on the paper and drew around my fingers." She pointed to the colorful crayon turkey. "See? My fingers made the tail and my thumb made the head."

"Wow. I'm impressed."

Jason's compliment brought a grin to Bonnie's face.

Beth shrugged her shoulders and brushed at her blond hair with one hand. "I learned how to do that in kindergarten."

Bonnie's grin faded.

"You must have attended more advanced kindergarten than I did," Jason told them, "because I never learned how to do this."

Bonnie's grin returned. "Do you think my daddy will like it?"

"Of course he will." Jason handed the card back to her. "He'll think you're a great artist."

Mandy's heart caught in an unexpected sweet pain at Jason's loving attitude toward the girls.

Beth walked to the counter where Grandma Tillie stood counting serving bowls. "Can Bonnie and me help, Grandma Tillie?"

The older woman wiped her hands on her terry-cloth apron and looked around the kitchen. "The dining room table isn't set yet. Come along. I'll show you where everything is." She took a couple steps and stopped. "I forgot to iron the tablecloth. Ellen, would you do that?"

As the four left the kitchen for the diningroom, Mandy heard Bonnie ask, "Will Daddy be here soon?"

Jason leaned back against the kitchen table and glanced at the oak wall clock. "Eleven-thirty. Surprised Zach isn't here yet. Thought he flew into Winston-Salem last night."

Mandy nodded. "That was his plan, and Winston-Salem is only a little over an hour from here."

"If he doesn't show up after promising those kids . . ." Jason stopped without stating the implied threat.

"I don't know whether to be angry with him for keeping them waiting or glad he's arriving late so there's less time we need to spend with him."

Jason grinned. "Why, Mandy. That's about the meanest comment I've ever heard you make."

She felt her cheeks heat. "Are you implying that I am a Pollyanna?"

"I think that's a pretty apt description." He reached for another olive.

"Just because I don't think it's necessary to say unkind things about people doesn't mean I'm not realistic."

"True. You must be realistic about business. That's a great store you created."

She debated a moment whether to allow him to so easily change the subject and decided carrying hurt feelings over such a small matter wasn't worth the effort.

He reached for a piece of celery. She brushed his fingers away. "One little compliment doesn't entitle you to more food."

He chuckled and crossed his arms over his chest. "I was surprised when Gram said you'd be spending Thanksgiving with us. I thought you'd spend it in Asheville with your folks."

Did he resent her spending the holiday with his family? She searched his eyes but saw no anger there. "My parents moved to Texas two years ago. My brother and his family live in San Antonio. My parents like it there, and my brother's family gave Mom and Dad the excuse they were looking for to move. They spend Easter with Ellen and me, and Thanksgiving and Christmas with our brother's family."

"Do you miss living near them?"

"Not as much now as I did at first. I don't feel cheated that they've chosen to live closer to my brother than to me and Ellen, if that's what you mean. In this day and age, it's easy to travel. I plan to make a trip to San Antonio this winter when the Christmas rush is past. Speaking of distances, how are your partners in New York getting along without you?"

She instantly regretted her question. His face looked suddenly tired.

"Neal, the senior partner, likes to complain whenever we talk, but I'm not worried about the firm. It's not like I'm the only knowledgeable player."

"No, of course not," she murmured. "Grandpa Seth said you were working on a major merger at the time of his heart attack. He's concerned that because you came here, your client didn't receive the best representation."

"The client's case turned out fine." Jason straightened and wandered toward the stove.

Mandy wondered whether he moved so she couldn't see his expression.

"I spent a lot of time on the phone and computer to the office until the deal was done," Jason admitted.

Worrying about his clients in addition to putting in fourteen- to eighteen-hour days here can't be good for him.

Ellen bustled back into the room. "Every five minutes all morning it's been 'How much longer until Daddy's here?' "

"Zach knows you're here at Gram and Gramps, right?" Jason asked.

"He knows. I even gave him the phone number here and told him dinner is at noon. He's just acting his usual unreliable self."

"There's still a few minutes left before twelve," Mandy tried to reassure her. "Zach will probably drive up right on the hour."

He didn't.

"We'll just keep everything warm." Grandma Tillie turned down the heat beneath the potatoes. "Won't hurt things to cook awhile longer. Won't be the first time we didn't sit down to dinner right on the minute we planned."

"Does Zach carry a cell phone?" Mandy asked.

Ellen shook her head. "I don't know."

At twelve-thirty, they still waited. Ellen's temper grew shorter. Everyone's stomachs grew hungrier.

Ellen called Zach's California number. "Just in case he never left." No answer.

Mandy hurried back to the Christmas barn and checked their E-mail and answering machine. No message.

By one o'clock, Zach still hadn't arrived. Bonnie's eager expression was changing to fear of disappointment. Beth's I-don't-care attitude had blossomed into outright belligerence.

Seated at the kitchen table with Grandma Tillie and Ellen, Mandy looked over at her sister. Ellen's lips were tight with fury.

Jason sat down beside Mandy. She gave him a tired smile, but his attention was on Ellen. "I think it's time we made some phone calls."

Anger drained away from Ellen's face, leaving it pale. "You think Zach's been in an accident?"

"I think it's possible. He lived in this area for years, so it's not likely he's lost. The weather's good for travel—no rain, snow, ice, or fog—but accidents happen."

Ellen took a deep breath and nodded.

Jason turned to his grandmother. "The girls are pretending to watch television with Gramps. Why don't you make sure they stay there? It's probably best if Ellen calls from the office. Less chance the girls will overhear her there."

Mandy kept her arm around Ellen's waist as they followed Jason. An office window looked out over a pattern of Christmas tree plantings on a distant hill. Maps of cities covered a large bulletin board on one wall, red tacks marking Christmas tree lots. The opposite wall held maps of the Always Christmas Farm, with indications of the types of trees and stage of growth in each area.

Jason first verified the plane Zach had been scheduled on had arrived on time. The state patrol knew of no accidents with a man of Zach's description. Jason's last call was to the local hospital. When he hung up, he shook his head. "Zach's not there."

Ellen, looking dejected, sat in the green leather desk chair, swinging it back and forth with a push of her foot.

Jason leaned against the old oak filing cabinet beside the desk. "I suppose we could call the California state patrol and see if Zach was in an accident there. Or call all the hospitals in Winston-Salem."

"Sounds like a lot of work," Ellen said.

Mandy stared at the ceiling. There must be a way to find him. "Where are his parents living now?"

"Iowa. Not exactly on the flight pattern from Los Angeles to Winston-Salem," Ellen clarified with a hint of sarcasm.

"We called our parents this morning," Mandy reminded her. "A lot of people call their parents on holidays."

Ellen stopped swinging the chair. "Zach does usually call his parents on holidays." She stood up. "I'll go down to the barn and get their phone number."

Jason dialed 4-1-1. "It's quicker to dial information." He handed Ellen the cell phone.

Mandy sent up a silent prayer as Ellen said hello.

When the call was over, Ellen set the phone down with exaggerated care. Then, fingertips on the top of the desk, she looked from Jason to Mandy. "Zach's spending Thanksgiving with his agent's family, who kindly invited him to join them since he hasn't got family in the area."

Her voice was sweet. Too sweet. A blowup Mandy could understand, but this? "Ellen?"

Ellen gave the desk chair a shove. It rolled across the room. "He could have called and told the girls something else came up and he's sorry—horribly sorry—to miss Thanksgiving with them."

Mandy slipped off the desk and slid her arm across Ellen's shoulder, wanting to give her a hug and share her pain.

Ellen stepped away and stormed to the door. "Buckshot is too good for that man."

Mandy felt Jason's hand on her shoulder and was grateful for it. She knew her sister was trying to stay strong, but Ellen's rejection of her sympathy hurt. Mandy tried to put it aside. Ellen and the girls' emotions were the ones that mattered now.

Ellen yanked the door open. Then she closed it slowly and leaned her forehead against it. "What am I going to tell the girls?"

13

nger at Zach's selfishness surged through Jason's veins. He crossed the room and cupped his hands about Ellen's shoulders. "Tell them the truth, at least part of it. Tell them Zach didn't make it because of business."

"They'll wonder why he didn't call."

"Say they can call him later. If you want to, that is."

"Want to?" Ellen gave a shaky imitation of a laugh. "I never want to speak to him again. But I won't stop the girls from calling him."

"Shall I go with you to tell the girls?" Mandy asked.

Ellen shook her head. "No. But I'd appreciate it if you'd tell Grandpa Seth and Grandma Tillie." Ellen gave another shaky laugh. "I'm sure Grandpa Seth is more than ready to eat his Thanksgiving dinner."

While Ellen spoke with the girls in the living room, Jason and Mandy told Grandpa Seth and Grandma Tillie in the kitchen. Anger and frustration registered on Grandpa Seth's bearded face. "Some men never realize it's a privilege to be a father and to spend time with their children."

Grandma Tillie, her lips tightened into a straight line, patted her husband's arm.

They're thinking about Mom, Jason realized. *Thinking how they'd give anything for another few minutes with their only child. I'd give anything for a few minutes with Mom too.* The remembrance made Zach's behavior appear even crueler.

"Guess it's time to get dinner on the table." Grandma Tillie picked up quilted, scorched hotpads. "Expect your heart won't keep you from carving the turkey, Seth." At the oven she turned around. "Those young-uns will be upset enough without lookin' at any more long faces. Let's try to keep things cheerful for them."

By the time the serving pieces were all on the table, Bonnie had cried herself out, though her eyes appeared swollen and red-rimmed. Beth's eyes looked suspiciously bright, but Jason doubted she'd allowed herself to cry over her father's change in plans. She carried the I-don't-care-what-my-Dad-does-he-can't-hurt-me look with which Jason had become familiar. She was one tough little kid. On the outside anyway.

"I'm sorry if your dinner's ruined," Ellen apologized to Grandma Tillie while everyone seated themselves.

"Don't you worry yourself about it. A little gravy and a lot of love makes anything taste good," Gram assured.

Mandy sat beside Jason, and when everyone held hands and repeated grace together, it gave Jason special pleasure to hear her sweet voice join with his in thanksgiving. It also brought back memories of holidays past he and Mandy had spent with Gram and Gramps, and a painful lump filled his throat when he acknowledged that today he and Mandy weren't here as a couple. He tried to push the pain away. He and Mandy had at least formed a tentative friendship in the last few weeks. He should be satisfied with that and grateful for it.

Gramps's mildly outraged voice broke into Jason's thoughts.

"What are you doing, Woman? I can dish up my own food. Been doing it since I was old enough to hold a fork."

Gram, seated beside Gramps, put a tablespoon of mashed potatoes on his plate. "I've watched you dish up your own food for over fifty years. I know the way you pile up the most fattening food. Need to watch out for those arteries of yours."

"I'll watch out for my own arteries." Gramps grabbed the serving spoon.

Gram gripped the spoon harder. "We've seen how well that worked out. Landed you flat on your back in the emergency room."

"I'm not apt to forget it. Let go of that spoon. You've fed me nothing but vegetables all week. It's Thanksgiving. One decent meal isn't going to put me back in the hospital."

Jason chuckled. "Might as well give in, Gramps. She's bound and determined to keep you around."

"Even though you're ornery as a mule." Gram released the spoon and the bowl of potatoes. "Just remember what the doctor said and see that you watch your portions."

"Like living with a nurse," Gramps grumbled. "Where's the candied yams?"

"Didn't make any." Gram handed him the turkey platter. "Enough other food today that's bad for your heart."

"Hardly seems like Thanksgiving without candied yams. Suppose you didn't make pumpkin pie and whipped cream either."

"Did so. Don't be thinking you'll get more than a sliver of dessert, though. Consider yourself fortunate your Thanksgiving dinner isn't turnip greens and nothing more."

Jason, Ellen, and Mandy broke into laughter. Jason knew Gram's nagging was her way of telling Gramps she loved him, and Jason knew Gramps knew it too.

"Why are you all laughing?" Distress and fear filled Beth's eyes. "Are you going to get sick again, Grandpa Seth?"

Seeing her terror, Jason disciplined his grin and saw Mandy and Ellen do the same.

Gramps handed the turkey platter to Gram and turned his full attention to Beth. "I'm going to do my best not to get sick again. It's true I need to eat healthy foods, but one Thanksgiving meal isn't going to hurt me, and Tillie knows that." He grasped Gram's hand. "Isn't that right?"

Gram darted him a sharp glance and pressed her lips together hard before answering. "Yes, but it's best to set good eating habits right off."

"I'll be careful." He turned back to Beth. "Another thing I'm doing to make my heart healthier is exercise. Jason bought me an indoor bike and a treadmill. Maybe you'll come up and exercise with me sometimes."

Beth's face brightened. "Okay. That sounds like fun."

"Can I exercise with you too?" Bonnie asked.

"Absolutely."

The girls grinned at each other.

Jason glanced around the table as the group ate and visited, watching the simple interaction between his family and Mandy's family, the sharing between generations. In New York he seldom spent time around children. His work brought him into contact with adults of every age, but he seldom saw them in their roles as parents and grandparents.

I've missed that. Missed being part of a family.

He'd dated a number of women through the years but no one other than Mandy whom he'd wanted to bring into his grandparents' home or with whom he'd wanted to raise children. Spending the last few weeks close to her only reinforced the correctness of his decision not to marry any of the other women. *A lonely thought, since marrying Mandy isn't in my future.*

He glanced across the table at Beth and Bonnie. *What was Zach thinking, leaving his family? If I had two fantastic daughters like these, nothing could tear me away from them.*

The Thanksgiving meal lived up to prior years' tradition in satisfaction in spite of overcooking. Everyone agreed they'd appreciate dessert more later.

Gram turned down Mandy's and Ellen's offers to help with dishes. "I've no intention of going from table to sink. The dishes will clean up just as well later. Go out in the living room and visit with the others. I'm going to start some egg coffee before I join you."

Mandy and Ellen wandered over to the Christmas tree, which stood in a place of honor by the front window. Gramps went from the table directly to his recliner. The girls checked on the dolls they'd left on the sofa. Jason leaned against the doorjamb between the dining room and living room and watched the others.

Mandy looked over her shoulder at the girls. "Did you check out the Christmas tree yet?"

"Yes," Bonnie answered. But she and Beth picked up their dolls and walked over to the tree anyway. Bonnie leaned against Mandy's side, gazing up at the tree, and Mandy gave Bonnie a hug with an arm about her shoulders.

He'd seen them that way together a dozen times in the last two weeks, Jason realized. Bonnie seemed as comfortable with Mandy as with Ellen, her own mother.

Beth held herself more aloof. Even when she ventured near Ellen, she kept a little distance. Trying to protect herself. She might take someone's hand or allow them to touch her or hug her for a minute, but she never leaned into someone with complete abandon the way Bonnie leaned against Mandy now. And Beth didn't allow a hug to last for long.

He recognized himself in her. He suspected Beth recognized herself in him too, though likely not at a conscious level.

Bonnie made herself more vulnerable. Bonnie trusted. And in doing so received both the physical and emotional comfort that Beth denied herself. Mandy and Bonnie were a lot alike that way.

Gram stopped beside Jason in the doorway. They stood together in amiable silence, watching the others.

A soft *plunk-plunk-plunk* sounded from the kitchen. Jason grinned at Gram. "Sounds like you got the coffee started." Gram always preferred egg coffee perked in a large old pot on the stove to coffee made in a modern coffeemaker. "You spoiled me with your egg coffee. Specialty coffees and coffee shops are big with my coworkers in New York, but I'd put your coffee up against any of the specialty coffees."

"Flatterer."

He could tell his comment pleased her.

She inclined her head to indicate the group in front of the tree. "They're a nice little family, aren't they?" She spoke low, her voice not meant to carry beyond the two of them. "I'm glad Ellen and the girls moved in with Mandy. Gives her someone to wrap her heart around."

Jason glanced from Gram to Mandy in surprise. Did Gram mean that Mandy might be lonely without her sister and nieces? Mandy always impressed him as the least lonely person in the world. Her sincere interest in others drew people to her, created a circle of warmth and welcome.

"I know you must feel Seth and I betrayed you," Gram continued, "letting Mandy move into the barn and us not telling you. But it's been good for us, having her there. Until she moved in, I didn't realize how quiet things had grown around here after you left."

Guilt slipped into Jason's chest with her words. She and Gramps had lost their only daughter, taken him into their home, then lost him when he moved to New York. For family oriented people like Gram and Gramps, that was a lot of loss. The guilt twisted tighter. What could he do? His career was in New York.

"I don't mind that you let Mandy move into the barn. Just don't expect us to get back together." He darted a glance across the room at Mandy, reassuring himself no one but Gram could hear him.

"Don't expect anything," she retorted. "But you can't keep me from praying the good Lord brings a woman into your life for you to love."

Jason grinned. "Hope that prayer's answered. Just as long as the woman loves me too."

"So what's not to love?"

"A little prejudiced in my favor?" He gave her a one-armed hug. "It's nice to spend time with you and Gramps again."

"It's nice to have you here again."

"Say, girls."

Jason and Gram quit talking at Gramps's attempt to gain Bonnie's and Beth's attention.

"Can you tell what kind of tree that is, girls?" Gramps leaned forward in his recliner and rested his elbows on his knees.

"I think so." Beth gently touched the needles. "Is this a Fraser fir?"

Gramps smiled. "Is that a guess, or do you have a reason for saying a Fraser?"

"J. P. taught us to look at the needles. These needles are green on top and silvery underneath. I think that's what he said makes it a Fraser."

"You're right. Very good," Gramps approved.

Beth beamed.

"How old are you now?" Gramps asked.

"I'm eight. Bonnie is six."

"You know, when Jason was a boy, he loved Christmas trees. He'd follow me all over the farm, just like a puppy, right on my heels all the time."

The girls giggled.

"Like a puppy?" Bonnie repeated.

"Just like my hound dog, Butch, used to do. Jason was a right smart boy. He could identify every kind of fir and pine tree on the place by the time he was five."

"That's littler than me." Bonnie pointed to her chest.

Beth sat on the arm of Gramps's recliner. "Tell us more about J. P. when he was a boy."

"Let's see." Gramps rubbed his fist across his bearded chin and appeared deep in thought. "There's the time he ran away."

Jason burst into a laugh. "I never ran away. Where'd you come up with a tall tale like that?"

Beth grinned at him, then turned to Gramps. "Did J. P. run away?"

"Seemed like. It happened on a cold November night."

"This is November," Bonnie interrupted, coming to sit on the floor in front of the recliner.

"That it is," Gramps agreed. "Jason and his parents had dinner with us. After dinner we adults sat around drinking coffee and visiting, the way adults tend to do."

The girls bobbed their heads and gave matching smirks, as if to say, "Yes, that's what adults always do."

"It was dark, it being evening and all. Jason was just a little whippersnapper."

"Whippersnapper." The girls repeated the word, exchanging grinning glances.

"Yep, just a wee tyke, no more than three years old. We thought Jason was in this very room, playing with his trucks—he especially liked a big yellow dump truck. Filled it with small Christmas trees a friend of ours carved out of wood."

Jason caught Mandy grinning at him and shook his head, embarrassment bringing a smile to his face.

Bonnie moved to her knees, all her attention focused on Gramps. "But he wasn't playing with his trucks, was he?"

"Nope. He sure wasn't. Well, we looked through the whole house. Looked in the closets, cupboards, clothes hampers—everywhere."

"Did you look under the beds?" Bonnie asked.

"Yep, sure did. Well, by the time we got done looking through the house, we were pretty worried."

Beth picked at the edge of the chair arm. "Mom says we're always s'posed to tell her where we go. She says some people steal kids, so we need to be careful. Did you think someone stole J. P.?"

Jason felt Gramps's hesitation.

The older man cleared his throat. "No, can't say we did. We fig-ured he went outside to find a real Christmas tree to put in his truck."

Bonnie giggled. "A real Christmas tree would be too big."

"A baby tree might fit," Beth suggested.

"A brand-new baby tree, maybe. As I was saying, it was dark out and cold. Jason wasn't wearing a jacket. We didn't know which direction he went."

Bonnie inched closer to the chair. "Were you scared?"

"Scared stiff."

Beth picked at the chair arm again. "Were J. P's Mommy and Daddy scared?"

Gramps darted her a curious look. "So scared they could hardly stand it." He cleared his throat. "Well, we looked in the barn and didn't find him."

"Our barn?" Beth asked.

"Yep. Wasn't a Christmas store then. He wasn't in the barn. We called our neighbors and the men who worked for us. Everyone came with lanterns and flashlights. We spread out and walked through the groves, calling out Jason's name. We walked for hours and hours. Almost all night. We had to walk slow so we wouldn't miss him, because he was little, you know."

Bonnie nodded, her eyes wide.

"Near dawn, I heard Butch howling."

"Butch your dog?" Beth asked.

"Yep. See, Butch wasn't more than about three himself at the time. He and Jason were buddies. So when Jason ran away—"

"I didn't run away."

The girls laughed.

"When Jason took off," Gramps amended, "he took Butch with him. When I heard Butch howling, I headed straight for that mournful sound. Sure enough, Butch and Jason were together. Jason was curled up snug as a bug in a rug, sound asleep beneath a Scotch pine. Butch was practically laying on top of him. Figure Butch probably saved Jason's life that night. Kept him warm."

" 'Cause Jason didn't have a jacket, right?" Bonnie asked.

"That's right." Gramps nodded. "You never saw a boy get as much attention as Jason the next day. Someone was always hugging on him: his mom or dad or Gram or me."

"Or Butch?" Beth grinned.

"Well, Butch didn't give hugs, just sloppy kisses. But we gave Butch lots of hugs."

Ellen walked across the room from the tree to the recliner. "Let that story be a lesson to you girls. There's a reason I always ask where you're going. I don't want to spend a night looking for you, scared out of my wits."

"Don't worry, Mom." Beth slid off the arm of the recliner. "Bonnie and I won't spend any nights under a Christmas tree. Not an outdoor Christmas tree, anyway."

Bonnie stood up and hugged Ellen around the waist. "Can we have a puppy like Butch for Christmas?"

"Can you imagine what a mess a puppy would make in the Christmas store?"

"We could keep it in the loft," Bonnie suggested.

"Yes," Beth chimed in.

"It would get lonely up there, don't you think?" Ellen nodded to encourage their assent.

Bonnie shook her head. "But—"

"No puppy this year," Ellen declared.

"There's a picture of Jason from the year he ran away on the Christmas tree." Gram headed toward the tree in an obvious attempt to divert Bonnie's attention from the puppy-for-Christmas idea.

"I didn't run away," Jason repeated, following Gram.

Amusement danced in Mandy's eyes. "I don't think you're convincing anyone."

"Here it is." Gram removed a crocheted ornament with a small picture in the middle. She handed it to Beth. "That's Jason when he was three. His mother made that ornament for Jason's Christmas present to Seth and me that year." She smiled, deepening her wrinkles. "It was our favorite present."

Mandy stood between Jason and Beth, and the floral scent of Mandy's shampoo blended with the pine scent of the tree. Mandy looked over Beth's shoulder at the picture, then back at Jason. The smile in Mandy's eyes when her gaze met his was so tender, his heart felt like it flipped over.

Beth held the ornament as though it were a fragile piece of glass. Bonnie stood beside her to get a look. "That's J. P.? He doesn't look like J. P." She looked up at Jason. "You had chubby cheeks."

"Flattery will get you nowhere."

Beth handed the ornament back to Gram. "Thank you for showing it to us."

Gram hung it back on the tree. "The woman who made it is the same woman who makes the crocheted ornaments you sell in your store, Mandy."

"I don't recall selling any photo ornaments like this among her items."

"Why don't you have pretty ornaments like we do at the Christmas barn, Grandma Tillie?" Bonnie asked. "All your decorations are old."

"Bonnie, you apologize," Ellen scolded.

"I'm sorry, Grandma Tillie. But it's true."

Gram nodded. "It is true. I wouldn't trade one of these ornaments for a whole tree full of new ones, no matter how pretty."

"You wouldn't?" Bonnie frowned.

"No. You see, these aren't just decorations. They're memories. Each one is a memory of a special person or a special time or a special love." Gram removed a cotton-ball snowman. "Jason made this for me."

The girls grinned over their shoulders at him.

He shrugged. "What can I tell you? The world lost a great artist when I went into finance."

"Oh, right." Beth's tone let him know she didn't believe him.

Gram removed another decoration. "Jason made this angel from a toilet paper roll."

"I can't believe you kept all these things." Jason spoke over the girls' laughter.

"Of course I kept them. You were very proud of this angel at one time."

"That's because you and Mom treated everything I made like it was a masterpiece and displayed it all. I was a college freshman before I discovered I wasn't the world's next Picasso."

"All children should be so fortunate," Mandy commented softly.

His gaze followed hers to Beth and Bonnie. Mandy was right.

Jason and Mandy watched while Gram pointed out more family heirloom ornaments and explained their history to the girls. Waves of memories washed over Jason, memories of Christmases before his parents died when he'd been too young and innocent to know how precious those times were as they happened.

"We need a tree like this."

Mandy's voice brought Jason from his memories. "There isn't space for one more tree in your store."

"Not in the store. In the loft. In our home. We need a tree Beth and Bonnie can hang their own ornaments on. Things that are important to them, not only beautiful or glittery."

"An ornament doesn't need to be made from a toilet paper roll to be special to someone. I expect a lot of the ornaments you sell will wind up being someone's treasures. Twenty years from now a grandmother will tell her grandchildren who gave her the handmade pottery ornament from your store and why."

Mandy studied his face. "That is unexpectedly sweet of you to say."

Sweet. Just the kind of compliment a man liked to hear from a woman. He shrugged. "Guess holidays put me in a saccharine mood."

Her gaze slid from his face back to the tree. He saw her eyes widen and glisten with sudden unshed tears, saw her mouth open in a soft gasp. Why? He turned to find out.

14

*J*ason immediately recognized the cause of Mandy's shock. Gram held another ornament, showing it to Beth and Bonnie. The ornament was a wooden bench with a white-haired couple seated upon it, holding hands and gazing at each other.

His throat tightened painfully. He remembered he and Mandy selecting that for Gram and Gramps's Christmas present the first year Mandy spent with him and his family. Mandy had held it in the palm of her hand, smiling up at him. "This will be us one day. Old and gray and still holding hands. Young couples will walk past us and say to each other, 'Will we still love each other that much when we're their age?' "

He cleared his throat and tried to push the memory away. "The couple on that bench look even more like Gram and Gramps today than when we gave it to them."

"Yes, even more in love." Mandy's smile looked tight. Her pain-veiled gaze held his.

He recognized that pain: pain at the loss of their own love which began with such intensity, such hope and promise. Her pain intertwined with his own sense of loss, leaching life from his heart like two vines twining about a branch.

"Anyone ready for pie?" Gram asked.

Her question brought a chorus of affirmatives.

Jason tore his gaze from Mandy's, glad for the interruption. The dream of their love had been beautiful and powerful once upon a time. But the dream was over. There was no retrieving it. Mandy had chosen that ending.

Zach's nonarrival hadn't affected the pumpkin and pecan pies. The only complaint came from Gramps.

"You call this a slice of pie? A pine needle is bigger."

He received no sympathy.

After dessert, Gram finally agreed it was time to do the dishes. While the women cleared the table, Jason retrieved his grandfather's old chess set. It was a holiday tradition for the men to play chess after the meal. Setting the chessboard on the dining room table, Jason felt guilty remembering they hadn't played since the previous Christmas. How had he allowed almost a year to pass without visiting Gram and Gramps?

Jason was opening the oak box containing the chess pieces when Bonnie leaned against his thigh. "Will you play with me and Beth, J. P.?"

"I'd love to play with you after Gramps and I finish our chess game."

Gramps's chair squeaked as he stood up. He waved one hand in dismissal. "Go ahead and play with the girls. We can play chess later. Besides, I haven't taken my Thanksgiving Day nap yet."

Jason glanced at him sharply. "Feeling okay?" He kept his voice light with an effort.

"Fine. Something about a Thanksgiving meal makes me want to sleep like a baby. I'll just take a snooze in my recliner."

I'm overly cautious, Jason told himself, closing the box. He smiled at Bonnie. "So what are we playing?"

"House." Bonnie's grin was bright with anticipation.

Great. I gave up chess for this? Jason thought as he stood up. "I've never played house."

"It's easy." Bonnie closed her little fingers about his hand and led him to the rose-print sofa.

That flowered material always seemed so unlike Gram with her tough spirit, Jason thought. Of course, he better than most knew her heart combined that strength with gentleness and compassion. Like Mandy's heart. He'd never before recognized that similarity between the women, but he knew instantly the truth of it.

Dolls, doll clothing, toy dishes and baby bottles, some of Gram's old shoes and hats, and other paraphernalia Jason couldn't readily identify covered the couch. "It takes this much stuff to play house?"

"Yes." Bonnie nodded emphatically. "It's lots of fun. You'll like it."

Beth carefully wrapped a pink blanket around a doll which was almost too large for her arms. "Daddy didn't like to play house."

Beth's expressionless voice and face didn't fool Jason. He knew her words came from a distressed heart.

"Too bad your dad missed out on the fun."

Beth's gaze met his, and he knew he'd said the right thing. He winked at her. She grinned in surprised delight and ducked her head, giving her attention back to her baby doll.

Jason sat down cross-legged on the floor, more determined than ever to be a good sport about this change in his plans.

Bonnie handed him a doll with curly blond hair and blue eyes that closed. It wore a short white T-shirt and a diaper. "This one can be your baby 'cause it's a boy."

"Thanks." He held it by the neck with his left hand and pretended to critically study the rubber face. "What's its name?"

"Ted." A look of disgust lodged on Bonnie's face. "You can't hold him like that. He's a baby. Hold him like this."

"Sorry," he mumbled while Bonnie tried to adjust his arms.

He heard a muffled laugh and looked up to catch Mandy watching from the dining room doorway, hand over her mouth, her green eyes dancing with laughter.

"Good for you, Bonnie," Mandy encouraged after removing her hand from her grin. "It's important for a man to learn how to hold a baby."

"Hold it like this, J. P." Beth cradled her own baby doll in her arms.

He copied her, laying the doll on its back in his arms. The doll let out a "Waaaaa!" as though in protest. Jason straightened his shoulders, sure he'd mastered the simple task. "How's that?"

Bonnie propped her little fists on her almost nonexistent hips. "Haven't you ever held a baby before?"

"Not for a long time. Last time I held a baby was . . . let's see." He frowned, trying to remember. "Beth, you were the last baby I held."

"I was?" Pleasure lit her blue eyes.

"Yes."

"As I recall," Mandy interrupted, laughter underscoring her voice, "Beth was the first and last and only baby you held."

Beth's smile grew. "I was?"

"I think so." Jason forced the words around his heart, which had taken up residence in his throat. How could Mandy remember such a minute detail from his life? Of course, he remembered everything about the time they'd spent together in love—at least, that's the way it felt.

He'd told himself all these years that she hadn't truly loved him. But would she remember so many things if she hadn't loved him as much as he loved her? The picture leaped into his mind of her tear-filled eyes at the sight of the ornament they'd picked out together for Gram and Gramps. Had he been wrong all this time? Could it be Mandy's love had been deep and true, in spite of the fact she'd turned down his marriage proposal?

Bonnie leaned against his shoulder, jarring Jason back into the present, her gaze imploring. "Didn't you hold me when I was a baby?"

Beth heaved an exaggerated sigh of exasperation. "He didn't know you then. He just met you a few weeks ago, remember?"

"Oh, yeah."

Jason chuckled again at Bonnie's disappointment. "Hey, I thought we were going to play house. Let's get this show on the road."

He gave himself to the girls' make-believe world and found himself enjoying it immensely—not the act of playing house but involving himself in the girls' imaginations and knowing his involvement increased their enjoyment.

The girls taught him how to change a diaper, how to hold a baby bottle, and how to test the milk for warmth—though of course the bottle didn't contain milk.

The girls soon tired of changing and feeding dolls, and Beth announced it was time to go shopping. He discovered this was the reason for Gram's old hats and shoes, for one evidently couldn't go to the store without dressing up properly. His ego protested loudly when he realized the girls' intention, but he stilled it and accepted a faded pale blue felt hat with a feather slid jauntily into the narrow band surrounding the rounded crown.

He did his best to act disappointed when none of Gram's awful, old high-heeled shoes fit him. He vocally admired the patent-leather monstrosities upon which the girls tried to teeter.

Too bad handbags aren't dependent on foot size, he thought, even as he accepted a blue handbag with tiny handles from Bonnie.

"It matches your hat." She looked delighted with her choice.

The girls weren't ready yet. There was plastic jewelry to don which stuck to the skin like stickers.

Jason drew the line at the pink stuff in a bottle with a golden-haired princess on the front.

"But it's perfume. It will make you smell good." Bonnie sniffed the bottle as if to demonstrate.

"It will clash with my aftershave. Where are we going shopping?"

"In the kitchen," Beth announced.

Jason swallowed a groan, but carrying the purse in one hand and the doll in the other, he gamely followed behind the girls, who teetered along on the high heels. A glance at the recliner reassured him Gramps was deep into his Thanksgiving nap and couldn't tease Jason about his outfit later.

The women's faces broke into wide grins when the threesome entered the kitchen. Jason caught the gurgles of strangled laughter.

"I loved that hat and purse when they were new," Gram told him.

"How long ago was that?" Jason asked.

"About 1950." Gram put one hand behind her head and the other on her hip and gave a Mae West pose. "I thought I was hot stuff. That hat was the height of fashion."

The girls broke into giggles.

Mandy grinned. "Feel like hot stuff, Jason?"

He imitated Gram's pose the best he could with a doll in one hand and a handbag in the other. "The hottest."

Mandy's grin erupted into laughter.

The girls' bodies jiggled with their laughter. Bonnie wobbled on her high heels. "I—I'm going to fall," she squeaked out between giggles. She sank to the floor, which caused her and Beth to laugh harder.

Beth put her hand to her stomach. "My stomach hurts from laughing."

"Mine too," Bonnie stuttered.

Jason helped the still-giggling Bonnie to her feet.

"Smile."

Jason turned toward Mandy's command without thinking.

Flash. Mandy lowered her camera, grinning.

Great, Jason thought. *My moment of glory is recorded for posterity.*

The front doorbell rang.

"I'll get that." Jason's tossed the hat to the kitchen counter and dropped the purse and doll beside it. "I'll get you for that picture too," he whispered as he walked past Mandy.

He strode through the living room, glad to get away from the women and playing house.

Cold air rushed in when he opened the door. Tom Berry stood on the porch, a wool plaid jacket warming his body, his heavy brown beard warming his face. "Happy Thanksgiving, J. P."

"Same to you. Come on in."

Tom stepped inside just far enough to allow J. P. to close the door. "I brought the nativity—the outdoor one I told you about. You still have time to help me set it up?"

"Sure. Let me grab a jacket and tell Gram where I'm going."

It took him longer than he anticipated. When he told Gram the plans to set up the nativity on the mountainside, the girls—always ready for a new experience—piped up. "Can we go too? Please? Please?"

"If your mom says so, but . . ." He hesitated, lifted his eyebrows, and looked at the girls' feet. "Not in those shoes."

The girls turned to Ellen. "You can go, as long as you do whatever J. P. and Tom tell you," she said. "Don't get in their way. And it will be dark soon, so don't wander too far from the men."

"May I join you?" Mandy asked. "A walk and a little fresh air would feel good before we get started on supper."

Do I mind? Hardly. "Sure, the more the merrier."

"You always say that," Beth told him.

"Do I?" He shrugged. "Guess I like a crowd."

Mandy set a bowl in a cupboard and shut the door. "Where he lives, there's always a big crowd, Beth. He lives in New York, one of the biggest cities in the world."

And lonelier than this little farm on a North Carolina mountain. Maybe I do like a crowd around, Jason thought, *but not the kind of crowds I'm used to in the city. This kind of crowd—family and friends who are close to the heart.*

The truth of this thought struck him. Of course Gram and Gramps were always close to his heart. He'd tried repeatedly and unsuccessfully to put Mandy from his heart over the years. But now Beth and Bonnie had slid inside his heart too.

He hadn't time to examine the thought in depth. He took his coat, gloves, and ASU hat from a closet and made his way back to the living room and Tom.

"We've acquired some helpers," he told Tom. "Ellen, Mandy, and the girls are coming, if that's all right with you."

"Fine by me." Tom tilted his head to one side. A puzzled frown scrunched lines between his heavy eyebrows as he studied Jason's face.

"Why are you looking at me like that?"

"What are those pink things on your earlobes?"

Jason clapped his hands to his ears. The plastic sticker earrings.

Mandy chuckled behind him.

Heat rushed up his neck and over his face. He peeled the earrings off. "I was playing with the girls."

"Ah." A grin split Tom's beard. "That female influence will do it every time. Plays havoc with a man's mind."

That it does, Jason agreed silently, *in more ways than one.*

15

he crisp nip in the air felt good to Mandy as she climbed out of Tom's extended-cab pickup truck on a rocky ridge overlooking a highway. Mandy recognized the road as the one which, a couple bends and half a mile farther along, ran past the Christmas barn. "Is this your land, Tom?"

"Yep. Just barely. Another fifty feet or so over, and you'll be back on Seth and Tillie's land."

Jason rested his hands on his hips and looked around. "You chose a good site. People will have a clear view of the nativity scene from the road."

Few trees dotted the hillside between the road below and where they stood near the top of the ridge. The wind raced across the mountainside undeterred, tossing Mandy's hair around her face. She tucked the strands behind her ears and turned her back against the wind.

A newly constructed platform of pine-fragrant wood stood on the uneven ground, and on the platform rested an A-frame structure Mandy knew must be the stable for the nativity scene. Inside the A-frame stood a simple wooden manger. A rectangular bundle of hay sat on one corner of the platform.

Jason nodded toward the platform. "Did you build this, Tom?"

"Yep. I worked on this project in my spare time for almost a year. Figure the platform will keep the figures from getting hidden by snow, should we get any before Christmas. Another of our former classmates who's now an electrician rigged some spotlights to light the display."

Tom pulled a heavy green canvas tarp off the items in the truck bed, revealing four statues: Mary, Joseph, the baby Jesus, and an angel.

The statues were large and heavy. Mandy, Ellen, and the girls watched while the grunting and puffing men moved the pieces from the truck bed onto the platform.

Mandy thought how natural it seemed that Jason was here on the mountainside helping Tom. The same way it seemed natural to see him among the Christmas trees with the schoolchildren and celebrating Thanksgiving in Grandpa Seth and Grandma Tillie's home with herself, Ellen, and the girls.

Her heart caught in a little twinge, then regained its regular beat. Sometimes it seemed the years Jason spent in New York never happened, that when their gazes met across a room or in a group of people, he'd give her the smile that meant he couldn't wait until they were alone, and give her the wink that always made her heart want to laugh.

Had she made a mistake all those years ago, believing he'd never be happy in the city working in finance? Maybe she'd only wanted to believe it because she wanted to stay in the mountains and wanted him to stay too.

Mandy's attention slipped back to the present at a question from Ellen.

"Tom, the statues are beautiful. Did you make these?"

"Yep." Pleasure filled his face at Ellen's compliment.

"They are beautiful," Mandy agreed. "You've surpassed yourself with these. I don't know how you found time to make them and also make the pottery you sell, to say nothing of all the other aspects of running your business."

He shrugged his massive shoulders and looked embarrassed. "Other than work and church, there's not much else to fill my time."

"You're too modest," Ellen said. "You do a lot to help your mother and take care of the house and lawn."

He shrugged again. "She's family. Besides, neighbors and church family help out when life gets too crazy-busy."

Jason cut the twine binding one of the bundles of straw. Pulling a good-sized chunk from the bundle, he placed it in the manager.

For all the world as though he meant to make the bed more comfortable for the stone child, Mandy thought. It brought a smile to her lips and heart. Most likely the hay was meant to ensure the statue of the baby could easily be seen rather than buried in the manager. Still, when Jason and Tom lowered the baby statue into the straw-filled manger, a lump appeared in her throat.

When Jason and Tom had the sculptures in place, Tom invited Beth and Bonnie to help spread straw on the floor of the platform. The girls scrambled up with alacrity.

Ellen leaned close to Mandy to stage-whisper, "I'll be pulling straw out of their hair and clothes for an hour when we get home." But Ellen's gentle expression as she watched her daughters work with Tom and Jason revealed that she didn't mind the thought of straw in the children's clothes at all.

"At least the girls seem to have forgotten for awhile that their father didn't show up today," Ellen continued, "between this and Jason playing house."

Mandy didn't know any words to ease Ellen's pain that she hadn't been able to prevent her daughters' father from hurting them. So Mandy simply squeezed Ellen's arm and stood silent.

The men teased with the girls while they worked. Seeing Jason with Beth and Bonnie brought out Mandy's maternal instincts and the memory of the dreams she and Jason once shared of raising a family together. Those memories made her heart heavy with longing.

Jason would make a wonderful father. She'd always known he would. It hurt deeply to think that when he became a father, she wouldn't be the mother of his children. She'd loved him for so long. Her attempts to move on, dating other men, looking for someone else with whom to share life and build a family, had been unsuccessful.

In a moment of clarity, she realized the Jason she'd loved all this time was the young man he'd been with the seeds within him of the man he was now. Those seeds were the faith and values he'd claimed and she'd believed in. Jason was no longer the man she'd loved before. In so many ways, he'd grown into the man she'd always believed he could be. Time, especially recently, had tested the values he'd claimed, and they'd stood true.

She loved the way he loved his grandparents and that without hesitation he'd taken a leave of absence from his work in the city to come to their aid. Loved the way he loved children, the care he extended to Beth and Bonnie in particular.

Jason would be a good man to share life with. Time-and-trial tested, he'd won her heart all over again without even trying. Or even saying he still wanted her heart.

Thank You for the gift of time spent near Jason again, Lord, and for allowing me to see the fine man he's become.

"What do you think you're doing?"

Ellen's sharp question brought Mandy from her reverie. She followed Ellen's glance to see what caused her outburst.

Beth was tucking her plum chenille scarf around the baby Jesus. Her face set firm with challenge, she turned toward her mother. "Baby Jesus is cold. He's only wearing that blue stone blanket-thing that looks like a funny diaper that's not fastened."

"It's not a real baby, Beth, and you know it. You insisted you needed that expensive scarf this year. You just put it back around your neck where it belongs."

"But—"

"No buts. Do it."

Beth obeyed, her face stormy.

Bonnie watched, wide-eyed and silent.

Tom moved close to the manger and picked up a large handful of hay from the floor. "I never noticed it before, but it does look like this little tyke might be cold, Beth. We'll stuff a little more hay in his bed. That will warm him up a bit."

Beth helped Tom tuck the hay around the small statue. When they finished, Beth stared at the manger, her lips in a sullen pout. "That helps some, but I think He's still cold."

Maybe it's Beth who feels cold, Mandy thought with a sad pang as the group climbed back into Tom's pickup. Cold at heart because her father didn't care enough to keep his promise and spend Thanksgiving with her and Bonnie. Didn't care enough even to call.

Gram had turkey sandwiches ready when the group arrived back at the farmhouse, and after the fresh air everyone was ready to eat again.

Ellen leaned back in her chair with a sigh when she'd finished the last bite of her pie. "Well, girls, you'd better pick up your toys. We'll head home as soon as the dishes are done."

"Can't we stay longer?" Beth pleaded. "We don't have school tomorrow."

"We adults aren't as fortunate," Ellen reminded her. "The Christmas store will be jumping, and Thanksgiving weekend is a busy time for the Christmas tree business too."

Jason grinned at the girls' forlorn expressions. He well remembered how he'd hated to see holidays end when he was their ages. Still did. "What are you girls planning to do with your day off?"

"Maybe we'll put them to work." Mandy nudged Beth. "What do you think?"

Beth shrugged. "Okay."

Bonnie's eyes widened. "That would be fun. But what can we do?"

Mandy rested her forearms against the table. "I thought we'd set out Christmas cookies and apple cider for the customers. It would be a big help to your mom and me if you two kept the plate filled and served people."

Bonnie gasped in delight and sat up straighter. "Can we dress up?"

Jason pretended to be aghast. "You mean, wear Gram's hats and shoes?"

Bonnie and Beth burst into giggles.

"No," Bonnie finally managed. "Our own pretty clothes."

"Then I'll need to stop by and see you."

Their instant smiles warmed his heart, and he knew immediately he'd be stopping at the store tomorrow no matter how busy his day. He refused to pull a stunt like Zach, getting their hopes up and then not showing, even for a simple promise.

The house felt quiet and still after the girls, Ellen, and Mandy had left. Jason and Gramps finally played their chess game. Gramps won hands down and in record time.

"You're hardly any competition at all tonight," Gramps complained while Jason put the pieces back in the chess box. "Brain fuzzy?"

"Guess I'm a little tired, at that." Actually, he'd found the quiet without their visitors distracting. "Not used to a whole day away from the trees anymore."

Gramps nodded. "Get in a man's blood, those trees."

Jason's heart tightened at the truth of Gramps's statement. He hated to think how he'd miss those trees when he returned to New York. He stood up and stretched. "I'm going to check our E-mail and make certain none of our men have any last-minute problems that can't wait until morning to solve."

"I'll go with you." Gramps was on his feet in a flash.

"Didn't Doc say you were supposed to stay away from work? Isn't that why I'm here?"

"It's not work if you love what you're doing. You're taking the stress of the work on your shoulders. That's the part that has the power to hurt a man."

As they walked across the living room, a corner of paper sticking out from beneath the couch caught Jason's eye. He stooped to pull the paper out.

He looked down at a turkey in crayon colors—Bonnie's Thanksgiving card for Zach. Had she forgotten it, he wondered, or had she pushed it beneath the couch intentionally, wanting to forget the pain her father inflicted?

Jason set the card down on the table beside the sofa and followed Gramps toward the office. Frustration at his own inability to help the girls roiled in his chest. *How long does it take little girls to heal from a father's neglect?*

16

$\mathcal{T}$he day after Thanksgiving proved as busy as anticipated. People started arriving at the Christmas tree farm's cut-your-own grove soon after eight o'clock. The number of customers grew steadily throughout the morning.

Jason didn't mind. The experience was a fun one for the families who came and fun for him and the others at the farm who provided the service.

He whistled "O Tannenbaum" as he headed for the house at one-fifteen. He'd take only enough time to grab a quick turkey sandwich for his late lunch. Gram would have one waiting for him, he knew.

His whistle cut off in surprise when he looked up and saw Beth sitting on the top step leading to the back porch. He smiled. "Hi there. Thought you'd be busy serving customers cookies and apple cider." He pointed to the long purple skirt below her jacket. "Looks like you're dressed for it."

Beth rested her forearms on her knees and looked at her fingers. "I wanted to be alone for awhile."

He started up the stairs. "I need to be alone sometimes too. You can stay here as long as you like." He moved past her. It disturbed him to see her so melancholy, but he'd respect her wish for solitary time. Besides, nothing could happen to her on the porch. When she grew cold enough, she'd go back to the store.

"I don't mind being alone with you, J. P."

He turned around and sat down beside her. "That's nice, because I enjoy your company."

She looked out over the yard, but he doubted she saw it. "You smell like a Christmas tree."

He chuckled. "Have a bit of pine tar on me."

"I like that smell."

"Me too." He hesitated. "Thinking about anything special?"

"Maybe."

He didn't push her. Almost five minutes passed before she spoke again.

"You know the stable Tom made?"

"The one we helped him set up last night?"

She nodded. "I'm thinking about that. I wonder why God let His Son be born in a stable. Why didn't He let Him be born in a hospital like other babies?"

Jason rubbed a gloved hand over his mouth and tried not to laugh. "Jesus was born a long time ago. I don't think any babies were born in hospitals back then. I don't know if there even were hospitals."

"God could make a hospital. God can do anything. The pastor at church said so."

"That's true, but it seems God usually leaves it to people to build hospitals."

"But it's not nice to leave a baby in a stable. In the stable Jesus would be cold. If God is Jesus' Daddy, He shouldn't let Jesus get cold."

Jason glanced at the thick, plum-colored scarf wrapped around Beth's neck. *So that's what this is about.* "God chose the best people He could find to look after His Son. He chose Mary and Joseph, remember?"

She nodded.

"Mary didn't let Jesus get cold."

"Are you sure?"

"I'm sure."

"Did she have a blanket for him?"

"I'm sure she did if she thought He'd need one. The Bible tells us that when Jesus was born, Mary wrapped Him in swaddling clothes."

"Are swaddling clothes like a blanket?"

"Not exactly. Swaddling clothes are strips of material that were wrapped around babies when they were little. The cloths covered most of the baby's body, so Jesus' skin wouldn't have been exposed to the cold."

He watched her face while she considered his comments.

"If I was born in a stable, my mom would have a blanket for me. She wouldn't let me be cold."

"I know."

"My daddy wouldn't care if I was cold, though."

Jason sighed. He felt completely at a loss. *What can I say, Lord? How can I help her?* "Sometimes our dads just don't know how to love us well."

"Did your daddy love you well?"

Jason hesitated. His father hadn't been perfect, but he hadn't left like Zach, and he'd never have promised to show up for a holiday and not kept his word. "He loved me the best he knew how."

"Mandy says God loves us and wants what's best for us."

"I believe that too."

"The pastor says God is our Father, like He is Jesus' Father."

"Yes."

"Would God ever divorce us, like my daddy did?"

"No, Beth. God's love is perfect. He'd never leave you."

"I think He might."

Shock rippled through Jason at her matter-of-fact tone. "People's love isn't perfect, Beth. Not even moms' love and dads' love. But God's love is perfect. I promise He will never leave you."

She considered his words in silence for a minute. "If God can do anything," she said slowly, "and He loves me, and He wants what's best for me, why doesn't He bring my daddy home?"

The walls she'd built around her heart crumbled instantly, totally. She burst into tears and hid her face against Jason's chest.

He wrapped his arms around her, rested his cheek against her head, and rocked slightly in the age-old comforting rhythm. His heart felt as though it would burst through his ribs in empathy for the dear girl. But he had no answer for her.

Jason carried a heaviness in his chest through the rest of Friday and all of Saturday. Even while talking and smiling with customers picking out their Christmas trees, he carried the burden of Beth's pain.

Saturday one of the tree-truck drivers came down ill, and Jason filled in to make runs to Winston-Salem and Charlotte to restock Christmas tree lots. On the way back to the mountains after the final run, he stopped at a truck stop to refuel and grab a cup of hot coffee. A stand displaying mittens and gloves for sale caught his attention, and he bought a pair of children's gloves.

The clock on the truck's dashboard showed twelve o'clock midnight when he turned into the drive to Always Christmas Farm. Lights still glowed through the Christmas shop's windows, though he knew the store had closed hours earlier. He parked the heavy-duty truck near a tree grove with the other trucks, then walked down the hill in the moonlight to the barn, carrying the newly purchased gloves.

He knocked lightly, not wanting to wake anyone who might be asleep in the loft. In spite of the lights, it surprised him when the door opened only moments after his knock.

"Hi, Jason. What brings you here at such a late hour?" Mandy's green eyes held surprise. Fear swept it away almost immediately. She clutched his arm. "Is something wrong with Grandpa Seth? Is it another heart attack?"

"Gramps is fine. Honest."

The fright in her face subsided but it didn't completely disappear.

"I brought a donation for your mitten tree."

Her expression relaxed into a friendly, fearless smile. "At midnight?"

He explained his tree-delivery trips and impulse purchase. "I saw the lights on when I drove in and took a chance you'd still be up." He handed her the gloves. The thumbs and each finger were a different color. "I know it's supposed to be a mitten tree, but I figured you'd accept gloves too. These made me smile. I thought they might make a kid feel the same."

Mandy grinned. "They make me smile too. They remind me of Joseph's coat of many colors." She stepped back, opening the door wider. "Would you like to come in for a minute? We'll hang these on the tree."

The mitten tree, a Fraser fir he'd selected for her, stood near the counter, only a couple yards into the store. Already the branches bent beneath almost two dozen mittens, he noted in surprise. "Wow. Looks like a lot of other people donated already. You'll need another tree by Christmas. Maybe by next week."

"I hope the donations continue that strong. We won't put up another tree, though. Just remove some mittens as new donations come in." She hung the gloves over a shoulder-high branch. "This is the only pair of its kind. Adds a bright spot of color."

No lights or garlands trimmed the tree—only mittens. He liked the look.

He hadn't needed to bring the gloves down tonight, but he'd been glad the lighted windows gave him the excuse to do so. He'd just wanted to see Mandy, he admitted to himself. Just a few minutes in her serene presence would end the day on a peaceful note.

Pale blue smudges beneath her eyes showed her fatigue, and her hair was slightly but pleasantly mussed—none of which distracted from her beauty in his eyes.

"The local newspaper ran a small story the Wednesday before Thanksgiving on our tree idea," Mandy told him. "That helped a lot." She pointed at a pair of bright red mittens attached to each other by a long red string of yarn. "An elderly woman brought these in. She lives in an assisted living complex. She liked the mitten tree so much that she's organized a group of women in the complex to knit mittens to donate."

"That's great." *Just like Mandy*, he thought. Come up with a simple idea and end up with the entire community involved—and make it look almost like an accident.

"It's not an accident. It's the way it's meant to be, the way God is able to work through a person who is true to His calling on their life."

The thought came to him full blown. He pushed it away to examine later.

"After Christmas I plan to invite all the women in the knitting group out to the store for a thank-you brunch."

"They should like that." He glanced up at the clock above the counter. "Why are you working so late?"

She brushed her bangs back from her forehead in a weary gesture. "I'm restocking displays. Too busy to do it during the day."

"Something feels different in here tonight." Jason glanced around the shop. The sights were the same as always. The familiar scents of Christmas spices filled the air. "There's no Christmas music playing."

"We try to remember to turn it off after the store closes. Sometimes we forget and wake up in the middle of the night to Christmas songs. If it's a hymn, it can be comforting. If it's a rollicking rendition of 'Rock Around the Christmas Tree,' it's jolting."

"I can imagine." He pushed his hands into the pockets of his jeans. "Can you spare a couple more minutes for me?"

She darted him a curious glance. "Sure."

"It's about Beth." He leaned against the counter. "We talked yesterday. Remember saying you thought she might be angry at God?"

"Yes."

"I don't think she's angry at Him. I think Zach's abandonment of the family has broken her image of God as a father."

Mandy frowned. "What do you mean?"

"Most of her life she believed a father was someone who would always be in her life, always take care of her and protect her. Someone she could rely on for anything and everything she needed and love her unconditionally."

Mandy nodded. "Someone who'd never break his promises to her."

"Exactly. Now she sees a father as a person who is no more trustworthy than a stranger. Someone who puts his own interests above her needs. A father is someone she can't trust. So when the pastor or anyone else tells her God is her loving heavenly Father, it's not an image she finds reassuring—because her image of a father is damaged."

"Wow." It was a quiet statement more than an exclamation. Mandy leaned against the counter beside him. "My heart is telling me you're right."

"Ever since talking with Beth, a Bible verse has been running through my mind. 'Which of you, if his son asks for bread, will give him a stone?' It goes on to say that if human fathers know how to give good gifts to their children, our heavenly Father will give good gifts to His children too. Jesus tries to make us understand God's love by comparing it to an earthly father's love. Trouble is, too many human fathers give their kids stones when they ask for bread—figuratively speaking, of course."

"Millions of children must feel like Beth about God."

"Sad, isn't it? And terrifying."

"I don't mean to imply that every child of divorced parents has this issue," she clarified quickly, "or that only absent fathers neglect their responsibilities. But think how common the deadbeat dad is who doesn't pay for child support. And how many children and their fathers who've left the family grow apart until they never speak."

"The single-parent family has become commonplace—the single parent usually being the mother. A lot of kids are growing up without any father figure around. How do they understand that when the Bible refers to God as a loving Father, it's comparing Him to one of the most loving relationships a child can experience?"

"My mind is trying to grasp the implications of this," Mandy said. "I don't even know how to help Beth with it, let alone come up with a solution for millions of other children."

He told her about Beth's concern that God allowed Jesus to be born in a cold stable without anything to keep Him warm.

Mandy smiled at Beth's misconception, but sadness mingled with the smile. "That's why she walked about the shop looking at all the nativities today. I just realized that most show the Christ child without clothing and with only a narrow strip of blanket across His body."

"Not in swaddling clothes."

"Definitely not in swaddling clothes."

It seemed like old times, talking like this. When they had been dating, they discussed anything and everything, eager to learn each other's thoughts and ideas. Such discussions weren't what normally came to people's minds at the term "romance," but to him such times were as much a part of his romance with Mandy as every other part of their relationship.

He missed those times.

He forced his attention back to the present with an effort. "Driving back tonight, I passed Tom's nativity with the spotlights on it. It's striking out there on the mountain where everything else is dark."

"I haven't seen it from the road yet."

Jason pushed himself away from the counter. "It's already Sunday. I'd better get some shut-eye."

"Me too." Mandy stretched her arms over her head, stifling a yawn, then let her arms fall back to her side.

At her movement, the lights sparkled off something in her hair. "There's a piece of gold tinsel in your hair."

She reached up. "Where?"

"I'll get it." With his thick fingers, it was difficult to grab hold of the tinsel and not pull her hair. "It's tangled. This might take a minute."

Her hair felt as soft as it looked. He could smell the gentle scent of a floral-based shampoo, although she must have washed her hair close to dawn, almost sixteen hours ago. He concentrated on the tinsel and tried to ignore the way his heartbeat quickened at her nearness.

Don't think about how good her hair smells, he commanded himself. *Don't think about how wonderful she'd feel in your arms. Don't think how you want to press your lips to her hair and then her cheek and her lips.*

"I guess there's worse things a person can wear than tinsel." Mandy's voice held a laugh. "Like maybe pink plastic earrings."

"I'll find a way yet to get you back for the picture you took of me in that getup."

"And here I was sure you'd want to pass that picture down through the generations."

Jason looked down and met her teasing green-eyed glance, then dropped his gaze lower to where her lips quirked in a smile, deepening her dimples. Those lips looked too inviting. He kissed them—a light, quick kiss.

When the kiss ended, he pulled back so their lips were only a breath apart. His heart hammered against his ribs. He heard her breath coming short and shallow. He looked into her eyes. At what he saw there, he kissed her again, drawing her close in his embrace. She came willingly, leaning against him.

Her kiss was warm and wonderful. It felt exactly the same as her kisses in his memories and in his dreams.

17

*M*andy leaned into Jason's kiss. It was warm and wonderful. Exactly the same as his kisses in her memories and in her dreams.

She relaxed against him as the kiss deepened, rejoicing in the gentle strength of his arms. It felt so right here, as though she'd never left his arms, as though the years she and Jason had spent apart had never happened. As though God created their arms to hold each other and their lips to kiss each other's lips.

The kiss became another kiss and another. And then Jason wrapped his arms more tightly about her, resting his cheek against her hair. His chest rose and fell in a deep sigh. "Mandy."

The word was a husky whisper, filled with reverence. Her cheek against his shoulder, she breathed a soft sigh of contentment.

They stood together that way for many minutes, speaking to each other without words, heart-to-heart.

Finally Jason moved to kiss her forehead. "I'd better go."

She nodded, too filled with emotions to speak.

They walked to the door with their arms around each other. Beneath the silent brass bells, which announced all comings and goings, Mandy accepted a half-dozen more kisses and returned them in the age-old, lingering good-bye manner of lovers.

When Jason finally left, she leaned back against the door and closed her eyes, still feeling Jason with her. Deep joy filled every cell of her heart. "Thank You, Lord."

Not a trace of Jason's earlier fatigue remained as he walked up the hill to the farmhouse through the crisp, pine-scented night air. His heart sang with the memory of Mandy's kisses and the sweet, willing way she leaned into his arms. He still felt her there.

When he climbed into bed, his mind continued reliving the wonderful minutes with her until reality pushed its ugly way into the memories.

"What was I thinking?" he whispered.

He planned to return to New York after New Year's. Every day—except Thanksgiving—since he'd arrived back in North Carolina, Neal had called or e-mailed at least once. Not twenty-four hours went by without a problem involving a client or case about which Jason's advice was sought.

He'd made a commitment to the company. Made a commitment to his father. He'd worked hard to reach this respected place in his career. It would be foolish and irresponsible to throw it away. His father hadn't raised an irresponsible son.

It was a God-given gift, this time back in the mountains involved in the work he'd always loved, spending time with Gram and Gramps and Mandy. He cherished every minute of it. But he couldn't chuck everything and move back here.

And he couldn't ask Mandy to move to New York with him.

He loved her more now than eight years ago. He loved the woman she'd become. He smiled into the darkness, thinking of her independent spirit, the cheerful manner in which she made her way through life without allowing problems and challenges and disappointments to trample her, the way Christ's love for others flowed so naturally from her.

He and Mandy shared a love for the mountains. He'd missed them horribly during the years spent in New York pursuing his father's dream for him. Eight years ago he'd asked Mandy to give up the mountains she loved for him. Now he knew he couldn't ask anyone he loved to give up something she loved that much—even if Mandy were willing. And what indication did he have that she was any more willing now than when he'd asked her to marry him?

He was jumping the proverbial gun, of course. Just because she returned his kisses tonight didn't mean she still loved him. Mandy wasn't the kind of woman who kissed a man unless she cared for him, but love—well, that might be a bit of a stretch.

One thing he knew for certain: There could be no more kisses. There was no place for their relationship to go if they moved past friendship. The more time they spent in each other's arms, the more painful the inevitable breakup.

He'd explain to her tomorrow. He hated the thought. It would be easier to just avoid her, but the easy way out was seldom the kindest.

He rolled over and buried his face in his pillow. He shut his mind to the memory of Mandy's kisses. The joy that filled him when he came to bed retreated, flooded out by the choice he'd made years ago to follow his father's dream instead of his own.

A thought nibbled at the edge of his consciousness. Something about following *God's* plan for his life. He couldn't get a solid hold on the thought and let it slip away.

He was wide awake but exhausted to the marrow of his bones.

Already he missed Mandy. Again.

Sunday morning sunlight poured through stained-glass windows, adding to the beauty of the Advent service at the one-hundred-year-old church. Mandy sat beside Ellen in the same oak pew they always shared—sixth row back on the left side. She knew Jason sat with Grandpa Seth and Grandma Tillie in their traditional Sunday morning spot on the other side of the church, three rows farther back.

The joyous spirit of the season filled the sanctuary. The smell of beeswax candles from the altar and the Advent wreath added an additional element of warmth and comfort.

Mandy's first conscious thought when she'd awakened was of the time spent in Jason's arms the night before. She didn't know where they were headed, but at least she knew now that he still cared.

As the service ended and the congregation rose to leave, Ellen leaned close to Mandy and whispered in a grumble, "How come you're so bright-eyed and bushy-tailed this morning when you got less sleep than I did?"

Mandy shrugged, smiling, intending to hug the secret to herself awhile longer. Then she changed her mind. The news was too lovely to keep to herself. "You know those kisses you keep asking me about?" she whispered back.

Ellen's eyes widened. "You mean you and J. P. . . . ?"

Mandy nodded, her grin growing.

"When? Where?"

"Last night. In the Christmas shop."

"I thought you were working. If I'd known you needed a chaperon—"

"We didn't, thank you very much."

"How did you two end up in the Christmas shop together?"

"I'll tell you later."

Ellen didn't look like she wanted to let it go, but she did.

The sisters exchanged greetings with numerous other church members as they slowly made their way with the rest of the congregation toward the sanctuary door. Mandy's gaze kept drifting across the sanctuary to Jason, but he was never looking her direction. It disappointed her only slightly. Other friends claimed his attention. She and Jason could talk later.

He certainly looked handsome in his obviously expensive gray suit, white shirt, and sapphire blue tie. Strange to think of him dressed in that manner every day in a fancy New York office instead of in the casual clothes he wore on the tree farm.

Mandy, Ellen, Jason, Grandpa Seth, and Grandma Tillie all reached the church vestibule at the same time. They were greeting each other when Beth, coming from Sunday school, pushed her way through the crowd to reach them.

She grabbed Ellen's arm. "Mom, guess what? We're going to do a Christmas play, and Teacher chose me to be Mary."

"That's wonderful, Sweetie." Ellen gave her a quick hug.

Mandy and the others added their congratulations.

Beth beamed at Jason. "I told the teacher I'll only be Mary if we have those swaddle things you told me about for the baby Jesus."

"Swaddling clothes?"

Beth nodded. "Yes, those. I told her we need a blanket for Him too."

"What did she say?" Jason asked.

"She said that would be fine if I bring the blanket. I'm going to find Bonnie and tell her I'm going to be Mary." She ducked between two elderly women and disappeared.

Ellen shook her head. "I better round up those two daughters of mine. We'll meet you at the car, Mandy."

Ellen had barely left when Jason took hold of Mandy's elbow. "Okay if I walk you to your car?"

Mandy smiled at him, thrilled at his closeness. "Of course."

At the coatracks, Jason helped Mandy into her red wool coat, then put on his own long black dress coat. Mandy thought it made him look even more the successful young executive.

They stopped beside the driver's door of her five-year-old white Taurus. "This isn't an ideal place to talk," Jason started. "I'm sorry about that."

"That's all right. What is it?" Looking up into his face, she thought, *He looks tired.*

"It's . . . about last night." His lips formed a tense line.

Did he think she was upset that he kissed her? She smiled at him, trying to reassure him. "Yes?"

He rubbed his hand over his hair and closed his eyes. "There's no easy way to say this."

Her stomach clenched. "You're sorry you kissed me."

He nodded, then opened his eyes, met her gaze, and shook his head. "No, I'm not sorry. Not exactly."

"What then?"

"I truly care for you, Mandy. But I'm returning to New York after New Year's. There's nowhere for a relationship between us to go."

Nowhere to go. Mandy's chest felt as cold and bleak as a snow-covered plateau. "So you'd rather stop before we start."

"Yes."

She swallowed the lump that suddenly filled her throat. "I suppose that's the intelligent thing to do."

"I think so."

"There's no chance you might move back permanently?"

He shook his head.

Mandy sighed, a sigh shaky with sobs she knew would demand release eventually. "I thought maybe you were reconsidering lately."

"No."

"Your work in New York—do you still do it for your father, or do you do it for yourself now?"

He didn't answer. The silence grew uncomfortable.

Mandy pulled her gaze from his face. "Is there anything else?"

"No. I just thought it only fair to tell you. . . ."

She nodded. She'd received the message loud and clear. He didn't want her back in his life. "I need to go. Ellen and the girls are coming."

She turned her back on him and opened the car door, then glanced at him over her shoulder. "You know, it's just possible it would make God happy to see you doing work you enjoy."

She climbed into the car. Tears burned her eyes. She tried to force them away. She had no intention of crying in front of the girls.

She heard Ellen and the girls calling good-byes to Jason, and then they were getting into the car. Ellen fastened her seat belt as Mandy backed the car up. "Now, about those kisses you started to tell me about—"

"Never mind. They were a mistake. Just one great big mistake."

Jason struggled to enter into the jovial spirit of the season with his workers and customers the rest of the day and evening. He and Gramps didn't like that Sunday work was common in the industry, but today it helped to push the image of Mandy's pain-bruised eyes to the edge of his consciousness.

There was nothing to push the image away when he was alone in his room that night.

He forced himself to think on other topics, starting with the Christmas tree business. Always a lot of worries there. More truckloads of trees to be sent to distant lots tomorrow. Course, he'd already arranged for those trips.

Mandy's eyes slipped back into his memory.

He grimaced. The New York office had only contacted him once today. Neal apologized, it being Sunday and all. Seemed a silly apology since Neal was working, and it was Sunday in New York too.

Mandy would hate life in New York.

He shut his eyes and rubbed the palms of his hands over his eyelids, trying to rub out the picture of the pain he'd caused her.

If only he could fall asleep, he'd find freedom from her eyes for a few hours. Sleep wasn't accommodating his desire.

What else could he think about? There must be something besides work in his life.

Gramps and Gram. Ah, yes, finally something cheerful—Gramps improving health.

His dad had never liked Gramps much. Jason hated the way his dad had ridiculed Gramps, simply because the older man found contentment in running a Christmas tree farm instead of pursuing a career guaranteed to bring wealth. Of course, the tree farm was large now and doing well financially. It was a small operation when Jason's dad met Gramps.

Jason didn't like this train of thought any better than thinking about Mandy. He sat up in bed, plumped up his pillows, and stuffed them between his back and the antique oak head-board, then turned on the bedside lamp. He reached for the Bible lying beside the lamp. If he couldn't sleep, he might as well read.

He turned to the Gospel of Matthew, searching for the verses which had nagged at his mind the last few days. He found them in chapter seven, beginning at verse nine: "Which of you, if his son asks for bread, will give him a stone? Or if he asks for a fish, will give him a snake? If you, then, though you are evil, know how to give good gifts to your children, how much more will your Father in heaven give good gifts to those who ask him!"

He sighed. It seemed to him too many fathers here didn't "know how to give good gifts to their children."

"Did your daddy love you well?" Beth's question from their discussion on the porch popped into his mind.

He loved me; he just didn't understand me. He loved the city and the world of finance and thought I should love them as much as he did. That I should love them instead of the mountains and Christmas tree farming.

I wanted bread, and he wanted to give me a stone instead.

Guilt and sorrow rushed through his chest. Guilt for thinking such a thing about the father he loved. Sorrow for believing the thought true.

The truth seared into his soul. He'd believed his father hadn't loved him because Jason didn't desire the same things his father desired. That's why he'd chosen to go into a financial career when his father died. One last, desperate attempt to gain his father's approval and love.

Father would be proud of my success. He'd think that stone he wanted for me is gold, through and through. He'd think that stone will buy me all the bread I need.

He and his father hadn't known each other at all.

He'd told Mandy that Zach's actions broke Beth's image of God as a Father. *I wonder if my image of God is warped because my father and I saw what constitutes bread and stones differently.* He didn't think so. *At least I understand that God is love.*

Jason set the Bible back on the table, turned off the light, and tried again to go to sleep.

(18)

*D*uring the next few weeks, Mandy felt certain Jason avoided her whenever possible. That was all right with her. It took all her emotional strength to keep up a facade of cheerfulness for her customers and Beth and Bonnie.

Only with Ellen did she let her defenses down and reveal her sadness. Even then, she refused to discuss Jason with her sister.

She'd lied to herself about those kisses Thanksgiving weekend. Told herself it was okay; she didn't know where they might lead. She knew exactly where she wanted them to lead—into Jason's heart and soul for the rest of their lives.

Eight years ago it sliced her heart when Jason left. Now she'd reopened her heart to the possibility of his love and been wounded again.

At least Beth appeared more cheerful. Her upcoming role as Mary and the normal childhood excitement of nearing Christmas apparently cast her untrustworthy father into the background of her mind.

"Did you ever see anyone so excited about a nonspeaking role?" Ellen asked Mandy with a grin.

"She seems less preoccupied with Zach, anyway."

"Yes. Maybe one day she'll heal from his selfishness."

The Christmas store became more of a blessing than ever for Mandy. Her longing for Jason was ever-present, but the demands of the store kept her from burying herself in self-pity.

December passed in a blur except for two events the week before Christmas. The first was a Christmas card that arrived—looking innocent and cheery in a bright red envelope—with a stack of other cards and advertisements. Ellen spotted it at the end of a busy day as

565

she went through the mail while Mandy checked the receipts against the register.

Ellen held the red envelope toward Mandy. "From Zach to me and the girls."

"Aren't you going to open it?"

Ellen scrunched her nose in distaste. "Suppose I better. He may be writing to say he's planning to spend Christmas with us." She slit the envelope with the letter opener, pulled out a card with a picture of Santa Claus, and opened it. "I don't believe it." Ellen's voice sounded strangled.

"What?"

Ellen handed her a wallet-sized photo. It was a picture of Zach and a woman with short brown hair.

"According to this signature, they're married."

"Married? He moves fast."

"I guess he hasn't changed his courting technique."

Mandy remembered the whirlwind romance between Ellen and Zach. "Are you okay with this?"

"I don't have another choice, do I?" Ellen's eyes flashed. "I don't mind for myself. I just hope it doesn't hurt the girls too badly."

"I guess this means he's not coming home for Christmas."

"Says they're spending it with the new wife's family in San Jose. At least the girls won't spend another holiday waiting for him to show up."

Mandy handed the picture back. "Will you tell the girls about his new wife?"

"I suppose they need to know. Maybe I'll wait until after Christmas. That news isn't exactly on their Christmas wish list."

The second event that stood out for Mandy was Jason's delivery of a burlap-bagged Fraser fir to the store. "You said you wanted the girls to have their own Christmas tree," he reminded Mandy. "I asked Beth if anyone had set one up yet and she said no, so . . ." He shrugged. "I know you prefer the live trees, so I brought this. Would you like me to carry it up to the loft?"

He placed it, at Mandy's request, in the loft's small dining area.

"We use the area in the store near the fireplace as our living room when the store's closed," she said, "but there are so many trees in the store. This one will seem more personal up here."

The girls jumped up and down in excitement when they saw the tree upon arriving home from school. Then they raced off to find and thank Jason.

Ellen insisted they wait until the store closed for the night before trimming the tree. "After all, it's Mandy's tree too. We all want the fun of trimming it." Ellen brought out red and green construction paper, children's scissors, and glue; and the girls filled the time waiting for Mandy by making paper chains for the tree.

When they grew tired of making chains, Beth asked, "Can we make cotton-ball snowmen, like Jason did when he was little?"

Ellen brought out cotton balls and improvised. Later she told Mandy, "I forgot children don't make Christmas ornaments in school anymore, the way we did when we were children."

Ellen dug out the small box of ornaments from the Christmases shared with Zach. She confided in Mandy her concern that some of the ornaments might awaken melancholy emotions in the girls, but that didn't happen. Beth's and Bonnie's favorite ornaments proclaimed "baby's first Christmas" for the years they were born.

There was no theme to the tree, as there were to those in the Christmas shop. The ornaments were a combination of sizes and shapes, some expensive and some recently handmade by the girls. It gave the children great joy, which caused Mandy to think it the loveliest tree ever.

The family Christmas tree became a constant reminder to Mandy of Jason's kind, thoughtful nature and of his love for children—Beth and Bonnie in particular. A constant reminder that one day he'd make some blessed children a wonderful father.

A constant reminder that she wouldn't be the woman sharing his life and future children.

So she poured her energy even more strongly into the store.

And, suddenly, it was Christmas Eve.

Mandy shared Beth and Bonnie's enthusiasm when the first snow of the season began around noon. The flakes were large and fluffy and lovely against the background of evergreens. Perfect for a white Christmas, yet light enough that Mandy didn't fear it might cause trouble for travelers.

She released a sigh of relief as she hung the "closed" sign on the door at three-thirty. Most likely a few last-minute customers would straggle by, knock loudly, and plead for an opportunity to take one more look for the perfect gift. Mandy knew she'd let them in as long as they didn't keep her from making it to church on time. She wasn't about to miss Beth in the Christmas play.

Ellen and the girls were already at the church, so Mandy had the loft to herself. She put on a new dark green velvet dress. It slid easily over the hips and waist, off which she constantly promised to whittle a few inches—and never did.

Viewing herself in the oak-framed standing mirror, she nodded approval. The simple, unadorned dress with its princess-cut flattered her figure and her hair. And matched the fir-green eyes Jason used to say were beautiful.

She'd reluctantly accepted Grandma Tillie's invitation to drive to the church with her, Grandpa Seth, and Jason. It seemed childish to say, "No, thank you. I don't even want to be in the same car as your grandson."

Grandma Tillie must know something had happened between her and Jason, but she hadn't asked questions. It was like her to allow people to work out their own solutions.

True to Mandy's expectation, two customers stopped by before she left for church. She warned them of her plans, but she doubted they'd have completed their shopping before midnight if Jason hadn't entered the store and announced he and his grandparents were ready to leave.

The snow was still falling when Mandy approached the car, and she thrilled to the winter beauty. The wind was still, and she loved the *sh-sh-sh* sound the snow made as it drifted down through the trees.

Jason held the front passenger door open for her. His grandparents sat in the backseat, so she climbed into the front seat beside him.

She smiled brightly at the older couple. "Blessed Christmas." When they'd returned her greeting, she explained, "I read that in the United States before the twentieth century 'Blessed Christmas' was the common Christmas greeting instead of the 'Merry Christmas' popular today."

"How lovely," Grandma Tillie exclaimed as Jason turned onto the highway. "I think I'll adopt it myself. Is Beth still excited about the Christmas drama?" she then asked.

"I think she's looking forward to it more than she is to opening her Christmas presents." Mandy's comment elicited chuckles from the others. "She brought her favorite life-sized baby doll to use as the baby Jesus. Also a blue wool blanket that was a gift when she was a baby."

"I thought people gave girl babies pink blankets," Jason said, his gaze on the snow-covered road.

"Babies get every color blanket these days," Grandma Tillie told him.

Jason grinned. "Beth didn't take swaddling clothes?"

"Oh, she did." Mandy shook her head. "You are in so much trouble with Ellen over those, Jason."

"Me?"

"You're the one who told Beth about swaddling clothes. Beth insisted the baby Jesus in the play needs them. Ellen tore an old sheet into strips and told Beth to use them for swaddling clothes. What the well-dressed baby doll wears in a Christmas play."

Gramps spoke up from the backseat. "Is Zach going to delay our Christmas dinner tonight?"

"Seth." Gram sounded for all the world like Ellen scolding the girls.

"What? I want to know if I'm going to eat on time."

Mandy told them of Zach's marriage.

"Lousy Christmas present for Beth and Bonnie." Anger clipped Jason's words.

"Ellen told them Zach's spending Christmas in California. She's going to wait until after Christmas to tell the girls he's remarried." Mandy sighed. "Beth's class drew pictures of their families in school this week. Beth's picture includes only herself, Bonnie, Ellen, and me."

Jason scowled at the road. "So Zach's out of the picture. That man doesn't know what he's given away."

The drive into town didn't take long. When the group entered the vestibule, they found Ellen and Bonnie waiting for them. They all sat together, but Mandy was glad that Ellen's presence made it a simple matter to avoid sitting beside Jason. She knew with him beside her, she'd have been distracted from the service.

The program was simple. The Christmas story was presented through the play. The children acted out the story as it was read from the Bible. Hymns—some solos, some sung by choirs, some in which the congregation joined—introduced at appropriate places in the story added to the beauty of the service.

Mandy, Ellen, and the rest of their group sat up a little straighter when Beth came onto the stage area in front of the altar.

Beth sat down on a stool behind the manger and carefully adjusted her white robe. Moments later, the narrator read the Scripture which told how Mary "brought forth her firstborn son, and wrapped him in swaddling clothes, and laid him in a manger"(KJV).

With a solemn expression, Beth picked up her doll from behind the manger. The doll was wrapped in sheet strips.

Mandy could hear the stifled chuckles from all the adults in her group. She longed to lean forward, catch Jason's glance, and share this moment with him, but she resisted.

Beth held the doll in her arms and gazed lovingly at it, then laid it gently in the straw-filled manger. Next she picked up the blue blanket from behind the manger and spread the blanket over the doll with exaggerated care.

The drama held a strong impact, in spite of the many times Mandy had heard the story, and in spite of the funny, endearing moments provided by Beth and the other players.

When the story ended, the pastor rose and walked to the podium, bringing the congregation back from two thousand years ago to the present. He smiled out at the people. "Well. There's so little that one can add to that story."

Murmurs of agreement came from the congregation.

"But maybe a reminder of the reason for Jesus' birth isn't out of line. I read from First John, chapter four, verses seven through eleven." He opened his Bible.

" 'Dear friends, let us love one another, for love comes from God.

Everyone who loves has been born of God and knows God. Whoever does not love does not know God, because God is love. This is how God showed his love among us: He sent his one and only Son into the world that we might live through him. This is love: not that we loved God, but that he loved us and sent his Son as an atoning sacrifice for our sins. Dear friends, since God so loved us, we also ought to love one another.' "

The pastor closed his Bible and looked out at the congregation. "Dear friends, this Christmas, may you go in love; may you go with God."

A gust of wind tossed Mandy's muffler and tugged at her hair as she left the church with Ellen and the girls. Mandy caught her breath in surprise. Blowing, stinging snow had replaced the large, lazy flakes that had drifted down when they arrived. In the light from streetlamps she saw snow thick in the air. Almost three inches of the white stuff covered Ellen's windshield. Mandy reminded herself Ellen's car had been parked at the church an hour and a half longer than Grandpa Seth's.

"I'm sure glad you're riding back with us, Mandy," Ellen said as she opened the back door of her car for the girls. "I hate driving in storms. Hope we don't slide into a ditch or something. I didn't bring a cell phone. Did you?"

Mandy shook her head. "No."

"There's a flashlight in the car. At least we'll have light if we need to walk for any reason."

"Cheerful thought." Mandy wished they were back at the farm, safe and sound.

A shadow came toward them through the swirling snow. It turned out to be Jason. "Roads might be slippery, Ellen. I'll follow you." Then he faded back into the storm.

The drive back was trickier than the drive into town had been. When they passed the area of the mountain where Tom's Christmas nativity was displayed, Mandy pointed it out to the girls. "See where that dim glow of lights is?"

"That's the stable?" Beth squinted, trying to see through the early evening darkness and the storm. "I can't see it."

"It's there. Probably covered with snow."

They arrived back at the farm, grateful they'd had no mishaps. Ellen parked beside Jason, near the farmhouse since Grandma Tillie had invited them to Christmas Eve dinner.

Beth zipped her doll inside her jacket before getting out of the car. She and Bonnie raced for the front door, followed closely by Mandy and Ellen. Once in the shelter of the porch, they and the Kramers brushed snow from their coats.

Jason undid Beth's plum chenille scarf and shook the snow from it. "By tomorrow there'll be enough snow to build snowmen. Let's have a contest."

"How do you have a snowman contest?" Beth asked as he settled the thick muffler back around her neck.

"We make up teams, and each team builds a snowman. You and Beth can be a team, and Mandy and Ellen can be another team, and I can be a team."

"What about Grandma Tillie and Grandpa Seth?"

"They can be the judges."

"I don't want to build a snowman," Bonnie announced, entering the house while Jason held the door. "I'm going to build a snow lady." Her eyes sparkled with laughter. "Then it can wear one of Grandma Tillie's hats."

Once they were inside, Mandy helped Bonnie out of her jacket. "Did I tell you yet how pretty you look in your red Christmas dress with its lace collar, Bonnie?"

"Thanks. When do we open our presents?"

"Bonnie." Ellen, on her knees beside them trying to unzip Beth's coat—still extended from the doll beneath—glared at Bonnie.

Ellen's scolding-mother tone didn't disturb Bonnie at all. "What? I didn't say anything I'm not supposed to."

"I told you tonight's schedule before we went to church."

"I forget."

Mandy intervened. "First we eat the great dinner Grandma Tillie prepared for us. Doesn't it smell good?"

Bonnie put her head back and took an exaggerated sniff of the tantalizing odor of roast beef.

Ellen groaned and gave Mandy a glance filled with frustration. "What's a mother to do?"

"Then we open presents after dinner?" Bonnie asked.

"After the dishes are done," Ellen reminded. "We left the presents at the store, remember? Grandpa Seth and Grandma Tillie and J. P. are coming down to the Christmas barn with us. We're going to light a fire in the fireplace and open presents in front of it."

"I wish we were opening presents right now," Bonnie declared with a pout.

"Me too." Beth, finally freed from her jacket, grasped Bonnie's hand. "Let's go play dolls." They headed off together, Beth still carrying her doll, safe and warm in its blue blanket.

Ellen reached for Mandy's hand and gave her an exaggerated smile. "Come on. Let's go play house."

Laughing, they headed to the kitchen to help Gram.

The meal tasted every bit as wonderful as Gram's Thanksgiving feast. Gram scolded at Gramps's portions and choices, and he scolded her back for nagging—bringing indulgent smiles from the other adults. The wind howled around the corners of the old house, but the sound only added to the warm and cozy family feeling. Mandy sensed the undercurrent of anticipation in the girls, eager to open their gifts. *I'm so glad this holiday isn't spoiled for them by waiting for Zach to arrive.*

Mandy avoided looking at Jason, who sat at one end of the rectangular table, opposite Gramps, whom Mandy sat beside. *At Thanksgiving, our kisses were still in the future. Now they're already in the past, and we have no future.*

She turned her mind purposely to the conversation around her, reminding herself that Jason wasn't the only person in her heart. Every person at this table was a loved one. *And that's a blessing worth waking up for every day.*

After the meal, the adults, to the children's chagrin, decided to linger over a cup of coffee before beginning the cleanup.

"We'll never get to open presents," Bonnie complained.

"When we grow up, we're going to open presents first," Beth announced. "Come on, Bonnie. Let's go play Mary and Joseph and baby Jesus."

"Can I be Mary?" Bonnie pleaded as she followed Beth.

"You can take some towels from the bathroom for your robes," Gram called after them.

When the dishes were cleared, Jason and Gramps set up the chess set on the dining room table. Gramps grinned across the table at Jason. "Let's see whether I can whip you at this before the womenfolk get done in the kitchen."

Forty-five minutes later, the women were putting the last of the dishes away when Gramps said, "Checkmate," and ended the game, chortling. As he and Jason put the chess pieces away, Gram removed her terry-cloth apron with its holly design and smiled at Mandy and Ellen. "Well, I guess it's time we head down to your place and let the little ones at their presents."

Anticipation at the girls' excitement gave off a warm glow in Mandy's chest as she went with Ellen to tell Bonnie and Beth that The Hour had finally arrived. At the door into the living room, Mandy and Ellen stopped. Beth's baby doll lay on the sofa alongside a doll of Bonnie's, but no one was in the room.

A small frown showed Ellen's minor annoyance. "I guess they're playing in one of the bedrooms. I've told them not to go in them without Grandma Tillie's permission."

"I'm sure they aren't getting into anything they shouldn't," Mandy reassured. "They're probably looking for Grandma Tillie's old hats."

Mandy and Ellen went up the narrow old staircase together. The girls weren't in the bedrooms.

Mandy and Ellen stopped in the dining room where Jason and Gramps were discussing the successful Christmas tree season over another cup of coffee. "Have you two seen the girls?" Ellen asked.

"Not since dinner." Jason stretched back in his chair.

"I bet they're in the basement." Gram started toward the basement door. "There's an old sofa and chair down there we've never gotten around to throwing out. The girls like to play down there sometimes."

But they weren't in the basement either.

Mandy tried to push away the fear edging into her chest. "They're probably playing hide-and-seek."

"That's right," Jason joined in. "They're probably in some closet right now, giggling at the trouble they're causing us."

The adults went through the house, calling to the girls, ordering them to appear, peering into every closet and cubby-hole and beneath each bed.

The last closet Ellen checked was by the front door. When she turned from it, her white face and panicked eyes shot dread through Mandy's veins. "Their coats are gone."

Mandy glanced at the rug before the front door. "So are their boots. Maybe they decided to start on their snowmen early."

"In this storm?" Jason reached past Ellen to grab his coat. He slid it on while stuffing his feet into his boots. "I'll check the yard. Mandy, you and Ellen check the Christmas store."

The storm had blown a thin layer of snow across the porch floor. The dim rays cast by the porch light revealed two sets of small boot prints crossing the porch to the steps. Mandy pointed to them, excitement threading through her. "Look."

A few feet from the bottom of the steps the prints were blown over. Mandy's heart sank at the unbroken snow. Their path was destroyed as surely as Hansel and Gretel's path. She cast a glance at Jason. He met her gaze, worry thick in his eyes.

Without a word to each other, Jason split off from Mandy and Ellen. For a short ways, Mandy could hear him calling the girls' names, as she and Ellen were doing. Then his voice disappeared, swallowed up by distance and the storm. *Or maybe he's found the girls. Think positive, Mandy.*

I never realized how many places there are for a child to hide in here, Mandy thought as she and Ellen investigated the barn, calling for the girls. It was maddening how much time it took.

Mandy had grabbed her cell phone before they left. No telling what the night ahead might hold.

The helplessness she felt at the growing terror she saw in Ellen's face added to Mandy's own fears. She slid her arm around Ellen's waist as they started back to the farmhouse. "Maybe Jason found them making snowmen behind the house."

He hadn't.

He, Grandpa Seth, and Grandma Tillie were pacing the living room. "Maybe we should call someone," Grandma Tillie said. "The sheriff or the police."

Mandy stood beside Ellen at the front door, her mind tossing about for ideas and coming up with nothing. Her gaze rested on Beth's doll, wrapped in Ellen's improvised swaddling clothes, and the memory of Beth's performance only hours earlier squeezed her heart.

Something clicked in her mind. The doll. Something wasn't right.

Mandy started toward the sofa, forgetting to remove her boots. Frowning, she picked up Beth's doll.

Jason came up beside her. "What is it, Mandy?"

"Beth wrapped the doll in the blue blanket." Mandy raised her troubled gaze to Jason's. "Where is the blanket?"

"The nativity." The realization hit Mandy and Jason at the same time.

Ellen stared at them from beside the front door. "What are you talking abut?"

Jason hurried toward her. "They've gone to the nativity to cover up the baby Jesus."

"In this storm?" Ellen's eyes showed she refused to believe it. "In the dark?" She shook her head. "They'd never go without telling me. It's the one rule they never break."

Jason snapped his fingers. "The card. Did you get the card Beth made for you, Ellen?"

"She didn't give me a card."

"On the dining room table." Jason crossed the living room with long, determined strides, Mandy and Ellen in his wake. "Beth came in during the chess game. She laid a folded piece of paper with your name on it in crayon. I asked if she'd made you a Christmas card. She just smiled and left the room. Here it is." He handed it to Ellen.

Mandy noticed the Christmasy red crayon in which the card was written. No wonder Jason thought it a Christmas note. She glanced over Ellen's shoulder. The note wasn't long and was filled with scratched-out and misspelled words which would otherwise have caused amusement.

The paper shook in Ellen's hands, and her voice trembled as she read:

Mommy,
    Bonnie and me are going to the baby Jesus. We took our jackets and a flashlight, so don't be scared like when J. P. was little.

Beth

Ellen pressed her fingers to her lips to stifle a sob.

A gust of wind shook the windows as the knowledge of the children's danger blew into Mandy's heart and chilled it.

19

*J*ason pushed his fingers through his hair. It chilled him to the marrow to find his and Mandy's assumption was correct. "I should have told you about that note right away, Ellen."

"You had no way of knowing what it contained," Gram reassured him as she hurried toward the kitchen. "I'll call the police."

But Mandy had already punched 9-1-1 on her cell phone.

Fifteen minutes later a plan was in place. The sheriff was on the way out to the farm. His office was making calls to volunteers experienced with hunting the mountains for missing persons. Everyone knew without it being said that it was unlikely the girls would find their way to the nativity in the storm. They could be anyplace on the mountain.

The farmhouse already felt like a command center. Gramps had dug out detailed maps of the mountains in the area, including an up-to-date map of the Christmas tree farm. Gram found the two-way radios used on the farm before the advent of cell phones. Mandy started coffee and hot chocolate for thermoses and collected blankets from the linen closet.

Ellen made a quick trip to the Christmas store for a change of clothes for herself and Mandy and for Beth and Bonnie. "They're out there in their Christmas dresses and tights," Ellen reminded Mandy.

Jason called Tom Berry and explained the situation. After hanging up, Jason turned to Mandy and Ellen. "Tom's heading up to the nativity from his place."

A shade of relief passed over Ellen's face at the realization one more person was looking for her girls.

Gram put in a quick call to the pastor and received his assurance he'd immediately arrange a prayer chain among the congregation.

Jason put chains on the tires of the farm's Jeep and attached a trailer behind it to carry a snowmobile. He made certain there was a first-aid kit, a flashlight, and extra batteries in the vehicle.

When he finished, he returned to the kitchen where Mandy was pouring hot chocolate into a thermos. A sense of urgency made his chest hurt. "I'm heading out in the Jeep. I think it's important someone is out there looking for the girls as soon as possible."

"I'm going with you."

"Don't you want to stay with Ellen?"

"Grandma Tillie and Grandpa Seth will be with her. And the sheriff will have others here."

It had already been agreed that after the sheriff arrived, Ellen and Grandma Tillie would go down to the Christmas store to wait in case the children returned there. Grandpa Seth would remain at the farmhouse where volunteers would headquarter.

Mandy changed quickly into jeans, a turtleneck, and a sweatshirt, then slipped into her practical winter parka. Jason and Mandy carried a radio, cell phone, thermos of hot chocolate, and blankets out to the Jeep. They took backpacks in case they needed to travel by snowmobile later. Ellen handed them the set of clean, dry clothes for each of the girls.

Jason's heart contracted. He took a moment to hug Ellen. "Keep praying."

She nodded, and he felt her tears hot against his cheek.

Tom would be headed up the path he'd made from his place to the nativity, but the girls started out from the farmhouse. Jason's plan was to approach the nativity as close as possible from the roads through the Christmas groves, go beyond as far as possible in the Jeep, then take the snowmobile.

At one point, Jason reached over and squeezed one of Mandy's gloved hands in an attempt to reassure her. He wished he could give her true comfort, assure her the girls were fine and would be found safe and sound.

He couldn't even hold her hand for long, let alone calm her fears.

Even with the Jeep's four-wheel drive and ability to travel over rough terrain, the way was difficult and demanded his full attention, with both hands on the steering wheel.

"I wish the girls had a dog with them, the way you had Old Butch." Mandy gave him a tight little semblance of a smile.

"Me too. Maybe we should override Ellen's veto and give the girls a puppy for Christmas, after all."

"A Saint Bernard might be a good choice."

He forced a chuckle. He didn't feel like laughing but appreciated her attempt at humor. "Can you imagine one of those in the Christmas store? Its tail would take out every Christmas tree in the place."

She gave him a small smile, then turned her gaze back to the windshield. "I've always liked a white Christmas, but I'd be just as happy without one this year."

Jason drove slowly, and they both tried to watch for the girls as they went along, but it was almost impossible to see anything but shadowy, lumpy shapes in the curtain of snow. They kept the windows partially down and stopped about every hundred feet to call to the girls and listen intently for an answer they never received. He sent prayers up constantly and knew Mandy did the same.

At one point they received a call on the radio from the sheriff, who'd arrived at the farmhouse. Jason told him where they were and reported they'd seen no sign of the girls. The sheriff told him the Highway Patrol was closing the highways and asked him to keep in touch.

When Jason could go no farther with the Jeep due to the thick growth beneath the snow, he stopped. "I figure we're within a quarter mile of the nativity," he told Mandy. "The snowmobiles are too noisy. If we walk, we can keep calling for the girls and have a chance of hearing them respond."

"Maybe Tom has already reached the nativity," Mandy said. "Maybe he's found the girls."

"Maybe."

"If he'd found them, he'd let the sheriff know, wouldn't he?"

"Tom took a cell phone with him, but he doesn't have a radio. He might not be able to keep in touch with the sheriff all the time. There are dead-air places in the mountains where the cell phones don't work, as you know."

They packed the thermoses, blankets, phones, first-aid kit, compass, extra batteries, and children's clothes into the backpacks and started out on foot. They each carried a flashlight, and Jason carried the radio in a holster over his shoulder.

The trees cut the force of the wind, but it was still hard going uphill through the storm, the tangled underbrush and rocks beneath the snow making their footing tricky. Jason and Mandy held hands as they trudged along.

His admiration for her grew. She was a trooper. No complaints from her at the conditions, though he could hear her labored breathing. The chill bit at his cheeks, and he pictured the girls' legs protected only by tights and high boots. He was certain Mandy had similar thoughts, but she didn't voice them. Likely she felt as he did, that expressing their fears wouldn't do any good. Better to put all their energy into trying to find the girls.

Twice he reconnoitered and changed their direction, and still he wondered whether they were headed the right way. Would they become lost and not find the nativity until the storm let up? He sent up a prayer of gratitude when Mandy leaned close and said, "There it is." He followed the direction she pointed with her flashlight, and saw a dim glow farther up the hillside.

Their pace quickened. They resumed their pattern of calling for the girls, listening, and calling again.

Soon they reached the nativity. The wind was stronger, coming up the ridge from the highway, which Jason knew lay below, though they couldn't see it. He climbed onto the platform and flashed his light around. Disappointment cut through him like a knife blade. He hadn't realized the extent to which he'd hoped to find the girls huddled in that makeshift stable in the hay behind the statues.

He concentrated the light on the manger. Snow mounded over the statue of the baby Jesus. No blue blanket covered it.

Jason jumped down off the platform. "Not there," he announced to Mandy unnecessarily.

Mandy shone her light beneath the platform, which stood two feet off the ground. They both bent down to look beneath it. The girls weren't there either.

A man's shout greeted them as they straightened up. It was Tom Berry, arriving on foot at the top of the rough path he'd cut through the woods for his truck.

It took only a couple minutes to exchange information. Tom's truck had become stuck a ways down the mountain, in spite of the chains on his tires. He'd seen no sign of the girls, though he'd kept a close watch and called for them regularly.

Jason pulled the radio out of his holster and called in to make his report to the sheriff. He slid an arm around Mandy's shoulders and pulled her close while he talked. The transmission crackled and the conversation broke up, but he was able to make out most of it. The sheriff explained a large group of volunteers had arrived at the farm and were ready to head out in an organized search pattern.

Jason's chest ached unbearably. The chances hadn't been great they'd find the girls here, but he'd kept a fierce hope up just the same. Now the area to search had expanded exponentially. An eight year old and a six year old in the middle of a snowstorm at night in the mountains. How could they possibly have any sense of direction?

They could be anywhere in the miles of dark and cold.

20

*J*ason was almost ready to end his radio contact with the sheriff when he felt Mandy straighten beneath his arm. He glanced at her, questioning her with his eyes.

"The highway."

"Hold on just a minute, Sheriff." He waited for Mandy's explanation.

"On the way back from church tonight, I pointed out the lights from the nativity to the girls as we drove by. I don't think Beth would have known how to reach here by cutting through the farm and woods like we did, but—"

"But she'd know how to follow the highway toward town," Jason interrupted, hope taking fire within him, "and look for the light on the mountainside."

Mandy nodded.

"And the highway's been closed off, so no one would have seen the girls," Tom added.

Jason explained Mandy's theory to the sheriff and signed off. "He's alerting the Highway Patrol," Jason told Mandy and Tom, "and sending some men out along the highway in a four-wheel drive and on snow-mobiles."

Jason had always prided himself on being quick and decisive under fire, but the dilemma before him now made him appreciate every leader who ever made a decision involving another human life. Should the three of them stay together or split up? Should they head down the ridge to the highway and search for the girls themselves? Or stay at the nativity in case the girls showed up there?

In the end, Tom offered to stay at the nativity. Jason and Mandy started down the ridge. It was steep and rocky with few trees. "Careful. Take it slow," Jason warned Mandy. "It won't help the girls any if one of us hurts ourselves."

Yet it was frustrating to take it slow. Once Mandy lost her footing and slid full length down the slope. His heart leaped to his throat until she came to a stop thirty feet down. He wanted to shout for joy when they reached the highway where they could walk without the burden of rocks and underbrush beneath the snow.

He and Mandy continued to call as they walked along the highway toward the farm. The wind seemed to delight in tossing their voices away. They flashed their lights across the highway and along the side of the road as they walked, hoping for a glimpse of something other than trees and rocks and snow.

They rounded a bend, and the ridge became less steep, with more trees. Mandy played her light along the lower part of the ridge, where pines with sweeping, snow-covered branches stood proud.

She stopped and grabbed Jason's arm. "I thought I saw something move."

He watched her light play back over the area she'd just covered. "There. Do you see it?"

"Yes." He started toward the tree, which stood about ten feet away. Something wide and long appeared caught on a branch and swung in the wind.

Mandy plowed through the snow beside him, keeping her light trained on the branch.

As he drew closer, his certainty grew. A scarf was caught on the tree. Could it belong to Beth or Bonnie?

He tried to call out the girls' names one more time, but hope formed a lump in his throat, and he couldn't shout. He ran the last couple steps and grabbed at the scarf. It was plum-colored chenille.

His fingers clutched about the material, Jason turned to Mandy. He saw the joy in her eyes. She recognized it too.

He pulled at the scarf, but it caught. Looking closer, he saw it had been tied around the branch.

Mandy grabbed the scarf beside the knot. "Beth." The name was barely a whisper on the wind.

Jason swallowed the lump in his throat. "Beth." It came out as soft as Mandy's, but they both kept trying. "Beth! Bonnie!"

Their voices grew louder.

"Here! We're here!"

The lower branches swung aside, dumping lumps of snow. Two red-cheeked faces peeked out.

Jason and Mandy dropped to their knees. Jason caught Beth to his chest, feeling his heart would explode through his rib cage in joy and gratitude. Beth clung to him. He saw Mandy drawing Bonnie into her embrace.

"I knew you'd come," Beth whispered between chattering teeth into his ear. "I knew you'd come."

Mandy dug the blankets and thermos from the backpacks while Jason radioed the sheriff. Shouts of rejoicing rang back over the radio waves.

A minute later the sheriff put Ellen on.

"We have a Christmas present here for you." Jason held the radio up to Beth's face.

"Merry Christmas, Mommy. Are you mad at me?"

"No, Sweetheart. Are you okay?"

"Yes."

Jason moved the radio to Bonnie. "Hi, Mommy. I want to come home. I'm c-cold."

A sob came clearly over the airwaves. "I know, Precious. Mandy and Jason will bring you home."

While Mandy and Jason wrapped the girls in blankets, Bonnie reported on their adventure. "I was c-cold. I told Beth I wanted to go home, but she said we couldn't until we found Jesus."

"I didn't think it was so far," Beth justified herself. "It didn't take very long in Tom's truck or Mommy's car."

Bonnie broke in again. "When I got really cold, I cried. Then Beth saw that tree and said let's pretend we were J. P. when he was little and crawl under it."

"The snow couldn't blow on us there," Beth explained. "But it was still cold."

Bonnie pulled the blanket closer about her throat, shivering. "I cried lots. I was afraid nobody would find us and we'd get lost like Hansel and Gretel."

"That's why I tied my scarf on the tree, so people would see it 'cause the tree hid us."

"Very smart, Beth," Jason commended, pouring a cup of hot chocolate and handing it to her.

Beth beamed.

"I wanted to pray and ask God to bring somebody to find us and take us home so I could be warm." Bonnie glanced at Beth. "Beth didn't want to pray. She said God didn't care if anybody found us. I told her she was wrong because my Sunday school teacher says God loves us. And then I cried harder, so Beth prayed anyway. And then you came."

Two snowmobiles pulled up, followed soon after by a red Jeep. Mandy and Jason quickly bundled the girls into the warm vehicle, where Mandy helped them change from wet tights to dry jeans and socks.

There was a knock at the window and Mandy opened it.

"I'm going back with the guys on the snowmobiles to get Tom," Jason said.

Mandy frowned. "Must you? You should get out of the cold."

"I'm fine. I don't want to take a chance on the men missing Tom. I know just where to find him."

Beth pushed her chin out from the blanket. "Where's Tom?"

"At the nativity," Jason told her. "He stayed in case you and Bonnie showed up." He waved one hand. "See you all later."

"Wait." Beth struggled to sit up straighter.

Jason waited.

"My doll blanket. I think we forgot it under the tree."

"I'll get it for you." Jason started to turn away.

"No."

Jason turned back. "Don't you want it?"

"Will you take it to the baby Jesus?"

Tears heated Mandy's eyes. After all Beth had been through, her first thought was still to protect the baby Jesus from the cold. Her determination could have cost her life and Bonnie's. One day, she'd tell her grandchildren about this adventure and laugh at what she'd perceive as her silliness. But Mandy suspected God would cherish the sweet, if misguided, desire in the little girl's heart to protect His Son.

Jason nodded solemnly. "Yes, I'll make sure your blanket covers the baby Jesus."

Beth heaved a sigh of relief. "It's a little wet. I carried it under my jacket to keep it dry, but we got cold, so when we were under the tree we put it over our legs."

"I don't think Jesus will mind that you used it first." Mandy shared a smile with Jason before rolling up the window.

The volunteers took Mandy and the girls back to the farm in the Jeep. Ellen waited at the Christmas store. Mandy watched the emotional reunion with a teary but happy heart. She called Grandma Tillie and assured her and Grandpa Seth the girls were truly home at last.

The sheriff came down to check on the girls himself before dismissing the last of his deputies and volunteers and heading home.

The girls wanted to open their Christmas presents right away—even though their pleas came between yawns—but Ellen stood firm. "It's late. You're going to take baths to warm you up and then crawl into bed. Besides, we can't open the gifts without Grandma Tillie and Grandpa Seth and Jason here. We'll have our Christmas party tomorrow morning."

Mandy was pleasantly surprised when Jason and Tom showed up half an hour after she and the girls arrived. "I thought you'd be out the rest of the night, finding your vehicles and driving them back."

"I left the Jeep, and Tom left his truck. We'll get them tomorrow. The volunteers brought us home on the snowmobiles. How are the girls doing?"

Mandy explained how the girls' hopes to celebrate Christmas yet that night had been dashed by Ellen's practical plans.

"Is Ellen holding up all right?" Tom's brown eyes looked anxious.

"She's doing fine," Mandy assured him. "She didn't even do the normal mother thing of throwing a tantrum once she realized the kids were safe. She just wants to get them warm and climb into their double bed and sleep with them."

Jason walked over to the fireplace area, picked out from the family

Christmas present stack two long rectangular packages wrapped in red paper, and handed them to Mandy. "Would you ask Ellen if the girls can open these before they go to bed?"

"What did you give them?"

"You'll see."

Ellen reluctantly agreed. She'd just gotten the girls out of the tub and into clean, warm flannel nightgowns. "I don't want them getting excited over Christmas presents again and waking up. They need their sleep."

She brought the girls downstairs, where they sat on the bottom loft step to open the packages. Gasps of delight greeted the gifts.

"A puppy!" Bonnie pulled a stuffed basset hound with ears almost as long as its body from the box and hugged it to her chest. "Thank you, J. P."

Beth pulled out a matching puppy from her box. "Thanks. I'm going to call mine Old Butch."

Jason grinned. "That's a perfect name."

Bonnie frowned. "I was going to call mine Old Butch."

"Why don't you call him Little Butch?" Mandy suggested. "After all, he is a puppy."

Bonnie, with her usual compliant nature, agreed.

Ellen sent the girls off to bed. "I'll be up in a few minutes." She waited until the girls reached the top of the steps before turning to Mandy, Jason, and Tom. "There is no way I can sufficiently thank you for all you did tonight, but I promise there will always be a special place in my heart for each of you."

"We didn't do it all ourselves," Jason reminded her.

She didn't argue, just gave each of them a hug and headed up to join her daughters.

Jason took Tom up to the farmhouse to arrange sleeping arrangements for him until morning, when the storm would hopefully abate. "Will you wait up for me?" Jason asked Mandy. "I know it's late, but I don't think I'm going to be able to sleep, and I'd like to talk to you."

So she waited for him.

There was still hot chocolate in one of the thermoses. Mandy brought two mugs down from the loft and set them on a table in the fireside area. Ellen had lit a fire in the fireplace earlier. Only glowing embers remained.

Mandy plugged in the lights of a Christmas tree near the hearth. Crystal icicles which glittered in reflected light decorated the tree. Beneath the tree, the unopened gifts were still piled, stacked in their brightly colored wrapping.

The other tree lights weren't turned on. The large, festive room felt unusually homey and comforting in the dim, mellow lighting, and the quiet was broken only by shifting embers.

She wandered idly about in the fireside sitting area, adjusting the placement of a china angel on a table or a gnome atop the mantel. A rag doll Santa Claus and his wife, dressed in red felt, sat on one corner of the hearth. Mandy knelt before them for a moment, tracing Mrs. Claus's red-stitched smile with a fingernail and running a hand over the soft white curls of the doll's hair. She pinched Santa's silky beard where it tumbled over the front of his red suit. These dolls always brought a smile to Mandy's face. Such an eternally happy-looking couple.

What did Jason want to discuss so badly he wanted to come back tonight to do so?

Mandy sat on the floor beside the dolls and stared at the embers. So much had happened inside her, in her heart and spirit, during the last few hours.

She heard the door open. The bells jangled merrily, their sound clearer and louder than usual in the night quiet.

"Mandy?"

"Over here, by the fireplace."

She could trace his movements by the sound of his footsteps on the wooden floor. In a minute he arrived at the fireside. He removed his jacket and hung it over one wing of the chair.

Mandy got up from the floor and sat down in the opposite wing chair. Only then did Jason sit down in the wing chair across from her. He rested his elbows on his knees and stared at the orange glow in the grate.

Mandy waited for him to choose his time to speak, studying his face and thinking about all the ways she loved him.

He sighed deeply. "Quite a night."

"Yes."

"Thanks for letting me come back tonight. I wanted to tell you—"

"There's something I want to say first. Please. I've been gathering my courage while I waited for you. If I don't say this right away, I might not say it all." Her heart raced as she met his gaze.

"I'm listening."

"Tonight when Ellen took the girls upstairs to bathe, I wandered through the shop. I love this store. I've loved Christmas stores from the very first moment I stepped into one."

She stopped, her gaze drifting over the shadows of trees in the dimly lit room, wondering how to put into words what was so clear in her heart. "Eight years ago when you asked me to marry you, I knew I couldn't. I knew God's place for me was in these mountains, involved in work I love."

"Mandy, I—"

She lifted a hand to silence him. If she didn't get this out, she might always regret it. "You thought I didn't love you if I wouldn't sacrifice everything for you. I did love you, but I didn't want us to end up like your parents. I only knew them through the stories you and Grandpa Seth and Grandma Tillie told me. But I know your father loved your mother so much he gave up his dreams to stay in the mountains she loved. Eventually, he grew bitter over his sacrifice. I don't know what that did to their marriage, but I know bitter hearts grow self-pitying and poison other lives."

"Our father images again."

Mandy frowned. She wanted to finish her own thoughts.

"Broken father images influencing our understanding of God," he clarified. "Remember?"

She nodded.

"I've been thinking about that a lot lately. One of the messages from my father's life was that perfect love sacrifices. And sacrifice entails giving up something we love. Suffering." His somber gaze held hers. "I was selfish to ask you to leave what you love. I don't want you to make that kind of sacrifice for me. I want you to be happy. You've been happy here, haven't you?"

"Mostly. I've loved following my dreams. But I don't need them or this place anymore to be happy." She took a deep breath and plunged on. "I don't know if there's any chance you still want me in your life, but if you do, building us is more important to me than building mountain Christmas stores."

"Mandy." With a swift, smooth movement Jason slid from the chair to the hassock in front of Mandy and gently framed her face with his hands. She saw the joy her words caused reflected in his eyes, and wonder curled through her just before his lips touched hers in a kiss so soft and so sweet it filled her with awe.

He folded his hands over hers and pressed a kiss to her fingers. "I'll never again ask you to give up your dreams for me, Mandy. But it means the world to me that you've offered."

Confusion swirled through her. When he kissed her she'd felt certain he loved her, but now . . .

"My turn to talk." He rubbed her hands gently between his. "The last couple months, seeing the way your life has played out because you stayed true to what you believe God called you to do has been a gift. You put love into your work, and that love multiplies. Following your path has allowed so many others doorways to following their own paths: Tom Berry and his mother, all the other craftspeople you've encouraged." He grinned. "The women who knitted all those mittens. You certainly gave those people a way to contribute to the world."

"You give me too much credit. People who want to contribute to the world always find places to do it." She sat up straighter, eager to share with him. "I forgot to tell you. The knitters enjoyed making the mittens so much that they've decided to work on them all year for next Christmas's mitten tree and make mufflers and hats to give away too. Isn't that wonderful?"

He laughed. "You see? You don't even realize the ways God works through your trust in the desires He puts in your heart." The laughter died away from his voice and eyes. "I realized recently that I chose the career I did because I believed my father didn't love and accept me for who I was. I fought with him until he died. Then, in a last-ditch attempt to gain his approval, I followed the example he gave me in life and sacrificed my dreams for his."

Mandy leaned forward and touched her lips to his forehead, her heart aching for the boy he'd been.

"How could I believe God wanted me to follow the dreams He put in my heart, when I couldn't believe my human father wanted me to follow those dreams? Then tonight—was it only tonight? It seems eons ago—out on the mountain in the storm, searching for the girls, everything became clear. I think my father did want me to be happy. He just couldn't see that he and I were different. He thought if I stayed in the mountains on the Christmas tree farm, I'd eventually grow as bitter as he had. He believed his only happiness lay in the financial world in a large city, so he believed that's the only place I could find happiness."

"He died young, only a few years older than you are now. He was probably just starting to figure out life himself."

"Yes." Jason splayed his fingers, touching his palms against hers. "I feel God's given me a second chance. He's given me glimpses— through you, Gramps and Gram, the girls, and Zach—into what my life might become if I make different choices. I'm not going back to New York. I'm going to tell Gramps I want to work with him."

"Jason, that's wonderful. I mean, if it's what you want."

"It's what I want." He picked up the Mr. and Mrs. Santa Claus dolls from the hearth and sat them on his knees facing Mandy. "These remind me of the Christmas ornament we gave Gram and Gramps, the old man and woman on the bench."

Mandy smiled. "They do look similar."

"Let's get married, Mandy."

She gasped, but he didn't give her time to reply.

"Let's raise a couple great kids like Beth and Bonnie. Let's grow old together. And when we're old and gray, young couples will walk past us and say to each other, 'Will we love each other that much when we're their age?' "

Joy engulfed her heart. He remembered almost word for word what she'd said that long-ago day when they'd bought the ornament for his grandparents. She rested her palms on his cheeks and smiled into his eyes. "If those young couples are very blessed, they will love each other that much when they're old."

This time she initiated their kiss, rejoicing in the freedom to do so.

When she pulled her lips from his, Jason raised his eyebrows. "Is that a yes?"

"Oh, it's a yes, Mister. It's a yes and a promise."

He drew her into his arms, and she snuggled her head against his shoulder.

"Deep in my heart, I think I always knew you'd come back, Jason."

His arms tightened around her. "Me too." Overwhelming gratitude for her love roughened his voice. In his mind Mandy's words echoed in Beth's voice—"I knew you'd come." *Thank God, I'm finally listening.*

ℰPILOGUE

𝒥 ason sat on Gram's rose-print sofa in the midst of Christmas Eve chaos. The tree with its memory-filled, humble
ornaments stood as always in front of the window, pine
scent filling the room. Beth and Bonnie played with new Barbie dolls,
sitting on the floor surrounded by colorful, crumpled Christmas papers. A lump thickened in Jason's throat at the remembrance of Christmas Eve two years ago, when he'd wondered whether he'd ever see
those two sweet girls alive again.

A slender golden retriever lay with its head touching Beth's leg.
Butch seldom let the girls out of his sight. Tom had given the dog—
only a wiggly puppy then—to the girls as a belated Christmas present
two days after they were rescued. It took only a gentle reminder of
the dog that played such an important part in saving Jason's life as a
boy to convince Ellen to let the girls keep the dog.

His gaze roamed the room. Gramps and Mandy's father played
chess on the small chess table that Gram had given Gramps for Christmas. Ellen and Gram sat on the floor with the girls, their own gifts
stacked nearby.

There was a stir in Jason's arms, and he looked down at his son
wrapped in a pale blue blanket. The bald, skinny boy, eyes closed,
yawned and stretched a two-month-old arm. Then Abe nestled in
again, his head resting against Jason's chest in perfect trust.

Jason's heart caught. *Don't let me ever give Abe a reason not to trust
me, Lord.*

Jason realized he'd break that trust someday. It was inevitable. It
was the way of humans to be imperfect. But he meant to love his

children the best he knew how every day and strive to be an example of the kind of father God is.

It worked the other direction too. He'd grown to understand that in the months during Mandy's pregnancy. He had studied God's love to see how a human father should love his children. He didn't know a better gift for them.

Beth leaned against his knee and smiled down at Abe. "Good thing Bonnie and me taught you how to hold a baby, huh?"

Jason nodded. "A very good thing."

"Can I hold Abe?"

"Sure."

She climbed onto the sofa and sat close beside him. Jason laid Abe gently on her lap.

A minute later, Mandy smiled down at them. "I think Abe likes you, Beth. He certainly looks comfortable."

Beth beamed up at her.

"How's Abe's brother, Sam, doing?" Jason looked at the baby wrapped in a green blanket and held by Mandy's mother.

"Dry and happy now," the grandmother replied with a smile.

He resisted the urge to reach for his son. Mandy's parents had made the trip from Texas just to meet their new grandsons. He was glad the couple had been able to attend the twins' dedication, held during the Christmas Eve service earlier.

Bonnie pulled a fold of Sam's blanket back and peeked at Sam. "Can I hold him?"

"Wouldn't you rather open the rest of your presents?" Ellen asked.

Bonnie shook her head until her curls bounced. "No. I want to hold Sam."

Jason shared a smiling glance with Mandy as Bonnie sat down beside her sister and held out her arms. While Mandy's mother settled Sam carefully in Bonnie's lap, Mandy seated herself on Jason's lap and slipped an arm around his neck.

Jason hugged her close. The light floral scent she wore teased his senses. His heart felt warm, filled with deep thanksgiving. He loved the extended family they lived among. A slight shiver ran through him at the knowledge of how close he'd come to missing it all by stubbornly following his father's dream instead of his own. He only wished his father and mother could have met his wife and their boys.

Mandy slipped off Jason's lap and picked up four small square boxes from beneath the tree. She handed one to each of her parents and to Gram and Gramps.

The older couples "oohed" and "aahed" appreciatively over the simple crocheted ornaments that framed pictures of Abe and Sam. Gram hung her and Gramps's ornaments on the tree, near the crocheted ornament picture of Jason when he was three and those of Beth and Bonnie from two Christmases ago.

Mandy sat down on the sofa's rolled arm and leaned against Jason's shoulder. Jason glanced down at Abe, who lay in Beth's arms as though completely unaware of the excitement in the room. Sam, in Bonnie's lap, looked equally unaffected.

He never looked at those boys without joy flooding his chest.

Jason squeezed Mandy's hand and whispered, "Think Abe and Sam would like sisters for Christmas next year?"

Her eyes widened in surprise, and color flooded her cheeks. Then a smile danced in her green eyes. "It's an idea definitely worth consideration."

Jason felt delightfully tangled in her gaze, embraced in contentment and peace. He'd never suspected life could be this good, and he thanked God for the joy He'd brought to their lives.